MYTHICAL ALLIANCE

PHOENIX TEAM

USA TODAY BESTSELLING AUTHOR
CLAIRE LUANA

Mythical Alliance
Phoenix Team: The Complete Season
Copyright © 2020 by Claire Luana
Published by Live Edge Publishing

eBook ISBN: 978-1-948947-10-7
Paperback ISBN: 978-1-948947-11-4
Hardback ISBN: 978-1-948947-12-1

Cover Design: MoorBooks Design
Editing: Amy McNulty

CLAIRE LUANA

MYTHICAL ALLIANCE

PHOENIX SELECTED

1

The guy at the bar wasn't my type. He was human, for one.

He threw back a shot as he and his buddy ogled the ass of a passing blonde. Strike two. He was stocky and thickly muscled on top—whereas I preferred a man lean and strong. Proportioned as nature intended. Strike three. Sad little goatee and too-tight Ed Hardy T-shirt. Strikes four and five.

It didn't matter. I was still going to go over there and pick him up tonight.

Because this ass-hat had something I needed.

I sucked in a breath, swallowed the rest of my bourbon, and stood, fluffing my dark curls up and tugging the neckline of my fitted dress down to show a bit more of my generous cleavage. Too obvious maybe. But was there such a thing as too obvious with guys like this?

I sauntered over to the bar, closing my sensitive glands to the overwhelming power of the man's Axe body spray.

I sidled in next to him and he turned to regard me.

"Buy me a drink?" I smiled widely at him.

He blinked twice as he took me in but only recoiled slightly. I had to give it to him. Most people stuttered or downright stared when they caught sight of my green slitted pupils and curved fangs. I supposed a man who worked security for MASC, the Mythical Alliance of Supernatural Creatures, the UN division governing all things supe, would have gotten used to a strange face every now and then.

His gleaming eyes drank me in. "Those scales go all the way down, honey?"

His skinny friend choked on his beer.

I let my hand drift to my neck, where a pattern of golden scales curved up to my temple. "Buy me that drink and maybe you'll find out." They did, in fact, go all the way down. And he would not, in fact, be finding out.

He grinned and I fought the urge to punch him in his tiny little teeth. "What are you drinking?"

"Martini?" I simpered. I lowered my voice half an octave. "Dirty."

His smile widened and he flagged down the bartender to order me my drink.

The friend stood, grabbing his beer. His eyes hadn't left me, and even with my glands closed, I could smell his fear. "I'm going to grab a round of pool, bro."

I waggled my fingers at him as he left before sliding onto the stool he had just vacated. Fine by me. I didn't need that one screwing up my plans.

A dirty martini was deposited in front of me and I picked it up. "What are we drinking to?" I asked.

He'd ordered himself another shot. The cinnamon tickled my glands. Fireball. The official drink of ass-hats. Or was that Jägermeister? He held up his glass. "To scales that go all the way down."

I giggled and took a sip, nearly gagging. I hated olive juice. But a dirty martini seemed like the type of drink a seductress version of myself would order.

"What's your name?" he asked.

"Veronica," I lied. This jackass deserved nothing real from me. "You?"

"Martin." We shook hands. "Your hands are as cold as ice."

I smiled. "Cold-blooded."

Martin's dark eyebrows shot up like two bushy caterpillars. "What are you?"

Rude. Didn't this guy know anything? You didn't ask a supe what kind of creature they were.

"Naga," I answered. "Well, half anyway." All right, I supposed I'd give him one true thing. Many mythical creatures—supes, as they're called these days—share kinship or at least a passing resemblance with animals. Nagas are snake supes. In ancient times, they were thought to be gods, and that suited them just fine. Nagas are capable of shifting between the form of a human and the form of a huge snake—or somewhere in the middle—human torso, snake lower half. Full-bloods have incredible power—they're strong, fast and agile. All their senses are heightened, and they have an extra one too: nagas can use their infrared glands to sense the heat of a nearby body one hundred yards away. Then there's the poisonous venom, and the fact that nagas can swallow someone whole. Though it isn't a particularly pleasant experience, from what I've heard. You're bloated as hell for days afterwards.

As a half-blood, I can't do most of that cool shit. My form is permanently stuck somewhere between a snake and a human. I have the slivered pupils and forked tongue of a naga, together with a pattern of golden scales that stretch up my neck to my temples as Martin so classily observed. I have much of my race's heightened senses: strength, speed, and venom. But compared to many supes, I'm weak.

His face went thoughtful. "I knew another naga once. At the office."

My gut tightened with anger as tears pricked my eyes. Impotent fury and soul-sucking grief, my two ever-present companions these past six weeks. I took a gulp of martini to hide my reaction, focusing on the disgusting tang of the olive juice. "You don't say," I managed.

Martin sipped his Fireball. "Well, he's dead now. Too bad. I liked the guy."

Me too, Martin. Me too. I wanted to slide off the stool into a puddle of myself. I wanted to rip his head off for even mentioning my dad, for thinking he knew anything about him when this useless human didn't even deserve to live in the same universe. But I'd tried rage, and I'd tried grief. Today, I was trying something new.

Action.

I set my drink down and dropped my hand to his hairy forearm. "Do you want to get out of here?" I could feel the clock ticking down, my ability to hold it together slipping through my fingers like sand through an hourglass. Tonight was the longest I'd been out of the house in weeks. The longest I'd carried on a conversation. The first time I'd showered in...well...it was probably best not to think about that.

"Fuck yeah," Martin replied, throwing back the rest of his shot and standing up.

"Great."

He dropped some cash on the bar and slung a beefy arm around my shoulders. The feel of him made my skin crawl, but I wouldn't have to stand it much longer.

We stumbled out of the bar into the warm night. I was taller than him, so there was an awkward angle to his arm and our stride. We started down the sidewalk and I caught sight of an alley.

Perfect.

"I don't want to wait," I said as breathily as I could, shoving him into the alley.

"Me, either, baby," he said, and pinned me against the wall, his hands cupping my ass. His liquor-breath was heavy as he crushed his lips against mine.

Oh, Martin, you are so predictable.

I had my first kiss—a human boy named Ryan—when I was thirteen. That was when I learned that it was pretty hard to kiss a human without my fangs getting into the mix. And the deadly poison they excreted. Ryan had ended up in the emergency room and I'd ended up with the tongue-lashing of the century from Dad. Needless to say, Ryan and I did *not* become boyfriend and girlfriend.

But right now, that was exactly what I was looking for. I surged against Martin's mouth and felt my fangs tangle in his tongue, pricking him. His body tensed and he froze, his eyes going wide, his pupils dilating.

"What—" His hands slid off me and flew to his chest. The venom was coursing into his bloodstream now. It would immobilize him, and if left untreated for more than fifteen minutes, would send him into cardiac arrest. "Don't worry, Martin," I sneered as I fished into his back pocket for his wallet. "It's not personal. Oh, wait. Yes, it is." I kneed him in the balls and he fell to the damp pavement with a wheezing groan.

I flipped through his wallet, desperately searching.

Please be here, please be here, please say this wasn't all for nothing...Yes!

His United Nations keycard, which provided access to all the secure levels of the MASC building. My ticket to the answers I needed. I pulled a card duplicator I'd bought on eBay out of my clutch and quickly scanned the card, duplicating it on one I'd made up with my own picture and fake identity.

I put the card back in the wallet and pulled his cash out, shoving it in my purse, before dropping it on his chest. Best if it looked like a simple mugging gone wrong.

I knelt over him, fisting his ridiculous T-shirt in one of my hands to pull him closer. "That naga who died, Martin? The one men like you were supposed to keep safe? He was my father. And he was worth a hundred of you, you stupid piece of shit." I didn't know why I was talking to him; he was totally out of it from the venom.

I stood, looking down at him. His color was leeching away as his vital organs shut down. I had a syringe of anti-venom in my purse, ready to bring him back. But I was stalling. Why? I wasn't a killer. I valued human life. I'd been going to med school, for God's sake, before I'd washed out two months from graduation. But I just couldn't bring myself to care. Why did this worthless douchebag get to live when Dad was dead?

Tears blurred my vision and I felt the despair closing in around me, cloying and suffocating. I didn't fight it. My hourglass had run dry.

The tears came unbidden now.

I was so tired.

So tired and heavy. I eyed the cobblestones beneath my heeled shoes, overcome by the urge to lie down and curl into myself in this filthy alley.

Some distant part of me spoke. *Move.*

Give him the anti-venom. Walk out of here and call an Uber.

One shot. Ten steps. Three taps of my finger.

I could do that.

I turned to find someone standing in the mouth of the alley. Three women, all clad in sparkly dresses and platform heels. Looking at the unmoving body on the ground behind me.

"Oh my god! Is he okay?"

2

───────

*F*uck.

Adrenaline burned through the fog of my grief, leaving the bright sun of panic. There weren't supposed to be witnesses. It didn't look good if I was found robbing and shooting up some guy in an alley...

The morose, self-destructive part of me pushed back. What the hell did it matter if I ended up in prison? My life had already gone to shit. Dad was gone, my medical career was over, I'd been living on cold DiGiorno pizza and boxed wine since Dad's funeral. That was no kind of life. But...a single thought shot through me, blazing bright. If I went to prison, I'd never find out who'd killed Dad. I'd never be able to avenge his death. It was enough to keep me going. That one shining purpose. After that, it was anyone's guess.

Damn it, I needed to save Martin.

"My date's gone into some sort of anaphylactic shock!" I cried. "I think he ate something he's allergic to! Call 911!"

One of the women, a brunette in a tight red dress, fished into her sequined clutch. "I have an EpiPen!"

Seriously? Those were some fucking odds. Well, hitting him with a jolt of epinephrine likely wouldn't hurt. "Help him!" I motioned her into the alley, crouching down next to Martin and quickly hiding his wallet beneath him. His skin had gone pale and waxy and his lips were tinged blue.

"This has never happened before." I played the helpless waif. "Where do we put it in?"

The brunette knelt down in her stilettos and jammed it into the side of his thigh like a meat thermometer in a turkey. I couldn't help but be impressed by her bedside manner. Cool in an emergency.

Martin's eyes went wide as he took a deep breath, one hand clutching his chest.

"I called 911," one of the other girls said, waving her phone. "An ambulance is on the way."

"Great." I tried to muster some enthusiasm. I needed this girl out of the alley so I could give him the anti-venom. This was going south faster than a sorority girl on spring break.

We helped Martin into a sitting position and I looked at her sideways. "Will you go see if the ambulance is coming yet?" I guessed I looked pathetic enough because she put a hand on my shoulder to comfort me. "He'll be okay."

She hurried back to her gaggle of friends, her heels clicking on the pavement.

I quickly pulled the syringe of anti-venom out of my purse and shoved the sleeve of his T-shirt up, injecting him. His color started returning instantly, his eyes clearing.

"What happened?" he groaned.

"Not all guys can handle their supes," I replied, praying that he didn't remember what I'd said about my dad. Naga venom had mind-altering effects, and he'd already been sinking when I'd spoken to him. I should be okay.

Flickers of red lights along the alley wall joined the whoop-whoop of a siren. "Ambulance is here!" the brunette announced.

The paramedics swarmed the alley and I stepped back, letting them go to work. An ache filled me as I watched their efficient motions. I was supposed to do that. Save lives. I'd wanted to be a doctor since I'd been ten years old. And I'd fucked it up.

They got Martin on a stretcher and into the ambulance. I followed them to the sidewalk, my arms crossed tightly over my chest.

"You coming with?" the paramedic asked. "Let's go."

I held up a hand to protest, but the EpiPen woman motioned me forward. "Go with him!"

"Yeah, go! He'll want you there." The other women joined in the guilt trip and I found my feet moving towards the back doors of the ambulance.

I stepped up into the vehicle, unable to believe that I was being bullied by a pack of party girls. What the hell had become of me?

The space in the back of the ambulance was suffocating. The two paramedics focused on Martin, checking his vitals, talking to him in low tones. They ignored me, which was just fine. As soon as we reached the hospital, I was fucking out of there.

The trip wasn't long, and I stepped out first to let them get the stretcher down. I trailed them into the emergency room as they whisked his stretcher away.

I let out a sigh.

He was gone.

It was over.

I reached for my purse to grab my phone and froze. It was still in the ambulance. I hurried back outside, but the vehicle was gone.

"Shit!"

I spun on my heel and ran back in, up to the front counter. "The ambulance. Where did it go? I left my purse in there. It has all my things..."

The portly middle-aged lady behind the counter pursed her lips, making it clear she had more pressing concerns than my lost handbag. "Which company was it?"

"What?"

"What did it say on the side of the ambulance? We contract with half a dozen providers in addition to EMS."

My mouth opened and closed as I tried to remember, to bring up the ambulance in my mind's eye. Nothing. "I don't know," I admitted.

"Then you're going to have to try each of the companies separately. They're independent from the hospital. We should get a bill within two days and could narrow it down for you then."

"Two days?" I sagged against the counter as I realized how much I had completely fucked up. In addition to my phone, keys, and wallet, my purse contained a used vial of anti-venom, the illegal card reader and the fake UN keycard with my face on it. *Fuck.* If anyone fished around in it...

I slumped on the counter, dropping my forehead to my arms. This night was a disaster. Why had I thought I could do some sort of 007 shit and find out who'd killed Dad? Like I'd ever actually successfully break into the UN and steal their classified report on the events surrounding his death. I'd fucked up every other part of my life; why had I thought this would be any different?

"Honey, you can't just stand there. I have other people to help."

I raised my heavy head. How was I supposed to get home? I didn't even have money for the subway. "Do you have a phone I can borrow?"

With a long-suffering sigh, the front desk lady showed me into an empty patient room. I thanked her and stared at the phone on the wall. I knew exactly three numbers by heart. One was my dad's. The second was my Auntie Temsula's, but she lived in New Jersey. Plus, I seriously didn't want to drag her into this. So I dialed the third number.

It went to voicemail, as I'd expected. No one picked up an unknown number these days.

A cheerful message answered. "*Hi. You've reached Kiki's phone. Leave a message. If you're a telemarketer, take me off your list or I'll make sure your personal data is blasted across the dark web like Halley's Comet. Have a great day!*"

A smile ghosted its way across my lips. Oh, Keeks.

Beep.

"Hey. It's Zariya. It's a long story, but I'm at New York Presbyterian Hospital and could use a ride home. I'm okay. Call me back at this number."

I hung up and waited about forty-five seconds. Long enough for her to listen to the message and call me back. Kiki was never far from her phone.

I picked it up on the first ring.

"Ohmygod, Zariya, are you okay?"

Kiki had been my best friend since we were eleven, and we'd lived together with our other roommate, Alviya, in a cramped apartment in Murray Hill for the last two years. She was one of the most talented hackers, excuse me, *computer prodigies*, I knew.

She could also read minds.

Kiki had taught me how to protect my thoughts, and I dropped what was left of my ragged mental walls, letting it all tumble out. I knew my thoughts were loud, jumbled. I didn't care. Kiki's gift worked even over distances, so long as she had a strong personal connection to her target or was connected by technology. And I didn't have the energy to explain right now.

"Oh, Zar..." She made a little *tsking* sound with her tongue. "I'll be right there."

"Thanks."

I was sitting on the sidewalk, my back to the brick wall of the hospital, when Kiki's Uber pulled up half an hour later.

She was wearing cute checked pants, platform black combat boots, and a Pusheen T-shirt. Her short, dark hair was pulled into a spiked ponytail, revealing her side-shave. Kiki had always had way more cool than me.

Her heart-shaped face was clearly worried as she settled down next to me on the ground. "What's wrong with the bench?" She nodded to an empty bench a few yards away.

"I don't deserve a bench." My words were flat.

She wrapped her arms around me and pulled me into a side hug, comforting me with her tiny body.

"I fucked up so bad."

"I hacked into the dispatch on the way here. Your purse should be headed back to EMS Station 10. We'll get it tomorrow."

Relief welled up in me. "What would I do without you?"

"Run out of DiGiorno pizzas?" she said with a grin. "Frankly, I'm just glad to see you out of the house and dressed in... Are these real clothes? Even if it was to execute an ill-planned heist."

I snorted.

"You just couldn't let it go, could you?" Her words were soft. She knew everything thanks to her supe heritage. Kiki was a satori, a mind-reading supe of Japanese descent. She looked human, but that brain of hers...it was anything but.

"You said you wouldn't get the report for me, so I had to find a way to get it myself."

She leaned back. "And you thought nearly killing some MASC security guy was the way to do it?"

"We're not all super-hackers," I shot back. "Some of us have to use the resources at our disposal." The pitiful, sorry excuse for resources.

"Was this guy with your dad when..." She trailed off. No need to finish the sentence. When he'd died.

"No, he's just some dude. He works out of Turtle Bay." If I'd had access to any of the security guys who'd been on my dad's protection detail, I wouldn't have rolled up with anti-venom, that was for damn sure. But most of them were out of country, working out of the offices in Turkey, where Dad had died.

Kiki pinched the bridge of her nose.

I felt a lecture coming on.

"Z, your dad wouldn't want this for you. He'd want you moving on with your life. I understand it was too hard to finish your last semester and study for your boards after he died, but...you put so much time and energy into becoming a doctor. Haven't you at least talked to Cornell about whether you could come back and graduate? This energy—you have to funnel it into something productive. It's what he would have wanted."

"I can't," I choked out. "I can't think of anything except him lying there, so...still. You knew Dad—he was tough as fucking nails. He was

Special Forces for a *decade*. And I'm supposed to believe he was in the wrong place at the wrong time? That some unstable building just happened to tumble over and land directly on his SUV? It's bullshit." I jammed the heels of my hands into my eyes, as if I could hold the tears in. "I've tried to let it go, but I just...can't."

Kiki was quiet for a long time while I cried.

"Okay," she finally said. "I'll do it."

I looked up, sniffling. "What?" The MASC report detailing Dad's death had been classified. I'd begged Kiki to get it for me, but she'd firmly refused.

She let out a long breath through her button nose, flaring her nostrils. "I said I wouldn't get you the report because I thought poring over it endlessly wouldn't help you. But maybe I was wrong. You clearly aren't letting it go. Maybe you need to see it. For closure."

"Yes," I whispered. "For closure." I was afraid to say anything else, for fear that she'd change her mind.

"Okay then." She tucked a lock of hair behind my ear. "Tomorrow we'll get your purse and the report."

A fresh wave of tears flooded over my cheeks. This time, tears of gratitude. I might have lost Dad, but I still had people who loved me. My Auntie. Kiki. Alviya. Why was it so hard to remember that sometimes?

Kiki stood, offering me her hands. "Let's go home."

3

———————

I slept fitfully and woke with a tight headache squeezing at my temples.

I dragged myself into the shower. Twice in two days—a new post-funeral record.

The shower's hot water ran over me until the snake in me cried out for cool. It was a sonofabitch to rely on external temperature regulation. Being a warm-blooded human would be so much easier.

I wrapped the towel around myself and stood on the cool tile. My reflection was blurry in the foggy mirror, but my scales were visible, glittering in the fluorescent bathroom light. I'd always been perched in the middle—not truly human, not truly supe. The only place I'd ever really fit had been with Dad. He'd had a way of filtering out the rest of the world; it hadn't mattered what anyone thought so long as he was proud of me. He'd always been a shelter to me. And now I was alone. Exposed.

"Zariya, you better slither your ass down here or your bagel is mine!" Alviya hollered up at me. She was remarkably peppy for a valkyrie, and I'd been avoiding her sunny presence since Dad had died. Two weeks in, she'd announced that she knew what I was doing and it would only make her try twice as hard to bring me back to the land of the living. She'd shown remarkable perseverance.

Today, for the first time, I found I didn't mind. Perhaps it was actually going outside yesterday, or maybe it was the prospect of finally getting the report... but I thought I'd be able to face her relentless enthusiasm.

I threw on a pair of old jeans and an oversized White Snake T-shirt—a gag gift from Alviya's boyfriend, Basirou, and headed downstairs, threading my thick dark curls into a braid.

A toasted bagel smeared in cream cheese and lox was poised between Alviya's perfect white teeth. Upon seeing me, she set it down on a plate and held it out to me. "You want?" After a year of rooming with her, I was used to Alviya's cavernous appetite. And her feathered wings—downy white as a snowy owl's, strong as an eagle's. The black caverns of her eyes, deep as the pit of Naraka... I wasn't sure I would ever truly get used to those. Even though I loved her like a sister, they were eerie as hell.

I eyed the bagel as a knock sounded on our door.

"That must be Bas. Come in!" she hollered.

The door opened to reveal a dark shadow filling the space. Wings, muscle, towering bulk. "I brought Starbucks!" Basirou stepped inside and flicked the door shut with his tail.

"You darling beast." Alviya retrieved the tray from him and gave him a ravishing kiss. Seeing the two of them side by side used to give me pause. Basirou was a seven-foot-tall gargoyle—ebony skin like dark marble, his wings membranous like a bat. Twisting horns protruded above an unfairly handsome face. Where he was dark, Alviya was fair, with her white wings, creamy pale skin, and bright copper hair. Where his muscles were roped like a Greek statue, she was as lean and long-legged as a ballet dancer. But they were actually good together. I supposed there had been stranger pairs.

"Chai latte for Zariya, Americano for you, some ridiculously sweet unicorn Frappuccino for Kiki that I nearly lost my man card ordering, and a flat white for me." Bas passed out his bounty, then cocked his head at me. He was always too discerning for his own good. "Good to see you up and around, Zar."

"Thanks." I took a sip of the latte, letting the warm liquid soothe me. He'd even gotten it with coconut milk, how I liked.

"What are you up to today?" Alviya asked me.

I shrugged, taking another sip. "The world is my unemployed oyster." A thought struck me. "Maybe I'll go see Dad."

Bas's dark brows knit together. "You sure that's a good idea?"

Kiki breezed into the kitchen, grabbing her Frappuccino off the counter. "Anything that gets my girl out of the house in real pants counts as a good idea."

"Har har."

Bas chuckled. "Suppose that's true."

"What about you guys? Anything wild and crazy at work today?" Alviya and Bas had met working at a PR company that focused on supe-run businesses and products.

Alviya hoisted her Americano in a faux salute. "You know us, saving the world one selkie sunscreen at a time."

I managed a smile.

"All right, we're out," Bas said with a little wave. "Have a good day."

Alviya and Bas angled themselves out the door, folding their wings to get through the opening. I loved them dearly, but those wings took up a lot of space. The apartment felt three times bigger with them gone.

Kiki turned to me. "I talked to the EMS guys. You can pick up your purse anytime after noon today."

"Thanks, Keeks," I said, waiting.

We looked at each other for a moment before she sighed. "I got the report."

My eyes fluttered closed. Finally.

When I opened them, she was gone, but she returned quickly with a manila envelope. I reached for it eagerly, but she tucked it behind her back. "Before I give this to you, you need to promise me something."

"Anything." I would promise her my firstborn in exchange for that report. Not that there'd ever be a firstborn, at the rate my life was turning into a dumpster fire.

"If you read this, and there's nothing there to find...you gotta let it go. Your dad was the most bad-ass supe I've ever known too, but even he was mortal. Accidents happen. Shitty things happen to good people. I need to know that you'll be objective about this. If there's nothing...just lay it to rest."

I pursed my lips together. I didn't want to let it go. I didn't want to believe a stray pile of bricks could take out my dad where terrorists and armed insurgents had failed.

But Kiki was right. I needed to read what was really there, not what I wished was. "I promise."

She handed it over and I cradled the envelope to my chest. "Thanks." I turned to go back up the stairs to get my shoes.

"You're not going to read it? After all of that?"

"I'm going to read it with Mom and Dad."

MY FATHER HAD BEEN full naga, born in the remote eastern corner of India, in Nagaland. I'd never been there. Auntie always told me it was a backwards and boring place, which was why she'd followed Dad when he'd left.

My mother had been human. A grad student accompanying her professor on an anthropological expedition. According to Auntie, the chemistry between my parents had been instant. According to Dad... well, he'd never spoken of Mom at all.

But there must have been some connection, because before they knew it, Mom was pregnant, and he'd accompanied her to America. Interspecies relationships weren't forbidden under the terms of the International Treaty on the Recognition and Protection of Supernatural Creatures (or just the Treaty, as we all called it), but they were frowned upon for all number of reasons. Religious intolerance, xenophobia... practicality. The human body wasn't designed to bear a naga child. As my parents well found out. Auntie said it was a miracle I'd survived. Mom wasn't so lucky.

Her gravestone had been here at Calvary Cemetery in Queens for as long as I could remember. Auntie would take me here on my birthday each year, which had felt like a morbid tradition, but she'd said it was important to honor Mom's sacrifice. As I'd grown older, I'd come to see there was a certain sweetness in that. Dad had never come with us; Auntie had said it was too hard for him.

Now, I wished I'd asked him why. Asked him about her. There were so many things I wished I'd asked him, but I'd been too chicken-shit. And now he was gone.

I stopped before two ebony headstones, hers weathered with age, his new and polished to a sheen. *Vizol Chanji*, it read. *Father. Warrior. Friend.* He was so much more than that, too, but everything my father was couldn't fit in this little space.

The flowers laid on his grave were shriveled and dry, and so I gathered them up, tossing them in a nearby trashcan. When I returned, I shoved my hands in my pockets. "Hi, Mom. Dad. I hope you guys are doing good. Getting reacquainted." My parents had only had a year together—I liked to imagine they were hanging out in the afterlife. Hopefully, they still had something in common. Me, at least.

I sat down, leaning my back against Dad's headstone. It was weird, thinking he was beneath me. Naga tradition dictated that a warrior be cremated after he or she died, but Dad's will had said he'd wanted to be buried beside my mom. I'd often wondered if his stony silence on the subject of Mom meant he'd forgotten her, but with that one action, I knew he hadn't.

I tilted my head back against the hard stone and closed my eyes. "I really fucked up since you left, Dad. It's just too hard..." The words tangled on my tongue. "It's too hard without you here. This isn't how it was supposed to be." He was supposed to be at my med school graduation, supposed to harp on me for working too much during residency, supposed to celebrate with me when I got that cardiac fellowship I'd been eyeing.

A choked laugh escaped me.

"The truth is, everything I did was to make you proud of me. To live up to your legacy. And now that you're gone, it just seems pointless."

Dad had always been larger than life. When he'd come to the U.S., even as an immigrant who hadn't spoken a lick of English, he'd charmed everyone. Nagas were warriors, and so he'd joined the Marines special supe division, rising up the ranks quickly. He'd been recruited for the Force Recon division, where he'd stood out even more, eventually leading his own team. He'd retired almost ten years ago to go work for MASC as a diplomat and consultant. Another distinguished career. Whatever Dad had touched had seemed to turn to gold. Except me, apparently.

I looked at the envelope. I didn't know why I was delaying after I'd been dying to get my hands on the report for the past six weeks.

I tore the envelope open.

I sped through the seven-page report once before turning back to the front page to read it again, slowly. I needed to take it apart piece by piece. Because there was something here that MASC leadership had missed. I knew it. There was something here that proved that Dad had been murdered. And it was up to me to find it.

4

———————

I pulled the report out and read it again on the subway. As if a fifth readthrough would magically help me find what I was looking for. According to the writeup, Dad had been visiting Syrian refugee camps on the Turkish border, checking on the treatment of supes and ensuring UN and MASC supplies were being appropriately distributed. He was traveling in an armored SUV with a Humvee military escort. The three-mile trip from town had been uneventful. The visit to the camp had been uneventful. But on the way back, just two blocks from his hotel, a condemned building three stories high had collapsed into the street. Directly onto my father's caravan. He'd been killed instantly.

MASC had conducted a full investigation. They hadn't uncovered any unusual activity, any sign of explosives or tampering. The building had been bombed in a terrorist attack the year prior and had become structurally unsound. Just an unfortunate accident. Wrong place, wrong time.

Bullshit.

I shoved the papers back in the envelope, drumming my fingers on the subway pole. They must have missed something. There must be *something* on the scene, something that no one found.

I was pondering the Turkish visa requirements when I remembered my promise to Kiki. *After you read this, if there's nothing to find there, you let it go...*

I let out an audible growl and the guy next to me scurried down the train car. *Damn it, Kiki.*

I let my forehead rest against my hand. She was right. I had what I'd been looking for—the truth about Dad's death. It just wasn't the truth I'd expected. Instead, it was proof that there was nothing to find. Maybe it *was* time to start picking up the broken pieces of what life I had left, rather than diving deeper down the rabbit hole of conspiracy theories and wild suspicion.

I didn't relish the conversation I'd need to have with the med school dean.

I MADE it back to the apartment a little before noon.

Kiki emerged from her room, which we called the "Keek-Cave," as it was piled high with computer monitors, external drives, and a million blinky lights I couldn't even begin to understand. "You okay?" she asked.

No. I nodded, though. "Sure."

"Nearly time for you to go get your purse. Want me to come with?"

I shook my head. I didn't think I could manage small talk, even with a best friend. I also really didn't feel like getting back on the subway. "Can I borrow your phone to call an Uber? I'll pay you back."

"Of course." She pulled her phone from her back pocket, handed it to me, and disappeared back into her cave.

I was halfway through calling my ride when a text popped up. I read it before I could help it. It was from a contact labeled as "K."

Vizol didn't want her involved.

The breath whooshed from my lungs. What the hell was this? Why was she talking about my dad with someone named K? I spun around so my back was to Kiki's doorway and quickly tapped the text to take me to the prior messages. I hastily remembered to raise my mental shields how Kiki had taught me, shielding my thoughts from her.

The text chain appeared on the screen. It was only four texts, all from the last few hours.

Kiki: I gave it to her.

K: Good.

Kiki: I feel bad. Doesn't she deserve the truth?

K: Vizol didn't want her involved.

My hands shaking, I quickly tapped on K's contact information and memorized the number. Then I closed out of the texts and called my Uber. I dropped Kiki's phone on her desk beside her. "All done. I'm going to wait downstairs."

She was already absorbed in her screens. "'K. Bye."

I hurried to the entryway table and wrote down the number on a slip of paper before I forgot it.

What the fuck was going on?

In the Uber I ran through the messages in my head, trying on different interpretations. Scenarios where Kiki hadn't just horribly betrayed me with some mystery person who'd known my dad. I kept coming back to one explanation. *"I gave it to her"* could only mean the report. *"Doesn't she deserve the truth?"* could only mean that the report Kiki had given me had been a fake. Or doctored somehow. Otherwise, she'd have been giving me the truth when she handed it over. And Vizol didn't want her involved... well, I didn't know what the hell that meant because Dad couldn't have been involved in the coverup of his own murder, could he have?

Adrenaline sang through my veins. I felt more alive and alert than I had in a long time.

Vindication tasted good.

I'd been right.

What I didn't know was what the hell I was going to do about it. Kiki wouldn't just admit that she'd lied and given me a fake report, right? I needed to find a way to catch her in her deception. Something more than the text messages.

The Uber driver, a young Ethiopian guy named Mehari, waited for me while I ran into the EMS station and retrieved my purse. I didn't get any particularly weird looks from the bored receptionist when she handed over my purse, which told me either she hadn't fished around in it, or she didn't know an illegal card duplicator when she saw one. Fine by me.

I pulled out the UN keycard with my face on it. I'd forgotten about it after Kiki had agreed to give me the report, but maybe it would come in handy after all. If I could get the real version of the report and prove that what Kiki had given me was fake, I'd have the evidence I needed to confront her and find out what had really happened to Dad.

Settled on a course of action, I relaxed back into the seat.

Until we got to the intersection just before my apartment, and I saw Kiki trotting down the stairs and into the back seat of a black car.

I surged forward between the front seats, pointing. "Follow that car!"

Mehari shot me an incredulous look. "This isn't a cab, lady. You have to book through the app."

I grumbled, fishing in my purse and pulling out some of Martin's cash. "I'll give you a hundred bucks if you follow that car. Off the record."

He blew out a sigh but took the money, sliding the car into gear. "You get half an hour, then you're out wherever we end up."

"I can live with that."

~

I wasn't sure what type of clandestine meetup I'd been expecting, but a trip to the park was not it. We followed Kiki's car across the Queensboro bridge, circled back around, and took the small Roosevelt Bridge onto Roosevelt Island, a long narrow strip of land between Long Island and Manhattan. At the very tip of the island was a triangular park called Franklin D. Roosevelt Four Freedoms State

Park (a mouthful, I know), which was where Kiki's car dropped her off.

Puzzled, and slightly irked that I'd just paid $100 bucks for a ten-minute ride, I hopped out and followed at a distance.

Kiki had never mentioned this park before. What was she doing here? Meeting someone? K, perhaps?

I'd never actually been to this park, either, despite living in New York most of my life. The tree-lined thoroughfare gave way to a stone monument at the tip of the island, and that was where Kiki was headed. I ogled the breathtaking skyline while trying to keep far enough back so she wouldn't see me.

Opening my glands wide, I took in her scent of coffee and coconut shampoo. It would be easier for me to track her at a distance this way.

I lingered behind the last tree before the open stone monument, as there was nowhere to hide from her if I continued. There were a few folks looking at the monument today, but they strolled back my way before too long. Kiki took a little set of steps leading down to the end of the island and stood there, looking out into the East River.

And then she disappeared.

I blinked twice. A third time. Flared my nostrils. But her smell was only a faint memory. She was gone.

What the fuck?

I jogged forward, no longer caring if she popped out from some-where and caught me. Where had she gone?

My steps stilled at the spot where she'd disappeared. Her scent was stronger—she'd definitely been here. And she was definitely not here now. I peered over the edge into the water. Had she jumped? Gone for a swim? That made no sense. Kiki didn't even like hot tubs.

There was definitely something fishy going on here. Something I didn't understand, and Kiki was in on it. I turned on my heel and walked back towards the trees, settling down on the ground, my back to a hard trunk.

I was looking for answers. And there were answers here to be found. I could feel it. So I would wait.

In the meantime, I couldn't help but gaze at the United Nations tower, glittering like a shining jewel in the afternoon sun. It was directly across the channel from here. Could that be a coincidence?

I used to love coming to visit Dad at work when I was younger. The whole city was like some alien world, and within it, the MASC offices felt like home. Filled with supes of all shapes and sizes, Auntie warned me not to stare half a dozen times before she simply gave up.

I could just make out the statue in the center of the courtyard from here. It depicted the moment that everything had changed. The Lupine Offensive. When a pack of French wolf shifters had saved an Allied battalion pinned down by enemy fire. The day the world had learned that supernatural creatures existed.

After World War Two, in those brief shining months when the world had resolved to find a better way and had still been naive to all the conflicts to come, the United Nations Charter had been signed, together with the Treaty, officially recognizing supes.

MASC had been created as a division of the UN, and over the next decades, supes had started feeling safe to come out of the shadows. Wanting recognition and the benefits it brought—employment, security, access to financing and resources. There were currently six hundred and twelve recognized races of supernatural creatures. And that number grew every year. It wasn't a perfect system, but it was still miraculous as fuck. I knew I was lucky to live in a time where I could walk through New York City without hiding what I was.

My thoughts were interrupted as a figure appeared at the end of the island—right where Kiki had disappeared.

But it wasn't Kiki.

It was a man.

I breathed in deeply. He smelled like the space between—night air and the nothingness of fresh snow. This man was like a black hole for my senses. No heat signature. There, but not there. I took pride in my tolerance of the diversity of all forms of supernatural life, but I couldn't help the thought that darted through my mind, bright as a comet. *Unnatural.*

This man was a vampire.

5

I pretended to be fiddling with my phone as he stalked past where I sat, his gait graceful as a jungle cat.

It took every ounce of effort not to examine him as he walked by, to keep my eyes fixed on my phone. His beauty was breathtaking—sandy-blond hair pulled back in a tight knot at the nape of his neck, sky-blue eyes framed by slanting blond brows, an aquiline nose, square jaw, and dimple in his chin—just a few of the gifts he was graced with. He was well over six feet tall and built of lean, roping muscle, and though he was dressed in dark jeans, a white collared shirt, and a charcoal sports jacket, my animal senses had no problem identifying him for what he was.

Dangerous. Predator. My snake sense withdrew, even as my human side was fascinated. Drawn like a moth to a flame. Vampires had that effect on people.

Could this be the person Kiki was texting? Did this man know my dad somehow? I shoved to my feet, watching him as he walked away.

Only one way to find out.

I pulled the scrap of paper with the phone number out of my pocket and ducked behind the trunk of the closest tree. I turned my call blocking on and tapped in the number, biting my lip as it rang.

As I watched him break his stride and pull a cell phone out of his pocket.

Holy shit.

"Hello?" His voice was a deep baritone. "Who is this?"

I wiped my sweaty palms on my jeans, first one, then the other. Damn, this was more nerve-racking than prank calling our history teacher in fourth grade. "I'm looking for Kiki."

Pause. "Wrong number." He had a hint of an accent. I couldn't place it. I needed to keep him talking. To find out something more about him. He was still moving in the distance, and I started to follow. I could track him on scent alone, or rather, lack of scent, but I wanted to keep him in sight.

"I have a job I need done."

"What kind of job?"

I was freewheeling into space here. But I figured this guy fell into one of two categories. Either he was government, like Dad had been, or he was a bad guy. I needed to know which. "I need...some intel from a high-level government target."

"Not exactly what we do."

"What is it you do then? I have a number of jobs I need completed, and I'm looking for...some special talent." I hardly recognized the bullshit coming out of my mouth, but I needed to get the guy talking. Anything. I needed a clue.

"We don't take third-party solicitation. Don't call this number again." The line went dead.

I frowned at my phone. His accent seemed European. German perhaps? Or Dutch?

Well, I hadn't learned much from the phone call, but I knew this was the right guy at least. Maybe he would lead me to my next clue.

I looked up and found him gone.

Damn it!

Shoving my phone in my back pocket, I trotted ahead, past a derelict stone building corralled behind a chain link fence. Where'd he gone?

I sniffed the air for his scent of starlight and black space. Emptiness, where the rest of the world was a tumble of smells. I smiled. *Gotcha.*

I jogged down the path after the mysterious Mr. K, my mind whirling to put the pieces together. I didn't have enough yet, that was about the only thing that was clear.

K was a vampire. He knew Kiki and my dad. He wasn't willing to access classified government data for me, which meant he could work for the government. Or he could just be a bad guy with a different skill set. I needed more—

A blur of golden darkness collided into me and my back hit the trunk of a tree hard enough to send a parade of stars dancing across my vision.

The vampire. He was attacking me!

Instinct kicked in and I spun and twisted out of his grip, thanking Dad for subjecting me to nearly two decades of mixed martial arts training. I ducked low and swiped my leg across the ground to knock him off his feet.

God, he was fast. He jumped and moved in close, grabbing one of my wrists.

But I was fast too. I flipped over him, freeing my wrist, and danced back, my pulse roaring in my ears.

The vampire was already coming at me again. He went for my wrists a second time, trying to restrain me. I darted back, but he was too fast.

His cold hand closed around my wrist like a shackle and when I went to spin—this time he was ready. He grabbed my other wrist and wrenched it up and over my head so both hands were pinned behind me, twisted at a painful angle. I kicked out at him but stumbled as he barreled me backwards against the truck of a tree, pinning me with his body—his powerful thighs pressing into and immobilizing my legs so I couldn't kick him.

I screamed with rage and struggled in his grip. No one had bested me like this in a long fucking time. Certainly not in twenty seconds flat.

"Who are you?" He growled, pulling my wrists tighter, straining my shoulders in their sockets. "Why are you following me?"

I bared my teeth at him, showing my fangs.

He did the same—revealing straight white teeth and two wickedly pointed incisors. "I won't ask you again."

Something about the sight of those two fangs brought me back to myself, clearing the red clouding my vision. Leaving something small and frightened. Mortal. *Of course this supe bested you—you've been fighting for eighteen years.* He could have been fighting for hundreds. Thousands. There was no telling how old he was.

The vampire's nostrils flared, and I could feel his hard body relax slightly against mine. "That's better."

I hated that he could smell my fear. Stupid human hormones.

I glared at him. With my draining anger, my awareness returned to my body. To my predicament. To the man pressed up against the length of me.

This close, he was even more breathtaking—surrounding me, gazing down at me with fury in his eyes. There was a ring of silver around his irises, surrounded by the blue of a glacier. His pale skin was as flawless as marble. His breath was cool on my cheek; his scent this close carried a hint of mint leaves and musky cologne.

My body responded in another way, my fear mingling with something new. An undeniable warmth deep inside me. Desire. Suddenly, I was glad he was pinning me to the tree because I wasn't sure my knees would hold.

No. No, no, no—

My cheeks heated as his nostrils flared again and I knew he could smell my desire. His chest heaved where it was pressed against mine and his eyes dropped, lingering on my lips.

"It's common," he murmured. "Human physiology interacts with vampire pheromones in a predictable way."

My mortification doused any semblance of sexy-feelings.

"But you're naga," he said. "Not human." Dear lord, his eyes were still on my mouth.

"Half-naga." My words were breathy.

His eyes flicked up at that and he recoiled slightly. Coming back to himself. "If I step away, can we talk? You won't run?"

I nodded and he dropped his iron grip on my wrists, taking a big step back.

I sagged against the tree. With the heat of the moment gone, everything hurt. Rolling my shoulders, I rubbed my wrists. I'd have a bruise where a knot of tree bark had jammed into my back.

"Who are you?" he asked again.

"I think you already know," I hazarded a guess. The way he'd reacted to the fact that I was half-naga, and the fact that he knew my father...

"Zariya Chanji."

"In the flesh." I gave a little fake bow with a twirl of my hand. "Your turn."

"The name's Bauer."

"Uh-uh." I made a little buzzer noise. "Try again."

He let out an exasperated sigh. "Konstantin Bauer."

"How did you know my father?"

"We worked together. In the past. I know it may be hard to believe when we met like this, but I cared about your father. He was a good man. His death grieved me."

I scrutinized Konstantin, trying to get a read on him. I could generally detect lying in humans, as my glands picked up their increased heart rates, their raised body temperature. But Konstantin was a black hole of cool, his body giving nothing away.

Yet his face did appear sincere. His annoyingly perfect face.

"What really happened in Turkey?" I asked. "How did he die? I know that report Kiki gave me is bogus."

"It's not bogus," he said. "I did edit out a few confidential details. You have to understand that much of the work your father did was classified. He wouldn't want you involved. Knowledge can be dangerous."

"I don't care! I know Dad's death wasn't an accident. Someone killed him, and I have the right to know who. I *have* to know who.

Don't you get it?" I hated the thickness in my voice. The tears that threatened to spill.

"I understand you're grieving—"

"You don't understand shit!" Oh god, the tears were coming now. My words wavered. "Nagas avenge our dead. It's my right. I won't be able to rest until I do. Dad won't be able to rest until I do."

His gaze hardened and certainty flooded me. This man knew something.

"Stop digging, Zariya. There's nothing to find."

I nodded, letting my shoulders slump. Pretending to be cowed.

He hesitated, and then stepped in, laid a gentle hand on my shoulder. "Be well, Zariya. Live your life. It's what Vizol would have wanted."

I tried to hide my shock as I caught sight of a mark on his palm— a mark I recognized. A brand that had graced my own father's hand. A circle, sliced diagonally by what appeared to be a cross.

This vampire had a matching one.

I stood silently as he walked away, disappearing around the bend.

And then I smiled. I'd gotten what I needed, and more besides.

Someone *had* killed my father. And this vampire knew who. Maybe he was protecting the killer, or maybe he wanted his own revenge, but either way, I'd find out whom the murderer was if it was the last thing I did.

6

———

Konstantin strode along the tree-lined path towards the other end of the park, where a wrought-iron fence separated it from the asphalt streets of Roosevelt Island. The base—"Tartarus," they called it—after one of the realms of the Greek underworld—sprawled beneath much of the island, five levels down at its deepest. You could access Tartarus through an emergency entrance near the UN building on the Manhattan side of the river, but the area was more heavily populated, so they were all commanded to use the island entrances unless absolutely necessary. It never ceased to amaze him that millions of New Yorkers could go about their lives ignorant of the secret military base right beneath their feet. But he supposed the set of highly-advanced magical safeguards protecting Tartarus from discovery had something to do with that.

Konstantin had been on the clock for over forty-eight hours, burning through intel to track down a group of supe-poaching assholes who called themselves "the Collectors." He'd been looking forward to heading home to enjoy the wagyu beef steak he had marinating, together with a glass of full-bodied red wine.

Zariya Chanji had thrown a wrench in those plans.

Vizol had spoken of his daughter often and with pride. Konstantin had heard about her growing up, winning Krav Maga competitions against kids twice her age. He'd bragged when she'd gone to Columbia, pre-med, and when she'd gotten into Cornell's medical school, which had one of the nation's leading supe medicine programs.

In his mind, Zariya had still been the gangly kid smiling out of the photos on Vizol's desk.

He hadn't been prepared for the reality of her in the flesh.

She was tall and lithe, with all the sinuous curves of her naga heritage. Her glossy black hair pulled into a thick braid, her smooth caramel skin unmarred but for two streaks of golden scales running up her neck to her temples. She was the picture of an Indian beauty—full lips, delicate cheekbones, thick black eyelashes framing arresting green eyes. Slitted, snake eyes. She'd moved with the same kind of sinuous grace Vizol had, though her moves were perhaps a bit rusty.

She'd been fierce and beautiful, and clearly falling apart over her father.

In his six hundred years, he'd lost more people than he could count. He'd seen war and hardship and the worst of human cruelty. He'd developed a thick skin—he'd had to. So he hadn't been prepared for just how much Zariya's furious grief would move him.

Konstantin stepped into the doorway of the vacant building, flashing his ring at the scanner. The portal's magic picked up the signature of his ring and whisked him down into the elevator bay. He pressed the button for the third floor.

The doors opened to reveal a utilitarian gray hallway. The base had been costly enough to build, so there hadn't been a lot left over in the budget to fancy it up.

He strode down the hallway, hanging a left into the Operations Center, a broad room filled with monitors and computers. Kiki, their technical wizard and resident hacker, was working at one bank of monitors, her noise-canceling headphones shutting out the world. Konstantin knew those headphones dulled more than noise; they were magicked to quiet the mental projections of those in the base, letting Kiki work without having to keep firm mental walls up at all times.

Konstantin tapped her on the shoulder, and she turned, pulling them down around her neck. "Thought you were heading home."

"I came back after I had an unexpected meeting in the park." Konstantin let down his own mental shields, letting Kiki see what had happened.

Her dark eyes went wide and she clapped a hand over her mouth. "Ohmygod, Konstantin, I'm so sorry. How..." She trailed off. "She had my phone. To call an Uber. It must have been when you texted... Damn it!" She slouched on the desk for a moment, her head in her hands.

Konstantin waited.

Kiki pushed herself back up. "What are you going to do? Maybe we should just tell her. This whole thing has me feeling like shit."

"You know the rules," Konstantin said, though he saw her point.

"Rules are made to be broken." Kiki waggled her pierced eyebrows. "Maybe she could help us with the investigation. Help us see something we haven't. She knew Vizol better than anyone."

Konstantin shook his head. "We need to respect her father's wishes. He didn't want her to know about this place. What we do here. I'm sure that would extend to investigating his own murder."

"But that was back when she was all happy and going to be a doctor. Now she's washed out and miserable and...I think she needs this, K."

"No daughter needs to know that her father was lying to her for half her life. I doubt that would help the grieving process," he said. Kiki started to open her mouth to object and he held up a hand. "Besides. It's not my call. The Director has to decide whether anyone's brought into the fold. I'm going to talk to him now. I'll let you know what he decides. Just wanted to give you a heads-up in case Zariya contacts you."

Kiki pouted. "Roger that, boss."

Konstantin headed down the hallway towards the Director's office. He passed a set of wide windows that looked into the gym and sparring room. The valkyrie Alviya was sparring with Strongroot, a sequoia dryad and her team leader. He towered over her, but she was fiercely maneuverable and darted around him like a hornet.

Konstantin frowned. He knew Alviya lived with Kiki and Zariya—marking yet another person in Zariya's life who was lying to her. He wasn't so sure that Kiki was right. Instead of giving the woman something to live for, revealing the truth of their operation to her might just be the thing that would break her.

Konstantin knocked on the thick door at the end of the hallway.

"Come in," came the muffled reply.

Konstantin found Cyriaque Broussard sitting behind his desk, a pair of reading glasses perched on his nose. He looked out of place, his slacks and blue button-down incongruous against his thick beard and wild shock of dark curls. Like he'd been domesticated.

"Konstantin," the werewolf said, motioning to the chair in front of his desk. "Thought you headed home."

"Was going to. But we've got a bit of a problem." Konstantin quickly brought Director Broussard up to speed.

Broussard took off his glasses and pinched the bridge of his nose. "That girl always was too inquisitive for her own good. I remember at one of her birthday parties—maybe she was nine? She rifled around her aunt's purse and swiped a scrying crystal so she could see through the wrapping of all her presents." He chuckled. "Vizol could barely keep a straight face while he was scolding her."

Konstantin sank into the chair. "I guess I didn't realize you were so close with the family."

"Well, Vizol didn't like to talk about it, make anyone else feel uncomfortable or like I got special treatment. But I think I was one of the first friendly faces he met when he moved to the States. I convinced him to join the Marines."

Konstantin nodded woodenly. Yet another person in Zariya's life whom wasn't who she thought he was.

"I wish he were still here. Then he'd be sitting behind this desk instead of me. If I'd known how much goddamn paperwork came with this job..." He growled. "Don't let them put you behind this desk someday when I'm gone."

"You've only had the job for six weeks. You're going to be sitting in that chair for a good long while, sir," Konstantin said. "Now, what would you like to do about Zariya? I've spoken to Kimiko, and she expressed an interest in bringing Zariya in. She had the interesting thought that she might be able to help us with our investigation—"

"That's a non-starter, Konstantin," Broussard said. "You know that."

He sighed. "Wasn't sure it was a good idea myself. I just thought it was worth mentioning."

"We've got better resources than every government in the world put together. We'll find the bastards who took down Vizol."

"Yes, sir."

"But Zariya is bound to keep digging. If she's anything like her father—and she is—she'll be a dog with a bone. We have to wipe the slate clean."

He frowned. "Wipe the—wipe her memory? But that can be dangerous—"

"Verte's been working on a way to make it more targeted. It won't take more than a few days of her memory. She'll be fine."

"I don't like it."

"Neither do I. I'm telling you, it's shit sitting behind this desk. But it's what needs to be done."

Konstantin ran his tongue over the tips of his fangs. It didn't sit well with him, but Broussard was right. "Fine. I'll get the potion from Verte. I'll administer it myself."

Broussard waved a hand. "Don't Alviya and Kimiko live with her? Have one of them do it. It'll be easy for them to slip the potion to her."

"Don't you think that's a little...personal? Asking them to wipe their friend's memory?"

"No one ever said this job was easy, Bauer. They can draw straws, but one of those two is dosing Zariya Chanji, and it happens tonight."

Konstantin stood. "Consider it done."

"Close the door on the way out," Broussard said, and Konstantin obliged, thinking all the while that Cyriaque Broussard was turning out to be a very different director than Vizol Chanji had been.

7

———

I sank to the ground under the tree where Konstantin had left me. I decided to stay here until I was sure my wobbly legs would cooperate.

A maelstrom of emotions threatened to overwhelm me. Anger. Fear. Desire. Resolve. They warred within me, leaving me sucking in deep breaths to ground myself. As overwhelming as it all was, after six weeks of nothing but numbness, it felt good to feel alive again.

My phone rang. I startled and let out a little squeal of surprise before pulling it from my back pocket.

It was my Aunt Temsula, Dad's sister. She'd called me every day since Dad had died, though I had gone for weeks without picking up. Finally, she'd stormed into the apartment for an intervention when it had gone on too long—bringing incense to dispel the bad spirits and homemade lamb curry to fill my belly. I'd started taking her calls after that.

"Hi, Auntie," I answered.

"Hello, my little curlicue," she replied, using the pet name she'd used since I'd been a girl. Snake joke. "You sound good today."

"I'm out," I admitted.

"Praise Manasa," Auntie trilled into the phone. "Tell me about your day."

Not likely. I cleared my throat, leaning my head back against the tree. "I ran some errands. Went to the park with Kiki." That was sort of true, right?

"Oh, Zariya, I am so pleased. I know you grieve, but it is a beautiful world. Life has so much in store for you." Auntie hadn't really raised me, but close enough. Every time Dad had been traveling for work, which was a lot, I'd stay with her. She believed that over-mothering and over-dramatics were her auntie birthright.

I swallowed. Auntie's unbridled optimism always made me want to cry. Sometimes I wished I could see the world the way she did. "Do you remember that mark on Dad's hand? The brand?"

She was quiet for a moment. "Yes. Why do you ask?"

"Tell me again how he got it?" I wanted to hear her version, to see if it matched my own memory. I remembered being cuddled up next to Dad on the couch while he'd read to me from *Grimm's Fairy Tales*. He'd always read the gruesome, old-timey versions of the stories, not the pretty, glossed-over Disney versions. My cheek was pressed against his bare chest, and I'd kept asking about his scars. Those were the stories I wanted to hear—our stories—not some stories from a world I barely recognized.

"Our clan consisted of renowned warriors around the continent," he'd said. "But before we were allowed to become full warriors, we were required to perform a feat of great bravery. To prove our worthiness. I was young and foolish and was determined to perform the most memorable feat in the history of our clan. There was a rumor of a dragon deep in the mountains, who protected the burial site of the great Naga King Vasuki. The tomb was supposedly filled with treasure. I knew if I brought back a piece of that treasure and bested the dragon that my name would go down in history. I found the tomb, but it fought me, even before I found the dragon. It was rigged with booby traps and terrible magics."

"Like Indiana Jones," I'd said. Those were some of my favorite movies.

"Exactly. But I found my way to the center—the tomb of the ancient king himself. But the dragon was not just a legend. He was there, in the flesh, and he was strong. I was in over my head, and before long, eager flames licked up around me, and I knew I needed to slay the beast if I had any hope of escaping with my life. So I seized a sword from the great king's treasure trove and plunged it into the creature's chest."

"But the sword was burning hot from the fire, and a symbol from the scabbard branded you," I'd finished for him. It wasn't the first time I'd heard the story.

"Exactly. I wear this brand with honor. It reminds me of that brave beast, which laid down its life guarding that which it had been charged to protect."

"A bunch of stuff?" I'd wrinkled my nose. "Did you at least keep the sword?"

"As the dragon fell, the temple began to collapse. I knew that I had meddled with something great, something beyond my under-standing. I left the sword, taking only my brand as proof of my worthiness. Some things are best left undiscovered, hatchling. Some magics are too much for the world."

Auntie's answer interrupted my memory. "He got it battling that dragon."

"Do you remember when he went for his quest?"

Another pause. "Yes, but I don't see why this—"

"And he said he lost the sword, right? That it was destroyed."

"Yes. He brought nothing back but that mark on his hand. Why do you ask?"

I chewed my lip. "No reason. I was just thinking about Dad's stories. Wondering how many of them were really true."

"They were all true, my darling. Your father was a great warrior. And a great naga."

"Thanks," I said. "I need to go, Auntie. Talk to you tomorrow?"

"Tomorrow, curlicue. I love you. And eat something!"

I rolled my eyes. "Love you too."

I hung up the phone and stared at it.

It didn't add up. The story—the identical brand on Konstantin's palm. How could a European vampire have been branded by a lost sword deep in the Indian jungle? I couldn't escape the unwelcome conclusion. Either Dad had been lying to me, or Auntie was.

I didn't know which was worse.

I WALKED off Roosevelt Island to dispel my nervous energy, but it still pinged about my veins like fireflies in a bottle. I wasn't ready to go home yet, to face Kiki when she returned.

Would Konstantin tell her I'd followed him? Would she say something? Or would she say nothing at all, pretending like there wasn't a huge fat lie between us?

An hour later, I found myself at the sparring gym, a large brick building where Dad and I had spent many nights. Even though I hadn't grown up among our clan, Dad had said all nagas were warriors and needed to learn to fight.

I'd loved those times when it had been just the two of us, Dad gently correcting my footing or the angles of my strikes. Even when he'd worked me until I'd wanted to vomit, I'd relished every minute with him. Here, I'd never felt like I was trapped between worlds. Here, we were nagas.

"Chanji!" the owner, Sal, a shaggy-haired cougar shifter, jogged over and wrapped me in a hug.

He rocked me back and forth, and I let myself relax against his muscled form. Sal had been like an uncle to me, overseeing my training when Dad had been traveling or working. "We've missed you around here, Cobra Kai." Another nickname. Another snake joke.

I pulled back, hastily wiping a tear that had gathered on my lashes. "I just...I haven't been getting out much."

He wrapped an arm around me and walked me towards one of the sparring rings. "Moving the body is good for the soul, Zariya. Emotions get stored in the body—stagnate there. I think coming back here more regularly could help, in its own small way."

Everyone had their advice, and I found most of it unwelcome. But Sal's carried a simplicity that resonated with me.

He continued. "But what do I know? I'm just a shaggy old cat a bit too long in the tooth."

"Hardly." I smiled wistfully. Sal was still muscled like a young Arnold Schwarzenegger, with neat sandy hair and a trim beard. "You're probably right. Sleeping my life away certainly hasn't helped much."

"What do you want to work on today?" he asked, all business. I appreciated that about Sal. Here, it was simple.

"Actually, I came across a vamp today who pulled some moves on me I couldn't get out of."

Sal's gold eyes flashed, and I could swear I could see his hackles rising. "What are you crossing vamps for?"

"It was a…misunderstanding. But do you think you could work with me on finding a way around his moves?"

Sal grinned, stepping into the ring. "With pleasure, Cobra Kai."

8

———

My mind was clearer than it had been in a long while when I headed home from the gym. I'd forgotten how good a hard workout felt—how it turned off my thoughts and filled me with endorphins. Sal had made me promise I'd return later that week, and I'd been happy to agree. I felt more like myself than I had since Dad had died.

I stopped at my favorite bodega for some falafel as I strolled home. I actually liked to cook—Auntie was a miracle worker in the kitchen and I'd always worked as her sous chef when Dad had been traveling. But our fridge was currently an empty black hole and my stomach was demanding something quick.

I sat at one of the little rickety tables on the street, pondering how the hell I would get into Kiki and Konstantin's hidden lair. I still didn't understand the connection between them or how they appeared and disappeared in the middle of a city park, but magic was obviously involved.

I closed my eyes for a moment at the thought of Konstantin Bauer, my mouth going dry, and not just from the falafel. I hadn't dated much in college, too focused on school and my studies, and med school had been even worse. There had been a fling or two, and a few ill-advised one-night stands, but the pickings had always been slim, as humans were off-limits. I hadn't been prepared for how my body had responded to his nearness.

Vampires had always been the celebrities of the supe world, and there were vampire groupies that got off on drawing a vamp's eye. It certainly didn't hurt that a few drops of vampire blood were all it took to turn a human into a glassy-eyed thrall who would do whatever the vamp told them. That was why the substance was strictly, aggressively banned.

But I'd never considered myself into vampires. If anything, I'd avoided them. They were ancient, dangerous, arrogant, unpredictable. Though somehow, when applied to Konstantin Bauer, all of those adjectives became downright delectable.

I shook my head, realizing I'd drifted into a dreamy fog, my fingertips lingering on my lips. "Cool it, Zariya," I muttered to myself, devouring another bite of falafel. He was the enemy. I didn't care if he'd known my dad and knew Kiki now. He was resolved to keep information from me that I needed. That made him my adversary.

I finished my pita and headed back towards the apartment. I wasn't sure what to do about Kiki. How I'd go about finding the key to whatever mysterious other realm Kiki had disappeared into. Maybe my glands would be able to smell something that would clue me in to the key.

But I wasn't prepared for what I found when I got home.

Alviya and Bas were posted up on the couch, watching Netflix and munching on a bowl full of popcorn.

"Hey, Zar." Alviya perked up as I came through the door. "Where've you been today?"

When a person doesn't leave their room for six weeks, I supposed that any trip out of the house was cause for celebration.

I sank onto the couch on Alviya's other side. "Went for a walk, then I went to the dojo and sparred with Sal for a while."

"That's great!" Bas said, baring his straight white teeth in a grin. "We should all work out together some time."

"That would be fun," I said halfheartedly, knowing that Alviya and Bas were in way better shape than I was.

"Popcorn?" Alviya offered me the bowl.

And I froze.

My glands flared.

I recognized the smell coming off Alviya. It was faint but undeniable. Starlight and empty space. Ice and deep water and stagnant snow. The smell of Konstantin Bauer.

I took a handful of popcorn to cover my shock. Alviya knew Konstantin. Or had at least met him. Encountered him. "How was work today?" I managed.

Alviya shrugged. "Business as usual. Office stuff. Boring."

"You meet any new clients, or have meetings out of the office?" Inwardly, I cringed at my inelegant questions.

"Naw." Alviya didn't seem to notice. "Just chained to my desk, as per usual."

I nodded, piling popcorn into my mouth. I had no idea how to fit this new piece into the puzzle. I was getting closer to something—but what—I had no idea.

Alviya, Bas, and I powered through two episodes of *Fixer Upper* before I headed off to bed. Kiki still wasn't home, which was okay by me. I needed to make my move quickly and try to find the real version of the report. I could keep my mental shields up for a while, but I wasn't great about mental discipline. If I let it go more than a few days without talking to her, she'd probably pick up my thoughts without even trying.

I had to confront her. It was the only way to get to the bottom of things. Kiki and I had been friends for too long to leave such a huge gulf between us. Besides, judging by the text to Konstantin, she'd felt bad about giving me a report that didn't have all the details. Maybe I could guilt her into telling me the truth.

After I made my mind up about how I'd handle Kiki, I finally fell into a deep sleep.

I woke to a prickle in my awareness.

Someone was in my room.

Moving only infinitesimally, I opened my glands. Not only did naga glands grant us an incredible sense of smell, but they worked as infrared sensors. I could smell the heat in the room, conceptualize the size, dimensions. It was a small body—familiar. Kiki.

What was she doing?

Curious, I kept my breathing still and deep. My eyes closed.

She crept closer, and I felt as she stood over me. Watching me.

Her heartrate was elevating, her heat increasing.

Something was wrong.

"I'm so sorry," she whispered.

I caught her hand before she struck and rolled her onto the bed, pinning her.

She didn't struggle against me, even when I caught sight of the syringe in her hand.

"What the hell are you doing, Kiki?"

She started to cry.

I plucked the syringe from her fingers and sat up slightly so I wasn't holding her down. "What is this?"

She curled into a ball. "I'm so sorry, Zariya. It's to make you forget. It wouldn't hurt you. The place I work, it's top secret. They know you'd just keep digging."

"Konstantin," I said. "The vamp. Do you work for him?" I looked at the syringe in disbelief. He'd actually erase my memory? So I forgot our conversation, forgot how close I was getting to finding the truth about Dad's death? Anger flared to life in me, bright and hot.

"Not him, not exactly. I can't—I can't say," Kiki said.

"We've been friends for over ten years, Kiki, and you've been lying to me this whole time?"

"Not the whole time, Zariya, I swear. I never lied about the stuff that mattered."

"Like who killed Dad?" I scoffed. "I'm going to find out. You can't stop me."

Kiki's eyes flashed and she sat up. She snatched for the syringe, but I was too fast and moved it out of her range.

Her mind flashed out, her thoughts barreling through my pitiful defenses. She was inside my mind, raining her will down upon me like a hailstorm. Kiki wasn't much of a physical fighter, but with her mind—she was deadly.

But I was ready. I lunged and stabbed her in the thigh with the syringe, emptying the vial with one quick shove of my thumb.

Her mental barrage stilled in shock.

"How do I get into the facility?" I asked her. I didn't have her satori gifts, but her mind was inside mine, her thoughts frozen in surprise. It was enough. A mental image flashed by and I caught it. She made an involuntary fist, curling her hand into her stomach.

Bingo. Kiki's ring was my ticket through the portal in the park.

She slumped back against the bed as the memory potion in the syringe went to work. I pulled a silver ring etched with a pattern of bamboo leaves from her middle finger and slipped it onto my own.

I stood, staring at her passed-out body slumped on my bed. A flurry of mixed emotions buffeted me.

"I'm so sorry too, Kiki," I said softly. I *was* sorry it had come to this. That she had pushed us to this. But I wasn't sorry for taking her ring. Because it was time to get the answers I deserved.

My guilt over leaving Kiki passed out in my bed, next to an empty syringe, was short-lived. *She was going to use it on me first!* Still, I prayed there weren't any negative side effects. If this ring didn't get my answers, Kiki was my best hope of figuring out what the hell was actually going on.

The ride to Roosevelt Island felt endless. When the Uber driver dropped me off at the entrance to the park, I practically launched myself from the car, jogging towards the island's apex. The city skyline was breathtaking from here—noble towers shimmering with endless lights.

I'd dressed in black jeans, an old gray tee, and my green army-style jacket. I'd threaded the sheath for the knife Dad had given me for my sixteenth birthday through my belt, but I really, really hoped I didn't need to use it. My muscles were already sore from my workout with Sal, and if my run-in with Konstantin had shown me anything, it was that these guys were good—whoever they might be.

The park was deserted except for a couple nestled under a tree, far too wrapped up in each other to notice me. My steps slowed when I neared the point where Kiki had disappeared. Would I know how to summon the magic that had whisked her away? Suddenly, I wished

I'd asked her more or had tried to rifle around in her thoughts when they'd been exposed to me. Maybe there was a magic password that I was missing and I'd just stand here in the cold, like an idiot.

I stepped forward. "Come on, come on—"

My stomach dropped out from under me as the world spun, shifting into something new.

"Yes!" I exclaimed with a pump of my fist. No magic password or spell. Then I flinched, realizing that my voice was now echoing throughout an enclosed space.

I looked around. I was alone in a gray concrete alcove, surrounded by walls on three sides. And before me, an elevator door.

"Looks like I'm going down," I whispered, pressing the button.

The door opened and I stepped in, turning to examine my options. Buttons for floors one through five stared mutely at me. I bit my lip. Which floor had the answers I sought? And more importantly, which floor opened to a nice empty hallway, rather than a mess hall full of soldiers?

I opened my glands and quested below me, seeing if I could sense bodies. There was nothing but cold stone and rock. Either there was no one home, or whatever materials they'd used to build this place blocked my naga senses. I suspected the latter.

On instinct, I pressed the button for the fifth floor. Might as well go all the way.

My heart seemed to race down before I did as the elevator started to move. Had my dad ever ridden in this elevator? Konstantin had clearly known my father, but in what capacity?

The elevator stopped moving and my hand gravitated to the knife at my hip. Not that it would be much use against automatic weapons.

The doors opened to an empty hallway and I nearly sagged with relief. A shaky laugh escaped me. I prayed my luck would hold.

Now that I was down in the bowels of the place, my glands could sense all the spaces of this floor. There were two people on floor five —in rooms lining the hallway. I'd skip those in my investigation.

I started forward, unsure what the hell I was looking for. Anything. Answers. I poked my head through a doorway and found a quiet room lined with filing cabinets. I perked up. Files were good. Files had answers.

The cabinets were arranged alphabetically, and so I opened up the drawer containing the C files. Chanji seemed a good place to start.

I thumbed through the files and my breath caught. There he was. Vizol Chanji. I pulled the file from the drawer and scanned it, my slitted pupils helping me in the low light. *MASC Veil Force Personnel File*, the title read. In the upper left-hand corner was a symbol—a circle bisected by a diagonal cross. A symbol I recognized as the one that had marked both my dad's palm and Konstantin's. It couldn't be a coincidence. "Veil Force?" I puzzled out loud. "What the hell is that?" My father had worked for MASC, the Mythical Alliance of Supernatural Creatures, as a diplomat. How could he work for this— Veil Force—also?

But it was undeniably my dad's much younger face gazing out of the photo. His roles were listed below.

2001-2011-Hydra Team Commander

2011-2020-Director

I sat my ass down in a chair before my knees gave out. According to this file, Dad hadn't just been involved in this organization, he'd been the fucking head of it. Not to mention he'd been involved in it for nearly my entire life—meaning he'd been lying to me for basically as long as I could talk.

A tear trickled down my cheek. It had always been me and him. I'd thought we'd told each other everything. How could he have kept something like this from me? Why?

My glands sensed movement in the hallway and I froze. Someone was coming. Maybe they'd just pass by this room, headed farther down the hallway. *Come on, come on—*

The light flicked on.

Shit.

I don't think he saw me right away. The incredibly handsome man in a white doctor's lab coat. He had strawberry blond hair, exotic golden eyes tilted up at the corner, and bronze skin that seemed out of place beneath the sad fluorescent lights flicking to life above us. He was tall and well-built and formed far too perfect a picture to be human. This man was a supe.

He blinked when he saw me and halted mid-step, a file in his hand.

It was the only opening I'd get.

I bolted from the chair and barreled past him into the hallway.

"Hey!" he shouted after me.

But I was already booking it towards the elevator, moving at a breakneck pace.

"Lock down the elevator," he said to whoever was at the other end of his comm. "We've got an intruder on the fifth floor." He had an Australian accent, I noticed, as I slammed into the open elevator and jammed the button for the ground floor. Maybe I'd get lucky and start moving before they managed to lock it down.

The button lit up and the doors started to close. I grinned victoriously.

Then the doors stopped.

My luck had run out.

"Stay there." He advanced on me, arms out in front of him. Why, so he could jab a needle in my neck like Kiki had planned to? Fuck that.

I darted out of the elevator and ran straight towards him with a naga war cry, my fangs bared.

I didn't know what my plan was. I had no plan. Knock him over and barricade myself in one of the file rooms before going down in a blaze of glory?

I was stuck inside a secret base and there was no way they'd let me out voluntarily. But at least I could go down fighting.

The air seemed to shimmer and shift around the doctor. I gasped as every hair on my skin raised. It was the feeling in the air right before a lightning strike. Or right before a shifter changed form.

Hot Aussie doctor was a shifter.

I zigzagged against the wall, trying to make space for whatever was about to manifest in this hallway.

And boy was I glad I did.

Magic exploded around me as he finished shifting. And then the hallway was filled with legs and talons and a sleek sinuous body covered in golden scales.

Holy fuck. A dragon shifter. He was a fucking dragon.

His roar rent the air and I clapped my hands over my ears, staggering to one knee. My fingers came away bloody as I scrambled to my feet and hurtled myself down the hallway, towards any sort of protection from the dragon.

He was big—too big to maneuver in the hallway, and I looked over my shoulder to see him struggling to turn around—his massive body smashing against the walls, cracking the concrete.

I wrenched open an iron door at the end of the hallway, slamming it shut behind me.

I looked about in a mad panic for anything I could use to defend myself. The knife on my belt was nothing more than a toothpick to a dragon. The room was some sort of treasure room—with art in glass cases on two walls, the other two covered with glass cabinets bearing ancient-looking antiquities. Weapons.

A sword. Prominently placed in one cabinet on the far wall was an ornate sword. That might be enough.

I yanked at the cabinet door, but it was locked. I smashed it with my elbow—once, twice.

The room's iron door exploded inward and I was thrown against the cabinet, my hands scrabbling against the broken glass.

The dragon shoved its head through the door and screamed, baring glistening white fangs as long as my forearm.

Pain exploded in my ears and my heart seized with fear, my limbs freezing, my mind numb. It didn't matter that the dragon was too big to get in the door. Dragons breathed fire. One shot and I was toast. Charred toast.

The sword.

My naga instincts screamed at me, singing life into my veins and overpowering the paralysis of my human fear. I wouldn't go down without a fight. I would show this pretender the true might of the serpent.

I reached into the case and seized the sword's scabbard, pulling it from its hooks.

And then the sword in my hand started to burn.

10

———————

I screamed as pain ripped through my hand and up my arm. The sword was magicked somehow—it must have been a protective enchantment. The sword clattered to the floor as I cradled my injured hand against me. I looked down at the burn and gasped.

The same symbol was burned into my palm as had been branded into my father's. And Konstantin's. I looked at the sword with new realization dawning. Somehow, this blade was the same sword from my father's story. He'd always said he'd left it in the dragon's lair. Another lie.

An explosion across the room startled me back to where I was. The dragon had broken through the wall, busting the concrete around the door frame to create a hole large enough for his body to get through. He advanced on me now, his fangs bared, his golden eyes ablaze with fury.

The fight drained out of me. I was trapped. This creature could snap me in one bite. Even if I somehow got past him, I would never get up the elevator and get free. Was Dad's secret worth dying for?

I held up my hands, the burn throbbing on one palm. "I surrender."

The dragon hissed at me, and then its eyes went wide. Its head snaked close, examining the burn, sniffing at me with huge nostrils. I knew he was intelligent, that there was a man in there, but still my stomach quaked with fear at his nearness.

The clamor of boots reached my ears and I turned to the gaping doorway just in time for Konstantin to appear, half a dozen armed men behind him.

"You." His weapon was trained on me. The dragon's body was still between us, but it vanished in an instant as the shifter returned to human form.

"She's surrendered," the shifter said as Konstantin approached in one fluid movement, the muzzle of his gun still fixed upon me.

And then he shot me.

The Chanji girl crumpled to the ground before him.

"God damn it, Konstantin! She surrendered." Oliver knelt down to feel her pulse. "You didn't need to shoot her."

"Quit your bitching. It was a tranq dart," Konstantin bit back. "I didn't need her making a last desperate try for freedom. You could've brought the whole fucking base down. Look at this place." Konstantin surveyed the lower level in dismay. The entire length of the hallway would need reinforcing, the framing and drywall into the Antiquities locker would need replacing—Broussard would be pissed as hell. While they had fairly generous funding thanks to some creative earmarking in the MASC budget, they all preferred using those funds on cutting edge technologies and research, rather than cleaning up their base. "What were you thinking?" he hissed at the doctor. "And will you put on some pants?"

Oliver straightened, standing proudly as naked as the day he'd been born. "I was thinking we had an intruder in our most sensitive level and I needed to do anything necessary to stop her."

"And you needed to shift to do that? You couldn't have used some of that Special Forces training?"

"She's a supe! A naga!" Oliver protested.

"She's only half-naga."

Broussard stepped into the room behind them, his thick arms crossed before him. If he was put out by the destruction, he wasn't showing it. "She's the daughter of Vizol Chanji and not to be underestimated. Get her to the medical bay and I want her restrained when she wakes. Oliver, put some fucking pants on. Bauer, with me."

"It marked her," Oliver called as Broussard turned to go.

"What?" The Director paused.

"*Caledfwlch*. The sword. She picked it up to defend herself and it marked her. She's been chosen."

Broussard nodded stiffly. "We'll deal with it."

Konstantin bit back a curse. This was a bigger clusterfuck than Gallipoli.

Konstantin fell into step next to the Director, who asked, "How did this happen? I thought we were settled in our course of action."

"We were." Konstantin ground his teeth. "Kimiko went home with the memory serum. I can only assume something went wrong there."

"Have we spoken to Nakamura?"

"You know as much as I do."

Broussard stormed into his office, bracing himself against the shelves. When he turned, his eyes were flashing, his fangs lengthened.

Konstantin held his ground. Vampires and werewolves had been historic enemies, but Konstantin had fought alongside many shifters in his day, especially the Rougarou—the Cajun wolves like Broussard. He respected the man and the position of leadership he was in, but Konstantin was an equal in power and skill. He wouldn't be intimidated.

Broussard sank into his chair, his head in his hands. "Vizol wouldn't have let something like this happen."

"We don't know that."

"Tartarus has never been breached."

Konstantin leaned down, his hands braced on the back of one of the chairs opposite Broussard. "With due respect, sir, I'm less concerned for how it happened and more worried about where we go from here.

That seemed to shake the Director back to himself. "Fair point. Send a Phantom to find out what happened to Kimiko. Let's get Alviya here too; they're friends, right? Perhaps it will calm Chanji to see a familiar face when she wakes." Konstantin wasn't sure knowing another friend had been lying to her would calm Zariya, but he swallowed the comment.

"What about the brand?" He found himself inadvertently fingering the mark on his own palm and stilled his hands.

"You know what it means, Konstantin. She's one of us. The sword chooses who is worthy."

"But we only let it test those who've trained. Who have fought. Our Phantoms are ex-Special Forces, ex-CIA—the mostly highly trained fighters, intelligence officers, and assassins from around the globe. We can't just let her in because the sword picked her. It was a fluke. She never should have been near enough to touch it."

"Wasn't King Arthur chosen by the sword when he was just a boy?"

"That's just in the Disney version," Konstantin said. "Caledfwlch was gifted to him by the fae to mark his sovereignty over Britain—marked him as protector and lord of the land. Just as it marked Vizol as protector of the supernatural races. As it has marked each of us."

"Including Zariya—"

"I'm not saying she shouldn't be a Phantom eventually if she wants to. I'm not denying that she has potential. But she would need to train. We only recruit those who are already fully capable, who've worked in the field for years. We should wait—"

"You don't have time to wait." A female voice sounded from the doorway.

Konstantin turned to find Signe Dirksen striding into the room. Signe was a norn, a Scandinavian fae with the power to see the threads of fate. And sometimes change them. Signe's knowledge of magic was incredible, just as her sister, Verte's, grasp of science and technology were beyond anything Konstantin could even hope to understand. The two of them both worked from the base at Tartarus but were integral to the success of Veil Force as a whole, and the teams' missions in the field.

"What have you seen?" Cyriaque leaned forward.

"Just snatches of futures," Signe said. "They started when Zariya breached the base. But enough to know that in each of them, Zariya is key to Veil Force's future. Perhaps all of our futures." She turned to Konstantin. "Yours especially."

Konstantin crossed his arms before him. He didn't see how one willful half-human could have any influence on his future, even if she was Vizol's daughter.

"So that's it," Cyriaque said. "She's in."

"No." Signe was still looking at Konstantin with those penetrating blue eyes. Though Signe was physically blind, it didn't stop her from seeing more than the rest of them put together. Her magic more than made up for any lack of physical ability. "Konstantin is right. If we ignore the rules with Zariya, it will undermine the Phantoms' confidence in her. We need to be united as one."

"But you said we can't wait," Cyriaque pointed out. "What are you suggesting?"

"A test," Signe said. "Make Zariya pass a test to show she's worthy of joining. It's the only way to prove to all of us, and herself, that she belongs here."

"Sounds like a circus," Konstantin protested. "We don't have time for this. There's intel that the Collectors are moving again shortly—"

"We make time." Cyriaque stood. "We have to. You heard Signe. When has she ever led us astray?"

Konstantin sighed.

Cyriaque nodded to himself, resolved. "We will have this test. I'll oversee it myself."

11

I came to in a rush. The dragon shifter...the sword. It had burned me. I pulled my hand up to examine my palm and found myself restrained. Handcuffed to a bed.

What the hell?

I rattled the handcuffs, pulling at them. I was in some sort of laboratory. Machines blinked around me, and two other beds sat empty beside mine.

"Hey!" I called. "Let me go!"

The dragon shifter appeared around the corner, striding into the room and pulling up a stool beside me. I tried to inch away from him, but I was held fast. He didn't look angry, though—his tanned face was pleasant. "Zariya, I'm Dr. Oliver Connell. I think we got off on the wrong foot."

"How do you know who I am?" I asked. Had Kiki told him? Konstantin?

"You're well known to our organization. Through your father," Oliver said. "I'm sorry for your loss."

"Thanks," I said grudgingly.

"There's someone here to see you. Do you think you're up for visitors?"

My curiosity overcame my wariness. "Sure." My eyes widened when Alviya appeared around the corner, her red hair twisted in a braid over one shoulder.

"Hey." She sat down on the bed by my knees. "How are you feeling?"

"Like I got attacked by a dragon and shot with a tranq dart," I snapped. "What the hell are you doing here?"

She patted my leg and cleared her throat. "I work here, Zariya. I have for the last two years."

What the hell? "You work for a PR company," I said lamely.

She shook her head. "That's just my cover. What we do here is secret."

"You're what, like a valkyrie James Bond?"

"Not exactly. Counter-intelligence is part of our mission, but not the main focus."

"What is your mission?" This was too weird. First Kiki, and now Alviya? I was starting to think I didn't know any of my friends at all.

"I think it's best if Director Broussard explains everything. Then we can talk more later."

"Director—wait, Cyriaque Broussard?" The Rougarou werewolf was an old friend of my dad's and had been around a lot when I was a kid.

"He took over as Director after your dad died."

Disbelief filled me. Cyriaque was in on this too? It was like the whole world was conspiring against me, all so sure I couldn't be trusted.

"Does Bas know what you really do?" I asked.

Alviya examined her fingernails. "Actually, Bas works here too. That's how we met."

I would have thrown up my hands if they hadn't been chained to the bed. "What the fuck, Alviya?! You're all just, what, laughing behind my back about what an idiot I was because I didn't know your big secret?"

"Of course not." Alviya grabbed my hand and I hissed. She pulled back, remorse written across her pretty features. "I wanted to tell you a thousand times, we all did. But our work here is top secret clearance only. Your dad recruited me after I became your roommate. Kiki too, although she'd already been here a few years when I joined. I met Bas here. Cyriaque and your father started this place. It wasn't purposeful; it just unfolded like that. You were so busy in med school..."

"That what, I wouldn't notice that everyone in my life was a fucking liar sneaking around behind my back?" I closed my eyes, fighting tears.

"Your dad didn't want you worrying—"

"You don't get to talk about him. None of you do. He should have told me. He robbed me of this whole...piece of himself. And now I feel like maybe I never really knew him at all." Dad had been my person. And I had been his. Or so I'd thought.

"You knew him. You knew how much he loved you."

I closed my eyes. "I think I'm ready to yell at Cyriaque now. If you can unchain me."

When I finally looked at her, tears shimmered in the corner of Alviya's obsidian eyes. "I'm so, so sorry Zariya. Please forgive me."

"Just get these fucking things off me."

ALVIYA LED me silently through the base. We passed a few rooms of interest: a dining hall where supes were sitting around a table and eating as well as a wide training room where two women sparred. I did my best to ignore it. My focus was on my anger. My rage.

Alviya knocked on the door and it opened to reveal Konstantin Bauer, filling the doorway in a black leather jacket and jeans. My breath caught in my throat, as if the air had been sucked out of the room by his mere presence.

"Zariya." He nodded, stepping out of the way and crossing his arms across his broad chest. "Created quite a mess down on the fifth floor."

"You can blame your dragon pet for that," I said. "I was just looking for some answers." I thought of the file I'd found with Dad's records. Who knew where that had gone in all this mess?

"And it's time you got some." Cyriaque came around his desk and waved a hand, ushering me inside his office. I crossed my arms. He better not be bullshitting me.

Alviya gave me a weak smile and walked down the hallway with Konstantin, leaving the two of us alone.

Cyriaque looked just as he had the last time I'd seen him—at my father's funeral. Tall and devilishly good-looking, with thick, chestnut hair and a full beard. His black Armani suit had been exchanged for a white button-down and slacks today, and he wore the sleeves rolled up, revealing strong forearms. I had a hard time reconciling this serious character with the man who'd played Marco Polo with me for hours at the community pool when I was eight.

"Have a seat, Zariya," he said with his southern drawl, settling down into his own chair. I wanted to be difficult and stand, but I was still feeling a little woozy from the tranquilizers, so I sank into the leather chair across his desk.

"I'm sorry you had to find out this way."

"You mean you're sorry I found out at all?" Clearly, me finding out hadn't been the plan.

He sighed. "How about we start at the beginning. You must have lots of questions. I'm happy to answer them."

"What the hell is this place?"

"This is Tartarus Base, the home of Veil Force. We're a covert, black-ops division of MASC. I report directly to the MASC Undersecretary myself."

"So all this time, when I thought Dad was a diplomat for MASC, he was what, a spy? An assassin? A special operator?" I guess I could see Dad in those roles, but I still couldn't believe that he wouldn't tell me. That he'd have this whole other life and lie about it.

"We are whatever MASC needs us to be. Our mission is to protect humans and supes alike from magical and supernatural threats. We investigate and stop terrorist threats, capture or eliminate individuals who have been deemed to be a danger to supernatural security around the globe, find and neutralize hazardous magical items...the list goes on. Our missive is flexible, because the threats are ever-changing."

"So you're like a supernatural global police force?"

"Of a sort. But we don't spend our time enforcing laws. Much of what we do operates in areas where there is no law."

"And Dad was the Director?" I said in disbelief.

"Your father and I started Veil Force. He was a team leader, and then Director for the last decade. When we served in the Marines, we realized that human military and counter-intelligence groups weren't equipped to handle many magical and supernatural threats. And, unfortunately, due to prejudices, ensuring supe safety and rights around the world was not a top priority. We pitched Veil Force to the Security Council, and they went for it. Our group is classified, as we've found much of our work is more easily done in the shadows. Not to mention humans still get nervous knowing that teams of powerful supes are running around beneath their noses. But our existence is known to a select few—we do collaborate with various UN and foreign government agencies on some missions."

That was all well and good. This place couldn't have been more like Dad if his picture had been on the damn brochure. But that wasn't what I really wanted to know. "Why didn't he tell me?"

Cyriaque cocked his head, his brown eyes kind. "You were seven years old when we started to build this place. It wasn't appropriate to discuss it with you and your father didn't want you worrying about him. You were all each other had, other than Temsula."

"Still, he should have told me when I got older."

"He worried. That if he did, it would put you at risk. Or that you'd want to join. He wanted you to follow your dreams, not his."

"A lot of good that did. My dreams have gone to shit," I muttered, guilt needling at me. After all the work I'd put into med school, I'd ruined it.

"I know. I'm sorry."

I crossed my arms over my chest, examining his office. Looking everywhere but at his sympathetic face. The framed photo of him and my dad. An ancient jeweled dagger in a glass box. A watercolor painting of a dark wolf silhouetted against a smoky sunset.

"How many of you are there?"

"We have four teams of six—Phoenix Team is led by Konstantin Bauer, whom I understand you've met. The other teams are Aquila, Hydra, and Draco. I led Draco team until your father...well, until I took this job. Then we have a few base support staff like Oliver and Kimiko. A few more."

"I want to know about Dad's death. Kiki gave me a fake report, didn't she?"

Cyriaque leaned forward, running his hands through his hair. "I'm afraid that was my idea, Zariya. I knew you would be like a dog with a bone if you got wind of foul play surrounding your father's death, and frankly, I didn't want that for you. He wouldn't have, either. Vizol would want you living your life, not chasing after revenge."

"Well, Dad's gone, so he doesn't get a say. Tell me the truth. You owe me that much. Dad was murdered, wasn't he?"

Cyriaque's pause spoke volumes. Finally, he looked up, meeting my gaze. "Yes, we think so."

The heat of vindication flooded through me. I knew it. I *knew it*. Everyone had told me to move on, that I'd been imagining things. But I knew that Dad hadn't died in some freak accident. "Do you know who did it?"

"Not yet. Believe me when I say we are all working on it. Everyone here loved Vizol; he personally recruited most of our team. We will find who did this, Zariya, and we will make them pay."

"I want to be involved," I said.

"I thought you'd might say that. But this is Veil Force business. We'll handle it."

Bullshit. They weren't cutting me out of this. "Then I'm joining."

"I thought you might say that too."

"I'm just as tough as anyone out there. I've been fighting for two decades. I'm a naga. We're warriors by nature. You owe me this, Cyriaque, you can't keep me out. Not any longer—"

"Easy, girl." He held up his hands. "Even if I wanted to deny you a place, that burn on your hand says otherwise."

I'd forgotten. I looked down at the mark on my palm and my eyes widened. Cyriaque held up his palm, displaying the same mark. "All of the Veil Force operators—'Phantoms,' we're called—have been marked by that sword. It chooses us. Marks us as worthy."

"I don't understand. Dad told me he was burned by some ancient sword in India."

"Not entirely accurate. Well, the India part, anyway. That sword is *Caledfwlch*, one of the legendary objects of power in Irish lore. Also known in some tales as 'Excalibur.' The sword has a long history of choosing those who are worthy to wield it. It chose your father first. And it's chosen each of us to fight beside him."

"So, what, Dad was King Arthur, and you're the Knights of the Round Table?" I offered a half-hearted joke.

He didn't laugh. "In a way. It has become the symbol of Veil Force—the sword and the shield. It's what we do, and who we are."

"But Kiki doesn't have one. Or Alviya," I pointed out.

"Most of our members have the mark healed after the sword chooses them. Some of us keep the brand. As a reminder. But whatever you decide, Zariya, that sword's choice marks you as one of us as surely as your Chanji blood does."

"Great. When do I start?" Was I really doing this? Joining some clandestine governmental organization with a secret base below New York City?

But it was one of the last pieces of Dad I had left. I couldn't just walk away from it without exploring what it meant. Plus, if I wanted to hunt down the men who had killed Dad, I needed these powerful supes at my side. And their fancy-pants resources.

"It's not so simple as that. Veil Force is an elite group. Phantoms are chosen after years in service—most have worked for counter-intelligence or in special operations."

I prickled. "I get it. You think I won't measure up."

"To the contrary. I'm sure you will. But I'm not the one who needs convincing. It's the rest of the Phantoms. The supes who'd be relying on you out in the field."

Like Konstantin Bauer. "Fine. What do I have to do to prove it to them?"

"It's funny you should ask…"

12

———————

Atest. I hated tests.

My head spun as I walked out of Cyriaque's office.

Cyriaque stood in his doorway. "We'll need a day to prepare. And a day of rest would do you good after tonight's...excitement. Report back here at 0600 on Monday if you want to take the test."

I ran a thumb over the burn on my palm. It throbbed, hot and angry. "I'll be here."

"I thought you'd say that."

"I want the real report."

"When you pass the test—"

"No, Cyriaque. Now. I deserve the truth, no matter whether I'm fit to join your little club or not."

Cyriaque sighed and started down the hallway, jerking his head for me to follow. "Fine. Konstantin has it."

We stopped at an office four doors down, and he poked his head inside. "Get her the real report."

I stepped inside, standing awkwardly. Cyriaque disappeared. I guessed he was done with me. Konstantin stood up from behind a large wooden desk, a pair of trendy, clear-rimmed glasses on his nose. He quickly took them off.

"Vampires wear glasses?" I couldn't help myself.

He strode past me to the filing cabinet at the back of the room, sending a whiff of his scent of cool breezes and night air my way. And giving me a good look at how his clothes clung to the muscles of his form—his broad back, his ass. My cheeks heated. *Stop staring at the vampire's ass, Chanji!*

"Vampires keep their human afflictions even after we're turned. I just need them for reading."

I ran quickly through what I knew about vampires. "So you're Derived?" I asked.

There were two types of vamps—Authentics and Derived. Authentic vampires lived in remote colonies and rarely mingled with human society. Authentic vampires had never been human—and they were the only type that could make a Derived vampire—a vampire who had once been human. Authentics also lived exclusively on blood while Deriveds could survive on a combination of human food and blood. It was why they were more easily Recognized. Authentics were Unrecognized—outside the protection of normal law, which was for the best. Because really, we needed protection from them, not the other way around. They were savage. Animal. Not members of polite society.

Konstantin inclined his head. The gesture was calculated, as if he had to remind himself to make such a typical human movement. "I am."

"When...?" I trailed off.

"1423."

Damn. He was old. I knew vampires grew in strength as they aged. I felt slightly better about the fact that he'd bested me in our sparring match.

Konstantin handed me a file from the cabinet. "The real report. I'll walk you out."

I followed him towards the elevator. "Don't trust me to find the exit on my own?"

"Just a precaution," he replied.

"You could have saved us all a lot of trouble if you'd just given me the real report when I asked for it."

"It wasn't my call."

We were at the elevator now and he pushed the button for me before turning. His expression was inscrutable. Devastating. It was hard to think when he looked at me full on like that, with those blue, blue eyes.

1423, I reminded myself. That made him... I didn't even know. If you needed a calculator to figure out a guy's age, you shouldn't be lusting after him, right? That seemed like a wise rule of thumb. "It wasn't Kiki's call, either. Don't be too hard on her."

"Why do you care?"

"I care about everyone here. Veil Force...what your father built here...we're a family. We take care of our own."

His words were a gut punch.

"Understood," I managed. I stepped into the elevator quickly and hit the button for the ground floor. I willed the elevator doors to close before I started to cry. I couldn't look at him—wouldn't look at him—and when the doors finally slid shut, a sob escaped me.

I crumpled to my knees, the folder pressed to my chest, one hand clapped over my mouth.

What your father built here...we're a family. The truth of it hit me like a semi-truck. It had always been Dad, Auntie, and me—they'd been the only family I'd had. But Dad had built a whole other family in secret, behind my back. Without me. All his business trips and travel took on new form in my memories. Dad hadn't been committed to his job; he'd been committed to his other life. The family he preferred over me.

I rose and screamed, punching the elevator door with my fist. My strike left a circular dent, and the pain startled away my tears. My chest heaved as the doors opened into the little alcove that would take me through the portal back to Four Freedoms Park.

Fewer than four hours had passed since I'd gone down this very elevator, but it felt like years. The weight of sorrow clung to me like an anchor. I felt worse than I had when Dad had died. I wanted to curl up in a corner of the concrete space and succumb to the blackness of sleep, but there was something else I needed to do. Someone else I needed to yell at. So I stepped through the portal and headed for a cab.

~

AUNTIE TEMSULA LIVED in a quirky Victorian in Montclair, New Jersey. She loved America, but she'd never liked the big city. Even New Jersey was busier than she liked, but she'd wanted to be close to us.

Everything about Auntie was as quirky as her home. She made her living as a psychic and a medium and was a damn good one at that. But right now I couldn't think about anything except that she *had* to have known about Veil Force. About Dad's secret MASC dealings and his other family. And she'd kept it from me too.

It was just after 3 A.M. by the time I arrived, but I didn't care. I banged on the front door and shouted her name. "Auntie! Wake up!"

I was about to bang again when she pulled the door open, a colorful floral robe haphazardly wrapped around her. "Curlicue? What's wrong? What's happened?"

I stormed past her into the foyer, rounding on her. I held up my burnt hand, showing her the brand. "We need to talk."

She stumbled back a step, her hand flying to her mouth. She recovered quickly, closing the door. "I'll make some chai. And I'll tell you whatever you want to know."

I wanted to yell at her to tell me now, but damn it if some of Auntie's chai didn't sound fucking delicious. So I led the way into the kitchen, dropping down into one of the chairs tucked into the island. The ceiling of her kitchen was painted like an Indian sunrise, and the cabinets each had mismatching hardware. Every corner and open space of her house was filled with color—carvings and wall-hangings, clustered altars to the gods. I felt my roiling anger draining away, leaving me spent and empty.

"You want an ice pack for that burn?" Auntie asked.

I nodded sullenly and took it, pressing it to my hand with a sigh. I thought Dr. Dragon back at the base had put some sort of salve on it, because my hand smelled faintly of camphor and hadn't been throbbing as badly as I would have expected. But still, the ice felt heavenly.

Auntie poured coconut milk into a pan on the stove, her back to me. "Why don't you tell me what's happened?"

So I did. Woodenly, I recited the events of the evening. Grappling with Kiki and shooting her with the memory serum, stealing her ring and breaking into Tartarus base, the dragon, the sword. Talking to Cyriaque and the test.

Auntie turned to me, her arms crossed before her. She didn't look a day over thirty, her black, curly hair wild around her shoulders. She was beautiful, her naga heritage hidden in her human form. I envied her—that she could pass as human. Whereas I actually *was* half-human and would always look *other*.

"Do you remember the Arcana Prep bombing?" she asked.

I blinked. That wasn't what I'd expected. How could I not? I'd been six years old, and we'd been here in this very kitchen, with the news on in the background. The image on the screen was burned in my memory—the bodies of children blackened and twisted. The news anchor explained in sober tones the details of the terrorist bombing that had ripped apart a private school—a school for children of supernatural creatures. One of those little bodies had had wings, another hooves. They'd been too far gone to see what type of supes they had been, but as I stroked the scales running down my neck, I knew it could have been me. I remembered Dad's fury, burning so hot, it scared me almost as much as the images on the screen. Auntie had taken me in her arms and rocked me until I stopped crying, her own tears mingling with mine. "Of course I do."

"That was the catalyst for Veil Force. Your father knew that things like that would keep happening unless someone did something. Unless someone cared. So he and Cyriaque started their campaign to the MASC Under-Secretary. Through sheer force of will, they secured the funding and approvals to start the project. It is his greatest legacy. Besides you, of course."

"Why didn't he tell me?"

"When it began, you were a child. And as you got older...he worried if you knew, you'd want to join. You always idolized him, wanted to do everything he did. And he didn't want that life for you."

"He was my dad. Of course I fucking idolized him!" Dad had always been like a superhero to me, ever since I'd been a little girl—strong, capable, commanding. I supposed he'd had the double-life thing down, too.

"You were doing so well in medical school—you'd found your own path—"

"He should have told me."

She sighed and turned to stir the chai. "Yes, he should have. For now through his lies, he's brought to pass the very thing he wanted to prevent."

"Did he think I wouldn't be good enough?" My voice broke.

Auntie whirled and crossed the kitchen in a blink, laying her hand on my cheek. "No, curlicue. He knew you would be too good."

I blinked back tears. "What do you mean?"

"You're a naga, and a Chanji what's more. You have battle in your blood. It sings to you, calls you to challenge and fight. That's why he put you in training when you were so young—he hoped to channel it. He wanted a normal life for you. An American life. A life like your mother should have had. Marriage. Children. Peace. A Veil Force Phantom has none of these."

"Dad made it work. He had me."

"But he didn't have peace. He constantly worried he wasn't a good enough father to you, that he wasn't here enough. And he worried when he was home that he wasn't giving his teams all they deserved. He was a man pulled in half, with one foot in two worlds."

"I know the feeling," I grumbled, running my tongue over my soft fangs, retracted in my mouth. I would never be fully human, or fully naga.

Auntie poured me a big mug of chai and placed it before me. "I am sorry for the lies. And I know he is too."

I gazed into the caramel swirl of the liquid. "I just feel…" I cleared my throat. "Like he wanted a different family. Like I wasn't enough."

"Nothing could be further from the truth." Auntie stilled, her hands braced on the cerulean tiles of the counter.

"Auntie?"

"Hold on a moment, curlicue." She disappeared into the hallway, leaving me to salve my raw wounds with the sweet spice of chai tea.

She returned a moment later, a long, black case in her hand. She set it on the counter before me, her hands on its lid as if to keep it from springing open. "Before he died, your father left this with me. He wanted you to have it, but only if you someday learned about his work with Veil Force."

Curiosity overcame my hurt. "What is it?"

Auntie unclasped the brass buckles and opened it for me.

I gasped. "Dad's talwar?"

It was a sword, a beautiful curving blade of shining silver. The hilt was wrapped in fine red leather, inlaid with gold, and etched with carvings of sinuous snakes. I'd only seen it a few times as a child—Dad had kept it under lock and key. The ornately detailed scabbard lay next to it in the case, both nestled in the black velvet.

"It's a family heirloom, passed to him by his father, and his father before that. Generations of Chanji warriors have wielded this blade."

I reached for it eagerly.

"Zariya—" Auntie held up her hand. "This blade is enchanted with strong magic. Do you smell it?"

I opened my glands and breathed deeply. Now that she pointed it out, I did—the loamy soil scent of ancestor magic. Earth and roots and old, ancient things. "What's the spell?"

"I do not know. But I suspect if you take up this blade, there will be no going back."

Good. I had nothing to go back to.

I seized the sword's hilt. And the world dropped away.

13

I stood in a dark room—a cavern of sorts. Yet not. It had no smell, no heat or cold—no dust or dank or dirt. It did, however, have another person.

When he turned around, my knees nearly buckled. "Dad?" I blinked and blinked again, disbelieving what I was seeing. But he was here.

I ran to him and threw myself into his arms, but instead of hitting the solid bulk of him, I stumbled through and out the other side. I fell to my knees hard, but it didn't hurt. No pain here, either. I held up my hand and found it ghostly and incorporeal. No body at all.

I turned, shoving to my feet. "Dad?" My voice wavered. "Where are we? What is this place?"

"This is my memory palace," he said. "I created it in case you ever needed my knowledge. The knowledge of your ancestors."

I shook my head. "What? How—"

"The Balsamic Moon coven specializes in memories and mind magic. A powerful witch owed me a favor, and this is what I asked of her." The North American witches were divided into eight main covens, named after the phases of the moon. The covens differed widely in philosophy, approach to magic, and their approach to flouting the laws. The Balsamic witches were considered to be on the "not evil" end of the spectrum.

"Why?" In its shock, my brain was moving like molasses.

"Because I knew a time might come when you'd want to follow in my footsteps. And if I was no longer around—I still wanted you to have my wisdom."

"You knew I might want to join Veil Force."

"Of course, my darling. How could you not? You are fierce and brave and detest injustice. Veil Force was made for supes like you."

"But you lied to me about it! If you thought I'd be so great at it, why didn't you tell me?"

"Because in my selfishness, I did not want you at risk."

I was temporarily stunned. Tears pricked my eyes. Great. Of course there were tears in this place. "That's a shit reason."

"I know. But you were always my greatest treasure."

"How can you say that when you spent your life building a secret base, a whole secret family?"

"I can only ask forgiveness for how I've wronged you. I did what I thought was best. I only ever wanted your happiness and safety."

"I was happiest with you," I managed to choke through the tears. I threw up my hands. "Why am I even arguing with you? What are you, a figment of some witch's imagination? You're dead."

"I am a fragment of your father's consciousness. Left here to guide you through the memories available."

I pressed my lips together. "So you're really...him? A piece of him?"

"The only piece left, it seems."

I wrapped my arms around myself, struggling to hold it together. Seeing him—it should be better, to have even the smallest piece of him right here before me. But it wasn't. It was worse. He was here, but I couldn't touch him, I couldn't hug him or pound my fists into his chest for what he'd done. It just reminded me of how much I'd lost. "I want to go now."

"Very well," Dad's form said, unperturbed. "If you ever wish to return, you have only to touch the sword and ask for a memory. I will supply it to you."

And then I was back, blinking away the light of Auntie's kitchen, my hand closed around the buttery leather of the talwar's hilt. She hadn't moved an inch. It was like I'd never been gone.

I dropped the sword back into the case like I'd been burned.

Auntie was there, her hand on my shoulder, her green eyes searching. "Are you all right?"

All I could do was shake my head as the tears poured forth. She wrapped me in her arms as I sobbed, feeling like I'd lost him all over again.

I THOUGHT I'd already reached the bottom of my well of my grief, but I'd been wrong. It went deeper than I knew—miles of dark and cold.

Auntie held me as I cried that night, her own tears perfuming my hair as we spooned in her big four-poster bed. The sun was rising when I finally fell into a fitful sleep.

I woke exhausted, my head tight and pounding, my heart rung dry.

She fed me coffee in the morning with dosa bread smeared with fig jam and ricotta cheese.

The folder sat on the countertop, next to the tightly closed case bearing the sword. I'd forgotten all about it. So I opened it and read while I ate.

"What is that?"

"The report on Dad's death," I admitted.

Auntie froze for a moment in the act of returning the creamer to the fridge but then recovered. "What does it say?"

I scanned it with a strange mix of eagerness and trepidation. "They found evidence of magical charges on the pillars of the building Dad drove by—C4 explosives with a spelled trigger. They said it looks like Black Moon Coven technology, but they're still investigating." The Black Moon Coven had been officially declared a terrorist organization by MASC two years back.

"So he was killed on purpose. You always said."

"You're the one who taught me to follow my intuition," I retorted.

"There's that sass. You must be feeling better." A ghost of a smile crossed Auntie's face. "I should have listened."

"It's okay. I get why you didn't want to believe me. *I* didn't really want to believe me."

"Any other clues?"

I finished scanning the report. "Just one. They discovered a strange circle imbedded on the concrete behind the facade that collapsed. Large—as if the stone had been imprinted upon, but the imprint was raised. Markings of some kind. Lettering? Runes? I can't make it out." I showed her the grainy black-and-white photo in the report.

We both peered at it, our heads together, as if getting closer to the image would make it reveal its secrets. "I have never seen its like," Auntie finally said. "You make them show you the details of these markings. We will find whatever magic did this."

"I will. If I pass, that is." My stomach flipped. The test would start tomorrow at 6 A.M. What had I gotten myself into?

"You will. You have your father's memories to aid you." My eyes flicked to the black case. It was beyond weird to think that I could access Dad's memories whenever I wanted. I was torn between desperate curiosity and my low-burning anger at him. "I'm not ready to go back in."

"Then you have friends who can help prepare you."

"I'm not asking Kiki or Alviya for help. I don't even want to see them."

Auntie clucked her tongue. "I know you're angry, but what did your father always say?"

I pursed my lips. "Use every resource at your disposal."

"There are times in life when the line between ally and enemy becomes blurred. In those moments, practicality must govern, not emotion."

"Thanks, Sun Tzu," I muttered. "I never thought I'd hear you advocating logic over emotion."

"We have both for a reason, curlicue. And I am still a naga. We keep to the three-fold path."

"I know."

For a second, I could see Dad in front of me. I was small, and he was down on one knee. I'd just gotten the crap kicked out of me by two human kids who lived three houses up, and green blood dribbled from my nose. He was wearing his fatigues, back before he'd started wearing business suits instead. When I sobbed at him that I wanted to learn to fight, he shook his head calmly and asked, "Do you think muscles make you strong? Training?" I nodded, wiping the back of my hand across my nose. He shook his head gently and poked me in the belly. "Nagas know that strength comes not from might, but from here. Your intuition. Let it guide you." He poked me gently in the breastbone. "Here. Your heart. Where courage and compassion lie. Let it guide you." He poked me between the eyes. "And here. Wisdom. Let it guide you. This is the three-fold path. Let it guide you, and you will always have what you need."

Tears pricked my eyes and I shoved them down. I wanted to scream at him, to flail against his memory. *I don't have everything I need, do I, Dad? Because you're gone.*

But as much as I felt wrung out and raw, I knew Auntie was right. I needed an edge if I wanted to pass whatever test they were planning for me. Using Dad's memories was the smart play, but I didn't know if I could see him again without falling apart. Kiki and Alviya were my other option. I didn't want to face them, either, though; I was still so furious about their lies.

Either way, I had fewer than twenty-four hours to decide.

Just after noon, I let Auntie wrap me in a hug and hand me a bag full of fragrant leftovers and called myself and Dad's talwar an Uber. I was still angry at her, but I was beginning to see that Dad had made a decision a long time ago that had shaped all of the lives around me. I couldn't cut out everyone in my life for toeing the line he'd set. Or I'd have no one left.

I went to wait for my ride outside in the fresh spring morning, closing my eyes to bask in the sun.

That was why I didn't see the car until it was almost upon me. Tires squealed and my eyes flew open to reveal a black SUV with tinted windows skidding to a stop directly in front of me.

Four black-clad soldiers with face masks and assault rifles burst from the car. Coming at me. Coming *for* me? Either way, it couldn't be good.

I launched into a run, sprinting down the street.

Something hit me from behind, square between my shoulder blades. I went down—hard. My chin scraped against the pavement, taking the brunt of my fall.

My lungs rebelled against me, unwilling to pull in breath. Had I been shot?

I hazarded a look over my shoulder.

Two sets of black-booted legs were approaching—their steps tight and precise.

I tried to push up to my hands and knees, but my muscles were frozen. Weak. Another tranq dart? Auntie's food had spilled over the sidewalk before me, and the case for Dad's sword had busted open. The talwar was lying just a foot from me. If I could reach it...

The men were almost upon me.

I rallied every last drop of energy and lunged forward. My hands connected with the hilt. And I was whisked away.

14

The memory palace was just as it had been. Dad stood calmly across the stone space, regarding me.

I, on the other hand, was freaking the fuck out.

I'd come in on hands and knees—I pushed to my feet. "Dad, someone's attacking me."

He frowned. "I'm sorry to hear that."

I growled. "That's it? You're sorry?" Where was Dad's fire? His righteous fury?

"The fragment that was preserved does not include emotion. But perhaps I can help you another way?"

Yes. I needed help. "Memories."

"What would you like to know?"

I didn't know what the hell was going on, or who the hell these people were. All I knew was that I was splayed out on the sidewalk like old take-out and when I returned to my body from the strange time of this place, I'd probably be loaded into that car. Or killed. Or loaded into the car and then killed. This might be my only chance to learn what Dad knew. To benefit from his wisdom. "Everything. Show me everything."

Dad shook his head. "That's unadvisable. The weight of that

many memories being added to your neural pathways at one time—it could overload your circuits, so to speak."

"I might not have any circuits left to overload if we don't do this. Give me the memories. Now."

He clucked his tongue. "Very well." He stepped in close, looking so much like Dad that it made my heart seize. The green of his eyes, the flecks of gray at his temples, the strength and authority that radiated from him...

He held out his hand, as if to shake mine.

"I thought I couldn't touch you."

"You may only during the transfer."

So I threw my arms around him. He was solid and real and *Dad*.

Then the onslaught began.

I CAME to in some sort of warehouse. Cold concrete floor beneath me, a tall ceiling with dim, buzzing lights above. Someone had hung plastic to section the space off into a sort of macabre room. Horror movie chic.

I took in the space, catalogued what I knew. Tried to ignore the fact that I was chained to a chair. That my chin smarted like hell from where I'd smacked it on the pavement.

My head felt like it might split apart from the weight of new knowledge. I didn't know if this was what it felt like to have my circuits overloaded, but I suspected it might. It was like there were two people inside me.

Zariya, who was practically peeing her pants in terror right now. I'd been *kidnapped*.

And there was Vizol. Calm. In control. He'd gotten out of situations ten times worse than this without breaking a sweat. Was this how Dad had felt all the time, supremely confident and sure of his own abilities? It was a heady feeling, especially compared to the stress ball of doubts and insecurities that was Zariya.

But Dad's fearlessness had gotten him killed. He hadn't been invincible, and neither was I.

I desperately wanted to explore my new knowledge, to swim through the waters of Dad's memories like a fish. Flashes of his memories of me surfaced—me with pigtails and a gap in my smile, me flying a kite on the seashore with a look of pure childhood delight on my face. I could feel his love for me. His pride. It was like oxygen to my suffocating heart.

I'd thought Dad had wanted another family because I hadn't been enough. I knew now how wrong I'd been. He'd built Veil Force *because* of me. Because other supes deserved safety too. Lives where their children could grow up and join the world as equals.

A man in black military gear slipped under the plastic, startling me out of Dad's memories.

I gave myself a mental kick. I should have finished analyzing my predicament, not taken a stroll down memory lane.

The man dragged a chair across the cement floor, dropped it across from where I sat, and settled into it. He was tall and muscular, with a chiseled, handsome face and chocolate-brown hair cut short. Though he looked human, he moved with a preternatural grace that cried *supe*. I wondered what he was. I didn't recognize him from any of Dad's memories.

I opened my glands and quested out to see what was around. The building was large, with six bodies within. It must have been located in a fairly deserted area, though, because I couldn't make out any other people or supes nearby. The building smelled faintly of oil and gasoline. So some sort of auto storage or repair facility. That was helpful but didn't exactly narrow the location down. That could put us in any one of a thousand places in the Tri-State area.

The supe in black was examining me, one booted foot resting on the other knee. His body language wasn't particularly hostile. More like curious.

The silence between us was itching at me, but Dad's memories said to stay silent. Let him take the lead. So I stared back, meeting his brown eyes.

"Zariya Chanji," he finally said.

"Gold star for you," I retorted.

I could practically feel Dad smacking his forehead in exasperation. I supposed antagonizing your enemy with futile snark was not part of the Veil Force handbook.

"I apologize for the force with which you were brought here. My men got a little...overeager. They have been disciplined."

"Who are you? Why am I here?"

"We are an organization that acquires objects of value." So... thieves. "We keep a close eye on what goes on in the supernatural law enforcement community. You came to our attention as the newest member of Veil Force."

Not if I didn't get the hell out of here and back to Tartarus base by 0600 tomorrow. "I don't know what you're talking about. I'm not a member of anything."

The man pursed his lips. "Now, Zariya, let's dispense with the facade, shall we?"

I said nothing, which I guessed he took as assent.

"We would benefit from having a woman on the inside. Someone who could help us understand where Veil Force was going to be next. Help us keep a few steps ahead."

I scoffed. This guy had a pair of *cojones* on him. "You want me to spy for you?"

"I understand it may seem distasteful, and so we're prepared to make it worth your while. Our clients pay handsomely for the items we procure for them. We would be willing to pay half a million dollars per year for you to serve as our eyes and ears inside Tartarus."

Half a million... My eyes goggled. Damn, that was a lot of money. *Corrupt, wrong, never!* Dad's memories practically shouted at me.

Well, yes, obviously, I wasn't actually going to do it. However nice a cool half a mil might have sounded. I'd never betray what Dad had built, what Veil Force stood for.

I shook my head. "No way. *If* I knew what you were talking about, and *if* I were a member, there's no amount of money that would turn me into your mole."

The man frowned, rubbing his strong jaw. "I urge you to reconsider, Zariya. You see, we will have you for our spy, one way or another. We'd prefer you to cooperate willingly. It's easier on everyone. But we're prepared to do this the hard way."

The hairs on the back of my neck rose. "You can't make me do anything."

"Unfortunately for you, that's just not true."

He stood and ducked under the plastic. My pulse roared to life, my senses on high alert. What was he doing? What was he getting?

Feeling out with my glands, I saw that he was returning with someone else. A smaller, female form. So not *what* was he getting... but whom. A supe.

I threw up my mental walls, forming them tightly around my mental space. Dad had been through serious anti-interrogation training from both human and supe adversaries, so I added his knowledge to my own, using the techniques he'd been taught to fortify my walls even stronger. Until they were as sturdy as steel. Impenetrable.

When the black-clad man reappeared, I was ready. For the woman at his side, not so much.

She was petite and lovely, clad in a suit of pink herringbone. Her platinum blonde hair cascaded in curls over her shoulders and her makeup was perfect. She looked like she belonged ruling the boardroom of a fashion empire, not in this dank place.

I wanted to laugh in relief.

But not Dad. He had known her. And for the first time since his memories had poured into my mind, a rare sensation surfaced from the depths. Fear.

15

———

Konstantin's phone rang for the second time. *Damn it.* He ignored it, pulling the pillow over his head. Didn't a man deserve a few hours of peace?

He felt a shudder against his mental shields, as if a giant were pounding on the door. That could only be Kiki. Which meant it was Kiki who was calling.

He dragged himself from bed and grabbed his phone. "What?"

Kiki sounded near tears. "Konstantin, I think you should get down here. Cyriaque...I don't know what he's thinking. This is super fucked-up."

The remaining fog in his mind cleared. "Calm down. What's going on?"

"The test Cyriaque is putting Zariya through. He called in the *mara.*"

He froze. "What test? Zariya's test isn't until tomorrow."

"No. It's happening right now. They took her to some warehouse. Konstantin, she's torturing her."

"I'll be right there."

Konstantin threw on jeans and a T-shirt and was out the door, wishing the elevator from his penthouse apartment was quicker.

Vampires in modern literature always had astounding powers like the ability to fly, to turn into a bat, or to run as fast as the speed of light.

The elevator doors opened to the garage, revealing the sleek lines of his Audi R8. While he did have incredible strength, speed, and stamina, if he needed to get somewhere fast, this was how he did it. He liked to think his true superpower was in having made six centuries of wise investments. The compound interest alone made him stupidly rich. As much as it galled him, in modern life, money was power. And freedom.

Konstantin shot out of the parking structure onto the streets of Manhattan. At this time in the early afternoon, traffic hadn't reached complete gridlock, and he maneuvered his way towards Four Freedoms Park.

His mind circled over what Kiki had said, again, and again. Cyriaque had told him the test was tomorrow. Had told Zariya. So what the hell was he playing at?

He shifted into high gear, the engine purring to life beneath him. He was going to fucking find out.

THE HALLWAY outside the Ops Center was filled with people—Oliver was talking with Signe and Verte in hushed tones. Alviya and Bas waited a little way down the hall, his hand on her shoulder.

When Konstantin approached, Oliver and the sisters turned to him. Verte and Signe, their two resident norns, looked nearly identical—tall, lithe blondes with bone structure a supermodel would kill for. While Signe was blind, Verte was deaf, both giving up a natural sense for the preternatural foresight their heritage had granted them. But it didn't slow either of them down—both were brilliant and an integral part of Veil Force's success.

"What's going on?" Konstantin asked.

The doors to the Ops Center were shut. Through the window, Konstantin could see that only Kiki and Cyriaque were inside.

Kiki flashed him a quick glance. Her eyes were red-rimmed.

"Cyriaque had a team pick up Zariya this afternoon," Oliver said. "Leilani's leading. Posing as an enemy of MASC to see if Zariya can be flipped." Leilani, number two on Corvus team, was a Hawaiian kapua shapeshifter who could take any form.

Signe shook her head. "When I said test, I meant of her skills, not her loyalty. The sword chose her. She's as honorable as her father."

"Any of my team on the mission?"

"He didn't call in any Phoenix members. I bet the Director knew you wouldn't like it."

"Damn right I wouldn't like it."

"Kiki said something about the mara?" The mara was a contractor they used when they needed someone broken—a supe with the power to control nightmares. After a few hours with the mara in his head, even the toughest sonofabitch was crying to give up his secrets.

"She's working Zariya right now," Verte said. Her voice was grave.

Emotions roared to life within him—outrage and burning anger. His vision narrowed at the thought of Zariya's delicate form wracked with the pain of her worst nightmares. And there was something else, too. A fierce desire to protect her and keep her from harm. *Ours*, it snarled.

He burst through the door of the Ops Center, going for Cyriaque. He barreled into the Director, driving him back against the far wall.

Cyriaque snarled, his fangs protruding. The air around him crackled with the electricity of a barely restrained change.

Konstantin bared his fangs right back, nearly nose to nose with the supe. Cyriaque was bulkier with muscle, but Konstantin was taller—and much, much older. "This test ends now."

"Stand down, Commander." Cyriaque growled. "Or I will have you removed from duty."

"You've gone too far. This isn't what Signe meant."

Cyriaque shoved Konstantin back, off of him. His chest heaved, his eyes dark with the threat of violence. "I'm the Director of this organization. It's my call. This test is designed to ensure she is loyal to us and can withstand the psychological pressures that she would face as a Phantom."

"Her dad just died. She shouldn't have to go through this. Vizol would be turning over in his grave at this bullshit."

Cyriaque bared his teeth. "Don't lecture me on what Vizol would or wouldn't have wanted. I knew him longer than you. What Vizol would want is for us to be sure that his daughter can handle the job. Coddling her won't do her any favors."

The sound of a scream ripped through the array of computer monitors. Konstantin risked a glance. Kiki's elbows were braced on the desk, her hands covering her mouth.

"This is what you call coddling her? Sending the mara to rip apart her mind?"

"Anyone can fight, Konstantin. Anyone can follow orders. We need more from her. We need her to be able to think her way out of an impossible situation. To face the worst and not break."

Konstantin let out a low growl, wishing he didn't see a sort of horrible sense in what Cyriaque was saying. The voice inside of him still wanted to strike out at the Director for what he was doing—put a stop to Zariya's suffering. Some part of him cared far too much.

He shoved that part down.

"I told the mara to be gentle. She's not going to turn it up to ten in there."

"Does that monster know the meaning of the word 'gentle'?" Konstantin muttered.

"Director," Kiki said. "Something's happening."

Zariya's screams had stopped. Leilani, sporting the skin of a random military-aged male, and the mara had retreated from the alcove where Zariya was chained.

"See, they're giving her a break," Cyriaque said.

Konstantin leaned in to examine the computer monitors. "What's she doing?" Zariya was frantically fiddling with the chains at her wrists.

She pulled her arms free, the chains falling to the ground. "Holy shit, she's escaping." How had she done that?

She was slipping out of the rest of her chains now. Running to the edge of the plastic sheets that had been hung, peeking out.

"Inform Leilani that she's escaping," Cyriaque told Kiki, who scowled. "Now we see how she fights."

Kiki must have followed orders because Leilani and two soldiers ran back towards Zariya. When Kiki worked communications in the Ops Center, she facilitated all communications telepathically. When she couldn't be available, using specs based on her brain-waves, Signe and Verte had rigged a similar communications device that any user could wear to stand in for her and assist a team's psychic communication. But it wasn't nearly as good as Kiki herself.

Konstantin watched as Leilani and her team faced off against Zariya. He inhaled a breath in the moment they all sized each other up. And then Zariya attacked.

She was a sight to behold, her moves executed perfectly and timed flawlessly. Strike, counter, strike—she danced in and out with the grace of a ballerina.

Silence fell in the Ops Center as the three of them watched Zariya move, watched her take down one adversary. A second.

Until she and Leilani faced off. Leilani was one of the best fighters Konstantin had ever faced, but she and Zariya appeared evenly matched.

"I thought you faced her, Konstantin," Cyriaque asked. "You didn't say she was *this* good."

"She wasn't." Had she been holding back when they'd sparred in the park? It hadn't seemed like it. And why would she have? His curiosity grew. There was clearly more to Zariya Chanji than met the eye.

Zariya executed a roundhouse kick that dropped Leilani hard.

Konstantin winced.

She leaned in and pulled the gun from Leilani's belt, standing over her. Then pointing it at her chest.

"Cyriaque—" Konstantin said.

The gun fired. Shock bloomed through him. Leilani...one of their best operators...

"They're rubber bullets," Cyriaque said with a shaky laugh.

"They're rubber bullets. I wouldn't send them in with real munitions."

Relief blasted through him like a tidal wave. Followed by anger. "This ends now, Cyriaque. Kiki, tell Zariya we're coming for her. That she can stand down."

Cyriaque didn't belay his order.

He headed for the door, but Kiki's words stopped him. "I can't reach her."

"What?" He turned.

"Her mental walls, they're rock hard. I've never felt this from her before. I don't know what's going on."

Neither did he. But somehow, Zariya had leveled up.

"Director," Kiki said, pointing to the screen. Zariya was now darting low through the warehouse, ducking behind a tall stack of black cases. The three remaining Phantoms were standing between her and the exits. "Those cases. Don't they contain real weapons?"

"Yes, they do."

"What warehouse is she at?" Konstantin asked.

"Seventeen," came Cyriaque's flat reply.

Seventeen... "Isn't that where we keep the Oblivion Charges?"

Cyriaque's tanned face had gone as white as a sheet. "Konstantin, get the hell in there. Now. Before she blows herself and our team off the face of the Earth."

16

The fight sang in my veins, a siren song of violence and vengeance. Dad's memories had shown me how to withstand the mara's nightmares, how to pick the lock on my chains.

When the black-clad men had come at me, I'd given my body over to his training, marveling as my limbs moved with a speed and a precision I'd only dreamed of.

If this was what it had felt like to be Dad, no wonder he'd been so supremely confident. I felt like I had fucking super powers.

I was holed up behind a tall pile of black crates. There were three more bad guys standing between me and freedom, but they appeared more afraid of me than I was of them. The mara had scuttled off as soon as the fighting began. Didn't want to get blood on her designer pumps, perhaps.

But before I made my break for freedom, I needed a weapon. I had the pistol I'd taken off my main interrogator, but I'd be exposed getting across the open floor to the door. I needed a distraction.

I pulled one of the cases down and crouched over it, opening the top.

Lying on a bed of black foam were four round glass balls, gleaming dully. My eyes shot open. Dad recognized these. They were called Oblivion Charges. MASC had confiscated some from a terrorist group of goblins who had planned to bomb the financial markets to up the value of their gold hordes.

I guessed there were more out there, and this terrorist group had them too. A plan was coming to life in my mind. I couldn't leave these charges here. They could be used for all manner of nefarious purposes. But the charges would level a city block. If Dad remembered correctly, I'd only have about a minute once I set the charge to get the hell out of the blast zone.

Which meant I'd need to take out the remaining tangos first. I couldn't risk getting held up when I was making my exit. I let out a little laugh. "Tangos" equaled bad guys. Even Dad's military lingo was rubbing off on me.

I peeked over the fort of crates and saw one of the black-clad men approaching. "Stop right there!" I shouted, leveling my pistol at him.

"Zariya Chanji," he said. To my shock, he held up his hands. "I have a message from the Director. This was your test. You passed. You can now stand down."

My brows drew together. What the hell was this guy talking about? I looked around—the warehouse, the chair I'd been chained to, remembering the missing but torturous mara. No way this was MASC-approved. Cyriaque wouldn't approve something this fucked-up. Which meant this guy was playing me.

There were two doors out of here. If I could get them out of one, I could leave via the other, after I'd set the charge. I'd take the remaining three out in one blow. I licked my lips. "Fine. Each of you put your weapons down where I can see them and step outside the building. Let me have a clear path to the exit."

The soldiers seemed to be complying. They walked slowly to the center of the warehouse and dropped their pistols in a pile. Then headed for the door.

I watched them until they were out of there, then picked up one of the charges. I examined it. Dad had never actually turned one on.

But there was a pattern of symbols on it that I recognized as runes. Which one was the trigger? And then I saw the rune *Hagalaz*. Destruction.

I pressed it firmly and the clear ball bloomed to life with glowing aquamarine light. It began a slow, blinking countdown. I set it back in the case.

Time to run.

I sprinted across the warehouse towards the other exit. I didn't know how big the blast would be, but better safe than sorry. I needed to get as far away as possible. *Sayonara, assholes*, I thought as I burst into the afternoon sun.

And barreled right into a hard body.

I tumbled to the ground but turned my momentum into a roll, coming up on one knee, my pistol pointed.

"Konstantin?" I lowered it a few inches. There was another man standing behind him, a thin twenty-something-year old with hipster glasses and a goatee.

Konstantin held up his hands. "Zariya, put the gun down. You're safe now."

I sighed and set it down, some of the tension melting away. MASC had found me. I stood. "We need to get the hell out of here—now. This place is about to blow."

Konstantin's eyes flicked to the ground, as if listening to something. Then his eyes went wide and fixed on me. "You set one of the Oblivion Charges?"

"Yes. I couldn't let these assholes have them. Who knows where they'd end up."

"These assholes are *us*! This is a MASC facility!"

"What?" If that was true, why hadn't I recognized it from Dad's memories? Maybe he'd never actually been here.

"Leilani is still in there," the hipster guy said.

"Fuck!" Konstantin ran straight back into the building.

"Konstantin!" My mouth opened in shock. The other man disappeared before my very eyes. *What the fuck?*

I let out a scream of frustration before heading back into the building after Konstantin. All the while, common sense shouted at me. He was a vampire. He might be able to withstand a massive explosion without dying. Me, little half-naga, not so much.

Inside, the guy with the glasses was standing next to the box of crates, examining the blinking charge. How the hell had he gotten here so fast? The teal glow was blinking much faster now. We didn't have much time.

"How do you turn it off?" the guy asked.

"I don't know."

He shot me an exasperated look. "How did you turn it on?"

"I hit the *Hagalaz* rune. That one."

"So which one says *off*?"

I took it from him in shaking hands, turning it around, examining the runes. "*Dagaz* maybe? It means happiness."

I pressed it. The ball kept blinking. Well, I supposed just because I thought not dying equated to happiness didn't mean the maker of these charges agreed.

Konstantin appeared with an unconscious female form slung over his shoulder. "What are we doing here?"

"Trying to not die!" I cried.

"If this goes off by these other charges, it will set off a chain reaction the size of a small nuclear reaction," goatee guy said.

"Who the fuck even are you?" I snapped at him.

"I'm Enigma, MASC's only teleporting warlock. And the one who will get you the fuck out of here if we can't figure this out."

Teleporting warlock? "Then why don't you teleport this glowy ball of death out of here and drop it in the ocean somewhere?" The charge was blinking even faster now. Tension climbed up my spine. I could feel our time running out.

Konstantin and Enigma looked at each other in surprise. Then Enigma grabbed the charge from me and disappeared.

He reappeared a moment later. His hair was wild, his glasses askew. He straightened the frames and cleared his throat. "Yeah, that was fucking close. Tell the Director I'm putting in for hazard pay."

"Tell him yourself," Konstantin barked. "If I see him anytime soon, I'm likely to rip his fucking throat out."

I staggered against the wall, my knees going weak as the adrenaline drained from me. I slid down to a seat on the cold floor, my face in my hands.

Konstantin transferred the unconscious woman to Enigma, who staggered a bit under her weight. "Take her to Oliver, will you?"

Enigma disappeared without a word.

Konstantin sat down beside me, his forearms resting on his knees, his head tipped back against the wall.

For a moment, we sat in silence.

"So those guys were telling the truth? This really was the test? The kidnapping? The torture? The highly deadly magical charges?" How could Cyriaque have done this to me? How could Konstantin? How could I trust any of them to be my teammates after they'd lied to me and then put me through hell like this? Was I supposed to *want* to be part of an organization that treated its own people like this?

"The Oblivion Charges weren't supposed to be part of it. That was your little improvisation."

"What was I supposed to think—"

"You did good, Chanji," he said, interrupting me.

His praise swept through me like warm sunshine, which just pissed me off even more. I didn't want to crave his approval. "This was fucked-up."

"I know." He took a breath and then let it out slowly. As if he wanted to say more but was restraining himself. "It's not what we're about. This." He gestured to the warehouse. "Veil Force is a family." He took my branded hand and swooped a thumb across my palm, sending a delicious shiver through me. "A family you belong with. I hope you give us a chance to prove that to you."

And as angry and hurt as I was, I knew I wanted to give him that chance. Not just because I'd be able to do good at MASC and find out who'd really killed Dad. Not just because I longed to be part of the secret life my friends had built.

But because if I was being honest with myself, part of me wanted to know more of Konstantin Bauer.

It was the one reason that should keep me far away. And it was the one I knew I'd give in to.

17

———

Konstantin stared at the file in his hand. It was thin, just one piece of paper. A photo of Zariya Chanji stared up at him. The newest member of Phoenix Team, if Zariya forgave them for the clusterfuck that had been her test. She'd said she needed time to think about it.

He hadn't felt this anxious in centuries. Not facing down demon hordes or Nazi battalions. What would she decide?

He didn't know why she disarmed him. Was it her beauty? He'd worked with plenty of attractive females. Perhaps it was that she seemed too delicate for this work—for the coarseness of his team. Could she withstand Luiz's sullen moods, Daevin's lewd jokes? Rex's bitter diatribes, and him... Could she face the ghosts that haunted him? Far too delicate. His fingers traced the line of her cheekbone. Far too beautiful.

But she'd passed that test, and what was more—he'd seen a strength there. The slitted eyes that stared at him were lovely, but they were something more. They were unblinking. Unyielding.

She'd faced down unknown enemies and bested one of Veil Force's most talented fighters. She'd confronted her own nightmares with hardly a blink. Her cool thinking had saved the situation. He was impressed.

But if he was honest, he knew it wasn't just that. It was the fact that Zariya had known loss and had pushed through. That was a special kind of strength.

But on the other hand, she was half-human. And he was undeniably attracted to her. Adding a woman to his team would add a layer of complication. They had enough complications already. Maybe he should insist that she join one of the other teams.

"What are you staring at, boss?" Konstantin looked up to find his second-in-command, Galu, leaning against the door frame, his tattooed arms crossed over his chest. The nereid, a form of water elemental, glided in and took the picture from him, examining it with glowing blue eyes. "Now she's a pretty fish."

"See, that. There. That's what I don't want," Konstantin said. "I don't want anyone distracted." Least of all himself.

Galu rolled his eyes, giving Konstantin a gentle punch with his webbed hand. "If you think the lot of us can't tell our ass from our elbow with a pretty face around, we've got bigger problems, right? And didn't she pass the Director's little test with flying colors? As I heard it, she got the drop on all of them."

Konstantin grunted his assent. He'd learned long ago to trust the little voice that whispered deep within him; it had never steered him wrong. But right now his inner guidance was going haywire. That voice wanted Zariya close. Needed her near. Which was exactly why he should refuse to let her join Phoenix Team, if she decided she wanted in on Veil Force. He was struggling to be rational when it came to her. "She's not even a full supe."

"I know you, boss. It's not because she's half-human and it certainly isn't because she's a woman." Galu waited calmly.

Konstantin pressed his lips together, the only sign of his displeasure. There was no hiding things from Galu. The supe navigated the waters of emotion like he'd sailed them all his life. He had to give him something. So a half-truth. "She's Vizol's daughter."

"And that's bad how? Means she's got some badass blood running in those veins."

"What if something happens to her? If I can't keep her safe…"

"From where I sit, there's no one better to look out for her than you and Phoenix. At least if she's close, you can protect her." The voice snarled within him at Galu's words. *Yes. Protect her.*

"I can't favor one of my team over the others. I need a sixth who can pull their weight equally."

Galu knocked his shoulder playfully. "We all know you favor me over the others anyway, so what's one more, am I right?"

Konstantin snorted softly.

"You already know what you'll choose, boss, so stop second-guessing. It'll make the boys nervous. They might start thinking you're not infallible."

"I'm immortal, not infallible."

"Don't let them hear you say that," Galu said with a chuckle.

Konstantin shook his head as Galu left, picking up the photo once again. There was so much of Vizol in her. "The fish is right," he muttered. "You'd want me to take care of her, wouldn't you, old friend? So that's what I'll do." The voice he could shove aside. Yes, Zariya was beautiful and there was something strangely compelling about her. But he was a professional. He could be her commander. A mentor. Nothing more.

His phone buzzed in his pocket. A text message from an unknown number. *I'm in. But you're all still on my shit list. Z.*

Konstantin couldn't stop the grin from stretching across his face.

"Look at you, all sunshine and roses. Good news?"

Konstantin looked up to find Signe striding into the room, her blonde hair streaming behind her. He struggled to check his emotions. "Chanji is in. Looks like Broussard didn't fuck it up irrevocably after all."

Signe gave him a smug little smile.

Konstantin shook his head. "You knew."

"I would be a pretty shitty demi-goddess of fate and fortune if I didn't. Timing is perfect."

"Why do you say that? You have something for us?"

"Sure do. You remember those unicorn poachers we've been tracking down? The Collectors? Well, we've got a lead. Orkney Islands. Scotland."

"Good work. When do we move out?"

"Under-secretary is still approving the mission package. Should be tomorrow."

"Good." Konstantin cocked his head. "Why are you grinning like the cat that ate the canary?"

"Satellite picked up something else on the island. A round circle, with symbols raised out of the stone."

"You're kidding. Like the circle we found where Vizol died?"

"Identical."

Now it was Konstantin's turn to smile, baring his fangs. "Looks like Zariya might get her revenge after all."

CLAIRE LUANA

MYTHICAL ALLIANCE

PHOENIX PROTECTED

PROLOGUE

Warrick Mason hated unicorns.

He stood just outside the pen, peering at the three shimmering white beasts. The stallion tossed its pristine head with a scream of displeasure. He stepped in closer and it shied back, its black eyes rolling wildly.

His presence made the beasts nervous—the bony stretch of his antlers, his tall, thin form. They could sense he was a predator.

He hung his hands over the railing, his long talons clicking together.

One of the mares reared away, her pearlescent spiral horn hitting the low ceiling.

He gave her a tight smile. "You're afraid. Well, you have every right to be. This isn't going to end well for you." Unicorns were beloved by the fool humans—some of the only supes that they cherished. Never mind that the creatures were no better than beasts, lacking in intelligence or true power. Perhaps that was why the humans liked them so much. They represented a type of magic that was safe. Controllable. Unicorns were recognized as Class H-NV. Herbivore, Non-Verbal. Just the way the humans liked it.

Well, unicorns were also worth a fucking fortune. And that was the way *he* liked it.

"Boss, I've got something on our back channel." Finn came up beside him, a laptop in his webbed hands.

"What's the word?"

"Looks like MASC is on to us. They're getting ready to spin up a mission. Contact confirmed they'll be headed our way in less than six hours," the green-haired merman said.

Warrick frowned. "Any word from the buyers for these nags?"

Finn grinned, revealing a row of shark-like teeth. "Affirmative. We have confirmation, and the wire transfer."

"What did they end up buying?"

"Only the horns. They said we can do what we want with the rest."

Warrick turned back to the pen with a grim smile, his cavernous stomach letting out a low growl. Looked like he'd be eating well this afternoon. "Let's leave a surprise for MASC."

"What kind of surprise?"

"The exploding kind." Then he launched himself over the fence, his talons outstretched.

1

I stood at the base of Franklin D. Roosevelt Four Freedoms State Park, soaking in the weak morning sun. There was a bite in the air, and my cold-blooded body needed a boost. I shoved my hands in my jeans to keep them from shaking. My nerves were going haywire.

I couldn't believe it. I'd agreed to join Veil Force, a covert unit of supe commandos run by the Mythical Alliance of Supernatural Creatures, or MASC. My life now would be weapons and intel and...I didn't even know. What had I gotten myself into? Today I was going on my first mission. I could get shot at. I could get *killed*.

When I'd agreed to be a Veil Force Phantom, I'd been thinking about my dad. The fact that these supes had been on the trail of the men who had killed him, and I needed to be on that trail too. But this decision meant so much more. It changed everything. Was I was ready for that?

The United Nations compound stood just across the Hudson from us. In the center of the cluster of tall buildings, I could just make out the statute of the Lupine Offensive, depicting a two werewolves fighting side by side with a human soldier. It was the moment the human world had first learned of us. Supernatural creatures.

We'd been fighting for our place at the table ever since.

I smelled him before I heard him. A smell like starlight and empty night air.

Konstantin Bauer. Ancient vampire. Veil Force Phantom. Friend of my father's. My new boss. There was no simple box to fit him into. Konstantin Bauer defied categorization, even setting aside the fact that his presence happened to make my insides go as gooey as grilled cheese.

Konstantin came to stand beside me. He wore dark-washed jeans and a soft gray sweater today, and his sandy blond hair was pulled into a knot at the nape of his neck. It wasn't fair, how effortlessly handsome he was. Blue eyes and long lashes and chiseled jawline and *killer* body. I mean, resistance was futile. "I was fewer than five kilometers away."

I looked at him with a blink of surprise. "During the Offensive? Really?" It didn't surprise me that Konstantin had fought in World War Two; he'd told me he'd been turned into a vampire in 1423. But to be that close to history...

He nodded. "I couldn't believe it, when the reports came out. Werewolves had revealed themselves and they were fighting for the Allies. We were sure it was a German trick designed to throw us into chaos. But it strengthened us. A sign that God himself was rallying nature for our cause. It was brave of them to take a stand like that."

"Did you reveal what you were?"

He paused. "Not for another three years after the war."

If I remembered my history, that meant he'd come out one year after vampires had been officially recognized by MASC. The delay surprised me, but I said nothing. Those were different times.

A smile curved the corner of his perfect lips. "Some might call it cowardly."

I doubted calling your new commander a coward on day one was a particularly good idea, even if he'd said it first. So I pushed back. "I imagine caution served you well over the years. It's not always wise to throw it to the wind."

He looked at me appraisingly. "Change can be hard."

I straightened, trying not to mind being appraised. Trying to ignore the way his glacial blue eyes made my knees weak.

"I can tell you're cold. Let's go inside. I'll show you the cages. And your special gear."

"I have special gear?" I shoved down my excitement as I trotted after him. Was it so obvious that I was cold? "It won't be a problem."

"I don't hold my team members' physiology against them," Bauer said. "We all have unique needs. Nagas like you are no different. It's MASC's job to accommodate them. Our Equipment Officer is excellent, if not a little…quirky. He'll ensure you have all you need."

We made our way to the tip of the park, where the portal would take us down to MASC's secret Tartarus base. Konstantin practically glided beside me. His gait was smooth and steady, every movement perfect. He was a marvel. A deadly, beautiful killing machine.

"This is for you." Konstantin held out his hand, revealing a slim silver ring. "I hope you…like it." He cleared his throat.

I picked it up, examining the engraving. A sinuous snake wound its way around the delicate band, a nod to my half-naga heritage. It was a delicate version of the ring Dad had worn. I hadn't known its true purpose back then. A lump grew in my throat. "It's perfect."

"It's your key into the base. There's the entrance here, but there are two more entrances as well that you can use if this is too crowded. I'll show you those when we get to the Ops Center."

"Thanks." I hesitated. "Should we go…separately?" I didn't know how the portal worked.

"Together is fine."

Konstantin stepped in close to me and as we moved into the portal, I did my best to steady my heartbeat, to ignore my rising desire. Vampires could smell human pheromones and the last thing I needed was my new boss knowing that my half-human side was seriously crushing on him.

The portal whisked us down together, into the alcove with the elevator down to base.

"The Ops Center is on the third floor. Today we're going to the fourth, where the team supplies are." He pushed the button and leaned back against the metal wall. His muscles rippled beneath the cotton of his gray sweater. "Is there anything you wish to ask me about vampires? I find that even with modern education, unhelpful rumors abound. I'd rather you ask your questions now."

I considered as the elevator opened and I followed him into the hall. He'd already told me that he was Derived, meaning he'd been human before he was turned into a vampire. "You eat..."

"I supplement my human diet with animal blood. It is one of our vulnerabilities—needing to eat frequently. One of the unique parts of my physiology we account for."

"So you get hangry when you haven't eaten?"

Not even a laugh. "My joints start to lock up and it becomes difficult for me to move."

Ah. Not a laughing matter then.

"I do feed on the job sometimes. It's a matter of practicality. Will that be a problem for you?"

I furrowed my brow at his question until I realized what he meant. That he sometimes ate the bad guys. Clearing my throat, I ignored the lurch in my stomach. "As long as they had it coming, no need to put a meal to waste."

"Precisely. Ah. Here we are." Konstantin shouldered open a door and flipped on the light. "The Phoenix Team cages."

The dingy yellow paint and the flickering fluorescent lights didn't dull my excitement. It was a large rectangular room, lined on two sides with three large metal cages each, one for each of the six team members to keep their gear in.

Konstantin walked to the end of the room and pulled open the last door.

"This is yours. Hamish provides and manages all our equipment, and he's made some special modifications to the standard kit. Take a few minutes to look through everything. Hamish will be in to answer any questions. Unless you have any now."

Poking my head in, I looked over the pile of weapons and black gear. I recognized everything thanks to Dad's memories—he'd used a spell to store his twenty years of military and intelligence knowledge in his talwar blade—and I'd soaked it all in like a sponge after I'd touched the weapon. Without those memories, I would feel like a fish out of water in this place. "Nope, everything looks in order," I replied.

If Konstantin was surprised at my competence, he didn't show it. At some point, I knew I'd have to share the leg up I had with Dad's memories, but I wanted to keep that little secret to myself for now. I didn't know how these tough supes would feel knowing I had extensive knowledge on each of them—some of it sensitive or even embarrassing. Best to cross that bridge later.

I ran my fingers over the name plate on the outside of the cage. *Phoenix Six*. No name. A reminder that supes cycled through these roles—there'd been a sixth member of this team before me, and there would be after. As the newest member, I was at the bottom of the totem pole.

The door burst open and I startled against the bars of the cage.

Konstantin didn't flinch a muscle.

I tried to recover my cool, but by the grin on the newcomer's face, he knew he'd surprised me. Shoving down my annoyance, I took him in.

Flaming red hair; two thick, curving horns; a flicking tail; and a cocky-as-fuck grin. From Dad's memories, I knew this could only be Phoenix Four. Daevin Ryan. Demolitions expert. Caco-demon. I shoved myself forward, surprised by the heat coming off him. He wore the black Veil Force uniform over his red skin—cargo pants and a tight tee—but somehow it looked impossibly cool on him, like he should be slouching against a building smoking a cigarette.

"Zariya Chanji." I stuck my hand out.

He closed my hand in his and I had to resist pulling back. His touch didn't burn me, but it was a close thing. He looked me up and down with a leisurely sweep and so I did the same—taking in all six and a half feet of him. Taking in his glowing red eyes. Gold earring. Toothpick tucked in the corner of his mouth. "Daevin Ryan," he finally drawled. "At your service."

He released my hand and crossed the room, dropping into one of the two rickety chairs flanking a table against the wall. "She doesn't look like much."

I prickled.

"Ms. *Chanji* was chosen by *Caeldwich*," Konstantin said, emphasis on my last name. A reminder to this fiery asshat that I'd come from a fierce bloodline. That their magical sword thought I was good enough to join the team. I looked at Konstantin in surprise. I didn't need him to fight my battles, but I didn't mind the backup.

"Great. She's good with long, thin objects." Daevin uncoiled and stalked to stand before me, too close. Anger kindled to life in me, and I stood my ground. "But can she hold her own in a real fight?"

"Ask Leilani," I replied, aware of Konstantin's eyes on me. In the mad test Director Cyriaque Broussard had devised for me, they'd sent in one of their best fighters, a shapeshifter named Leilani, to pose as a bad guy and turn me. I'd kicked her ass.

"Daevin, have you lost all your manners?" a new voice called.

Daevin stepped back. "Figure you got enough for the both of us, mate."

My rescuer was tall and bronzed, with a shock of blue hair and a tapestry of glowing blue tattoos covering his hands, neck and temples. He was handsome, with big features and an even wider smile.

"Galu Leota." This was Konstantin's second-in-command. When he shook my hand, his touch was cool and soothing. "If that fireball-for-a-brain gives you trouble, you come to me, you hear?" His voice was lilting, with what I thought I recognized as a Caribbean accent. Dad's memories told me Galu was a water elemental from off the coast of Jamaica.

The door opened again and two more men walk into the door.

The first was fae, and hot damn—even better-looking than Konstantin. His ebony black hair was cropped neatly around his pointed ears and his tawny skin spoke of Latin descent. I couldn't help but stare, my eyes tracing the impossible beauty of his features and his tall, well-muscled body.

I swore I could hear Dad chuckle in my mind as his memory

informed me that this was Luiz Archileta, a Brazilian incubus. Great. A sex fae. Like I didn't have enough to deal with already.

Galu made the introduction because apparently I was too dazed to speak. "Luiz Archileta."

"Pleased to meet you," Luiz purred in a dulcet Latin tone, giving me a nod of acknowledgment before striking a pose against his cage that would make a Calvin Klein model jealous.

Galu finished the introductions. "And this is Rexsis Ahmad. But we all call him 'Rex.'"

Luiz's allure fled from my mind as I took in my last teammate. I didn't think I would be calling Phoenix Five "Rex" anytime soon. I wasn't sure what it took to get on a nickname basis with a demi-god, but I knew I wasn't there yet.

Rexsis was a descendant of the Egyptian god Anubis, and he bore Anubis's signature jackal head. His black, furred snout was long and narrow, his ears tall and delicately pointed. His eyes were as black as Alviya's, except for the two glowing irises shining like gold nuggets. His presence charged the air with magic, making my skin feel tight.

He stalked to the other chair across from Daevin and sank into it without a word.

Suddenly, it felt suffocating in here—the air was thick with magic and male ego. Panic lanced through me. This was crazy. Dad would have fit in here, no problem. He would have had these men, these creatures, laughing and telling war stories in a matter of minutes.

Me? I'd never felt so out of place, even surrounded by a crowd of humans. I felt distinctly female. Distinctly human. Distinctly like joining Phoenix Team had been a huge fucking mistake.

The briefing room was full already.

My roommate Kiki was lounging at a desk with two computer monitors in the corner of the room, and she offered me a small smile when we all filed in.

I didn't return it. I was still mad as hell at her for lying to me about her job with Veil Force for the last several years of our friendship—not to mention the fact that she'd tried to jab me with a memory serum when I'd started getting close to the truth. Things had been awkward as hell at the apartment last night.

Thanks to Dad's memories, I also recognized Sergeant Chris McMichael and Signe Dirksen, both standing at the front of the room. McMichael, a clean-cut guy in his early forties, was Veil Force's MASC liaison. That organization did much of the intelligence gathering for Veil Force, verifying the teams' missions and target packages. He was also the only human in the room.

Signe was a norn with the power to see the future. She was also gifted with in-depth magical knowledge. Dad'd had mad respect for that particular supe, and her sister, Verta. In fact, he'd been a little in awe of them both, and so I figured I should be too.

Konstantin and the rest of the team filled in around the table. I took my seat, trying to ignore how weird this was. I was getting briefed for a real, live mission. What the hell had I gotten myself into?

McMichael started the briefing. "As most of you know, we've been tracking a group of poachers called 'the Collectors' for some time. They've been targeting supes for the last year, but the flavor of the month seems to be unicorns. The horns are renowned for their medical and magical properties."

Daevin grinned and waggled his eyebrows. "Help a fella in the bedroom, they say."

"Need more than a unicorn to help you," Galu shot back.

I pressed my lips together to keep from smiling.

McMichael ignored them both. "Yes, unicorn horns are known for their aphrodisiac properties."

"Why are these guys suddenly on our radar?" Galu asked. "They've causing trouble for months, right?"

"The Collectors crossed the wrong herd. A week ago, they broke onto a game reserve in Norway. They took three unicorns belonging to the Norwegian royal family."

"God forbid some princess loses her pretty pony." Daevin rolled his eyes.

"MASC doesn't work for the European royal houses," Luiz said, his deep voice made even sexier by his accent. I found myself wondering which of the rumors about incubi were true. Hours-long endurance? Knowledge of secret erogenous zones? I'd have to do some Googling when I had a chance. Just for curiosity's sake, I reminded myself. Not like I'd ever get involved with a teammate. And in a hypothetical world where I *did* get involved with a teammate... Konstantin was still top of my list.

"We do when they have friends at the head of the department." McMichael replied to Luiz's comment, which I'd already forgotten. *Focus, Chanji!*

"Anything unique about these unicorns?" Galu asked.

"Just their important owners. Although..." McMichael looked at Konstantin, who gave a quick shake of his head.

I frowned at the exchange. *What was that?*

McMichael continued. "That's all you need to know for now."

If the others had taken note of the unspoken conversation, they ignored it. "And we think they're still alive, do we? With all their..." Galu made a corkscrew gesture from his forehead.

Kiki flicked the screen to an image that looked like a fortress on a remote island. "Our intel puts them on a remote island in the outer Hebrides, in Scotland," she said. "Satellite imagery shows, that at least as if this yesterday, the unicorns were whole and alive. We suspect they're arranging buyers, though, so that won't stay the case for long. You're going in today."

"What sort of opposition can we expect?" Konstantin asked.

Kiki answered. "The compound is heavily fortified, but they're not expecting visitors. Half a dozen guards. A few more Collectors. Automatic weapons. Likely not the most impressive operation." Damn, it was weird to see my friend like this. Advising military commandos on their dangerous ops?

"We think an amphibious entry is best," said McMichael. "There's no other way to get you on the island undetected. We've arranged a local fishing vessel that can get you approximately a quarter mile out without detection. You'll swim the rest of the way. The water's choppy and frigid, but there's a beach you should be able to land on. Here." He pointed. "Shouldn't bang you up too bad."

"Galu, maybe you can find some friendly porpoises to do the hard work for us." Daevin waggled his dark eyebrows.

"Naw. You could use the workout," Galu shot back.

Konstantin ignored them both. "Wheels up in two hours."

The room mostly emptied out when the briefing was over but for me and Signe, who glided over to where I stood, waiting for the rest to file out. She navigated the world so easily, I could hardly tell that she was physically blind.

Daevin paused at the door, eying us. "You two plotting the overthrow of the patriarchy over there?"

Signe smiled sweetly. "It's already crumbling around you. We just have to stand back and watch it burn."

I snorted. "You seem like a man who appreciates a good bonfire, Daevin."

His glowing eyes narrowed.

"Go." Signe shooed him. "I just need to fill Zariya in on a few lady things. Where the bathroom is, which of you has the smallest dick, etcetera."

His eyes widened as she stage-whispered to me, "It's Daevin."

He was grumbling to himself about the girth of his tail as he disappeared through the door.

I laughed out loud. "That was amazing."

"I don't really know how big any of their dicks are." She turned to me. "But you've got to give as good as they do. Better. They'll respect you for it."

I nodded, grateful for any ally I could get.

"Konstantin is shit at introductions—well, at most niceties—so I wanted to make sure you know you can come to me with anything."

"Thank you." My life had been steeped in lies for so long, it was surprisingly refreshing to encounter such a straight shooter.

"You should meet with Hamish before you head out. He should be in the cages by now, complaining about something. He'll make sure you have the gear you need." She held a hand out for me to head out before her and I obliged. "Oh, Zariya?"

"Yes?"

"You should be honest with Konstantin."

I paused. "About what?"

"Everything. Your father's memories. Your feelings for him. You two will need each other, before the end."

My blush scalded me right up to my hairline. Perhaps Signe was *too* straight a shooter. "Noted," I croaked out.

SIGNE'S WORDS chased me all the way back to the cages. Was my crush on Konstantin really that obvious? But no, there was no way she could have known about Dad's memories without her supe powers. It must have been her norn abilities revealing all my secrets. Still invasive as fuck, but not quite so alarming. As long as Konstantin didn't know. It was one thing for my human physiology to react to his vampire hotness, it was another for my commander to know that I was drawn to him like a moth to a fucking flame. I think I'd prefer the earth to open up and swallow my mortified self whole.

I thought the room was empty, but the door to my cage opened, startling me back. My hand flew to my chest as a tree popped out. Or should I say...a creature that looked like a tree. His wizened skin was cracked like bark and stark branches grew from the crown of his head like antlers. Soft moss dusted the cracks and twists of his arms and neck. But he moved quickly and efficiently. I didn't think he was as old as he looked.

"You must be Hamish." I catalogued what I knew about spriggans. They were some sort of supe from the British Isles. They like to collect things. *The end.* That was all I had.

"Zariya Chanji! Yer most welcome indeed." His accent was both thick and adorable, though I couldn't quite place it.

I fought back a smile.

"Come see, come see what I've gathered fer ye."

He gestured me towards a pile of weapons and tech sitting on the desk, and I couldn't help but feel like he was inviting me to look at his trove of gold. He showed me my gear with the pride of a young father introducing his firstborn son.

He held up a suit that looked like black Lycra covered with threads of dulled onyx. "This is a special uniform fer ye—special fabric Verta designed. It'll regulate yer temperature perfectly." I ran my fingers over the soft fabric. They'd found a solution for the inconveniences of my cold-blooded nature—that was pretty sweet.

The other items twisted the knot in my stomach even tighter as I realized I was potentially going into fucking battle. AK-15, sidearm, grenades, body armor, helmet. Everything was magically enhanced to protect it from cold and wet and basic malfunctions. The communication link was a neural connector that tucked into my ear, letting Kiki communicate directly into my head from a distance and allowing the team to communicate telepathically to each other when the comms were activated. That would be interesting. He showed me the med kit equipped with healing draughts. At least I knew my way around the medical supplies from my own med school training, rather than just from borrowing Dad's memories.

"Here are some of yer special things." He lifted a belt fitted with half a dozen little cylinders that look faintly like grenades. He pointed to them in turn. "Neutralizes the magic in the area. Glamours and such. This one's a protective enchantment. Ye each get one, so use it wisely, eh? Containment spell. Rescue beacon. This—" He pointed at the last cylinder. "Ye better be about to die if ye pull this pin."

"What does it do?"

"This summons Enigma, our resident warlock—"

I held up a hand. Ah, Enigma, the hipster warlock who could teleport in and out of Tartarus base. "Say no more. We've met."

"He's our only teleporter," Hamish lectured. "So if ye summon him to rescue ye when ye don't really need him, ye could be keeping him from another team who's dyin'. So think on that before ye pull the trigger." No problem. I hoped I wouldn't have to see the warlock again anytime soon.

"Weel, I think that's it. I'll leave ye to try it all on, get familiar." He moved past me and I leaned back, out of the way of his branch-horn thingies. "Okay. Thanks." I offered him a smile. I could use all the friends I could get.

Hamish looked at me and his face seemed to *crack apart*. It was mildly horrifying. A smile? "Me pleasure."

3

———————

My gear was on by the time the rest of the team returned to the cages. Everything fit like a glove. I'd braided my thick hair back, and I could tell from my reflection in the window that I looked hella badass. This Lycra suit thing hugged me in all the right places, displaying my curves in a way that even a fashion model would be willing to pay a small fortune for.

Konstantin entered the cages first, freezing in the doorway as he took me in, top to toes.

I gave him a curt nod, trying not to be pleased by the flash of what I thought might be desire in his ice-blue eyes. I reminded myself, for what seemed like the tenth time that day, that vampires could detect human pheromones. I'd be better off not thinking about Konstantin like that, or things were going to get real awkward between us. Signe's suggestion flashed to mind and I shoved it aside. Tell him how I feel? Not fucking likely. I had to *work* with this guy.

After the rest of the team filed in, and gave me their own once overs, I stepped out of the door to give them all privacy to change. I was sure we'd all be seeing lots of each other changing, but for now, I'd rather do without Daevin's snark.

The door opened, revealing Konstantin looking devastating in a black uniform. The other Phoenix Team Phantoms filed out after him. They looked even bigger and more menacing in their gear—bristling with weapons.

"Grab your gear, Chanji," Konstantin said. "We're headed to the airfield."

~

IT IS one thing to know your job will involve jumping out of airplanes and navigating frothing, angry seas—it is quite another to experience it.

The Veil Force airfield was in New Jersey, accessible by a portal on the second floor of the base. From there, we piled onto a state-of-the-art V-22 Osprey helicopter that was outfitted with long-distance flight capability. The guys weren't real talkative on the flight, so I did my best to ignore the testosterone fest around me. In North Scotland, we landed and quickly piled onto a sketchy-looking fishing boat that would take us the rest of the way.

We caught our first glimpse of the island when we were less than a mile away. The sky was so heavy and gray that it felt almost like twilight. Normally, we would go in at night, but we feared that another eight hours could find us there too late.

A gust of cold wind splattered rain across my face. My suit was getting its first test, and I was pleased to find I was toasty warm inside it, despite the bone-breaking chill around me. I would have to give Hamish and Verta my compliments.

Konstantin stood stock-still despite the rolling of the boat, his eyes fixed on the monolith of white rock in the distance. He looked like a painting—*Vampire at Sea*. He was as foreign to me as the depths beneath our vessel—as enigmatic as the ocean itself. Between our battle at the park and his rescue of me at the MASC warehouse after my test, I was almost starting to feel like we were friendly. But now that we were on mission, it was like he'd barricaded himself inside the fortress that was Commander Bauer. He seemed impossibly distant.

Galu sat at the bow, trailing a hand over the side into the frigid surf, like he was petting a puppy. Luiz and Rexsis both sat staring silently at our target—contemplative or zoning out, I wasn't sure.

Daevin was smoking a cigarette and chatting with our boat driver, whose Scottish brogue was so thick, I would barely recognize the words as English.

I was beginning to wonder if Daevin talked so much to make up for all the rest of them. Was this my life now? To sit in a tense, sullen silence with five deadly supes who wanted nothing to do with me? Was it always like this, or did my presence make it worse? I suspected the latter.

Dad's memories were filled with jokes, war stories, and pranks between the guys on his teams. Bonds of friendship and brotherhood forged in unbreakable links. Maybe making friends was just one more thing that Dad had been better at than me.

Daevin crossed the deck to speak to Konstantin, but his words were snatched by the wind before I could hear them.

"Five minutes," Konstantin announced.

My stomach lurched. *God, help me.* This was really happening.

"Comfortable with the amphibious entry, are you?"

I looked up to find Galu standing next to me, his chin raised to the wind. Konstantin had moved slightly. He was listening.

It was a fair question, as I hadn't told them about Dad's memories inside me giving me an edge when it came to all this commando stuff. "I'm a fast learner," was all I said.

"I believe it. Your dad was one of the most proficient supes I've ever known. There's nothing he wasn't good at."

I looked into the roiling surf, fighting the thickness in my throat. I still couldn't talk about Dad—even think about him—without the tears coming.

"He recruited me, you know."

I did know, but I wasn't about to admit that. "Seems like he recruited most everyone." I didn't really want to talk about Dad, but Galu was my only teammate who was giving me the time of day, and I didn't want to offend him. "So...you can...manipulate water?"

Galu leaned over the railing, looking down at the water below. The network of his tattoos lit up a glowing aqua blue. I startled but watched as a ball of water floated up out of the sea into the air before us. He held out his palm and the water settled onto it before forming into the tiny glistening form of a coiled cobra.

I breathed out in amazement. "Cool."

"Showoff," Konstantin said, still not looking at us.

"Some of us were built for more than killing, boss. We were built for wonder, you know?"

Konstantin stalked across the boat to us and I gripped the rail. My senses misfired when he directed that steel gaze on me. The animal in me called out in warning. *Danger.* "Some of us have to do the killing so the rest of you can make pretty water art."

I looked from Galu to Konstantin to get a read on the situation. Galu was grinning, his posture at ease. So they were joking around, not really at odds. But something about what Galu had said lingered with me. *Some of us were built for more than killing.* Which was I?

Konstantin turned to me. "Are we close enough for your infrared…?" He gestured, clearly unsure what to call it.

"My glands," I offered. My naga glands operated like an infrared sensor, allowing me to sense heat or cold.

"Your glands, right, to evaluate the hostiles on the island?"

I gauged the distance. "Should be." I turned and opened my senses, sending them questing towards the island. The gusting wind didn't help, but I struggled to focus.

Nothing. I couldn't sense any life on the island. I turned back to Konstantin with a frown. "It's possible that between the wind and the rock, I'm too far. But I'm not detecting any signs of life on the island."

"That's consistent with what Ops told us. We might be too late."

We'd gotten an update from the Operations Center? I resisted touching the communication chip in my ear. It was weird to think Kiki was so close.

"We're still going in to check it out, right, boss?" Galu asked.

"Affirmative. We need to gather any available intel on where they might have gone."

"Any chance Angus here can drive right up and drop us off?" Daevin looked about as excited to get in the water as I was. Which was not very.

"We stick to the plan. If our intel is wrong, we can't risk it," Konstantin said. "We go in two."

My stomach flipped nervously as I opened the oxygen valve on my tank and put my respirator in my mouth.

Splash.

Galu was over the side, happy as a fat kid at a buffet. Konstantin tossed him the dry bag with our weapons and he threaded his arms through the straps.

Luiz was over next, followed by Rexsis and Daevin, who didn't hesitate, despite his earlier bitching.

"You ready, Six?" Konstantin asked me.

I jerked my head up. That was me. My callsign. Phoenix Six. I nodded at him. His chiseled profile was the last thing I saw before I dove over the side and the sea swallowed me up.

The cold of the water hit me like a physical thing. I could feel my lungs constricting and seizing up. I fought against it and my blessed suit kicked in, the fabric compensating for the frigid temperature, heating around me. I took a shaky breath from my respirator and kicked towards the other forms I saw floating in a loose formation.

Galu glowed softly underwater, like the teal and aquamarine of the tropics. He was a comfort in these stormy seas—a beacon.

Konstantin joined us and motioned for us to head in.

The swim wasn't long, and Galu calmed the surf for us as we hit the beach, making it relatively easy to pull ourselves up onto the rocky shore and regroup behind a boulder. Galu handed out our rifles and pistols and we checked them for water. I buckled on my holster with my pistol. Everything looked good.

"*Ops to Phoenix Team.*" Kiki's voice sounded in my head. *Weird.* "*Have you made landfall?*"

Konstantin touched the comm chip in his ear. "*Affirmative.*" Konstantin's thought flashed quickly after, like a firework in the night. I shivered, ignoring how much I liked the feel of his thoughts in my head. *"We're about to head up. Any change on sat view?"* He touched the chip again, turning it off. *Note to self: Turn the chip off, unless you want your thoughts blasted through the entire teams' minds.*

"Negative. Island looks dead."

"Rex, Zariya, anything?"

Rex lifted his jackal snout and sniffed the air, his black nostrils flaring. After a moment, he shook his head.

I felt out with my senses. Again, I didn't sense any heat or life on the island. "Looks like they're gone."

"Let's see what we can find."

Despite the island's apparent emptiness, we proceeded cautiously, guns trained ahead, clearing each area as we went. The fortress was old and crumbling; its stone hallways and chambers were cold and dark. Here and there were signs of modernity—a few bags of trash, bootprints crisscrossing the dirt floors, a smashed hard drive that apparently had not make the cut when these Collectors turned tail.

"Looks like they left in a hurry," Luiz said, toeing aside a tall lamp that had been abandoned and broken in a hallway.

"Think they knew we were coming?" Daevin asked.

"Don't see how," Konstantin replied as we summited a set of stairs at the top.

Next to me, Rexsis's nostrils flared. "Hold," he said, his golden eyes gleaming.

We all froze on the stairs. "Do you smell that?" Rex asked.

I sensed nothing with my glands, but I flared my nostrils.

Konstantin's gun went up. "There's something dead up there. Move slowly."

The top of the fortress was a large, open room with a view of the sea. In the corner was a makeshift paddock, strewn with straw. And something else.

4

———————

My hand flew over my mouth to keep down the bile rising in my throat. All that was left of the unicorns was three mangled corpses, half gnawed through, blood and entrails splattered on the wall.

Daevin swore under his breath in a language I didn't recognize.

Konstantin walked forward and knelt down, surveying the scene with a calm I envied. "Horns are gone."

"What did that?" I asked. The violence of it was staggering. As if whatever had eaten those poor creatures had reveled in the destruction and inhumanity.

"What do you smell?" Luiz asked Rex. "Can you tell what it is?"

Rex's jackal snout was curled back in a snarl, as if whoever had done this was too animal even for him. "I smell...a wendigo." He had a British accent. Huh. Dad's memories didn't have much about Rex. He was one of the few supes he hadn't recruited himself.

A wendigo... Wendigos were Recognized but restricted—Class X —meaning they ate...humans.

"They are evil motherfuckers," Daevin said, which I imagined coming from a caco-demon really meant something. "From north-eastern Canada. Their hunger drives them. However much they consume, they always want more."

"I wonder if this one is just working for the Collectors, or leading it," Galu asked.

"Either way, it's our next lead. There aren't too many wendigos in the world. We'll find this bastard," Konstantin said.

Galu hurried into the room. "Boss, I've got something around the back of the island you should see."

Konstantin nodded. "All right, listen up. We're not going to leave these poor supes here. We'll bury them. Galu, you're with me. Zariya, I want you to go check out those trash bags in the hallway and see if you can find anything."

I stifled my grimace. Rifling through trash bags seemed like a *new girl* task, but I far preferred it to digging and burying unicorn parts. "Yes, sir."

I followed Galu and Konstantin out the door, leaving my other teammates looking down at their task with distaste.

I glared at the three black trash bags when I reached them, my mind filling in all manner of disgusting items I could be about to find in a wendigo poacher's trash. Ugh. At least I was wearing gloves.

I tore open the first bag, upending it on the stone floor. I toed through it—mostly banana peels, protein bar wrappers, and other food scraps. I saw a piece of paper and snagged it, trying to make sense of the numbers written on it. Account numbers maybe? Buyers? I tucked it into my belt (this suit needed pockets—I'd have to talk to Hamish) and tore into the next bag.

Something hard and metal tumbled out. It settled onto its side, blinking its big red numbers at me. An alarm clock, but it wasn't an alarm it was about to announce.

59

A timer.

58

My heart froze and stuttered back to life.

57

There's a bomb. Somewhere in this building, there's a bomb.

56

Oh, fuck.

I grabbed the timer and hurled myself back up the stairs, throwing open the window.

Konstantin and Galu were below me, bending over something embossed on the rock courtyard below.

My mouth dropped open as I saw it. Forgetting the urgency.

They were kneeling over a broad circle made up of strange symbols indented in the stone. I'd seen a circle like that once before in my life. In the report on Dad's death.

"Zariya?" Konstantin looked up. "Report."

I held up the timer.

42.

41.

"Oh fuck," Konstantin said.

Konstantin touched his comm on his temple, shouting his order directly into his team's minds.

"Everybody, out now!"

His thoughts raced. They hadn't spotted the explosives, which meant they could be anywhere on the island. And they had only—36 seconds to clear the place.

But his team was well trained. They exploded into action. Out of the room and down the stairs faster than any human being could move. They were supes after all—preternatural speed was their birthright. Konstantin was relieved to see Zariya was keeping up with the rest of them—she may have been half-human, but she was fast as a full blood.

They ran together from the courtyard down to the beach, their boots pounding through the sand. Galu thrust his arms out before him and made a splitting motion—parting the water before them easy as Moses had split the Red Sea. They were a hundred yards past the surf line, the dark ocean forming a strange semi-circle around them, when the bomb went off.

It shook Konstantin to the core, rattling his teeth. Zariya staggered against him and he steadied her with one hand on her trim waist in that skin-tight suit, the other catching her arm. He righted her and withdrew his hands, turning to watch the wall of flame licking towards the sky. The entire fortress had gone up.

Galu twisted his magic so the water formed a roof over them, blocking them from raining dust and debris.

"Musta been a mountain of C4 in that place." Daevin's eyes were bright, flames dancing in his irises.

"No one smelled the explosives when we went in?" Konstantin asked.

Rex shifted uncomfortably. He had the best nose; he should have caught it. Should have known something had been amiss. Maybe over the stink of dead unicorns, he'd missed it.

"Zariya just saved all of our asses. Guess we should promote her from provisional status," Konstantin said.

"I was on provisional status?" she asked.

"We can heap praise on Zariya later." Galu groaned. "But can you all move your asses so I don't have to keep holding up the whole damn ocean?"

THE ISLAND WAS TOO BADLY DAMAGED for their helicopter to land, so the team had over an hour to kill until the little fishing vessel could return to pick them up.

Galu swam while Daevin paced the shore, clenching his hands in and out with every other step. He didn't like confined spaces.

"Konstantin?" Zariya stood before him with a piece of paper in her hand. Did that suit have to be so form-fitting? He knew it served a purpose in regulating her core temperature, as she was cold-blooded, but in it she looked so... female. It showed every bit of her form—

lean muscle running into soft curves. How was he supposed to treat her like one of his men when it was so obvious she wasn't?

Konstantin took the paper and frowned at the numbers written on it.

"Might not have been a total bust. I found it in the trash. I was thinking bank account numbers maybe? Too long for phone numbers."

Konstantin nodded. "Good find. I'll get it to Kiki when we return. Maybe she can piece it together."

Zariya nodded and bit her lip, flashing a glimpse of a fang. Her fangs were different from his—long and curved like a snake's. "That circle on the stones. It was the same as the one they found in Turkey, wasn't it? Where Dad was killed."

"I think so."

Zariya looked up at the wreckage of the island. "There's no way it survived."

Konstantin shook his head. "No. I'm sorry."

"Did you get any photos?"

"Galu and I had just started examining it. But we have some sat photos. We can do our best to enhance them and compare them to the circle in Turkey."

Zariya's smooth brow furrowed and he realized his mistake. "Sat photos?" She held up her hands. "Wait, you knew when we were coming that the ring was here?"

"We spotted it before the mission, yes. It was part of our interest in the island."

She let out a little grunt of disbelief. "Why didn't you say anything?"

"It was need-to-know."

Zariya stuck her jaw out, crossing her arms over her chest. "That's bullshit and you know it."

I didn't want to get your hopes up, is what he wanted to say. But his other team members were perked up, watching their exchange with interest. Watching to see if Konstantin would let this upstart talk to him like that.

"Phantom Chanji," Konstantin barked, advancing on her.

She held her ground, her hands balling into fists. God, she was beautiful this close up.

"I am your commanding officer, and you will not question my authority. If I say something is need-to-know, then it's need-to-fucking-know. Am I understood?"

Zariya took a step forward until they were almost nose to nose, though he towered over her by a foot. "Yes, sir. I will follow your orders without question."

He relaxed slightly. She smelled of cinnamon and C4, her pheromones a potent mix of desire and anger.

But she wasn't done, apparently. "But when it comes to my dad, every fucking detail is need-to-fucking-know for *me*. I will not be kept in the dark. Ever. Again. Am *I* understood?"

Anger smoldered in him at her insubordination. Anger and a desire to tackle her into the sand and kiss her until those plush lips were swollen. He blinked away the thought. "It seems we understand each other perfectly." He didn't move. He was her commander; he wouldn't stand down first.

She spun on her heel and stalked off across the beach. It was all he could do to not sag with relief. Tension crackled through him.

Konstantin's sensitive ears caught Daevin's whisper to Luiz: "I'm going to bring popcorn on missions from now on."

He frowned. Konstantin himself would have to bring something more. Because he'd just gone head-to-head with Zariya Chanji, and he had the distinct impression he'd lost.

5

———

The plane ride back was subdued. We hadn't accomplished our mission, those poor unicorns had died, and we'd almost gotten blown up. What if I hadn't found the timer in the garbage bags? What if I'd opened that third garbage bag first, taking the time to rifle through it before I'd finally moved on to the last? We'd all be smeared across the Scottish stones right now.

How many missions had Dad gone on that had been so close—a hair's breadth the only thing separating life from death, success from failure? I'd known what he'd done had been dangerous...but in an abstract way. Now I really *knew*. Understood deep down to my core. I found myself glad for my prior naïveté.

I closed my eyes and the image of the stone circle came to mind. I wish I'd had more time to look at it, to take pictures of the inscription. The script must mean something—must presented some clue as to the circle's purpose. A clue to who'd killed Dad.

Konstantin was on the phone, arguing quietly with someone back at command. Cyriaque, maybe? I caught snatches of conversation. Whoever had owned those unicorns was not pleased with our failure. No, the intel hadn't shown any movement off the island. How had the Collectors escaped?

We landed and took the portal back to Tartarus. Suddenly, I was bone-weary. The thought of getting myself home, feeding myself, and collapsing into bed felt like a Herculean task.

The team parted once inside Tartarus with fist-bumps and shoulder pats.

"Nice job, Zariya." Galu flashed me a broad smile. The mood of the rest of the team didn't seemed to affect him at all. Maybe it was his swim, but he was as chipper as a blue jay. I could tell I was going to be forever grateful for his presence on the team. The only one willing to talk to me, apparently. Unless you counted Konstantin's lecturing, or Daevin's snarky comments. Which I didn't.

Konstantin paused, his pale skin shadowed in the light of the fluorescent bulbs above. He didn't appear worse for wear—unbothered by the close call or the politics that had followed. He was everything I expected a vampire to be, and a Veil Team leader. Powerful. Unflappable. Deadly.

Dad had exuded those traits in spades. An unexpected bolt of jealousy lanced through me. Would I ever be so self-assured, so capable? Dad had said it was in my blood. My birthright. But right now, I just felt tired.

Konstantin examined me for another second and I struggled not to squirm under his inspection. "Unless I call sooner, be back here tomorrow at 0900 hours."

"Are you doing further investigation into the numbers I found?"

"I was going to give them to Kiki to run through the pattern recognition software, to see if we can find a hit."

"I'd like to stay then, if that's all right. Sir. In case something comes back quickly?" Never mind that I also wanted to peruse the database for any mention of the imprinted stone circle.

"Fine. But grab some food and get some rest. We need you fresh if we get a new mission."

"Roger that."

It wasn't a bad idea. I followed Konstantin's advice and found my way to the gym for a shower and then headed to the cafeteria. I felt like there were eyes on me wherever I went, though I wasn't sure if it was because I was new and had busted half the base apart breaking in or because I was Vizol Chanji's daughter.

I was just about to brave my way into the cafeteria when a red braid and tucked pair of white wings caught my eye. I hadn't really talked to either of my roommates since I'd joined Veil Force. Since I'd learned they'd been lying to me for years. But I found I missed them. "Alviya?" I called.

She turned and her black eyes lit up. She hurried over to me. "Hi."

"Hi," I replied.

"You had your first mission, right?"

I nodded.

"Wanna tell me about it?" she prodded. I hated it, this weirdness between us. I wanted hugs and gushing and jumping up and down with excitement like we used to have. Maybe those days were gone.

"We went to rescue some unicorns those Collector guys had stolen. They were already dead." My stomach flipped at the thought of the mangled corpses we'd found.

"Oh, Zariya, I'm sorry. That's rough."

"The place was rigged to blow. We barely made it out in time."

"What?" Alviya's black eyes went wide. "I'm so glad you're okay."

"Me too."

"Helluva first day."

I smiled despite myself. "That's an understatement."

"How's your team?"

I glanced around and then grimaced. "They're...an acquired taste, I think. Clearly, they're all tough as hell and good at their jobs. Not a real friendly bunch, though."

Alviya patted my shoulder. "They'll warm up to you. Must be weird. The last Phoenix Six was injured and couldn't return to duty. Hard to have someone new come in and take your buddy's place. Must feel like they're betraying him if they're too nice to you."

I nodded. I didn't know much about the last Phantom who'd had my place. Dad's memories said it was a fae male who'd been injured. "I hadn't thought about it that way, but you're probably right."

"You'll win them over in no time," she said encouragingly.

"I did alert everyone to the bomb today," I admitted.

"There you go! Nothing like saving someone's ass to make them like you." Alviya nodded approvingly.

My phone buzzed in my jeans pocket, and I glanced at it. "It's Konstantin. They must have found something."

I looked up to find Alviya with a knowing smile on her face.

"What?"

"You call him 'Konstantin.' Everyone else calls him 'Commander' or 'Bauer.'"

A blush crept up my cheeks. "I dunno. I met him before he was my team leader. Besides, his head's big enough without me 'yes, sir'-ing and 'no, sir'-ing him all the time."

Alviya's smile broadened. "You'll be good for them. For all of them. Shake this place up a little."

"I hope so."

"Well, you should go. It was...good talking to you," Alviya said.

"You too," I admitted grudgingly. I felt like our conversation had dispelled some of the awkwardness between us. Now I'd just have to figure out how the hell to do the same with Kiki.

I ran into the cafeteria and grabbed a banana and a protein bar before heading back up to the third floor.

I found Kiki and Konstantin hunched over a computer screen, her fingers flying furiously. She looked over her shoulder and gave me a small smile. I returned it.

"What'd you find?" I peeled my banana and took a bite.

Konstantin gave me a withering look and I shrugged. "You told me to eat. Just following orders, boss."

Kiki saved me. "The computer found a match to the numbers you found. It's the website information for some sort of illegal hunting site. The second number is the log-in code."

"What kind of hunting?"

"Supe hunting," Konstantin said. "There's quite a black market in supe products, but some sick fucks like to take their own trophies.

Selkie pelt rugs, elf ears, mounted dragon heads... Humans love to exploit other creatures for their own pleasure."

My stomach flipped at the thought. *Bastards.*

"Does the website have any information about who's running the hunts? Or where they're located?"

"Why, yes it does." Kiki's fingers flew as she navigated to another page. "There's a name. One we know already. The Collector. Looks like the events happen all around the world, but the next event is taking place in...Scotland again. Inverness. Looks like you guys will be getting your frequent flyer miles."

"What's the target of the hunt?"

Kiki leaned into the screen and then hissed. "It looks like they're offering a guided hunt for...Nessie."

"Nessie? Like the Loch Ness Monster? It's real?" As soon as I asked the question, I realized how dumb it was. Of course Nessie was real. Ninety-nine percent of the legendary creatures were just shy supes who had the misfortune of being caught by some human camera.

Konstantin's hands balled into fists. "Of course. Nessie is a rare sea dragon. There are only a few in the world. She's a gentle, ancient creature. Wouldn't hurt a fly."

She? I mouthed, and Kiki pressed her lips together to keep from smiling.

Konstantin was shaking his head. "Fuck no, not on my watch. Kiki, tell the team I want them in the briefing room in ten minutes. It's the end of the line for these assholes."

6

Galu stood under the showerhead for far too long, letting the water soothe away his tensions from the day. It had felt good to swim in a real ocean again. Fierce and wild and untamable.

He had found a sort of home here with MASC and Veil Force, but he would never get used to living in a city as big as New York. Not really. So much concrete and *so* many people. The only thing wild here was the fight for a cab on a rainy afternoon.

He came out of the shower into the communal bathroom with a towel wrapped around his waist. Luiz was at the mirror, freshly showered, working on getting his hair just right.

"Dunno why you even bother," Galu said. "Don't the women just fall into your lap no matter how you preen?"

Luiz paused, looking at him in the mirror. "Do I detect a hint of jealousy?"

"No. I could get all the companionship I wanted. *If* I wanted."

"Ah, yes, your self-imposed exile from the female gender in penance for the one who got away."

Galu scowled, putting toothpaste on his toothbrush with a bit more force than was strictly necessary. He didn't like talking about Melusine.

"You know, maybe you should just rip the Band-Aid off. It's been, what, two years since you moved here? Since you enjoyed female companionship? If I had a dry spell like that..." Luiz shook his head.

"A week is a dry spell for you," Galu shot back around a mouthful of toothpaste.

"Don't hate the incubus, hate the game." Luiz flashed a dazzling grin and Galu rolled his eyes. "Speaking of the female sex, what'd you think of our newest recruit?"

"Zariya?" Galu spit out his toothpaste. "I was skeptical, but I like her. For a civilian, she's surprisingly competent."

Luiz nodded. "She moves like Vizol. It's almost like..." He shook his head. "I don't know. Except for her ass in that suit." He whistled. "Nothing about Vizol there."

Galu shook his head. "Don't let Konstantin hear you say that."

Luiz raised one dark eyebrow as a delighted grin spread across his face. "You think our ancient, fearless leader has...a crush?"

"I know I've never seen someone tell him off the way she did on the beach, and he just...took it. Like he was flustered as hell."

"In all the years I've been on Veil Force, I've never seen Konstantin interested in anyone, let alone a Phantom. This would be an extremely interesting development."

"Maybe you're not his type."

"I am everyone's type," Luiz purred.

Galu shrugged. He regretted bringing it up. He respected Konstantin. He didn't want to undermine his authority within the team. "Just don't say anything. Maybe I'm reading something into the situation that isn't there."

"Don't you worry, my fishy friend. I'm nothing if not subtle," Luiz said with a grin.

Right. Subtle as a freight train.

Daevin appeared in the door, his red eyes glowing. "When you two are done painting your nails, boss has called us in for a briefing."

"Already?" Galu asked.

"Looks like they found something. Briefing Room in five."

GALU DRESSED in a fresh Veil Force uniform and poured himself a cup of coffee before he found his way to his seat. The rest of the team had already filled in around the table. Konstantin and Kiki stood in front before the projector screen.

Galu had lost count of how many briefings like this he'd attended, how many missions, in his two years on the force. But they got his adrenaline going every time, even now. He'd never get tired of this.

He'd fled Port Royal thinking he'd never find another family, another place to call home. He'd been wrong. Vizol had found him living homeless on the beaches of the Florida Keys and given him a second chance. A purpose, in a time when he'd had none. Vizol Chanji had saved his life.

"Listen up," Konstantin said. "Zariya found evidence on the island that Kiki has used to find the Collectors' next stop. It appears that in addition to slaughtering innocent unicorns, these assholes run illegal supe hunts around the globe. The next event takes place in three days. In Inverness, Scotland."

"What's the target?" Rex asked.

"The Loch Ness Monster."

Galu spluttered into his coffee cup. "What?"

"If we don't stop this, in three days' time, Nessie will be a trophy on some asshole's wall."

"A bloke would need a real big living room for that head," Daevin remarked.

Galu shot him a disgusted look. Sometimes Daevin didn't know when to shut the hell up.

"Our intel shows that the hunters will be gathering at nearby Aldourie Castle, which has been rented out for the hunt," Kiki said. "Unfortunately, the Collectors' website doesn't have details about how the hunt's going to go down. So you'll need to pose as hunters, infiltrate the castle, and figure out exactly what the hunt's going to look like."

"We authorized to kill these bastards?" Daevin asked.

Konstantin crossed his arms over his chest. "I spoke with the Director. The mission objective is to stop the hunt and save Nessie. Our secondary objective is to take any Collectors into custody and collect as much intel as we can about their operations. We have the opportunity to take down their organization for good."

"Didn't answer my question," Daevin replied.

"Capture if you can, kill if necessary."

"How are we infiltrating the castle?" Zariya asked. She'd been quiet, apparently taking it all in.

"The hunt is capped and at capacity," Kiki said. "So I can't just buy your way in. You'll need to take the spot of hunters who are already signed up. I'm in the process of evaluating who's best, and I will have that intel for you by the time you land in Scotland."

"So we'll have to take out these other supes first?" Zariya asked.

"Affirmative," Konstantin said.

"Quite a few unknowns on this one," Rex said. "Lots of potential for error."

"So we'll improvise," Galu said. "We always do."

"You're both right," Konstantin said. "But we have no choice but to move on this. So let's move."

THEY WERE an hour from landing in Inverness when Kiki pinged the team over their mental comms.

Galu had been dozing, dreaming about Melusine. She was all he ever dreamed about. The cerulean blue of her hair, the musical cadence of her laugh, bright as a bubbling stream.

Galu stood and made his way to the metal table where they conducted their in-air briefings.

God, he missed her. Two years later, he *still* missed her. But he'd never see her again. He'd ruined what they'd had. He'd ruined everything.

Daevin snapped his fingers in front of Galu's face and Galu shook off the memories. The melancholy. He put on the face he wore here, that had come to feel true most days. His team needed him now. They needed his optimism and cheer. He needed it too.

"What do we got?" he asked. They could all communicate mentally with Kiki, and each other, through their comms, but it was easier to speak out loud when they could. None of them liked spending more time in each other's heads than was strictly necessary.

Kiki's voice crackled over the speaker in the plane. "First, I think I have a name on our wendigo target. Warrick Mason. He's wanted in three countries for a whole slew of charges. He was last seen in Europe, cozying up with some pretty bad guys. He's mostly referred to by a nickname."

"Let me guess," Zariya said. "The Collector?"

"Ding ding! Someone give the girl a prize."

"Good work. Kiki. Let us know if you get any more intel on him that could help," Konstantin said.

"Will do. Second, I found you some hunters. There's a group of six that landed in London last night. They'll be driving up to Inverness today. You'll be able to intercept their vehicle, take their identities, and proceed to Aldourie Castle."

"Are we going to just leave them tied up under some bushes somewhere?" Luiz asked.

"Broussard's been in contact with the Supe Unit at MI-6. They're going to meet us and take the hunters into custody, allowing us to proceed with the mission."

"And MI-6 doesn't want in on this particular bit of action?" Daevin asked.

"Broussard convinced them to let us handle it. They'll be in the wings if we need assistance."

"Not fucking likely," Daevin said. "We don't need babysitters."

Kiki cut in. "I'm sending you the information on the hunters now."

Konstantin turned on an iPad and placed it on the table between them. Six pictures came up, and they all leaned in to examine the faces they'd be impersonating for the next forty-eight hours.

Kiki cleared her throat. "As you can see, there's a bit of a wrinkle—"

Daevin let out a bark of laughter. "There are two women." He held up his hands. "Not it."

Galu started to chuckle. Daevin was right. Zariya would impersonate one of them, but which of them would play the other?

"Obviously, it should be Luiz," Daevin said.

"Whoa, just because I'm the prettiest, you assume I should play the girl?" Luiz countered.

"Yes," Galu said.

"Precisely," Rex added.

Zariya had a half-smile on her face and was leaning in, examining the photos. "This guy's a merman. And looks a bit like Galu. You could play him without a glamour, probably."

"And I could be this imp." Daevin pointed to another image.

"Luiz could pass for this human," she said. She looked at Rex with an apologetic smile. "It seems like you'll have to wear a glamour. You're too distinct. It should be you."

Rex's black, furred jackal head shimmered and transformed into his human form—that of a handsome, Middle Eastern man with a pronounced nose and a wolfish look.

Zariya took a step back, shock written across her face. "What? How...? You can do that?"

Rex crossed his arms, a smug expression on his face. "Of course. I prefer my human form."

"Then why have you been all scary jackal face since I've met you?"

"What do the youths these days call it? Hazing?" Rex gave her a toothy grin. In Rex's proper London accent, it sounded like a game aristocratic lords would play on their sprawling estates. Possibly with polo horses.

Zariya put her hands on her hips, cocking her head at him. She didn't seem angry, more amused. "Okay, I clearly underestimated you, Ahmad. Game on."

Konstantin was staring at the photos, looking slightly ill. "Rex does look a lot like this djinn. He wouldn't need to use a glamour."

Kiki chimed in. "That's what I concluded. Glamours can be detected or neutralized, so it's best to use them as little as possible. That's why I selected this team. This way, only one of you will need to use one."

Galu picked up the iPad with a chortle, turning it around to face his commander. "Konstantin, looks like you'll be playing the part of... Rebecca Spire, vampire."

Zariya patted Konstantin on the shoulder. "Don't worry, boss. I'll give you a lesson in how to walk in heels."

7

———

Konstantin had always liked Scotland. The stark, spartan beauty of its countryside, the grit of its inhabitants, the faerie magic that permeated the place like a subtle heartbeat. Even in this modern era, it hadn't lost its wildness. He admired that. Especially when he himself was starting to feel domesticated—softened by modern life.

They had set up an ambush point along the narrow one-lane road that turned off the B862 from Inverness and led down to the Aldourie Castle. The main roads from London were too large to risk a vehicle intervention. This spot was closer than he liked to their final destination, but it was isolated, with forest on one side and fields on the other. It was their best option.

Daevin and Rex were crouched next to him in the bushes, Daevin silent for once. The demon was a chatterbox unlike anyone Konstantin had ever known in his hundreds of years of existence. Zariya, Galu, and Luiz were positioned at a cross street fifty meters ahead and would pull out to block the road when the vehicle with their supe targets approached. Their MI-6 help had another SUV that would block the supes' exit—giving Konstantin and his team time to incapacitate the bastards.

He craned his neck, searching through the trees for the other team's van. He could just make it out. He'd checked three minutes ago. They were in position. He flexed his fingers, keeping them limber. The calm he normally felt before battle was eluding him.

He looked back to the road and found Daevin watching him with a twisted smile of amusement. "What?" Konstantin said.

Daevin raised his eyebrows. "Nothin', boss. Been a while since I've seen you this wound up on a mission."

"I'm fine."

"Wouldn't have anything to do with our pretty new teammate?"

"I'm fine," Konstantin snapped.

Daevin grinned. The supe delighted in pushing buttons. It seemed to be one of his favorite pastimes. But damn it, Daevin was right. He was on edge with Zariya around. He was fucking *worried*. Between the "test" Broussard had given her and their last mission, she was two for two of almost getting blown up. That was an impressive record for any Phantom.

"No need to worry," Rex said. "She moves like one of us. She thinks like one of us. It's peculiar, but it's like she's been a Phantom for years. We just have to get used to the dynamics of the new team."

Konstantin frowned. "She does seem...surprisingly competent for a civilian, doesn't she?" He wasn't worried about Zariya's competence. So what was he fretting about like a mother hen? *Keep her safe*, the voice deep within him growled. There it was. That was the problem. He was drawn to her in a raw, animalistic way that he hadn't experienced in...decades. Centuries? He was worried about what the hell *he* would do if the voice got too strong. Emotion was dangerous in battle. It overpowered training, reason, all else. He couldn't let it control him. Even if he felt a deep throb of need when she was around.

God, I wish you were here, old friend. Vizol's presence would have been enough to douse even the most tenacious feelings for Zariya. Vizol Chanji had recruited him a decade ago, back when Konstantin had been leading Austria's special ops teams. They'd been tasked to protect an Italian siren who'd been on tour throughout Europe and who'd received death threats before her concert in Vienna. The singer hadn't thought the Austrian military was up to the task, and so she'd called MASC.

Back then, Konstantin couldn't even hear the acronym without snorting. Mythical Alliance of Supernatural Creatures? A branch of the United Nations under the arm of the Security Council designed to protect supe rights around the globe? Everyone knew it was a joke. A political dog and pony show designed to mollify the supe world—to quiet the complaints about rising violence and discrimination against supernatural creatures. *Look, we're doing something. Things are going to be fine.* Well, Konstantin had lived and fought through countless wars, including World War One *and* Two. Humans had a remarkable capacity for hating those who were different. Things didn't always end up fine.

The only organization he'd had less respect for than the Mythical Alliance had been its Veil Force, its black-ops group of highly-trained supe special operators. The UN, MASC—all of it had seemed like a fawn surrounded by wolves.

And then he'd met Vizol. A supe larger than life. He'd been a magnet of a man—when he walked in a room, you looked. When he spoke, you found yourself leaning in to hear more clearly. Vizol'd had a fire about him—a drive to better the world. An unwavering belief it could be done. An unflinching warrior's spirit. And something else...something Konstantin had thought lost in himself. Humanity.

Four days that mission had been. Four days was all it had taken for Vizol to convince Konstantin to upend his life, to leave his men and career and the country he'd called home for six centuries.

And he'd been right. Veil Force was a place to make a difference. A place where they were doing something real.

"Satellite shows them five minutes out." Kiki's voice permeated his mind. His thoughts skittered away in surprise and he resisted a shudder. There was no doubt that Veil Force's telepathic communication was effective on mission, but there was some part of him that would never get used to someone else's voice in his head. He knew that his thoughts weren't broadcast to the team unless he activated his comm,

but they still ran for cover whenever a message came in. His subconscious clearly didn't trust the tech.

He touched the comm in his ear. "*Phoenix Two, you in position?*"

"*Ready as we'll ever be, boss*," Galu said.

The air charged with electricity and anticipation, and the calm fell over him. He breathed it in deeply. *Finally.* Life was messy, but this was a place he understood. A place he embodied. The calm before the storm. Where *he* was that storm.

"*You've got a clear road. No more vehicles between you and the target*," Kiki said.

"*Galu, move into position*," Konstantin ordered.

The van rolled out, blocking the narrow road. There were thick trees and underbrush on the left, and a stone fence on the right.

"Nowhere to go, assholes." Daevin grinned.

He heard the vehicle before he saw it, his ultra-sensitive vampire hearing registering the purr of the SUV's engine. He checked his rifle. They'd loaded special tranq bullets that contained a toxin excreted by the mara, the same supe whom Broussard had hired to fake-torture Zariya during her test. The tranquilizer sent the recipient into a swift, if not terrifying, sleep. He suppressed a shudder. He'd come across a lot of frightening supes in his day, and though he'd never admit it, the mara frightened him more than most. He'd lived through enough nightmares for one eternal lifetime.

"Here we go," Rex whispered.

The black SUV with tinted windows slammed on its brakes as it caught sight of the truck blocking its path.

It sat for a moment, quiet but for the idling of its engine. No doubt as those inside took stock of the situation.

Their MI-6 partners pulled out of the gravel turnout behind them. "*Everybody, move*," Konstantin ordered.

First, he had to find and neutralize the djinn, whose magic was the most unpredictable and who posed the greatest threat to their mission. Konstantin tore out of the trees with lightning speed and wrenched the driver's door open, warping the metal hinges. He tossed in a smoke bomb filled with cardamom and anise combined with microscopic gold flakes and shielded behind the door as it went off. It was one of Verte's ingenious inventions, designed to come out swinging with all of the djinn's natural aversions.

Cries and expletives sounded from inside the smoke-filled vehicle, which Konstantin's team surrounded.

With a nod from their commander, Phoenix Team moved as one, pulling four doors open and shooting with tranquilizer darts. There were five individuals inside, and he took it all in in a blink as darts made contact. Human, human, merman, imp—but the djinn vanished before the dart hit him.

"Fuck!" Konstantin cried. He backed out, away from the vehicle. "Find him. He couldn't have gone far." They fanned out away from the vehicle, onto the road.

Konstantin felt the tug of magic in the air before he heard Zariya's sharp inhale.

He turned to find the djinn behind her, his arm wrapped around her throat, a Beretta M92 pressed to her temple. The supe was tall and thin, with jet-black hair and golden skin. "Stay away from me or I'll shoot her!" the djinn cried. His dark eyes were red and watering—clearly, Verta's smoke bomb had done its work.

"Easy now," Konstantin said. "We don't want to hurt you."

"Fuck you!" the djinn cried. "You shot them all!"

Konstantin took a slow step forward. "They're just sleeping. We just want to talk." The rest of the team was arrayed in a semi-circle around Zariya and the djinn, rifles trained on the supe. Someone had a shot, but it was too risky. The djinn could reflexively pull the trigger and shoot Zariya in the head.

Konstantin reached up to touch his comm, but the djinn's eyes widened. "Don't fucking move! Put your guns down! All of you!"

Galu's voice swam through his mind. *"Hold your fire. We don't want to risk him pulling the trigger as he goes down."*

Relief flooded Konstantin. His second had made the same assessment.

Konstantin held up one hand and carefully lowered his rifle to the ground. "We're putting our guns down. Just don't do anything crazy." He didn't need a gun, and neither did his team. They were twice as dangerous without weapons. He struggled to stay calm in the face of the animal rage that flooded through him, singing in his veins. He'd rip this supe's throat out for laying a finger on Zariya.

The djinn's eyes were watering now, and he shook his head, scrunching up his nose. As if he were about to sneeze.

Zariya's eyes captured Konstantin's as she tried to communicate something. Her hand strayed up slowly, ever so slowly, to her comm. Her reassuring voice flooded his mind. "*Nobody move. This fucker is mine.*"

The djinn sneezed.

And Zariya moved. So fast that even Konstantin's vampire sight could hardly keep up. She knocked the pistol up and away and flipped the djinn clean over her head.

He crashed hard on the pavement.

Zariya grabbed the rifle that she'd dropped at her side and popped the djinn in his chest with a tranq dart.

The supe started to flicker in and out of space. He was trying to teleport away. But the flickering stopped as the djinn's eyes closed. As the tranquilizer took over.

Konstantin blew out a breath.

Luiz whistled and started a slow clap. "Phoenix Six, you don't disappoint."

Zariya gave a shaky laugh. "Couldn't get shot and miss Konstantin glamoured to look like a woman, now could I?"

Daevin let out a bark of laughter.

Konstantin had to hold in a smile as a surge of pride overtook him. His Zariya was fierce and strong and—his thoughts stuttered as he realized where his mind had gone. *His* Zariya?

She met his gaze and grinned, displaying those curved fangs and devastating smile. His heart squeezed.

God help him, he was in deep fucking shit.

8

I buried my hands under my armpits to keep them from shaking. Damn this suit for not having pockets.

I stood safely off the side of the road as our MI-6 contacts and some of the team loaded the unconscious supes into the MI-6 SUV. We'd take our targets' vehicle the rest of the way to the castle.

Galu trotted back towards me. "Hop into the van and pull it off the road, will you?"

I was glad to be given something to do. Anything to distract me from the shitstorm of emotions raging inside me.

I pulled myself into the driver's seat and turned the key. Dad's memories and training had taken over in the heat of the moment, when the djinn had pressed the cold butt of that pistol to my temple. I'd been calm. Unafraid. I'd known exactly what to do—wait until a moment when he was distracted, and then pounce.

But now, in the aftermath, I was jumpy as fuck, the adrenaline leaving me feeling strung out. I'd never been in a life-or-death situation before, and now I'd been in two in fewer than twenty-four hours.

"*Zariya?*" Kiki's voice brushed softly against my mind.

I touched my comm. "*Yeah?*"

Hesitation. "*I saw what happened on the satellite feed. Are you okay?*"

A thick knot formed in my throat. I'd almost died. For the second time in so many days, I'd almost died and Kiki and I still weren't speaking, other than official MASC duties. My eyes stung with tears. Kiki had lied to me, and that would take a long-ass time to get over. But...I wanted to forgive her. It had only been a few days and I already missed her. *"I'm fine. Do you think we could talk when I get back?"*

"Of course." Her mental voice sounded hopeful.

"Thanks."

I stopped the van far enough off the road that Galu could pull the other vehicle in behind me. I got out and leaned against the side.

"How are you doing?" Galu propped an arm against the van beside me. "You did great back there, but that sort of thing would shake anyone up."

I let out a little laugh. "I think I'm okay, but it's like my body won't catch up. I think it keeps expecting someone to jump out from every tree."

"Deep breaths," Galu said. "Your sympathetic nervous system is in charge right now—fight or flight. Deep breaths tell it that the danger has passed."

"Thanks." I followed Galu's instructions. My med school classes had taught me as much, but learning something in a book and applying it in the field were two very different things, as I was learning.

"So what are we going to do?" I asked.

"About what?" Galu crossed his arms over his chest.

Konstantin approached, looking like an angel of death with his pale skin and dark tactical gear. He'd been beyond impressive as he'd gone for that SUV, nearly tearing the door off its hinges. *"About the fact that we're missing a supe. Kiki, any ideas where our last lady is?"*

So I wasn't the only one who'd counted five instead of six supes. Good. "If she's coming late, she'll blow our cover," I said. "We may be able to fool the front desk staff at the hotel, but she'd be on to us in a hot minute."

"Looks like she's sick. Not coming," Kiki chimed in.

"So we don't get to see Konstantin in drag?" Daevin drawled.

"Sorry to disappoint all of you." Konstantin couldn't keep the smirk from his face.

"What's the plan, boss?" Galu asked.

Konstantin's jaw worked as he thought for a moment. I couldn't take my eyes off him. *It's just cuz he's a vamp. They're literally supernaturally attractive*, I told myself. At least I'd been able to keep my desire under wraps on our missions, or, under wraps enough to keep my half-human body from betraying how bad it wanted to jump his bones at least.

My face was heating. *He's your boss. Your boss.* I needed to distract myself. I looked at Daevin's horns. Rex's little goatee. The undulating lines of Galu's tattoos. Luiz's...nope. Luiz was just as hot as Konstantin. No help there.

"All right. Here's what we do. You five proceed with the plan. I'll travel overland and sneak into one of your hotel rooms tonight."

"The castle has surveillance," Daevin pointed out.

"If I can't outsmart a few cameras, it's time for you all to put me out to pasture. I'll come in from above. You just let me know what your room numbers are after you check in. You can find me someone to glamour myself as, and we'll go from there."

"You've got a vehicle incoming on your position," Kiki said. *"Five minutes out."*

"Everyone, get changed—now," Konstantin said. "I want you in the vehicle and gone by the time that car drives by."

I opened my mouth to ask about the van, but Konstantin was already gone.

I shook off my surprise and took the pile of clothes that Luiz handed to me—they'd been stripped off the supe prisoners. It would be creepy as hell to wear some human chick's clothes. To take her identity. But it was the mission.

"You need help peeling yourself out of that suit, Six?" Luiz asked.

I snorted. "Not even in your dreams, incubus."

Daevin cackled and I suppressed a smile. I was starting to like these guys.

I went around the other side of the SUV and stripped out of my suit, pulling on the human woman's black jeans, chambray shirt, and leather jacket. Her pants were *reeeally* tight, and definitely too short, but by some miracle, I got them buttoned. Her knee-high boots were definitely too small, but I could wear my combat boots with this outfit and look decent. Not sure what the hell kinda footwear I would wear with the rest of her outfits, though. Couldn't wear combat boots with a cocktail dress. Although, with this crowd of murderous supes, who the hell cared?

I came around to find the guys in various states of undress. Luiz buttoning up an oversized plaid shirt over a truly glorious six-pack, Galu fighting to get on a white T-shirt that was stretched so tight across his muscles that they screamed for help, Daevin looking like a couch potato trying to pour himself back into his high school jeans. Only Rex looked perfectly put together, adjusting the crisp cuffs of a charcoal suit that fit him like a dream.

As Daevin let out another string of expletives, I couldn't help myself. I started laughing.

"Oh, yuk it up, honey," Luiz said, pulling the shirt away from his body. He looked like a kid playing dress-up in his dad's clothes.

"Yeah, seriously, you're one to talk. Those jeans tight enough over that ass, Kim Kardashian?" Daevin said.

"At least I could get them buttoned," I said sweetly.

Daevin growled.

Galu leaned forward and flexed his back, trying to get the shirt to fit better. The sound of ripping fabric startled a nearby bird off a branch.

I doubled over and started cracking up. It was too much. These were MASC's toughest, most terrifying operators, and they looked absolutely ridiculous.

The guys started chuckling, their laughter joining mine. "Well, I think we look great. We'll fool anyone," Galu said.

"Look at this proper English fuck." Daevin pointed to Rex. "What, do you have your tailor on speed dial? You have a tiny elf in your pocket? How'd you get that to fit so perfectly?"

Rex's mouth twitched, as if he were holding in a smile. "You know my abilities include manipulating matter."

"Yeah, you've moved rocks and stuff—wait, you can just change the size of clothes?" Daevin goggled.

"What the fuck, man?" Luiz said. "Hook a brother up!"

"You just going to let us all suffer like that?" Galu said, with mock hurt.

I straightened, wiping tears from my eyes. Wow, I didn't realize how much I'd needed that.

Kiki's voice filled our minds. *"Vehicle one minute out."*

"Are you on the move?" Konstantin's voice came a second later. Damn, he had a sexy voice—dark and velvety, with that hint of an Austrian accent. But fun time was over.

"In the car," Rex said. "I'll fix everyone's wardrobe on the move."

I grabbed our discarded tactical gear and threw it in the van and we all piled in, Galu behind the wheel. He threw the SUV into reverse and gunned it.

Rex attended to each of the guys as Galu took the narrow road that curved down towards Aldourie Castle and Loch Ness.

It was my turn last, and I breathed a sigh of relief when my jeans magically increased in size and stopped cutting painfully into my stomach.

I groaned in relief. "Rex, every woman needs one of you."

He just nodded, turning back to the front. I thought I'd made him blush.

We quickly identified whose luggage was whose, making sure we knew our names and information. Rex magicked our IDs and passports, transforming the pictures to look like us. For the next two days, I would be Catherine Richardson, from Los Angeles, California. "You can call me 'Cat,'" I said.

Luiz made a purring noise, complete with a clawing motion directed my way. I rolled my eyes.

The trees opened up before us and Aldourie Castle came into view.

My mouth dropped open. It was beautiful—with creamy tan

brick siding and soaring spires. It was the type of castle you'd expect to see in a Disney movie.

Galu pulled into the parking lot and turned off the car. A frazzled-looking valet in a white jacket jogged out towards us.

"All right, team," Galu said. "It's go time."

9

Konstantin crouched beneath the shadowed eaves of the roof of Aldourie Castle. The view from here was incredible—the loch stretched flat and gray into the distance, nestled against the somber hillside. A cold wind tugged at the edge of his coat, sending its icy fingers down his collar. It didn't bother him. One of the perks of being a vampire. His body was incredibly durable now, nearly invincible. Regular heat and cold didn't bother him. It would take far greater extremes to even touch him.

Konstantin had watched the SUV with his team pull up, observed them carrying their bags inside. They had looked the part—clad in leather and dark denim, mirrored sunglasses and sneers on their faces. He hated being left outside like this, especially with Zariya so new to the team. But he trusted them. Galu and the others were experts. They would take care of her.

His hand strayed to his ear and he forced it into his pocket. He wouldn't ping them on comms. He would wait and trust them.

But he couldn't help but let out a deep breath of relief when he heard Galu's voice. "*We're checked in. Heading to rooms now. There are some real dangerous mofos here, boss.*"

"*Including us,*" Konstantin replied. They'd come head to head with some of the worst in the supernatural world. They'd busted ISIL's wyvern nest and tangled with the panther shifters who ran the Pantera drug cartel. This would be no different. Veil Force protected supes from assholes like the Collectors. They'd do so here. And hopefully get some answers about Vizol's death, too.

Galu's voice crackled to life again. *"I'm in room 24 with Rex, Daevin, and Luiz are in 25. Zariya's in 26, with a window facing the lake. Should be easy to get into, and you can hole up there."*

Konstantin's heart skipped a beat. Stopped. Restarted. Sharing a hotel room with Zariya was a bad idea. Far too familiar. He needed to see her as a Phantom—a team member—not as a woman sleeping in a bed just feet from him.

But he couldn't think of a legitimate reason not to follow Galu's suggestion. It made sense. If he truly was to treat Zariya like just another member of his team, that meant he had to act normal. Maybe if he acted like he wasn't attracted to Zariya, his body would get the idea. So he responded with *"Roger."* God help him.

He crept over the dark tiles of the castle's roof, making his way towards room 26. He was grateful that he'd studied the castle blueprint before they'd landed. The window was already open, and it was an easy maneuver to swing himself off the roof and into the room in one lithe motion.

Zariya whirled and let out a little squeak as he landed on light feet inside the room. She pressed a hand to her chest. "Konstantin. You surprised me. Galu said you'll be staying here."

He surveyed the room quickly. Only one bed. "I'll take the floor," he said gruffly.

She opened her mouth to protest, but Konstantin pressed on. "Any trouble with check-in?"

"None. There's a welcome party tonight at 7 P.M. downstairs in the ballroom. I suspect they'll announce the rules and details for the hunt there."

"All right. We'll make our plan after that."

Zariya unzipped the suitcase on the bed and started transferring clothes to the dresser. She was tidy. He would have done the same.

She pulled out a short, black dress that looked barely big enough to cover her long legs, holding it up before her. "I guess I'll have to wear this tonight; it's the only thing she has that's even remotely party-appropriate. Hopefully, Rex can make it bigger; otherwise, it'll be way too tight."

Konstantin's mouth went dry at the thought of Zariya's luscious body poured into that tight little number. He took a breath, trying to steady himself. *You're over six hundred years old. You've been with the finest French courtesans and wealthy heiresses and even a fucking queen that one time. It's Just. A. Dress.*

He headed back to the window before she could see the molten expression on his face. He needed some air.

I sat by the window, flipping through the room's sole magazine for a tenth time—an outdated volume that was little more than an advertisement for Inverness's restaurant scene.

Konstantin was laid out on the bed like a knight in a ballad, fast asleep. Taking a goddamn nap. *The only bed in this room that I'm sharing with Konstantin Bauer, holyshit, holyshit.*

His feet were bare, and damn it, he had nice feet, with long toes and graceful arches and strong ankles. What the hell was wrong with me? Who was I, some prudish Victorian dude catching a flash of ankle? Why the hell were Konstantin's bare feet so disarming?

Maybe because it felt too real—hinting at other types of intimacy I really shouldn't have been thinking about. The last thing I needed was Konstantin's sensitive nose smelling my attraction again. Now that he was my boss...I'd die of mortification. But damn, if I couldn't even look at the guy's bare feet without getting turned on? I was so screwed.

I flipped the page of the magazine with more force than was strictly necessary.

"You can't possibly be reading that again."

I froze. "I thought you were asleep." Though...did Derived vampires even really need sleep? I didn't know.

"Not with you constantly rustling over there." Konstantin opened his blue eyes and regarded me.

I swallowed but did my best to shake it off. "It's not my fault you have superhuman hearing."

He pursed his lips. "I suppose that's true."

"Is this commonly how these missions go?"

"You expected...what? A shootout every ten minutes, a car chase on the hour?"

"I'm just...bored." Right. Bored. Better that than *wound up with enough sexual tension to send me to the moon*. I hoped sitting by the window would cool me off, steal the scent of my pheromones before they reached Konstantin's sensitive nose.

Konstantin sat up, draping his strong forearms over his knees. "That's the problem with supes these days. You expect instant gratification and have the attention span of goldfish."

I rolled my eyes. "Do not go all '*in my day*' on me now, Bauer. Are you going to regale me with tales of how you had to be up at dawn to sheer the sheep, spin the yarn, and knit yourself a sweater before you could get dressed every morning?"

The corner of his mouth twitched, as if he were holding back a smile. "I mean, I didn't sheer the sheep myself—"

I stood hastily. "All right, Gramps. Point taken. I think it's time for me to get ready, anyway."

Konstantin closed his eyes again, laying his hands beneath his head. "Knock yourself out."

I'd already traipsed over to Rex's room to make him magick my dress and Cat's black heels into my size, so I locked myself in the bathroom and riffled through Cat's toiletries bag. I looked at her toothbrush with a frown, then set it down. That was too much sharing. Hopefully, the front desk had extras.

I changed into the dress and then did my best to make myself look presentable, putting on the basics: mascara, eyeshadow, lipstick. I'd never been much of a makeup girl. I remembered with a pang the times Kiki and Alviya and I had gone out dancing, blasting tunes in the apartment while we got ready. I didn't think my life would ever be that carefree anymore.

I fluffed up my hair, which looked okay as it was, curly and bouncy. I buckled on Cat's shoes—pretty cute strappy heels—and surveyed the look. Not bad, if I did say so myself.

What would Konstantin think? I banished the thought. He was my boss. My commander. Nothing more. Could not be anything more. Despite the way his blue eyes seemed to bore into me, sending energy straight down to my lady parts.

I came out of the bathroom and was rewarded by Konstantin's eyes going wide as he choked on the water he was drinking. Just because he was my boss, and I couldn't ever act on my attraction, didn't mean that wasn't an ego boost.

"What do you think? Do I look like an evil hunter of rare and treasured supes?"

"You look..." He paused. "A different type of dangerous."

"I'll take that." I held in a smile. "What time is it?"

"7:05."

"Shit. I better get down to the guys."

"You remember all their cover names?"

"I do."

"And you're going to avoid talking to anyone if you can? If someone did know you—know Cat, I mean—we want to avoid any interaction."

"I remember the rules you laid down an hour ago."

"Okay. Sorry. I'm not used to staying back while the rest of the team goes into the field."

"We'll be fine. It's just a party."

"Famous last words," he grumbled.

Waggling my fingers over my shoulder, I headed out the door. "Bye, Dad. I'll be home by eleven."

He scowled as I shut the door, and I paused for a moment, leaning against the door frame. Suddenly conflicted. For the first time in a long time, the word *Dad* had left with my mouth without being accompanied by the crushing sorrow I'd come to wear like a second skin. Sure, I'd said it as a joke, and hadn't been referring to my real dad, but somehow, it was still okay. Being with Phoenix Team... knowing the truth about Veil Force and Dad's role in it...I think it was good for me. I think it was starting to help me move on. Battle was a strange place to find some semblance of healing, but I was a naga. And a Chanji.

The interior of Aldourie Castle was a breathtaking throwback to past centuries—the vaulted ceilings framed by intricate crown molding, the richly wallpapered hallways hung like a museum portrait gallery. The glittering light of crystal chandeliers guided my way down to the main floor, which held the majority of the common rooms.

The murmur of voices and music greeted me as I reached the bottom of the stairs. My stomach flipped nervously as I neared two open doors that led to the main hall. Even though I'd put on a brave face to Konstantin, I was nervous as hell to walk through those doors.

But like always, Dad's memories steadied me. He'd done missions like this dozens of times. The key was to give pieces of truth and weave the lies deftly around them.

The main hall was filled with supes of all shapes and sizes, but there was a definite thread running through them. These supes were Class C—carnivorous—and Class X—those who consumed humans. There were a lot of Class X supes here. More than I'd ever seen in one place. A leggy chupacabra, a gorgon with sinuous snakes writhing about her head, and several I didn't even know the names of. The supes in this room were bad motherfuckers. They were those who operated in the shadows. Those who skirted the rules MASC had lain down to protect humans. And to protect us from human backlash. Humans didn't like getting eaten very much. It really ratcheted up the inter-species tension.

I caught sight of Daevin and Luiz over by the bar and hurried to their side. I felt eyes on my body as I navigated through the room and wished this dress had a little more fabric.

You're not prey, I told myself. *You're a predator. You're just as dangerous as these supes.*

Luiz let out a low whistle as I reached the bar. "Buy you a drink, m'lady?"

For once, I didn't have any quips for him. I was too nervous.

Luiz raised an eyebrow as if noticing my lack of comeback, but he didn't ask. "What do you want?"

"Something strong."

"She'll have a vodka soda. Make it a double," he told the goateed human bartender, who looked like he was about to shit his pants. I didn't blame him. I hoped he was getting hazard pay for this.

Luiz handed me my drink and I took a big swallow. I shouldn't have been drinking, but I needed something to soothe my nerves.

All of a sudden, the murmur of voices stopped and the room fell silent but for the background music. The crowd seemed to be parting as a new supe walked through the front door.

Goosebumps broke out on my body as I took him in. My skin went cold. This was him, I knew it to my bones. Warrick Mason. The wendigo. The Collector.

10

————

The supes around the room regarded Mason warily. I opened my glands, taking in their scents. And yes, they regarded him with fear. For these badass supes to fear this creature spoke volumes. Mason was responsible for the gruesome deaths of those poor unicorns. For leaving that bomb for us. And I was sure for death and destruction we didn't even know about. But most importantly, this supe had had something to do with my dad's death. Anger flared through me, banishing fear and common sense. I started forward.

"What are you doing, Six?" Daevin caught my arm.

"Going straight to the source," I replied. I shook off Daevin's arm and stalked across the room.

Galu's voice sounded in my head. *"Zariya, what are you doing?"*

Then Konstantin's. *"Someone, report."*

"Zariya's going to talk to Mason," Daevin said.

I navigated through the crowd, adrenaline singing in my veins. I needed to get the measure of this supe, to find out what he knew about Dad's death.

"Zariya, stand down. That's an order," Konstantin barked.

I touched my comm gently, ducking my head so my hair covered the motion. *"Get out of my head, Bauer."*

And then I was in front of him. With the broad stretch of his antlers, he was at least seven feet tall, his skin a chalky white. He was thin and long—all hard angles and sharp corners. And sharp talons—damn, those things looked lethal. His face was skeletal, but for two black eyes, shadowed by reddish bruised skin beneath. I swallowed. This supe was the stuff of nightmares.

"Konstantin, give her a minute," Galu said.

"Mr. Mason," I said.

In a languid sweep, he took me in.

My skin crawled. What the fuck was I doing here? *Abort, abort!* my mind cried. But it was too late. I'd let some fool urge carry me here. "I wanted to thank you for the invitation."

"And you are?"

"Cat Richardson."

"Cat...Catherine Richardson? I thought you were human."

My heart stuttered. "Half."

He cocked his head but didn't question me further.

"Quite an impressive gathering you have here," I said to fill the silence.

"Thank you."

"When are we going to hear the details of the hunt?"

"Once everyone's enjoyed their beverages, I'll make the announcements."

"I have to ask. Something like this—so public—how do you keep off MASC's radar?"

He threw his head back and laughed, deep and booming. Others turned to look at us.

"Those bumbling idiots? They couldn't find a fly in their own honey jar."

I gave him a simpering smile, swallowing my outrage on Veil Force's behalf. "Why do you say that?"

"Let's just say that the only threat they ever posed to me has been neutralized."

My smile faltered, my nostrils flaring. Was he talking about my dad?

He continued. "It's all about who you know, Cat. The Collectors was founded on that principle, and we'll continue to thrive because of it." All about who you know... Did that mean he had a contact at MASC? Someone who was helping him? A mole in the organization?

I forced my smile to hold. "Wise words."

Another supe was standing just beyond us, a nervous-looking vampire with Mediterranean coloring. "I won't take up any more of your time. Nice to meet you," I forced out, grinding my teeth together.

He smiled then, displaying a terrifying row of little fangs. My heart stuttered in my chest. "Be careful tomorrow."

I froze and turned to look at him.

He bared his sharp teeth farther in a macabre smile. "With this many supes, all after the same prey...tempers run hot. Accidents happen. That waiver of liability isn't just a formality."

"Thanks. But I can take care of myself."

I pressed my glass to my stomach as I walked back towards Luiz and Daevin to hide the shaking of my hands.

"Little meet and greet go well?" Davin hissed. "Did you get his autograph?"

"Hardy harr." I rolled my eyes, downing half my drink, reveling in the burn of the vodka as it slid down my throat. Holy shit, that supe was scary.

"*She's back,*" Galu said over comms. "*Not eaten.*"

Konstantin's voice exploded in my mind. "*Zariya, if you ever disobey orders again, you are off this team in a fucking heartbeat. You jeopardized the whole mission. I don't give a fuck who your dad was, or whether King fucking Arthur himself branded you with his sword. You will be done. Do I make myself clear?*"

Wow, Konstantin was pissed. Like, really pissed. I knew what I'd done was a little reckless maybe, but had I really jeopardized the whole mission? If something happened to Nessie because of me... Guilt bloomed heavy in my stomach. "I need some air."

I hurried out onto the patio, which overlooked the flat, gray expanse of the Loch. The chilly air hit me like a slap in the face, and I shivered. It was still better than the inside of that room, filled with the oppressive breath of predators.

Luiz and Daevin stayed inside, but Rex and Galu joined me, taking up positions on either side of me against the railing. Galu shrugged out of his coat and draped it around my shoulders.

"Thanks."

I breathed in the cool air, letting its faint scent of heather and sage calm me. I owed Konstantin an explanation. I touched my ear. *"I'm sorry, Konstantin. It was reckless to talk to Mason. But as soon as I saw him, I started thinking about the fact that he could have been behind the explosion that killed Dad. I just...needed to look him in the eyes. It won't happen again."*

The silence stretched in my mind. None of the other guys said anything, though I knew they'd heard our conversation. This was between me and Phoenix One. Konstantin's voice was gruff but no longer shouting. *"I understand emotions can run high. But you have to control them. None of us can go off script for this to work."*

"Roger that. I did learn some things that could be useful."

"Like what?"

"His claws definitely match the tears in the unicorn flesh we found. Same for the bite marks on the bones. That asshole ate those unicorns."

Next to me, Rex put down the crab puff he'd been about to eat with an expression of disgust.

I hurried on before Konstantin could tell me that intel wasn't worth the risk. *"And he said he neutralized the only threat MASC posed to him. I think he was talking about Dad. And he implied he had a contact at Veil Force. I think he might have someone on the inside. That could explain why they were off the island by the time we got there. Why they rigged the bomb. They knew we were coming."*

Pause. *"That's not possible."*

"Just telling you what he said."

Galu swore softly next to me, turning back towards the castle. "If that's true, this whole mission could be shot already."

"What do we do? Do we abort?" I asked.

"We can't abort. It's the fucking Loch Ness Monster. She's like the...Madonna of the supe world. We can't leave her to these wolves."

"*We continue as planned,*" Konstantin said. "*But watch your backs. And minimize information going back to base for the time being. Assume we six are the only ones we can trust. I'll have to bring this up with the director when we return.*"

"Great," I said. "Galu, shouldn't we, like, switch rooms or something? I feel like we're sitting ducks in there."

But Galu was staring into the distance, as if he'd been frozen in space and time.

"We'll be ready for any assault," Rex replied for him. "We'll institute added precautions, just in case."

"Galu." I grabbed his muscular shoulder and gave a little shake. "Earth to Galu?"

He didn't look at me. "I-I'll be right back."

GALU'S THROAT was as dry as a desert. It couldn't be. There were plenty of undines in the world, there had to be one out there who looked like Melusine. When he'd run two years ago from the turquoise waters of the Caribbean, he'd known he'd never see her again. But Poseidon's balls, it looked like her.

The same sheet of glistening blue hair, undulating like a wave. The same delicate face, with sharp cheekbones angling towards her tiny chin. The same plush mouth, lips tinted blue like the waters of his homeland.

She was wearing the white and black uniform of the party's waiters, but why was she out here, crouching behind a set of bushes tucked against the castle wall?

It was only luck that he'd seen her at all, as his eyes had been idly sweeping back towards the party.

His feet moved as if on their own, drawn towards the supe like the pull of the tide. God, he'd missed her. He dreamed about her. He'd never stopped loving her, even when he'd had to run. Even knowing that she'd never be able to forgive him for what he'd done. He'd just resigned himself to the fact that he had loved and lost, and the ache would be a constant feature of his supernaturally long life. But damn it, it *was* her.

As he drew closer, he saw that she was unzipping a black case on the ground. A black case containing—a large gun. Was that an UMP-45? What the hell was she doing?

She was loading it hastily, crouching over the gun on the ground.

He was just feet from her now. "Melusine?"

She stood and whirled, the gun tucked against her shoulder and trained on his chest. Then her eyes went wild. She took a staggering step back. "Galu?"

He surged forward, pulling the gun from her grip and pushing her behind a tall set of ornamental hedges, flush against the rough stones of the castle.

"What the hell are you doing here?" he hissed.

"What the hell are *you* doing here?" she shot back. "Are you one of these assholes? These supe killers? I know you're a coward, but I never took you for a sadist."

Galu winced. He deserved that. "I'm not part of this. Not like that. I'm trying to stop it. What are you doing?"

"I'm trying to stop it too. Stop him," she hissed, her eyes sparking like embers.

"Who?"

"Finn Xara," she spat.

"Who?"

"The merman! Warrick Mason's righthand man. It was him, Galu. It's taken me two years, but I tracked him down. The other supe who killed Liandine. So now I'm going to kill him. And finally get my peace."

Galu's mind worked slowly as a red hot rage filled him. "That merman in there drinking a fucking Corona was the third supe?"

"That's what I just said."

Galu's fingers curled into fists. It was time for a reckoning. Time for that merman to pay for what he did. He would stake him out in the hot sun until his gills strained and flapped, until he was gasping for water—

Daevin's voice cut in. *"Mason's starting his little speech in here."*

Right. The mission. Hadn't Konstantin just torn Zariya a new one for letting her personal vendetta get the better of her? Galu did his best to wade through his anger back towards calmness. It sucked at him like quicksand, but he fought it. Steadied himself. "You can't kill him."

"Like hell I can't."

"Not yet. There's more going on here. Another mission we need to ensure succeeds."

"I don't give a shit about your mission, Galu. This is my chance. He's right there. I'm taking my shot." She pulled the gun up against her shoulder and Galu moved to stand in her way.

"I can't let you do that. Not yet."

"Get out of my way, Galu. I *will* shoot you," Melusine said through gritted teeth. But there were tears shimmering on her lashes.

"No, you won't," he said softly, pushing the barrel of the gun down slowly. Inch by inch. He couldn't believe it. His Melusine. Here, in the flesh.

"I have to do this." Melusine's voice broke. "For her."

"Give us twenty-four hours. And then I'll help you kill him."

Tears slicked her cheeks, salty as the sea they'd once loved together. She looked at him, her sapphire eyes shimmering. "Do you swear?"

"On my life."

11

We rendezvoused in Luiz and Daevin's room. The minute the door shut behind me, I sank into a chair, taking off my borrowed stilettos and wiggling my toes in relief. Torture devices. "Worse cocktail party ever," I grumbled.

"I don't know. I think Galu did all right," Luiz said as Galu slipped through the door, followed by the willowy supe who had been lurking on the patio. She was lovely—lithe and lean, her coloring painted in dark shades of blue. She was clearly some sort of water nymph or nereid like Galu, though she didn't bear his same tattoos. A distant relative, perhaps?

Luiz continued. "Picking up a lady in less than three minutes flat. That might be a record, even for me."

"Shut it, Luiz," Galu barked.

The supe pressed herself into the corner of the room and folded her arms over her chest. She was clearly uncomfortable, but I supposed the guys were an intimidating bunch. I gave a soft snort through my nose as I realized I'd already grown used to them. That was fast.

A rapping on the window drew our attention and Rex pushed the window open, allowing Konstantin to swing inside. The hallway had cameras to avoid.

The supe started, shrinking farther into the corner.

"Can someone please tell me what the hell is going on here?" Konstantin barked. "And who the hell this is?"

The supe jutted her chin out stubbornly, straightening. So she did have a little fight in her.

Galu moved next to her, placing a soft hand on her shoulder. "This is Melusine. She and I... knew each other back in Port Royal."

I raised an eyebrow. There was definitely more to this story. Not a distant relative. I rifled through Dad's memories, summoning what I could from Galu's file. Dad had singlehandedly recruited most of the Veil Force Phantoms, including Galu. He'd found Galu living on a Florida beach, drinking away his days and brawling away his nights. He'd been a wreck. But Dad had never asked for the story about what had happened. He'd just helped him—given him a purpose and a second chance.

"Nice to meet you, Melusine." Konstantin softened, though it did little to take away his hard edge. My heart tap-danced in my chest. His gentleness was just as disarming as his anger. Perhaps even more so. "Now, why are you here?"

"I'm here to kill Finn Xara. The merman who works for Warrick Mason. And I would have, if Galu hadn't gotten in the way." She glared at him.

Even Daevin raised an eyebrow at that.

Konstantin pinched the bridge of his nose, looking down. "Shall we start at the beginning?"

Galu and Melusine exchanged an uncomfortable glance, as if drawing straws to determine who would have to recite their obviously complicated history. It seemed Galu lost. He cleared his throat. "Melusine and her little sister, Liandine, are undines. From Athens. They came to visit relatives in Port Royal, the nereid colony where I grew up. Melusine and I met, and well..."

"We were stupid kids." She crossed her arms beneath her chest, looking away from Galu.

"Port Royal is located in a reef off the coast of Jamaica, for the geographically illiterate among you"—he looked pointedly at Daevin —"and I took Melusine to show her the island. Liandine tagged along." Galu ran his hands through his hair and rubbed his face. I shifted uncomfortably in my chair. I didn't think this story had a very happy ending.

"I took them to this waterfall in the middle of the island. We swam and played. It was great. The island wasn't exactly the safest place for supes, but the dangers were minor. Pickpocketing, the occasional asshole human supe-hater. We went back to the sea, and we thought nothing of it."

"Until Liandine disappeared." Melusine's throat bobbed. Her blue eyes fixed on the carpet now.

"We looked everywhere for her. The city leaders started a search party in the waters surrounding the island. Melusine and I realized she might have gone back to the island proper..." Galu cleared his throat. "We found her near the waterfall. Staked. Staked in the sun. To dry out and die."

I couldn't help the gasp that escaped me. Why were people so fucking cruel? To do that to a little girl?

"Let me guess." Konstantin's voice was measured but as deadly as a cobra strike. "Humans."

"Actually..." Melusine let out a harsh laugh, fighting tears. "It was supes. She was conscious enough to describe the three supes who had done it to her. A goblin, a wolf shifter, and a merman."

"That's beyond fucked up," Daevin said. No joke to offer.

Murmurs of agreement rounded the room.

"I found two of them," Galu said. "They were meeting with drug lords on the island, working on distribution. I found the goblin and the wolf and I killed them."

"And got yourself arrested," Melusine hissed. "If you had told me, we could have dealt with them together. Could have kept it off the cops' radar."

"You were grieving. And you're not a killer, Mel. I wanted to spare you that. I thought I could give you that much."

"Bullshit," she shot back. "You weren't thinking of anything but your own fury. Your need for vengeance. Because if you had been thinking of me, you would have realized that the one thing I needed wasn't to lose you too."

Galu's jaw dropped.

I met Rex's eyes across the room as we shared an uncomfortable glance. Was I the only one who felt like this was getting a little too personal? Like maybe Melusine and Galu should continue this discussion privately?

But Konstantin stepped in. "I take it Finn Xara was the merman."

Melusine nodded. "It's taken me two years to track him, but it's him. I'm here to finish what Galu started. What Galu left me to finish." She seemed to spit these last words.

Galu winced.

I think we all did.

"I understand your grief and your need for vengeance," Konstantin said, "but you've put us in a difficult position. Setting aside the issue of whether or not I can allow you to kill a supe in cold blood, stopping the hunt takes precedence."

"Who the hell are you to *allow* me anything, vampire?" Melusine sneered.

Konstantin rose, suddenly looming tall and foreboding. "Let's just say I report to the Under-secretary of MASC himself, so if you don't want to find yourself in a MASC detention cell—"

"Stand down, Konstantin." Galu stepped between Konstantin and Melusine. "There's no need for threats. If we explain the situation, Mel will understand our mission comes first. She can be reasonable. Can't you?" He turned to her. "The supes here are going to hunt and kill the Loch Ness Monster. The hunt begins tomorrow."

Melusine froze, the color draining from her face. "That's impossible. Nessie is... She's an ancestor. A national treasure. Surely, no one would..." She trailed off.

"I assure you it's quite possible," Konstantin said. "And we're here to stop it."

"Let us do this," Galu pleaded. "And then we can talk about bringing Finn to justice."

She pressed her lips together. "Fine."

"Good." Konstantin sat back down. "Now did anyone catch the details of the hunt, or were you all off galivanting and disobeying orders?"

"Daevin and I heard it," Luiz said. "Hunt starts tomorrow at first light. Mason has brought in six state-of-the-art personal submersibles that can hold up to four supes each. One for him, I assume, and the rest for his guests. Some supes will be hunting on their own—water supes and those with spells to help them breathe underwater. It's going to be a nightmare to try to stop everyone."

"Maybe we should consider calling in another team. More manpower," Luiz said.

"The other teams are on missions right now. I don't want to pull them in unless absolutely necessary." Konstantin rubbed his jaw. "Do those subs have weapons capability?"

Daevin nodded. "Affirmative. Plus, each has a unique firing solution, so Warrick can tell who should get the prize at the end." He scoffed.

"So let's take out the subs," I suggested. "Sabotage them. Except one, which we keep for ourselves. Then we take out the individual supes who still go for Nessie. Easy peasy." I knew that in reality, it would not be so easy or peasy.

Konstantin considered. "You're entitled to at least one sub, as hunters. Galu, they'd assume you'll be in the water. Can we sabotage the others so the engines give out after a few minutes or so? So they'll be dead in the water, away from shore?"

"Don't see why not," Daevin said. "They'll need some sort of cooling system for the engines. If that goes, they'll overheat."

"Perhaps Warrick will call off the hunt if the majority of his clients can't partake," Rex suggested.

"We can't count on that, though. Or the fact that we could take them all out. We need another reason for them to scatter."

"MASC raid should be enough," I suggested.

Konstantin looked at me like an idiot. "I just said the other teams—"

"I'm not saying there needs to *be* a raid. Just word of one. Enough to send the rats scrambling back into the shadows."

Konstantin's eyes lit up. "Vizol and I pulled a similar stunt in Morocco."

I pressed my lips together. No need to tell him that was where I'd gotten the idea.

"I like it. All right. Here's the plan. Daevin, you and I are going to go down to those subs for a little midnight sabotage. Galu, Luiz, and Rex, I want you to head down to the common room and play some pool and poker and plant some rumors. I want these supes shitting their pants thinking MASC is going to drop a fucking battalion on them tomorrow. We'll have Kiki send similar intel to our UK partners. I can't imagine they're not intercepting that traffic."

"What do you want me to do?" I asked.

Konstantin looked me dead in the eyes. "I didn't like how close you got to Warrick Mason, and I don't need him asking more questions about you. You're benched. Stay in the room. Melusine, you can stay with Zariya too."

My mouth dropped open. Did he just *send me to my fucking room*?

But Galu caught my eye and shook his head slightly. I didn't need to speak nereid to interpret that message. Drop it. You disobeyed orders; take your licks.

I stood, grabbing my heels. "Fine. Can't wait to get out of this dress anyway." I offered my elbow to Melusine. "Come on. You can tell me all the embarrassing stories you know about Galu."

Melusine looked about as pleased with the situation as I was, but she said nothing, taking my arm and following me out the door.

"Is he always that...?"

"Alpha? Bossy? Infuriating?" I supplied, pulling my keycard out of my bra where I'd stashed it. Nowhere else to put it in this dress.

Melusine smiled. "Exactly."

"Yes, unfortunately. He has a few good qualities, though."

"Such as?" I opened the door and we stepped inside.

I flicked the light switch. It didn't turn on. "Huh," I said. "Weird—"

And then a set of strong hands grabbed me and clapped a sweet-smelling cloth over my nose and mouth. I didn't even have time to struggle before consciousness slipped away.

12

———————

I came to with a boot to my ribs. "Wakey wakey." A gruff, male voice.

I blinked, the world coming into focus. A bookshelf. A desk. The smirking face of the merman—Finn. His webbed ears were tucked back among his dark hair.

I flared my glands and froze. Yes, Melusine was here too. And another. A tall figure with antlers. With a smell like dirt and death. Warrick Mason.

Fuck.

I tried to push myself up and found my hands were tied tightly behind my back. "What the hell?" I croaked. I used an elbow and got myself up into a seated position. My change of perspective brought the room into focus. Warrick was standing as still as a lion before his prey, watching me.

Melusine was tied up next to me. She groaned and her eyes fluttered open.

"What the hell is this?" I barked, trying to still my panic. If I were Cat Richardson, I'd be confused as hell right now. "Is this how you treat your guests, Mason?"

"You aren't guests. You are trespassers," Mason said softly. "Isn't that right, Zariya Chanji?"

My name was like a gut punch. The breath whooshed from me. Stupid. Stupid. I never should have confronted him. I should have stayed in the background, done my job. My hands were tied too tightly for me to be able to reach my comm, so I tried to reach it with my shoulder, vainly pressing my shoulder to my ear. I didn't know if I could reach it—

"Looking for this?" Mason held up a tiny flesh-colored earpiece. *My* earpiece. Shit. No help from Kiki.

"Get her up," Mason said, nodding to Finn.

"Don't touch me," I cried, but Finn's hands were under my armpits too fast, hauling me painfully to my feet. He dumped me into a chair behind the huge desk. My feet were still bare, and I was wearing the stupid, too-tight dress that had hiked up *waaay* higher than I liked.

My heartbeat thundered beneath my skin as Mason leaned in closer and placed his hands on the two arms of the chair. He encircled me—I couldn't back away. I could only stare at his skeletal face. His razor-sharp teeth and red-rimmed eyes. I gagged on the scent of carrion on his breath. "Now, I'll only ask this once. Who are you working for, Zariya Chanji? Why are you here?"

I scrambled through Dad's memories, willing them to take over like they had before, to fill me with his calm detachment. *He doesn't know why you're here, and he doesn't know you're with MASC. The guys are safe. You just need to divert him.*

"I'm looking for my father's killer," I spat out. I wished my voice didn't sound quite so choked. "And I think I found him."

Mason smirked, leaning back, releasing the arms of the chair. I let out a shuddering sigh. It was then that I noticed that a necklace had fallen out of the collar of his shirt when he'd leaned over me. A silver amulet with strange markings. Markings that I recognized. The same as the stone circle we'd found on the island with the unicorns. The same found at the scene of Dad's death.

"That amulet," I said. "What language is it?"

Mason looked down, amused. "You admire my Chinvat Key? Well, you have good taste in antiquities."

"What is it?"

"I'm afraid I'm asking the questions here, Ms. Chanji. Now, tell me about your friend here." I shoved down my disappointment. It had probably been too much to hope that I could get him monologuing.

Finn pulled Melusine to a seat, and she snarled at him and lunged, gnashing her teeth. Finn shoved her down, and her back hit the wall hard.

I scrambled for a lie to protect the undine. "She's just a waitress here. She and I... We were just going to enjoy a night in. She has nothing to do with this. Let her go."

A warped smile drifted across Mason's frightening visage. "Well, we can hardly let her go now that we've tied her up. Can't have her filing a complaint with HR, can we? No, I think we'll keep her." He bared his teeth at Melusine. "I do love seafood."

My skin went cold. "You leave her the hell alone."

"I'll do whatever the hell I like, Ms. Chanji. Because even if MASC or the human governments delude themselves into thinking they've created a utopia for supes and humans to co-exist, I know the truth."

"And what's that?" I shot back.

He bared his teeth again. "That we are the predators, and they are our prey. No law or technology or even magic will change that simple fact. This world is ours for the taking."

"You're a monster," I spat. Not exactly my most creative insult, but I was struggling here.

"Thank you." Mason crossed his arms over his chest. "Now, let's finish our questions. Who are you working for?"

"I told you. No one."

"Then who is the vampire who's been pitter-pattering around our roof? Sneaking into your room?"

Fuck. They'd seen Konstantin?

"He's my boyfriend," I said. "I told him I wanted to do this on my own. But he worries. He wanted to stay close."

Mason said nothing. Not moving. But Finn snorted. "Boyfriend on the roof, but sneaking this one in for a good time?" He pointed to Melusine, who was glaring at him with the wrath of an avenging angel. "Girl sure keeps herself busy."

Shit, yeah, I hadn't thought that through. Apparently, I was a shameless hussy in all my cover stories. "We have an understanding," I managed.

"You're still lying to me," Warrick said. "Perhaps you haven't been properly motivated."

Stepping forward, he leaned over me once again as I struggled not to gag. He grabbed my hair and yanked my head to the side painfully, baring my neck. I hissed.

"You know, ears are one of my favorite snacks," he said. "The best little hors d'oeuvres. And you have such pretty ones, Ms. Chanji. It would be a shame to lose them."

Sweat prickled my body as a tidal wave of fear coursed through me. But Dad's training kept me calm. Kept my mind from spiraling. I wouldn't give up my teammates. I wouldn't give up MASC.

"For the third time," I grit out against the pain. "I'm...working... alone. I'm here for myself."

Mason sighed and released my hair. He started to roll up the sleeves of his white shirt. "Yes, yes, to avenge your father. Afraid you won't get to do that."

"So you admit you killed him?"

Mason stared at me.

I didn't avert my eyes. I only stared into the dark abyss that was Warrick Mason. Daring him to tell me the truth.

"It was a rare pleasure," he said. "My only regret was that I didn't get to rip him apart limb by limb."

Red stained my vision. This monster—this murderer—had admitted to killing Dad. I didn't care if my hands were tied behind my back. I didn't care if he was more powerful than me even on a good day. I didn't care if this creepy fuck ate ears like bruschetta. In that moment, I didn't care about anything except killing him.

I exploded towards him, spinning my body and crashing the chair I was tied to into his bulk. It sent him reeling, but I staggered to my knees too. The chair hadn't exploded apart like it did in the movies. I was still stuck.

Mason surged to his feet and I went to smash him with the chair again. He caught it this time and tossed me bodily across the room.

The world spun and I hit the ground hard on my side. Pain exploded through my forearm as the chair and my weight landed on top of it. Oh gods. I might have broken something.

I blinked to find Mason standing over me, his chest heaving. Shit, shit, shit—

"Everything okay, boss?"

I blinked to take in a vampire—another of Mason's lackeys—standing at the door.

"Yes, everything is fine, thank you," Mason purred. As if he didn't have a battered, bound supe groaning at his feet.

"I know you're busy, but there's an issue with the submersible vendor. He's saying the ammo isn't included in the price, and I know you negotiated that with them—but he's being a real dick about it."

Mason let out a long-suffering sigh. He looked down at me. "To be continued, Ms. Chanji. You get to enjoy those pretty ears for a few more hours. Finn, put them in the wine cellar. I'll be back to finish this."

13

Konstantin tossed and turned on the sofa, tangled in the blanket Galu had thrown him. God damn it, he couldn't stop thinking about Zariya. Zariya in that dress. Zariya's voice over the comm as she'd stalked towards one of the most dangerous predators on this planet without backup. *"Get out of my head, Bauer."* Even while he and Daevin had snuck out to the row of submersibles floating darkly at the shoreline, sabotaging the air intakes, she filled his mind. She was impetuous. Foolhardy. Beautiful. Damn impressive.

But none of that mattered. She was his teammate. He was her commander. And if she didn't start following orders, he'd need to discipline her. Transfer her. Do something other than stand there like a limp-dick weakling. On Veil Force, you followed orders. On Veil Force, lone wolves and outlaws got their teammates killed.

The sky was just starting to lighten when Konstantin finally got up. Showered. Dressed. Tried to get the electric kettle working. Failed. Swore.

Galu turned over in bed, squinting at him. "The fuck? You battling a tiny hobgoblin over there, boss?"

Konstantin scowled. "This thing doesn't work for shit."

"Just pop downstairs and get a cup," Rex said. "Let us get another hour."

"I can't go downstairs," Konstantin said. "I'm not supposed to fucking be here, remember?"

"Then go ask Zariya. Or Luiz."

Yes. Ask Zariya. Konstantin looked at the clock. Five. It wasn't too early. He'd just check if the women were sleeping—if they still were, he wouldn't bother them.

Konstantin slipped out the window onto the roof, a stiff breeze grasping at him with greedy fingers. It was freezing out here. He could sense it, though it hardly registered through his toughened exterior. He looked into Zariya and Melusine's room. The light was off. He squinted through the glass. Was that... A lamp was knocked onto the ground?

The world narrowed to a pinprick. To that lamp. He moved to the other side of the window so he could see the beds. Made. Like they hadn't been slept in at all.

He was through the window in a heartbeat, his nostrils flaring wide. The faint smell of brine and salt lingered. But not Melusine's sweet sea breeze scent. This was male. Someone had been in here.

Konstantin tore out the window, launching himself back inside and flipping the lights on.

"You mind?" Rex put his pillow over his head as Galu held up a hand against the light. "A little warning, please?"

"They're gone," Konstantin said. "Zariya and Melusine are gone."

He tapped his comm. "*Zariya, come in. Report. Daevin, Luiz, I need you up and in here now.*"

Galu was sitting up, one hand to his ear. Waiting for Zariya's reply. That didn't come. "Melusine is gone too?"

"*Zariya, I repeat, report. What is your location?*" Konstantin asked. His mind spun out over the possibilities. Zariya had been taken. On his watch, just feet from him. *Damn it, damn it.*

"Fuck!" Konstantin resisted seizing the nearest object and smashing it to pieces. They didn't need to attract the attention of the hotel.

Galu and Rex were up and hopping into pants, pulling on boots.

Konstantin touched his comm again. "*Kiki, come in. I need you to find Zariya.*"

It was a moment before her voice responded. He could practically hear the yawn when her reply came. "*What do you mean, find Zariya?*"

"*I think she's been taken. She's not answering comms. Start in the castle. Hopefully, she's still here. Fan out from there.*"

"Konstantin, the hunt begins in an hour. We might not have time to find Zariya before it begins," Rex said.

"We sabotaged the subs. It should be enough. Finding Zariya has to be the priority."

"Agreed," Galu said.

Luiz and Daevin slipped through the door, mussy haired, but dressed.

"The water supes will be hunting outside the subs. And we left one for us. That's enough firepower to terminate Nessie permanently. We can't just abandon her," Rex pointed out.

"What the hell are we talking about?" Daevin asked.

"So we abandon our teammate?" Konstantin snapped.

"Zariya and Melusine have to be the priority," Galu agreed.

"We don't know where they're located. I'm not saying to abandon them. All I'm saying is we need to proceed with the mission until we get more intel about their position," Rex said. "I shouldn't have to remind you of this, Konstantin."

"Rex is right," Luiz said. "We can't abort the mission."

Konstantin ground his teeth. "I'm not going to leave Vizol's daughter to the wolves."

"I'm only suggesting—" Rex began.

"I know what you're fucking suggesting!" Konstantin went nose to nose with Rex.

Rex didn't move an inch, simply staring him down. Then he slowly transformed into his jackal form—his snout elongating and covering with dark fur, his ears thinning to points atop his head. He grew taller, his eyes flashing gold. Not a threat. A fact.

Some part of him knew Rex spoke sense. But that wasn't the part of him howling for action right now. The part of him screaming that Zariya—*his* Zariya—was in danger.

The thought was enough to shock Konstantin back to himself. *Fuck.* Zariya wasn't *his* anything. Not like that. Konstantin stepped back. It wasn't like Rex to challenge him. He was quiet and loyal. If he was opposing him, Konstantin was way the fuck off-kilter.

"*I've got her.*" Kiki's voice shot through his thoughts like a comet.

Everyone looked up. She'd broadcast her thought on their team channel. "*Where?*"

"She's in the castle still. Locked in an office somewhere. She says —I'll just patch her through."

They must have taken Zariya's comm, which enabled them to communicate telepathically without the use of Kiki's powers. Without it, they needed Kiki to connect them.

The sound of Zariya's voice was like a balm for his ragged soul. "*Miss me, boys?*"

Daevin let out a snort, rubbing his hands over his face. Luiz blew out a slow breath. Konstantin felt the tension uncoiling from his spine. "*Are you all right?*"

"Ask her about Melusine," Galu said.

"*I'm fine. Melusine is with me,*" she said, as if anticipating his question. "*We're okay. Mason roughed us up a bit, but we still have all our parts.*" Konstantin thought he could detect strain there. What she wasn't saying. *For now.*

"*We're coming to get you now,*" Konstantin said.

Zariya cut in. "*No, you can't. I've had a lot of time to think, shoved in this closet. If you free us, they'll know you're here and it will jeopardize the mission. We only get one shot at saving Nessie.*"

"*We don't leave teammates behind—*"

"*This is the job, Konstantin,*" said Zariya. "*None of us would be here if we weren't willing to risk ourselves for vulnerable supes. Mel agrees. We're not in immediate danger, but Nessie is.*"

Konstantin ground his teeth. If it were Daevin or Luiz, or even Rex, he wouldn't be debating right now. They were trained to handle themselves. Tough as nails. And Zariya was too, if he was honest with himself. She'd withstood torture from the mara during Broussard's fucked-up test. He needed to get his head on straight to lead this team effectively. He needed to treat Zariya like the Phantom she was, not some fucking damsel in distress his male ego was screaming at him to protect.

"*Fine. We stick to the mission. Kiki, you keep an open link with Zariya. The second, I mean the second, your situation changes, we need to hear about it.*"

"*Roger that,*" came Zariya's reply.

"*Got it, boss,*" said Kiki.

"We better get down there if we're going to do this," Daevin said.

Konstantin nodded. "You know which sub we left untouched. I'll meet you a bit down shore and hop in. And, Phantoms... Let's make sure nothing else goes wrong."

A grumble of agreement was all he got in response.

I LEANED my head back against an aged bottle of Merlot, trying to adjust my aching body. Finn the asshole merman had shoved us in the wine cellar hours ago when he and Mason had been called away to deal with whatever sort of micromanagey bullshit evil master-minds had to deal with. They hadn't returned.

"God, I have to pee," Melusine complained, rolling her head to stretch her neck.

"You water supes can't just like...absorb it back into you or some-thing?" I asked.

"Ew," was all Mel said in reply.

"Yeah, I guess that would be gross."

"It was the right call," she said softly. "About Nessie. We can't let them get her. Can't let them take another..." She trailed off, her voice thick.

"I know. They'll come for us if we need them. He'll come."

"Must be nice to have a boyfriend who'll move Heaven and Earth for you," she said wistfully.

"What? Who?" I sat up a touch.

"The vampire?"

I let out an awkward laugh. "Konstantin? He's not my boyfriend. Commanding officer."

"Oh." Her blue eyebrows drew together. "The way you two were looking at each other... Sorry, I just thought... Sorry."

How were we looking at each other? "It's okay. I mean, the man is gorgeous. If the situation were different, I wouldn't mind getting a piece of that." Gods, it had been a long time since I'd gotten a piece of *anything.*

She let out a tired laugh.

"What about you and Galu? Am I wrong to think there's some history there?"

"We were inseparable. I thought... Well, for a while I thought he was it, you know. But then Liandine died, and he just took off."

"I haven't known the guy long, but that doesn't really sound like Galu."

"I know. But that's what happened. He didn't care enough to stick around when things got hard."

"Maybe there's an explanation. You should talk to him when this is all over."

"Maybe."

I knew I shouldn't have been prying, but what the hell else was there to do when you were locked in a cellar? "Do you still have feelings for him?"

Melusine shook her head, her sheet of hair glimmering in the dark. "No. Yes. I don't know. I think some part of me will always love him."

"Then you should talk to him. Unsolicited advice."

"How you guys holding up?" Kiki spoke into my mind.

"We're both hungry and have to pee."

"Sorry, Z," Kiki said softly. *"The guys have reached the submersible. They'll be headed out soon."*

"Good." I remembered the strange amulet hanging around Warrick Mason's throat. *"Hey, can you do me a favor? Can you look up a*

Chinvat Key? Mason had something around his neck that had markings that looked like the stone circle."

"*I'm on it."*

The door swung open and Melusine and I squinted against the sudden influx of light.

Warrick Mason stood tall, the silhouette of his antlers casting skeletal shadows on us. "Rise and shine," he rumbled.

Finn and a vampire stalked in and grabbed us, hauling us to our feet. "Feel like a little swim, ladies?"

"*Uh, Kiki?"* I thought. "*We have a bit of a problem…"*

14

———

The dock before the castle teemed with supes shouting and gesturing to each other. Warrick Mason stalked before us like a goddamned king descending upon his subjects.

I looked sideways at Melusine, but she was staring daggers into Finn's back.

Warrick held up his hands as we came to a stop, and the bickering silenced. "What seems to be the problem?"

A red-skinned imp spoke, his forked tail thrashing. "One of the teams snuck in and grabbed a sub. This is bullshit, Mason. We were all supposed to be evenly matched. Start the hunt together."

Mason stepped forward, into the imp's personal space, towering above him.

The imp stepped back hastily.

"The cheating team is fair game. Anyone can take them out."

"What about the rumors that there's a MASC team about to descend on this place and arrest everyone?" someone else called out.

"Every creature must decide for himself," Mason bellowed, turning in a slow circle, "whether he is a true predator, or mewling prey! No one is forced to be here. You may scurry back to your holes if you wish. But you paid for the privilege of hunting. So proceed to your submersibles. And let the hunt begin!"

A moment of stillness lingered, and then the supes exploded into action, scrambling towards their subs. Others—mermen and a creepy long-haired set of twins and a supe on a waterhorse—dove into the water, rifles and harpoons strapped to their backs.

Mason turned to me. "The submersible that was taken. Friends of yours?"

I shrugged, struggling to keep my face neutral. So the guys had taken off into the lake before the rest of the crowd. Good. "Gather together a bunch of supes like these, no surprise you'll have a few who flout the rules."

Warrick bared his teeth. "You two will be coming with us. Our personal guarantee that our submersible isn't attacked. Not unless whoever you're working with wants you to die a very watery death."

"I told you," I managed. "I'm not working with anyone."

"We'll see."

KONSTANTIN DUCKED his head and made his way to the final seat in the submersible. It was a sleek gray-and-white machine, with a wide plexiglass screen before them. Daevin was at the controls, Luiz at the guns, and Rex was sealing the hatch he'd just come down.

"Well, this is cozy," Konstantin said.

Daevin scowled. "I've done a lot of stupid shit, but voluntarily trapping myself inside a wet tube of death may top the list."

Luiz jumped as a glowing aquamarine body flitted in front of the windshield. *"Jesus Christ, Galu,"* he barked. *"A little warning, you fucking lurker."*

Galu's laugh echoed in his mind. *"Why's everyone so jumpy?"*

Daevin just grumbled.

"You want me to drive?" Rex sat down calmly across from Konstantin. Little fazed the Demi-god. He was still wearing his dark jackal face, as he always did during battle.

"I got it," Daevin said.

"Take us down," Konstantin directed. "Head back towards the castle. We need to be prepared to take out anyone who tries to get by us."

"*I found her,*" Kiki said. "*Nessie. Her mind is primitive, but I sent her some images of the hunters. She's headed into the deepest part of the lake to shelter.*"

"*Good.*"

"*Also, Zariya's on the move,*" Kiki added. "*Mason has her and Mel in his submersible.*"

"Fuck," Konstantin said. "*Is she all right?*"

"*So far.*"

"It should be fine," Luiz said. "The engines should stall before they get too far past the castle. They'll be dead in the water. Once we're done taking out the rest of the hunters, we can deal with them."

"*I don't think that's going to work,*" Kiki said.

"Why?"

Zariya's voice filled his mind. "*Mason had his own submersible kept separate. It's larger, with more weapons. And it's fully operational.*"

Double fuck.

"*And some of the hunters were pissed you got a head start. Mason just made you guys a second target.*"

Konstantin hissed. *Triple fuck.*

A shadow darted in front of the window. "What was that?" Daevin asked.

Galu's voice joined Zariya's. "*Guys? I think the competition is here.*"

A TRIDENT WHIZZED BY, just inches from Galu's head.

Galu caught sight of the gray-skinned merman who'd thrown it, barreling down upon him with a battle cry. He rode on a dark horse, its mane streaming behind it like ribbons of seaweed. It was a kelpie, a Scottish waterhorse, a supe that lured travelers into lochs like this one—and to their deaths. It was a Class X-NV supe

—human-eating, non-verbal. He'd never actually seen one in person.

Galu shoved down his awe and braced himself in the dark water as it barreled down on him. He swirled to the side at the last moment, sending the merman and his mount galloping past him.

Galu didn't waste time. There were more coming. He fired his weapon, hitting the merman between the shoulder blades. This was no time for gallantry or valor. This was war. He would have to remember to thank Hamish for rigging this special rifle for him that functioned underwater.

The echo of another creature was all that warned him of the next attack. The water of the loch was dark and cold, nearly black. He didn't understand why Nessie would want to live in a place like this, so different from the balmy, crystal-clear waters of his home. But to each their own.

The creature that came howling at him next was unlike any he'd seen before. It had a monkey-like, saucer-shaped head, and the yellow-green skin of an overripe squash. It wielded a curved samurai sword, and it moved fast—too fast. Galu barely had time to get his rifle up to block the blow of the sword and then the creature was in his face, snarling in the dark water, snapping at him.

Galu punched the creature clear in its hooked nose and it went reeling. "*What the hell is this thing?*"

"*It's a—ohmygod, what is it doing here?*" Kiki asked.

"*Helpful, Kiki,*" Galu thought as the creature slashed out with its sword. Galu pulled free the long knife he kept in the holster at his side and feinted at the creature. It dodged back, wary.

"*It's a kappa. It's a Japanese water demon. They never leave Japan, though.*"

"*Maybe this one got a bargain on airfare.*" Galu sent a jet of water at the creature, tumbling it backwards, giving him enough time to get his gun up and shoot at the creature.

His bullet hit the kappa straight in the torso, but it just grinned with ragged teeth. "How do I kill it?"

"*The top of its head. It has a soft spot.*"

"Enough of this shit," Galu said, wrapping the creature in bands of ice. The kappa thrashed against bonds, but Galu didn't hesitate. He pulled a knife from the sheath at his hip and with a powerful blow, stabbed the creature right through its creepy flat skull. It fell still instantly.

Galu let the ice dissolve.

A lance of pain shot through his arm. Someone had shot him! Galu whirled, taking in his opponent. Scratch that. *Opponents.*

They were arrayed before him—armed to the teeth and sporting maniacal grins like *he* was the next target on the hunt. Two Russian Rusalkas, their dark hair undulating over their pale faces; a nereid male, turquoise tattoos covering every inch of his muscled bulk; a trio of mermen with tridents in one hand and...did that one have a harpoon gun? Another creature—with wicked, curving tusks jutting from its jaw and flippers for limbs—leered at him. He tried to remember his cryptozoology lessons. Was that a bunyip? An indigenous creature from Australia. The Collectors had supporters far and wide.

For the first time, a curl of fear snaked through him. He couldn't fight all these creatures himself. "*I need backup,*" Galu said.

"*We're a little busy ourselves,*" Konstantin said. "*Mason's headed for Nessie.*"

Shit. A blast of bullets flew towards him and he swiped them aside with a swell of water. "*Kiki, any ideas?*"

"*I don't—I don't know, Galu. I'm sorry. Fight like hell.*"

Awesome. With a cry, the hunters charged.

But Galu was strong, and his training had honed him into a weapon. So he fell into the calm of battle. Shoot, slash, surge. He sent everything he had at them—bullets, icicles, eddies of water—to send them tumbling away, to give him enough time to grab weapons from flippers and fins.

One down—one rusalka felled by a geyser of hot liquid—which only sent the sister barreling at him with vengeance in her black eyes.

He dodged and parried against her furious strikes. He could tell in his peripherals that another hunter was sneaking around behind him. He jetted down, deeper into the depths, sending bullets into his wake. He couldn't get himself surrounded.

A blow out of nowhere knocked him sideways, sending stars kaleidoscoping through his vision. The nereid had appeared beneath him, ready for his escape.

They grappled in close quarters, tumbling up and down, side to side in the darkness. Another predator lurked. They were closing in around him.

With a bellow, the nereid shouldered him in the stomach, knocking the water from his gills, and his gun from his hand. *No!* It fell quickly into the dark depths.

Galu could feel his magic waning, the last of his strength spent. He needed help. He wasn't going to be able to take them all.

Please, someone—

HELP.

The desperate plea went out from him like a shock wave, born on the last surge of his magic. Hopefully, it would reach some creature that could help, some protection innate to this mythical place. He needed a miracle.

Galu shook his head to clear it and pulled a knife from his belt. His last weapon, and a woefully inadequate one. He turned slowly in a circle. There were four opponents left. The rusalka, the bunyip, the nereid, and one more merman. This would be his last stand. But he'd go out like a warrior. A Phantom.

"*I want to say it's been an honor serving with you,*" Galu thought through the bond.

"*What?*" Konstantin barked. "*Galu, report. Kiki, can we get him out of there? Where's Enigma?*"

"*I don't think he can transport this deep.*" Kiki's voice was choked. "*Galu's on his own.*"

"*Get to the surface!*" Konstantin cried. "*We'll get Enigma in there.*"

"*It's all right, boss. Tell Melusine I never stopped loving her.*"

With that, he tapped off his comm. They didn't need his last moments echoing inside their heads.

"Come and get me, motherfuckers." Galu bared his teeth.

And they would have. But for the brilliant white lights that bloomed around him suddenly, a circle wreathing him as bright as Christmas lights.

He gaped. Ashrays—translucent water ghosts that were said to guard the lakeshores of Scotland. They were a myth of myths, as far as he knew. Their existence hadn't been confirmed in modern times.

But here they were. And they'd answered his call.

Their bodies were eerie and warped, their long hair floating in the dark. But the anger in their skeletal faces was clear as they regarded the hunters—their backs to him. It was evident they knew who the interlopers were. The threat.

Galu grinned at the hunters, a last wave of adrenaline surging through his veins. "This isn't going to end well for you, friends."

15

———————

The space inside the sub was cramped—the air taut with Warrick Mason's rage. His hunt was falling apart, and it was all I could do to keep the satisfied smile off my face. How much had these supe hunters paid for a chance at bagging the head of the legendary Loch Ness Monster? It couldn't have been cheap. And now they were all bobbing in the water, stranded in personal submersibles with overheated engines. He'd have a PR nightmare on his hands for his little Collectors. That was if we didn't kill him first.

But I was getting ahead of myself. Because right now, Melusine and I were both tied to chairs in the submersible. And there was a very real chance that Mason would turn his fury on us very soon.

But for now, his attention was fixed on the glass windshield before him, where Phoenix Team's submersible faced off against his. Konstantin was at a distinct disadvantage, as they couldn't fire on Mason's sub without risking us.

Mason had no such hesitation. Finn was firing off automatic rounds like it was going out of style. The sounds of the machine gun and Mason's shouts echoed through the metal tube of the sub, clanging in my ears.

My imagination filled with horrors—each bullet launched could be the one that took out my friends. My teammates. I couldn't allow that to happen. Warrick Mason had already stolen my father from me. I wouldn't let him take anyone else.

"Zariya?" Kiki's voice. "*How are you doing?*"

"*Oh, you know, tied to a chair, trapped inside an iron coffin of death with the carnivorous monster who killed my Dad.*"

Pause. "*So...just another day on Phoenix Team?*"

I had to keep myself from barking out a laugh. "*Why didn't someone warn me?*"

"*We all tried. You know you were too stubborn to listen.*"

"*Fair point.*" Gods, I missed Kiki. I really needed to have a beer with my friends when this was all over. *If* this was ever all over.

"*Well, I'm not sure what I can do about that, but I thought I'd tell you what I found out about the Chinvat Key.*"

I perked up. "*What is it?*"

"*The Chinvat Bridge is from Zoroastrian mythology, said to separate the world of the living from the dead. It's just a legend. But there are some ancient sources that talk about a key.*"

"*Does it activate this bridge?*" I frowned. "*Please tell me we're not talking about a zombie apocalypse. I am so not down for a zombie apocalypse.*"

"*Luckily, no. According to the texts, the key opens a gateway.*"

"*Like a portal?*"

"*Exactly like a portal. But this one, instead of bridging the world of the living and the dead, bridges points between our world. I think it's how Mason travels quickly from place to place. There would be another artifact, I think, the Chinvat Gate. The key activates it. It would probably look like—*"

"*A stone circle that leaves raised markings on the ground?*"

"*Bingo. It's probably how they got that bomb on site in Turkey without detection. And how they got away from the Orkney Islands so fast before we could get there.*"

"*So with this thing, he can move between any two points on Earth?*"

"*I think so.*"

Meaning if things went south here, Mason would probably try to use the key to make a quick getaway. I couldn't let that happen. *"Do we have any idea what the Gate looks like? It shouldn't be hard to find if it's as big as the circles we found on the ground."*

"The texts are murky, but I suspect the Gate enlarges when it's activated. It could be a smaller object, like something you'd hold in your hand."

I looked at Mason. He could have it with him. But it didn't seem like there would be room to activate the Gate inside the sub. So he'd have to get to land before he could flee. *"Thanks, Kiki. This is huge. How are the guys doing?"*

"Daevin's behind the wheel, swearing like a drunk sailor. Luiz's at the guns bitching that he can't shoot. Konstantin is pissed as hell and wants to rip someone's head off. Rex is taking it all in calmly."

I smiled. That sounded like them.

"Galu...Galu was in a tight spot, but he's good now. He's headed your way, though his powers are weak. Hold on, Zariya."

If we could get free before Galu got here...we could fight.

"Zariya," Melusine whispered.

I looked at her from where I was struggling to free myself from my bonds, chaffing my already raw wrists on the ropes. If only I could turn into true naga snake form, like Dad had been able to do.

She turned slightly in the swivel chair and revealed where her hands, tied behind her, were loosening. "Can you get this?"

I looked at Mason and Finn. They were intent on the screen.

If Daevin was behind the wheel, he was doing a hell of a job dodging those bullets.

"Maybe," I whispered back. I turned in my chair as well so we were back to back. The chairs were bolted to the floor, so I couldn't scoot closer, but I stretched my arms back as far as I could, straining my shoulders in their sockets. I just brushed skin. Yes! I could reach.

It was strange, fumbling with the knots of her bonds without being able to see. But my fingers knew what to do. I tugged at the knots with my fingernails, watching Mason hunched over the windshield. He was too big for this space, his antlers banging against the ceiling.

A shout of triumph came from Finn. "I took out one of their props. They'll be unable to maneuver."

"Finish them," Mason growled.

Shit! The guys were in trouble. Mel's hands were free. "Get your feet," I whispered.

Something darted by the windshield and Mason pointed, the roar of the sub's guns falling silent for a moment. "That. What's that?"

I saw it again.

"It's a nereid," Finn said. "I think he's with them."

A clanging sounded outside the sub and they both froze, looking up. Mel froze too. If they saw she was freeing herself—

But they weren't paying attention to us.

"He's probably trying to take out our engines like they did for the other subs. If he does that, we're sitting ducks."

"Do we still have our guns?"

"Yes, sir."

"Destroy him." Mason's words chilled my blood. Galu... Kiki had said he was weak.

"I can't get at him with the guns without risking hitting our sub. I don't know where he is."

"Then surface and get out there! Take him down and I'll handle the other sub."

"Yes, sir," Finn grumbled, and the submarine started to rise.

Mel and I looked at each other with wide eyes and she resumed working on the ropes around her feet with a frenzied pace. This was our chance to escape. He'd have to open the hatch. If we could take them by surprise, we could get out there. Help Galu.

My ears popped as the sub rose. Mel almost had her feet free...

The submarine lurched as we surfaced, sending me jerking forward against my bonds.

Mason unscrewed the hatch above them.

"Hurry!" I hissed. Melusine still had to untie me.

Finn started climbing up the ladder into the daylight beyond.

Melusine looked from him to me, her eyes wide. Then back to him.

"Mel—" I growled.

"Sorry," she whispered. And then she darted for the ladder, scaling it so fast, she was almost a blur.

Mason realized what was happening too late, letting out a roar of fury, grabbing at her foot.

But she was gone.

Leaving me alone, tied to a chair, with Mason glaring balefully at me. *Bitch!*

My anger quickly quelled, transforming itself to fear as Mason stalked towards me, pulling a curved knife from a sheath at his hip. He was going to kill me.

I thrashed against the ropes, but they held me firm.

But to my surprise, he just sliced through the ropes, grabbing me by my arm and hauling me to my feet, his curving talons digging into my arm.

"This ends now."

Mason dragged me to the front of the sub and punched a button. He pulled me taut against him, pressing the knife to my throat so hard, I could feel a drop of hot blood ooze down the column of my throat.

A view screen bloomed to life. Konstantin filled it. My heart seized at the sight of him, the fury written across his face.

"To the captain of that submersible," Mason said. "I have your pet snake. If you do not stand down immediately, I will skin her alive."

16

———

Konstantin's rage burned so hot, he thought he might implode. The sight of Zariya with that *monster*'s knife to her neck...

"You harm her and it'll be the last thing you ever do, you sick fuck," Konstantin said. Not a threat. A promise. It was hard to think through the voice in his head snarling. *Zariya, Zariya.* He had to get to her.

Zariya was staring at him, her green, slitted pupils shining with fear, but something else too. She was trying to communicate. She needed a distraction. He had to keep Mason talking.

"I'm afraid you're not in a position to make demands," Mason said. "Your submarine is damaged. You're dead in the water. I would have already taken you out, but I didn't want to deprive you of the pleasure of watching your friend here bleed out before I killed you."

Zariya's voice sounded in his head. Kiki must have connected her. *"I need a distraction. Just a second."*

Luiz's voice. *"Rex, could you turn that knife into a banana?"*

"Not over this distance, or through water," Rex replied. *"But—"*

"Say your goodbyes," Mason said.

"Wait!" Konstantin cried. "Killing her's a big mistake, Mason. You don't know who she is. *What* she is." He was bullshitting, stalling. But this supe was a Collector. Of creatures, of magical objects. Maybe the prospect of power would make him pause.

"You're bluffing." Mason narrowed his ebony eyes.

"*On the count of three, everyone, close your eyes,*" Rex said.

"She's been inhabited by a powerful demon," Konstantin said.

"*One...two...three!*"

Konstantin squeezed his eyes shut, but even then, his retinas burned with the bright of the light Rex emanated. The pure golden sunlight of an Egyptian Demi-god, as powerful as a star.

Hopefully, it bought Zariya enough of a shot.

GALU HAD NEVER FELT SO heavy. His limbs hung like weights as he clung to the top of Mason's submersible, his eyelids drooping. He had drained every drop of power fighting the other supes, and most of his physical strength as well. But he could do this last thing. He could disable this sub and give his teammates a fighting chance.

He felt the rising of the sub in his body before his mind registered it. They were surfacing. They must have detected him. Must have known he was here.

He had lost his rifle. Lost his knife. The glowing ashrays had disappeared after they'd dispatched the remaining hunters. He was all but defenseless against whatever would come out of that submersible.

But it didn't matter. He would fight it anyway.

He only wished he'd had more time to talk to Melusine. He would have told her how much he regretted leaving Port Royal. He'd escaped from the human prison and had been on the run. But he could have been on the run *with* her. They could have hidden out together, if she'd been willing. But he'd run *from* her. From his guilt. Instead of staying and facing it like a man.

It had been his fault Liandine had died. His showing off—taking them deep into the island to show them the waterfall. If he hadn't done that, Liandine never would have snuck back onto the island by herself. Never would have come across the hunters. Never would have been left to die, scorched by the sun like an animal.

He hadn't been able to face Melusine after Liandine had died. His love of her was mixed up with his grief, his shame. How could she want him, knowing what he'd done? So he'd run. Like a coward.

They'd reached the surface, and the submersible's hatch popped open. Finn climbed out, two handguns holstered at his hip. No doubt enchanted to withstand the water.

Anger and adrenaline roared to life within Galu, filling him with energy. A second wind—a third wind.

This supe had killed Liandine—laughed at the prospect of leaving a little girl to die. If Galu had an ounce of strength left in his body, he would use it to take his revenge.

Finn caught sight of him and grinned a shark's grin, stalking towards him across the slick top of the submarine.

Not seeing that someone had followed him up the hatch. Someone whose dark blue hair tangled in the Scottish wind. Someone else with revenge in her eyes.

Melusine hit Finn from behind in a tackle that would have made a linebacker proud, sending them both splashing into the water.

Galu dove after them, submerging into the murky depths.

Finn spun and had his gun out, shooting at her.

"Melusine!" Galu cried, which only turned the guns on him. He kicked out, shooting out of the way of the bullets, putting the bulk of the submarine between him and the barrels of those guns.

Finn whirled around, both guns out, searching for Melusine.

Galu had always loved seeing her in the water—graceful as a ribbon, her limbs elongating and morphing until she curled and spun effortlessly as water itself. Seeing her swim—glistening like quicksilver as she frolicked with a pod of dolphins—was when he'd first fallen in love with her.

She was still just as devastating.

Melusine ripped up out of the black depths, tearing around Finn like a cyclone, knocking one of the guns from his hand. Three shots rang out as Finn kicked for the surface, firing back wildly at her.

They needed to get that other gun from him.

Finn was searching for Melusine, his head swinging wildly as he darted in erratic, evasive patterns.

This was Galu's chance. He shot off the sub, straight towards Finn. Barreling down on him...

But Finn swung around, his eyes going wide. His gun went up, pointing straight for Galu's heart.

An explosion of light burst through the dark waters, burning Galu's eyes. He threw up a hand against the glare—

And a shot rang out.

I MOVED FASTER than I'd ever moved before, my eyes still squeezed shut. The moves were so rehearsed from Dad's memories that it was like dancing. A dance I'd known all my life.

I whirled out of Mason's grip, ducking under his arm and knocking the knife against the ceiling. It clattered to the sub's metal floor.

Mason was still screaming, one hand over his eyes. I needed to subdue him.

Dropping, I grabbed the knife and buried it in the side of his ribcage, under one arm.

Mason bellowed with rage and pain and swung out with his fist, connecting with my sternum.

The wind rushed from my lungs and I hit the floor hard, bright pinpricks like snowflakes blinding in my vision.

The bloody knife had fallen to the floor, just a foot from me.

Mason stood above me, blinking away the glow of Rex's flash, one hand to his dripping ribs. His baleful eyes fixed on me.

I lunged for the knife, but Mason was too fast. His boot connected with my temple and everything flashed white.

Then went black.

17

———

Galu felt his stomach, his chest. Prodded for the wound—for where the bullet had struck him—but there was nothing.

Blue blood bubbled out of Finn's mouth as he looked down in disbelief. As he took in the gaping wound where his heart should have been. If the merman had such a thing.

Galu met Melusine's eyes as she lowered the gun slightly. She was ready to finish Finn off with another shot if necessary.

But the merman was beginning to sink. His eyes fluttered closed as his limbs became heavy and his head lolled to the side. Slowly, they watched as he sank away, stolen by the deep.

Melusine let the gun slip from her fingers then, and it disappeared after Finn. She floated in the faint movement of the loch's waters, her face gone slack.

Galu swam to meet her and raised a tentative hand to her face. He caressed the cheek of the woman he'd dreamed about every night for the last two years. "Are you all right? Are you hurt?"

She looked up at him with a hollow laugh. "I just...can't believe it's over. I did it. I finally fucking did it."

She tipped her head forward against his own with a soft sigh and closed her eyes.

"You did. You were amazing. If you hadn't been here..."

She leaned back slightly, opening those turquoise eyes. But her body didn't move, it hovered just inches from his. "You would have been royally screwed."

"I would've been so screwed." He grinned. "I was always lost without you, Mel. I've been so lost. I never should have left. I was a coward and a—"

Her lips cut him off—firmly, resolutely. Warmth bloomed inside him as bright as daybreak, banishing the chill of the loch, dispelling the exhaustion weighing his bones.

He leaned into her kiss, eager and enthusiastic, wrapping his arms around the body he remembered. Relearning every curve and dip, the fresh, crystal-clean taste of her.

"Does this mean you forgive me?" He broke off the kiss with a gasp.

"It was never me who had to forgive you, Galu. You had to forgive yourself."

He blinked in surprise at that. Perhaps she was right. Perhaps his time with Phoenix Team, protecting those who couldn't protect themselves... Perhaps it had been part of his penance. Part of what he'd needed to prove to himself he was still worthwhile. "When did you get so wise?"

"I've always been this wise. You were just too young and stupid to recognize it."

"Well, I'm slightly wiser now."

She arched a brow. "Yet apparently not wise enough to know when to shut up." She claimed his mouth again with a kiss, and this time, he was wise enough to take the hint.

I woke to the pain of a blinding headache. I stifled a groan, trying to get my bearings. Was I still on the sub?

Drip.

Drip.

I looked around for the sound, the world coming into focus.

Mason was standing at the controls, one hand pressed beneath his armpit, where I'd stabbed him.

I felt a shudder beneath us as the submarine lurched to a halt.

Land. We'd run aground on the shore. Mason was running for it.

I couldn't let him do that. But I was also in no condition for another fight inside this submarine. Even injured, Mason was strong. And I was injured too. I needed to level the playing field. I needed a weapon.

Closing my eyes, I slumped down as Mason turned towards the ladder. I could hear his heavy footsteps. The hatch being opened.

I could feel the weight of his scrutiny on me, no doubt as he decided whether I was dead enough or whether he needed to make me deader. My skin prickled and it took all my restraint not to spring to my feet—to defend myself.

Drip.

Drip.

He started up the ladder. He must have decided his own condition was more important than my death.

I waited a few seconds and then shoved to my feet. I grabbed the ladder to stop the world from swaying around me. And then I started climbing.

We had run aground on the shore of the loch just past the edge of the castle grounds. I could see Mason trekking towards the castle. I knew where he was going. To his precious Chinvat Gate—which would take him far from here. He would escape.

Determination flared in me. No fucking way I was going to let that happen. I had Dad's killer in my sights. Mason was going down. Today.

"*Zariya, come in.*" Konstantin's baritone flared in my mind. I couldn't resist the shiver of desire that his soft, accented syllables sent through me. Inconvenient as fuck. I shoved the thoughts down.

"I'm here," I responded. *"Mason is headed to the castle. He has a portal that will allow him to escape. I'm going after him."*

"Stand down, Zariya. I can see you're hurt. You are not to go after Mason without backup."

I looked over my shoulder. He could see me? Where the hell was he?

There. Bobbing in the loch, a few hundred yards offshore. I could just barely make out a blond figure standing on the top of the submersible. Damn, his eyesight was good if he could see the blood on my temple from here.

"I'm going after him, so if you don't want me to go alone, you better get your asses over here."

"Negative. Our submersible's engine is damaged. We can't get to shore. Not yet."

"Can't Galu push you or something?" I asked as I stalked after Mason. They could come up with something.

"Galu's power is depleted from the battle."

"Then fly over here."

I could hear the exasperation in his voice. *"Derived vampires can't fly, Zariya. Only Authentics."*

"Well, I'm hearing a lot of excuses and not a lot of ideas. I'm headed for the study on the first floor. Join me if you want."

"Stand down, Zariya. That's an order."

"I told you, Konstantin, I'll obey your orders except when it comes to my dad. And this bastard admitted to killing him. I'm not letting him go. Kiki, will you get Konstantin out of my head?"

He went silent. *I'm probably going to get kicked off Phoenix Team for this,* I thought with a pang of regret. As crazy as the last few days had been, I was kinda good at this. And the guys were starting to grow on me.

But it didn't matter. Only avenging Dad did.

I vaulted over the railing onto the back patio of the castle grounds. My head was starting to clear. I needed to find a gun. And then it was time to end this.

"That little…" Konstantin bit off his expletive. He wasn't one to use derogatory names for women, but damn it if Zariya Chanji didn't test his resolve.

"We need to get to shore." Daevin crawled out of the sub and inched out onto the roof.

"Any bright ideas? Can demons fly?"

"You know we can't. Coulda impressed a lot of chicks with that little trick if I could."

"Then we swim." Konstantin pulled off his leather jacket and dropped it down the hatch.

Daevin looked at the black water, his mouth twisted with distaste. "I fucking hate swimming."

"Boss!" Galu popped out of the water next to them, Melusine's sleek head appearing at his side. "Need a ride?"

"Yes!" Konstantin cried. "How? Where?"

"I found us some help." Galu grinned. "She's awful grateful for what we did today and wanted to return the favor."

Konstantin didn't have time to question his second, for a glistening, smooth, *giant* head surfaced next to them. Awe filled him.

"Great balls of fire." Daevin's eyes went wide. "Nessie herself!"

The supe's head lengthened out of the water as she seemed to blink the water off her long, dark eyelashes. The hump of her back appeared and sidled up alongside the submersible.

"Get on, boss!"

Konstantin didn't wait. He climbed down onto the Loch Ness Monster's broad back, Daevin quickly following. Her hide was thick and rubbery, and Konstantin dropped to his hands and knees to keep from slipping off.

"Ain't no one going to believe this," Daevin said with a grin.

"Hang on!" Galu cried, and Konstantin gripped his fingers into her slippery hide just as Nessie took off, cutting through the water with the grace and speed of a dolphin.

Luiz popped his head up from the sub and shouted, "we'll get her towed into shore. Go get our girl!"

They reached the shore in thirty seconds, and he and Daevin splashed out into the water. "Thank you," Konstantin called back to Nessie, even as he pulled his gun from his holster and sprinted towards the castle. He caught a bob of the creature's head before she headed back into the lake. She understood.

They ran through the castle at blinding speed, startling servants and waitstaff out of the way.

Hold on, Zariya. We're coming.

The room at the end of the ornate hallway was pulsing with a lavender light emanating from the doorway. "He must have the portal open." Daevin panted.

They burst through the door and Konstantin took in the scene in a blink. A round stone circle the size of a Volkswagen rested on the plush carpet. Purple light burst from within, sending dancing patterns on the gilt of the ceiling. Zariya stood at the far edge, blood matting her hair to one temple.

She was poised to jump into the portal.

"Wait!" Konstantin shouted.

She looked up sharply. Took in Konstantin with his hand outstretched, Daevin with his pistol gripped in two hands.

But she didn't wait. She jumped.

CLAIRE LUANA

MYTHICAL ALLIANCE

PHOENIX CAPTURED

1

———————

There's something about falling sideways through space and time that makes a person question their life choices. And I was no exception.

I'd barreled through the Chinvat Gate after Warrick Mason, the wendigo supe who'd killed my dad. I'd known that if I didn't follow, I'd lose him—maybe forever. I hadn't had time to think about what would happen when I came through the other side.

That thought was now stark in my mind. Whatever happened, I had to come out fighting.

The dark space around me shuddered and compressed, and before I had a chance to brace myself, I was through, popping up through the floor as the Gate tossed me over its threshold like last week's leftovers.

I rolled to a crouch, taking in my surroundings. I was alone in a corridor made of weathered stone—some sort of castle or fortress. A trail of blood led away from the gate and around the corner. Mason. Injured—and headed somewhere.

I bit my lip as a shiver wracked my body. It was fucking *cold* here, wherever *here* was. I was still clad in the ridiculous cocktail dress I'd been kidnapped in back at Aldourie Castle—God, that felt like an eternity ago. My feet were bare. My cold-blooded naga half was not pleased with this situation.

I either needed to go forward, securing warmer clothes and a weapon, or I needed to go back.

The Gate flared to life, a surge of purple light nearly blinding me. I staggered back in time to see Konstantin and Daevin pop out of the Gate and crash onto the stone in a tangled pile of muscled limbs. *Thank Manasa.* My relief at seeing them bowled into me with hurricane-force winds.

The Gate began to shrink—dimming and contracting until it was little more than a stone bracelet lying still on the stone. But the imprint—the raised stone circle with telltale markings, was hewn into the stone. Just as it had been in Turkey and in Scotland.

Konstantin pushed to his feet, offering Daevin a hand. Even after flying through a magic portal he took my breath away—a modern Viking with his sandy blond hair pulled into a ponytail, his ripped torso clad in a black leather jacket and black T-shirt. Worry was written across his chiseled features. "Zariya, are you all right?"

I nodded and wrapped my arms around myself, fighting off another shiver. "Got a headache, but I'm okay."

Worry turned to anger. Konstantin took a step towards me and I couldn't help it—my human side prickled with fear. "Coming through the gate by yourself was one of the stupidest, most idiotic moves I've ever witnessed in my six hundred years."

"I couldn't lose him," I explained lamely. "He admitted to killing Dad."

Konstantin's broad shoulders drooped slightly. "I don't care, Zariya. Putting yourself at risk puts the entire team at risk—"

"Boss?" Daevin broke in, smoothing his black hair back between his two curving horns. He didn't look remotely concerned, he braced himself against a stone wall with one red-skinned hand, his forked tail flicking lazily. "Maybe we should save the lecture. Figure out where the hell we are. I've been trying to get Kiki on comms, and I've got nothing."

Konstantin blinked his sky-blue eyes and tapped his comm. "Tartarus Base, come in. This is Phoenix One, can you read?"

Silence. "Fuck," Konstantin swore. "They must have some magic neutralizing our comms. I think they're fried."

My eyes had fluttered closed against the cold, and they snapped back open at his curse.

"Six, you're not looking so hot." Daevin cocked his head as he examined me.

I gave him a ghost of a smile. "Funny choice of words. I'm cold-blooded. It's too cold here. I need more clothes—"

Konstantin took off his jacket and draped it around my shoulders. It smelled of him—starlight and glacial ice and the black of space. I resisted the urge to close my eyes to take in the scent.

A blast of heat hit me as Daevin's hands burst into flame, as he directed the controlled fire towards me.

I nearly groaned in relief. Sometimes it came in handy to have a caco-demon as a friend.

He let the fire go out and ushered me towards him. "Come here. I'm as good as a heated blanket."

I was too frozen to be shy, so I threaded my arms into Konstantin's jacket and then stepped in and leaned against Daevin, my head drooping against his chest. He was like a heater.

"Gettin' blood all over my good shirt," he said, but when I looked up in apology, he was grinning. He wrapped his arms around me, sealing in the warmth.

Konstantin snorted, his eyes narrowed at Daevin. "You don't have any good shirts."

Daevin's grin just widened. "So, what's the plan, boss?"

"Besides you feeling up our sixth?"

"I believe you mean *keeping her alive*. But yes."

Konstantin looked down the corridor. "We evaluate. If we can take Mason safely, we do so. Otherwise, we retreat."

"Retreat?" I protested. "We can't leave without taking him down."

"I didn't stay alive the last six hundred years by running into situations with impossible odds like some stupid American cowboy. And if you'd known your father in the field, you would know he didn't, either."

I pinched my lips together. That was a low blow, but he was right. Dad's memories, nestled safely within my mind, told me that Konstantin's approach was the right one. This was an unknown situation with no base support. Caution was key.

I quested out with my naga glands, evaluating the maze of halls and passageways around us. Looking for lifeforms through their infrared heat signatures. The place was a maze. Huge, multiple floors. Outside was cold. Cold, cold, cold. But inside—there were a lot of heat signatures. Perhaps fifty scattered throughout the levels. But that wasn't what concerned me. It was the concentration of a dozen. Headed our way.

I pushed back from Daevin, mourning the loss of his delicious warmth. He was like a one-man space heater. "We have a group fast incoming. We need to get out of here, now."

Konstantin stilled. Switched from our grumpy commander to deadly killing machine in a moment. "Where?"

"Down that hallway. I'd give them...about a minute."

"Do your senses give you any indication of a way out of here?"

I closed my eyes, trying to picture the blueprint of the building. Based on the location of the people, and the temperature fluctuations outside, I thought we were on the second floor. "That way." I pointed away from Mason's bloody footprints. "We need to get one floor down and then find an exit."

Konstantin gestured. "Lead the way."

We took off running. Damn, I wished I had a pair of shoes. I felt like a heroine in the action movies that Kiki, Alviya, and I would always make fun of. Like, why did the guys get to be fully dressed and the girl always ended up scantily clad, running for her life? Wasn't that some damn irony.

My heart squeezed. I really hoped I got to see Kiki and Alviya again. I slowed. "There's someone in the corridor up ahead."

Konstantin stopped beside me. "They could be armed."

"In here?" Daevin nodded to a door beside us.

"There's a window," I whispered. "We could get out that way." The person was about to round the corner.

"Go," Konstantin ordered, and we piled inside the door. Konstantin shut it quietly and we listened as bootsteps passed by. Crates and black cases were piled high around us. We were in some sort of storeroom.

I flew to the window, looking out and getting the first true glimpse of our predicament. My heart sank into my stomach. We were surrounded by a field of white snow, crowned with jagged, snow-peaked mountains.

"Well, ain't that some shit." Daevin appeared beside me.

"We need to find you some warmer clothes before we go out in that," Konstantin assessed.

"And some shoes. Unless Daevin wants to carry me piggyback the whole way."

Konstantin let out a soft growl, but Daevin laughed. "Now you're getting it, six."

"Start looking in these," Konstantin said. "Maybe they have clothes. Or weapons. Or something we can use to communicate with base."

Daevin's eyes went wide as he opened the first crate. The look on his face was one of pure delight—a child on Christmas morning shredding the wrapping paper to discover his most-wished-for toy.

Konstantin's nostrils flared. "That smells like—"

Daevin held up a brick with glee. "C4, baby. Don't know if we have shoes, but we've got explosives."

2

———————

Bombs were simple. One objective, one purpose. A symphony of destruction, and Daevin was the maestro.

Daevin hummed as he worked, connecting the blasting cap and detonators. To the block of explosive. They had no way to remote time the bombs, so they'd have to set the charges and get the hell out of Dodge.

Konstantin and Zariya were rifling through boxes and crates, calling out as they found various items that might be useful for their quick retreat from here.

Wherever *here* was.

He had to give it to Chanji. Diving through that gate after that creepy-as-fuck wendigo all by her lonesome took some serious balls. He might have underestimated her.

Out of the corner of his eye, he caught Konstantin helping Zariya into a thick jacket. It was obvious Konstantin had underestimated her too—obvious precisely how quickly he'd become wrapped around her little finger.

Daevin didn't particularly think it should matter what Veil Force Phantoms did on their own time, but Konstantin had always had a stick up his ass about matters of rank and propriety. Maybe it was a vampire thing. Or an Austrian thing. Or just a being-super-fucking-old thing. It was going to be fun watching their fearless leader tie himself in knots over Zariya, that was for damn sure.

Daevin attached the final detonator and stood, waving the bomb at them. "All done. Where do you want—" He froze, the words gone to dust in his mouth as something buzzed through him. A feeling both foreign and as familiar as the back of his hand. A feeling he hadn't felt in a very, very long time.

No, it couldn't be. He shoved down his panic. He was imagining it.

Konstantin was talking to him. Daevin focused on the words. "Three, are you all right?" he was saying.

"Yeah—thought I heard something." Daevin shook his head. "Must be going nuts."

"You sure you're all right?" Konstantin offered Daevin one of the snow parkas they'd found, but Daevin shook his head. "Make my own heat."

Zariya cut in. "Mason's men are close. Can you rig one of those at the door, and another at the window? One after the other? Hopefully, we can catch them in the hallway and then in the room?"

Konstantin gave a quick nod.

"You got it." Daevin crossed to the door, setting up the charge on the floor by the doorjamb. His hands were shaking. He cursed under his breath. It was that damn buzzing. It was the way it felt when a queen was near.

He couldn't help the memories that tumbled over him. Daevin was a caco-demon, which made him an impossibly-strong, near immortal, fire-and-explosive wielding badass, and also...a slave. Demons were like bees—pledged to a queen. More than pledged. Enslaved. When a queen was near, her will was law—a demon was incapable of disregarding her commands. As a caco-demon, Daevin was pretty high in the food chain—in the warrior caste, just beneath the queen. But it didn't matter. If he was back home, he'd still be a slave. A drone.

You didn't find many demons on Earth, as they hailed from a parallel realm that had been known throughout human history by many names. Hell, Hades, Hel... The ancient Hebrews had called it "Sheol." They'd actually gotten it right because that was what his people called it, too. Magic wielders and certain supes could open gates between the realms, but not many demons came through. They were too busy fighting the wars between the various demon sects as the queens battled for position and land.

Occasionally, a queen would lend a drone to a magic wielder or black witch on this side of the barrier between worlds. It was how he'd ended up on Earth, how he'd ended up in a MASC holding cell. And how, eventually, he'd ended up free. He didn't know of any other free drones. He didn't think he ever would.

Something touched his shoulder and he whirled with a wild cry, flame dancing on his fingertips.

Zariya stumbled back, pulling her hand back like she'd been burned.

He doused the finger-flames. "Sorry. You startled me."

"We're ready to go." Zariya's words stretched sideways as a buzzing filled his mind. Drowned out his thoughts. His free will.

This time, there was no mistaking it. There was a queen here. And she was coming for him.

Daevin shot out a hand against the wall to keep himself up, but it wasn't enough. His knees buckled as he clapped his hands over his ears. They'd found him. Somehow, the queen knew. Was it the queen who had once commanded him? Xyana? No, it couldn't be. She'd never leave Sheol.

Zariya and Konstantin stood over him, matching expressions of worry on their faces. "What is it?" Konstantin asked.

"There's a demon queen here." Daevin gasped. Konstantin would know what it meant.

Konstantin swore, but Zariya hissed in a breath too. "We have to get you out of here. Come on, Konstantin!"

The buzzing was coalescing into words. Commands. *Stay where you are. Restrain your companions.*

"I can't—" Daevin gritted his teeth, fighting the urge he had to tackle Konstantin to the floor. "I can't go. She wants me to stop you from leaving. You have to go now."

"I'm not leaving you," Konstantin growled.

"She's got a hold already." Daevin shook his head. "I won't come...willingly."

"Then I'll make you come." Konstantin leaped for him, his vampire form nothing but a blur. But Daevin was superhuman too, and he dodged out of the way, his body moving of its own volition. He understood what Konstantin was trying to do. Incapacitate Daevin and get him out of range of the queen. But it was too late for that.

Konstantin darted left as Daevin tried to go right, but his commander twisted in the air with impossible speed. He tackled Daevin—the vampire's bulk slamming full on into Daevin's stomach. They tumbled together and thunked hard against the stone wall. Konstantin palmed Daevin's head, smashing it once against the stones.

Stars exploded in Daevin's vision, but his body had a mind of its own. His flames roared to life as he seized Konstantin's head between his hands.

Zariya screamed in the background as Konstantin twisted in his grip, desperate to extricate himself. Fire was one of the few things that *could* kill a vampire.

Konstantin smashed Daevin in the stomach with a booted foot and scrambled back. Daevin collapsed to the floor, his breath whooshing from him. When he pushed to his hands and knees, Konstantin was standing against the far wall with Zariya, his pale skin blistered.

"They're almost here." Zariya sounded near tears. In some helpless pocket of Daevin's mind, he regretted what he'd done to Konstantin, regretted that Zariya had had to see their battle. But that part was so far from in control it was laughable. Zariya was right. The queen was close now. Her control was near complete. It was all that he could do to choke out through gritted teeth, "It's too late. Leave!"

Konstantin bared his teeth, his fangs flashing, his fists balled. But

Zariya grabbed his arm. "If we don't go now, they'll capture all of us. We'll come back for him."

Konstantin let out a roar of frustration but met Daevin's eye. "Stay strong. We will come for you." And then he pulled Zariya up into his arms and dove through the window and out into the frozen freedom beyond.

Daevin flew to the window, about to launch himself after them. He'd been ordered to hold them here, and he'd failed. He had to go after them—

"Stop." A single word from an imperious female voice.

Daevin tightened his hands on the windowsill, not caring that the glass bit into his palms and drew black blood. His last bit of rebellion before he turned to meet his new queen.

3

———

Konstantin's feet hit the snow with bone-jarring force. He held Zariya tightly in his arms, but even so, the two-story drop nearly ripped her from his grip. He straightened and set her down gently on her feet, ignoring the twinge of regret as her warm form left his arms. He looked back and got his first glimpse of the building they'd been navigating. It was a huge stone fortress—hewn into the rock of a craggy mountain peak.

Zariya was squinting into the expanse of ice before them, a long, open stretch leading to the foothills of more mountains before them. "Where are we?"

"I don't know," Konstantin admitted. "But we need to get out of here and make contact with HQ."

Konstantin heard the bullet slicing through the air from a hundred yards away. He moved with all the speed his supernatural form was granted—diving at Zariya to knock her out of the way of the bullet's path.

They tumbled across the snow together, both coming up ready as a spray of bullets ricocheted off the snow to their left.

"Run!" he cried, and run they did.

Zariya was fast, but not as fast as him. He sent up a silent prayer of thanks to whatever gods might be out there that they'd found snow gear that fit Zariya. The cold didn't bother him, but Zariya wouldn't have lasted long out here without it. Frigid air burned in his lungs, the wind sending snow into his face like tiny stinging barbs.

Wherever they were, it was an unforgiving climate. They wouldn't last long exposed to the elements.

The spray of bullets from the castle window stopped. They must have been out of range.

"Head for those foothills," Konstantin gasped.

"Okay," was all Zariya could say through her labored breathing.

They'd put serious distance between them and the fortress, and so he didn't hear the click of the sniper rifle as its bullet clicked into the chamber. The ticking of the gear as the shooter adjusted for the wind velocity.

There was only the bullet as it exploded through Zariya's shoulder.

She tumbled to the ground in a tangle of limbs and dark curls, leaving a smear of emerald blood on the pristine expanse of snow.

"Zariya!" Konstantin spun around, his feet slipping on the ice beneath him. He scrambled to her side and pulled her up into his arms. It wouldn't take long for the sniper to reload.

Then he was off and running again, hazarding a look over one shoulder. They had to be close to three thousand meters from the fortress now. Almost out of the sniper's range. He kicked his legs into his highest gear, zigzagging right and left in a dizzying dash that would hopefully leave the sniper without a shot.

Zariya was blinking in confusion, as if her mind didn't yet understand what had happened. She'd been shot. And she was bleeding out.

"Can you use your glands?" Konstantin asked. "Is there any shelter around here? Can you find anything? Anyone? You've been shot. I need to tend to your wound."

Zariya's caramel skin had gone pale, the golden pattern of her scales standing stark against her skin. She opened and closed her mouth as if to speak, but then her nostrils flared. She'd understood.

She craned her head and pointed, then hissed. "To the left—those hills. There's a heat signature underground. It must be a cave."

"Perfect." Konstantin headed straight for it. There was no way the shooter could get them from this range. They were out of that danger, anyway.

"The signature is big." Zariya coughed, and green blood flecked her full lips.

His heart seized. She didn't have much time. "We'll deal with it."

Her eyes fluttered shut, and Konstantin squeezed her leg with one hand. "Stay awake. I need you to navigate. Where's the entrance?"

She squinted, struggling to lift her head. "I don't—" She blinked. "I don't know. I'm having a hard time—"

"Come on, Zariya. Try to focus. When we get inside you can rest. But I need you right now, okay? I can't do this without you." The words were said for her benefit, to rally her strength. But Konstantin realized how true they were. Zariya had only been on Phoenix Team for a few days, and already he'd come to rely on her. Her unusual gifts. Her fresh perspective, her vibrant presence. He couldn't lose her.

"There." She gasped. "There's an opening..."

Konstantin saw it with his superhuman sight. Just a crack in the rock, nearly indecipherable. A refuge for them, away from the certain pursuit that would be pouring out of the fortress.

Away from a known danger—and towards an unknown.

It didn't matter. Getting Zariya healed did.

The cave was dark at first, but then a dim, pearlescent light bloomed above him. Some sort of glowworm, nestled into the cracks above them.

He set Zariya down on the hard ground. Her eyes were closed and green blood dribbled from her lips.

He felt for a pulse. It was faint. He took quick stock of her wound. The bullet had gone through her shoulder cleanly. In one side and out the other. But she'd lost a lot of blood, and it continued to gush freely. It looked like it had nicked her brachial artery.

Konstantin pressed at the wound and her eyes flashed open, her slitted pupils unfocused with pain. The wound was severe. She wouldn't last much longer. And he had no medical supplies.

There was one solution. The only solution he had to give. He rebelled against it, even as he knew it was the only way. Vampire blood. It had remarkable healing properties when ingested. Miraculous, really. But it came with a price.

Vampire blood changed a person. It transformed humans from free-thinking individuals into devoted, mindless thralls. Acolytes desperately in love with their vampire masters. He'd only fed his blood to humans a few times, each time in circumstances as desperate as these. Each time, he'd regretted it.

Some thought it was worse than death.

But perhaps he could find a solution. He'd heard there were spells that would free a person from the hold of the blood. Perhaps MASC had the resources to find such a thing. And what was more, Zariya was half naga. It wouldn't affect her supe side. She would retain her free will—her self. It was an acceptable risk, considering the alternative was to watch her bleed out—to let her die in his arms. To break the promise he'd made to himself and to Vizol's memory just days ago when he'd agreed to let her join Phoenix Team. He'd promised to keep her safe.

Zariya had grown still. Her pulse was weak in her veins.

No choice. He had no choice.

Konstantin bit into his wrist, tearing open the skin. Crimson blood welled up.

"Zariy." He cradled her head and tried not to think how silky soft her hair was. He held his wrist to her mouth, letting blood dribble into her lips. She wasn't drinking. With his thumb, he gently smeared the blood across her lips, tenderly probing into her mouth and touching the velvet surface of her tongue.

She reacted. An inadvertent swallow.

"Come on, Zariya. Drink." He dripped more blood into her mouth. "Come on."

Her throat bobbed again.

Her eyes flew open and she latched on to his wrist with sudden fierceness. Her fangs dug into his skin.

In his surprise, he almost pulled back. Her venom coursed into his veins, sending a pleasant warmth tingling through him. His eyes fluttered closed as she sucked at the blood pulsing through his delicate vein.

The power of his vampire physiology could repel any intruder, but he hadn't been prepared for this—intimacy. His blood, inside her. Her venom inside him. He forced his thoughts back to Zariya. "That's enough." He wrenched his arm away from her. Her lips were tinged a bright shade of scarlet. It was as erotic a sight as he'd seen in decades, and he couldn't account for how it moved him.

He smeared blood on his own wrist, and the wound began to close.

Zariya's eyes were sharp as he gently probed at her wound. It was already closing. A huge sigh left him and his head drooped slightly towards hers. She would be all right. "Welcome back."

Her eyes were fixed on his, as if she were a starving woman and he a feast for the taking.

"What did you do?" Her voice was breathy.

"You were dying. I fed you my blood. You might be feeling some... effects," he said carefully. "We'll find a way to counteract it when we're back. In the meantime, fight it. It's not really you."

"How can you be so sure?"

Her words stunned him. What was she saying? She didn't mean—

Then her eyes flicked behind him, her nostrils flaring. Her fingers dug into the flesh of his arm.

And then he smelled it too. The wet musk of fur and magic.

We're not alone, she mouthed.

4

———

My body was on fire with awareness of Konstantin's presence.

Something was coming towards us—something big and smelly and definitely supernatural. But that didn't even rank in my list of concerns. Every fiber of my being was fixed on the fact that Konstantin crouched over me—his finely-wrought mouth close enough to touch. *He would protect me.*

The simpering thought came out of nowhere. So apparently the vampire blood had me appreciating his heroism, in addition to his rugged good looks.

I groaned, forcing myself to sit up. My shoulder no longer burned where the bullet had ripped through it. That was something, I guess.

The ground shuddered beneath me. Once. Twice. Footsteps. The beast was drawing nearer, whatever it was. And we had no weapons other than our hands.

Konstantin leaped to his feet and offered me his hand. I allowed him to pull me up but didn't release his fingers. He didn't pull back; he only angled his body slightly in front of mine in a fighting stance.

I fought against the flurry of butterflies that buffeted me. *I'm holding Konstantin's hand.*

A shadow appeared in the low light, and my glands showed me its form. It was shaped like a humanoid—two arms, two legs it stood upon. But it was big. Maybe eight feet tall. And shaggy—with thick fur to keep in its warmth.

"We don't mean you any harm." Konstantin's deep voice echoed through the cave. "We only needed shelter. Do not attack."

The creature shifted, cocking its head. "What are you?" Its voice rumbled in a deep, scratching tone—the sound of ancient glaciers sliding infinitesimally slowly over stone. I got the distinct impression that this creature was old. Older than even Konstantin perhaps.

"I'm a vampire. My name is Konstantin Bauer. I'm a representative of the Mythical Alliance of Supernatural Creatures. This is my teammate Zariya Chanji. She's a naga." Konstantin left out my human heritage, which was just fine by me. No way of knowing if this creature was Class X.

The creature seemed to consider and then finally said, "Come with me." It turned and began to amble back into the passageway.

Konstantin started after it and my fingers tightened on his in a vise grip as I pulled him back. "What are you doing?" I hissed.

"Following."

I let out an incredulous laugh. "Have you never watched a horror movie? You don't just...follow! We could be following him to some sort of torture chamber where he'll string us up and eat us!"

"I suspect if the creature wanted to attack us, he would have already. We have few alternatives. Outside this cave, we have the Collectors on our tail, including our own enslaved teammate, with no supplies and no way of contacting base. My comm remains inoperative. Maybe he has something that can help."

"Or maybe he has a giant, person-sized cooking pot!"

Konstantin's mouth quirked, and I thought maybe he was resisting a smile. "Or maybe you watch too much television. Come on." He tugged on my hand. It had not escaped my notice that I was *still holding Konstantin's hand*. "I'll be able to defend us."

I let him pull me forward, the still-sane naga side of me bristling at the suggestion that I needed him to protect me. My vampire-blood-addled human side didn't give a shit so long as it ended up with me and Konstantin horizontal.

I shook my head, trying to clear it. "Your blood—is it strong? Because you're old, I mean? It seems strong." I rifled through Dad's memories, but I couldn't find one where Konstantin had ever used his blood to heal a teammate. It seemed he really did avoid it, if at all possible.

"Yes," he admitted. "I wouldn't have used it unless I was desperate. It's an inconvenience, I'm sorry."

An inconvenience. That was an understatement. Having my moderate crush on my boss turn into a raging, fae-mate style obsession? Big fucking inconvenience.

"You said there might be some sort of cure?"

"Signe and Verte are pretty damn inventive. They'll rise to the challenge, I'm sure."

"So...hypothetical cure."

He grimaced. "I'm sorry, Zariya, I really am. I should have foreseen the possibility of a long-range shooter. I was distracted by the loss of Daevin, and I took my eye off the ball. And you got hurt."

"It's all right." I ran my other hand down his forearm, reveling in the strength of muscle and sinew. "I'll need to get a T-shirt. *I jumped through a portal, got shot, and all I got was this raging crush on my boss.*"

He did smile then. "I suppose if I was stuck with a thrall, you wouldn't be the worst."

"Was that a...compliment?" I pretended to gasp. "You must be going soft."

"Never." Dim light was blooming before us as the tunnel opened up into some sort of larger cavern.

I reluctantly released Konstantin's hand, readying myself to fight if necessary. But as we came out of the tunnel, I found my mouth dropping open instead.

Hundreds—no thousands—of glowworms decorated the glittering cavern roof above us, interspersed among what looked like quartz crystals.

Before us stood what looked like an albino Sasquatch—our

host was tall and thick, covered in snowy white fur. It had eyes as blue as Konstantin's, and a soft muzzle covered in a bristle of whiskers.

"You're a yeti," I said in surprise. They were Recognized, through extremely rare and shy. Class O-V. Omnivorous. Verbal. *Not human-eaters*, I thought in relief.

The yeti nodded. "My name is Bunko. This is my cave. You are welcome to rest here before you continue on your journey." He turned and crossed to a large stone fire pit stacked with wood and began to light it with a little red Bic lighter, like you'd find in a convenience store. The cave was surprisingly cozy. The floor was strewn with thick furs, and there were two ancient-looking chairs, a stack of crates and supplies against one wall—even a fur-covered ledge that I suspected served as Bunko's bed.

"How do you get wood out here?" I couldn't help my curiosity. When we'd been running—granted, I hadn't had a lot of time to check out the territory—it had seemed pretty desolate.

"There are townsfolk a few miles into the hills that I trade with for supplies. Apparently, yeti tears are a potent aphrodisiac. The Chinese go nuts for them. I can trade one bottle for a year's worth of supplies.

"The Chinese?" Konstantin asked. "Where exactly are we?"

Bunko raised an eyebrow but didn't ask. "We're in Bhutan. Don't get a lot of visitors. How'd you get here, anyway?"

Konstantin shot me a sidelong glance.

"I impulsively jumped through a magic portal after a dangerous supe poacher who killed my father. We ended up in that fortress."

"We need to get word back to our base. One of our team has been captured, and the rest will be worried sick about us. Do you have any sort of communications device?"

A stab of guilt needled me. I'd been so focused on myself and how good Konstantin's muscles looked under that parka that I hadn't even been thinking about Galu, Rex, and Luiz, whom I'd totally abandoned back in Scotland. Or poor Daevin. Who knew Mason was doing to him right now?

"I do not. There is a village about a three hours' trek west of here that has access to a satellite phone."

"Perfect. If you could give us directions, we should head out immediately."

Bunko frowned slowly. "Not that I'm trying to force you to stay here, but there is a storm blowing in, and night is falling fast. I would recommend eating and resting and commencing your trek in the morning."

"I appreciate the concern, but I'm built for pretty tough weather —" Konstantin began, but then he trailed off as he looked at me. Realizing my inconvenient cold-blooded nature.

"The storms bring worse than frostbite. Angry wind elementals roam the higher mountains, and they come down when the storms roll in. It's best you shelter here," Bunko said.

"I know you're anxious to get in touch with base. I am too," I said. "But I think we should listen to Bunko."

"I will put a soup together," Bunko offered. "You can bathe in the hot springs if you wish to clean yourselves, in the meantime."

"Hot springs?" I squeaked.

5

———

She was beautiful, this demon queen. They always were. Beautiful, and terrible.

Daevin stood by the window, watching helplessly as a pale vampire sniper calmly set up the weapon that would take out his fleeing friends.

But there was nothing he could do. His body—his will—was no longer his own.

She watched him with amusement—enjoying the white knuckles of his fists, the feathering of muscle along his jaw as he ground his teeth. It was all the rebellion he could muster.

She was almost dainty—this queen—lean and long-legged, with delicate cloven hooves leading to slim hips and a trim waist. Membranous wings sprouted from between her shoulder blades, and her horns twisted upward in a spiral, like some sort of gazelle. But there was nothing dainty about the expression in her dark eyes—feral delight at his predicament.

She stalked across the room towards him and seized his chin in one surprisingly strong hand. She turned his head left, then right, as if examining prize livestock.

Daevin's outrage was impotent within him.

"How delighted I was to discover an unclaimed warrior drone right beneath my fingertips. I've so missed having someone to play with."

"Maybe you should go back to hell," he managed to spit out, his rebellion sending wracking pain through his head.

She raised one dark eyebrow, stark against her crimson skin. "Your freedom has made you strong." She smiled. "That will make you even more fun to break."

A shot rang out and Daevin winced at the sound.

"Got one!" the sniper said with delight. "The girl."

"Quit celebrating and get the other one," the queen snapped.

Daevin's mind was whirling. Oh god...Zariya. Konstantin... He looked at the sniper, flexing his will against the queen's order to stay put, like a bodybuilder struggling to lift a weight. It was too heavy. Too much. He let out a groan of frustration.

The queen let out a delighted laugh.

Another shot rang out.

Daevin's eyes closed. No. Konstantin. After all they'd been through—the battles and firefights—to stand here and do nothing while the man he respected more than any other was gunned down like an animal—

"Damn. I missed him," the sniper said. "He's too fast."

"Well, get him," the queen said simply.

"He's out of range." The vampire stood and turned. His face went pale as he saw who was blocking the doorway to the room.

Warrick Mason. Standing tall and healthy once again; whatever wound Zariya had inflicted upon him had apparently healed.

Daevin's eyes flicked to the explosive he'd planted by the base of the door, just a mere foot from where Mason stood. God, if he could just get—

Stars exploded in his vision as Mason backhanded him across the face with the force of a thunderbolt, sending Daevin reeling.

"Warrick!" the queen snapped, stepping between them and placing a hand on Mason's chest. "This one is *mine*. He is under my control."

"Then have him tell us where his little friends scurried off to." Mason glowered at him.

Daevin straightened, wiped the black blood from his lip, and glowered right back.

"What's your name, drone?" the queen asked.

"Daevin Ryan," he gritted out.

"Where are your friends going?"

He wanted to resist, to give her nothing. But he had nothing to give, and fighting her took too much of him. He needed to save his strength for the questions that mattered. "I don't know. We followed Mason through that bloody portal. They're probably trying to get to shelter so they can be picked up."

"Where might they shelter?"

"How the fuck would I know? I don't even know what bleeding country we're in."

Mason's face blackened and he took a step forward.

The queen moved to block him, her wings opening wide. An obvious challenge. "I will question him further. In the meantime, I suggest you busy yourself finding the two who got away. Or getting your story straight to explain the debacle in Scotland. We have a call with the Authority in an hour."

Mason bared his needle-sharp teeth at the demon but spun and stalked out of the room. The vampire sniper quickly followed.

Daevin struggled to keep his expression neutral. Now this was an interesting development. They'd thought Mason ruled the Collectors with an iron fist, but it seemed this demon queen was at least equal with him in status. And they both reported to someone else. This Authority. He couldn't wait to tell Konstantin. If he made it out of this alive.

The queen turned back to him, her smile growing wide. "Finally alone. It's time for us to get to know each other."

THE QUEEN SHOWED him to a holding cell deep within the stone fortress. It was galling, the fact that she didn't have to restrain him. No shackles on his wrist and no gun at his back. He walked into the cell like a lamb to the slaughter. Stood limp-dicked as she closed the door.

He'd noticed with mild interest another demon who stood guard at the entrance to the cellblock, a curvy female with deep violet skin who wore black tactical gear. Soldier caste? He couldn't tell. Their eyes had met as he'd passed, and hers had widened in surprise. He wondered if she was here against her will, too. They all were, to some extent, but the queens' holds were tighter on some. Others didn't mind the simple life of a drone. There was comfort in being told what to do, never having to take responsibility or make decisions. For the weak-minded, it suited. Somehow, he didn't think that purple demon fell in that category. Too much intelligence in those dark eyes.

The queen stepped into the cell with him, settling onto a rickety stool like it was a fucking throne. She crossed one slim leg over the other and folded her hands on her knees primly. "So. Daevin Ryan. Please sit." She pointed to the stone shelf against the wall that served as a bed.

He crossed his arms and leaned against the wall. "I'll stand."

"SIT." Her command echoed through his bones and he found his ass thunking on the stone bench before he even registered moving. *Bitch.* "Who are you?" he asked, trying to recover some semblance of dignity. He at least needed to know the name of the demon enslaving him. Whom to direct his hatred towards.

"I suppose that's a fair question. My name is Xarianne."

Daevin wracked his memories. He'd tried hard to put his time in Sheol behind him. But he had lived most of his life there. "You were queen of the Eastern Crags. Before..." He trailed off. There had been a coup. Xarianne had been killed.

"I assure you, rumors of my death were greatly exaggerated. I am queen in exile. Soon I will return and reclaim my lands and my drones. But I have some tasks to complete first."

"Like doing Warrick Mason's bidding?"

Her lip curled. "I warn you, Daevin Ryan. My time on this earthly plane has robbed me of my patience. We have not even reached the hard part yet."

"Oh yeah? And what's that?" Daevin said with a bravado he definitely did not feel inside.

"The part where you tell me everything there is to know about MASC's Veil Force. Right down to the type of coffee in the Phantom break room."

"I'm more of a tea man, myself," Daevin managed. Her compulsion was like a vise grip, choking his free will, his ability to think or do anything except desire to please her.

Her lip quirked. "It's been so long since I've come across a warrior with such spirit." She stood and crossed the space between them, laying her hands softly on his shoulders. "You and I both know, Daevin, that you are going to tell me the information I want to know, one way or other." In a lithe motion, she straddled him, her knees about his hips, her arms circling his neck.

It was all he could do to suppress a shudder. She was beautiful, true, but she was evil incarnate. All the queens were. She was the last thing he truly wanted. Though his body was already telling him otherwise. He could feel her compulsion wrapping around him, fueling his desire for her.

She continued, leaning in so her lips hovered just inches from his. She whispered, "The question is whether we're going to do this the easy way or the hard way?"

His conscience warred within him. Part of him wanted nothing more than to stand up and send her tumbling off his lap onto her ass on the dirty stone floor. But that would stoke her anger towards him —and she would use her direct compulsion to force him to spill all of MASC's secrets. Either before or after she forced him to inflict torturous agony upon himself. But if he could distract her until Phoenix Team came for him...he might be able to hold out. He might even be able to gain information from her.

So he shoved his revulsion down and grabbed her ass, wriggling her closer so she could feel the hard length of him. With a brash grin, he said, "Who says the easy way isn't the hard way too?"

Xarianne let out a throaty laugh and claimed his mouth with her own.

Daevin shoved down that part of him that belonged only to himself, that free supe who he'd fought so hard to become. Missing it even as he donned the mantle of the mindless slave he'd once been. The thrall he swore he'd never be again.

His last thought before he turned off his brain completely was for his team. *Hurry, mates. Please, hurry.*

6

____

Bunko led us through a dark tunnel deep into the mountain. I wished I had my comm—I was getting used to being able to communicate telepathically. I wanted to tell Konstantin that if Bunko had wanted to win our trust before luring us deeper into his lair to eat us, this would be a pretty good way to do it.

But I didn't think our host really had that in him. He seemed neat and kind, if not a little lonely. Besides, Konstantin and I together should be able to take one yeti, if it came to that.

But the tunnel widened into a long, low cave, the ceiling filled with glowworms. The faint smell of sulfur tickled my nose, but the gently bubbling waters laid out before us made me want to weep with delight.

Despite the bump I'd gotten from Konstantin's blood, I was sore and cold and covered in dried blood. Bunko pointed to a stack of furs in one alcove. "If you need to dry off, feel free to use those. The tunnel will bring you back when you're done."

"Thank you," I said, suppressing the urge to grab his furry middle and squeeze him in a hug. Definitely not a murderer.

He ambled back down the passage, leaving Konstantin and me alone.

Me and Konstantin. Alone.

There was nothing I could do to stop the desire from coursing through me. I only hoped the mineral smells from the hot springs would disguise my pheromones.

"You can go alone, if you want," Konstantin offered, rubbing the back of his neck. I didn't think I'd ever seen my fearless leader look so out of sorts.

"It's fine," I said. "It's a big pool. We can just take...separate ends."

"I think that's best."

Without another word, we turned our backs to each other and started stripping out of the black parkas and snow pants we'd stolen.

The chill air pebbled my skin and I hurried over and slipped into the deliciously warm waters of the pool. I couldn't help myself, I hazarded a glance over my shoulder at where Konstantin was taking his pants off. My mouth went dry. His body was in a word—exquisite. Sleek, bulging muscle, rippling abs, an ass a Greek statute would be jealous of... Dear God in heaven, the vampire was a work of art.

"Eyes to yourself, Chanji," Konstantin said, and I turned scarlet, whipping my gaze away from him, allowing him to slip into the waters.

"Sorry," I croaked. "It's...your fault."

"How do you figure?"

"Your blood made me do it."

Konstantin let out a bark of laughter. "That's what they all say."

I turned around carefully and settled into a seat on a low shelf against one wall of the pool.

Konstantin unthreaded the tie on his hair and let his blond strands fall around his shoulder. It was disarming as fuck, seeing him like that. It softened him. As if I were catching a glimpse of the real him—the one beneath the armor and mantle of command. I couldn't look away.

"How are you feeling?" he asked.

Like I'd give my left kidney for one unrestrained hour with you... "What do you mean?" I managed.

A knowing smile. "Your shoulder. You were shot, remember?"

"Oh, right." I tried rotating it. "Good as new."

"Good." He sighed. "Zariya, what you did, coming here…"

Here it came. The lecture of the century. "It was reckless, I know. I'm sorry. I never meant for anyone to get hurt. For Daevin to get captured."

"We never do. But acting like a lone wolf, when you're a part of a team, will get people killed."

"I know," I said quietly. "I'm sorry. What… What are you going to do?"

He raised one eyebrow and my heart skipped a beat. Damn, he was sexy when he did that.

"Are you going to…reprimand me?" I couldn't voice my true fear. That he'd kick me off the team. I'd only spent a short time with Phoenix Team, but already it felt like I'd been here for ages. Already it felt like I belonged.

"I should. I should kick you off Phoenix Team for what you did."

I winced. "But?" Please let there be a *but*…

"*But*…you performed admirably on our missions, insubordination aside. You're a good Phantom, Zariya. And I can't help but feel like you belong with us."

"I feel that way too. I'll be better. I won't be so reckless next time. I can follow orders."

Konstantin smirked. "Don't make promises you can't keep."

I laughed ruefully. "Fair. I don't know what came over me. When I saw Mason was going to escape…I just couldn't lose him."

"Part of being a soldier is knowing when to retreat. So you can live to fight another day."

I smiled. "Dad said that."

"It was one of his favorite phrases."

"I wish I had been part of this when he was. I wish I could have seen him in action."

"He was a magnificent warrior. And an even better person." Konstantin paused, closing his eyes to bask in the heat. "Like you."

Konstantin's words soaked through me, touching me with a heat even stronger than the waters surrounding me. Could it be so bad, to have one moment with him? To run my fingers down the angles of his cheek—over his strong chest?

I found myself drifting closer—closing the distance between us. Common sense, propriety, rank—it was all echoes and dust. Maybe in this place, we could just be Zariya and Konstantin.

And then I stood before him, my hand reaching out. His eyes were still closed, his head tipped back in sublime relaxation. I just wanted to touch him. To feel his skin—

My fingers connected with his cheekbone and he startled—his eyes flew open and his hand captured my wrist. The glacial blue of his eyes shone in the low light. "What are you doing?" he whispered.

"What do you think?" I replied. I was beyond thinking. Beyond right and wrong. Desire coursed through my blood—a siren song with a melody of only three notes. Konstantin.

I surged forward through the water and captured his mouth with mine. He stiffened beneath me, his mouth firmly closed against my assault. He still held one of my wrists, but I wasted no time with the other. I trailed it over the hard planes of his chest, the ripples of his perfect stomach—yes—to capture the impressive length of him in my hand.

He let out a groan, parting his lips, and I pounced, darting my tongue against his. Fire burned in me, deep in my core. Touching him was even better than I'd imagined.

And then all of a sudden, his resistance melted. With a growl, he wrapped his arms around me, tangling one hand in my hair, the other pulling my chest flush against his. He claimed my mouth, his lips taking mine with bruising expertise.

My heart thundered within me—I could feel that throb deep in my most intimate parts. Gods, it had been so long since I'd been with someone, and I'd never been with someone like Konstantin. I couldn't think because of how badly I wanted him—I wanted every hard inch of him inside me, taking me past the point of oblivion.

I pressed myself tighter against him, wrapping my legs around his waist—

He broke off our kiss, pulling my head back with a gentle tug of my hair. "Zariya—" He panted. "We can't do this."

"I beg to differ." I tried to kiss him again, but he held me firmly, pushing me away by the shoulders. His head dipped down, his chest heaving. "This is the vampire blood talking. You're not yourself. If I allowed this to happen right now, I'd be taking advantage of you."

"I assure you," I said, desperate to close the space between us, "that this is definitely me. The blood might have...lowered my inhibitions a bit, but I'm not doing anything I haven't wanted to do since the first day we met." The confession tumbled out of me. "Signe said I should tell you, but—"

Konstantin looked up sharply. "Signe said what?"

"Just that it was important I was honest with you—that you and I needed each other, or something like that. I don't know, I don't really want to talk about Signe right now."

A strange expression crossed his face, and he surged out of the pool. He stood before me—dripping, steaming—the glorious length of him at full attention. Holy shit, if I didn't fuck him, I thought I might implode. I would literally beg—

That thought slapped away some of the haze. Wait. That wasn't me. I *wasn't* myself. I had just literally thrown myself, butt ass naked, at my boss. Horror filled me. What had I done?

Konstantin had already wrapped a fur around himself like a towel, and he held one out for me. "I think it's time we head back."

I swallowed thickly. "I think you're right."

I stepped out and took the fur from him, wrapping it around my shoulders. Feeling suddenly shy and confused and humiliated beyond belief. Tears stung my eyes. I felt like Dr. Jekyll and Mr. Hyde. Who was that person back there? "Thanks. For...stopping things."

Konstantin reached out and took my chin gently. As if he could read my thoughts. "You have nothing to be ashamed of. Okay? It was the blood. As far as I'm concerned, this never happened."

I nodded. Right. We'd pretend it had never happened. Everything would go back to normal. That was totally possible, right?

7

———

Konstantin slept like shit that night. Between the snores of their host and the fact that he had the worst case of blue balls he'd had in years—not a lot of shut eye.

He should have known better than getting in a pool naked with Zariya less than twenty-four hours after she'd drunk his blood. Of course she'd come on to him. It had been a virtual guarantee. You'd think in his six centuries of life he would have learned some fucking common sense. He should have *insisted* she go alone. Because apparently, he had no fucking self-restraint. And *he* didn't even have the blood to blame it on.

He shifted in the musty furs, letting out a long-suffering sigh. There was a sharp stone poking him between his shoulder blades. When had he grown so soft? He used to sleep on the ground all the time. It should have been no problem. Maybe it was time to stop working in the field. Was he getting too old for this shit?

But when he thought about sitting behind a desk like Broussard, it made him twitchy as hell. He'd been stuck in sedentary jobs a few times in his existence—military service didn't always give you a choice. He'd always hated it. No, best to be where the action was. Uncomfortable, but at least you were living.

And uncomfortable he was. He couldn't stop thinking about Zariya—how damn good that kiss had been. The feel of her mouth on his—her full, slippery breasts pressed against him—it had sent him over the edge. He almost hadn't been able to hold back. As it was, he felt like he deserved a medal for pushing her away when he had.

It had been a long time since he'd been pulled towards a woman like this. And it seemed, if her confession was true, that she felt the pull too. But what did that matter? Did he expect some fucking award for being attracted to someone and having them reciprocate? They were adults. Just because they felt something didn't mean they acted on it. It would be way too complicated with her working on his team. It'd screw up the team dynamics something fierce. And besides, everyone who got too close to him ended up dead. He couldn't add Zariya to that tragic tally. No, it was best to keep her at arm's length.

His thoughts spiraled and chased each other until morning, though there was no real way to mark time in this cave. But Bunko rose and put some wood on the fire, followed by a dented old tea kettle. The cave had stayed fairly warm. Zariya still slept.

"We owe you a lot," Konstantin admitted as Bunko poked the fire with a stick. "We would have been really screwed out there."

"I don't like the supes in the temple," Bunko admitted. "I stay out of their way, but they smell of death. It was my pleasure to help you escape them."

"It's a temple? The place we came from?"

"*Was* a temple. For wind elementals. They were kind and peace-loving. Those supes slaughtered them all and took the temple, about three years back. It's why the elementals ride the storms now, angry and aimless. Taking revenge on any who are near."

Konstantin shivered. "They're bastards. We'll be coming back to take them down. They have one of our teammates."

"The temple is heavily fortified," Bunko said.

"I know. But we have a lot of firepower. We'll come in, guns blazing. They won't know what hit them."

"That does sound impressive. However, there are tunnels that run all beneath these mountains. Carved by my ancestors. If you wanted to take a quieter approach, I could show you."

"There's a back way in?

Bunko's furry muzzle parted in a smile. "There is."

THE STORM HAD BLOWN through in the night and the morning sun shone brilliant on the white of the glacier. Konstantin and Zariya had followed Bunko through a maze of tunnels that appeared to let them out on the other side of the foothills.

Zariya looked well-rested, her coloring good. She had fully recovered from her wound. She made every effort to avoid his gaze, but that would pass as her embarrassment dimmed. He hoped. She spent the time instead chatting with Bunko, asking him increasingly personal questions about yetis and his life. Had he always lived in his cave? No, he'd been born in Nepal. How had he ended up here? A spiritual pilgrimage. What did female yetis look like? About the same, but they smelled better. Did he mind living alone? Not most days, he enjoyed his solitude. To his credit, Bunko answered everything without a frown. It was probably nice to have someone to talk to for a change.

They followed Bunko though icy trails that gave way to sharp stone and scrubby plants as they descended from the mountain. Just before a curve in the path, Bunko stopped, his shaggy form blending in with the snow behind him. "I'll leave you here. The village is just another mile down this path. You can't miss it."

"You're not coming?" Zariya asked.

"There are only a few of the townspeople who know of me. It wouldn't be smart to walk into town in broad daylight. I wouldn't want to instill fear."

Zariya smiled. "You're a good supe, you know that, Bunko? I'm glad we met you." And then she wrapped Bunko in a hug, leaning her head into his snowy chest.

Bunko startled in surprise but then softened, giving her back a gentle pat. When she released him, he pointed back the way they'd come. "When you wish to return to the temple, meet me in my cave. I will lead you through the tunnels."

"Is there anything we can bring you?" Zariya asked. "You're all alone out here. Books? Food?"

He considered. "I am partial to poetry. And Spanish wine."

Zariya barked out a laugh. "You're a girl's dream, Bunko. A book of poems and a bottle of Tempranillo it is."

Konstantin shook Bunko's huge hand, and then they left him, leading down towards the village.

"Maybe I should take the lead when we get to the village," Zariya said. "You can be kind of...*intimidating* when people first meet you."

"I'm perfectly polite," Konstantin countered.

"You smashed me into a tree."

"You were following me."

"You were texting my roommate secret conspiracies about my dad!"

Konstantin pursed his lips. "Fair point."

She fell silent. "Do you think Daevin is all right?"

"I think he will be. He's withstood a lot. He can get through this."

"At least he'll have his shield of snark and bad jokes to get him through it," she mused.

"Always. He'll probably drive the torturer out of the room with the sheer force of his sarcasm."

She stopped short. "You think he'd being tortured?"

Konstantin's heart squeezed. Zariya seemed so competent, it was easy to forget she was new to all this. This world and the ugliness that lived in it. "Look, a building." Konstantin pointed. They'd reached the outskirts of the village.

"Don't think I didn't see what you did there."

"Whatever do you mean?" Konstantin asked innocently.

A tanned villager in thick furs caught sight of them and called out a warning. The village was little more than a few thick stone buildings with tiled roofs, perched right into the hillside.

"Hello," Zariya called, waving a hand. "Does anyone speak English?"

"*Or Mandarin*?" Konstantin called out in Mandarin.

One of the villagers, a younger boy, called out something, and then ran off. Hopefully in search of someone.

Zariya shot him a sidelong glance. "Showoff," she grumbled.

He shrugged. "Living so long, I've had a lot of time on my hands."

"Just how many languages do you speak?"

"Eight," he admitted. He actually loved learning languages and had a bit of a knack for it.

"Just eight? In six hundred years?" Zariya snorted. "Slacker."

He smiled. It seemed the awkwardness of yesterday was already passing. Thank god.

An older couple walked up the path towards them, with the young boy at their side. "Hello," the boy said. He had wide, dark eyes and a friendly face. "Welcome."

The older woman, the tanned skin of her face deeply lined, said something, and the boy rolled his eyes. "My grandmother asks if you would like to have tea."

"Hello. We're looking for a telephone." Zariya held her thumb and pinky up to her ear in the universal signal for phone. "And yes, we'd love some tea."

The woman grinned, revealing a warm but gap-toothed smile. She gestured for them to follow. Zariya shrugged at Konstantin. So they did.

It turned out the old couple was unofficially in charge. That meant they had custody of the village's one satellite phone.

It was all Konstantin could do to restrain himself from yanking it out of the old man's gnarled hands when he saw it. Finally. Contact with base. They could get reinforcements, rescue Daevin, and redeem this clusterfuck of a mission.

They sat down on cushions on the floor, at the old woman's insistence. She put a kettle on and offered them some hard little wafers. Zariya took one.

The old man offered Konstantin the sat phone, and he nodded his thanks, punching in the number for Tartarus Base.

Please connect, please connect…

"Hello?" It was an operator. A supe he didn't know.

"Patch me through to Kimiko. This is Commander Bauer. Command ID Victor Foxtrot 216."

"Hold please."

Konstantin drummed his fingers on his knee.

"Hello? Konstantin?" Galu's voice. The tension running up his spine unraveled slightly. God, it was good to talk to his second-in-command.

"You back at base?"

"Yep. But where the hell are you? Broussard's practically ripping the walls down. He's not pleased you guys went off-grid." Konstantin glanced at Zariya, who was smiling at the old woman around a bite of cookie and pretending not to listen.

"We're in Bhutan."

"The fuck—"

"We need backup here. Daevin's been captured by a demon queen. I have a way back in, but there are a ton of supes in there. We need more firepower than just me and Zariya. Two teams, maybe."

"Zariya's with you? She's safe?"

"She is."

"Okay. Kiki's got your location. We're pulling up satellite now. But Konstantin, the director's ordered you back here. We're already spinning up the plane."

"Negative," Konstantin said. "Daevin has been captured. Rescuing him comes first."

The sound of a brief scuffle crackled over the line. Director Cyriaque Broussard's voice exploded out of the phone, "You get your ass back here now and that's an order, Bauer. I'm not sending more Phantoms off on some half-cocked rescue mission. We do this right. You return to base. We'll prep the target package while you're in the air. But I need you back here."

"Director, we should stay onsite. It'll just take more time—"

"You're not a fucking superhero, Bauer, you're a soldier. Which means you take orders. From me. So if I say you get your ass back here, you get. Your ass. Back. Here."

Konstantin's face heated. In his ten years as director, Vizol had never once spoken to him like that—and his team had done more than a few half-cocked things in their day. Broussard had no right to lecture him. They'd completed their mission in Scotland. They'd seen a chance to terminate Mason—

"Uh, Konstantin?" Galu said. Broussard must have given the phone back. "We have you on satellite. You're in a little village, right?"

"Right." He heard the warning in Galu's voice. "What is it?"

Zariya looked up sharply at his tone.

"You have multiple enemy combatants converging on your position. I think Mason found you."

8

———

I could tell from Konstantin's face that it was bad.

"Can you send Enigma for us?" he asked.

I couldn't make out what was being said on the other end.

"I don't care if it's his fucking day off. We're going to be pinned down soon," Konstantin growled.

Shit. Mason must have found us. I looked at the smiling old woman who was offering me a teacup. "Konstantin, we have to go or we'll bring Mason down on these innocent people."

Konstantin looked around, split between whatever Galu was saying and my comment. "You're right. We need to move. Galu, can you find us a defensive position to the south of here? We don't want to bring a firefight down on these people."

I handed my teacup back with a smile and a small bow and spoke to the boy. "Thank you for your hospitality. We need to leave; there are bad men after us and we don't want them harming your village."

His eyes widened, but he nodded.

Konstantin hung up the phone and handed it to the old man, pulling me out by my elbow without a look back.

"Thank you!" I called back and I narrowed my eyes at Konstantin as I jogged at his side. "That was rude. Not even saying goodbye."

"We don't have time for manners, Chanji. They're less than three minutes out. We need to be gone from here by then."

We broke into a sprint, dashing through the small main street of the village and up into the hills beyond. "Galu found us a good spot to wait and watch. They're trying to find Enigma. It's his day off, so he's not on base. No missions were supposed to go down today." He looked sidelong at me, and I knew it was a not-so-subtle jab at my improvisation in diving through the portal.

We settled into a crevice between some rocks, startling a chubby little rodent who had already claimed the spot. From here, we had a decent vantage point over the village.

"I wish I had a sniper rifle," Konstantin said as the skeletal expanse of Warrick Mason's antlers appeared over the rise.

"You don't think they'll hurt the villagers, do you?" I bit my lip.

"I wouldn't put anything past supes like that."

Mason was clad in black tactical gear, and half a dozen other dangerous-looking supes followed him, all bearing assault rifles.

The sight of Mason, strong and healthy yet again, set my blood boiling.

Konstantin's strong hand gripped my arm and I looked down. Then into his eyes—leveled on me. "I know he's the red waving cape to your bull when he's around, but you do not move until I tell you to. Is that understood, Phantom Chanji?"

"Yes, Commander Bauer," I said softly. Wishing I could kiss him again.

He cleared his throat and turned back. Had he been looking down at my lips? I must have been imagining it.

I turned back and hissed as one of Mason's lackeys pulled the old man out of his house, tossing him to his knees on the dirt. He leveled his weapon at the man, clearly questioning him. Another held the old woman by her throat, keeping her from coming to her husband's rescue.

My jaw clenched and I turned to Konstantin. "We can't let them kill those poor people. They helped us. We can't just watch and do nothing."

Konstantin's words were tight, his mouth a thin line. "We don't have any weapons. There are six of them with automatic rifles."

The supe rammed the butt of his rifle against the man's temple, and he slumped to the ground. They dragged the woman forward next, and the young boy who had found us. "Please, Konstantin. We're MASC's Veil Force. We help supes who can't help themselves."

Konstantin groaned and shook his head. "Damn it, you're right. When I say run, you run."

"Okay—"

Konstantin stood and waved his arms. "Hey, assholes!" he shouted. "Why don't you fight someone who can fight back, you fucking cowards?"

There was a moment of stunned silence and then I knew their guns would be swinging up. Sights trained on Konstantin. "Run!"

We both darted away down the hill, gunfire peppering the rock behind us.

"What's your plan?" I panted, careening over boulders and cracks in the rock.

"This *is* the plan."

Splinters of rock exploded to my right and I shied to the side with a flinch. They were getting closer. This wasn't going to end well. I was going to get shot again—

The sight of Enigma appearing just feet before us in his thick rimmed glasses and a gray hoodie startled a scream out of me. Konstantin and I were moving too fast to stop, and we bowled into him, bearing us all forward—

I hit the ground hard, rolling out of Enigma's wiry arms onto a rough concrete floor.

I coughed, catching my breath. Fluorescent lights buzzed above me. I looked around. We were in a small room with no furniture. Little more than a closet.

"Are we back?" I rubbed my face, pushing onto my knees with a groan.

Enigma *tsked*. "You're back. And you're welcome." And then he disappeared.

"Is it just me or is that guy kinda a dick?" I asked.

Konstantin offered me a hand and I let him pull me to my feet. "Wouldn't you be if people kept bothering you, needing you at a moment's notice?"

I supposed so.

"Don't worry. We pay him a ridiculous salary to be on call." Konstantin opened the door into a familiar Tartarus Base hallway.

"Why'd he transport us into a closet?"

"It's his teleporting room. Always empty. So he doesn't accidentally teleport into someone else who happens to be standing in the wrong place at the wrong time."

I wrinkled my nose. Ew.

"Zariya? Konstantin?" Kiki rounded the hallway and sprinted towards us. The rest of the team followed—a grinning Galu, smirking Luiz, enigmatic Rex.

Kiki threw herself into my arms, and I squeezed my eyes closed, soaking in the presence of my tiny best friend. "Let's never fight again," she said, her words muffled in my curls.

"Deal." I set her down gently.

Galu and Konstantin clapped hands, doing some sort of cute little bro handshake. The sight of Phoenix Team's blue haired, tattooed second-in-command couldn't be more welcome. "Welcome back, boss."

My heart seized as I looked around and realized who was missing. It wasn't right to be here without Daevin. We needed to rescue him ASAP.

"Director's on the warpath—" Galu began, but was cut off by a sharp bark at the end of the hall.

I turned to see Cyriaque, his handsome face like a thundercloud. "Bauer. Chanji. In my office now."

I winced as I extricated myself from Kiki's arms.

"*It'll be okay,*" she whispered softly in my head. "*I'm glad you're safe.*"

Galu and the other guys gave us pats on the back and encouraging grins. "I want you ready to start planning Daevin's extract as soon as we're done," Konstantin murmured to Galu.

Cyriaque paused at the end of the hallway. "Right fucking now, Bauer."

The muscle in Konstantin's jaw ticked, but he replied, "Yes, sir."

Konstantin and I followed after Cyriaque like two busted kids getting called into the principal's office.

"Close the door," Cyriaque said, and Konstantin obliged. He rounded on us, his sizable arms crossed before his chest. Cyriaque's canines had elongated, a sure sign that the wolf shifter was really pissed. I mean, in case I wasn't totally sure by the furious expression on his face. "Do I even want to know what the fuck went wrong in Scotland?"

"The mission was a success." Konstantin kept his eyes straight ahead, his chest puffed out. "We defeated or apprehended the majority of the Collectors. Warrick Mason, the leader, was about to escape through a portal that matches the signature found at the site of Director Chanji's death."

Cyriaque raised a dark eyebrow at that but didn't interrupt as Konstantin continued. "Given his status in the organization and the importance of the intel, I made the call to follow."

I couldn't help but look at him, letting in a sharp inhale. He was lying to Broussard. For me. Taking the blame for me jumping headlong into the portal.

"Do you have some dispute with that version of events, Phantom Chanji?" Cyriaque scrutinized me.

"No, sir." If Konstantin was willing to take the fall for me, he must have a reason. I wouldn't fuck that up, especially since telling the truth would very likely get me kicked off Phoenix Team for insubordination.

"It was the wrong call, Konstantin." Cyriaque sighed and set his hands on the desk. "Daevin Ryan is in enemy hands. Subject to mind control of a powerful demon queen. He could be spilling all our secrets right now. We have to assume Tartarus Base is compromised. Possibly our whole organization. Our secrets are likely being auctioned on the dark web to the highest bidder right now. We have plenty of enemies who are gunning for a little payback."

"Don't count Daevin out yet. He's had experience resisting demon control; it's how he broke free and joined us in the first place."

"That was at a distance, Konstantin. What I've heard of demon hierarchy says that it's impossible for a drone to resist a queen in person."

"We don't know that. Give us a chance to rescue him. He could be resisting."

"He's been in there almost a day."

"Then time is of the essence." Konstantin leaned forward. It was impossible not to feel the pull of his gravitas. He was like a black hole of power and force. "Let us do this. Let me make it right. We can save him. We can save Veil Force."

"You have twenty-four hours," Cyriaque said. "The base will be on red alert, ready to evacuate. Phantom Chanji, you are dismissed."

I looked between Konstantin and Cyriaque. Clearly, there was something they needed to talk about without me there. But I found myself reluctant to leave Konstantin. After everything he'd done for me, he deserved the same kind of backup. Not that there was much I'd done except stand there as moral support.

Konstantin gave me the slightest of nods. *Go.*

I shoved my curiosity down and headed into the hall. If the last few days had shown me anything, it was that Konstantin Bauer could take care of himself.

9

———————

Daevin lay on the bunk in the cell, his stomach growling, his skin crawling. Only the twitch in his pointed tail betrayed his upset.

He'd sworn he'd have nothing to do with his kind ever again. And here he was, drawn back in. A queen's plaything.

At least he wasn't spilling MASC secrets. As long as he was keeping Xarianne busy screaming his name, she wasn't questioning him about Veil Force's capabilities and weaknesses. If he could just hold on a little longer, Konstantin would be back for him.

If he and Zariya had managed to escape. Surely, they had. If not, Mason and Xarianne would have come down here and gloated in his face. His teammates were coming for him. He just had to hold on.

The sound of a tray clattering to the floor roused him.

He turned to find the guard glaring at him. She'd dropped a tray of food on the floor. She toed it through the slot in the cell, sending half of it slopping over the side onto the stones.

"I might want to eat that, lavender." Daevin uncoiled to his feet. He walked over and stood on the other side of the door but made no move to pick up the tray. She was quite beautiful, this guard. Delicate horns and high cheekbones with tilted eyes framed by impossibly long, dark lashes. She wasn't winged; only the queens were. But her lovely face showed nothing but contempt. It roused Daevin's curiosity.

"Did I step on your tail or something, darlin?" Daevin drawled, leaning one forearm against the bars.

"A free demon, and you consort with her? It's pathetic."

Daevin tapped a fingernail on one of the bars of his cell. "Do I look free do you?"

"I heard her talking. You came here with the other supes. Unbound by the compulsion of a queen. And yet you run right back into her arms. It's pathetic. If I had broken free—" She bit her lip, no doubt aware of the dangerous words she spoke.

"Not sure if you can hear this through your cloak of disdain, but sometimes you have to lose the battle in order to live to fight another day." Daevin gave her a cocky-as-fuck grin. "Something I learned out there. Free."

Emotions flashed across her face. Anger. Disgust. But something else. Curiosity. She was desperately curious about him.

"What caste are you? You don't look like a grunt. Scholar?"

"Priestess," she replied.

"Ah, a magician," Daevin said. Priestesses were powerful magic-wielders. It made sense why Xarianne would want this one as her drone, but not why she kept her in a backwards posting on Earth, rather than back in Sheol in a more strategic location. Daevin willed a tendril of fire from his index finger. "I'm a bit of a magician myself." It was rare for guardians to have magic as well. It was part of why he'd been so valuable to his queen. Why he'd been sent to Earth. And why he'd been able to escape.

The guard seemed little impressed by his display. "Child's play," she said. And all at once, dark shadows exploded from her, spinning around them, engulfing the entirety of the cellblock. Shouts of surprise and fear echoed farther down the dungeon. And then in a blink, as quickly as it started, it was gone. As if he'd imagined it. It was all Daevin could do to hold his ground. A shadow weaver. They were rare indeed.

"Well. Aren't you full of surprises," he managed.

She smirked.

"What I don't understand," he said, "is why Xarianne has you hidden away in the corner of bumfuck-nowhere Earth."

The guard's face darkened with anger. "She invaded our land and killed my queen. Then my people rebelled and took our land back. She keeps me here because she worries I would foment rebellion if they knew I was still alive. But I am too valuable to kill."

Interesting. "So I take it you're no fan of our current master."

The guard spit on the ground. Roger that.

"Maybe we can help each other," Daevin suggested.

She laughed, letting out a little snort that was kinda cute. *Easy Daevin*, he cautioned himself. *Do not fall for the alluring guard. Keep your eye on the prize here. You might have to kill her on the way out.*

"You're in a cell. Even more of a prisoner than I."

But I've got friends coming for me, he thought, though he kept that fact to himself. This one could be compelled to tell Xarianne. "Am I?" he said instead. "I know how to resist a queen's compulsion. Even break free of it."

"Bullshit," she responded, but there was a breathiness in her voice. She wanted to believe him. But she didn't dare let herself. Oh yeah, it was on. This demon wanted out. They could help each other.

"I've been free for the last two years. No one in my head. No one compelling me. No more demon queen infighting. No more darkness and rock and sulfur. Just the sweet fresh air of freedom."

"I don't believe you. It's impossible."

"Nothing is impossible. My queen farmed me out for a mission on Earth, and I was captured. I was stuck in a cell, much like this one, granted with nicer accommodations and much better food."

He'd never forget it as long as he lived. The day Vizol Chanji had walked into his cell. Tall and strong, with that air of authority and command. His dark hair had been flecked with gray at the temples, and lines had pinched the corner of his green eyes, but Daevin'd had no doubt that the supe was deadly. Powerful. Vizol had sat down in a metal chair across from Daevin. Calm, almost friendly. Daevin had braced himself for torture—interrogation. He'd been trying to break into one of MASC's magical storage facilities to steal some seriously deadly weapons for his queen's Earthly allies. But Vizol had just asked him—all matter of fact—"Are you here on Earth by choice?"

Daevin had been so taken aback by the question that he'd answered honestly. "Demons don't have the luxury of choice."

And Vizol had responded with four words that had changed his fucking life. "What if you did?"

The guard cleared her throat, bringing Daevin back to the present. Her violet eyes were wide. Waiting.

"I had help, and the distance from my queen helped. Her power over me was weakened. But I was able to break free of her hold completely. You could do it too."

"If you could be free from here, then why are you still here?"

Daevin grinned. "I'm waiting for my ride."

She scoffed, rolling her eyes.

In truth, he didn't think he could break free on his own. His magic had helped back then—giving him a link to something besides his queen. A tether to hold on to. But Kiki had also helped untangle the web of compulsion in his mind, and Signe had cleansed the last of it from his thoughts with a powerful norn spell, designed to free someone from a dark fate. He didn't think his own will was strong enough. Was it? He remembered what Kiki had done, remembered the spell Signe had used.

He looked the guard up and down. Perhaps this priestess could help. If she could perform the spell, maybe, just maybe, he could dismantle the web around his mind. But could he trust her? She was in the queen's thrall, just as he was. If he shared too much, the queen could just order her to spill his secrets. She might be doing reconnaissance on Xarianne's behalf right now.

Could he risk it?

"What would you do if you were free?"

Her eyes flashed. "I would seek vengeance."

That could be helpful. "Against Xarianne?"

"She slaughtered my family. My sisters. My mother. My little brother was just two years old, and she..." Her hand flew to her mouth.

Daevin's stomach dropped in anticipation of whatever horror she would share. The queens were ruthless.

"She forced me to drop him into a chasm," she whispered.

His mouth went dry. Slaughtering children? For what purpose? Though did the queens need any purpose but cruelty? "And after your vengeance?" He cleared his throat. "What then?"

"I suppose I'd want to see the ocean. Have you seen it? Is it as large as they say?"

"Larger," he said, understanding. There was nothing close to an ocean in their realm. Something so vast and unclaimed. Something so free. "And more beautiful."

The wistful expression on her face made up his mind. It resonated with him—sung out in a tone he recognized. He'd felt it before, the longing to be free. If he could, he'd take her with him. She could have a good life, on Earth. A free life.

"What's your name?" he asked. Telling her the secret of how to extricate himself from the queen's compulsion would be a risk. But a calculated and necessary one.

"Yara," she said.

He held out his hand through the bars. "Yara, I'm Daevin Ryan. And we're going to get the fuck out of here."

10

Konstantin knocked on the door frame of Oliver's office.

The dragon shifter swiveled in his chair, raising a golden eyebrow. He wore his white lab coat over jeans, like he did most days. "Bauer, in the flesh. Word of your adventures has been buzzing around base. Or should I say, Zariya's adventures?"

Konstantin dropped onto the faded sofa nestled in the corner. "She is...a handful."

Oliver tapped his dimpled chin with an index finger. "With those curves, I'd estimate two handfuls least—"

Konstantin was across the room in a moment, his hand closing around Oliver's neck. "Don't ever speak of her that way," he snarled.

Oliver *tsked*, though his expression was still friendly. "You are well and truly wrapped in her coils, aren't you, my friend?"

Konstantin released Oliver, shoving down his shock at himself. He'd attacked his friend at the slightest mention of Zariya. He hadn't felt this sort of drive to protect a woman since he'd first been turned. He dropped back onto the sofa, smoothing back his hair. "Sorry."

"It's no shame. She's quite lovely."

"She's on my team."

"She won't be forever. Phantoms move on, switch teams. You two are adults. You can keep things professional until the time is right."

Konstantin shook his head. Was he really admitting to Oliver that he had feelings for Zariya? He'd hardly admitted it to himself. "I gave her my blood. She was dying."

Oliver's eyes widened. "Oh shit. Shit, mate. Well, that complicates things. How's she handling it?"

"Fairly well, all considered. There was an *incident* in Bhutan, but it didn't get too far."

Oliver pressed his lips together, clearly trying not to laugh.

"It's not funny," Konstantin snapped.

Oliver held up his hands. "It's just...you're normally so fucking proper. You have it all figured out. I can't help but enjoy seeing you sweat a little bit. I think it's good for you."

"I don't have the luxury of worrying about my fucking feelings, Oliver, when one of my teammates is probably being tortured right now."

Oliver's face went slack. "Right. You're right. Daevin takes precedence. How can I help?"

"Is there anything you've heard about how to neutralize vampire blood in someone's system? We need Zariya focused. A transfusion? Or an antidote?"

"I haven't heard of anything. The magic from the blood permeates the native tissue, so even a blood transfusion wouldn't eliminate it once the blood has circulated. But maybe there's a magical solution. I know a witch in the Half Moon Coven. I can ask her."

"Please. Anything."

"Are we interrupting?" Signe Dirksen, future-telling norn and magical genius, leaned against the doorframe.

"Never," Oliver said. Even after years of working with the norns, Konstantin thought everyone at base was still in a little bit of awe. It was always wise to be respectful of a being with that much power.

Signe's sister, Verte, followed her into the room. The two leggy blondes looked nearly identical, though if you looked closely, you could see the differences. Verte's face was longer, her cheekbones more angular. Her wit was sharper, too.

Oliver placed a hand to his heart. "Am I to believe we are being graced with the presence of the elusive and mysterious Verte Dirksen?"

"Har har," she said in her lilting tones, mussing up his perfect blond hair. "I'm not elusive."

"Word is she hasn't been spotted outside her lab in, what... months?" Konstantin said, careful to keep his face tilted towards her so she could read his lips. Verte was deaf, through it was easy to forget, with how proficient she was with lip reading.

"Years," Oliver countered.

She crossed her arms over her chest. "Yes, well, I've been perfecting my formula for turning sarcastic Veil Force members into toads. I'm ready for some test subjects."

"Roger that." Oliver rolled back in his chair slightly. "How can we help you fine Demi-goddesses today?"

"It's how *we* can help *you*," Signe said. "Konstantin in particular."

Oliver pouted. "Konstantin has all the fun. He gets to go outside the wire, gets to make all the interesting magical discoveries..."

"Feel free to trade places with me. I'd be happy to let someone else get shot at for a change, while I strut around in my lab coat flirting with the new recruits."

Oliver leaned forward in mock outrage. "I serve as a mentor to those young Phantoms. They need someone to show them the ways of the force."

"Focus, boys." Verte drew them back. "Konstantin, we understand you've come across a most interesting relic of Zoroastrian decent."

"Zariya did," Konstantin admitted. "Mason called it the 'Chinvat Gate.' It's a portal."

"Sure is hard to chase the bad guys when they keep skipping off across the realm," Oliver said.

"I don't think Warrick Mason has ever skipped in his life," Konstantin said. "But yes. I'm afraid if we get close again, he'll escape through the portal and elude us. I don't fancy an epic game of cat and mouse. Can you track the portal?"

Signe and Verte looked at each other. "Track it, no."

Konstantin's shoulders wilted slightly.

"But disable it, maybe."

"Really." He leaned forward.

"If we can isolate the magical properties used by the gate, it's possible we can generate an inhibitor of sorts. Mason will try to open the Gate, but you block the magic."

"That would be fantastic. But how do we identify the specific type of magic it utilizes?"

Verte pulled a vial from her back pocket. "Tada."

Konstantin leaned closer. There was a swab inside.

"You've been through the portal, so some of its magic likely still clings to you."

He eyed the swab warily. "Where do you need to put that...?"

I JUST HAD time to eat, shower, and change into a fresh uniform before our mission briefing. I was in the cage, lacing up my boots, when Kiki and Alviya burst in. Kiki was wearing skinny black pants and an oversized Hawaiian shirt, half-buttoned over an orange cut off top. Alviya sported black camo pants and boots and a gray tank, her white valkyrie's wings a stark contrast to her bright red hair. They rushed across the room and skidded to a stop before the cage.

I stepped out, feeling tongue-tied as emotions warred within me. My friends had lied to me about working at Veil Force for years—keeping Dad's secret life from me and more of their own besides. I *should* never trust them again.

But being here, being a part of Phoenix Team, I thought I was starting to understand. The work we did here was important. And the feeling of being on the inside of something like this was compelling.

"Bas heard from Leilani, who heard from Oliver that you were shot and Konstantin used his blood on you," Alviya blurted out. "Is that true? Are you okay?"

I rolled my eyes. "This place has more gossips than the high school cheerleading squad." But I didn't shield my mind.

Kiki's eyes widened as her mental powers skimmed over my thoughts. I knew it was as natural as breathing for her, given her satori heritage. It had stopped feeling invasive a long time ago. "Ohmygod, Zariya!" Her hand flew to her mouth.

Alviya looked between us. "What?"

My lips were twisting into a smile as I thought about the kiss Konstantin and I had shared. It was a terrible idea—I needed to keep a professional relationship with him...*and* I was still mortified that I'd thrown myself at him like that, but there was no denying that the kiss had been *hot*. Like, the best kiss of my life. Hands down. That kiss was like an Olympic Gold kiss compared to the amateur league kisses I'd had before.

"*What?*" Alviya shrieked.

Kiki shook her head. "She kissed Commander Bauer."

"What?" Alviya's voice reached near sonic decibels.

"In a hot tub," Kiki said. "Naked."

Alviya's wings shot out in surprise as she clapped her hands to her mouth. "How, what? You were on a mission...where'd you find a hot tub? Girl, you've got game."

I couldn't help it. I started to laugh at the shock of her staccato words. "Technically, it was a hot springs, not a hot tub—"

"I want to see," Alviya said. "It's not fair. Kiki got to see."

"Ew, voyeur much?" Kiki said. "Bas not taking care of business?"

"This is not about Bas," Alviya countered. "Bas is a business-*man*, if you know what I mean. But I just think, as one of your best friends, I need the complete intel." She paused then, her face falling. Realizing what she'd said. "I mean...I'd really like to still be your best friend. If you'll have me."

"Me too," Kiki said, her tone growing serious. "Zar, I am so, so sorry. I hated every moment I had to lie to you, and I swear as long as I live, I will never do it again. Please forgive me."

"Same." Alviya's black eyes were wide.

I chewed on my lip. Thinking. They had betrayed my trust. But I already knew that I wanted them in my life. I needed my best friends back. "I forgive you both."

They both screamed and jumped on me, throwing their arms around me. I laughed, even as I was smothered in an effusion of best friend love. "But no more lying."

"Never," Kiki vowed.

"I swear it on Odin's right ball," added Alviya.

"Just the right one?" I raised an eyebrow.

"It's the fertile one," Alviya said. Dead serious. "Now can I please know what happened with you and you-know-who?"

I rolled my eyes. "Fine!" In truth, I wanted their read on the situation. Yes, I'd made the first move, but Konstantin had kissed me back. I hadn't imagined that.

Kiki put a hand on Alviya's temple, transferring the memory to her. Not strictly necessary, but easier for her. Their arms were still around me, Alviya's wings encircling us in another layer.

Alviya's pitch-black eyes widened to saucer size. "Holy shit. Holy shit, holy shit. Zariya..." She fanned herself. "He is into you. It is *so on.*"

"I concur completely," Kiki said.

I pursed my lips, struggling not to grin. Konstantin Bauer was a bad idea. He was my boss. He was ancient, and enigmatic...but damn, if it didn't feel good to hear them say that.

All of a sudden, a new head poked up between my arms and Alviya's, breaking into our circle.

It was Luiz, with a cocky-ass grin on his face. We hadn't even heard him come in. "Girl talk. I want in on this."

We shoved him away with shouts and waves. "Get out of here, you creeper!" I said through my laughter.

He just waggled his eyebrows, walking backwards towards the door. "If you have a sleepover, you know where to find me."

"So creepy." Kiki shook her head. "What are you even doing here?"

"This is my cage," Luiz said with mock hurt. "Also, Z needs to get that fine ass to the briefing room. We're going to go get our boy back."

"I'll be there in a minute," I said. As Luiz left, I turned back and wrapped my arms around Kiki and Alviya once more. I pulled their foreheads against mine, in a tight little triangle. "I really missed you guys," I admitted.

"Same," they said in unison.

And I couldn't help but feel that despite everything going on—Dad gone and Daevin captured and Konstantin's sultry blood singing in my veins—a critical part of my life had just clicked back into place. For the first time in a long time, I felt something new. Optimism.

11

The briefing room was filled with the usual suspects: Chris McMaster, Kiki, Konstantin. The rest of Phoenix Team. With one notable exception. Daevin. It felt wrong without tongues of fire dancing across his red fingers, the gesture nimble as a magician with a gold coin. Without his sarcastic comments making all of us roll our eyes. I shoved down the guilt I felt at the fact that he wasn't here. He'd been following me when he'd gotten captured. It was my fault.

We'd get him back.

They outlined the mission. It had already been planned and mapped out, I assumed with Konstantin's input from the fortress. I struggled to pay attention, my thoughts swirling. But when I heard Konstantin say, "parachuting," I looked up sharply.

"Wait, what? I'm sorry, you said we're parachuting into the fortress?" I raised an eyebrow.

"Yes," Konstantin responded, his blue eyes boring into me. "There's no other way to get in undetected."

I opened my mouth to object. To ask him about the tunnels Bunko had told us about. The yeti had promised to help us. It was a far stealthier way to get inside. But something in the intensity of Konstantin's stare kept me quiet.

"The decision's been made, Six. This is the only way in."

I recoiled slightly. Konstantin was purposefully keeping intel... from who? The rest of the team? Or HQ? Whoever it was—he was imploring me with those glacial blue eyes to keep the secret too.

I crossed my arms over my chest. "Okay. You're the boss."

They quickly outlined the rest of the mission details. Kiki couldn't contact Daevin in the fortress due to wards around the place, so we had no way of knowing what was going on, or if he was all right. We had to assume the worst and move fast.

Before I knew it, I was heading back towards the portal that would take us to the Veil Force airfield.

Konstantin fell into step beside me.

"What about—" I began, but he seized my elbow. I stiffened. "Why all the secrecy?" I hissed.

"Not yet," he murmured.

I narrowed my eyes at him. I didn't like being left out of whatever was going on. But at least it appeared that everyone else was being left out too.

We were bundled into the plane and it wasn't until we were thirty thousand feet over the Atlantic that Konstantin put his hands flat on the table we gathered around.

"The mission has changed."

Luiz arched an eyebrow. "How so?"

"The specs that were laid out in the briefing were for the benefit of MASC HQ. What I'm about to say is for our team only. Because the only people I trust right now are in this plane. In Inverness, Mason bragged to Zariya that someone is feeding intel to the Collectors. We can't risk that there's a mole inside MASC. Especially within Veil Force."

"You think someone's really feeding info to the enemy?" Galu asked.

"They've been two steps ahead of us the whole time. I'm not going to risk it. Not with Daevin's life in the balance."

"If they move Daevin, we might never find him again," Rex pointed out.

I frowned. He was right. "How do we know that they won't just head through the portal when they hear we're coming? Even if they think we're coming by air, we might have just guaranteed Daevin will be gone when we arrive."

Konstantin looked at me. "After the way we fucked up his plans in Scotland, I have a feeling that Mason will be itching for a little payback. Especially against you, Zariya. If there really is a mole, I think it's more likely that they'll be waiting for us with an ambush."

"So if there's a welcoming committee at the back of the fortress, where we were supposed to land, we'll have confirmation of a mole," Luiz said.

"Exactly. But we'll be coming in another way."

"How?" Galu said. "From what you two said, this place is a frozen Fort Knox."

"We have a way in," Konstantin said. "An inside man."

"You'll like him." I grinned. "Very cuddly."

"Cuddly?" Rex mouthed to Galu.

DAEVIN SAT STRAIGHT UP, rocketing out of the shallow sleep he'd fallen into.

Xarianne was there, standing at the door to his cell. A wicked grin on her face. "I would have thought more of you."

"Back for another ride?" Daevin stood, stalking across the cell. He gripped the bars above his cell, displaying his broad chest and a cocky grin.

"I have better things to do than engage in another subpar round with you."

Daevin scoffed. "Subpar? Your screams said otherwise."

"Clearly, I'm not your type."

"What do you mean?" he asked warily. The last thing he wanted was to subject himself to more of the queen's attentions, but he needed to keep her distracted. If she was distracted, she wasn't asking him questions he didn't want to answer.

Two shifters, one weaselly and dark-haired, the other brawny and fair, entered the hallway, dragging a struggling Yara between them. She flailed and thrashed, trying to break free of their grip. "I haven't done anything," she cried. "I've obeyed every command."

"Do you think I don't know when rebellion is brewing in your souls?" Xarianne asked. "Do you think I can't feel it in my bones? It is a poison. A weed I must pull out at the roots."

"I've never been much of a gardener myself," Daevin said.

"I've been far too lenient with you." Xarianne sneered at Daevin. "I planned on returning for more information, but I bet you would try to resist. Try to keep your secrets as long as you can. We don't have time for that. I need confirmation on a few key points of intel. And then we're going to take down your little organization when they least expect it."

"I happen to know they're always expecting it."

She examined her black fingernails. "They won't be expecting the doors to be open wide. Opened from the inside."

He frowned. "You're bluffing. I won't give you anything."

"Are you sure? Your time among the humans has made you soft. Compassionate. Empathetic. I've never understood the way they feel for other beings. It is weakness. There is nothing more than survival."

"That's a very demonic way of looking at the world."

"It is the only way to look at the world," she bit out, her tail thrashing once. She snapped to the guards. "Strap her down."

They dragged Yara down past his cell, towards another room.

"Hey!" Daevin surged against the bars. "What are you doing to her? Take your fucking hands off her!"

Xarianne took a ring of keys off her belt and unlocked his cell door.

Daevin tensed.

"Come with me. Don't make any sudden movements." Her voice was syrupy with compulsion. It was a command that he couldn't disobey.

The door opened and he walked out into blessed freedom, knowing her command held him just as tightly as the cell bars did.

"Follow me."

They walked to a large room at the end of the cell block. There was a metal table in the middle. Daevin's stomach dropped. He didn't need to smell the tang of stale blood and fear to know what this room was used for.

The two shifter guards had already tied Yara on the table with leather straps.

Behind them, a new shadow fell. Tall and thin, antlered and ghostly. Warrick Mason. Come to enjoy the show.

The queen nodded to him, and he nodded back, leaning against the far wall, his bony arms crossed over his chest. His eyes glowed with a hunger for vengeance. They'd made a powerful enemy in Inverness. And now those chickens were coming home to roost.

"I won't let you do this," Daevin growled.

Xarianne laughed a trilling sound that grated against his bones. She walked across the room and picked up a knife stained with hardened blood. She tapped the point of the knife against her fingertip, turning. "Oh, Daevin. It is so delightful to connect with one who has forgotten our ways. I will not be doing anything. *You* will."

She flipped the knife in her palm and held it out to him, handle first.

He took a step back.

"Take it."

His fingers closed around the worn wooden handle before he registered the movement.

Yara thrashed against her bonds. He looked over at her and their eyes met. Her jaw was set. There was resolve in her. She gave him a small nod. She understood. She knew it wasn't him. It was the queen. It was always the queens.

"Now, Daevin, tell me what I want to know, or you will carve up beautiful Yara, piece by piece."

Daevin's teeth ground together as he struggled against the

compulsion that gripped his body. It was drawing him closer. He stood above Yara now. "I won't do this."

"Don't make me make you. Tell me what I want to know, and no one gets hurt." It was a lie. A pretty lie. The demon queens—all they knew was cruelty and violence.

But...could he really keep MASC's secrets, at the cost of Yara's life? Did he even have a choice? The queen's compulsion was too strong. Without Signe's spells, and Kiki's mental help, he would spill it all. If he tried to resist, he would take Yara down with him.

The knife in his hand inched closer to Yara, shaking as he tried to resist. He couldn't. Horror filled him. Where would the blade land? What would she make him do first?

The knife came to a stop on Yara's cheekbone, her soft, violet skin almost yielding beneath the blade.

"She's so pretty, isn't she?" Xarianne cooed. "I can tell you appreciate her. So I think we'll take her face first."

Yara's lips were pressed together, her breath punching in and out of her nostrils in quick bursts. But she didn't scream or beg. She held strong. She was so strong. Stronger than he'd ever been.

Daevin hung his head as his shoulders slumped. "I'll tell you everything you want to know."

12

———

Daevin was wrung dry by the time they shoved him back in his cell. He'd squealed like a pig—told them all of MASC's secrets. Identities of Phantoms and their abilities—government contacts, location of safehouses and weapons caches. If this information got out, he'd singlehandedly set Veil Force's operation back a decade.

But he felt—he knew deep in his bones—that Yara was his key to getting the fuck out of here. And if he'd carved her up, she never would have helped him. Now, he'd proven his loyalty. She wanted free of Xarianne's influence. Together, they could take the queen by surprise.

He lay on the hard stone bench for what felt like an eternity, his eyes closed, his mind searching desperately for a way to control the damage to Veil Force that he'd wrought. When he heard the soft shuffle of a step, he resisted a smile. He'd known she would come.

Because he used to be just like her.

"You gave up everything. Your friends, your secrets. All to protect me? Why?" Yara whispered.

He sat up on the bench and saw her standing, her violet fingers wrapped tightly around the bars. "Because I wasn't going to let her use me to hurt you."

She shook her head. Her stare seemed far away. In the past, most likely. "Demons...we don't sacrifice ourselves to help someone we barely know."

"Why not?" he countered.

"It's just—not done."

"That's what the queens want you to think. That we are savage and selfish and evil. But that's not what we are." He stood and walked to face her so only the bars separated them. "Without their control—we're capable of anything. Kindness. Generosity. Beauty." At that last word, he reached a hand up slowly and ran the back of his fingers across the soft contour of her cheek. Her long eyelashes fluttered closed.

When she opened them again, her dark eyes flashed with resolve. "I can't be a slave anymore. I won't be."

"Then let's kill her and get the hell out of here."

A harsh laugh escaped Yara's lips. "Just like that?"

Daevin grinned. "Well, you brought the key, didn't you?"

"How did you—How did you know?"

"Call it intuition."

She cocked her head. "Are you just using me, Daevin Ryan?"

"Not *just* using you..." His grin widened.

She took a step back.

"Yara." He reached out a hand. "I'm not going to lie; I need your help. But I think you need my help too. We can end this. Together."

She looked from his hand to his face and back again. Then with a sigh, she fished the key out of her pocket and shoved it into his open palm.

Adrenaline surged through him, powered by his need for vengeance. How many people had Xarianne destroyed? Her reign of terror ended today.

"I still don't see how we're going to kill Xarianne when she can sense our rebellious thoughts and stop us where we stand."

"Simple," Daevin said as he unlocked the cell door and stepped out. "We're going to need a lot of C4."

THEY STOOD deep in the shadows of the tunnel, Bunko's huge, furry form blocking most of the light from the glowworms on the ceiling.

For the third time, Konstantin checked his belt, where the device Signe and Verte had given him was securely clipped. They had been able to isolate the magical signature of the Chinvat Gate and were fairly certain that when he pressed the button on this little black box, it would emit a frequency that would neutralize the magic of the Gate. Rendering Warrick Mason's getaway plan inoperable.

God, he hoped so. If not, he'd have to keep a tighter rein on Zariya. He couldn't have her diving unassisted through the portal to an unknown destination again. He didn't think his nerves could take it.

They moved quietly through the tunnel, and he tried to ignore how good her curves looked in that fitted suit Hamish had made her. It was functional—it regulated her body temperature in the field so her cold-blooded nature wouldn't shut down—but did it have to look so damn good on her? Being back in these tunnels didn't help, either —the luminous light of the glowworms only served to remind him of the glisten of her tan skin in the hot springs, the swell of her full breasts in the water. The slick feel of her against him—

A groan escaped him, and Galu looked sideways at him. "All right boss?"

"Fine," he replied. *Pull your head out of your ass, Bauer. This is a mission, not a fucking prom night.* He needed Zariya out of his head. Maybe it had just been too long since he'd enjoyed the company of a woman. His vampire nature was more insistent about all of its primal needs than a human body was. Yes, that must have been it. When this was all over, and he was back in New York, he'd pick up some pretty advertising exec and show her the time of her life. That would get Zariya off his mind.

Bunko stopped and turned. There was a door hewn into the rock before them. "This was a tunnel the monks who built the temple fortress used to get to the sacred hot springs. "

Zariya's eyes flicked to Konstantin, but he kept his gaze straight ahead.

"Do we know where in the fortress it comes out?" Galu asked.

"Not exactly. The lower levels somewhere."

"That could be good. If there's some sort of dungeon in there, it could be where they're keeping Daevin," Zariya suggested.

"Agreed," Konstantin said. "We'll look there first. Zariya, can you see anyone with your glands yet?"

She shook her head. "Not through the rock. Hopefully, when it opens I'll be able to get the lay of the land."

"And we'll be able to see if we have a welcome party waiting for us on the upper levels," Luiz added.

"It would be helpful to have a majority of their fighters converging elsewhere. Perhaps we'll get so lucky," Konstantin mused.

The others exchanged a look.

"Do I have to say it?" Galu said. "Is it considered lucky to be betrayed by a traitor in our midst?"

Zariya sighed. "I miss Daevin. He would have been all over that with some sort of witty quip."

"Don't let him hear you say that or there'll be no living with him," Rex said.

"We'll get him back, Six," Luiz said.

"Not if we keep standing here cackling like a bunch of hens in the chicken coop," Konstantin said. "Rex, can you shrink that rock blocking the tunnel? Then I should be able to push it aside."

Zariya raised an eyebrow to Galu. "Hens in the chicken coop?" she whispered.

"All Konstantin's metaphors are as old as sin. Kinda like he is. Wait until you hear the one about the broken wagon axle."

"You two are welcome to wait here while the rest of us go save Daevin," Konstantin said without looking their way.

"We wouldn't miss it for the world, gramps." Galu clapped Konstantin on the shoulder, stepping up beside him as Rex's golden magic filled the tunnel around them.

Luiz laughed as Konstantin's scowl deepened. "I like this new Galu. I told you all you needed was to get laid, my friend."

"Galu got laid?" Zariya leaned forward, looking between the two supes.

Galu's face turned scarlet. "Sometimes you're so fucking crass, Luiz."

"I'm a sex fae, bro. It's literally what I do," Luiz shot back. "And yes, you didn't see how Melusine and Galu were making googly eyes at each other after they speared that asshole merman working for Mason. The couple that slays together stays together."

"It's not like that." Galu rubbed the back of his neck.

"Good for you, Galu," Zariya said. "I like Melusine. Except tell her she owes me a beer for totally ghosting me in the sub with Mason."

"Yeah, she felt bad about that—"

Konstantin stepped forward beside Rex. "Do they ever stop talking?" he murmured, though in truth, he didn't mind his team's banter. It meant they were in good spirits. And good spirits made for good teamwork in the field.

"I could seal their mouths shut," Rex offered as Konstantin grasped around the side of the boulder and heaved. The huge rock moved, leaving a narrow passageway into the dark beyond.

"You can do that?" Konstantin asked, dusting his hands off.

"I can manipulate all types of matter. Including flesh."

"Let's keep it as a last resort." Konstantin turned. "If you three are done painting each other's toenails, do you think we can go rescue our teammate now?"

"With pleasure." Luiz grinned.

"You are a strange group," Bunko rumbled. "But the good kind of strange, I think."

"Bunko, we are indebted to you for your help," Konstantin offered his hand, and the yeti closed his large paw around it, engulfing it as they shook. "If you ever have need of us, you have friends in Veil Force."

"If you rid my mountains of those monsters above, allowing the ghosts of the wind spirits to return to their ancestral lands, you will more than repay any debt you owe. Good luck, Konstantin Bauer."

13

———

I was ready for the fortress this time. Likely, it was the fact that I was fully clothed, armed to my teeth and surrounded by four of the deadliest supes I'd ever known, but whatever it was, I was feeling optimistic. Ready to kick some wendigo ass.

My anticipation grew as we silently moved up through the tunnel into the bowels of the fortress, our weapons trained ahead of us. Warrick Mason wouldn't escape us this time. Dad would get justice today. And I would get my revenge.

I opened my glands and quested out ahead of me, through the stone hallways and floors above. "I think there's a dungeon up ahead," I whispered.

"There are a few bodies, but I don't think Daevin is in there. No one is hot enough."

Luiz snorted softly. "Totally going to tell him you said that."

I rolled my eyes. "Temperature wise."

"Rex?" Konstantin asked. His pale face was implacable, his jaw set. God, he looked good in his tactical gear, his rifle gripped in his strong hands.

Rex was wearing his intimidating jackal head, and his nostrils flared beside me as he tested the air. "She's right. Unwashed bodies...

blood. Definitely the dungeon. I smell faint traces of him, and another demon." He cocked his head. "Maybe two more? But he's gone."

"Can you track him?"

Rex nodded and pointed straight ahead.

Konstantin fell back until he walked beside me, his eyes straight ahead, peering through the sights of his weapon. "Can you sense all the way to the top courtyard? Where we would have parachuted in?"

"Give me a sec." It was too hard to use my glands to conceptualize that much of the building complex while moving and trying not to get shot.

Konstantin nodded and stopped, acting as lookout for me. "Hold," he whispered, and the other guys stopped before us, falling into defensive positions.

I closed my eyes, questing out with my senses, imagining floors and bodies, the borders and boundaries of walls and windows. I could sense the cold of the upper courtyard, where the fortress was exposed to the bracing wind from the mountains. Positioned in two towers in flanking positions and several on the hillside behind were at least a dozen supes. Waiting exactly where we would have landed. Which meant someone at Veil Force had given our mission plans to the enemy.

I opened my eyes and blew out a slow breath.

Konstantin met my sober gaze. His mouth tightening into a thin line was the only gesture that betrayed his disappointment. "At least now we know."

"We'll catch them," I said.

"Daevin first."

I nodded.

We made our way quickly up a flight of stairs into the main floor of the fortress. My heart galloped in my chest with each room we passed. I tried to keep my infrared senses open, laid over my sense of sight—so I knew when two bodies were approaching around a bend in the hallway. "Two are coming," I hissed.

Konstantin motioned sharply to Galu, and then to himself. Then he put a finger to his lips.

Galu nodded.

Luiz and I pressed ourselves against one side of the hallway, Rex to the other. Luiz placed a hand on my rifle, gently lowering it. No guns. We were trying to stay incognito as long as possible. What were Konstantin and Galu going to do?

The two heat signatures were almost around the bend now and I pulled in an involuntary breath as my hands tightened on my weapon.

Konstantin attacked so fast, I could hardly follow his movement —one moment he was pressed against the stones, then next he was wrenching a man's head to the side, his fangs burying into the soft flesh at the base of the man's neck.

Galu had the other man in a chokehold and had magicked a bubble of water over the man's nose and mouth. The guard tried to shout and struggle, but Galu held him fast. He was drowning in the middle of the corridor.

Bile rose in my throat as I watched these two supes I'd playfully joked with become lethal killing machines. It was so...ruthless. Those guards had never had a chance.

Luiz must have seen the expression on my face. "It's them or us, Six. You'll get used to it."

I swallowed the lump in my throat. Did I *want* to get used to it? But I didn't have time to ruminate on philosophical questions right now. I had a teammate to rescue and a father to avenge and an evil Collector to take down. That was all I could focus on.

Rex's nose led us on. I stepped over the bodies of the two guards, willing my stomach to hold. We found ourselves back before a door that looked familiar. "Isn't this the stock room where we jumped out the window?" I asked.

Rex opened the door and we all slipped inside. They'd put a piece of plywood over the broken window we'd leaped through, but it was still cold as fuck in here. The crates and boxes appeared mostly untouched. Except...

"This is where we were separated from Daevin. Where the queen's power began to influence him," Konstantin said. "Are you sure it's not an old trail?"

I walked over to one particular crate against the wall, kneeling down to open it. I gawked at its contents. Or lack thereof.

"There's a fresh trail overlaid over your old scents. He was here less than thirty minutes ago," Rex said.

"Why would he have come back here?" Konstantin mused.

"Uh, Konstantin?" I said. "Wasn't this crate filled with C4?"

"Yes, why?" Konstantin took a step towards me.

"Because it's all gone."

Konstantin whirled around.

"If Daevin got himself free, he's going to blow this place sky high," Luiz said.

Galu added, "And if he doesn't know we're here, he could blow us to kingdom come with it."

Konstantin motioned for the exit. "We need to get out—"

But it was too late. A concussive force rocked the building and threw us off our feet. The lightbulbs above us shattered in a shatter of glass and sparks, and the world went dark.

"Yeehaw." Daevin coughed, waving in front of his face to clear away the dust.

Yara sat back on her heels next to him, wiping the grit from her features. "What the actual fuck—"

"Honey, bombs are like 80's mullets. The bigger, the better."

"I don't know what an 'eighties' or a 'mullet' are, but you could have killed us."

"I had it all under control." A huge chunk of stone chose that moment to break free from the ceiling above and crash to the ground just feet from them, sending Yara scrambling back, her tail thrashing wildly.

When the shower of dust and stones settled, Yara glared at him.

She looked like a deranged miner, covered in fine dust from head to toe. But still as beautiful as hell. "Remind me never to trust you when you say you have it under control."

"It worked, didn't it?" Daevin grinned. He took a finger and scrubbed at his front teeth. He could feel the dirt and grit between them. "Do you feel her influence anymore?" He and Yara had known they couldn't get close enough to kill the queen by conventional means. So he'd decided blow her to kingdom come. There was a simplicity to it. An elegance. A certain Daevin Ryan signature.

Yara paused, cocking her head. As if feeling for the queen's compulsion—the buzzing within her skin and in her thoughts that would signal a queen was near.

He himself felt nothing. Nothing but blissful, peaceful free will. Daevin let his eyes close, reveling in it. It was only a temporary victory. He still needed to figure out how the hell to get out of here and reach Tartarus Base.

Buzz.

It was just a flicker. A flash of consciousness.

Buzz, buzz.

His eyes flew open.

The horror on Yara's face mirrored his own. "She's still alive," she whispered. Almost a whimper.

Daevin surged to his feet and threw out his hand to help her up. Yara was brave and strong. He wouldn't let Xarianne steal her freedom again. "Not for fucking long."

14

———————

Daevin scrambled over rubble and fallen stone, Yara hot on his heels. His explosion had taken out the western corner of the fortress, where Yara had said that Xarianne's quarters were located.

But somehow, despite a shit ton of C4, the bitch was still alive.

The buzzing in his veins was growing stronger—tendrils of compulsion licking against his mind.

Yara's breath came in panicked bursts behind him. "She's coming to. She'll be strong enough to seize our will and then—"

"That's not going to happen." Daevin leaned forward and heaved a boulder blocking their path. It was too heavy. "Help me with this."

"Daevin!" Yara's eyes were glassy eyed with panic. "We should run."

"So she can keep enslaving our brethren?"

She shook her head wildly. "I'm not brave like you. I can't go back. I'd rather die. I know it's selfish, but—"

Daevin took her face in his hands. "You are and you can. We can do this together." On a whim, he pulled her face to his and kissed her, reveling in her taste of cinnamon and lavender, mingled with dust and mortar.

When he pulled back, her eyes were clearer—fixed upon him. "What was that for?" she whispered.

"I don't want to die with regrets. And I definitely would have regretted not kissing you."

Her lips twisted in a smirk.

"Now help me with this rock."

She crouched down next to him and together, they heaved, sending the boulder off its axis and tumbling down the hallway, where it came a thundering stop.

Buzz, buzz.

Daevin shook his head, wishing he could claw at his brains to rid his mind of the queen's incessant influence.

"I have an idea," Daevin said as they jogged down the ragged remnant of the hallway. "I saved one bomb. A small one. I'm going to set it. If shit goes sideways in there... If she's able to take control of us, she won't know to order me to disarm it. It'll take us all out, but at least we'll die free. If we finish her off, I'll disarm it." He looked at her then—her twisting horns, her smooth, lavender skin. "Are you okay with that?"

Yara nodded. Resolute. "It's perfect. That's her room. At the end of the hallway." The door was barely visible beneath rubble and dust. But he could feel Xarianne just beyond.

Daevin quickly activated the bomb. "We have four minutes." He gingerly tucked the trigger and the brick of C4 into the pocket of his cargo pants.

Yara handed over the rifle they'd taken off the body of a guard felled by the rubble. She held a sidearm. "Let's end this."

They moved into position before the door. He looked at Yara.

She nodded back.

He counted silently.

One...

Two...

Three...

The door exploded inward off its hinges under the force of

Daevin's powerful kick. He and Yara poured into the room, both searching desperately for Xarianne.

There! Xarianne leaned against the windowsill across the room. Black blood coated one side of her face and her normally perfect glossy hair was wild with dust and rubble.

She narrowed her eyes at them and lashed out with a web of compulsion to trap them both. But she was weak, and Daevin was desperate.

He started firing. Semi-automatic rounds flew at her and Xarianne dove behind the bed, moving with remarkable speed. He knew he'd clipped her at least once. He and Yara moved forward, their footsteps in unison, pumping round after round in the demon queen's direction. Shadows exploded out from Yara, searching and seeking for the demon queen.

But when he rounded the bed, Xarianne was nowhere to be found, only a smear of blood leading under the huge, wooden bedframe.

"She's under it!" Daevin cried.

Or so he thought.

Xarianne scrambled out from under the bed and danced across the once-white sheets in breathtaking speed. She dodged the grasping shadows and leapt onto him with a carnal scream, her fingernails digging into his face, her mind into his mind.

A guttural cry burst from him as she enveloped him, as panic seared his vision and his thoughts. He was helpless again—a slave—a pathetic thrall with no will or mind of his own.

With a snarl, Xarianne turned her attention to Yara. The pistol fell from Yara's fingers with a clatter, the throbbing power of Yara's shadow magic dissolving in a puff.

The bitch had Yara too! Daevin surged against the barbs in his mind, thrashing and fighting. He had to get free—

Stars exploded in his vision as Daevin struggled to make sense of what was happening. Xarianne had full on clocked him in the face. Even crushed and riddled with bullets, the demon queen's power was breathtaking. Terrifying.

Daevin stumbled to his knees, the metallic tang of blood in his mouth. The queen's compulsion in his mind was an iron cage fixed tightly around him. She loomed over him like a dark shadow.

Yara stood with her shoulders slumped and her arms hanging slack beside her.

He looked up, blinking away stars, and met her violet eyes. As lovely as the night sky. She gave him a tiny nod, resigned.

He nodded back. How many minutes had passed? Two? Three?

The queen was railing at them both for their audacity and disobedience, promising torture and vengeance. But he barely heard her.

A strange sense of peace had settled over him. They'd done their best and come up short. But at least they'd take this bitch with them when they went.

The sound of gunfire startled him from his strange reverie. He looked down at himself, then at Yara. No, both of them were fine.

Then he looked to Xarianne. She was being annihilated with gunfire, the bullets exploding through her chest. How—who?

Xarianne fell with a crash, her torso a mess of blood and carnage. He felt her grip on his mind loosen, then slip away completely. Until nothing was left but stillness and freedom.

Konstantin stepped through the door first, his rifle still trained on the queen's body. Then Galu, Rex, Zariya, and Luiz. They'd come for him. His team. His family. They'd bloody come for him. Daevin's eyes tightened with the sting of unfamiliar tears.

"Took you long enough," Daevin said through the thick lump in his throat.

"Didn't want to miss your fireworks show." Konstantin offered him a hand.

Daevin clapped it and let his commander pull him to his feet. "God, it's good to see you guys."

"Glad to see captivity and torture didn't rob you of your flair for the dramatic." Galu looked around at the rubble.

"Daevin," Yara said, her voice laced with urgency.

"Right, I'm sorry. Everyone, this is Yara. Yara, this is—"

"Daevin, the bomb!" she cried.

Fuck.

His heart froze in his chest. Had he just killed his entire team? Daevin fished into his cargo pocket and pulled the bomb out. Eight seconds left.

Seven.

"What the fuck is that?" Zariya cried.

"Everybody down!" Konstantin shouted.

Disarm, disarm, disarm... Daevin pressed the buttons to turn the detonator off, his mouth gone bone dry.

Four.

Just four. It stopped.

Daevin blew out a shaky breath.

His teammates looked up from where they'd crouched or dove for some semblance of cover.

"If that's the kind of thanks I get, remind me never to rescue you again," Luiz said as he ran a shaky hand through his black hair.

"Seconded," Rex added.

"Do you want to tell us what the hell that was about?" Konstantin demanded.

Daevin looked at Yara. "Not really."

"As much as I hate to interrupt our reunion, are you guys okay to move? Because we aren't out of bad guys yet," Zariya said.

15

———————

We stalked in unison through the fortress, taking out four more guards in quick succession. My naga heritage hissed within me, my snake ready to strike. Warrick Mason had gotten away before. No way in hell was I going to let that happen again.

We were stopped in the hallway by a pile of rubble and debris that must have been shaken loose by Daevin's explosions.

"Let's clear this quickly," Konstantin said, and everyone moved in to help.

"And you're sure the dampening device Signe and Verte made is working?" I whispered to Konstantin.

He responded, "I said I'm sure it's on. Your guess is as good as mine if it's working. The heat signatures haven't moved?"

"No. They seem to be clustered in a room at the top floor," I said. "I bet it's where the Chinvat Gate is. They're all trying to get the hell out of Dodge and wondering why their getaway car won't start."

Daevin pinched the bridge of his nose. "So many mixed metaphors."

"I've missed you too, Sparky." I ruffled Daevin's hair.

"Sparky?" He quirked an eyebrow.

"Yeah, I've been working on nicknames for all of you." My nerves were jangling at the delay, and I was finding it helped me to talk.

Galu sidled up after dropping a huge rock on the ground behind us. "Do tell."

"Well, he's Sparky, Luiz is Spicy, you're Swimmy, Konstantin is Broody, and Rex is...Rex."

Daevin rolled his eyes. "Great, she has the naming capabilities of a five-year-old."

"Why do we sound like the seven dwarves?" Galu demanded to know.

Luiz flashed a grin from where he was digging. "I don't know, I kind of like mine."

"Of course you do." Daevin scoffed.

"I don't mean to interrupt your little gab-sesh," Konstantin snapped, "but are we going to kill this fucking wendigo or not?"

"Classic Broody," Luiz stage-whispered.

Yara looked to Daevin. "Your friends are strange."

"You have no idea," he muttered back.

"Move. The. Fuck. Out." Konstantin enunciated each word like a gut punch. We'd opened up enough of a path to scramble over the remaining rock.

The lightheartedness drained from me. Konstantin was right. This was my shot to kill Warrick Mason, the supe responsible for Dad's death. I needed to get my head on straight.

I fell in next to Luiz, the cool metal of our rifles pressed to our cheeks.

"What's your nickname?" Luiz whispered.

"Obviously 'Sexy.'"

"Obviously."

My smile fell as we approached a thick closed door. There were at least eight supes inside, presumably sporting some heavy firepower.

"We move fast," Konstantin whispered. "Rex, use your magic to shield us as best you can from any bullets. Yara, you stay here."

"I can fight," she hissed. "I have shadow magic."

"I don't doubt you can, but we have a way of doing things on

Phoenix Team. We can't have any unknown elements when we get in there."

She bared her teeth but nodded.

"I want Mason," I said.

"And I want a fucking pony," Konstantin shot back. "But we don't always get what we want. We shoot to kill everyone in that room. Am I understood?"

Now it was my turn to growl.

Konstantin turned the knob slowly, and we exploded into that room like a fucking tornado of destruction.

It was an operations room of some kind, furnished with two rows of desks. One wall was lined with monitors and TV screens. Had we found the nerve center of their whole operation? The Chinvat Gate lay yawning wide on the ground between them, but it lacked the glowing purple light that must have signified its magic was working.

Warrick Mason was standing beside it with half a dozen other lackeys—it looked like shifters and vampires, mostly. He wasted no time when we burst through the door.

Mason and the other supes scattered, diving behind the desks. Our spray of bullets left trails of destruction through the room as computer screens shattered and sparks flew into the air.

The air charged with magic and one of the wolf shifters bounded towards us in wolf form, leaping into the air with a snarl.

Rex took him down with a burst of gunfire from his rifle.

A compact black object sailed through the air towards us. "Grenade!" Konstantin shouted, and we all dove out of the way.

I hit the ground hard and rolled away, covering my head with my hands.

A whoosh of air swept through the room as the device went off in a strange shock wave that rattled my bones.

I looked up, gingerly raising my hands. It hadn't exploded. What was it?

Another wolf, this one with fur as black as pitch, leaped out from behind a desk, gunning towards Daevin. Daevin got his weapon up and pulled the trigger, but nothing happened.

What the hell?

The wolf barreled into him, its jaws snapping at Daevin's face and neck as he struggled to hold it off.

"Guns are disabled!" Konstantin shouted. "Take them down by hand!"

The grenade must have been a magical device designed to neutralize human weapons. Well, luckily, none of us needed guns.

Daevin's hands flamed to life and the smell of charred fur filled the room as Konstantin and I both went for Warrick Mason.

The wendigo swung to his feet, his dark eyes blazing, his talons bared and ready to rip us limb from limb.

Konstantin reached him first—little more than a snarling blur. But Mason was impossibly fast too. His fist connected with Konstantin's jaw, hard enough that I thought I heard the crack of bone.

My knife was in my hand, though I couldn't remember pulling it from its sheath on my leg. The madness of the room—Galu grappling with a vampire, the golden glow from Rex's vengeful eyes bathing another combatant who lay prone on the floor—it all faded away as Warrick Mason stood before me. This monster who had killed and robbed and taken the freedom and life from so many supes. Including my dad.

I slashed at him twice in quick succession, but he danced back and sliced back at me with his five razor-sharp talons. "We have unfinished business, Mason," I said.

"Happy to take out the entire line of Chanji mongrels," he spat back.

Konstantin had regained his footing and fell into a fighting stance a few feet from me. I knew we were supposed to fight together, but Mason's words filled me with a fiery anger.

With a scream, I whirled in close, slashing him across the torso, the arm, going for his throat. Mason twisted out of the way and surged for me with a roar that bared his sharp teeth and gaping maw, but Konstantin was there, like a fucking bulldozer that bore Mason into the back wall.

Konstantin seized Mason's antlers and smashed his head against the wall. Again and again and again until red slicked the concrete behind him.

Konstantin dragged in a ragged breath and stepped back, letting gravity take Mason's body sliding down the wall. The wendigo slumped onto the ground. He spat blood onto the floor before him and blinked heavily as he looked up at us with pure loathing in his blood-red eyes.

Konstantin looked at me. "He's yours, Zariya."

He was giving me the kill. I still held the knife so tightly in my hand that my knuckles ached. This creature had stolen my father from me. Had kidnapped, beaten, and tried to kill me. Had no doubt done so many other awful things that he himself had lost count.

But when it came time to kill him, I found myself faltering. He was unarmed. Defeated. This wasn't me. Did Mason deserve to be punished? Absolutely. But death was too good for him. Too easy. He deserved to suffer. To rot in a prison somewhere for the rest of his semi-immortal days, hungry and caged like the animal he was.

"Let's take him in," I said.

Konstantin raised an eyebrow. "Are you sure?"

"Do we have enough evidence to put him away for what he's done?"

"Absolutely. Especially with what we'll find on the computers here."

The rest of the team had gathered around in a loose semi-circle. The rest of Mason's guards and henchmen were dead.

"You're going to pay for your crimes for a very long time." My voice sounded cold. Dispassionate.

"Kill me." Mason coughed. Blood dribbled from his mouth. Konstantin has broken off one of his antlers with the force of his blows. "Just fucking kill me. Like I killed your idiot father! He thought he was better than all of us, just because he pretended to play nice with the humans."

"My father *was* better than you," I said, grinding my teeth.

Konstantin laid a steadying hand on my shoulder.

I continued. "We all are. Which is why we're not going to kill you. We aren't monsters."

Mason let out a bubbling laugh. "Yes, you are. To the humans, we're all monsters! All the same. You think you'll find a place among them? Acceptance? Because you do their fucking dirty work? I'm willing to face the hard truth that none of you are willing to. The only place for supes is the one we take for ourselves. Through force." He tightened his claws into a fist.

I looked at Konstantin, at the rest of my team behind me. "You're wrong," I said softly. "I've found my place." I turned away from him, meeting the nods and grim smiles of my teammates.

"Then you're just as naive as your father," Mason snarled. He surged to his feet and leapt at me with talons wide and bloody fangs bared.

I reacted without thinking—Dad's memories and my naga heritage seizing control. I spun, brought my knife up, and buried it in the side of Warrick Mason's neck.

16

Konstantin surveyed the scene, his breath slowly returning to normal.

Mason was dead. Despite a close call at the end, saved only by Zariya's lightning reflexes, they'd done it. Rescued Daevin and taken down the Collector. Without an injury to his team. It was a good day. Tonight, after they returned to base and he completed his mission report, he'd go home and enjoy that bottle of Dalmore Selene scotch he'd been saving and watch the city lights.

Zariya's jubilant laugh from across the room drew his attention, and he felt a pang of *something* as he watched her talking to Luiz. Where a quiet evening sipping scotch had once sounded lovely, now it felt—lonely. A scene in black and white, where he now saw in color. He didn't want to go home and be alone. He wanted her with him.

"I found this, boss." Rex appeared before him and offered him a black laptop case. "Smells like Mason. I think he was taking it with him."

"Good find." Konstantin banished his prior thoughts. "Listen up, everyone," he called. "We're going to do a sweep of this fortress, fast and efficient. We need to find a way to neutralize whatever wards are protecting this place from psychic interference. Or, if we can't find that, at least a radio that'll work. Once we've renewed contact with Tartarus, we can go home. Gather any evidence you find or any magical devices or weapons."

"Evidence of what?" Galu asked. "I thought Mason was our head honcho."

"After seeing this place, I'm not so sure. A fortress like this is expensive to equip. The Chinvat Key, the wards, the demon queen as their ally... This operation must be costing a fortune. Based on what we know of the Collectors, they make good money, but not *this* good. There's a decent possibility that someone else might be bankrolling them." Not to mention buying the loyalty of someone inside Veil Force. Konstantin hoped at least the traitor in their midst had held out for a good paycheck.

"Konstantin's right. The queen mentioned someone called 'the Authority,'" Daevin said. "I don't think we can put a bow on this one yet."

"Meet back here in twenty. And don't let your guard down. We're still in enemy territory."

THEIR SWEEP of the fortress uncovered an interesting trove of magical and human weaponry. Galu had found the communications center and called Tartarus Base. They'd been picked up, and now they were on the plane on the way home.

Konstantin sat against the hard inner wall of the cargo plane, Mason's laptop on his knees. He peered through his reading glasses, scanning the emails he'd found in Mason's file.

Rex, Luiz, and Galu all slept in swinging hammocks, while Daevin and Yara talked softly, their heads bowed together. Konstantin examined her thoughtfully. She'd handled herself well under pressure, and Daevin clearly trusted her. Maybe she could be recruited.

Zariya plunked herself down next to him and offered him a beer. He examined it. Bud Light.

"I saw that," she said.

"What?"

"That grimace. Sorry the beer wasn't like, craft brewed by thirteenth-century monks in an ancient Belgian abbey and sprinkled with angel dust."

"I've never understood that expression, 'angel dust.' The angels I've met aren't particularly dusty."

Zariya leaned forward, bracing her forearms on her knees and turning her head to goggle at him. "Wait—I'm sorry. Are angels real? Have you actually met one? I thought they were just a myth?"

Konstantin quirked an eyebrow and grinned.

Zariya recoiled, one hand to her chest. "I'm sorry, was that—a joke? Did Konstantin Bauer make a funny?"

"You should have seen your face. You'd believe anything, wouldn't you?"

She pursed her plush lips crossly at him. God, he wanted to kiss those lips again. "It just happens to be more plausible that angels are real than Konstantin Bauer is messing with me."

"I'm actually very funny," Konstantin said lightly. "Daevin takes all the punchlines, though. I thought it better that I settled into my role as brooding commander."

Zariya cocked her head. "Was that...another joke?" She shoved his shoulder and hollered, "Get this guy a microphone! The Konstantin Bauer show, one night only!"

Daevin and Yara looked over, and Rex cracked an eye open but quickly closed it again.

"Are you done?" he asked.

"Yep." She settled back against the seat, her shoulder brushing his. As if she were as comfortable with him as anyone in the world. "But I'm going to take your beer since it's beneath your noble tastes."

Zariya reached for it and he pulled it away from her. "I make exceptions for victory beers," he said. "They taste good no matter what."

She took a swig of her own, settling back. "They do, don't they?"

Zariya was silent for a moment. "Find anything on that?" She pointed her bottle at the laptop.

"Unfortunately, yes."

Her green eyes popped open. So mesmerizing. Slitted and vibrant. She was unlike anyone he'd ever met. "Tell me."

"I couldn't go full Kiki on it, so I'm sure there's more information to gain. But I've been reviewing his emails, and there are months of conversations with someone who just goes by the title 'the Authority.'"

"Like Daevin said. The Authority, the Collector, these guys really love their generically threatening nicknames, don't they?"

"From the emails I've skimmed, the Authority was giving Mason his marching orders. He worked for this supe. Or person."

Zariya tilted her head closer so she could look at the screen. Her scent of cardamom and jasmine wafted over him. "Does that include the order about killing Dad?"

Konstantin clicked into an email from just before Vizol's death. Laying out the plan. Ordering it done.

Zariya skimmed it. Her throat bobbed. "So this isn't over," she whispered.

"No, it's not." Konstantin took off his glasses and tucked them into his pocket and closed the laptop. "We'll find this person, Zariya. We'll avenge your dad."

She met his gaze with a promise of her own. "I know."

"I still can't believe I'm free," Yara said with a shake of her head. "How long did it take you to get used to it?"

"A year, maybe?" Daevin thought about it. "Before I really relaxed. Before I stopped expecting a queen to show up and take it all away."

"Xarianne tried to," she said softly. "It must have been terrifying, when you realized a queen had found you again."

"I was not pleased, no." Daevin gave a husky laugh. The terror he'd felt at that buzzing in his bones…he shivered. "I hope I never feel it again."

"With a team like this, you won't. You protect each other. Freely. It's kind of extraordinary."

"You'll find lots of extraordinary things in this realm. Earth isn't a perfect place, but it's home."

"I'm excited. And nervous. Nervous-excited."

"Is there any other kind?" Daevin paused, examining his finger-nails. Speaking of nervous-excited… He wasn't good at this part. Kissing the girl before it all went to hell, yes. Having a sane, adult conversation about feelings and the future? Hell no. "Where will you go?"

"So eager to get rid of me?" She arched a brow. God, she was beautiful. The sorceress caste demons always were—as lovely and finely-wrought as statutes. But even among her caste, Yara was special. Her delicate features belied a strength that took his breath away.

"Not at all. I bet I could find a spot for you in Veil Force, if you're interested. Konstantin mentioned it to me."

She bobbed her head as if considering. "Maybe. But there's some-thing I have to do first. Do you think you could help me find someone?"

Please don't be a man, please don't be a man… "Of course. Who?"

"There was this girl—"

Yes! Daevin wanted to pump his fist. Unless Yara was into girls… but no, she'd kissed him back. Unless she was into guys and girls… that could be hot. Wait. Better listen.

Yara continued. "She was at the fortress for at least two months before they took her away. We had gotten to know each other. I considered us friends. I'd like to help her, if I can. She was so kind to me, even though she was treated horribly."

"She was one of Mason's prisoners?"

Yara nodded.

"Human or supe?"

"Fae. Her name's Rheanan."

"Any enemy of Mason is a friend of ours. I'll help you find her. On one condition," Daevin said.

"And what's that?" Yara cocked her head.

"You let me help you get settled in the human world. And when you are, you let me take you out."

"Are you bargaining for a date?"

Daevin rubbed the back of his neck. "When you put it like that, it sounds pretty tacky, but yes, I suppose I am."

"That's a bad bargain, Daevin."

His heart sank. "Why?"

She leaned forward, capturing him with those stunning violet eyes. "Because I would have gone out with you for free." Her lips met his, and he drank her in—all Yara—beautiful and powerful and free. He didn't think it was a bad bargain at all.

17

———————

I stood on the sidewalk in front of Konstantin's building, a cup of fancy finely-brewed coffee in each hand. My heart in my throat.

I looked up. This place was swanky as all get out. What was I doing here? I muttered to myself, "It's fine. You're just stopping by, checking to see if he found anything else on the laptop. Casual. Breezy."

"Ma'am, are you all right?"

I looked up to find the uniformed doorman holding the glass door open, his wrinkled brow scrunched.

"Yes," I said with forced cheer. "Absolutely. I'm here to see Konstantin Bauer."

"Ah." He nodded, gray hair sticking out from beneath his cap. As if that said it all. As if now he knew why I was pacing the sideway like a rabid raccoon. A scary, ancient, hot-as-hell vampire could make anyone a little jumpy. The doorman gestured inside with a sweep of his hand.

There was another uniformed older man inside at a gilded desk. I repeated my request and gave him my name. I tapped my toe as he gave me a snooty once-over before calling up to Konstantin. Security in this place was as fierce as Tartarus Base.

"Yes sir." He hung up the phone and regarded me with what I thought I recognized as regret that he wouldn't get to throw me out on my ear. "You can go up. Top floor."

I paused halfway through the door. "Top—top *floor*?"

"Yes, ma'am." Barely restrained eyeroll. "The penthouse. I've buzzed you in."

Of course. It fucking figured. Like Konstantin Bauer wasn't already out of my league enough, he had to be a bazillionaire too? Meanwhile, I was still letting Auntie pay my cell phone bill. A harsh laugh escaped me. "Of course."

I jabbed the button to the fortieth floor with my knuckle and let the sleek, silver doors glide shut. I sucked in a huge breath. I needed to get my shit under control before those doors opened or Konstantin would be able to smell my human desire like I'd just doused myself with a can of Axe body spray.

I took deep, calming breaths and did a little cross over myself with one of the coffee cups, hoping the aroma would stick. Non-sexy things. Think of non-sexy things. Melting ice caps. Images of those sad, skinny polar bears. Picking up a dog's poo with one of those little plastic bags, but you can feel it's kinda warm and you know that there's only a thin sheet of plastic between you and poo that literally *just* came out of that dog—

The doors slid open. I was calm. Cool. Collected.

Until I saw Konstantin's place. My jaw dropped. Damn it, this place was *nice*. Floor-to-ceiling windows displayed a spectacular view of the city. Stylish leather furniture that likely cost more than my entire med school tuition yet somehow managed to look cozy filled out the space.

Even the art on the wall was classy. I turned to examine a stunning abstract piece by the elevator, the huge frame filled with swooping lines in ombre shadows of cerulean and ochre.

"Zariya?"

I whirled around to face Konstantin. "Hi!" I said brightly. Damn it, he looked hot. He was wearing dark wash jeans, a soft flannel of gray buffalo check with the sleeves rolled up, and leather moccasin slippers. "I brought coffee!" I hoisted the cups up, desperately thinking about bagging warm dog poo.

"Thanks?" he said. "I'm just surprised to see you."

"I know, I'm sorry, I didn't mean to intrude. I was just nearby"—*lie, big fat lie*—"and thought I'd see if you found anything else on Mason's computer? Since you can't take it to base, because of the mole—"

"Got it. Sure, come on in."

I smiled in relief and hurried forward. "Coffee?"

"Why not?" He grabbed one of the cups and took a sip. "This is good."

Yes! European coffee snob approval. Check. "Your place is, like... really nice. I love the decor," I said. Did my voice sound high? Was I squealing these words out? I cleared my throat. "Did you have help?"

"Furnishing it?" He looked at me with amusement. "No, actually, I did it myself."

"Wow."

"Surprised that I have good taste?"

"You're European." I waved a hand. "It's, like, impossible for you not to, right?"

He chuckled. "I suppose. Come with me. I did find something else."

I followed him through his impossibly huge loft into what must have been his bedroom. A sprawling bed with gray impossibly-soft-looking sheets dominated one wall. And dominated my mind. This was where Konstantin Bauer slept. All the thoughts of warm dog poo couldn't keep my body from revving into high gear.

We were alone. How easy would it be to push him onto that bed, to rip off that flannel shirt and push his jeans down over his hips? I desperately wanted to see his body again—he was achingly beautiful. I wanted the freedom to run my hands over his skin—to savor him like a fine wine—drinking in every luscious inch of him until I was dizzy with need.

A sharp clap broke my reverie. I jumped, looking over to the corner of the room, where Konstantin stood next to a desk with an amused expression on his face. "Earth to Zariya." He clapped again.

My face went scarlet. Ohmygod, I'd just been staring at his bed. It was so obvious what I'd been thinking—

"Oliver said he's got a lead on a cure for my vampire blood. We'll get you over this, I promise," he said gently.

"Right," I said, a bit too brightly. "The blood. It sure has a mind of its own." I let out a shaky laugh.

"You want to come over here? Are you safe?" He was fighting a smile.

"Har har. Yes. I can resist my baser urges." Barely. I walked over to the desk. He pulled out the chair and I sat down in it, taking a gulp of my coffee.

He leaned over my shoulder to navigate with the little track pad on Mason's laptop. I let my eyes flutter closed for just a moment, breathing in Konstantin's crisp, clean scent of starlight and fresh fallen snow.

"So I found this email from a few months back. It looks like the Chinvat Gate is in fact owned by this Authority person. It's quite an important relic. They'll want it back."

I scanned the email. The Authority was loaning the artifact to Mason for his use but stressed how important it was.

I risked a glance sideways at Konstantin. He'd put his reading glasses on. I didn't know why that made my heart melt a little more. He'd explained before that being turned into a vampire didn't fix bad eyesight. "We have the Gate now. So you're thinking we use it to bait this Authority?"

"I think we use it as bait for our mole." Konstantin leaned against the desk and faced me. "If the Authority has a contact in Veil Force, they would be the logical person to use to get the Gate back. We find whoever tries to steal the Chinvat Gate, and we find our mole."

"Where is the Gate now?"

"I locked it into our evidence locker on the fourth floor."

"There are cameras on all the floors. But whoever is within the organization will know that. They'll likely also know how to disable the cameras to get in and out undetected."

Konstantin closed Mason's laptop and slid a sleek MacBook forward, opening it. It revealed a black-and-white image of a quiet room. I recognized it. The evidence locker. "That's why I set up my own camera. One undetectable and hidden. This camera is going to catch us our mole."

Cyriaque stared at the phone, willing it to stop ringing. It didn't. It just kept ringing, and ringing.

With a hiss, he snatched the receiver off the table. "Broussard."

"We have a serious problem, director."

Cyriaque leaned forward and massaged the bridge of his nose. "I'm handling it."

The voice on the other end was scathing. "My entire Collector operation has been dismantled. One of our best facilities has been blown to hell. Warrick Mason is dead. I've lost countless artifacts. Do you know how much fucking money you *handling* it is going to cost me?"

More money than he was worth, that was for damn sure. "I'm not sure what happened. We had everything under control. We were going to neutralize the team before they entered the fortress, but they changed their infiltration plan without telling base."

"Maybe because you're so incompetent that it took your loyal little soldiers less than two months to make you."

Cyriaque froze. No, that wasn't possible. If Bauer suspected anything, Cyriaque would know it. The vampire was a lot of things, but he wasn't subtle. He would march right into Cyriaque's office and start pontificating about duty and honor. "Our relationship hasn't been compromised. I would know."

"Would you?" The voice hissed. "Because I'm beginning to think you don't know a damn thing that goes on under your fucking nose.

First that Chanji girl waltzed into your base and onto one of your teams, now this—"

Cyriaque held the phone away from his ear as the caller lectured on.

He ran a hand through his hair. Fuck him. When had everything had gotten so out of hand? Well, he knew the answer to that question. When Vizol had died. He'd never deserved a friend like Vizol Chanji.

"Broussard!" the voice barked.

He cleared his throat. "Yes. I'm listening."

"I want my fucking Chinvat Gate back, do you hear me? It's one of a kind. Deliver it to me in the next forty-eight hours and I will look past your recent streak of disastrous incompetence."

"It's in the evidence locker. There are cameras and surveillance—"

"ARE YOU THE DIRECTOR OR ARE YOU THE FUCKING—"

He held the phone away from his ear again as the screaming continued.

When the other line went quiet, he put the phone back to his ear. "I'll figure it out. Consider it done."

"Good," the voice purred. "You have forty-eight hours."

CLAIRE LUANA

MYTHICAL ALLIANCE

PHOENIX TRAFFICKED

1

____

I snuggled deeper under the covers, trying to muffle the incessant knocking at the door.

My roommate Kiki's mental voice resounded through my head. *"Zar, get the door."*

"It's so early," I moaned back, sending her a mental message. *"Make Alviya get it."*

"Traitor," came Alviya's sleepy mental reply. Kiki, through her supernatural satori powers, had connected our minds.

"If we ignore it, they'll just go away." I pulled my pillow over my head, which was pounding like a mofo. Kiki, Alviya, and I had hit the town a little hard last night in honor of our renewed friendship, now that I'd forgiven them for lying to me for years. I sure as hell wasn't going to get out of bed for someone collecting signatures or raising money.

"It's your auntie. She's not going anywhere."

I sat straight up and then groaned, regretting the sudden movement. "Auntie Temsula?"

"Do you have another one?"

Kiki was right. Auntie was as determined as a honey badger. Getting up was now inevitable. I swung out of bed with a sigh of regret and stepped into my fluffy slippers. A shiver wracked me and I grabbed a gray hoodie, threading my arms through it as I walked. It was chilly this morning and my cold-blooded naga side needed to warm up.

I pulled the door open and stepped aside in one quick motion, letting Auntie explode inside. "I've been out there knocking for hours! The least you could do when I came all this way was let me in!"

I swallowed my retort that I had, in fact, let her in, and she had not, in fact, been knocking for hours. "Good morning, Auntie." I leaned in and gave her a kiss on the cheek. "I was still sleeping, I'm sorry."

Auntie's thick, black curls were tied back with a colorful scarf, and she wore a cute denim dress cinched at the waist with a braided leather belt. But that wasn't what I zeroed in on. It was the fact that she carried food.

My nostrils flared. "What'd you bring me?"

"I made Aloo Paratha. They're probably cold by now, as I had to wait—"

I pulled her into my arms and spun her around, planting a kiss on her cheek. My mouth was already watering. The dish of pancakes stuffed with spicy mashed potatoes was one of my absolute favorites. "Did you bring pickles?"

"Of course. And mangos to make lassis. You're too skinny."

Kiki poked her head out her room, her dark hair mussed and wild, sticking out above her sleek side shave. "Do I smell Indian food?"

"Auntie brought us breakfast," I sang.

Alviya appeared from the third bedroom, her red hair in wild curls and her white wings wrapped around her like a fluffy hotel towel. "Auntie, if I'd known, I would have rolled out the red carpet."

Auntie beamed with pride. Sometimes I thought the only thing she liked more than bossing me around was cooking for grateful people.

"Well, everyone get dressed and make yourselves presentable. I'll get the food ready," she said.

"Yes, Auntie," Kiki and Alviya said in chorus, disappearing back in their rooms.

I rolled my eyes as I slid into one of the chairs at the little kitchen table.

Auntie shooed me with a dish towel that she had purloined from our kitchen. "That means you too."

I crossed my arms. Sometimes I liked to engage in petty insurrection against her Auntie-style tyranny. It was good for her. "I'm fine."

She rolled her eyes. "You smell like that vampire your father used to know. What was his name—"

"Konstantin?" I sat up. She could smell him? On me? I resisted a shiver of delight at the thought. If only his smell of starlight and open skies came from what I really wanted to be doing, not just me visiting his apartment on business.

"Yes, that's the one. Very handsome. Very dangerous." She waggled one of our wooden spoons.

"He's my commander. I have to spend time with him. Besides, he's only dangerous to the bad guys." I struggled to keep my tone light. Never mind that he was very dangerous to my resolve not to jump his bones.

"Mm-hmm." She sounded unconvinced. "I know that you have your father's memories, but you are still new—"

I hissed, looking at Kiki's and Alviya's rooms. They hadn't returned yet.

Auntie looked up. "What?"

"Keep it down," I murmured. "About the talwar. Dad's memory palace. They don't know. No one does."

"You haven't told anyone?" She cocked her head in puzzlement. "Why?"

I shrugged. How to explain that I wanted them to think I, Zariya, was worthy of being on Phoenix Team, not just the part of me that acted as a storage device for my dad's memories?

Auntie clucked her tongue. "Secrets cause trouble, curlicue. Be careful."

"Really? *You* are going to lecture *me* about secrets? You, who kept from me that Dad was the head of a secret supernatural special forces operation for decades?"

"And see? Look at all the trouble it caused." She leaned down to look in a cabinet. "Now where is your blender?"

My phone rang down the hall in my bedroom, and I bolted upright. "Blender's to the left of the oven." I jogged and grabbed my phone. My heart backflipped. Konstantin. It was probably work. It was definitely work. "Hello?" I tried to sound nonchalant. Wasn't sure I quite pulled it off.

Konstantin's light Austrian accent caressed my ear through the phone. "I know I promised the team two days off, but I think we have something."

"On the Chinvat Gate?" I whispered. Konstantin had planted a trap for the mole we suspected was lurking inside Veil Force. We knew the ancient portal artifact we had confiscated was important to the Authority, the shadowy figure who controlled the Collectors and its head, Warrick Mason. We hoped the Authority's inside man would try to grab the Gate and reveal themselves.

"Nothing on that yet," Konstantin said. "But we've found another operation connected to the Collectors. And, we think, the Authority."

"Do I have time to eat breakfast? I have company."

"Company?" Konstantin's tone was strangled.

Then I realized how that sounded and I hurried to explain. "No, no, my auntie is over. She brought food."

"Ah." Was that a sigh of relief? Surely, I was imagining it. Konstantin went on. "I still remember those spicy potato pancake things she makes. Heaven."

"You've had Auntie's paratha?" It was still so weird to think that Dad and Konstantin had interacted before I'd even known he existed. I'd have to spend some time going through Dad's memories of Konstantin. Not in a creepy way. Just, you know, to have all the info.

"Just once. But once is enough to ruin you for all other pancakes."

I laughed. "I'll bring you one."

"Really?"

"It's the least I can do."

"See you in two hours?" Konstantin asked.

"See you then."

I walked back into the kitchen with a whistle on my lips and froze when I saw Auntie, Kiki, and Alviya all looking at me, my two room-mates with Cheshire Cat grins on their faces.

"Who was that?" Auntie asked. "You sounded familiar with them."

"Just a work thing." I shrugged and set my phone down on the table.

Auntie'd never had trouble reading through the lines. "That vampire is dangerous, Zariya. Be cautious."

Alviya, sitting in one of the chairs at the table, rested her chin on her hand and batted her long eyelashes at me. "Oh, Auntie Temsula, you have *no idea* how dangerous."

I pointed at her with wide eyes. *I'm going to kill you*, I mouthed as Auntie whirled around. "What does she mean, curlicue?"

"She's just being an overly-dramatic valkyrie, *aren't you*?" I said pointedly.

"Of course. We're just teasing Zariya. She's way too smart to get involved with her boss." Her black eyes glittered with amusement.

"He really liked your cooking," I said, desperate to distract Auntie from further questioning. "He asked me to bring him some."

Auntie perked up. "Well, good to know the vampire has some sense."

Kiki's lips were pressed together to hold back her laughter. I tapped my temple and Kiki opened up a mental link between herself, Alviya, and me. *"You both better shut it about Konstantin Bauer or I'm revoking your breakfast privileges."*

Alviya just grinned and started chanting in a singsong voice in her mind. *"Zariya and Konstantin, sitting in a tree. K-I-S-S-I—"*

I picked up my phone and pretended to start searching. *"Siri, how do I send a pain-in-my-ass valkyrie back to Valhalla for good?"*

Kiki and Alviya both started laughing out loud, and Auntie turned back to us, amazement on her face. "What are you three giggling about?"

"Nothing, Auntie," Kiki said. "That smells amazing. How do you get the layers so flat?" Kiki moved into the kitchen, and I sank into a chair across from Alviya, sticking my tongue out at her.

Kiki was right. We were laughing about nothing, but somehow, to me, it was everything.

2

———

Konstantin stared at the lush tropical island on the screen, trying to run through its strategic and defensive features. But all he could think of was Zariya in his apartment yesterday. How good it had felt to have her there. How well she'd fit.

It had been so long since he'd imagined a woman in his life on more than a superficial level. For decades—centuries—he'd been pushing potential partners away, certain that they would get hurt if they got close to him. Better to focus on the mission. His life was helping people now. That was enough.

But Zariya—she ran into the fire. If anything, warning her would only make her want it more. Want *him* more.

He gave himself a little shake. But she didn't want him. That kiss —that fucking amazing kiss—it hadn't been real. It had been the vampire blood in her system taking control. A reflection of his own desire for her.

"Bauer." A pair of fingers snapped in front of his face and Konstantin snarled.

Chris McMaster took a big step back, his hands up. "You back with us?"

Konstantin gave himself a little shake. "Sorry. Deep in thought. What do you have?"

McMaster, a trim middle-aged military man, was their human liaison to the Mythical Alliance of Supernatural Creatures, or MASC, and worked with most of the human governments to gain approvals for their operations. "I've got the green light from Costa Rica. They've been aware of suspicious activity on the island but haven't had the resources to check it out. The president is running for re-election on some anti-corruption campaign, so he's eager for us to take out some bad guys."

"And hand him a nice PR moment." Daevin snorted. The horned, red-skinned caco-demon lounged against the table in the briefing room. It was good to have him back. Konstantin hadn't been able to focus with one of his team captured in the field.

The door opened and the rest of the team filed in, all clad in black camouflage pants and gray T-shirts. Standard Veil Force fare. Galu, Rex, Luiz, and Zariya all settled into the chairs around the table. Konstantin couldn't help the flash of pride. Phoenix Team was his, and setting aside Zariya's occasional rebellions (which she promised wouldn't happen anymore), they were running like a well-oiled machine.

"Are we waiting for Kiki?" Galu asked.

"Giving her the day off," Konstantin said. "We've been working her too hard."

"So does this mean you fleshed out this target package all by yourself?" Luiz asked.

"Daevin and I did," Konstantin said. "With McMaster's help."

Luiz exchanged a look with Rex. "And...we're all going to die," the ebony-haired incubus said.

"I don't know." Rex pointed at Daevin. Rex, the Egyptian demi-god, wore his human face today, olive-skinned and handsome. "Look at him. He's like a proud papa home from the hospital. He'll make sure his *t*s are crossed and his *i*s are dotted."

"If you fuckheads would shut the hell up," Daevin said, scowling, "we can get on with the briefing."

Konstantin swallowed a smile, looking sideways at Daevin with an arched eyebrow.

"What?" Daevin replied. "They were pissing me off."

"Welcome to my life every time I'm up here and you're sitting there," Konstantin pointed out.

Daevin winced. "Ah. Yeah. Perhaps it's time to reconsider my role as captain of the peanut gallery."

"Am I the only one who actually wants to know what the mission is?" Zariya asked. "Because I have a pancake in my pocket with Konstantin's name on it, and it's getting colder by the minute."

Everyone froze for a moment, looking at each other. And then they burst out laughing. Konstantin couldn't help but join as Luiz howled with laughter, his head teetering onto Zariya's shoulder.

"What?" Zariya cried over the laughter. She shoved Luiz's head away. "It's not—you guys are fucking gross. Grow up. It's an actual pancake." She fished a Ziploc bag out of one of her cargo pockets with an Indian pancake inside. She threw it on the table towards Konstantin. "See, actual pancake."

It just made everyone laugh harder.

Finally, when the howls died down, Konstantin gave himself a little shake and wiped a stray tear from his eye. God, he hadn't laughed like that in—centuries.

Zariya had long since given up trying to keep a straight face and was hiding her features in her hands, shaking her head.

"All right, Phantoms," Konstantin said. "Play time's over." He reached forward and took the pancake. "Thank you, Zariya."

"Remind me never to do you any more favors," she grumbled, crossing her arms over her chest.

Konstantin cleared his throat and pointed to the screen. "This is a remote island off the Caribbean coast of Costa Rica. The locals call it 'Quiribri Island.' Based on the intel on Warrick Mason's laptop, this is where they sent Yara's fae friend."

They all straightened at that. Zariya leaned forward and squinted at the pixelated image on the screen. "It looks like some sort of resort."

"Actually, supposedly, it is. Some very high-end resort for the rich and powerful called Siren's Quay. Invitation only."

"That sounds exactly like the sort of place we'd find the Collectors," Galu said.

"From what we know, by taking down Mason and the fortress in Bhutan, we've crippled the Collectors network. They're effectively done. But we know they were bankrolled by another individual, known to us as 'the Authority.' It's possible, likely even, they were part of a larger criminal organization."

Zariya frowned. "Someone who calls the shots. Like putting out the hit on my dad."

Konstantin nodded. "Unfortunately, yes. Mason was a big fish, but not the biggest. Right now, this island is our best clue about this larger organization."

"But we don't know what they do in there?" Galu asked. "I'm guessing not just massages and scuba diving lessons."

"That's what we need to find out. To start, our mission is intel only. Depending on what we find, we may be able to engage."

"And we're also looking for Yara's friend, right? The other prisoner from the fortress?"

"She's a fae female named Rheanan. If we can find her, it'll be a bonus," Daevin said.

"I'm surprised Yara doesn't want to come," Zariya said.

"Oh, she does." Daevin grimaced. "But she's not a Phantom yet. It'd be too dangerous. I convinced her to let us go and look around."

"Whoever these guys are, we have to assume they are at least as dangerous as the Collectors, likely more. This one won't be a tropical holiday, team," Konstantin cautioned.

"And I'd already packed my Speedo." Luiz pouted.

I STOOD up from the briefing room, trying to ignore that damn pancake that had just disappeared inside Konstantin's pocket. In that moment, I had wanted the pit of Naraka to open up and swallow me whole.

"Zariya," Konstantin called out, following me into the hallway. "Would you mind coming with me?"

"Sure." I shoved my hands in my pockets and fell into step with him. I couldn't focus when I was this close to him. My mind kept flitting from little detail to little detail. The way his shirt stretched over the hard planes of his muscles, the little scar he had just underneath his jaw. The casual predatory nature of his walk. Even the man's walk was sexy. "Where are we going?"

"Thank you for the pancake." He shot me a sideways look. "I do appreciate it."

"Let's just forget about the fucking pancake," I managed.

"I thought we could see Oliver before we go so he can take a blood sample from you. He's going to work on finding something to neutralize the vampire blood in your system. Verte is going to help. If anyone can figure it out, those two can."

Great. The super-hot dragon shifter doctor was going to work on finding a solution to my very embarrassing, very public crush on my commanding officer. My cheeks flamed. "Sure. Sounds good."

Suddenly, I felt like an idiot for gushing to Kiki and Alviya about the kiss Konstantin and I had shared. Konstantin was as proper as the Queen of fucking England. He would never indulge in a relationship with a subordinate Phantom. It violated protocol. *Of course* Konstantin wanted his blood out of my system; it was probably inconvenient to no end that the blood he'd used to save me now filled me with desire for him. Had I *really* thought there could be something between us? He was a billionaire gorgeous centuries-old vampire commander. Some days I forgot to brush my teeth.

We walked into the clean, white-washed space that was Oliver's lab. A pang of regret stabbed me, hitting me out of nowhere. I'd been planning to be a doctor, once upon a time. I was going to help people —work in a space like this—rather than running around getting shot and stabbing evil supes in the neck.

But a lot of things were supposed to be different. Dad was

supposed to be here, for one. What was that cheesy saying? Life's what happens when you're making other plans? Too fucking right, Hallmark.

Oliver pointed to a leather examination table. "You mind having a seat?" He looked devastating in his white lab coat over jeans and a blue button-up today. But honestly, the golden-haired shifter could wear a burlap sack and make a woman's knees weak.

I obliged and Konstantin leaned against the doorjamb, crossing his sizable arms. Sometimes when he stopped moving, he looked like a statue—a beautiful, breathtaking piece of art. I looked away, hating how my eyes were drawn to him. He wasn't for me. I'd always been more of a modern art girl, anyway.

Oliver efficiently took my blood, making soothing noises as I looked away from where the needle went in. But before I knew it, he was pressing a cotton ball to my elbow and putting a Band-Aid on it. I looked down at the Band-Aid, then at Oliver.

"Teenage Mutant Ninja Turtles?"

He grinned his thousand-watt smile, rolling his chair across the room to his microscope. "I didn't have any snake ones. Thought the reptile connection would have to be enough."

I shook my head with a little laugh. Oliver was all right, I supposed. We'd gotten off on the wrong foot, what with him trying to eat me and all after I'd broken into the Tartarus Base, but he seemed like a decent guy.

He put a drop of my blood onto a slide and inserted it under the microscope.

I leaned forward. What was he looking for?

"Hmm. Extremely curious," Oliver mused. He rolled back. "Konstantin, come take a look at this."

I hopped off the table and came to the other side of Oliver as Konstantin leaned in and peered through the microscope. "This can't be right."

"What? What is it? Am I dying?"

Konstantin looked up in amazement. "Am I interpreting this right, Oliver? There's no sign of vampire blood cells at all. They're gone."

"That's right. Zariya's blood somehow completely neutralized the vampire blood. I'm assuming it's thanks to her naga heritage." Oliver turned to me. "Zariya, you're completely cured."

Konstantin and Oliver started talking excitedly about the possibilities this presented for a cure to the compulsive effects of consuming vampire blood.

But all I could think about was the fact that if Konstantin's blood was gone, I had zero excuse for my huge, fat crush on him. I was totally and completely exposed.

Luiz loved flying. It was said that centuries ago, incubi had had wings and would flit from town to town, seducing the most beautiful maidens and darting off into the night before their fat fathers had been any the wiser.

Likely, that was an overly optimistic version of the truth. Whatever the incubi had done to lose their wings, they'd probably deserved it. Most of his brethren were real dicks.

But man, wings *would* be nice.

He surveyed his teammates in the plane around him. Rex and Konstantin were both reading, Rex with his long jackal nose in some leather-bound tome, Konstantin swiping on his iPad, likely going over the mission details a third time.

Daevin was napping and Galu had his earbuds in.

Only Zariya, their sixth, was unencumbered. She sat across the plane, staring glumly at her fingernails.

Luiz cocked his head. That was weird. He hadn't known her long, but other than her dark silence when someone mentioned her father, she was actually quite upbeat. Before he knew it, he found himself striding across the plane to plop into the seat next to her. He felt Konstantin's eyes watching his movement, but he ignored him. None of his boss's damn business if he wanted to get to know their pretty new teammate. It'd be good for Konstantin to sweat a little.

"Hey." He nudged her shoulder with his own.

"Hey," Zariya replied.

"Why the long face?"

She looked up at the ceiling. "Am I that transparent?"

"If you were in a movie, the scene would be in black and white, with tragic background music playing."

Zariya snorted.

"Want to talk about it?"

She shot him a sidelong glance. "No offense, but I'm not sure I want to spill my guts to you."

Luiz pursed his lips. He was used to it. Everyone expected him to be the brash playboy incubus who didn't give a shit about anything, and most days, it was just easier to slip into that role. But that wasn't the whole of who he was. He actually cared about his teammates. This job. What they did was important. Helping people was important. "I'm a surprisingly good listener."

"I'm sure you tell all the ladies that." Zariya rolled her eyes.

Luiz ignored the stab of pain her comment brought on. It wasn't like he wanted to be an incubus, like he would have chosen it. People glamorized his fae heritage, and he admitted he played into the stereotype, but in reality, there were some seriously shitty parts. He was reliant on human sexual partners for his energy, but being with him drained their life forces. He always made up for the exchange with multiple, mind-bending orgasms, but it wasn't a formula for monogamy. If he ever let himself love someone, he wouldn't be able to stomach slowly draining their vitality, day in, day out. It was a Catch-22. But...no need to burden anyone else with that. "You're not *all the ladies*, you're Phoenix Six, and if you've got a problem, we've all got a problem."

Zariya looked back down at her fingernails. "It's my problem. It's...It's stupid." Her slitted eyes flicked across the plane to where Konstantin sat. Luiz didn't have to be a master in the art of love to see the longing in that glance.

"Ah," he said.

"I just..." She sighed and leaned in slightly. "I can't really talk about it here."

Right. The noise from the plane was loud, but vampires had freakishly good hearing. Luiz tapped his comm and opened a direct link to Zariya. *"We can talk freely here."*

She perked up. *"How did you do that? They can't hear us?"*

"No. You just tap your comm and imagine clearly which teammate you want to speak to, and that you want the link to be private."

"They seriously can't hear us?"

Luiz shook his head. *"No. Look. Konstantin's accent is fake,"* he shouted through the mental link. *"He's really a redneck from the Deep South. He thinks salad is made of Jell-O with marshmallows in it."*

Konstantin didn't look up.

Zariya's lips curved up in a smile. *"That was...weirdly specific."*

"I have a cookbook on the cuisines of America. Some are quite disturbing."

"You can cook?"

"Food is like, a quarter of the art of seduction. What kind of master of romance would I be if I couldn't whip up a delicious meal?"

"I didn't mean to question your seduction skills," Zariya said drolly.

"It's fine. We're getting off track here. The recipe swap can wait. We're talking about the undeniable chemistry between you and Konstantin and what you're going to do about it."

Zariya turned scarlet, from her neck all the way up to her temples, setting off the glittering gold of her scales. She truly was beautiful. And undeniably unique. She dropped her head into her hands. *"I feel like such an idiot."*

"Why?"

"He gave me his blood in Bhutan, and I was kind of blaming that for how I was feeling, and then right before we left, Oliver told us that my naga system had neutralized the blood somehow. It's gone. So now he knows..." She shook her head. *"I shouldn't be telling you any of this."*

So, she was feeling embarrassed because Konstantin could tell she was attracted to him? Couldn't she tell he reciprocated? *"There's really only one obvious solution here."*

"Fake my death, change my identity, and open a food truck selling delicious baked goods?" Zariya suggested.

Luiz snorted. *"You guys have to bone."*

"Luiz!" Zariya shrieked out loud, smacking him on the shoulder.

Konstantin looked over with a frown.

Zariya crossed her arms and settled back into the seat. *"Why did I think I could get a straight answer from an incubus? Of course that's your solution for everything."*

"It's definitely my solution when the problem is rampant sexual tension!"

"It's not rampant."

"Yes, it is. It's so thick around here, you could cut it with a knife."

"I'll try to do better," she mumbled.

"I'm not just talking about you, Zariya. Konstantin's practically tripping over his dick for you."

"That's...graphic." But she was fighting a smile.

"I'm serious. I haven't seen him flustered, like ever. Until you. This thing could be good for you both."

"What, just, to hit it and quit it?"

"If that's what you both wanted. But honestly, I don't think that's Konstantin's style. Think of how long he's been around, how much he's seen. It must be...kind of lonely." Luiz knew for damned sure that was how *he* felt, anyway. Not that he'd ever admit it.

"Right. It must be so hard to be ancient, rich, handsome, and powerful. Poor guy."

"What good is an immortal life if you don't have someone to share it with?" Luiz struggled to keep his mental voice even. It would be good, if he could play matchmaker. Help Konstantin and Zariya find love. Galu had reunited with Melusine, and Daevin seemed really chummy with the guard from the Collector fortress, Yara. At least he could help his friends find happiness. That would have to be enough. He'd just have to find Rex some pretty little...huh. He had no idea what Rex's type would be. The demi-god was enigmatic as fuck.

Zariya was scrutinizing him in a way that felt far too exposing. *"Luiz Archileta, I think you just might be a good guy."*

He forced a bold grin. *"Don't tell anyone."*

Zariya looped her arm through his and leaned into him, settling her head on his shoulder. *"Your secret's safe with me."*

4

———————

Despite having a globetrotting father, I'd never traveled much. Dad had always been working, and Auntie was more of a homebody than she cared to admit. A trip to Cancun for my sixteenth birthday was as far afield as I'd gotten before Phoenix Team. One day Dad and I had taken a tour to see the great Mayan pyramid at Chichen Itza, then gone swimming in the sparkling waters of a cave-like cenote.

As I stood on the beach waiting for the guys to secure our rubber boat, that day came to mind. The wall of dense jungle before me, the symphony of the insects chirping and buzzing, the thickness of the humid air, heavy as a cloak about my shoulders. I unzipped the high neck of my black suit to let in some air. But Hamish seemed to have thought of everything—the suit was already starting to cool, its advanced fabric wrapping like an icy embrace around my body. I couldn't help but groan in relief.

Daevin came up beside me, quirking his head in my direction.

"My suit has AC," I explained. "Remind me to buy Hamish a bottle of scotch. Or...maple syrup? Whatever trees drink."

"Whatever you say, Six."

He started forward and I grabbed his wrist. "Daevin—"

He turned back.

I bit my lip. "I'm sorry that I got you caught. It was reckless of me to jump through that portal and—"

"It's part of the job." Daevin's jaw worked. "Everything turned out for the best. We got Mason and the Collectors."

"But—"

"None of us is perfect. You came for me. That's all that matters."

I released his arm. "So we're good?"

"We're good."

Daevin continued ahead and I stood for a moment as a huge weight lifted from my shoulders. One I hadn't even realized had been there.

WE HIKED into the interior of the island, heading for Siren's Quay, the opulent resort cradled on the island's southern side.

The jungle was thick with vegetation, seeming to grab and snarl at our path. At one point, I opened my glands to quest out about me, but it only made me stumble to a stop. The forest was teeming with life around us—birds, insects, scurrying rodents, and something bigger far off that I couldn't quite make out. I hastily closed my glands.

Dad had plenty of memories of places like this, but somehow, being here in person was more disconcerting than I cared to admit. Shouldn't I feel at home amongst all these wild creatures? Or perhaps I'd become too domesticated. Too human.

I felt a soft hand on my shoulder and turned to see Rex's golden eyes glowing in the recesses of his furred jackal head. "You should keep moving," he said softly. "Don't want to get separated."

"Do you smell it all? There's so much out there."

He nodded. "There are plenty of wild places left in the world."

A surprised shout sounded ahead and we dashed forward, our rifles in our hands. We found the guys arrayed in a semi-circle, Galu dancing from foot to foot, like he'd just walked through the biggest, creepiest spiderweb.

"What is it?"

"Ugh!" Galu pointed, and I saw, camouflaged on the dark ground, a huge, thick snake slithering away.

Luiz had his gun up, trained on the snake.

"Hey!" I surged forward and laid my hand heavily on the barrel of his rifle, pulling it down. "It's just a boa constrictor. They're not aggressive."

"Tell that to Galu," Luiz said.

"It fell on me." He shuddered.

I took a few steps and crouched down. The snake stopped and turned, curling around to regard me.

"Is she going to speak Parseltongue or some fucking thing now?" Daevin half-whispered.

I looked back at him crossly. "That's not a real thing."

I couldn't talk with snakes, not in so many words. But I could impress emotions upon them in an intuitive, primal form of communication. I did so now, questing my emotions out, conveying apology for startling it, that we were friendly, and not a danger. But also not food.

The snake seemed to nod at me before turning and slithering away.

I stood and turned back to the guys, and they were all looking at me.

"What?"

"You are full of surprises," Konstantin murmured. "Let's move out."

We resumed hiking. "I'm impressed you know what Parseltongue is," I called out to Daevin.

He looked back with a grin. "I *can* read, you know."

"He listened to the audiobooks," Luiz whispered.

I WAS SWEATY, tired, and hungry by the time the jungle started to thin as we approached the compound of resort buildings.

"Traipsing through the jungle is so much more glamorous in the movies," I grumbled. Freezing my ass off in Bhutan was no fun, but this hothouse of hell was not endearing itself to me, either.

"I really could go for a caipirinha right now," Luiz agreed.

"It's ten in the morning," Rex pointed out.

"I stand by what I said."

"There's a ridgeline over there," Konstantin pointed out. "We should be able to get a good look at everything that's going on in there."

I held back my whine. Now we had to hike up a hill? Stupid Konstantin and his stupid vampire endurance.

By the time we reached the top, I sank to the ground, pulling my binoculars and a protein bar out of my pack with a groan of relief.

"I think we tuckered out our human." Daevin leaned down and patted my head.

I swatted at his hand. "Don't make me sic a boa constrictor on you in your sleep."

He just smirked at me. Oh, yeah. Back to our normal banter. Ignoring Daevin, I took a ferocious bite of protein bar and peered through my binoculars.

There wasn't much to see from the back of the resort. It was designed in a semi-circle, with courtyard, pools and the balconies facing the ocean. We could make out the docks, though, and the helicopter pad was on this side, with a sleek black helicopter parked to the side. It had a logo on the side that looked familiar. "What's that logo on the helicopter?" I asked.

"PharMagus." Konstantin's voice was low.

"That's right. They make pharmaceuticals using supe stem cells, right? Cutting edge research and such?"

"The owner, Parker Kensington, is progressive in incorporating magic and supernatural compounds into his products. That company is worth billions," Konstantin said.

"So what's he doing here?" Luiz mused.

"It looks like there's a vessel coming in." I pointed.

A boat was cutting through the aquamarine waters, approaching the dock. It was a large yacht, the type of pleasure cruiser I imagined dotted the aquamarine waters around Cannes or Saint Tropez.

I munched the rest of my protein bar as we watched it dock.

My binoculars went up as the first person emerged from below deck. It was a slender woman in a short magenta dress. Her hands were tied behind her back, and her feet were bare. A man shoved her forward, and she stumbled, shying away from him. "Whoa. What the hell is this?" I asked.

Another woman came into view, a brunette in jean shorts and a tank top. Also bound. Her slender legs tapered to delicate hooves. She was herded off the boat after the other, onto the dock. Marched up towards the main resort. "She's a supe," I observed.

"I have a bad feeling about this." Luiz's voice was low.

A tall man came up from below deck, with a woman thrown over his shoulder. She appeared unconscious, her blue-tinged limbs dangling loosely. They were offloading women. Supe women.

I let my binoculars fall. "What the fuck is going on here?"

"Yara said the prisoner she knew, the fae woman, had been taken from the cells in Bhutan. Maybe she was brought here. Maybe this is another of the Collectors' prisons?"

"Nice fucking prison," Konstantin remarked. "Why would they keep them somewhere this fancy?"

"And why only women?" Galu asked.

Luiz surged to his feet, spinning in a circle. "I know what this place is." He paced away for a moment and then back. He leaned over, suddenly putting his hands on his knees.

"Hey." I stood and laid my hand on his back. "Are you okay?"

"No." When he straightened, his normally caramel skin was ashen. "I know what this place is."

"What?" Konstantin asked.

"This is a trafficking operation."

5

────────

Low-boiling fury thrummed in Konstantin's veins. He was pissed at the situation, at the Collectors, at whatever fucking monsters were running this trafficking operation. Slavery was inexcusable. It was reprehensible. It was—

"Are you okay, boss?" Galu asked.

Konstantin's head snapped up. "Of course. Why?"

"You looked like you just swallowed a whole tuna and it's not going down well."

Konstantin shook his head. Sometimes Galu's marine metaphors were just...nonsensical. "I just want to get these bastards. It feels like whack-a-mole. We hit one, and an even worse villain pops up somewhere else."

"We'll get 'em."

"All right, everyone," Konstantin called. "Circle up. We need a plan."

The team drew into a circle around him. Konstantin did his best to not look at Zariya in that tight black suit, her thick curls braided over one shoulder. She'd unzipped the neck of her suit to let the air in, but now it displayed her stunning cleavage. He needed to focus. Not think about how badly he wanted to get her naked in his bed.

"Boss?" Galu raised an eyebrow.

"Ideas. Give me your ideas," Konstantin barked.

"We need to get inside," Zariya said.

"Thank you for that stunning assessment, Six," he replied.

She frowned and crossed her arms before her.

All these unknowns were making him crazy. Normally, he knew exactly where he stood, had everything under control. His team, his life—it all felt like it was spiraling out of control. He needed to get his shit together. "Ideas for *how* to get inside?"

"We could disguise ourselves as rich assholes and walk in the front door," Daevin suggested.

"The back looks poorly guarded. I believe we could get into the lower levels undetected," Rex proposed.

"We could go in as some sort of maintenance staff? Security guards? Waiters? They have to have servants," Galu suggested.

"There have to be cameras inside," Zariya said. "If we can tap into their feed, we can have eyes in the place. You know, like you and Dad did in Vienna."

"That's...a good idea," Konstantin admitted. "Wait, how'd you know about Vienna?"

Zariya froze. "He must have mentioned it to me."

"But—he didn't tell you about Veil Force," Konstantin pointed out.

"He told me plenty of half-truths and war stories. I must have heard it sometime."

Konstantin's brow furrowed. There was no way Vizol would have told her about a Veil Force operation. So how did she know?

"It's not important. What *is* important is that my idea rocks," Zariya said.

"What do you think, Luiz?" Konstantin asked. The incubus had been strangely quiet, a distant expression on his face.

Luiz looked up sharply. "I think we go in guns blazing, take the girls, and burn the fucking place to the ground."

"Easy there, cowboy." Daevin held up his hands. "You sound like...me. Wait, is that what I sound like?"

"Usually," Zariya said, as Galu nodded and Rex added, "To a T."

But Luiz wasn't laughing. Such aggression was unlike Luiz, as was the smell of fury that radiated off him in waves. Something about this place must have struck a nerve.

"It may come to that," Konstantin said. "But we need intel on the resort before we can mount an assault, let alone a rescue mission. So we follow Zariya's suggestion first."

"Fuck yeah, we do!" Zariya gave a victorious smile, along with a little fist pump.

Konstantin shot her an exasperated look.

She winced. "I mean, right, boss."

LUIZ GLARED at the palatial building below them. Konstantin was talking with Kiki over comms, strategizing about the probable location of the resort's AV wires.

But he couldn't focus on that. His memories pulled him back, back, back, crashing over him like tumbling waves on the shore.

Zariya crouched down next to him. "Are you all right? You look like you've seen a ghost."

"Places like this...they're a true evil."

"You have experience?"

Luiz didn't respond.

Zariya looked at him sideways. Not asking, just...available. If he needed to talk. He was beginning to appreciate that about her.

He sucked in a breath and blew it out slowly. "I grew up in a place like this."

Her face paled. "I can't imagine. Were you...a prisoner?"

"Not in shackles and chains, but they owned me just the same. Incubi and succubi are highly prized in those circles...for our skills."

"How did you escape?"

"The Federal Police approached me, wanting me to spy on the cartel that controlled everything. I had a lot of access, as many people came through the brothel. I agreed, if they promised to get me out. Three years I did that, thinking that every day I'd be caught and tortured to death. I was eighteen when Veil Force finally arrived to help run the final takedown operation. The head of the cartel was a panther shifter, and his whole pack was deep in the organization. But Veil Force kicked ass. Arrested most of them, killed the rest. Your dad…" He swallowed thickly. "Your dad saved me."

"That's what he did best." A wistful smile drifted across her face.

"We flew back to the United States and he got me set up with an apartment in Miami, with work for a security company. A few years later, he approached me to see if I wanted to join Veil Force. I never looked back."

"I'm so sorry, Luiz." She laid a gentle hand on his shoulder.

"It's in the past." Though right now, as it all came rushing back, it felt like just yesterday. When he'd left that place behind he'd sworn to himself that he'd never, *ever* be with a partner who wasn't his choice. That he'd never connect with anyone in that intimate way without making damn sure that there was one hundred percent enthusiastic consent from both parties.

"That doesn't make it all right."

"No, it doesn't. But I've helped a lot of people since, and I never would have gotten the chance if not for what I went through. So I can't regret it all."

"All right. I think we have a location where we can tap into the resort video feed," Konstantin said.

Zariya gave Luiz's shoulder a squeeze.

Luiz sucked in a breath and stood. He could do this. He was no longer the timid young man who had cowered from cartel bullies and allowed others to dictate what happened with his own body. He was strong and powerful and confident and ready for some fucking payback. He controlled his own life now.

They moved down through the dense jungle off the ridge they had summited. The afternoon heat was relentless, even through the shade of the thick foliage. The heat and humidity of this place reminded him of home.

But he forced himself to stay in the present, forced his mind to stay focused, rather than flitting back.

As they neared the resort, they slowed. A wide stretch of grass separated the building from the encroaching forest, but there didn't appear to be any guards. They must have been counting on the remote nature of the island to keep enemies at bay.

A gray electrical box was nestled in the shadow of the building's stucco wall. "Zariya, with me," Konstantin said. "Everyone else, stay here and keep a defensive position."

Luiz held back a snort. Of course Konstantin wanted Zariya with him. It was so obvious their fearless leader was head over heels. How long had it been since he'd felt like that? Like he needed someone by his side every moment? Maybe not ever. Not for real.

Luiz settled himself against a tree, scanning the open stretch of grass and the jungle around. It was quiet. Clearly, all the action was happening on the sea-side of Siren's Quay.

A shimmer caught his eye at the far corner of the building.

Konstantin and Zariya were heading out of the underbrush, about to make their dart across the open lawn.

Luiz hit his comm. *"Anyone see a shimmer over there by that corner?"*

"What do you think it was?" Konstantin asked.

"I don't know. Not a reflection. More like...magic."

But as much as he searched for it, it was gone.

"I don't see anything on infrared," Zariya said through comms.

"I don't smell anything, either," Rex added.

"I must have imagined it." Luiz shook his head. *Head in the game, man.*

Konstantin motioned Zariya forward and they went for it.

The wind swirled, shifting the dry leaves about their feet.

Rex's black nostrils flared. *"Wait—I do smell something. Konstantin, Zariya! There's a dark magic around the—"*

But a shimmer rippled in the air as Zariya crossed over the spell. It was too late.

6

———

The magic wrapped itself around me with a vise grip, settling through my skin and into my bones like a deep, cold chill.

I fell to my knees and gasped for air.

Konstantin stayed back, hovering just past the line where the perimeter spell stretched.

Idiot! I thought. Rex had called out, and I should have waited. I should have known to look for it. Of course a place like this had wards.

"Zariya," Konstantin urged. "Come back here. I can't cross."

With a cough, I staggered to my feet. I shook my head, trying to clear it from the fog of the spell. I stumbled forward, into his open arms.

His hands flitted up my arms, my shoulders, my neck and face, examining me with desperate fervor. "Are you all right? How do you feel?"

"I—I don't know," I admitted. "I feel all right, but there was definitely a protective perimeter around this place. I tripped it. I don't know what it did." I was sublimely aware that Konstantin's hands had settled on either side of my neck—his blue eyes still searching me for some flaw, some consequence of the magic I'd crossed.

He let out a groan and let his hands fall. "I haven't been doing my job as your commander. This can't keep happening. You've gotten into trouble or injured on every mission. You're still new to this."

"It's not your fault, Konstantin. We all should have thought to look for magical booby traps. We didn't."

"I should have known. I'm getting sloppy—"

"We should get out of the open." I grabbed his arm and towed him back towards the others. At this rate, his self-flagellation could take all morning.

We jogged into the shadows of the palm fronds, where the rest of the team waited. "I probably should have just stayed inside the perimeter. We didn't even get eyes inside."

"We need to focus on evaluating that spell," Konstantin said.

Luiz was looking at me with a strange look in his eye, but I ignored him.

"Rex, can you smell it?" Konstantin was asking. "Can you tell what it is?"

Rex's black nose whuffed over me with gentle breaths as he tried to smell the magic on me. "Dark...like molasses and charcoal and ink. I think it's Black Moon Coven work."

My heart sank. The Black Moon Coven was comprised of the worst of the witches. They supplied spells for unspeakable things. MASC had officially declared them a terrorist organization. "That's bad."

Luiz still hadn't stopped staring at me.

"Take a picture, lover boy. It'll last longer," I snapped at him.

He ignored my childish outburst. "Did your hair have a streak of white in it before?"

"No, of course not. Gold... Wait, why?"

"Because now it does." Luiz cocked his head. "Does she look older? No offense, Zariya...but more wrinkly?"

I backed up a step as they all peered at me. My hands flew to my face. "What? What is it?"

Konstantin pulled his phone out of his cargo pocket, hit the camera and held it out to me. "I think I know what this is."

I looked into the camera, and horror filled me. I did look older. Almost as old as Auntie Temsula. My dark hair was mixed with strands of silver, and the beginning of crow's feet bracketed my green eyes.

"It's an aging spell," Konstantin said.

"I'm getting older?" I gasped. I mean, I didn't mind being a feisty old lady who could say whatever the hell crossed her mind—someday. But I was only in my mid-twenties!

Konstantin nodded grimly. "And rapidly. Too fast. Whoever set that spell...it was a nasty one. You've already aged a decade or more."

"If I've aged a decade in a few minutes, what happens when I get really old?!"

"I've read about this before. How long do nagas live?"

"Pretty long. We're not immortal, but like, five or six hundred years?"

"And you're half-human, so we have to assume your lifespan will be half that. Two hundred and fifty years, maybe."

I nodded nervously. I wasn't digging where this conversation was going—at all.

"If you're aging, say, a year a minute, then we should have about three hours before..." Rex trailed off.

"Before I'm dead?" I screeched. "We need to find a counter-spell!"

Konstantin was already on his comm. "Kiki, we need Enigma here —yesterday."

"Why do these things keep happening to me?" I shook my hands before me. As if that was all it would take to rid me of this foul magic.

"Hey, I got kidnapped last mission," Daevin said.

"But I got kidnapped the time before that," I pointed out.

"Fair point," he conceded.

My breath was coming in short bursts. I couldn't die. There was so much left for me to do. I wanted to see my homeland. I wanted to go skydiving while Alviya flew next to me. I wanted to do drugs and dance till dawn at Burning Man with Kiki. Goddammit, I wanted to fuck the living daylights out of Konstantin Bauer.

The hairs on the back of my neck rose, and we all turned to find

Enigma standing a few yards away, looking infinitely out of place in dark washed jeans, a Dr. Who T-shirt, and Birkenstocks. His thick-rimmed glasses were already starting to fog up from the humidity. "What's going on? You need a ride?"

"No, we need a counter-spell." Konstantin shoved me forward. "Zariya's tripped a Black Moon Coven aging spell."

Enigma whistled. "You have some shit luck, don't you, new girl?"

I hissed.

"We estimate she has less than three hours to live," Konstantin added.

Enigma paled.

"Please tell me this isn't above your pay grade."

"Aging spells are complex work. That coven often works with demons—black magic. Without access to those same ingredients, even if I could figure out the counter-spell, it wouldn't stick."

"We have a demon. Can you use him?" I pointed at Daevin.

He shook his head. "It's like a disease. Without knowing the precise strain, you can't prescribe the right medicine."

"Well, can you reverse-engineer it or something?" I pleaded.

"Not in three hours."

"Try," Konstantin barked.

Enigma huffed and stepped up, keeping a good foot of distance between us.

"I don't think it's contagious," I snapped.

"Can't be too careful," he said under his breath. Enigma closed his eyes, and I felt a wash of smooth, cool magic, like a soothing balm. It was so unlike the tight ache of the other spell gripping me that I let out a sigh of relief.

"Is it working? Is he doing something?" Galu asked.

Enigma opened his eyes. "No. I was just scanning. It's as I thought. The spellwork is too complex. I think I know what the witch did, but there's a signature...a lock, if you will. It requires her magic as the key."

"So the only person who can undo this spell is the witch who cast it?" Konstantin asked.

"It's really quite clever," Enigma admitted.

I glared at him.

"I'm sorry. If I could do something, I would."

A lump was growing in my throat. This had just gotten way too fucking real.

"Is there any way of identifying who this witch is?" Daevin asked. "The signature? So we can find her?"

"It's not like she left her name. If I were with her, I'd be able to be able to recognize the magic, but she could be anywhere."

"Then what the fuck good are you?" Konstantin exploded and spun away, stalking deeper into the forest.

My eyebrows flew up. Damn, I had never seen Konstantin lose his temper like that.

Galu gave Enigma an apologetic smile. "I think what he means is that we really appreciate your help. He's just disappointed we haven't found a solution."

Enigma pushed his glasses up. "Right."

My thoughts spun like a top, desperately seeking a solution. "We have to find her," I said. "What if...?" My mind was working feverishly. "Whoever's inside that resort might know the witch who did this."

"What are you suggesting?" Konstantin stopped and turned back.

"They must. It's their hideout. What if I give myself up? They can take me prisoner; maybe they'll want me alive."

"It's too risky." Galu shook his head. "We don't know that they wouldn't just let you die. We can't just give up our only chance to find the counter-spell."

"Whoever's inside that resort is the best chance I've got. Maybe the witch is even here right now."

"Can you tell that?" Konstantin was back. "Enigma, can you detect her signature inside?"

"It's hard to identify one witch's magic from that far away, but I can try." Enigma closed his eyes and concentrated. This was the most accommodating I'd ever seen him. I thought he might feel a little bad for me.

When he opened his eyes a few seconds later, there was excitement there. "It's faint, but I do detect something similar. There are at least half a dozen witches inside, but the most powerful magic feels similar. It could be just an echo, but there's a real possibility she's inside."

That settled it for me. "I have to do this. It's my only shot."

"We're not letting you turn yourself in." Konstantin growled, stepping before me. "Especially to a place bristling with dark witches. It's out of the question."

"So you're just going to let me die?" I stuck my chin out.

"We'll find another way. We always do."

"What if she didn't turn herself in, per se?" Luiz stepped between us. "This place traffics in beautiful supernatural women. We have a beautiful supernatural woman right here."

"Go on..." I said.

"What if she pretends to be a lost supe who stumbled into the wrong place at the wrong time? Tripped the perimeter spell. They would see her as valuable, someone they could potentially sell, or use. They'd lift the spell."

"This island is in the middle of nowhere," Konstantin pointed out. "She's in a fucking tactical suit. They're not going to buy that."

"Rex can change her clothes to something touristy. We could say she was out...cruising with her boyfriend and her boat went down. She washed up on the island and looked for any sign of habitation. Voila!"

"It's pretty fucking farfetched," Daevin said.

"But not impossible," Galu said.

"I'll do it," I said. "We need eyes inside anyway. It's perfect. Once I've scoped out the place and gotten the counter-spell, you can come in, guns blazing."

"It's too dangerous," Konstantin insisted.

"We're way past dangerous," I countered. "It's the only way."

Konstantin was shaking his head and growling under his breath.

"Come on, boss," Galu said. "It's her best shot."

"Fine." Konstantin growled. "Do it. Just do it before I change my mind."

Rex made quick work of my clothes, transforming my tactical suit into cut-off jean shorts, a pink tank top, and a striped bikini.

"This is cute, Rex," I said, trying to ignore the fact that the ends of my curls were showing even more gray. "You have good taste."

His ears perked up. If his face weren't totally covered in fur, I swore he would have blushed.

Konstantin leaned down and took some dirt and smeared it on my cheek, then my forehead, almost tenderly. "Perfect."

My mouth went dry. Without my suit, I was already sweating like a stuck pig, and Konstantin's nearness only set my blood boiling all the more.

"I'll need your comm. We can't risk that they'd recognize it."

I pulled it out of my ear and dropped it in his hand. "Kiki will be able to keep in touch."

"Hopefully," he said. "Their wards could block telepathic communication, like in Bhutan."

Doubts were rushing in, fast and furious. This might be it. If I didn't find that witch...today could be the last day I spent on this earth. It could be the last time I saw any of them. My last chance with Konstantin. Damn the consequences, if I was going to die, I was going to have one last kiss.

I grabbed his face in my hand and pressed my lips to his. Pouring every unfinished thought, and dream, and hope into that kiss. When it broke off, he looked a little dazed. "Before I change my mind," I said.

I waved to the other guys, Rex and Daevin, Galu and Luiz, who was grinning like a fool. "Thank you..." A lump grew in my throat even as I walked backwards towards the resort. If I lingered, I'd start to cry. "It's been an honor to be your teammate. And friend."

"We'll see you soon, Six," Galu said.

"Those witches won't know what hit them," Daevin added.

"We're with you, Zariya," Luiz added. "Every step of the way."

Rex put his hand on his heart and gave me a little bow. "This is not goodbye."

And Konstantin...Konstantin just looked at me, his devastatingly handsome face a storm of emotions. Fury, helplessness, worry. "I'll come for you," he said through clenched teeth.

I believed him. All of them. So I did all I could do. I turned and jogged off into the unknown.

7

———

I didn't really have to fake being a sweaty, simpering mess. I felt all of those things. As I ran back through the shuddering perimeter of magic, the wards washed over me yet again.

My joints were hurting and a low ache had settled in my back. Was this what it felt like to be old? It was fucking awful.

I staggered around the side of the palatial resort, getting my first glimpse of the fine side where a few women lounged. Were they guests or witches? A huge infinity pool overlooked the crystal blue of the Caribbean while palm trees swayed in a soft breeze. It could have been a Sandals resort, if not for the two guards with automatic rifles stationed at the two entrances.

"Hey!" one guard shouted as he caught sight of me. He was a burly, dark-haired man with a thick beard, probably some kind of shifter.

"Ohmygod," I shouted. I was drawing the attention of the few women by the pool, but none of them moved to help me. I headed for the guard. "Thank God I found someone. I thought I was going to die out there." I fell against his chest like a whimpering mess, letting some of my real fear seep out. My final minutes were slipping away like sand through an hourglass. "My boyfriend—my boyfriend's boat sank, and we got separated, and I washed up on this horrible island and I thought I was going to die," I babbled, forcing tears to the surface. "Thank God I found you. But...I feel...I feel funny. Like something's wrong."

My legs started to go out from under me and he caught me. A whimper of real fear escaped me. I wasn't faking anymore. I was as weak as a mewling lamb.

My commotion had attracted the other guard, a sandy-haired man built like a Mack truck. "What the fuck is this?"

"I'm so thirsty," I whimpered.

Mack truck guy shrugged. "Take her inside. See what the boss says."

The dark shifter, my original target, handed his rifle to the other guy and scooped me up in his arms. "Come on."

I let my head fall against his chest as ragged breaths of relief pounded from my lungs. He carried me inside. Into the lion's den.

I tried to keep a sharp eye out while maintaining my damsel in distress persona. There were cameras in every corner of the marble lobby, and another two guards flanked a silver elevator. That was four so far.

"What is this place?" I said. "It's so beautiful."

"Private resort, honey. Siren's Quay. Don't worry. You're...safe now." His gentle tone carried no hint of malice. He really seemed to feel bad for me.

"I'm so worried about my boyfriend. Do you think you could call the mainland so they can look for him?"

"Of course. Once we get you checked out. You've been through a lot." He didn't ask me any details. Not about the boat, or my boyfriend's name or even what port we'd come from.

We passed a tall, solidly-built woman with silver hair, and the shifter turned. "Hey, Maribella, would you be able to check this girl out? She just washed up. I think she's sick."

Maribella turned her keen eyes on me. "No shit. She's crossed the wards. Only Naeve can undo that." Yes! It took every bit of self-restraint not to heave a huge sigh of relief. The witch who had set the wards—this Naeve person—was here.

"But if I take her to Naeve—" The guard who held me glanced at me and trailed off. Why was he hesitating?

"It's what we do here, Cameron, you know that." Maribella turned and stalked away.

He grunted.

"Everything okay?" I asked, batting my eyes.

"Yeah. Of course. Let's go find some help."

We navigated through another corridor, Cameron's boots squeaking on the polished marble. "I'm going to put you down," he said, gently lowering me to my feet before a thick mahogany door.

He knocked.

"What?" came a sharp bark from inside.

"I've got something I think you should see," he called back.

The door whipped open, revealing a tall blonde beauty in a skintight white dress. She wore an embarrassment of high-end jewelry—diamonds at her throat and around her wrist and large, dangling earrings. She looked like a WASP at a country club, not at all the type of woman I would have pictured here. Was this our witch? Naeve? She must have been.

"Cameron, what is this?" she said with disgust.

"She just stumbled in from the mainland." Cameron kindly explained my story so I didn't have to. "Her boat sank. She tripped the perimeter defenses."

"I feel so funny. I don't know what happened..." I didn't have to pretend. I did feel funny. It was getting much, much worse.

The witch cocked her head. "How old are you, honey?"

"Twenty-six."

"And what are you?"

"I'm half-naga," I gritted out, trying not to bristle at the rudeness. "Can I have some water?"

The woman rolled her eyes and nodded inside. "Bring her in."

Cameron, who was actually kind of endearing himself to me, despite being an armed guard for sex traffickers, helped me to the couch and then crossed to a little mini fridge to get me a bottle of cold water.

"You're a lifesaver," I simpered to Cameron as he handed me my water.

The room was an office, complete with a sleek wood desk and an overstuffed couch of damask silk. A tray of tropical fruit sat on a side table next to a silver tray with coffee service. It was all so...normal. Where was the raven familiar, the dripping candelabras, and the ancient grimoires bound with dried human skin? Maybe I'd just watched one too many horror movies. Evil in the real world accessorized with power and money, not cauldrons and kitschy gothic jewelry.

The woman leaned against the desk, crossing her impossibly long, tanned legs at the ankle. "You just...happened to be here?"

"My boyfriend and I were fishing and the boat went down. I made it to this island..." I let out a fake sob and buried my face in my hand. "I thought I was going to die. Once I saw this place, I thought everything would be okay, but now I feel so funny. Maybe I drank too much salt water. Or maybe I ate something? I had some berries, maybe they were poisoned? Do you have—"

The witch cut me off. "It's not something you ate, my dear. We have a strong security system here. You tripped the wards."

"Wards?" I simpered. "Oh no. What's happening to me?"

"Never fear." She flashed perfectly white teeth in a predatory smile. "Now that I see it's just a lost traveler, I'm happy to remove the spell."

"Thank you so much!" I didn't have to fake my gratitude. I really didn't want to die of fucking old age at twenty-six. I was going to live to fight another day. Another thought hit me like a gut punch. Live to face the fact that I'd kissed Konstantin in front of the whole rest of the team. *Shit.*

The witch crossed the room with an easy, sashaying stride. The hairs on the back of my neck rose. I could feel the power radiating from her—the wrongness. Despite her Malibu Barbie appearance, this woman was dangerous.

As she reached out to lay a hand on my forehead, I caught a glimpse of the tattoo on her wrist. A single circle filled in with black. The sigil of the Black Moon Coven. I was definitely in the right place.

The witch murmured under her breath and my skin tingled as the spell disintegrated around me. I let out a gasp of relief. It was like the force of gravity had been pressing heavily upon me, squeezing my bones, and now it had suddenly lifted. "Thank God," I groaned. I looked at the backs of my hands, at the ends of my curls. I was young again, blessedly, wonderfully, young.

She stepped back and cocked her head at me. "You're quite lovely. Those scales...I've never seen anything like them."

"Thank you," I managed. "I'm Abigail. What's your name?"

A smile quirked on her bright red lips. "You can call me 'Naeve.'"

I smiled widely. Better than Mistress of Darkness, or some shit like that.

"Now, can we call someone for you? Surely, someone back home must be looking for you."

It took all my power not to glare at her. Clearly, she was testing the waters to see if they could take me captive without any pesky strings attached. I'd expected as much. But was that what Cameron had been trying to avoid? Had the guy been looking out for me? I glanced at him and saw his lips were set in a thin line. So he didn't exactly approve of what was going on here.

I shrugged helplessly. "It was just me and my dad. But he died a few months ago. My boyfriend was on the boat with me, but it sank and I don't know where he is. Cameron said he'd call the mainland to see if they found him?"

"Absolutely." Naeve smiled. "You must be hungry. Do you want something to eat?"

That pineapple did look good. And I didn't think Abigail, my cover persona, would refuse. "That would be nice, thank you."

Naeve retrieved the platter and a napkin and held it out for me. I grabbed a few slices of pineapple and mango, feeling a little bit like Persephone in Hades's lair. She set the tray down. "You've had quite an ordeal. We have plenty of rooms here. After a shower, some food, and a change of clothes, you'll feel like a new woman. Promise."

I forced a smile and took a bite of mango. It was juicy and tart and downright delicious. "I can't thank you enough for your kindness." I smiled. *Bitch, I'm going to take you down hard.*

She smiled right back at me, fake as a cardboard cutout. "Why don't I have Cameron show you to a room? You must be exhausted from your ordeal."

"Thank you." I stood and blood rushed to my head.

Cameron was at my side in an instant, catching my elbow.

"Whoa." My hand flew to my temple. I felt even funnier than I had when I'd tripped the wards. I honed in on the fruit. Had she poisoned me?

Naeve let out a dark chuckle. "Don't you worry, *Abigail*. We know just what to do with you."

The world spun out and blackness swallowed me.

8

Konstantin peered through the foliage, unable to look away from the hulking back of Siren's Quay. He needed to know what was going on in there. His fingers twitched at his side—desperate to pull something limb from limb. How had this happened? Zariya had been put in jeopardy—again. Had she found the witch? Was she receiving the counter-spell? Or was she still aging, her supple skin sagging, her ebony curls turning to gray? Would she die in there? Alone?

What if watching her jog away was the last time he'd ever see her? If that kiss was... He couldn't believe she'd kissed him. Full on, in front of everyone. But of course she had. She was bold and fearless and so *alive*. He needed to protect her. He needed to see her again. Needed to make her *his*.

Desperate, hopeless fury coursed through his veins. This couldn't happen, not again. He couldn't lose another woman he cared about. This was why he'd sworn off romance. It was complicated, messy, and god damn, it *hurt*.

But things were different this time. It wasn't too late for Zariya. He wouldn't lose her. He couldn't. Not if he was alive to stop it.

Against his better judgment, against his own orders, he found himself starting to move towards the treeline. He was immortal. The wards shouldn't affect him the way they had Zariya.

"Whoa, boss, where are you going?" Galu put himself before Konstantin, placing a hand on his chest.

"Out. Of. My. Way." Konstantin growled.

"You do this, you could jeopardize her," Galu said. "Give her time. Zariya is smart. She'll be all right."

"Why haven't we heard from Kiki then?" Konstantin pointed out.

"Kiki said she was going to have to work through the wards to make contact. Let her do her job. We're going to have a hard enough time taking those witches down even with intel on the inside."

"Galu's right," Enigma said. "If there're multiple Black Moon Coven witches in there, you're going to be seriously outmatched. We'll need help if you want to stop the people running this place."

Konstantin ground his teeth. He didn't want to talk and plan. He wanted to surge into that place and start ripping heads off. But some part of him still saw the wisdom in what they were suggesting. He couldn't risk busting in there half-cocked if Zariya could get caught in the crosshairs. But he didn't like having her in there, not for one second. These people trafficked in supe women. They were the worst kind of monsters.

"The Crescent Moon Coven," Enigma suggested. "They're experts in battle magic. If you could get a few of them to help out, the witches in here wouldn't stand a chance."

"Can you get them for us?"

Enigma adjusted his glasses. Uncomfortable. "I'm not sure. By joining with MASC, I technically broke my affiliation with my own coven. The Crescents are very territorial. All about loyalty. Purity. I'm not sure me being there would help your case much."

"Then what do you suggest?" Konstantin stepped forward. "What would get through to them?"

Enigma licked his lips and looked at Luiz. "Him."

"Me?" Luiz pointed to his chest.

"The head of the Crescent Coven is known for having

certain...*appetites*. She loves handsome men. I bet an incubus would peak her interest."

Daevin chuckled and slapped Luiz on the back. "I guess it pays off to be a man whore."

Luiz's face darkened, but the expression passed quickly. He hooked his thumbs in his belt loops. "With great power comes great responsibility."

"I can't ask this of you," Konstantin said. It was one thing to run into gunfire and the madness of war, but he would never ask a member of his team to sacrifice their body. A person's sexual choices were sacrosanct.

"Good thing you don't have to then, boss," Luiz said. "You think I can let our girl go in undefended to that place and not be willing to turn on my charms to get her some backup? No way."

Konstantin sighed. "Where is the Crescent Moon Coven located?"

"Russia," Enigma said.

"Daevin, you're going with Luiz. Enigma, you're on transport. This is top priority. Bring back whatever firepower we need to burn this place to the ground, and those dark witches with it."

"With pleasure," Luiz said.

Luiz and Daevin stepped in close to Enigma, and then they were gone.

Konstantin tapped on his comm. "*Kiki, tell me you've gotten through those wards.*"

"*Not yet,*" she replied. "*I'm sorry. I'm afraid they might be too power-ful. Comms should work once you're all inside, but I can't get through to Zariya via telepathy alone.*"

Konstantin bared his teeth in a snarl. "*Try harder.*"

"*She's my friend too, Konstantin. I'm trying as hard as I fucking can.*"

That was true. It wasn't entirely fair of him to suggest she needed added motivation.

"*But I think I have something. Several people are coming onto the resort tonight for an event. It looks like a private auction. These witches' physical wards are good, but their encryption isn't the best. I've added one name to the guest list. You'll be going in as Anton von Steiner.*"

"What about Galu and Rex?"

"I've noticed something interesting about this place. Most of the clientele are humans or vampires. I think Galu and Rex would stand out too much. You'll have the best chance of staying incognito if you go alone."

Galu and Rex exchanged a look. "I don't like how they're separating us," Rex said. "It feels deliberate."

Konstantin frowned. He couldn't help but agree. The team was strongest together. This situation felt off. Like something bad was coming.

"Don't see how you have a choice in the matter," Galu pointed out. "Zariya needs backup inside."

"Agreed. I'll be careful," Konstantin said. "Galu, you'll be leading the mission from here, and Luiz and Daevin will be back with reinforcements before we know it. I want you two to keep your guard up out here."

Galu nodded sharply. "If you get into trouble in there, we'll have no way of getting you out before those witches come."

"Then I better not get into trouble."

WHEN I WOKE UP, I immediately regretted consciousness. My head was throbbing like a back-alley rave. I tried to sit up and found my wrist handcuffed to a bed. A groan escaped me.

"Hey look, new girl's up," a soft female voice said.

I squinted and tried to blink the world around me into focus. "Who said that?" I was in a long, gray room. Lined with cages.

I maneuvered to sit up, closing my eyes for a moment against the surging pain pounding inside my temples.

"Hi. You all right?"

I peered through the bars to the next cell and found a beautiful fae woman looking back at me with concern in her wide green eyes.

"Not exactly the Ritz-Carlton, is it?" I managed.

She offered me a soft smile. "That sleeping draught is a real ass-kicker. You'll start to feel better in a few minutes."

"Will I wake up from this nightmare?" I asked. I needed to keep up my cover in case any of the prisoners in here were friendly with the guards. Or the witches. "Because last time I checked, that woman promised to put me up in a room and call the mainland. What the fuck is this?"

She pursed her lips in sympathy. "It's a lot to take in, I'm sure. But it's really not so bad. They aren't unnecessarily cruel to us. We're well fed and kept clean."

"We're in fucking cages," I pointed out. "Like animals."

"Trust me. The last place I was at..." She shivered. "Disgusting dungeon."

Could this be Yara's friend? Was it possible I'd gotten lucky enough to end up right next to her? I'd see what I could find out, but right now I needed to confirm what we were dealing with.

"I'm Abigail."

"Rheanan."

I schooled my features to stay still. It *was* Yara's friend. How long had this poor fae been a prisoner of the Collectors? But I didn't want to spook her by making her think I knew a whole bunch about her. Not until I knew she could be trusted. "What are they going to do with us?" I rattled the handcuff. It was enchanted—much stronger than regular metal. *That* I would have been able to rip through, no problem.

The fae sighed. "I'm not going to sugarcoat it, honey. This is a market. I think some of us are sold for medical research, others for... private collections."

A shiver wracked me. Private collections? Like some sort of messed-up menagerie? "Slavery of Class V supes is illegal under the Treaty. They can't do this."

She threaded her hands together. "We're a long way from the authorities. Out here, the strong make the rules. And the rest of us..." She gestured down the row. "We just try to stay alive."

"So we take back the power." I looked down the room. Every cage was full. There were at least ten powerful supes in this room, and a few humans. The witches were strong, but we weren't helpless.

"It's not possible," Rheanan said sadly. "The sooner you accept your predicament, the easier it's going to be for you."

My hands balled into fists. "We'll just see about that." Maybe I was in a predicament now, but I wouldn't be forever. I trusted my teammates. The cavalry would arrive, and when they did, we *would* burn this place to the fucking ground.

9

———

Luiz, Daevin, and Enigma materialized in a snowy field just beyond a soaring ornate gate. Through the twisted wrought iron sat a compound that looked much like a palace—a dozen buildings of buttery yellow, creamy peach, and tangerine, topped by black tiled onion domes.

Luiz's gut was twisted like a pretzel; Enigma's words echoed in his head. *"Certain...appetites. She loves handsome men."* He pressed his lips together. Why did it always fucking come back to this? He couldn't just be a Phantom, a teammate, a friend. He was always an incubus first. It was all people saw in him.

He shook it off. It didn't matter. It was what it was. And he was here for Zariya. He could flirt, seduce, beguile. He could do any of those things and not break his promise to himself. And who knew? Maybe this witch would be a knockout and the chemistry between them would be electric. Maybe he'd jump into bed with her gladly. Maybe none of it would be necessary and the witches would help voluntarily. He owed it to Zariya to find out.

"What is this place?" Daevin asked.

Enigma rubbed his arms against the chill. "It used to be a monastery. Now it's Crescent Moon Coven HQ. Their training grounds, too. The best battle witches in the world come out of this facility."

"Good," Daevin said. "We need 'em."

"What else can you tell us about the High Priestess of this coven?" Luiz asked.

"She's Russian, which is why they picked this facility. She's ex-KGB. Smart. Ruthless. A lot of covens tolerate unaffiliated witches in their territory; they just kind of ignore them. Not the Crescents. You're with them—or against them."

"So let's be with them." Daevin grinned.

"How many witches do you think we need to infiltrate the resort grounds and defeat the other witches?" Luiz asked.

"Crescent Coven? Likely only one. They're legendary."

"Why hasn't Veil Force been recruiting these chicks?" Daevin mused.

"They're loyal only to their coven. And to each other. The witches have a code. Even when they fight amongst themselves, they believe they are superior to all other creatures. Human and supe."

"Great. This ought to be fun," Luiz muttered.

"I'll be here when you guys are finished." Enigma forced a smile.

"You don't want to come in out of the cold?" Daevin asked.

"I'd rather brave a blizzard than what's in there," Enigma replied.

"Suit yourself," Daevin said. But as they walked through the open gates, he added, "Why is that not particularly comforting?"

Luiz stumbled to a halt as five women materialized in a semi-circle around them, each with silver wands like swords pointed their direction.

"Easy, ladies." Daevin put his hands up.

The five witches wore identical gray-and-silver uniforms—stark but well-tailored to fit their trim forms. They all looked young—in their early twenties at the latest, and all of them were lovely. But none of them held a candle to the woman in the center. She had ebony black hair with a streak of silver swooping back from one temple, and her eyes were the steel gray of hematite. She was petite and slim—her heart-shaped face barely came up to his chest. But there was a fire in her that startled him, a power that seemed to charge the air around them. This witch was a force to be reckoned with. "You're trespassing on private property. I suggest you turn around and go back from whence you came. Unless you fancy living out the remainder of your immortal lives in the forms of small rodents." She had a staccato, lilting way of speaking. Even her threat sounded like poetry.

"We're here to see Svetlana Morikova," Luiz said. "We're from MASC."

"If you're from MASC, you know that MASC has no jurisdiction over witches. We're not supernatural creatures. We are unto ourselves."

"It's not a matter of jurisdiction," Daevin replied. "It's a matter of mutual interest."

"We've heard the Crescent Moon Coven is the best, and we need the best," Luiz said.

A smirk flitted across the black-haired witch's face and she crossed her arms before her. The other witches kept their wands up. He noticed each wand had a different color at the tip. The leader's wand was tipped in the deepest black. "Perhaps. But we want for nothing."

Time to turn on the charm. Luiz purred, "At least hear us out. I'm sure we can come to a mutually beneficial arrangement."

She met the challenge of his gaze with a step forward. Evaluating. Weighing. He prickled under her scrutiny even as his skin buzzed pleasantly at the proximity to her magic. It took all of Luiz's willpower not to put space between them.

"Two Veil Force Phantoms admitting they need help? Today must be a cold day in hell. But...fine. We will hear your proposal. Follow me." She nodded inside the fence and turned without another word. The rest of the witches dispersed—walking away or downright vanishing.

Luiz and Daevin quickly followed.

"Actually," Daevin said, "hell has a surprising range of temperature variations. Especially in the south. It frequently freezes."

The witch looked back with a roll of her eyes.

"Not a fan of trivia?" Daevin said with a grin.

"Not a fan of idle prattle," she snapped in response.

"Awkward silence it is," Daevin muttered.

Luiz shot Daevin a sideways glance, in a universal "Be cool, bro, be cool."

"What's your name?" Luiz asked.

She didn't look back. "Isobel."

"I'm Luiz, and this is Daevin."

No reply. Isobel led them inside one of the buildings topped with a tiled onion dome. The space inside was wood on wood with a soaring circular ceiling. He could imagine that this room had once been a place of worship.

A pair of younger women in white uniforms trotted by, eyeing them with curiosity. One held a thick leather tome tucked under her arm. Trainees, perhaps?

"This is first and foremost a school," Isobel said, in response to the question they hadn't asked. Isobel led them through hallways of white plaster and dark wood, flanked by alcoves lined with books, candelabras, statutes, and paintings. The place was clean and orderly, not lavish or extravagant. For the most powerful battle witch in the world, Svetlana had simple tastes. So perhaps money would not be an incentive.

They reached the end of a hallway and she pointed to a velvet couch set against one wall. "Wait here. I'll see if Svetlana has time for you. She doesn't normally accept uninvited visitors."

"It is a matter of some urgency," Luiz replied.

Luiz and Daevin settled onto the couch to wait.

"She was a real firecracker, eh?" Daevin raised an eyebrow.

Luiz nodded his assent, not wanting Daevin to see how much his exchange with Isobel had rattled him. He wasn't used to encountering humans with such power. Her life force was vibrant. Enthralling. Sexy as hell. "Can't wait to meet the head honcho." Maybe Svetlana would be as stunning as Isobel. She must be, if she compelled the loyalty of such powerful women.

"How do you think Zariya's holding up?" Daevin asked. He left the other questions unspoken. Was she even alive? Had she found the witch who could lift the spell?

Luiz tapped his comm. *"Any word?"*

"No," came Konstantin's sharp bark in response. *"But Kiki got me an open door inside. I'm going to see what I can find out."*

"Roger that," Luiz said.

He exchanged a frown with Daevin.

"She's fine." Daevin bobbed his head. "She's tough. If something had happened, we would know."

"She's not invincible," Luiz said quietly. Vizol had seemed invincible; they'd all viewed him that way. A man of mythical stature. And the Collectors had killed him. "Even if she's alive, I don't want to think about what they're doing to her."

"This hits close to home for you, doesn't it?"

"Yes," Luiz admitted. He rubbed his temples. "People who buy and sell other people—supes like the Collectors, Mason—they have no conscience. You cut them down, but a newer, more disgusting version just reappears somewhere else."

"Evil motherfuckers are exactly like weeds."

"I'm sick of it. We need to rip them out at the root."

"Vengeance." Daevin looked at him. "It's a strange color on you."

He could never tell Daevin, or anyone, about parts of his past—the things he'd done. The way that place had broken him. Veil Force had put him together as something different, but he'd never be whole. Not truly.

Isobel opened the door and motioned them inside. "Svetlana will see you. She doesn't want your kind lingering here any longer than necessary."

"How magnanimous of her," Daevin drawled.

They walked into a warm office with a stretch of bay windows framing the snowy meadows beyond.

Svetlana Morikova sat behind a massive wooden desk. She wore the same gray uniform as the other witch, but her blonde hair was threaded in an intricate set of braids, the only extravagance in the room. She was beautiful but severe, the type of beauty that burned like liquid nitrogen. As she turned her dark eyes on them, his mouth went dry. Too cold. He had the sudden sense that she would devour him.

"Luiz Archileta and Daevin Ryan. Esteemed Phoenix Team Phantoms." Svetlana didn't get up, and she didn't offer them a seat. It was a clear power play. Her house, her rules. "What can I do for you?"

"We have need of a battle witch." Luiz ignored the rapidly-growing knot in his stomach. It was clear that she was as mighty as Isobel, perhaps more so. But her magic didn't sing to him in the way Isobel's did. No, her magic was like a boot to the throat. "We're infiltrating a location protected by the Black Moon Coven. We need your assistance."

"And why would I ever get involved in such matters? Naeve of the Black Moon Coven and I aren't exactly friends, but I wouldn't call us enemies. We keep to our respective corners. Why would I upset that balance?"

"These witches are capturing supernatural women—intelligent, verbal creatures—and selling them. Fae, naga. The practice is illegal."

"And fucking despicable," Daevin added.

"Wards and curses and dark magic is one thing, but trading supernatural lives is another. We can't stand by," Luiz said.

"Again, you haven't told me how this is my problem."

"Maybe it could be your problem," Daevin suggested. "For the right price."

A small smile curved on her lips. "Now you're getting warmer. But you assume that I don't have enough money."

"No one has enough money," Luiz pointed out, though he knew it wouldn't be enough to sway her. A wave of cold sweat washed over his body. He couldn't sleep with her—he knew it deep in his bones. There was a darkness in this woman that repelled him. *Please, let us find something else to bargain with. Please, let there be some other way for him to help Zariya.* Because if it came down to it...he didn't know what he'd do.

Svetlana stood and paced to the window, looking out over the bleached landscape for a moment. She turned. "There is something I believe you can do for me. In exchange for borrowing one of my battle witches for a time."

"Name it," Daevin said.

Luiz shot him a warning look. There was plenty they couldn't promise.

"I've heard that Veil Force has recently come into possession of a certain object of great power."

"You're going to have to be more specific. We have plenty of objects that would fit that description."

"An ancient portal device."

"The Chinvat Gate?" Luiz asked.

"That's the one." She pinned him with those piercing eyes.

Luiz held back his frown. They'd acquired the Gate just days ago, from the Collectors' headquarters in Bhutan. How had word already traveled to these witches that they had possession?

Daevin answered. "We give you the gate, and you give us enough witchy firepower to defeat the Black Moon Coven?"

She nodded slowly. "One operation. Then our deal would be complete."

"I'll have to check with our director. Giving up the Gate... It's not my call," Luiz said, even as he seized on this solution. He'd convince Cyriaque to give it up. What good was it to have something sitting on a shelf when it could save one of their operators?

Svetlana's eyes narrowed. "Then what good are you?"

Her comment prickled his pride. "Oh, I'm plenty good." The words were out before he could stop himself. Stupid, baiting her like that.

Svetlana braced her hands on her desk, taking him in with a leisurely sweep that set his blood running cold. "Maybe I should ask for you to be thrown in, too."

"Our supes aren't for sale, your witchiness." Daevin clapped Luiz on the shoulder. "Now if you don't mind, we need to make a call."

10

─────

I lay on the hard bed, trying to keep my spirits up. I wasn't dead. Sure, I wasn't digging my current predicament, but I could have been dead. This was definitely preferable to that.

I'd busied my mind taking stock of every detail of the room where I was being held, just as Dad's memories reminded me to do. A round, red-haired woman I assumed was a witch stood watch at the door, though she was scrolling on her phone, not paying particular attention to anything. That was a useful tidbit. Access to Wi-Fi would be huge.

The supes in the cages around me were all females, with the exception of one brawny, good-looking guy who could have been an extra on a Viking period drama. I thought I placed him as a dhampir —half-human, half-vampire. Other cages held a lavender-haired nix covered in shimmering scales, a lovely shifter of what I thought was some avian variety, a satyr with slender legs leading to delicate hooves... It was a disgusting supe-lover's wet dream in here. And, strangely, the two women caged together at the end looked distinctly human. One paced the short length of their cage like a wild beast while the other sat on the bed in apparent meditation. Why would they be here? But why were any of us here?

A sharp clap broke me out of my melancholy. I craned my head and found myself baring my teeth in a snarl at the newcomer. Naeve. She had changed into a sleek black pantsuit and wore nothing beneath the plunging V of the jacket. A silver cross studded with winking rubies nestled in her perfect cleavage. Two witches flanked her—the silver haired one Cameron had pleaded with in the hallway, Maribella—and a raven-haired Asian woman with a network of intricate tattoos running up both arms.

The pacing human at the end crashed against the bars, snarling at Naeve. "You aren't fit to call yourself a witch, you greedy corporate sellout. Our coven will come for us, and they will make you pay."

My eyes widened. So these two humans were witches? That could be helpful.

But Naeve just smiled. "You Full Moon witches, bloated and as useless as the moon phase you worship. You've forgotten how it used to be." She took a step closer to the cage, her black patent Louboutin heels clicking on the stone floor. "We used to take what we wanted. Beauty, money, influence. We were given this power for a reason. Not to cower and pretend to be lesser to make the humans feel safe. But to rule them. This world is ours for the taking. Any witch who is too weak to see that doesn't deserve her magic."

"You mean to take our power for your own," the other caged woman said. I thought she'd been meditating, but she now regarded Naeve with a steely eyed glare.

"You're not really using it." Naeve smiled. "Now, if you don't mind—"

"I'd rather die than give my power to you," the witch clasping the bars spit at Naeve.

"That is your other option." Naeve flicked a finger and Maribella raised a hand.

The witch standing by the bars choked, her hands flying to her throat. Her eyes grew wide, and she began to shake.

I craned my neck, trying to get a better look. Maribella was doing it. Killing her.

"Stop it!" the other witch in the cage flew to her friend's side, holding her up while she spasmed. "We're more valuable to you alive!"

Naeve shrugged, examining her black-painted fingernails with a bored expression. "I'm only giving her what she asked for. Words have power. A witch should know better."

"Please!" Tears were running down the cheeks of the other witch now. "She didn't mean it. Stop! She's sorry!"

My own fingers gripped my bars as I ground my teeth. But there was nothing I could do. I was going to have to stand here and watch this woman die. I wanted to attack the bars with a fierceness that made Naeve stop, but more than that, I wanted to shrink and hide and be small. With every minute I stayed in this place, I was feeling less like Phoenix Six and more like Zariya Chanji. Young. Inexperienced. Half-human. Out of her fucking league.

Naeve gave a dramatic sigh and snapped her fingers. Maribella dropped her hand, and the witch in the cage stopped shaking. Her friend maneuvered her body to the ground through her own sobs, putting an ear to her mouth to see if she was breathing.

For a moment, the room was perfectly quiet. Even Naeve watched with a detached curiosity to see if the witch was dead.

But then she let out a heaving gasp. Her friend fell over her with a sob of relief, and I found tension uncoiling from my own body. I let my head rest against the bars. Thank God.

But my relief was short-lived, for now Naeve turned her attention to the rest of us. "Show's over. Or shall I say, it's just beginning. We need to prepare you for tonight. If any of you steps out of line, what just happened to this coven bitch will look like a day at the fucking spa. Do I make myself clear?"

Silence. A few murmured acknowledgments.

Questions choked me, but I was too chicken-shit to ask. I didn't want to draw her attention. Prepare for what? What was tonight?

~

As THE BLACK Moon witches led us, minus the dhampir male, into a long bathing chamber that bubbled enticingly, my emotions warred within me. We were being prepped for something that I was pretty sure I wanted no part of. But damn if a hot soak didn't sound really good to wash off the dirt and sweat and mosquito spray. If I was the lobster going into the pot, I might as well enjoy the soak before the end, right?

I dutifully undressed and filed into the pool with the rest of the supes. The two witches had been left in their cage. I closed my eyes briefly, my mind fleeing back to the last hot pool I'd been in—with Konstantin. Screw the vampire blood, I shouldn't have taken *no* for an answer. I'd felt too mortified after he'd stopped things between us, totally humiliated that I'd come on to my boss. But honestly, that hierarchy felt less and less important. If I was going to risk my life for Phoenix Team on a daily basis, I at least deserved to be with the man I wanted. Konstantin Bauer should be my hazard pay. If he wanted *me*, that was.

I went to work shampooing my hair. The pretty nix was next to me, already rinsing out her long tresses.

"Psst." I leaned over. "Do you know what they're preparing us for?"

She gave me a gentle smile. "You just got here, right?"

"Yeah," I replied warily.

"I convinced a guard to tell me. One of the men, not these soulless bitches. Once a month, they hold an auction. It's tonight. We'll be sold."

I blanched. Luiz had said this was a trafficking operation—I knew it was. But I hadn't fully wrapped my head around the fact that I could be sold. And tonight? What if whoever bought me took me out of here before the guys came to rescue me? What if I couldn't reach the team?

"I'm sorry," the nix said. "I've had some time to come to terms with it."

"Okay," I murmured. I needed to get word to the team somehow, tell them about this timeline. Bribe a guard maybe? That Cameron guy seemed halfway decent...for a shifter working in an illegal trafficking operation.

My mind spun as I finished bathing and got out of the pool. As we were lined up in a row of chairs like pigs for slaughter. Though I didn't think they bothered doing the hair and makeup of the pigs first.

I examined myself as a silent blonde woman went to work drying my hair. My green slitted eyes, pattern of golden scales at my temples. It had taken a long time, but I'd come to terms with how I looked. Not human, not naga. Unique. Now, once again, I didn't want to be unique. I wanted to blend in and keep a low profile.

I didn't want to be paraded like an animal. Bought and sold. I looked down, and my eyes caught on the brand on my palm. Where *Caeflwich* had marked me. I traced the contours of the brand with my other thumb, and a dogged determination filled me. I was Veil Force now. A Phantom. And I was naga. The blood of warriors sang in my veins. I would not be cowed. I would not go easily. When it came time, I would fight. If anyone tried to lay a hand on me, I would take them out. I had my venom.

A smile curved my lips. Oh, yes. They would rue the day—

The silver witch Maribella appeared behind me, and before I could react, she clicked a matte black ring around my neck. When it settled onto my skin, every hair on my body raised on end. This thing was magic. "What is this?" I raised my hand to it.

Maribella held up a black leather band with a gold face, almost like a watch. But the face didn't have hands or marks—it had a sort of dial. "This ensures you don't get any bright ideas. Like escaping." She flipped the dial to the side and an excruciating pain coursed through my body, singeing every nerve ending. A scream ripped from my mouth as the pain overcame all rational thought and reason and logic.

She flipped it back and I slumped in the chair, panting. I'd never felt such pain in all my life. "I think you get the picture." She handed the dial to the woman who'd been doing my hair and makeup, who fastened it on her wrist.

Rheanan caught my eye down the line. Each woman now wore a similar collar. She gave me a sad little smile.

I looked back at the mark burned in my hand as despair pulled me down. So much for the blood of warriors. So much for ruing the day. With one move, they'd stripped me down to a scared girl, all alone.

11

Konstantin peered through the window of the helicopter as it neared Quiribri Island. The landing pad was just beyond the resort's walls. Konstantin adjusted his silk tie, trying to give himself some breathing room.

It had been a mad dash to get him ready to attend the auction tonight—Rex had adjusted his clothing, Enigma had shepherded him to the mainland while Kiki arranged a private helicopter ride back to the island so he could appear to be arriving as a high-value guest.

This op was going seriously sideways. He didn't like his team divided like this, didn't like relying on outside help that may not pan out, didn't fucking like that Kiki hadn't been able to break through the wards to contact Zariya.

"*Boss?*" Luiz's voice over comms. "*We think we can wrangle us a battle witch, but they have some demands.*"

"*What?*" he replied. He needed to be done with this conversation before they landed. Once they did, he needed to own the role of Anton von Steiner, vampire oligarch. Kiki had found him the identity of a vampire who was known throughout less virtuous circles but who was also reclusive. Didn't like being photographed. Perfect.

Pause. "*They want the Chinvat Gate.*"

"*What is it with this thing?*" Konstantin said. *Shit.* The gate was currently his only lead to the mole within MASC.

"*I don't know. Traveling portals are rare. I don't know of any other witches and warlocks who can do what Enigma does. Maybe it's just the convenience factor.*"

"*Maybe.*" Or maybe there was something else going on. "*There's nothing else they'll take?*"

"*Svetlana doesn't seem like a real enthusiastic negotiator.*"

"*Roger that. I'll give Cyriaque a call.*"

"*Thanks.*"

The comm link went dead.

He taped his comm again. "*Kiki, can you connect me with Cyriaque?*"

"*Just a sec.*"

"*Bauer?*" Cyrique's deep drawl bloomed in his mind. "*Report.*"

He shut his eyes briefly. "*We've hit a snag. The property is protected by Black Moon Coven magic. We need a battle witch to help us get inside.*"

Cyriaque gave a little whistle. "*That is quite a pickle. I don't imagine you're calling for permission to approach Svetlana Morikova?*"

"*Luiz and Daevin are already there. It's what they want in exchange for helping us. The Chinvat Gate.*"

"*What?*" Cyriaque barked. "*What the fuck do they want that for?*"

"*I don't know, sir.*"

"*Well, we can't let them have it. The witches are a powerful, independent organization not under MASC jurisdiction. We can't let them grow too strong.*"

Normally, Konstantin would agree. But Zariya was inside there, and she needed rescuing. They didn't have time to dick around with debates and political posturing. "*Sir, Zariya's inside the compound. We need to get her out. I need you to approve this.*"

Silence stretched long inside his mind. Too long.

Konstantin glanced out the window again. They were almost to the island. He needed to wrap this up.

"*How the fuck did Zariya get inside a compound the rest of you incompetents can't breach it without a battle witch?*"

"*She's a prisoner, sir. It's not a good situation. We need to get her out of there.*"

"*Let me get this straight. For the second time in as many missions, Zariya has gotten herself captured and cozied up along with the Collectors and their witch bitch friends? You used to be my best Phantom, Bauer, but you've been off your game.*"

A spark of indignation shot through Konstantin, followed by guilt. As much as he hated to admit it, Cyriaque had a fucking point. He was off his game. So he swallowed his pride and gritted out, "*I understand, sir. My mission, my team, my responsibility. But we can't abandon her. Are you going to give us the Gate or not?*"

"*Fuck no, Bauer. Getting Chanji captured is your shitstorm, and so you're going to have to clean it up. I'm not giving up a dangerous ancient artifact that we know so little about. Frankly, the fact that the witches want it makes it all the more important that we keep it.*"

"*Cyriaque, you could be dooming Zariya—*"

"*Despite your recent failures, you are my best operator. Ancient. Deadly. Scourge of the fucking night. So figure it out. I'm confident you will.*" The link clicked off.

"Fuck!" Konstantin pulled off his headset and tossed it across the helicopter.

The pilot looked back with alarm.

Konstantin tipped his head forward into his hands. He was going to have to rescue Zariya himself. The rest of the operation would have to wait. He tapped his comm again, directing his thoughts towards Luiz. "*Bad news. No Gate.*"

"*What the fuck?*" came Luiz's angry reply. "*He's just going to leave Zariya to rot in there? It's not a good place, Konstantin.*"

"*We need to find another solution. See if there's anything else Svetlana wants. Luiz—I would never normally ask this of you...*" He trailed off. If what Enigma had said was true, perhaps Luiz could convince the head of the coven that he had something else of value.

Luiz sighed. *"Roger that, boss. For Zariya. Time to turn up the charm."*

"Thank you. Deeply."

Konstantin touched off the comm and leaned back in his seat as the helicopter landed. It was showtime. Time to put on his persona as Anton von Steiner. Rich-as-sin billionaire with zero moral compass. Konstantin wasn't sure how he was going to keep his cool amongst these monsters. He'd dealt with a lot of awful people in his day but those who enslaved other intelligent beings were a special kind of evil.

He stepped down out of the helicopter, and found a thick-set shifter in a black suit hurrying across the grass towards him. "Mister von Steiner," the shifter said. "Follow me."

Konstantin stalked after him until they were out of the noise and wind of the helicopter's rotors.

The shifter turned back to him with a smile. "Welcome to Siren's Quay, where you can find all manner of creatures. My name is Cameron. If you need anything, you just let me know."

"Thank you." Konstantin let his accent come through a bit more thickly than normal. "When is the auction?"

"In just a few hours. It begins at 8 P.M. I'll lead you to your room, where you can rest or work until it's time."

Konstantin followed Cameron through the opulent resort, mentally taking tally of its security, its blind angles and escape routes. They reached a room on the second floor, and Cameron handed him the key. "There's a menu inside. So you can peruse and better make your...selection." The shifter coughed, looking away.

Konstantin just looked at him. He wasn't sure what the man was talking about, but he didn't want to give up that fact.

Cameron looked at the ceiling, refusing to meet his eye. "Anything else you need, sir?" Strange. The shifter was obviously uncomfortable with something here. This menu? But why would fucking room service bother the supe?

"No. This is sufficient."

With a nod, the shifter strode swiftly back down the hallway.

Konstantin entered his room and was greeted by a wall of floor-to-ceiling windows revealing a stunning vista of turquoise water. He'd never been much of a beachgoer, preferring to vacation in more rugged locales, but it was undoubtedly a lovely place.

He walked across the room and loosened his tie. His eyes fell on an elaborate parchment folder on the coffee table. The menu. He *was* a little hungry. He should probably eat something. Who knew how the rest of the day would go down?

He picked it up and flipped it open to the middle page.

Anger exploded through him like a nuclear blast, annihilating all rational thought. For staring up at him, from the pages of this folder, was a picture of Zariya.

12

We sat in a quiet row, perfumed and coifed, polished and preened. Under threat of magical electrocution, I'd been forced into an elaborate bra and panties of glittering gold. Topped with chandelier jewelry of gold and emerald, gold stilettos, and a green snakeskin robe, I would have felt like an absolute stunner if I'd put this on for someone of my own volition.

As it was, I felt vulnerable—and exposed. And frankly freaked the fuck out.

Not that I'd let them see that.

I'd be fierce to the end.

From whispering with the other supes, I'd gathered that the "auction" would be a sort of twisted Victoria's Secret fashion show where worthless pieces of shit would bid on us while we pranced around like peacocks. It was less than fifteen minutes to showtime.

And as much as I desperately longed to hear Kiki's voice in my head or see the team bust through the door with guns blazing, I didn't know the situation outside. I needed to prepare myself in case they weren't in a position to rescue me.

So I'd come up with a plan.

My plan was simple.

Step one. Bide my time and go along with whatever stupid bull-shit they wanted me to do.

Step two. Get bought.

Step three. Once alone with my new "owner," bite the shit out of him and stop his heart.

Step four. Seize the remote control device that controlled my collar, remove it, and go seriously scorched earth on these mother-fuckers.

It was not a foolproof plan. But it was all I had.

Rheanan sat next to me, her dewy skin dusted with powder that shimmered in iridescent waves. "It'll be okay."

"You never told me what you did to end up here," I said. I still desperately wanted to tell her that we'd come here looking for her—that I'd come here to rescue her. (That had gone a bit sideways). But I didn't want to risk compromising myself if they forced her to talk.

"These witches work for the same boss as this other gang, called the Collectors. I started dating a new guy. He seemed so great...but he turned out to be a total psychopath. When I tried to break things off, he had his Collector friends scoop me up."

I wrinkled my nose. "God, like the dating world isn't enough of a minefield. That's awful."

"My only regret is that I won't be able to stop him from catfishing some other poor unsuspecting woman."

"That's your only regret?" I raised an eyebrow.

She let out a little laugh. "Okay, yeah, I also regret not slicing off his favorite part and feeding it to the neighborhood chimera."

I grinned. "There you go. I think in another world, we would have been great friends."

A sad smile flitted across Rheanan's lovely features. "I'll take being new friends in this one." She reached out and threaded her fingers through my own with a squeeze.

A lump grew in my throat, and I squeezed her fingers back. Mentally, I amended my plan to add a step five. Rescue every one of these prisoners and help them find their way home.

～

LUIZ TURNED TO FACE DAEVIN, whose red-skinned face was uncharacteristically serious.

"What the hell are we going to do?" Daevin asked. "You heard Svetlana. They'll only go for the Gate."

Luiz chewed his lip. They stood in the hallway outside Svetlana's office. There were likely magical listening and recording devices throughout this school.

Cyriaque either didn't understand the gravity of the situation Zariya faced inside that resort, or he didn't care. Either way, he didn't deserve to be director if he wouldn't move Heaven and Earth to protect his operators. If Cyriaque wouldn't play ball, they needed to go around him. Besides, they couldn't leave those other helpless supes inside that place. It was abhorrent and wrong. It went against everything they stood for at Veil Force. They needed a battle witch.

Luiz tapped his comm and directed his thoughts towards Daevin. *"Cyriaque won't give us the Gate. So we take it."*

Daevin raised one eyebrow, but then nodded. *"Damn the consequences. Right is right."*

"Exactly."

"How do you propose getting back to HQ without being detected?"

"We can't. We would need Enigma, and Cyriaque won't approve that. We need a man on the inside. Or a woman."

Daevin's other eyebrow rose to meet the first. *"You have someone in mind?"*

Luiz put his hand on his hip, letting his head hang for a moment. Cyriaque would have his eye on Kiki or Signe, but there *was* one other person whom he thought he could trust with this. Not that he wanted to involve her. *"Alviya."*

"The valkyrie? On Aquila Team? I didn't know you two were—" Daevin's eyes went wide and he let out a chortle. *"Are you serious? You and the valkyrie?"*

Luiz rubbed his forehead. Even sharing this info went against his strict no-kiss-and-tell policy. "*Just one time, after the Christmas party last year, we were both way too drunk…*"

"*Isn't she dating Basirou? You dog—*"

"*They weren't exclusive yet.*" Luiz held up his hands. "*I don't do cheating. Neither does she. She's a good person. I trust her with his. She's Zariya's friend too. She'll do it for her.*"

Daevin crossed his arms before him and grinned. "*What other delectable Veil Force fruits have you tasted?*"

Luiz rolled his eyes. "*None you'll hear about, creeper.*" He felt a weight in his gut from conversations like these. People expected something from him—the carefree incubus, sowing his seed far and wide. It was easier to just be that male than to explain that after a few hundred years, the whole "no strings attached" thing had started to wear seriously thin. That he wanted connection. Intimacy. Something more. But the guys would tease him to no end about going soft.

Luiz pulled up Alviya's number on his list of contacts. They were always friendly and polite to each other. But there was something about a shared secret that made it easier to ask for another one.

"Hello?" came a breathy voice on the other end. "Luiz?" Alviya was undeniably lovely. Had been a dream in the sack, too. But she and Bas seemed good. He would never want to upset that.

"Do you have a minute to talk privately?"

"Yeah, I'm in a good place."

"Are you at base?"

"Sure, why?"

"I need a favor…"

❧

KONSTANTIN SAT ON A CUSHY COUCH, drumming his fingers against his leg. The room was large and dimly lit. White drapes hung on either side of him, separating him from the other attendees, who appeared to be arrayed in a semi-circle around a raised stage.

When Konstantin had been a young human, before he'd been turned, he'd thought little about the practice of slavery. It had been a fixture—and in those days, no one's life had seemed to belong to them. By joining the army, he had signed himself up for a sort of indentured servitude, after all.

And then he'd been turned, and he'd seen how free he'd truly been. Authentic vampires exercised near absolute power over their Deriveds in the first decade after they were turned. The older he'd gotten, and the farther away from his Maker he'd run, the more autonomy he'd regained. But those early years had been a nightmare branded deeply into the fabric of his soul. He'd never be the same.

He wouldn't let that happen to Zariya.

The auction catalogue he'd been given proved that she was alive and healthy, and that was the most important thing. But he wouldn't let her stay in chains one moment longer than necessary. No mission was worth that, no job or rescue or even selfless deed. Nothing was worth that.

A tall, blonde woman strode onto the stage before them, wearing a satiny black pantsuit—the sleek jacket buttoned only over her generous cleavage. She was stunning—but in that kind of manufactured way. Was there anything truly real about her? "My name is Naeve," the woman said. "And welcome to Siren's Quay. We have some delectable offerings for you tonight, and I'm sure each and every one of you will find something extraordinary." She smiled wide, revealing blindingly white teeth. The woman made his skin crawl. There was an aura of magic about her—but of wrongness. Like she lacked a soul. This must have been one of the witches running the coven here, if not *the* witch. Had it been her wards that had pulled Zariya into this mess?

"To cover the mechanics quickly, you will each find your bid card on your table, along with wiring instructions for our bank account, in the event you make a purchase tonight. Bidding is in increments of $50,000. Good luck!"

Konstantin picked up his paddle, and the routing instructions. That would be helpful in tracing these assholes' accounts, maybe all the way back to the Authority. Freezing those funds would be satisfying as fuck.

The blonde witch had disappeared back behind the curtain, and a little, red-haired man in a tux came out and perched on a stool at the side of the stage. He held a microphone in one hand. He was a leprechaun, and apparently, the auctioneer.

A swell of music came on and the curtain parted, revealing the first auction item.

The blood froze in Konstantin's veins. It was Zariya.

13

———

On some level, Konstantin had known he would see her. He'd thought he had prepared himself. Now he understood how wrong he'd been.

She was dressed like Shahrazad on her wedding night, like a desert princess from some story. Gold and emeralds, her supple skin draped in jewels and lace. But he couldn't even think about how stunning she looked—and she did look stunning—for all he could think was how these monsters didn't deserve to see her like this.

He wanted to rip out their eyes for even looking at her.

Konstantin found himself standing, the paper with the wiring instructions clutched in a tiny ball in his fist. He wanted to explode in a fury of vengeance, to tear limb from limb. But that wasn't what Zariya needed right now. She needed him calm. And fucking bidding.

He sat down and raised his paddle. The Leprechaun pointed to him. "We have $50,000 from bidder number eight."

The bidding began in earnest.

Zariya walked farther onto the stage and stood, her slitted eyes gazing out into the distance. Not exactly strutting, but not cowering, either.

His respect for her swelled even greater. Even in this terrible situation, she stood tall and proud. Not knowing the future, not knowing if anyone was coming for her. He could see it in the set of her slim shoulders, the resolute tilt of her chin above a strange black necklace that encircled her throat. She would not be cowed.

Look at me. He tried to send the thought to Zariya, borne on some whispered psychic wave. *I'm here. I'm coming for you.* But the bright lights illuminating the stage no doubt blinded her from seeing any of the bidders. She kept her eyes fixed in the distance. As if envisioning her future vengeance. He would help her seize it.

The bidding was up to near a million dollars now, and it was narrowed down to just him and another bidder. Number five. The man didn't seem to be slowing down.

Konstantin scowled, peering around the curtain and trying to get a look at him. It was impossible to see with the lights as they were.

This needed to end. Now. Konstantin held up his paddle again. "A million!" he shouted.

The Leprechaun blanched. "We have one million—"

Konstantin was already in motion, moving with the lightning quick speed of a six-hundred-year-old vampire. He was behind bidder number five in an eye blink, the human's neck between his hands as he crouched low, out of the line of sight. "You bid again, I snap your neck like a twig."

The man's body went as stiff as a board beneath him.

The leprechaun peered their way. "Bidder number five? Do I hear one million fifty?"

Konstantin's hands tightened.

"No." The man voiced a simple mangled word.

Konstantin eased his grip slightly.

"Our first item is *sold* to bidder number eight, for one million dollars. All bidders, your items will be brought to your rooms after the auction is complete."

Konstantin disappeared from behind bidder number five, heading out the door. If he had to watch another second of this, he might explode. He needed some air.

Konstantin found his way to the roof of the resort, looking over the quiet sea. He breathed in the humid warm air, pulling it into his lungs in shuddering gulps. Too close. It had been too close for Zariya. What if he hadn't been here, what if he couldn't buy her for some reason? He couldn't keep sending her into danger like this. It messed with his head, left him ragged and worn.

He cared too deeply about her to risk her like that.

He gripped the railing tightly as the realization sent a wave of heat through his body. It wasn't just attraction to Zariya. It wasn't just his vampire male ego wanting something to protect and call his own. He cared for her. Deeply.

Seeing her in his apartment in a T-shirt and jeans, coffees in hand... Something about that moment had resonated deep in his soul. He'd resigned himself to being alone for so many years, and the thought of change was terrifying. But the thought of not giving voice to what he was feeling... That was scarier still.

A crackle sounded in his mind as a voice flickered and cleared. "*Bauer?*" He recognized Luiz's voice.

Konstantin tapped his comm. "*Report.*" They hadn't expected comms to work through the protective wards. But maybe the wards only protected the lower levels.

Galu's voice chimed in. "*Man, is it good to hear you, boss.*"

"*Is she okay?*" Rex asked.

"*She's okay,*" Konstantin said. "*I should able to talk to her soon. I just...bought her.*"

Silence.

"*And you didn't even get a me fucking Christmas present,*" Daevin drawled.

Konstantin let out a bark of laughter as some of the tension uncoiled from his body. His team was okay. They were in contact. Everything would be all right. "*Where are we on the witches?*"

"*Since the director said no on the Chinvat Gate,* Luiz said, "*we decided to help ourselves to it.*"

"*Steal it from the evidence lockup?*" Konstantin asked.

"*Desperate times, boss. But—*"

"*Let me guess. It was already gone.*"

"*How did you know that?*"

"*Educated guess,*" Konstantin replied. Damn, the Gate had already been stolen? He prayed that the camera he'd hidden had caught the thief red-handed. "*So where does that leave us with Svetlana?*"

"*With jack shit.*"

"*We're about to go back in there. Luiz's sexy body is about the only bargaining chip we've got left,*" Daevin said.

Konstantin shook his head. "*I don't expect you to do that, Luiz. Not if you're not comfortable. I'm done putting my team in positions that compromise their integrity.*"

"*Maybe it won't come to that.*" Luiz's voice was thick.

"*Zariya and I will be together soon. We should be able to escape,*" Konstantin pointed out.

"*But what about the other prisoners?*" Luiz asked. "*There are others in there, right?*"

"*Yes,*" Konstantin admitted, thinking back to the catalogue he'd flipped through. "*About ten supes, two witches. They're being auctioned off as we speak.*"

"*We can't just abandon them. I'll figure something out.*"

I SAT NUMBLY backstage as the other collared supes were paraded outside for their turns before the bidders.

My emotions refused to leave me be. Should I be glad that some asshat was willing to pay a million bucks for me? I didn't know. It kind of made me sad that there was a place where the value of a person could be captured in dollars and cents.

Strangely enough, it made me think of Dad. He'd been a tough taskmaster, but even when I'd failed to live up to his near impossible standards, he'd never made me feel small. He'd made sure I'd known my worth. No matter what, I was always his daughter, and he'd loved me.

His love had been like a warm, protective blanket. Would I ever find that again? Something that unconditional?

I shook my head. I should be worrying about how the hell I was going to bite and poison the dick who'd bought me, not indulging in existential ennui. But try as I might, I couldn't seem to tame my thoughts. They raged as they pleased.

Rheanan forced a smile as she came back through the curtain, shimmering like a rainbow. The leprechaun auctioneer followed her back. The auction was over. She gave me a quick hug. "Good luck to you," she whispered.

I clung to her. I couldn't help myself; I found myself promising, "Someday soon, I'll come for you."

She lay a soft hand on my cheek. "That'd be nice." It was clear she didn't believe a word I said.

Well, I would be happy to prove her wrong.

"Come!" Our horde of witch mistresses dispersed among us. I glared at the blonde who wore the little remote that controlled my collar. She handed me my robe, and I slipped into it gratefully. "Come on." She nodded.

I followed her through the quiet, marble hallways of the resort, up to the second floor. To the door of the man who had purchased me.

My stomach clenched and unclenched, and a flush of cold sent prickles across my body. It was go time. Once inside, I couldn't give him time to gain the upper hand and figure out the collar. I needed to attack.

"Wait here." The witch tapped the remote control to remind me of what would happen if I didn't obey.

I just nodded, the memory of that shock of magical current making my knees weak.

The witch knocked on the door and it opened. She stepped inside for a moment and I heard a low, male voice speaking to her.

I looked down the corridor, gauging if I could make a run for it. There was no way I'd get anywhere. She'd zap me before I was to the elevator bay. My best chance was incapacitating my purchaser, getting the remote, and making a stealthier getaway. Somewhere in that jungle, the rest of my team waited. I desperately wanted to get to them.

The witch reappeared and gestured for me to go in. The device was off her wrist; she must have transferred it to my purchaser.

My heart sank. If he understood how to use the device, he'd be waiting for me to make a move. I might need to bide my time and bite when he wasn't expecting rather than attacking outright.

It's okay. The plan could still work.

"Go." The witch jerked her head towards the door.

So, mouth dry, palms sweaty, a lump the size of Texas stuck in my throat, I walked through the door.

14

———

Luiz normally enjoyed negotiating, especially when sexual chemistry sparked between him and his opponent. But going back into Svetlana's office...that he was dreading like a fucking root canal.

"Are you good?" Daevin cocked his head to look at him. "You look like you swallowed something rotten."

"I'll be fine." Luiz put his hands on his hips and squeezed his eyes closed. He could do this. He would do this—for Zariya.

"The Gate was only an opening offer." Daevin clapped him on the shoulder. "We'll find something else she wants."

Luiz looked up sharply.

"Other than you. I can tell this is rattling you, mate. But you gotta nut up and head in there. No one's telling you to do anything you don't want to do."

Luiz's skin felt hot, and there was a tightness in his chest he couldn't quite break, even with the deepest breath. "I can't let Zariya and the other prisoners down. If this meant the difference between her life and death, I'd never be able to forgive myself."

"We're fucking Phantoms. When we don't like our options, we find a new option."

Isobel opened the door to Svetlana's office and peered out at them. "Svetlana has another meeting. Your window is closing rapidly."

"We're ready," Luiz said.

Isobel pointed at him and a flicker of distaste crossed her lovely features. "She says just you."

Daevin gave Luiz's shoulder a squeeze.

Luiz sucked in a breath and walked back into Svetlana's office. The door closed ominously behind him. Did it have to be so fucking hot in here? He felt like he couldn't breathe. He looked down and found his hands were shaking. He quickly shoved them behind his back, settling into what he hoped looked like a relaxed stance.

Svetlana turned from where she had been standing, looking out the window. "Well? I see you have not brought me a Chinvat Gate. Am I to understand our deal is off?"

Luiz ground his teeth. "The Gate is too important to our operation. I couldn't get it for you. But there are plenty of other powerful items in Veil Force's possession that we could pay in trade for your assistance. There must be something else you want."

Svetlana came around the desk and leaned back against it, openly admiring him. Her gaze raked from the top of his head to his toes, sending a shudder of wrongness through him. The room swam around him for a moment before he pulled his focus back.

Was this how women felt when they were ogled by some gross guy at a bar or on the street? Suddenly, he wanted to apologize to the whole female gender on behalf of men everywhere.

"Incubi and succubi are unique creatures with remarkable physiology," she said softly. Her steely eyes never left him. "You pull power and vitality from your partners. You take their life force energy. Do you know where it comes from?"

Luiz wanted to roll his eyes. He didn't need an Incubus 101 lesson from this witch. But he didn't want to offend her. "Of course. The sacral chakra, a human's energy center that contains their creative and sexual energy."

"Very good." Her eyes flicked down to his groin and even the psychic contact was like jumping into a cold lake. Little Luiz wanted to run for the hills. This witch, though she wasn't physically unattractive, was abhorrent to him. He couldn't do this. He couldn't.

"Did you know that witches also draw our power through the sacral chakra? Our magic comes from this creative well, drawn from the power of the universe itself."

Luiz blinked in surprise. "I didn't know that. Witches keep such information closely guarded."

"We do." She clucked her tongue. "But I trust you can keep our little secret, as it may be of interest to you."

"Why would it be of interest to me?" He couldn't help but take the bait.

She pushed off the desk and came to stand before him. She was almost as tall as him, and so she only had to look up slightly. He looked into the distance, his eyes on the window. If he looked down at her, it could be seen as an invitation. "When an incubus couples with a witch, a certain peculiar alchemy happens. Instead of draining the witch's life force, the witch's connection to her innate magic is opened farther. And she grows stronger."

The fuck? Luiz did look down then. "You're shitting me."

Her self-satisfied smirk rattled him. Was it truly possible this witch knew something he didn't about his own people? Was she telling the truth?

"I never . . . *shit* anyone. I am Svetlana Morikova, High Priestess of the Crescent Moon Coven, and my word is my bond. This is why witches and incubi make such an excellent match. And why I am willing to trade the assistance of one of my battle witches for a night with you."

His saliva turned to chalk in his mouth.

Luiz stepped to the side and rested his hands on the back of the chair that flanked her desk. He was suddenly afraid his knees would go out. Prickles of hot and cold rippled across his skin. What the fuck was happening? He felt like he was going to pass out.

What was wrong with him? Had Svetlana poisoned him?

Or was he having a fucking panic attack?

He had to do this.

He couldn't do this.

Memories flooded into his mind with the force of a tidal wave, memories he'd spent years burying. The faces and hot breath of men, women, supes—a parade of faces and pawing touches... He squeezed his eyes shut against the onslaught, sucking in short breaths. He'd sworn he'd never go back there. Never be that version of himself again. Never let anyone else use him like that. Never let himself be used.

I'm sorry, Zariya.

Maybe he was dooming her by refusing. But he'd be certain to doom himself if he agreed.

As soon as the decision was made, the heat left his body, the vise grip around his lungs released.

Luiz looked up, meeting Svetlana's predatory gaze. "I am not for sale," he growled.

"But perhaps...for rent?"

He straightened. "No. Never. There must be something else Veil Force can give you."

Svetlana frowned. The expression twisted her face into something frightening. "Am I so distasteful that you cannot stomach a night with me?"

"No, that's not it." Luiz held up his hands. "It's me. It's personal. I have a history. I swore—"

She scoffed, striding forward, forcing Luiz to step back towards the door. "An incubus with principles? It's as perverse as a baby with two heads."

A flood of anger filled him. "And I suppose a witch with basic empathy would be too much to expect."

She scoffed. "I did not claw my way to my position as the most powerful battle witch on the Goddess's green Earth by indulging in weak emotions like empathy. Now get out, and take your demon pet with you."

"With pleasure," Luiz snapped as he yanked the door open. He strode out, past where Daevin and Isobel stood, wide-eyed.

"Follow them, Isobel. If they are not off my property within two minutes, turn them into frogs," Svetlana snapped.

Daevin and Isobel jogged to catch up with Luiz as he strode through the hallway like a bat out of hell. "So...how'd it go?" Daevin asked.

"How the fuck do you think it went?" Luiz shot back. Already, he was cooling off. He shouldn't have lost his temper with Svetlana. Even if she didn't help them, Veil Force didn't want the Crescent Moon Coven as an enemy.

"We'll find another way to help Zariya and the rest of the prisoners," Daevin said. "We always do."

They were nearing the gate, and Luiz turned to Isobel. He found himself reluctant to leave. Surely, he'd never see her again. "I behaved poorly back there. I'd like to send Svetlana something in apology. Do you have any ideas?"

Isobel blinked. "You want to apologize?"

"We don't need her as an enemy."

"I don't get it. Why didn't you just do what she asked?"

Luiz sighed. "I made a promise to myself I'd never...be with anyone if there wasn't enthusiastic consent from both parties."

Isobel shook her head in amazement. "What kind of incubus are you? You say *no* to sex and then you want to apologize for not indulging someone's perverse demands?"

Daevin put an arm around Luiz's shoulders and grinned. "We raise 'em right at Veil Force."

Luiz scowled and tapped his comm. He couldn't see Enigma in the field beyond the gate. "*Kiki, can you tell Enigma to get his skinny ass out here to pick us up?*"

Pause.

"*He says three minutes.*"

He looked up to find Isobel still examining him. She was biting her lip. "How many supes are being held at this facility?"

"Besides our teammate? Maybe ten. Konstantin said there are two humans there, too. Witches."

"Wait, what?" Isobel recoiled. "They're holding witches?"

"Holding, selling into slavery," Daevin said. "That's kinda the whole operation."

"And why we're trying to stop it."

"Fuck." Isobel swore under her breath. "Damn it. Okay, I'm coming with you."

"What do you mean?" Luiz didn't dare hope.

"I'll help you...infiltrate or whatever the hell you boys do. I'll help free your teammate. And the other supes."

"You will?" Luiz and Daevin exchanged an amazed look.

"Yes, it's beyond fucked-up they're doing it to supes, but I can't stand by and let my own brethren be sold like cattle."

With a whoop, Luiz seized Isobel around the waist in a bear hug and spun her around. Then, realizing what he was doing, he quickly set her back down on the snow-packed ground. "Er, sorry."

Isobel gave herself a little shake, but she didn't seem angry. "That was...unexpected."

Daevin frowned. "Won't Svetlana be, you know—"

"Pissed as fuck that I'm helping you against her orders?" Isobel filled in.

"Right."

Isobel grinned, her dark eyes sparkling. "I find it's better to ask forgiveness than permission."

Luiz laughed. "Isobel, we're all going to get along great."

15

———————

I've never been the fainting type, but when I saw the face of the highest bidder, my knees went out.

He was there in a blink, catching me, his arms tight around my waist.

Konstantin.

It was Konstantin.

He was here. He had come for me.

I started to bawl. I fisted my hands in his suit jacket and buried my face against his chest. I clung to him like a lifeline. Because that was what he was.

This horrible nightmare was over. If Konstantin was here, I was safe.

"Hush," he murmured into my hair. "It's all right now." He wrapped his arms around me and rocked me gently as I cried. Asking no questions. Needing nothing from me, just being everything I needed in that moment.

His scent of starfall and winter snow settled over me like a balm. The tears started to slow. I took a shuddering breath and pushed myself back just a touch, just enough to wipe my eyes and my nose.

I didn't want to let him go. But I needed to eventually. So regretfully, with a hiccupping sniff, I leaned back a touch. "How'd you get in here?"

"Kiki." He gave me a wry grin and it tugged on my heart like a fish on a line.

"Are the other guys here?"

"Not yet. Soon."

"I don't understand." I looked down and found that he was stroking my hair back with a gentle motion. Like he didn't want to let me go, either.

"Luiz and Daevin have been working to secure the aid of a battle witch so we can defeat the Black Moon Coven. But we couldn't leave you in here alone, not even knowing if you'd found a cure to the aging spell. So Kiki set me up with a fake identity as a buyer."

I made a mental note to get Kiki a *really* good birthday present this year. "But how'd you fool them into thinking you bought me?"

He looked down. With these insane platform heels on, we were almost the same height. I was close enough to take in every detail of him—the porcelain stretch of his skin, the fine feathering of his eyelashes, the angles of his brow bones, his jaw.

He met my gaze, and I felt frozen to the spot by those glacial blue eyes. Frozen—and yet melting too. One look from him could steal the breath from me. "We didn't *fool* them." Konstantin cleared his throat. "I really bought you."

"What?" I recoiled a touch.

"It's bullshit, of course. I mean, you're free. I free you."

"The high bid was a million dollars," I said incredulously.

He looked down again with a rueful smile. "I have...a lot of money. Compound interest really works in your favor over an immortal lifespan."

"You just shelled out a million dollars to make sure I was okay?"

"Of course. I would do anything to secure the safety of my team."

Disappointment flooded me. "Right. Your team. Of course." I stepped back, heading for the bed. I needed to sit the fuck down. The adrenaline was draining from me, leaving me feeling woozy and weak.

"Wait." He caught my hand, and I turned back. Konstantin closed his eyes and inhaled a deep breath. "I didn't mean that. I mean, I did. I would do anything for my team. But that's not why I'm here." When we locked eyes again, there was a steely resolve there. A heat I didn't dare hope I recognized.

"What do you mean?"

"The truth is I was desperate with worry. I haven't been able to think about anything else since you crossed those wards. Fuck, I haven't been able to think about anything other than you since you joined Phoenix Team." His words were spilling out faster and faster and it was all I could do to keep my face neutral when a fucking Fourth of July parade's worth of happy fireworks were going off inside of me.

"I haven't felt like this about anyone for a long, long time. I tried to shove it aside because I'm your commander, and it will totally mess with the team dynamic, and it's unprofessional, and you're Vizol's daughter—" He trailed off, looking at the ceiling with a strangled laugh. "But I don't think I can fight it anymore."

My body trilled with energy—it coursed through our hands, which were still clasped. It wasn't nearly enough closeness. I needed every bit of him pressed against every part of me. I wanted to drown in Konstantin Bauer. Forget this nightmare, forget the Collectors and Dad and the Authority. Just live in these feelings. Because hearing those words was the best, most exquisite, toe-curling, soul-shimmering feeling I'd ever experienced. And he hadn't even kissed me yet. But he was waiting for an answer. Searching my face for a clue— a tell.

"Then don't," I said.

"What?" Konstantin's voice was hoarse.

"You said you can't fight it anymore." I pulled him towards me. "So don't."

Our lips crashed together with the force of centuries. This kiss was different than the kiss we'd shared in the hot springs—that had been a question—and this kiss was the answer. Every answer to every question I'd ever asked.

For this was all I needed. He was all I needed. I could live and breathe, sleep and die in the magic of Konstantin's kiss.

His lips were demanding and dominant and *holy hell*, he was a good kisser. My body melted against his, yielding and ready and demanding its own kind of satisfaction.

He broke off for a moment as we both gasped for air, our foreheads pressed together. He took in a deep breath through his nose and let out a rumbling growl. "You smell—" He seized me and half-jumped, half-flew onto the bed, moving with such speed that I let out a startled yelp as his weight settled on top of me.

Oh God, I'd known Konstantin was going to be a good lover, but even my over-active imagination could not have come up with this.

A moment of self-doubt snaked through me and my body stiffened. Konstantin had enjoyed centuries of lovers—he was like one hundred times more experienced than me. I'd had a few half-decent flings, but nowhere near the level of regular practice that a man like Konstantin must have had. I mean, my partners had always seemed satisfied, but anything involving a naked chick probably would have done the job for those men.

Konstantin pulled back, caressing one hand from my forehead to my neck, following the path of my golden scales. "Where'd you go?"

I shook my head and seized his face, angling up to kiss him again. "Nowhere."

He pulled back farther. "Zariya—" He let out a sigh. "Shit. I'm a fucking idiot."

This was going sideways. "What? No, you're not."

He climbed off me and sat on the bed next to me.

I did my best not to let my expression show how much I mourned his absence.

"This is not the time or place to be doing this. You've just been through an incredibly traumatic experience that must have left you feeling extremely vulnerable, and here I am like a walking cock just taking advantage of you."

I let out a little snort of laughter at the image. I pressed my hand to his chest and trailed it up around the back of his neck. I couldn't believe I got to touch him. I'd wanted to touch him from the first moment I'd seen him. And now I could. Explore every inch of him. Every bulging muscle and lean plane of his body. I didn't want this to end. "It's fine," I assured him. "You bought me, you should get your money's worth." I froze as I realized what I was saying. "Okay, yeah, that's fucking weird."

He chuckled. "Not how I want to remember this moment." He reached out and fingered the collar around my neck. "Not with this on you."

I scooted up against the head of the bed. "I'm just afraid..."

He cocked his head.

I shut my eyes. It sounded stupid.

"Hey." Konstantin seized my chin gently and turned me to look at him. "Tell me."

I didn't like the waver in my voice. "We still have to get out of here. I'm just afraid that if we don't do this now, we may never get to."

He nodded. "I'm not going to tell you we're out of danger. Because we're not. But Galu and Rex are out there in that forest. Luiz and Daevin are securing us allies as we speak. I'm here now, by your side. I didn't live six hundred years through countless wars just to get popped by some witch bitches now."

I snorted.

"Besides, I haven't even told you our secret weapon."

"Kiki?"

Konstantin rolled his eyes. He took his forefinger and tapped me on the nose. "You, Zariya Chanji. You are the fiercest, bravest, most beautiful warrior I have ever known. Our enemies will quake before you."

A lump grew in my throat. I hadn't felt like that Zariya in the last twenty-four hours. I'd felt small and afraid. But somehow, with Konstantin here to remind me, I felt my snake rising up inside me. My power. My naga heritage. I would not be chained or stopped or —"Wait, did you just boop my nose?"

Konstantin burst out laughing.

I couldn't help it. I started to laugh too.

When his laughter died down, Konstantin put a hand on my knee. "You know, there's no better incentive for me to get you out of this place and home safely." His hand slowly slid upward. "I'm going to worship every inch of this body. I'm going to make you feel things you've never felt before." Heat pooled in my core at his words—at his hand. Pretty sure his hand on my thigh was all it took to meet that criteria.

"I'm going to—" he started.

A knock sounded on the door.

Konstantin and I looked at each other in alarm.

Another knock. More insistent.

"Stay here," Konstantin whispered. He pressed a quick kiss to my lips and crossed to the door. The Konstantin I knew was gone in a second, leaving in its place an arrogant, imperious vampire with a look like thunder on his face. I didn't envy whoever was on the other side of that door.

He yanked the door open. "We're a little busy in here—"

My stomach seized as I saw who was on the other side of that door. Naeve, the Black Moon Coven high priestess. And from the look on her face, this wasn't a social call.

16

Naeve stalked into their room like a pageant queen. Behind her trailed two witches and a man Konstantin recognized. It was the human bidder he'd grappled with in the several-thousand-dollar suit. He looked triumphant. Which didn't bode well for Konstantin and Zariya.

But for the time being, Konstantin needed to bluff like the devil himself. "What are you doing interfering with my private time with my purchase?" Konstantin barked. "Is this the kind of operation you witches are running? When I pay over a million dollars to—"

Naeve held up a hand, made a strange chopping motion, and Konstantin's voice...stopped. One minute, he was speaking and the next, his voice was gone.

His hands flew to his neck as he glared at Naeve.

"Let me just stop you right there, Mr. von Steiner. Or should I call you 'Mr. Bauer'?" She raised an eyebrow.

Well, fuck. His cover was blown.

"Mr. Kensington here has filed a complaint. Apparently, he was primed to purchase this lovely specimen when you physically assaulted him, preventing his next bid. I assure you, that's not how we do things here."

An explosion of motion drew his eye. But it was over as soon as it began—Zariya was frozen in mid-stride as Naeve held up her other hand. She'd been going for the remote control tied to her collar, which he'd left on the side table. Damn it. They should have taken that thing off when they'd had the chance rather than necking like a pair of teenagers.

"Ah, ah, ah," Naeve chided. "Your new owner will want that on. He has some fascinating research underway in need of a specimen just like you. I'm sure he'll make you comfortable. As long as you live, that is."

Konstantin made the connection. The PharMagus helicopter parked outside. The human was a pharmaceutical billionaire named Parker Kensington. He made supe- and magic-derived products and medicines. That meant he wanted to use Zariya as some sort of...lab rat?

Red colored his vision. No fucking way. He gauged the distance between himself, Naeve, and the billionaire. Naeve probably had some sort of magical enchantment, but he could rip the human's head off. That was the least he could do in revenge for what the man would have done to Zariya. And had no doubt done to countless other supes.

"Now now, Mr. Bauer." Naeve strode across the room and seized the remote device. "You move a muscle and your little friend here suffers worse agony than you could ever imagine."

Konstantin's muscles bunched as he evaluated the situation—just a split second. But Naeve was already wrapping him in magical bonds like those that held Zariya.

Bitch!

He struggled against them, roaring his fury. But nothing came out. She'd neutralized him in seconds. Her magic was just too powerful.

Naeve tossed the remote to Kensington and released Zariya from her frozen position. She stumbled to one knee and then righted herself.

"Take your naga prize, Mr. Kensington. I have business with Mr. Bauer here."

"Come on." Kensington jerked his head towards the door, buckling the remote on his tanned wrist. "Don't make this harder on yourself."

Zariya looked desperately back at Konstantin as Kensington towed her by an elbow out the door.

Zariya! He tried to shout. Tried to tell her to fight. But how could she when he was so completely hamstrung himself?

The door clicked shut and he turned the weight of his fury on Naeve. How dare she put Zariya at risk? How dare she think she had the right to act like a god, buying and selling supes and humans like animals? She'd caught him unawares, but he was not without resources and power. He would find a way out of this.

"Save your righteous fury, Konstantin." Neave chuckled. "There's someone who'd like to speak to you."

She motioned to one of the witches, a silver-haired woman, who pulled a laptop out of a briefcase. She set it on the desk, powering it up. The other witch, a petite dark-haired woman covered in tattoos, stationed herself in the corner, looking out the window.

Konstantin couldn't help the curiosity that filled him, blunting his anger. What was this? Some game?

Naeve tapped on the keyboard with her long fingernails, pulling up a video chat that showed nothing but a dark room.

She set down a chair before the desk. "Sit."

He felt the bonds release from around him. But Konstantin didn't move.

She huffed and flicked a hand. His legs jerked forward, like he was a cursed puppet on a string. His ass *thunked* into the chair and the bonds wrapped tightly around him again, holding him in place.

He glared at Naeve, but she just rolled her eyes and gestured to the screen. "Talk." Then she chuckled, a low purr. "Oh, wait. You can't."

His voice returned, and he turned every ounce of venom on

Naeve. "When I get free, I will rip your throat out and gorge myself on your blood, down to the very last drop—"

"Konstantin, haven't I warned you about letting your anger control you?" A voice came through the computer and Konstantin froze.

No. It couldn't be.

He couldn't breathe as he craned his head as far as the bonds allowed and squinted to make out the figure in the dark. The figure leaned forward slightly, and an outline of features came into view.

His stomach dropped into his feet.

There was no mistaking those red eyes.

It was his Maker.

AFTER THE ICE cold of Russia, the heat of the jungle hit Luiz like a slap in the face.

Daevin let out a sigh of relief, his tail uncoiling.

Isobel looked around the dark forest with a frown on her face.

A rustle sounded in the trees to their left and her wand went up in an eyeblink.

"Wait!" Luiz held up a hand.

And thankfully, she did, for it was Galu and Rex who ducked through the foliage into the clearing. Galu put his hands on his hips. "About fucking time. I worried I was going to die of boredom by the time we got this op rolling."

Luiz grinned and strode forward, clapping hands with Galu. God, it was good to be back with the team. Now they just needed to reunite with Konstantin and Zariya. He turned back. "Galu, Rex, this is Isobel, of the Crescent Moon Coven. She's agreed to help us here."

"Nice to meet you, Isobel." Galu shook her hand. "Very grateful for your assistance."

Rex followed suit and gave Isobel a respectful nod of his jackal head. "It's an honor to work with someone of your caliber."

Isobel's white teeth gleamed in the darkness. So flattery worked on this one. Good to know.

They fell into a line and moved through the night until they reached the perimeter of the forest, where the foliage faded away to landscaping and ornamental grass.

They crouched down in a row, surveying the target.

"There are wards surrounding the place. Nasty ones," Luiz said.

"I can see them," Isobel said. "They're the Black Moon High Priestess's work. Naeve Blackthorn. I can bring them down, or I can get us through. I recommend the latter; she'd know the second I dismantled them, and we'd lose our element of surprise."

"So you can get us through without triggering them?"

"Yes. If I disguise our magical signatures to mirror the wards, we won't trigger it. It will think we are a part of it."

"Clever," Galu said. "That sounds like complex magic."

"I didn't train under the fiercest witches alive for the last twenty years to chew bubble gum and paint my fucking nails," Isobel said.

Luiz and Daevin exchanged a grin. She was a fiery one.

"So, our next problem will be locating Zariya and Konstantin inside. Rex, do you think you'll be able to smell them?" Galu asked.

"Shouldn't be a problem. I should be able to smell the witch too, now that I've tasted the scent of her magic."

Galu nodded. "Okay, then we have our plan. Get inside. Zariya first, then Konstantin, then we take out this witch. Kill anyone who resists, but arrest anyone who doesn't. Recover the prisoners. Any questions?"

Isobel cleared her throat. "Not a question, but I thought you should all know, my battle magic can be...*unpleasant* to watch."

Luiz raised an eyebrow. "As long as you're pointing it at them, honey, you can unleash all the wrath and pestilence you want."

"Good. And I'm not your honey."

His grin widened. Yes, a fiery one indeed.

17

———

Konstantin blinked at the dark image on the computer screen, as if squinting harder could bring his Maker into focus.

He knew that eternal voice anywhere; it resonated in his blood, his bones. They hadn't spoken in over five centuries. Since he'd fled her clutches and hadn't looked back.

And now she'd found him again.

"Konstantin, my sweet pet," she purred.

He let out a low growl of warning.

"I've let you be these last few centuries, though it pained me greatly that you weren't at my side. But you have forced this confrontation by interfering in my operations."

Logic was piercing through the fog of shock clouding Konstantin's mind. "*Your* operations... Are you the Authority?"

She *tsked*. "I never liked that name. It's far too melodramatic. But it stuck."

Konstantin shook his head. "So you—you ordered the hit on Vizol, even knowing that he was my boss? My friend?"

"Do not flatter yourself that my world revolves around you, dear Konstantin." Her voice hardened. "Vizol Chanji took something precious from me, and he paid the consequences for that mistake. I hardly thought it necessary to restrain my hand due to your relationship to him. Why should I show you deference or loyalty when you've made it crystal clear that you show me none?"

"I've been living my own life. Making the most of the situation you placed me in," Konstantin spat.

"You haven't been living, Konstantin." She leaned forward, and a sliver of pearlescent light illuminated one of her red eyes, framed by long, ebony lashes. "Bowing and scraping to the humans, to supes who are inferior to yourself... What you call 'a life' is a waste of everything I gave you. I can no longer abide you frittering away the gifts of eternal life. I made you a god. It's time to fucking act like one."

Konstantin ground his teeth. "It's *my* life. I live it how I please."

"Not anymore," she snapped. "It's time to come home. I will see you here, standing before me in person, before the next new moon, or I will kill each and every supe on your sorry excuse for a team."

I GLARED sideways at the human who now held the key to my captivity. He was handsome in an obvious way—tall, fit, tan, his auburn hair perfectly cut, his clothes perfectly tailored. It probably cost him millions just to keep up his appearance. It made me want to rip the douchebag's throat out all the more.

He stood back a few feet from me and waggled his wrist, his fingers on the dial, his eyes on me.

The shifter who'd first found me on the island, Cameron, was standing guard by the elevator.

"You," Kensington barked at him. "Escort us to my helicopter. Your job is to ensure she doesn't get near me. Do you have restraints?"

Cameron frowned but reluctantly took a pair of zip-tie restraints out of his pocket.

"Put them on her," Kensington said, as if he had every right in the world to order us around. To own me. Well, I was going to show him the true natural order if it was the last thing I did. Nagas didn't bow to humans, and definitely not piece-of-shit humans like him.

But I couldn't risk making a scene in Naeve's earshot. She'd shown her power back in that room—if I played this wrong, she'd yank open the door and incapacitate me in a second. I needed to bide my time. So I held out my wrists and Cameron put on the restraints. Not that tightly, I might add. His frown hadn't lifted.

"All right." Kensington sneered. "Let's go."

I dragged my feet through the halls of the resort. My mind was swirling. What was going on with Konstantin? What was Naeve doing to him? Was he okay? The memory of his kisses buoyed me, even as it sent a thunderstorm of worry swirling through me. I'd voiced my secret fear, and now it was coming true. Konstantin and I had been ripped apart. What if this world was too shitty a place for happily-ever-afters? Especially for Veil Force Phantoms?

I wished that I had my comm. I wished I hadn't walked through that ward. This was all my fault. If I hadn't bumbled into it, I'd still be with the team, in my gear, with a gun in my hand, ready to kick some ass. I hated being away from them. Cut off. Whatever happened, I couldn't get on that PharMagus helicopter with Parker Kensington. If I left this place, who knew if I'd ever find my team again? If I'd ever see Konstantin again?

We turned the corner, and a rattling noise startled me. It was the flicker of gunfire.

"What was—" Kensington began, and I seized my chance. I whirled and kicked the remote device on his wrist with my stiletto heel. The glass face shattered with a crunch, and Kensington howled in pain. It looked like I'd gotten some of the delicate bones in his wrist, too. I dove behind him, wrapped my bound hands over his head. and seized his neck.

I hissed at Cameron, who had his gun up, pointed at the both of us. "Make one move and I bite him."

Doubt flickered across Cameron's face. And then he lowered his gun and heaved a sigh. "This job is so not what I signed up for. I thought I'd be working security at a private resort, not this shit."

Relief flooded me. So there was at least one decent guy left here. "Do you have another of those zip ties?" I asked.

Cameron fished one out of his pocket.

"Bind him."

"You're going to regret this, you little bitch—" Kensington started.

I hissed and seized his neck in my jaws, just shy of biting. He froze, and Cameron quickly slipped the ties on his wrists.

"Good boy," I said. "If you need me so badly, I'm guessing you don't have a naga for anti-venom yet. And our venom is particularly painful." I unthreaded my arms from around Kensington's neck and shoved him to a seat against the wall.

"Cut these." I held out my hands, and Cameron pulled out a pocket knife and sliced through the zip ties. "Now give me your gun," I instructed. He handed it over, just as obligingly. "You're free to go. There's an empty helicopter you could take." I grinned balefully at Kensington.

Cameron was just shaking his head, his eyes wide with awe. "The moment I met you, I knew you didn't belong in a cage."

Another volley of gunfire sounded in the distance.

"No one fucking belongs in a cage, Cameron," I snapped at him. "But I'm going to take that as the compliment you meant. Now get the hell out of here. Some shit's about to go down."

Cameron nodded and jogged away.

I hauled Parker Kensington to his feet, shoving the barrel of my gun into his ribs. "How do you fancy being a human shield, Kensington?"

LUIZ TOOK out another shifter guard with a bullet to the shoulder, while Galu sent a volley of icicles through another.

They'd made it through the exterior wards without detection but had had the misfortune of coming across two guards. The gunfire must have alerted another witch to their position.

Isobel... Well, Isobel hadn't been kidding. Her powers were

fucking terrifying. And disgusting. She'd pointed that black-tipped silver wand at the spikey-haired witch and the woman had doubled over, retching black bile from her mouth like her body was turning inside out.

Luiz had had to look away and throw an arm over his nose to keep the stench from turning his own stomach.

Isobel had just faced all of them—fierce Phantoms turned pale and green. "You ride with me and you don't get a pretty, made-for-TV kind of battle. War is ugly. I warned you."

Galu motioned them forward and they hurried by the poor witch, who was moaning and sobbing on the ground. When they'd turned the corner and a gust of fresh wind carried the scent away Luiz let out a sigh of relief. "There are some things that you can never be prepared for."

"Remind us not to get on your bad side," Daevin remarked.

"Consider yourself reminded."

Rex's nostrils flared. "I smell Zariya."

Galu perked up. "Is she all right?"

"I do not smell blood or injury on her. There is a human scent as well. A captor, perhaps."

"Well, let's go rescue our girl," Luiz said. "What are we waiting for?"

"She's approaching." Rex raised his rifle.

They scattered to defensive positions around the courtyard—behind large potted plants and ornate columns.

A human appeared around the corner first. A brown-haired man, well-coifed, bound, mad as hell. Zariya appeared behind him, wearing what looked to be a silk bathrobe, gold stiletto heels, and a determined expression. She had a semi-automatic rifle pressed against his ribs.

"Zariya?" Galu called. "Are you all right?"

"Right as rain, boys." She grinned, relief written plainly on her face. "Took you long enough."

"There were complications," Daevin offered.

"There always are."

Isobel pointed to Zariya. "*This* is your damsel in distress? I like how you guys roll."

Luiz couldn't help the surge of pride at her praise. Yes, their team *was* badass.

"The only one still in distress is our fearless leader," said Zariya. "The Black Moon High Priestess has him in a room down the hall."

"Then let's pay her a little visit." Isobel cracked her knuckles and twirled her wand in her hand.

Luiz and the others shied away instinctively, Daevin going so far as to shield his head with his hands.

Zariya raised an eyebrow. "I'll let you go first."

KONSTANTIN JUMPED as the door smashed open and an unfamiliar woman in gray strode forward, a wand outstretched in her hand like a fencing foil. "Naeve Blackthorn, High Priestess of the Black Moon Coven, I, Isobel Rosethorp, charge you with crimes committed in violation of the Laws of the Lunar Conclave of 1693. How do you plead?"

Konstantin's eyebrows floated up almost to his hairline. This Isobel person sure knew how to make an entrance. His nostrils flared as familiar, welcome scents reached his nose. The rest of his team was hovering just beyond the doorway. Including Zariya. Now was his chance. He looked between the two witches, poised to make a move. But—maybe he should let this play out. Maybe there was a plan in motion.

Naeve sneered at Isobel, crossing her arms under her ample chest. "Leave it to Svetlana to force you to wear the most hideous uniforms possible. The woman has the fashion sense of a block of wood. Come work with me, honey, and I can show you what real power is."

The two other Black Moon witches had made their way to stand on either side of Naeve, and they glowered at Isobel with disdain on their faces. He hoped their new ally knew what she was doing. Because it looked like it was going to be three against one.

"Any power that rests on the back of innocent witches and supes is corrupt to the core." Isobel's dark eyes flashed. "Now how do you plead?"

Naeve heaved a sigh, twirling a hand. "Not guilty."

"According to the bylaws of the Conclave, your guilt or innocence will be determined by single combat. Defeat me, and the goddess will have proven you—"

Lightning snaked from the ceiling, piercing the spot where Isobel stood.

Konstantin blinked. Where she *had* stood. The witch had spun out of the way.

"Get her!" Naeve screamed to her two lackeys.

Mayhem exploded inside the hotel room.

Konstantin dove out of the chair, rolling into the corner, where the desk partially shielded him. He came up crouching.

"The bylaws call for single combat," Isobel cried as she held up one hand, the space around her fingers crackling with a sort of shield spell.

"I make my own rules," Naeve screamed over the second charge of electricity she called down.

One of Naeve's witches, the silver-haired woman, was circling behind Isobel. If Naeve could play dirty, then so could he.

Konstantin reached out, grabbed the witch's leg, and pounced, sinking his teeth into the tender flesh of her ankle. She screamed and tried to turn her magic on him, but it ricocheted off some sort of magical barrier. Isobel had thrown a shield between them, even as she was defending herself against attacks from both Naeve and the tattooed witch.

One of Isobel's attacks hit the tattooed witch square in the chest and the woman doubled over, vomiting foul-smelling liquid on the floor. It splashed all over Naeve's stiletto shoes. The High Priestess's eyes went wide, but instead of throwing a counter-spell or helping her sister-witch, she dove for the window—shattering the glass and disappearing into the night.

Isobel wasted no time. She dove after her.

Konstantin ran to the window, joined by the rest of Phoenix Team. Isobel's gray uniform was just visible in the darkness as she sprinted across the lawn towards the treeline.

Rex positioned himself at the window and raised his weapon. He squinted into his scope. Rex had excellent night vision, but to hit a moving target that far away—

The crack of a single shot rang out.

Followed by the muffled thunk of a body hitting the grass.

Isobel slowed to a jog, then stopped. She turned to look at them. "I had her!" she shouted.

Luiz whistled. "Nice shot, Rexy."

Galu clapped Rex on the back.

Zariya's shoulders slumped. "Is it over?"

Konstantin looked behind him to where the two other witches had fallen still, soaked in puddles of their own bodily fluids. His nose wrinkled. It was unfortunate, but they had backed the wrong horse.

"It finally is." Konstantin wrapped an arm protectively around Zariya's waist.

She leaned into him, her scent of caramel and jasmine filling his nostrils. "Good, because these shoes are killing me."

He forced a laugh. The team filed out of the room, and Konstantin tried to banish the lump of dread that had settled deep within his stomach.

His Maker's words rang in his ears. *"I will see you here, standing before me in person, before the next new moon, or I will kill each and every supe on your sorry excuse for a team."*

No, it wasn't over. Not by a long shot.

18

______

Luiz walked along the row of prisoners and glowered at each and every one of them. They'd taken five guards and eleven buyers prisoner. They'd be taken to Tartarus Base for processing and then make their way to a MASC prison pending trial.

Except Parker Kensington. Somehow, when they'd all been distracted by Isobel and Naeve's showdown, that piece of shit had weaseled free of his restraints and made it to his helicopter. The billionaire was gone. No doubt with a huge chip on his shoulder. It likely wouldn't be the last they'd see of him. But it didn't matter. They'd be ready.

Isobel strode into the room like she didn't have a care in the world. Like she hadn't just tangled with some incredibly powerful witches and turned several others inside out.

"How'd it go with Svetlana?" he asked. She'd wanted to find a quiet place to update her High Priestess.

Isobel shrugged. "There was some yelling and some swearing. But once I explained to her what was really going on here, and that Naeve had broken a number of coven laws by holding witches in order to steal their life forces… Well, she'll get over it."

"Good. I would feel bad if helping us screwed things up for you back home."

She eyed him shrewdly. "I think she was angriest that I was helping *you*. You really ruffled her feathers."

Luiz grinned. "What can I say? I'm a hard man to get over."

Isobel paused. "Is it true what she said?"

"About what?"

She looked over his shoulder thoughtfully. "About witches and incubi. The...power exchange."

"Oh." He hadn't been sure that Isobel was interested in him, but the gleam in her eye now told him otherwise. But...maybe she was just interested in him for what he could do for her power. "I'm not sure."

"Perhaps someone should look into it. You know, for scientific purposes." Her lovely features were neutral.

She was hard to read. Did she want something casual? Just sex? He tried it on for size, weighing how it felt. If that was the case, he'd find himself disappointed. Isobel was fierce and beautiful and fucking intimidating. But he liked her. Respected her. And now knowing that being with a witch could be mutually beneficial—that the potential for a long-term relationship was actually possible—he didn't want something casual. He wanted to explore the possibility that there could be something more between them.

He looked at her plainly. "I'm not interested in scientific experiments."

Disappointment flitted across her face as quickly as a butterfly. She waved the air. "Of course not, that was—"

"But what about dinner?" Luiz suggested.

"Like...a date?"

"Exactly like a date."

She cocked her head at him, considering.

He held his breath.

And then she smiled, bright as a sunrise. "Dinner sounds great."

∾

Konstantin eyed Zariya, who sat on the floor next to a lovely fae woman, their hands intertwined. Their backs were braced against the wall, their long legs stretched out before them. The fae female's head rested against Zariya's shoulder while they talked quietly. He didn't know what they were saying, and he didn't care to intrude. He was just glad that Zariya had found a friend when she'd needed one the most during this awful ordeal.

Galu approached. "We found the keys for that big boat. We can head back to the mainland whenever you're ready."

Konstantin frowned. "Let's give them ten more minutes to rest. Get the prisoners moving. Then we can come back for the rest."

"Roger that, boss."

His guilt was like a thrashing tiger within him—sharp jaws, lashing tail. He'd balked at the idea of allowing Zariya to join Phoenix Team because he'd been afraid something would happen to Vizol's daughter. But now he was falling in love with her, and the thought of her running into danger day in, day out terrified him. He'd done a shit job of keeping her out of harm's way.

Especially now that his Maker had his team, Zariya included, in her sights. He'd as good as put a target on their backs.

He had to go. She'd demanded his presence, and as much as he wished it, he couldn't refuse. He wouldn't put them at risk anymore.

There was just one thing he needed to do before he left.

Konstantin found Rex standing on the balcony, looking out at the night. "Can I borrow the laptop?"

"In the backpack," Rex said without looking his way.

Konstantin fished around the pack that sat by Rex's feet and retrieved the laptop. He took it to a table and logged into the resort's Wi-Fi, then his own cloud storage.

Someone had taken the Chinvat Gate from evidence while they'd been gone. He'd arranged for the camera to upload to his cloud storage every six hours. He pulled up the files and cycled through the footage.

As he saw the culprit come on the screen, plain as day, his eyes narrowed in rage.

That bastard.

Cyriaque Broussard.

I SHUFFLED ONTO THE YACHT, bone tired and soul-weary. On the one hand, we'd done it. We'd shut this place down and rescued the poor prisoners who'd been destined for god-knew-where.

But we still hadn't found a lead on the Authority.

That asshat Parker Kensington had escaped, and who knew how many other places like this were out there?

I stationed myself at the railing and watched as everyone else was ferried onto the boat. Konstantin came last, casting off the lines and striding up the gangplank with those impossibly sexy legs of his.

"Hey." Luiz appeared next to me. "You hanging in there?"

I leaned against his arm. "How do you stand it?"

"What?"

"This? All the time? Facing this much evil, day in and day out? How can you see it all and still have hope?"

He wrapped his arm around me. "I guess...fighting it is the only thing that gives me hope. It's when I stop fighting that I know they've really won."

I nodded, swallowing a lump in my throat.

"Come on, Six. Things will look brighter after a good night's rest. And a good lay."

I chuckled. "Leave it to an incubus..."

"Yeah, yeah. Got to keep up appearances."

I had to give it to him, though, the prospect of picking up where Konstantin and I had left things did cheer me significantly. A surge of desire tugged at my core and suddenly, I *needed* to see Konstantin. I needed to bury my nose in his scent of winter and night and let him kiss the rest of the world away. "Where is Konstantin?"

Luiz angled his head. "Not sure. Below deck, maybe?"

"I'll go find him."

"Get it, girl." Luiz feigned giving me a slap on the ass, and I laughed, heading below deck.

I walked through room after sleek room of the yacht. Where the devil was he? It wasn't like there were a lot of places to hide on this boat.

I frowned and put my hands on my hips. I opened my glands and quested around me. Konstantin's signature was unique—the coolness of his body hardly registering as more than an outline on my sixth sense.

I searched around, widening my scope, until I was holding the visual of the whole boat around me. I could account for every body *except* his.

When I opened my eyes again, my stomach clenched. What the hell was going on? I barreled back up the stairs to the main deck. "Galu! Guys!"

I turned to find Galu stalking towards me, holding his phone in his hand.

"What's up, chicka?" Daevin asked as he, Luiz, and Rex gathered around.

"I can't find Konstantin," I said. "I don't know what happened, but he's not on the boat."

"That's not possible. I saw him get on," Luiz said.

"Me too," Rex added.

"Zariya's right," Galu said grimly. "Konstantin is gone."

USA TODAY BESTSELLING AUTHOR
CLAIRE LUANA
MYTHICAL ALLIANCE
PHOENIX REVEALED

1

———

The desert heat hit Konstantin like the bellows of a forge.

Next to him, Enigma pivoted slowly, a hand held up to block the sun. "What are we doing here?"

Konstantin examined their surroundings—the expanse of mustard sand behind them, the imposing ochre cliff that seemed to touch the heavens before them, broken only by a narrow, shadowed slot canyon. It did look like the middle of nowhere. And it was.

If you didn't know what was here, hiding just out of sight.

"*I* am here to see an old friend," Konstantin said. "You're heading back to Base."

Enigma's eyebrows raised behind the thick rims of his glasses. "You want me to just...leave you out here?"

"I'll be fine, I assure you," Konstantin replied. He needed the warlock gone.

"Do you want me to get you a water bottle or something?"

"Go, Enigma," Konstantin growled.

Enigma wiped his brow, which was already glistening with sweat. "Okay, your funeral."

Konstantin did his best to remain calm. It wasn't Enigma's fault he was in this predicament. "One last thing before you go. You are not to mention this location to the others. That's an order."

Enigma frowned but shrugged. "Off the books. I get it. Be careful."

"I'm always careful—"

But Enigma had already disappeared.

The knotted tension in Konstantin's shoulders relaxed. Finally. Every step from here was one he had to take alone.

The high, twisting walls of the canyon provided a blessed respite from the oppressive heat of the sun. He had taken this route once before, several lifetimes ago. He'd been searching for death back then, too. Though death of a different kind.

He shoved thoughts of his team to the back of his mind. Thoughts of Zariya—fierce and breathtaking and *breakable*. He couldn't risk having his Maker targeting her or the rest of Phoenix Team.

As good as his team was, they couldn't be on guard all the time. Eventually, someone would let down their guard, for just a moment, and someone he loved would end up dead. He couldn't be responsible for that. No, he had to confront this problem head-on. Even if it meant vanishing and leaving only questions in his wake.

Konstantin had done this for them. Galu, loyal and stalwart. Daevin, brash and brave. Luiz, who hid his tender heart beneath that layer of cocksureness. Rex, enigmatic, brilliant, and more powerful than he suspected even Rex knew. And Zariya. Undeniable. Who'd walked right through all his defenses and stolen his heart.

He shook his head. If they'd known where he was headed, they'd never have let him go alone. Which was precisely why he'd left.

At least an hour passed before Konstantin found himself at a dead end—a wall of undulating rock that stretched hundreds of feet above him. He could climb it; he was strong and nimble enough.

But he didn't need to. There was another way through. So he knocked on the stone, the rough rock scraping his knuckles. "Merhzad! *Mitunam biyam tu?*" Konstantin's Farsi was rusty, but he knew enough to ask to come inside.

No answer.

He looked up, then around. His old friend was watching from somewhere. He must be.

Konstantin's stomach clenched in doubt. It had been hundreds of years since he'd last visited. What if Merhzad no longer lived here? Or if something had happened to him? Manticores were rumored to live for thousands of years, but Merhzad had already been old when he'd come last time—

A rumble deep in the rock set his teeth vibrating. Konstantin let out a sigh of relief as the rock face before him began to morph, pulling back to create a narrow opening.

Konstantin stepped inside and made his way through a dark passageway. When he came out the other side, it was like he'd stepped into a different world. A world of green leaves and fragrant blossoms and *life*.

He closed his eyes for a moment, taking in the rush of sensory input—the chorus of birds singing, insects humming about their business, the gentle burble of a crystal stream. The heat of the desert was filtered through the shade of the canopy, leaving the air sluggish and warm, smelling of jasmine and hyacinth.

A shadow fell across him, and he opened his eyes to find a beast that some might find terrifying. The muscled body of a brindle lion melded into wide golden wings, and the tail that twitched softly was topped with the sharp barb of a scorpion. The face was strangest of all—that of a wise old man, with silver eyes and a mane shot through with gray. "Merhzad," Konstantin said with a grin. "You don't look a day over a thousand."

Merhzad mirrored his smile and opened his wings wide, curving them to pull Konstantin into an embrace. "You are a sight for sore eyes, my boy."

Konstantin chuckled. "No one's called me that in six hundred years."

"Well, if anyone can, it's me. Now, come inside and let's have some refreshments. No one comes here without a story to tell."

Chattering monkeys watched as Konstantin followed Merhzad through the pathways of the lush oasis. This hidden valley was a place of legend. Preserved, protected from the world by the very myth that made it infamous.

The Garden of Eden.

As they walked into a cool entryway carved into the rock of the canyon wall, Konstantin recognized a series of carvings on the wall. They told the story of this place—Adam and Eve, the first man and woman. And Lilith. The first vampire.

He'd been certain, back then, that the birthplace of Authentic vampires would hold the key to killing them. And he'd been right.

Merhzad led him into a large room with a soaring ceiling that let in streams of sunlight from above. They settled onto plush cushions around a short, carved table. Konstantin's mind flashed back to centuries ago.

"Will you pour the nectar?" Merhzad nodded to a pitcher on the table.

"It's like nothing's changed," Konstantin marveled as he picked it up and poured the nectar into his cup and Merhzad's bowl. The manticore had large, lion-like paws, but he was amazingly dexterous with them. He could hold a bowl and drink as well as a man.

"You've changed." Merhzad nodded. "That much is clear."

Konstantin took a sip and the sweetness of the nectar hit his tongue. It was squeezed from one of the fruits that only grew here in the garden. "I have."

"Yet you are here for the same reason. Are you not?"

A flush heated his cheeks, and he looked down into his cup. Merhzad had always been uncomfortably observant.

Merhzad placed his own bowl back on the table. "When you came here to me, some six hundred years ago, there was a rage in you that burned so hot, I feared it would destroy you from the inside out."

Konstantin let out a dark laugh. "She'd stolen everything from me."

"Iona?"

Konstantin's gaze jerked up. "Don't say that name."

Merhzad shook his head briefly. "She holds power over you, even after all this time. She is your Maker, yes, but you have always had the power to break free of her."

Konstantin exploded to his feet, storming across the room. "She robbed me of my life. After she turned me, she let me escape, knowing I would run home to my family, knowing I would be unable to stop myself around them. Knowing I would..." Images flashed in Konstantin's mind that he'd spent centuries shoving down. His wife's throat, torn and bloody. The glazed eyes of his little boy—

"Yes, she wanted to mold you into as much of a monster as she was," Merhzad said. "To unleash it in you. But you didn't yield to the monster inside, did you?"

Konstantin shook the images from his mind and paced across the room again. "No, I tried to kill it. I tried to kill..." Konstantin balled his hands in his fists to fight the numbness overtaking him. Remembering all the ways he'd tried to end himself. To kill the monster inside, even if it meant killing the shell of the man. But Iona had kept bringing him back. She wouldn't let him die. Wouldn't let him be free.

"And so you escaped and found your way to me. Obsessed with the legend of Lilith, convinced that this place would have the answer you needed."

"The way to kill an Authentic vampire." Konstantin rounded on him. "And it does. You do have it. And—"

"Sit." Merhzad pointed. "At least do me the honor of telling me the rest of your tale before you start asking."

Konstantin's cheeks burned as he made his way back to his cushion. Goddammit, he'd forgotten that way Merhzad had of making him feel about ten inches tall. He sucked in a breath and let it out. "After you made me stay here, for months—"

"Helping you heal from your trauma," Merhzad volunteered.

"Yes." Konstantin softened. Merhzad had saved him. Perhaps not his body, but his soul. The manticore, through stories, and the quiet wisdom of nature, had started putting him back together. "After you showed me that I could free myself from Iona's influence, I went into the countryside, as you suggested."

"Yes, where was it?" Merhzad asked.

"Back home. Austria. I lived as a hermit for decades. I wasn't exactly happy, but I found a sort of peace. One winter, I was out hunting when I heard a commotion on the king's road. A group of brigands had attacked a caravan and were killing and looting. I had to do something. So…I intervened. I killed the brigands. There was only one survivor, a merchant's daughter. But when she looked at me, covered in their blood and gore…she wasn't afraid. She thanked me. She fell over herself with gratitude." Konstantin shook his head. Even now, he remembered that moment. The feeling of helping someone.

"And you knew you had found the reason you had been Made."

He met Merhzad's amber eyes. "Yes. I fought as a vigilante for a while, then joined the Austrian army. I've been fighting ever since. Now, I work for an organization called the Mythical Alliance of Supernatural Creatures. We protect supes from threats around the world. I have a team. A family. And…there's a woman…" He looked down at his fingernails. Zariya must have been so worried right now. He hated that he'd had to leave without explanation. But he was doing this for her. For all of them. They'd understand in the end.

When Konstantin looked up, Merhzad wore a soft smile. "You've made a good life for yourself, my Konstantin. Now why would you upset it with the need for vengeance and death?"

"She found me. She said she'll kill them all unless I come back and serve her. You have to understand. I can't do that. I'd rather die."

A troubled expression crossed over Merhzad's lined face. "I see." The manticore's muscled body shifted as he stood, his wings tucked into his back. "Thank you for your story. I needed to understand why you sought this poison. It is my sacred charge, and I cannot give it to just anyone."

"I understand. And I wouldn't be here if I didn't need it. Iona must be stopped. She's reached a position of great power. Who knows what other harm she's doing?"

Merhzad nodded. "Yes, she must be dealt with. Very well. Come with me."

2

———————

I sat in Cyriaque Broussard's office, Galu at my side. Cyriaque paced before us like an angry wolf in a cage.

The Rougarou wolf shifter was Veil Force's Director. Our fearless leader. Also, a traitorous asshole.

Konstantin hadn't explained his mysterious disappearance, other than leaving Galu a message saying he needed to "Take care of some personal business." But he had seen fit, on that same voicemail, to tell us the identity of the Veil Force traitor who'd been working with the Collectors and the Authority. Konstantin's camera had captured *Cyriaque* stealing the Chinvat Gate.

It was all I could do to hold myself back. To keep from launching myself across the desk and clocking Cyriaque in his stupid square jaw with every bit of force my supernatural naga half carried.

"Konstantin has to answer to me for that disaster of a mission in Costa Rica," Cyriaque raged. "He's not allowed to go AWOL."

"He's not AWOL, sir. He's attending to some personal business." Galu, Phoenix Team's acting leader, seemed cool as a cucumber beside me—not a strand of the nereid's blue hair was out of place. How Galu was keeping his cool was beyond me. Not when looking over the desk at this traitor. Cyriaque had been my dad's best friend.

For decades. And he'd betrayed him. My nostrils flared as I dug my nails into the arms of the chair.

Cyriaque seemed to settle for a moment, pausing behind his chair, bracing his hands on its leather back. "Someone has been feeding information to the Collectors and this Authority person. And now Konstantin goes off the grid? Are we sure they're not connected?"

I couldn't keep the shock from my face. He had the nerve—the *audacity*—to try to shift the suspicion onto Konstantin when he knew full well that *he* was the traitor in the Authority's pocket?

Fury billowed through my veins like a burning inferno. I found myself on my feet, my hands braced on the desk, facing off against Cyriaque. I could barely speak. "I'm sorry, are you suggesting that Konstantin in the mole?"

Galu's cool hand closed around my wrist, and I looked down to find his turquoise eyes imploring me. *Don't fuck this up.*

That look managed to quench some of my fire. I could do this. We had agreed. Konstantin may have told us that Cyriaque was the mole, but we had no damn proof until he returned. We couldn't risk clueing Cyriaque in to the fact that we knew until we had enough evidence to walk him out in handcuffs. I wouldn't let him escape. No, he needed to pay for what he'd done.

So until then, we had to play nice. Like everything was normal.

"I'm sorry," Galu said. "Zariya has had a particularly rough twenty-four hours. I told you this briefing should wait until she got some rest."

"I'm not saying anything conclusively." Cyriaque shook his head. "It just doesn't look good for Konstantin."

"Konstantin...is not the mole," I ground out through my gritted teeth.

"I know you feel close to your commander, but you've only been on Phoenix Team for a few weeks, Zariya. How well do you really know—"

I held up my hands. "This briefing is over. We'll tell you when we hear from Konstantin." I spun and jerked open the door, stalking out.

Galu jogged after me, falling into step beside me. "I think that went well."

"How could you be so...*calm* in there? Knowing he's smearing Konstantin's name? Knowing..." I trailed off. I was infuriated. I was exhausted. I was worried sick. Where was Konstantin? Why had he vanished without even telling us where he was going? It wasn't like him. What if something was wrong? What if that voicemail had been left at gunpoint? What if he was captured, or dying, and we were just sitting here with our thumbs up our asses?

"I'm calm because that's what Konstantin needs most right now. He doesn't need us rushing off without thinking and he doesn't need us"—he lowered his voice—"clueing in Cyriaque that we're on to him. This is delicate."

"I've never been very good with *delicate*," I grumbled.

"Daevin and Rex are talking to Enigma as we speak. Let's see whether he knows anything."

Ugh. I hated that that smug warlock held the key to the whereabouts of my...commander? Boyfriend? God, I didn't know what Konstantin and I were. Where we had left things—we'd both admitted we had feelings for each other, and that we wanted to give in to those feelings. But he was still my commander. Were we going to ignore all the complications and skip happily into the sunset?

I groaned in frustration, ignoring Galu's sidelong look. This was why I needed to fucking find him!

Galu opened the door to let me into a small interrogation room. Enigma and Rex, wearing his black-furred jackal head, complete with glowing golden eyes, sat across a metal table from each other, while Daevin sat on the table itself, looming over Enigma, his forked tail lashing.

Worry flashed across Enigma's face when I entered the room, followed by relief when he saw Galu. If anyone was going to stay even-keeled, it was Galu.

"Galu, you can't let them hold me," Enigma said. "I'm a member of Veil Force. This is bullshit."

"No one's holding anyone," Galu said. "This is just a friendly chat."

"Then I can go?" Enigma stood. Normally, Enigma would be able to teleport anywhere, but the Tartarus Base interrogation rooms were warded against that sort of magic. Most of the base was. It wouldn't do to have anyone just popping in or out.

"No." Everyone sang in chorus. Daevin reached out a red-skinned hand and shoved Enigma back into his chair. "Sit down, fly boy. When you tell us where you took Konstantin, you can leave."

Enigma removed his thick glasses and rubbed his eyes before putting them back on. "Here's the thing. You're all scary, but you're not *Konstantin scary*. He told me not to tell you where I took him, and I'm not going to."

"But you forgot the difference between us and Konstantin," the demon purred.

Enigma leaned away from Daevin. "What's that?"

Daevin leaned in and bared his teeth. "We're here."

A knock sounded on the door, and by the time it opened, Daevin was standing nonchalantly against a wall.

It was Signe, mythical norn and member of Tartarus Base's support staff. "Would you all leave poor Enigma alone and come with me?"

I exchanged a look with Galu.

"It's about Konstantin," she said.

I practically rocketed out of that room.

I managed to hold my tongue until Signe led us into her office. Her sister, Verte, was sitting at her desk, her feet up as if she hadn't a care in the world. I pressed my lips together. It would not do to insult Verte's commitment to the job. If the sisters knew anything, we needed to know, too.

We'd come across Luiz, Phoenix Team's resident incubus, in the hallway, so all of Phoenix Team, minus our fearless leader, piled into the office.

Signe closed the door.

Once I would have been intimidated by these muscled, enigmatic supes, but I'd so quickly come to love each of them like brothers. We'd been through some shit together, and that had formed a bond like I'd never known.

I had a feeling we'd be going through some more shit side by side before this was all said and done.

"Do you know where Konstantin is?" Galu asked. "Have you seen something?"

Signe and Verte exchanged a glance. "We have." Signe rotated her computer monitor to display a photo of a stunning auburn-haired woman with alabaster skin. But it wasn't her beauty that drew my attention. It was her blood-red eyes. I tried to shove down the curl of jealousy that churned my stomach. What did Konstantin want with this woman?

"An Authentic vampire?" Luiz asked. "I thought Konstantin steered clear of them."

"Not just any Authentic vampire. This is Iona Haas. She's his Maker."

Stunned silence blanketed the room. Dad's memories flooded me —snippets of conversations with Konstantin about his Maker, how he'd fled her influence, how her cruelty had nearly driven him to madness. "Why the fuck is he seeing her?"

"That, we do not know."

"And why did he leave without telling us?" Daevin asked. "If he needed to take down the original bitch, we'd gladly go with him."

"Unless he's not going to take her down," I choked out. What if Konstantin had gone back to her? My mind started to replay all my interactions with Konstantin. Our frantic kisses in the hotel room, our conversation after. Had I done something? Said something to drive him away?

"You think he has returned to her?" Rex asked.

Silence fell over the room again.

"Nah." Daevin waved a hand. "Boss is all in with Veil Force. With Phoenix Team. It doesn't make sense that he'd just up and leave. We're missing something."

"Zariya, did anything happen at the resort? When just the two of you were there?"

My mouth fell open as I heard Galu voice my deepest fear. "You think this is my fault? That I drove him away?"

"No, not at all." Galu held up his hands. "But something shifted between when we went to Quiribri Island and when we returned. Did he talk to any of the buyers? Have conversations with anyone?"

I frowned, trying to remember. "I think he had a run-in with Parker Kensington, the CEO of PharMagus, during the bidding. But when Naeve and Kensington showed up, Kensington took me, and Naeve and her witches stayed with Konstantin."

"So they separated you," Luiz said.

I shrugged. "I guess. But does it matter why? We have to get him." I turned to Signe. "Do you know where he is? Where this vampire is?"

Signe and Verte exchanged another look. Did they have to keep doing that?

"We have tracked Iona's known whereabouts. But you're not going to like it."

"Just give it to us straight," Daevin muttered.

"She is imbedded deep within heart of the DRC. The Democratic Republic of Creatures."

I barely found a chair before my knees gave out beneath me. *That* was going to be a problem.

3

———

Konstantin stood at the threshold of what Merhzad had called "the Ways." He wasn't normally one to hesitate, but stepping into something so strange would make any man pause.

He looked back at Merhzad. "Explain how this works again?"

"It is an ancient network of magic, woven into the very fabric of our world. The veins or arteries, if you will. It connects the ancient places of the world."

"Like a magical subway system," Konstantin muttered. "But how does it work?"

"You don't need to know how something works to utilize it. Do you understand how electricity works? Combustion engines?"

"Yes," Konstantin replied.

"Nuclear fusion?"

Fair point. Not that he *used* nuclear fusion in his daily life.

"So long as you wear my talisman, the doors will open for you."

Konstantin fingered the ivory pendant threaded around his neck. It was carved in a small image of a manticore. It wasn't the only gift Merhzad had given him. Konstantin had changed into tan cargo pants, a white linen shirt, and soft leather boots. In the pocket of his pants nestled a small vial, enclosed safely in a traveling case. What he'd come for. The way to free himself from Iona's influence for good.

"And how will I know which doorway leads to the DRC?"

"I have spelled your talisman. There should only be one door. A...*direct flight*, if you will."

Konstantin looked back with a smile. "I'm impressed that you're keeping up with technological developments of the outside world."

"I'm on Facebook." Merhzad shrugged.

Konstantin let out a bark of surprised laughter. "No, you're not."

Merhzad chucked. "No, I'm not. But I am tapped in to the collective mind of human and supernatural consciousness on this planet. Very busy. Very loud."

Konstantin couldn't imagine. His own thoughts were loud enough most days. But he was stalling. "Thank you for your help, old friend. You have saved me again." He closed the few steps between them and pulled Merhzad into a hug. The manticore's fur was as soft as goose down.

Merhzad patted his back with his great gentle paw. "Nonsense. I only gave you a safe space to heal yourself. Now go and fight this battle so you can return home to the one you love."

Konstantin's face heated. "Is it so obvious?"

Merhzad placed his paw on Konstantin's shoulder. "She must be very special."

"She is," Konstantin admitted. His stomach clenched in guilt at leaving her. Zariya had voiced her fear that something would happen, and they'd never have their chance to be together.

And now, he was going to face the most powerful Authentic vampire he'd ever known, one who had a magnetic hold on him. He shoved down his doubt. He had a plan. He had a weapon. He would end this and return to her.

"Now go." Merhzad nudged him gently, and Konstantin reached out and turned the handle of the sandstone door.

A wave of vertigo washed over him. Beyond the door, it was like the night sky. A starry expanse of eternity—nothing solid at all. Wait, no, that wasn't right. He could see the door beyond.

He peered forward, looking down. There was no solid footing. If he stepped out, he'd fall into nothingness.

He turned back to Merhzad. "I think something's wrong! There's nowhere to stand."

Merhzad's face was serene. He motioned Konstantin forward with a casual flick of his paw. "Trust me. It's there."

Konstantin hadn't considered himself a religious man for centuries, but he couldn't help it, he made the sign of the cross over his chest before he stepped out into blackness.

But Merhzad was right. There was something solid beneath his feet. The door to the Garden of Eden swung shut and a kind of infinite silence washed over him. As if there were a sound to creation that he hadn't even realized. Until it was gone.

But this wasn't a place to linger, no matter how remarkable. His heart hammered as he hurried forward, relief washing over him as his fingers made contact with a firm brass doorknob. He turned it and nearly threw himself through it, stumbling to a stop on the sunbaked stones of the Democratic Republic of Creatures.

He heaved a sigh of relief. If Merhzad was correct, which he seemed to always be, Konstantin now stood in the heart of the DRC's capital city of Antares. This nation, if it could be called that, was carved out of several North African countries—a crossroads between east and west, Europe and Africa. Human and supernatural creature. This place was something entirely its own.

Konstantin had traveled extensively, but fate had never brought him here, to this tangled nest of criminals and opportunists. It was one of the few places in the world in which MASC had no jurisdiction. The DRC refused to be recognized, refused to be party to the system that categorized and catalogued mythical creatures like animals. This country was run by a loose coalition of six leaders— who had once been the heads of street gangs but had risen to far greater power. Those factions now controlled significant firepower and military resources. Not to mention money. Lots and lots of money.

Supes came here to hide, to swindle, to hunt, to live on the edge of a chaos that many thought had been lost—had been civilized out of them. This was the Wild West of the supernatural world. And he suspected his presence would not go unnoticed for long.

Merhzad's gate had let him off in a dark alley, shaded from the noon sun by a bright cloth awning strung between buildings. He didn't know where Iona was located, but he suspected she would not be hard to find.

He checked the sidearm on his hip. It was old, a relic of some treasure hunters lost to the desert. Its weight was a comfort to him. He was fast, but no one knew him here. Guns, on the other hand, were universally respected.

Konstantin headed towards commotion and movement—it seemed the alley spilled into a broad street. He immediately lunged back out of the way as some sort of blue-skinned horned supe whizzed by on a rickety motorcycle. He couldn't help the smile that crossed his face as the heat and sound and smells hit him. There was something about being in an unfamiliar city that was fodder for the imagination. It was easy to imagine grand adventures and new acquaintances.

His smile fell.

He was no tourist here, and this town was devoid of photo ops and friendly faces. This place was cutthroat, not to be trifled with. And neither were its inhabitants. If he walked around with his head in the clouds in this place, he was likely to end up as someone's dinner. No, he needed to focus.

Konstantin had worked out his plan while resting with Merhzad. It was simple. Present himself at Iona's. Pretend he was playing nice with her and had come back to stand by her side. Then poison her drink when she wasn't looking. How hard could it be? With his Maker gone, Konstantin would be well and truly free. He would belong only to himself. And maybe, someday, to Zariya.

But first, he had to find his way through this godforsaken town.

Konstantin threaded his way into the hubbub of the larger street, following the majority of traffic. Hopefully, it would lead him to a town center or market or some sort where he could acquire the information he needed. Including the location of his Maker.

A large man with violet skin stepped directly into his path. Konstantin drew to a stop, meeting the man's challenging gaze. The supe wore dark clothing and a checked scarf around his throat, and his hair and goatee were as black as night. An ifrit or some sort of demon, perhaps?

"Excuse me." Konstantin tried to step to the side, but the supe mirrored him, remaining in Konstantin's path. The fine hairs on the back of Konstantin's neck rose and he glanced over his shoulder to find two more intimidating supes—a large shifter of some kind, perhaps a bear, and a stone elemental, blocking his retreat.

"I don't want any trouble," Konstantin said.

"That's too bad," the purple supe said with a grin, revealing two golden front teeth. "Because we do."

4

I sat in Signe and Verte's office, my head in my hands. What were we going to do?

"Cyriaque is never going to approve a mission to the DRC," Galu said. "It's against MASC policy. There's a strict non-interference agreement."

"At least now we know why Konstantin went off on his own," Daevin said.

I looked up, my curls still threaded wildly through my fingers. "Not really. It explains why he went off book, but not why he didn't take us with him."

"Perhaps this is something he truly needs to handle alone," Rex suggested. "If we show up, it could make the situation worse."

"Or we could save his ass."

"He doesn't seem to think his ass needs saving," Rex pointed out.

"Because he's a stupid man who thinks he can do everything himself!" I threw my hands up. "Signe. You told me my first day here that Konstantin and I needed each other. What do you see? Does he need me now? Or should I..." I choked on the words. Should I leave him be? On some unknown and likely dangerous mission, with no friends, no backup, where he could be bleeding...dying...

Signe bit her lip. "The magic of Authentic vampires is powerful and old. It twists and warps the possibilities around them. It's difficult for us to see the possible futures."

"But," Verte added, "we do know that difficult situations are always better with friends. We may think we need to go them alone—"

I rocketed to my feet. "See!" I pointed at Rex, perhaps a bit too forcefully. "Better with friends. We go, even if you don't want to."

Rex flattened his ears back. "It's not that I do not want to go. I only think it is important to consider all sides of the issue."

"Konstantin doesn't need a devil's advocate right now," I snapped. "He needs the fucking A-Team."

Daevin's tail thrashed. "Ooh, can I be Mr. T?"

"Dibs on Face," Luiz chimed in. "Because—"

"Because he's the best-looking." Daevin rolled his eyes. "Yes, thank you for reminding us."

"I guess that makes me Hannibal," Galu said, "which means I'm the one who has to ask: How the hell are we going to get to the DRC? The Chinvat Gate is gone, and Cyriaque won't approve a flight."

"We could steal the Veil Force helicopter," I suggested.

"Do you know how to fly?" Galu asked.

Dad had taken some flying lessons—so he'd sort of known how to fly, but that had been on a little prop-engine Cessna. I didn't think I was qualified, even with his memories, to fly the Veil Force helicopter. "No," I admitted.

"Anyone else?" Galu asked.

The team responded with murmured *nos*.

"I think I know someone who can help." Signe clapped her hands. "You five, meet me at the portal to the airfield in one hour."

I'D SWALLOWED my questions about whether or not we could trust Signe's mysterious pilot and made quick work of getting ready for another mission. I was exhausted and strung out from my time on

Quiribri Island and worried to death about Konstantin, but I knew I needed to take care of myself on a basic level.

I showered, put on a fresh uniform, and wolfed down a huge meal of waffles, bacon, and eggs in the cafeteria. I texted Auntie to say *hi* and tell her that I was heading out for another mission, then I quickly put my phone away before I got her myriad responses about how Veil Force was working me too hard. Veil Force could be putting me up at the Ritz-Carlton penthouse suite for an extended holiday and Auntie would still find something to complain about.

I managed to navigate the halls of Tartarus Base without encountering my roommates Kiki or Alviya, or more importantly, Cyriaque. The fewer people who knew about our little off-book mission, the better. Soon enough Cyriaque would realize we stole the plane, and there would be hell to pay when we returned. But hopefully by then, we'd have Konstantin back, together with proof that Cyriaque was our mole. He'd be slapped in handcuffs before he could dish out our punishment.

I smiled grimly. That would be satisfying as fuck.

A memory of Dad's swam to the surface—him and Cyriaque taking a surfing lesson after completing a mission in Australia. Cyriaque had been a terrible surfer. He'd kept getting tumbled by the surf, looking like an angry wet dog after a bath every time he'd clambered back onto his board.

Dad had been laughing so hard at Cyriaque's frustration that a rogue wave had taken him out at the knees, popping his board out from under him. They'd both crawled to shore—wet, sandy, and cracking up at how ridiculous they'd looked. Two dangerous predators, lain low by a few waves and some balance issues.

They'd shared a bucket of Coronas and talked about life, love, and loss as the sun had slipped over the horizon. Friends. Brothers. What the hell had happened? What possibly could have turned Cyriaque against my father—

A hand on my shoulder made me yelp. I turned to find Oliver grinning at me. He wore a leather bomber jacket over his lean physique and had a pair of silver aviators sitting atop his head, nestled in his golden hair.

"Wait, are you—"

"Your pilot, reporting for duty!"

"Do you just keep that outfit in the closet for what...flying emergencies?"

"I *am* a dragon." His grin widened.

I rolled my eyes. "So long as you can keep us in the air and your mouth shut about this, you'll do."

Oliver put a hand to his chest. "Your tender words warm the cockles of my heart, Ms. Chanji."

I put my hands on my hips. "Hearts don't even have cockles. That's not a thing. They have ventricles."

He put an arm around my shoulder and led me towards the portal. "Actually, cthulhu hearts do. And certain other mollusk-like supernaturals—"

~

Dad only had one memory of the DNC, and I let myself sink into it as the plane took off. In truth, I thought he'd been a little enchanted by the place.

A bastion where supernatural creatures could be free from human interest and control—a place that was raw and colorful and as varied as the supernatural world? What wasn't to like?

He hadn't liked the crime, corruption, and relative lawlessness quite so much.

He'd traveled there two years ago. Cyriaque had been leading Hydra Team then, but for some reason, Dad had come along. I searched the memory. A critical rescue mission. The daughter of a high-level MASC diplomat had been kidnapped and held for ransom by a group of shifter extremists. They'd brought her here for the exchange. The MASC Under-secretary herself had charged my dad with overseeing the mission to make sure things didn't go wrong.

And it was a good thing he had because things hadn't just gone wrong, they'd gone off the rails. Cyriaque had disappeared for over twenty-four hours. The heat of my dad's fury made me cringe, even in the memory.

He'd found Cyriaque tied naked in a cell, about to be strung up for a gambling debt.

I frowned. Cyriaque had a gambling problem? That fact hadn't been prominent in Dad's other memories, but it was an interesting piece of intel. Maybe he'd owed money to the wrong person and that was how they'd first gotten him to turn on MASC. I wished Konstantin were here so I could tell him. I just wished Konstantin were here.

"We should talk strategy once we land in the DRC." Galu unbuckled his seat belt and stood, now that we'd reached cruising altitude. "Does anyone have any contacts there?"

"One." Daevin stood and stretched, his tail curling around his left leg. "But he'd just as soon slit our throats as help us."

"Mental note, avoid parties at Daevin's house." Luiz shook his head.

"You assume you'd be invited," Daevin shot back.

"Dad mentioned someone a few years ago. I think he could be considered a friend." I considered for a minute the prospect of telling them about Dad's memories in my head. It would be a lot easier to explain that this contact had helped out with a MASC mission two years back. I did plan to tell them, but I wanted to tell Konstantin first. I didn't want him to be the last to know.

"Could you locate this person?"

I rubbed my jaw. "I think so. He can't be too hard to find."

Galu cocked his head. "Why do I suspect there's a story there?"

"How do you guys feel about trolls?" I offered a weak smile.

5

Konstantin had known Iona would find him. But even so, he was surprised at her speed. It had quickly become evident that the three muscled supes who had stopped him weren't common street thugs. They'd been sent to retrieve him.

So now he rode in a sleek black Mercedes, the purple-skinned ifrit sitting next to him in the back seat. Konstantin took the opportunity to gaze out the window at the speeding-by scenery. Antares was a city of hills, like the ancient cities of old. Iona's compound sat high atop one of those hills—a stone fortress reminiscent of the Moorish architecture of southern Spain and North Africa—graceful arches topped by ruddy tile roofs. It sat as a watchtower over the labyrinthine roads or dusty sandstone and adobe buildings that sprawled below it.

"How long has Iona served as Authority?" he asked. His captors weren't talkative, but he had learned that Iona's title as the Authority wasn't just a self-aggrandizing nickname. Antares, and the DRC beyond, was ruled by several crime-lords-turned-governors. Iona was one of them and held some sort of quasi-judicial role.

"There has always been an Authority," the bear shifter said from the front passenger seat without turning around.

Konstantin rolled his eyes. It was useless talking to these goons. Perhaps Iona herself would give him a straight answer. If she was in the mood.

Konstantin's stomach clenched as they drove through the elaborate arched gateway into the courtyard of Iona's palace—as the car stopped and his escorts got out.

He hadn't seen Iona in person in centuries. Hadn't been in the oppressive fog of her presence. Even the prospect of seeing her brought it all back—the man he'd been—and the young vampire, even worse. The things he'd done before he'd found his way to Merhzad. The helplessness.

His fingers clenched into fists. He wouldn't let himself go back there. He wouldn't allow it. She might always be his Maker, but he was a different man. A different vampire.

They walked through a courtyard carved with intricate detail, past a babbling fountain and rows of ornamental grasses. It could be the grounds of a fine Middle Eastern hotel. None of it was Iona.

Until he stepped inside.

The inside of the fortress was as dark as night. Authentic vampires were harmed by daylight, and Iona wouldn't allow the offending presence of the sun anywhere near her. She had always swathed herself in a cocoon of darkness and sycophants. It seemed little had changed in six hundred years.

Though as he followed the ifrit through the quiet halls, he did see some semblance of modernity—instead of the dripping wax candles and tapestries he remembered, sleek electric sconces lit the stone corridors here, and the art was modern and classy, though all in hues of gray and black and red. Always red.

"Iona has asked you to join her for dinner," the ifrit said. "Come on."

His stomach clenched again. He was hungry—starving, in fact—but dining with Iona was bloody. Savage.

The supe opened a set of broad double doors before him and Konstantin stepped in, shrouded by dread and tension. It took all the self-restraint he had not to blanch at the sight of her. To keep his face impassive. Uncaring.

Clad in an emerald gown of satin, Iona lounged in a high-backed chair at the front of the room. Her face hadn't changed, from her creamy pale skin to her heart-shaped face to the shadowed red eyes, set off by dark makeup and thick lashes. Her ebony hair was different, straightened, cut in a short style that brushed her sharp jawline. But the smile on her blood-red lips was one he recognized—hungry, delighted. Her favorite toy, returned.

By Iona's stiletto-clad feet sat a handsome, young Middle Eastern man with the glazed and adoring eyes of someone dosed with vampire blood. A thrall. What Zariya could have been, if her naga blood hadn't protected her and purged it from her system.

Konstantin quickly shoved aside the thought of Zariya. Iona was like a bloodhound with personal secrets. He couldn't let her learn of his feelings for Zariya; it would make her even more of a target than she already was.

Iona's soft, scratching voice set his teeth on edge. "My dear, sweet Konstantin. How I have longed to see your face! You have been gone for too long."

"Hello, Iona," Konstantin ground out.

"You must be hungry from your travels. Come, eat." She motioned to the boy.

His stomach let out a growl. "I don't eat innocents anymore."

A scowl darkened her face for just a moment. "This one?" She ran a hand through the young man's onyx hair. "He chose this freely. He gives willingly."

"Perhaps once he did. There's nothing free about him now."

Her mouth pinched together in a frown and he hurried on. It could go poorly for the boy if Konstantin continued to insist on abstaining. Iona's cruelty grew creative when she didn't get what she wanted. "I'm not here to argue about vampire ethics. I have chosen a different life. You know this. Yet you demand I come to heel like a dog, threatening my allies. What do you want?"

She rose in a fluid movement and stalked across the marble floor towards him. She peered up into his face, cocking her head, scrutinizing. She was quite petite, as most Authentics were, coming only up to his chest. But what they lacked in stature, they made up for in power. And darkness. "So. Right to business? We can't even share a meal? I raised you better than that. Your time among the humans has made you rude."

He sighed, closing his eyes for a moment. "Iona, I've come a long way and I'm tired. Out with it."

She seized his chin in her hand, her lips pulling back in a snarl, revealing her long, sharp canines. "I gave you everything. Don't forget it."

"You *took* everything." He stared unflinchingly into those unnatural eyes. "You may be frozen in time, but time has changed me. I'm no longer a young pup, terrified of a nip from my bitch mother. I've faced the worst of this world and won. Maybe you could take me down, but maybe I'd take you down with me. And besides, you clearly need me for something. So why don't you tell me what it is?"

She released his chin with a little shake of her head. "That is why I need you, Konstantin. You were always my fiercest child. And my loveliest." She looked at him with open admiration.

"Iona—" Would the vampire not keep on point?

"Yes, yes, why I summoned you." She stalked back to her chair and settled into it like a throne, throwing one leg over an arm, revealing an expanse of her creamy thigh.

Konstantin kept his eyes fixed on her face, doing his best to fight against the roiling memories of the...*times*...they'd shared when he'd first been turned. The power of her magic had driven him mad with desire for her...had blinded him to everything or everyone beyond her. But as time had passed, her power over him had waned. Now, the thought of sharing a bed with her disgusted him.

"The DRC is growing lawless—"

"Antares has always been lawless. I thought that's how you Governors wanted it."

"There can be chaos swirling around us, but the word of the Governors must be obeyed. We must be respected. I am the Authority, and I have been charged with securing peace in this place, with securing justice."

More likely charged with collecting taxes and securing the funds that paid for these pretty palaces. If the citizens of the DRC weren't paying up...Konstantin would bet his left kidney that was why Iona wanted more firepower. "What does this have to do with me?"

"I need a commander. A leader to whip my new recruits into shape."

"You want me to train your...private army?" He'd been in training roles before. Perhaps this wouldn't be so bad. From what he'd heard, the DRC *could* use more law enforcement.

"I've watched your illustrious career. You're perfect for the job. I understand perhaps I cannot keep you here forever, but I do need you for a time."

"How much time? And how many troops?"

"However long you think it will take. A hundred vampires. All my children."

Konstantin's eyes flew open. "A hundred? Unleashing a hundred brand new vampires on this place...it will bring it to its knees."

"That's where you come in. Only you can teach them the contours of your precious *morality*," she sneered.

No one could teach a brand new vampire morality. They were creatures of pure instinct and violence. Lust and destruction.

Konstantin turned and paced the room. It didn't matter. He was going to slip the poison in her drink and kill her. That would put an end to this madness as well. But he had to keep up his act. Appear reluctantly cowed. "Do I have a choice in this matter?" Konstantin finally asked.

"Not if you care for your teammates," Iona said primly. She was looking down, caressing the neck of the young man who still sat by her feet.

It wasn't like he would really have to do it. So Konstantin nodded, feeling nonetheless like he was making a deal with the devil. "I'll do it on one condition. You tell me everything. About all your operations."

It was worth a try. Might as well see what he could find out while he was here.

She bared her teeth. "So you can take down the empire I've worked so hard for the minute you run back to your little Veil Force? I think you overestimate your bargaining power here, *kostlich*."

Konstantin ground his teeth together at Iona's use of her old nickname for him. *Kostlich* meant "delicious." She'd always been the predator, and him the prey. "Fine. Then at least promise me that my team will be safe. If I do this, it's to secure their protection. No going back on your word."

She nodded, sending her sharp bobbed hair swishing about her face. "Do as I say, and I promise your team will be safe. Now, there's another task I need you to do for me."

God, there was always something more with her. Another layer to the rotten onion. "What task?"

"I'm hosting a round of fights tonight. The Coin-keeper has challenged me to put forth my champion. You will serve, and you will win."

Konstantin threw up his hands. "Isn't it enough that I'm here? That I've agreed to your ridiculous little scheme?"

"It is not enough!" Iona leaned forward, her lacquered nails digging into the ebony arms of her chair. "Because you made me a promise once, and then you left. You must prove your loyalty."

Konstantin strode across the chamber and seized the arms of the chair, looming over her until she was forced to lean back into the carved wood behind her. "I will not be paraded about like your prize pony," he hissed.

Iona grinned, sliding her pink tongue across one of her fangs. "You will indeed. What do the Americans say? Giddy-up?"

It took all his strength not to try to throttle her right then. "Why do you do this?" he gritted out.

She reached out and gave him a sharp slap. "Because the only thing more beautiful than you, *kostlich*, is watching you bleed."

6

I'd seen a lot of strange supes in my day, but Yani the troll might have been the strangest. And he was definitely the biggest.

We'd landed in the airfield outside of Antares and hired a car to take us into town. Dad had an excellent memory for directions and recalled right where Yani lived. But I couldn't think of a way to explain to the guys how I knew his address. So I directed our driver to a nearby coffee shop. It only took a few strategic questions of the clientele to get Yani's location, as apparently he was pretty well known in Antares. I got a cappuccino and a freaking amazing orange blossom scone out of the stop, so all in all, I was feeling pretty smug.

We'd walked the few blocks to Yani's and knocked on the huge, oaken doors to the walled compound. A nervous little brownie opened a tiny door the height of our knees, peering up at us with open suspicion. But when I'd given him Dad's name, he'd let us in. Grudgingly.

Yani lounged in a broad courtyard in the shade of a fragrant jasmine trellis. He was huge—at least eight feet tall when standing, with sage green skin stretched over the roping bulk of colossal muscles. His hair was black and bound in long dreadlocks tied with silver beads and bright leather ties. But he wore linen pants and a white T-shirt, rather than the animal skins and human skulls I'd somehow expected him to accessorize with. He held a newspaper in one hand and a coffee cup dwarfed by his massive fingers in the other.

He folded his newspaper when we approached, a wide smile displaying surprisingly white teeth. I surreptitiously eyed the name of the paper. *The Wall Street Journal*? Color me surprised. Yani was actually...kind of hot...if you went for the intellectual-crossed-with-steroids look. Never thought I'd actually think that about a troll. Somehow that hadn't translated in Dad's memories.

"This must be the daughter of Vizol Chanji." Yani stood, his massive bulk even more impressive when towering above me. But he held out a friendly hand and I shook it. His size made me feel a little like a child meeting a grown up, but I squashed that feeling as I introduced the rest of the team.

"How can I help?" He gestured to the classy rattan sofa set and we settled onto couches and chairs.

Luiz sat a bit too close to me on the sofa; his sharp gaze hadn't left Yani for a second. I suspected he was feeling protective of me after Quiribri Island, a sentiment I didn't exactly mind. Except that Konstantin was the one who was supposed to hover like an overprotective mother hen. I forced myself to take a breath. "We're looking for a friend. We think he's been picked up by the Authority."

Yani winced. "That's bad luck. Those Authentics are strange. Not right in the head, if you ask me. The Authority is ruthless and unpredictable. Rules this place with an iron fist. Though one could argue that's necessary to keep this pack of wild animals in line."

"We don't know that he's in trouble with her," Galu said. "They're...old friends."

"The kind of friend that refuses to die, eh?" Yani said. "The kind that sucks you back in for just one favor, and before you know it, your life's gone to shit and you're on the run from the law?"

I arched an eyebrow. That sounded like the voice of experience. "Exactly that kind of friend."

Yani picked up his coffee cup and took another sip. "If you need information about the Authority, I know a guy who runs in her crew. Timing's perfect, actually. Once a month, she hosts a set of fights. It's tonight. We can talk to him there."

"So these fights are legal, I assume? If she's running them?"

"Only two laws here in the land of the free. Don't cross the Governors and their crews. And whatever you're up to, don't get caught."

"Survival of the fittest, eh?" Daevin said. "I can respect that."

"It's more like *divine selection*. Or so the Authority says. The fights aren't just for entertainment; they're how the Authority metes out punishment. Trial by combat. If you can beat one of her thugs, you'll be judged innocent. If they beat you into a pulp...well, you're as guilty as they come."

"Barbaric." Rex shook his jackal snout.

"We're not in Kansas anymore," I remarked. "You can get us into the fights tonight? So we can talk to this friend of yours? See if our friend has shown up and what she wants with him?"

"Can do."

"And what do we owe you in return for this favor?" Luiz asked.

"Consider it on the house. I liked Vizol; he helped me out of a tough pinch. And I'd like even more to have Veil Force on speed dial."

"That's not exactly how we do things."

Yani grinned and cracked his massive knuckles. "Well, it's how we do things 'round here. So if you want my help, that's the price."

THE FIGHTS WERE LOCATED in a claustrophobic stone building known to the locals by the charming nickname "The Gauntlet." The main floor was strewn with sawdust, spilled liquor, and god-only-knew what else, while three rings of rickety balconies soared high above, with rowdy supes hanging over the sides.

I felt a few drops of something fall from above and held back my shudder of distaste. I needed an umbrella in here. I didn't even want to think about the possibilities of what might be dripping on me.

To his credit, Yani seemed as comfortable as a cucumber in this place. He was met by handshakes and slaps on the back as he navigated us through the crowded space. Dad had reached out to the troll for his original mission because he'd heard Yani was the supe to go to if you needed information or connections in Antares. Clearly, Yani's little empire had only grown in the last few years. Impressive.

I, myself, was not enjoying the attention I was getting from the mostly male patrons of this place—the up-down looks and even a few catcalls. Luiz and Daevin flanked me closely, and I found myself both grateful and missing Konstantin. He should have been the one at my side breaking the fingers of the greasy shifter who'd just tried to pinch my ass as I scooted through the crowd. I could break the shifter's fingers myself, but it was the thought that counted.

I needed him back with me. I needed answers. *Where are you, Konstantin? Are you here? And if you are, what the hell are you doing in a place like this? Why did you leave? And what does it mean for us?* And what was more, I needed to pick up where we'd left off in that hotel room—

A hand on my elbow startled me and I jumped. It was Luiz, leaning in close to whisper, "I don't know what you're thinking about, but you smell delectable right now. You're going to draw the wrong kind of attention."

My face turned scarlet as I realized he was talking about my human pheromones. Even thinking of Konstantin had ratcheted my desire up to ten. "Konstantin," I half-whispered, half-groaned.

Luiz slung an arm around my shoulder, pulling me tight against him. "We'll find him and you'll get your happily-ever-after sex. But right now, you've got to be on your guard."

I nodded. He was right.

A deafening cheer went up around us and bright light punctured the space from above, illuminating a ring in the center. My stomach dipped. I didn't mind fighting, but I didn't want to sit through state-sanctioned murder under the guise of combat. This would be hard to watch.

Yani leaned in close. "You five stay here. I'm going to see if I can talk to my friend. I'll bring him over here if I can, and you can ask him your questions."

"Isn't there anywhere more private?" Galu looked around at the mass of bodies pressing in around us, shouting and hoisting up money to place wagers.

"Best not look suspicious. She watches things closely. Best that it seem like we just ran into each other and are having a chat."

I was about to ask him when the fights would start when an absolute hush fell over the crowd.

I looked around in alarm.

But then I saw what had caused it. A figure had stepped into the spotlight in the center of the ring. She was small and petite, her figure almost girlish. Her eyes were the unnatural round shape of a baby doll, but this was a doll built for nightmares, for they were bright, blood red. She wore a necklace of glittering black stones and a slim-cut black dress that displayed her smooth, alabaster skin.

"That's her," Yani whispered, just the softest sound under his breath.

Iona Haas. The Authority.

This creature had been forged from an ancient fusion of human and bat. She subsided on pure blood and thrived in darkness. Authentics lived in complex and ruthless social networks in elaborate underground palaces. Almost all of the literary tales about vampires had been based on these Authentics. They were incredibly powerful, and they avoided sunlight, as it pained them. But it didn't kill them. Nothing did.

But she was more than just an Authentic. She was Konstantin's Maker. The reason I was here, rather than cozied up in Konstantin's palatial bed after a two-day shag session

My eyes narrowed. Everyone else seemed to look away, but I stared right at her, willing her to look at me. Daring her. Somehow, she had stolen Konstantin from me.

I would take him back.

Her red eyes met mine, and she sneered, revealing two shining white daggers for fangs. Then she looked away, dismissing me, looking out at the crowd. "Citizens!" she called. Her voice was velvety and deep, incongruous to her tiny body. "Today I have a special treat for you. We have six criminals who will face their fates by combat today—"

The crowd roared with excitement, and Iona basked in it a moment before holding up her hands for silence. "But that's not all. I have a new enforcer here today. One of my fiercest warriors. Ancient and deadly. One of my children come home, ready to dispense divine justice on the lawbreakers who would seek to exploit our fair city."

One of my children come home...

My eyes widened. *Ohmygod, was she talking about—*

Konstantin.

He stepped up into the ring beside her.

My Konstantin. But not.

He was clad entirely in black leather, his hair tied back and secured with black leather straps. It was Konstantin...but he looked nothing like himself. The expression on his face was imperious as a Caesar. Cold as the darkness of space. Sharp as the axe blade he was allowing himself to become.

This was worse than I could have imagined. We were too late.

What had she done to him?

7

There was a simplicity to the fight. Kill or be killed. During the fight, the world fell away and Konstantin became something purely animal. Unburdened by morals or ethics. Heroism or chivalry.

But this...this was no fight. It was an execution.

Konstantin looked at the cowering dryad before him. How had this poor woman ended up in a place like this? She held her hands up before her in some semblance of a defensive posture, circling him warily.

His stomach heaved. He couldn't do this. He wasn't a murderer. Especially not for something as simple as theft, which was apparently this poor supe's only crime.

"Take her out!" someone heckled from the crowd.

"What are you waiting for?" called another.

He glanced over at Iona and found her imperious face twisted in a frown. She was not pleased about his delay.

He never should have agreed to this. *Fool!* He had to buy her trust long enough to slip her the poison. If he was successful in his plan, he would put a stop to this in the future. Iona wouldn't be able to force any more helpless supes into the ring under the guise of a "trial." But he wouldn't get to that point unless he ended *this* poor creature's life. He circled nearer, his mind still racing, running through the angles and permutations. Was there a way he could save this creature's life and still end Iona's? If there was, he didn't see it.

"Do it," his opponent whispered. Her face was pale with fear, her loam-brown eyes wide. Her dark hair was threaded through with ivy and ferns, her skin tinted with the soft green of chlorophyll. Dryads were gentle, peace-loving supes, protectors of the natural places in this world. How had this poor woman ended up in a place like this?

The crowd was growing increasingly restless.

"Only one of you is leaving that ring alive, my new enforcer," Iona called. "So if you want it to be you, you better fight."

"If you don't, someone else will," the dryad pleaded.

This was no fight, he wanted to shout. But he felt the walls closing in around him. At least he could make it quick. Painless. It was more than anyone else in this hellhole would give her.

So he pounced. Fast as lightning—the strike of a predator. Banishing his mortal thoughts and letting instinct take over, even while he sent up a prayer to an unfeeling God for his immortal soul.

She didn't struggle against him, but rather yielded in his arms like a lover. He stroked her cheek as he drank her lifeblood, trying to give her some last, small moment of kindness.

A desperate idea burst through him. Maybe he could give her more than the comfort of a kind death. He was almost full; he could feel her life slipping away. She was on the precipice, her skin gone sallow.

And so he stopped. Just short of the moment she was gone. To give her one last chance. Perhaps they would think her dead and she could escape. Konstantin prayed for a miracle, even as he surged to his feet, blood slick on his lips, and roared into the crowd. "Who's next?"

His eyes caught on a face in the masses and it was all he could do to disguise his shock. Rex. He would recognize that that furred jackal snout and those glowing golden eyes anywhere. And Daevin. He scanned the faces desperately. No, tell him they hadn't all come. That they hadn't brought her to this place. Luiz. Galu—

No. Zariya. Wearing an expression of horror and disbelief on her lovely features.

The crowd roared and it took all of Konstantin's reflexes to duck a swing that came at him from behind. In his moment of shock, they'd cleared the ring of the dryad's body and let his next opponent in. Konstantin whirled to face the ferocious snarl of a wolf shifter.

With a cry, he threw himself into the fight. Anything to forget what he'd just done. And the fact that Zariya had seen it all.

Konstantin fought until his muscles ached and his lungs barked for air. Eight opponents he faced, each progressively more deadly. Antares was a dangerous place, and it bred dangerous criminals. Those unlucky enough to be caught in the Authority's net were no lightweights, with the exception of the poor dryad. By the time the last opponent, a stringy-haired leyak with bulging eyes, hit the red-stained floor of the ring, Konstantin was swaying on his feet.

He hardly registered Iona's words, or the crowd's chants, or the missing faces of his team as he dragged himself out of the ring and down a cramped hallway to the room where he and Iona had waited prior to the fights.

He opened the door and collapsed onto the black leather sofa, not caring if his blood and sweat smeared the furniture. He hadn't been in a knock-down, drag-out fight like that in years. Vampires strengthened with age, but somehow he just felt old and tired.

"Excuse me," a simpering female voice said.

Konstantin shot up, adrenaline spiking once again.

A petite brunette in an even smaller black cocktail dress was sitting in a chair in the corner, one long leg crossed over the other, displaying ridiculously high platform heels. "Iona thought you might be hungry." She stood, swaying towards him.

"Get out," Konstantin growled. Iona had done enough. He'd been here a day and already he felt like he was losing himself. Doing things he'd sworn he'd never do again. He'd drank enough from that poor dryad. He wasn't about to start indulging in the blood of human women again.

"But—"

"Get out!" he roared, and the girl trembled in fear as she darted out of the room, slamming the door behind her.

Konstantin dropped his head into his hands. He needed to find a way to slip Iona the poison. And *soon*.

The hinges of the door creaked softly, announcing another intruder. "I said, *get out*," he growled, every syllable a threat.

The door clicked closed. "And here I was, thinking you'd be happy to see me."

Konstantin's head jerked up at the voice. There was no mistaking that sass. "Zariya!"

"In the flesh." She quirked a half-grin. Her hands were on her hips, and the expression on her face was as cocky as ever. But she kept her distance. Unsure. The distance pained him more than he could have imagined.

"You shouldn't be here," he said.

"Neither should you. But here we are."

"It's too dangerous—"

Zariya held up a hand. "Let's just skip the song and dance, shall we? We're here, and we're not leaving without you. You could have made this a lot easier if you'd just told us why you wanted to come visit your dear old mom rather than all this cloak and dagger."

They'd figured out he was here to see Iona, and what she was to him. Of course they had. But they didn't know the danger they were in. Maybe it was his fault for not telling them. But they never would have let him go alone. And they'd come anyway. His team was wonderful—and infuriating. "She threatened you. Phoenix Team, all of you. Unless I came. So I came. But I have a plan to free myself of her. For good."

Zariya frowned. "What does she want with you?"

"She says she wants me to help her train some new police force? I don't know. I won't be around long enough to do it. *She* won't be around."

"You're going to kill her?" Zariya crossed her arms beneath her chest. God, it was good to see her. He wanted to go to her, to take her in his arms and never be parted from her. But Iona might be able to smell a foreign supe on him. He couldn't risk it.

"The less you know, the better."

"Let us help you, Konstantin. I never thought I'd say this, but seeing you out there...it seems like you're in over your head. I mean, you killed a defenseless girl."

He bristled. The observation was too spot-on for his liking. "I didn't kill her. I just made it look like I did. And I've got it under control. You all need to lie low until I finish this. Where are you staying? I'll come find you when it's done."

"With a troll named Yani. But we're not letting you do this alone, Konstantin."

He stepped closer. As close as he dared. "Don't you see? I *have* to do it alone. Just seeing you in the crowd..." He shook his head. "I almost lost myself. I need you safe."

"That's a nice dream, but it's not the world we live in. I'm a Phantom. I'm on Phoenix Team. And we don't abandon our own. You all taught me that—"

Konstantin held up a hand as his sensitive ears caught the clicking of heels down the hallway. He knew that gait. Iona was coming.

"Hide!" he hissed. "She's coming!"

There was a closet in the corner and Konstantin hurried Zariya across the dingy room, nearly shoving her inside. He whirled just in time for Iona to glide into the room.

"Well," she said, her red eyes piercing him through, "you got off to a slow start, didn't you? But once you got the hang of things, you performed rather admirably."

"I didn't sign up to kill innocent supes."

"She was not innocent," Iona snapped. "She stole valuable property from me."

"What, a pair of earrings?'

"Slaves, Konstantin. She helped some of my most prized and valuable slaves escape. Some of my favorite vintages."

Konstantin paled. The dryad had been working *against* Iona to help other innocents? He prayed she was still alive and would make it out of this mess.

"Luckily, I still have some of the best. Like Amber, whom you so rudely dismissed. You need to eat, Konstantin. Regain your strength." Iona's nostrils flared, and her eyes searched the room.

Konstantin's stomach somersaulted. Could she smell Zariya?

"Unless you had something more exotic on the menu? Something sweet...Caramel and spice..." Her eyes closed. "Delectable."

"A lingering scent from earlier. Besides, food is not what I have in mind after a fight." He stepped closer to Iona, his stomach roiling. He needed to distract her. She couldn't find Zariya. She would rip her limb from limb. Then find the rest of his team and do the same.

"Nonsense. Appetite is on everyone's mind after a fight." Iona opened her eyes and blinked rapidly at finding him so close. "Unless, a *different* appetite is what's on your mind?"

"We could see where the night takes us." Konstantin brushed Iona's hair back from her neck with the back of his hand. It took all his acting not to shudder. As soon as they were gone from the room and Zariya was safe, he'd make an excuse to stop this from going further.

A smile curved onto Iona's inhuman face. He'd done it. She was moving towards the door. Relief filled him.

A muffled clunk from across the room snapped Iona's attention back.

So he did the only thing he could think of. He kissed her.

8

I was numb. Hands. Feet. Heart. Konstantin was kissing that
—*thing*. I couldn't. I just couldn't.

I stood in the broom closet, my face flaming with humilia-
tion, my heart twisted with agony. Iona broke off the kiss with a
smirk, brushing a lock of Konstantin's blond hair back from his
temple. A closeness that I thought Konstantin had reserved for me
alone. I stood there in helpless fury as she took his hand and led him
out the door. As he didn't even look back my way.

I swiped tears off my cheeks with the heels of my hands and then
kicked the cursed bucket I had accidentally nudged with my foot,
resulting in the noise that had almost gotten me caught.

Konstantin was acting. He had to be. Right?

But the vampire in that ring—the vampire with Iona... I hadn't
recognized that vampire. How well did I really know Konstantin?
What if it wasn't just an act? What if being here was letting free some
savage part of himself he'd kept chained for too long? What if part of
him *wanted* to let it free?

I slipped out of the room back into the hall to join the guys, my
mind spinning like a top. Among it all, I latched on to one fact. He'd
spared the first "competitor" in the ring. The dryad. Her takedown

had looked ruthless—vicious—but he'd said it had been an act. She was still alive. We could help that supe. And maybe she could help us.

The main floor of the arena was emptying out as the crowd collected their winnings or went to grab drinks at other establishments. The rest of the team was huddled in the corner, shadowed by Yani's huge bulk.

The troll had been quiet ever since the savagery of the first fight. I would have expected him to be used to this sort of thing, but now that I really looked, Yani's face was drawn, his eyes distant. Was he all right? He'd gone off at one point during one of the later fights, but I'd assumed it was to talk to his contact. But he hadn't returned with anyone.

"Are you okay?" Galu asked. "The Authority went back the same way you did. We worried you might get caught."

"Almost," I admitted. "But I talked to Konstantin. He said he's trying to kill her. He wants us to let him handle it. Lie low."

"Screw that," Daevin said. "He's obviously in over his head. Otherwise, he wouldn't have been up there draining defenseless girls dry."

"Also, about that," I said. "Konstantin said he didn't kill her. Not all the way. "

"What?" Yani rounded on me and seized me by my shoulders, lifting me bodily, his face inches from mine. "Don't fuck with me."

"Whoa, whoa, easy." Galu laid a hand on Yani's huge shoulder. "We're all on the same side here."

His thick fingers were digging painfully into the flesh of my upper arms, but I struggled to keep calm. I examined his face. "You knew her, didn't you?"

Yani's features crumpled. He set me down with a jarring move. "Yes. She was a...a friend."

I patted his forearm. "She sounded special. She helped smuggle slaves out of the Authority's compound," I explained to the rest of the team. I turned back to Yani. "If there's even a chance she's still alive, we should go get her."

"There's no way. Your *friend*"—he said the word with venom —"drained the life from her."

"He said he didn't. Isn't it worth finding out? Do you know where they might have taken her? Maybe we can save her."

Yanni furrowed two huge eyebrows. "I imagine the bodies will be loaded in a truck to go to the city morgue. Maybe we can intercept her before then."

"Let's go."

Yani nodded and motioned for us to follow him deeper into the building. We fell in behind him.

"Did he seem all right?" Luiz asked. "Are *you* all right?"

I pressed my lips together, refusing to meet his eyes. "He and the Authority seemed...*friendly*. We have to hope it's an act." I shook my head and closed my eyes briefly to banish the image of them kissing. But it was burned into my retinas. "He was convincing."

"Have some faith," Galu offered. "Veil Force is everything to Konstantin. Protecting supes is what he does. He has a good reason for all of this."

I didn't mention what he'd said about the Authority targeting us. It might make them object to my next suggestion. "I think we need surveillance on the Authority's fortress. We need to know what's going on in there, and we need a plan to get Konstantin out if things go south."

"It's a wise course of action and shouldn't jeopardize Konstantin's primary mission," Rex said.

It was all I could do not to pump my fist in triumph. I'd been learning that if Rex went for a plan, it was definitely a good one.

Yani led us down a set of rickety stairs and into a dim part of the building. He paused before a thick door. "The loading dock lets out from this storeroom. I've done a few exchanges from this location."

I motioned him forward and he opened the door and ducked inside.

My heart squeezed at the sight inside. Amongst crates of liquor and shelves of boxes sat eight black body bags stacked on top of each other against one wall.

Yani's big hand was to his mouth, and I thought I glimpsed tears glimmering on his lashes. Wow, this dryad must have meant a lot more to him than he'd let on. "I don't think I can look," he said.

"I'll do it," Daevin offered quietly, and he walked across the room to unzip the first bag.

I shuddered to think of the bloody remnants inside those containers—evidence of Konstantin's true potential for violence.

"It must have been hard to watch," I said.

Yani nodded, his eyes fixed on Daevin.

"But you came tonight, with us. Did you know she would be in one of the fights?"

"No." The word was barely a whisper. "I hadn't heard from her in a few days. I was worried, but I didn't know. Not until I saw her up there."

"I found her," Daevin said. He reached a hand in to search for a pulse.

Silence swallowed us as we stood, watching. Waiting.

"I think..." Daevin looked up with amazement. "I think I feel something. It's really weak—"

Yani moved faster than I could have imagined anyone with his bulk capable of. He lifted the dryad's body gently out of the body bag. "Come on. We need to get her to a healer." He turned to look at us, anguish on his face. "And you all need to run."

My eyes widened. "Yani, what did you do?"

He looked away. The ceiling, the floor, anywhere but me. "I saw your friend kill her—or I thought I did. I was angry. When my contact came to talk to me...I may have mentioned you were staying with me."

"Yani, what the fuck?" Daevin exploded.

"I'm sorry! Now that I know he spared her, I feel terrible. Go find a hotel to stay in and I'll still help you. I'll make this right, I swear. You just shouldn't stay at my place. They might come for you there."

Goddammit. Less than a day in Antares and the Authority's thugs were already on us.

I sighed. "Fine. Lead the way."

We made our way outside and waited for one of the sleek black vans that served as the city's taxi service. A cab pulled up and Yani hopped into it, still tenderly cradling the dryad to his chest. "I'll fix this—"

"Just go," Luiz snapped as I waved him off. It had been too much to hope that we would have help here. We were on our own.

The street was quiet, but it was only a few moments until the next cab pulled up. We piled in and Galu told the driver to head to the nicest hotel in town. I guess he figured it was a good idea to get us into a good part of town so we could regroup.

But then two vampires with machine guns climbed into the cab after us, and I realized that we were in deep shit.

One of the vampires, a dark-skinned male with a head full of short dreadlocks, pointed one of the guns at me. "The Authority has requested the honor of your presence at her home."

Fuck. It seemed that Yani's betrayal had already come home to roost.

The other man, an older vampire with silver hair, waved to the driver. "There's been a change of address."

I looked between the two vampires. It wasn't worth risking a fight in the confines of this vehicle. Someone would get shot. "We'd be honored."

"Excellent," the older vampire sneered.

It wasn't long before we were gliding through the gate to the Authority's big-ass fortress and into a tree-lined courtyard. Honestly, who needed a castle these days? Tacky.

Our vampire "escorts" got us out of the vehicle at gunpoint and directed us through the ornately-carved front doors.

Galu sidled up next to me as we walked, whispering, "Stay calm. We don't know what she wants with us. This could be routine. We're strange supes in her city."

"I...forgot to mention..." I murmured back. "The whole reason Konstantin is here is because she threatened to off all of us if he didn't come to heel."

An explosion of quiet curses sounded behind me. Even Rex let out a disgruntled, "Bloody hell." I looked over my shoulder.

"No talking." The older vampire prodded Galu between the shoulder blades with the butt of his AR. As Galu crossed the threshold into the castle, a shiver wracked his body and he nearly staggered to his knees.

"What just happened to him?" I drew to a stop. "Galu?"

"The threshold washes away enchantments," the old vampire said. "All must come before the Authority as they truly are. No magic." He shoved me next and I stumbled forward over the lintel.

A wave of enchantment washed over me, like I had been dunked in cold water. My mind—my memories—stretched and tore as Dad's memories were ripped from my mind like a plant pulled out at the root.

I fell forward to one knee with a gasp, my hands clutching my pounding head, as if I could keep the magic inside my skull by pure force of will. But the enchantment was too strong. Every memory imparted by Dad's memory palace was torn from me.

Leaving barren emptiness in their wake.

My breath came in ragged gasps as, for the first time, my own fears and inadequacies washed over me. I had relied on Dad's memories—his strength—to make me into a Phantom. Without them, without *him*, I was alone.

9

———————

Konstantin sat at the impossibly long dining room table, wishing everything on the plates didn't look so...raw. He'd spent so much time living among humans that he'd come to like his meals a little more cooked. He glanced at the lovely young redhead sitting demurely by Iona's side. Or a little less *alive*.

He only drank blood from a live person during battle these days, and that was often out of necessity. Drinking from an innocent human no longer felt right. Even if the human said they were willing, vampire magic and the unequal power dynamic made him question whether that could ever be true.

He hadn't realized that these days Iona was only drinking blood right from the vein. That made his task here infinitely more complicated. Perhaps he could slip the poison in a drink? Her wine? But she was always surrounded. Someone was always watching.

He would need to get her alone. There was one way he thought he could do that, but the thought made his skin crawl. Kissing her had brought back a maelstrom of memories he'd done his best to lock away.

And poor Zariya. What must she have been thinking? The way

she'd looked at him after seeing him in the ring—almost convinced he was the monster he was pretending to be.

Besides, the line between acting and reality was a hazy one. He *had* committed those atrocious acts, even if he hadn't wanted to. He'd almost killed a defenseless dryad. Or maybe she was dead by now.

He couldn't stay here much longer. Iona had a way of corrupting everything around her. She was a plague. A cancer. She needed to be terminated.

One of Iona's lackeys, a scarred Derived with a black fauxhawk, crossed the room and whispered something in Iona's ear. Her bored expression twisted into something...delighted. Her eyes flicked to him. Konstantin licked his dry lips. What was going on?

"Konstantin, we have guests. Shall they join us for dinner?"

"Whatever you think is best," he replied. What game was she playing?

"Yes, bring them in. Find chairs for them. She'll sit here." Iona patted the table by her left hand.

She?

Konstantin did his best to suppress his curiosity.

But when the first "guest" walked in, his blood ran cold. Galu. No. Daevin—Rex—Luiz—no, no, no.

Zariya emerged through the doorway, a vampire guard directing her steps with a heavy hand on her shoulder. She was looking at the ground, her face as white as ash. What had they done to her?

Konstantin exploded to his feet, his chair crashing to the floor behind him. He was around the table in an instant, his hand grasping Iona's throat. "What is this?" He growled into her face. "I did what you asked. I came here. This is not the deal."

Iona was smiling widely, her delight at his outburst evident. She'd always loved his savagery. It was why he'd worked so hard to over-come it. He loosened his grip slightly.

"I've done nothing except invite your dear friends to dinner. I figured if they were here, we should all meet."

"You figured wrong. They leave here. Now. Or I won't help you."

"But, Konstantin, you already have." Iona grinned.

"What are you talking about?"

"You brought me her." Iona pointed at Zariya. Her lip drew back in a scowl, her sharp fangs flashing.

Zariya was still looking at the ground, shock written across her lovely features.

"Why? What did you do to her?"

"Release me or you'll never find out."

Konstantin begrudgingly uncoiled his fingers from the column of Iona's throat and backed up. Red fingerprints marred her neck, but she knew as well as he did that his threat had been a bluff. He couldn't kill Iona by strangling her. She was too powerful. She was practically immortal.

His Maker rose from her chair. Her vampire servants had quickly filled in chairs for his team around the table. "Why don't we all sit? You've all come such a long way, and this one has clearly had a fright."

No one moved.

Iona frowned. "*Sit!*" She shouted the word in a voice as deep and as ancient as the grave. Shadows splattered the walls as the candles guttered at her command.

Even Konstantin found himself taking a step back. Iona didn't often show her full power as an Authentic. When she did, it was terrifying.

His team settled into chairs around the table. He wished he had his comm and could communicate with them. They needed to play this very carefully. Iona was unpredictable and dangerous. But they were ready for that. Except Zariya. She didn't seem herself. Something had happened since he'd seen her last.

"They're all sitting." Konstantin growled, perching on the edge of his own chair, his muscles coiled. "Now tell me what's really going on."

"My protective enchantments around this place are quite powerful. A web, capturing any magics or spells that may try to sneak through. The spell delivers them all to me for inspection."

Konstantin banged the table with a fist. "It's not story time. I asked you what the fuck is going on."

"Konstantin, don't be petulant. I'm trying to explain what the fuck is going on, as you so crassly put it. This one tried to bring a spell with her into my castle." Iona pointed at Zariya, who was still staring mutely at the table, her arms wrapped around her waist protectively. He longed to go to her, to take her face in his hands and kiss away her shock and fear. But he couldn't draw extra attention to her. If Iona knew that Konstantin had feelings for Zariya...it would become her special delight to torment her.

Iona took the silver plate from before her and poured a bit of water onto it. Then she reached in the air above her and twisted, as if plucking an apple off an invisible tree. But what materialized in her hand was no apple, but a pulsing ball of iridescent light, the colors twisting and darting like the surface of an oil slick.

Konstantin couldn't help it. He found himself leaning forward. His eyes flew open as he caught an image flickering across the surface of the ball. Another. Pictures were undulating around the strange thing at impossible speeds. Too fast to capture with his eye. But there were definitely pictures.

"What is that?" His words were hoarse.

"Would you like to tell him, Zariya Chanji? What you have been hiding in your mind all this time?" Iona's macabre smile was wild with delight.

Zariya looked up at her name. Tears shimmered in her eyes as she regarded the glowing magic held in Iona's deft fingers. "It's..." She cleared her throat. "It's all my father's memories."

Silence.

But for Iona's quiet chuckle.

All her father's...all of Vizol's memories? How was that possible? She'd carried his memories with her? In her mind? Konstantin's thoughts were like quicksand, but still, the bolts of insight began to reach him.

The sudden change in Zariya's skill level—from when he'd first fought her in Four Freedoms park to when she'd passed her test. Her uncanny skill as a Phantom despite her lack of training. Her casual knowledge of certain missions that should have been top secret. A picture was coming into focus.

Zariya...had all of Vizol's memories.

And that meant all of his memories of Konstantin, too.

Konstantin's failures, his fears, his doubts. He'd confided in Vizol more than anyone in centuries. And the rest of the team, too. As she'd been getting to know them all, pretending to become their friends, one by one, she'd already known it all. She'd had *all* the inside information. Had she been using it to befriend them? To get them to trust her? Had *Caelfwich* even really picked her to be a Phantom? Or had she known what a brand from the sword would mean? Had she sought it out? Marked herself to become one of them for her own purposes?

He looked at the shocked expression on the faces of the rest of his team and knew their thoughts mirrored his own. Did any of them really know Zariya?

Tears were flowing freely down Zariya's face now. "I didn't mean to keep it from you. At first, I just wanted some extra help fitting in, completing the missions. And then as time went on...I didn't want to ruin anything." She looked around. "Konstantin, this team, you all... you mean so much to me. Everything between us is real. I'm still me. I just...had some of my dad's memories in my head."

"You should have told us, Six," Luiz murmured.

There were mutters of agreement.

Zariya stood, her chair screeching on the cold tile floor. "I can't do this." She whirled and started across the room, but two of Iona's guards seized her by the arms and spun her back around, shoving her back into her chair.

"As much as I've enjoyed this little scene of domestic discord, that isn't why you're here." Iona flashed her teeth. "You're here because you wronged *me*."

"I've never even met you," Zariya protested.

Iona plucked a single strand from the ball of memories she still held and dropped it into the water-covered plate. She twirled her finger and an image bloomed into life in the air above the table.

It was Vizol. In black tactical gear, moving through the twisted, dusty streets of Antares. His team followed close behind. Konstantin recognized Cyriaque. They were fleeing someone. Something.

"Though MASC has no jurisdiction here in this free city, your father and his team came here two years ago to execute a mission. A rescue. They performed poorly and were being chased through the city. In order to get away..."

The scene showed Vizol stopping, setting a bomb below a gate, and then running for it. But it seemed that the pursers didn't come that way. Instead, a silver Jaguar turned directly through the gate.

From the back of a black SUV, twisted in his seat, Vizol watched in horror as the bomb detonated and annihilated the car.

The memory flickered and died, leaving only silence.

Iona's skin was even paler, her face pinched in rage. "Do you know who was driving that car?"

Zariya gave a tiny shake of her head.

Alarm bells were going off in Konstantin's mind. This was wrong. All wrong—

"My dearest daughter. My Persia, who was with me for some two hundred years. You see, Konstantin, you were once my favorite son, but then you left, and after a time, I was content to let you have your life. But I made more children. Persia was my most cherished offspring. She made this immortal life worth living. Until Vizol Chanji murdered her."

Dear Father in heaven. The truth spread out before him, vast and wide. It had never been about training a police force. It had always been about this. Iona had threatened his team, knowing he would force them to stay behind. Knowing, somehow, that they would come for him. That Zariya would come. Iona had played him so completely. Played them all.

"I'm so sorry," Zariya managed. "It was an accident."

Iona drew herself up to her feet, her hands pressed to the table.

"There is no excuse! She's dead because of him. And so I made sure to repay the favor."

Zariya's green eyes flashed. "You had Warrick Mason kill him."

"I did. But that revenge was hollow. Distant. It wasn't enough to calm the ache inside my heart. This hole that eats at me each day." Iona stalked around the table and seized Zariya by the hair.

"Iona!" Konstantin moved around the table, but another of Iona's vampires, a muscled Derived with a shiny bald head, appeared before him and pressed an AR-15 against Konstantin's chest.

"It wasn't until I saw the footage from Bhutan that I realized why my revenge was so unsatisfying. You see, Vizol Chanji stole my daughter from me. My vengeance won't be complete until I take his daughter in return."

10

Fear roared through me, as loud as a jet engine. It drowned out all other thoughts and emotions. No, that wasn't true. There was one other emotion.

Loss.

I hadn't realized how much of a comfort Dad's memories had become. Though he was gone, in a way, he had always been with me. And now that was gone too. It felt like losing him all over again.

I couldn't find it in me to summon anger or outrage over what Iona had done. Iona was hungry for vengeance, but I was tired of it. It had fueled me, but in doing so, had twisted me too. I'd lied to my team and to the man I loved. I'd thrown myself into harm's way with reckless abandon. I hardly recognized myself.

At least now I had answers. Iona had been behind Dad's death—all because a mission had gone sideways. Because of an accident. She was grieving. And that kind of sorrow did strange things to people.

I should have been on alert, readying myself to fight, but I all I wanted to do was cry. Those weeks following Dad's funeral tugged me back, the grief an insistent lover that wouldn't let me go.

The scene around me moved as if in slow motion—as Iona's

vampire goons closed around us—as my team leapt to my defense with snarls and threats.

The tears started flowing freely then. I didn't deserve them. I had lied to them from the very first day. And still they were protecting me? They should just let her take me. I couldn't let Konstantin and the rest of my team risk themselves for me.

"Don't you fucking touch her," Konstantin roared. His blue eyes were wild and unfocused, his face purple with rage. "This was all a setup, wasn't it? You lured me here knowing my team would follow."

"You're all so predictable, you Phantoms, with your honor and loyalty. So trite. It will be your downfall," Iona sneered.

Konstantin pointed at me. "She is under my protection. They all are."

Iona tightened her fingers in my hair, twisting painfully. "Peculiar. I think you care for this one more than you care to admit. How perfectly the fates align. When I kill her, I'll be avenging your betrayal of me as well."

"You'll have to come through all the five of us, bitch!" Luiz shouted.

Iona just smirked. "Have you ever fought an Authentic, fae? No, I thought not. You don't understand what it is you face. You're children, playing at being soldiers."

"If we're children, we're those freaky twins from *The Shining*. Because we're your worst fucking nightmare," Daevin snapped.

I couldn't help the tiny smile that flicked across my face. I didn't think we could fight our way out of this, or talk our way out, though Daevin and Luiz would give it a good try. But I wouldn't let them die for me. "Don't hurt them," I said. I raised my hands. "Let them all go, including Konstantin, and you can have me."

"I think you overestimate your bargaining power. I can have you *and* them," Iona snarled.

"No, you can't." Konstantin looked up. Triumphant. "Because I've Claimed her."

I looked at him sideways. What the hell was he on about?

Iona's lip curled back. "You can't do that. It only applies to humans."

"She's half-human," Konstantin said. "And I invoke it."

"Then I'll only kill half of her," Iona countered.

"That's not how it works and you know it."

Iona released her grip on me and stalked forward to stand before Konstantin. She only came up to his chest, but she glared up at him with such fierceness that I was surprised he could hold his footing. "It doesn't apply."

"It does."

She looked between me and Konstantin. "You haven't Claimed her fully. I can tell."

"I have," Konstantin said, though his voice wavered ever-so-slightly.

I opened my mouth and then closed it again. I hadn't ever heard of a vampire Claiming someone. But if Iona wasn't happy about it, it meant it was probably good for me. So I was going to keep my mouth shut. I wished I had Dad's memories. Maybe he'd heard of this law.

Once again, I felt the painful realization of how much I'd come to depend upon his knowledge. Without it, I felt ill-equipped to navigate through this dangerous world.

Konstantin continued. "I call on the Matriarch to discern the truth. And to make the final determination regarding the validity of my Claim."

Iona hissed and whirled, stalking away. "That old bag? She's gone senile."

"She's still the highest authority over our kind. Higher than you."

She turned back, her blood-red eyes blazing. "Fine. Keep your pet for now. I'll kill the rest of your team instead." She raised a hand to gesture to the vampires that surrounded us—but never made it.

Konstantin launched himself across the room and barreled into her.

They tumbled across the room together, grappling for the upper hand with movements so quick, my eye could barely track them. But

Konstantin came out on top, his hands around Iona's throat, one knee pinned across her chest. "Call them off," he gritted out.

Iona just smiled at him, half-glowering. "I've missed you, *kostlich*. There was never another like you. As I'm sure your snake pet knows."

I wished in that moment that I could transform like my ancestors, like my people. I knew Authentic vampires were notoriously difficult to kill—nearly impossible—but swallowing her whole still sounded pretty fucking satisfying.

Konstantin ignored her. "You will leave them alone. They are innocent. They've broken no laws."

"The DRC is a lawless place," Iona spat. "Unfortunate *mishaps* occur."

Konstantin's knuckles turned white as he tightened his grip. "You will not harm them." I didn't know if he was really hurting her, but she seemed to relent.

"Fine. They will stay here until we return from visiting the Matriarch. They will be safe until I am certain you will not double-cross me."

Konstantin released his grip and stood quickly, walking back to where we huddled in a circle, ready for a fight. "You better not harm a hair on their heads. Or there will be hell to pay."

Konstantin schooled his face to remain an impenetrable mask. He shouldn't have Claimed Zariya, but in the moment, it had been all he could think of. Claiming was an ancient act of subservience and ownership, whereas most modern vampires approached their relationships as partnerships. He didn't want Zariya to think he looked at her in that way, and he had never intended to treat their relationship in that manner. But in the moment, it had been the only way he could think of to keep her alive.

Konstantin and Zariya sat across the table from each other as the rest of the team was marched out of the room at gunpoint. Iona promised to make them "comfortable," and he trusted that she would not harm them, at least not yet. If she did, she'd want him to watch. To maximize his suffering. The team should be safe at least until they returned from visiting the Matriarch.

He wished he could say as much about him and Zariya. He met her gaze across the table and could read the apology written there.

She had a lot to apologize for. For risking herself by coming here. For not telling him about Vizol's memories.

But despite her lies, he found he wasn't angry. God, he'd made mistakes too. He should have told the team the truth, should have told them his plan and insisted they stay behind.

The vampire with the fauxhawk, who appeared to be Iona's vampire second-in-command, returned to the room bearing a silver inlaid box.

"Ah, our transport is here." Iona stood and opened the box, retrieving a familiar stone circle.

"The Chinvat Gate," Konstantin said. "You took it."

"It's always been mine. It was on loan to Warrick Mason, and when he so hopelessly bumbled things in Bhutan, I needed it back."

"Cyriaque is your pet?" The fire flared in Zariya's eyes.

A smile curved on Iona's blood-red lips. "So you figured it out. Bravo. It only took your little organization two years to realize they had a snake in the grass." She laughed once, but her face grew cold. "He has indeed been brought to heel. I'm surprised you didn't see it in your father's memories."

"You took them from me," Zariya snapped.

"So I did. What the memory would tell you is that Cyriaque Broussard was second-in-command on the mission that killed my daughter. In searching out the men who killed her, I found him first. After making him suffer a great deal, I was going to kill him. But he convinced me he could be more useful to me alive. And for the most part, it's proven true."

Konstantin ground his teeth. Cyriaque had been spying for two years? What sensitive information had he leaked in that time? What missions had he ruined? Though he knew how torture could warp a man...he still couldn't find sympathy within him. Cyriaque had helped Iona kill Vizol. He'd helped kill his best friend. That was unforgivable.

"Come," Iona said. She set the gate on the ground and threaded the key around her neck. "You will make your plea."

"What's so important about the Gate, anyway?" Zariya muttered as she went to stand on the other side of the stone circle.

It was the question he'd been wondering as well. There were thousands of ancient objects of great power scattered throughout the world—many even in Veil Force's evidence locker. Why was this one so important?

"Freedom," Iona said. "This Gate can transport you anywhere. Through any enchantment or spell. Such a device is precious."

Konstantin frowned as he went to stand beside Zariya. It was a non-answer. Zariya's pinky finger brushed his, and he took her hand. Gave her what comfort he could. Took her comfort for himself.

Iona scowled at the sight, but he didn't care. He had Claimed her. To convince the Matriarch, they better look the part.

So he took a deep breath, and they jumped.

11

———————

Falling through the Gate was just as I remembered it last time
—a strange sensation of stretching and separating. And then
coming back together all of a sudden. Dense and solid and
somewhere else.

A loud caw startled me as I stumbled out into a dark wood, shadowed with tree branches clutching at us like spindly fingers. We stood
on a cobblestone road leading to an ancient wall covered in moss.
Before us, a wrought-iron gate stretched tall. And behind it, a castle.

It looked like Dracula's castle, straight from a Hollywood movie.
This was a place of vampires of old, not the sleek, cosmopolitan type
that Konstantin had become. Coffins and candelabras and blood. What
the fuck were we getting ourselves into? Who was this Matriarch?

Iona strolled forward like she were a celebrity checking into a
five-star resort, and Konstantin and I trailed after, our hands still
clasped. That connection was more steadying than I could say. I was
still feeling the painful absence of Dad's memories, and my courage
was in short supply. I was going to have to rely on sarcasm and my
acting skills, apparently.

"Authentic vampires live in colonies." Konstantin spoke quietly, his voice a velvet rumble in my ears. "The social structure is matriarchal. The females live together, with whatever males they've deemed worthy. The rest of the males wander or live solitary lives."

"It's why there are so many vampire tales focusing on the male variety," Iona added, though she didn't look back. "You won't find Authentic females lurking in some remote village taking defenseless maidens. People come to us. Humans, supes, males alike. We are magnetic." She did look back then, raking her crimson eyes over me from top to toe. She sneered, clearly finding me wanting.

I set my jaw. *Don't let her rattle you.*

The gates let out a rasping squeal as one of the large doors opened of its own accord. Iona smirked and sauntered through.

Trepidation filled me as Konstantin tugged me forward through the gate. This had been his idea—Claiming me—whatever the hell that meant. So why did I feel like we were falling right into Iona's clutches? She'd taken Dad's memories and isolated us from the rest of the team. I didn't even know where I was. If they split Konstantin and me up, I'd be totally screwed.

Iona led us through the front gate, past vampire guards and guests with pale, imperious faces. Their nostrils flared as they saw me, no doubt my human blood calling to them like a siren song. I did my best to squelch my fear; I knew the intoxicating scent of my terror would reach them otherwise. From some of the hungry looks I got, I didn't think I'd been entirely successful.

"I won't let anything happen to you," Konstantin murmured. "Trust me."

I trusted him, but I didn't trust *her*. Iona had outmaneuvered the most brilliant, powerful supes I knew—my dad, Cyriaque, Konstantin. She'd known Konstantin would come to protect his team and she'd known we'd follow. We'd been pawns on her chessboard before we'd even realized she was a player. Was I supposed to just hope that we wouldn't be so naive next time?

A voluptuous vampire woman with flame red hair stopped us before a set of double iron doors. She was dressed in black leather with way more buckles than seemed necessary for functionality. "She's in an audience. You'll have to wait."

"I'd like somewhere private to rest and wait with my Claimed," Konstantin said.

"You don't make demands here," the vampire sneered.

"Please." He inclined his head respectfully.

"Very well." She flicked a hand and another vampire hurried over. "Take these two to the Emerald Suite." She turned back to Konstantin. Never to me. Me, she didn't even acknowledge. Snobby bitch. "We'll summon you when it's time."

"Thank you."

Iona waggled her fingers over her shoulder at us and followed the red-haired witch.

Our escort led us to a set of gold-encrusted doors, opening one without a word and disappearing back down the hall.

We hurried inside and Konstantin slammed the door, collapsing back against it, his eyes on the ceiling.

Then on me.

Words were stuck like cotton in my throat—all the things I wanted to say, now that we were alone. But I didn't know where to start. Things had spun out of control so fast.

The electricity between us on Quiribri Island felt like a distant memory. Replaced by...I wasn't sure. Whatever this was, it was awkward as hell.

"I'm sorry," I finally forced out. I sat down on the ornate damask bedspread with a bounce. "I should have told you about Dad's memories."

"Yes, you should have."

"I didn't mean for it to happen. When Cyriaque kidnapped me for my test, I thought it was real. I grabbed all the memories he'd left for me in one giant download. I don't think it's what he meant to happen."

Konstantin crossed the room and sat on the bed next to me, a careful space left between us.

"I wanted to tell you guys, I meant to. But it just felt so good to be competent. To be able to keep up on the missions. Dad's memories helped me so much. I was afraid sometimes, but not like I would have been if it was just...Zariya."

"We threw you in the deep end. Our missions have been incredibly tough. Nothing's gone according to plan. I don't blame you for using the resources you had. It's just hard for me to think that there was a part of Vizol preserved in you." Konstantin shook his head.

"It's not like I had a split personality. Just...memories. It helped me decide to join Phoenix Team. Dad really admired you as a leader. And a person."

"I felt the same."

"Konstantin, what's going on here? What's going to happen? Please tell me this is all part of your master plan?"

He leaned forward, his elbows on his knees, his head hanging. "None of this is going according to plan. I had no idea that Iona was using me to get to you. That she was behind Vizol's death. I shouldn't have Claimed you, but it was all I could think of at the moment."

"What does it mean? Am I like your vampire blood slave or something?" At the thought of the collar around my neck on Quiribri Island—walking down that stage with bright lights and a dozen eyes heavy on my skin—my gut twisted. I didn't think I could pretend to be anyone's slave, even to save my life.

"It is a public claim that the human is precious and has great value to you. That you will defend them to the death and consider harm to them as a mortal offense against you. That they are bound to you for the entirety of their mortal life. But vampires believe humans are inferior to us, and the law is antiquated, so there is an element of subservience. It's why I would not have Claimed you if I had a choice. I consider us equals."

I was still stuck on the first part. A lump grew in my throat. "I'm precious and have great value to you? You want me to be bound to you for the entirety of my life?"

"Of course." His blue eyes met mine, so filled with hope and helplessness and a hundred other things I didn't think I could decipher.

"We've only so recently declared our feelings for each other, and I do not even know what you want. But it is how I feel. Yes."

Disbelief filled me. He was doubting...whether or not I wanted him? I reached out and put my hand on his cheek. "I want you. Now and in the future. I don't know what forever holds, but I sure as hell hope it's you."

He leaned against my hand. "I feel the same. But it's not that simple. The magic of the Claiming will test our hearts and our bond. It is what Iona hopes will reveal a deception."

I let my hand fall. "So Iona's rooting for our true love to be a big sham? What happens if we don't pass this test thingy?"

"Likely, she will attempt to seize her revenge by killing you. I will have offended the Matriarch with my false petition, and my life will likely also be forfeit."

I rocketed to my feet. "What the hell? Konstantin, we're in deep shit."

"Only if our love isn't pure."

"We haven't even been on a date," I pointed out, spinning in a circle. This wasn't happening. I knew I was really, really into Konstantin, but I'd only dated losers and douchebags up until this point. Was this really true love? Forever? How the hell was I supposed to know? We were supposed to have time to figure it out.

I looked up and found Konstantin standing right before me. His hands seized my face, gently but firmly, and he walked me back until I bumped into the wall, his body pressed against mine.

"Zariya," he said, the word alone sending a curl of desire through me. "Do you remember what you said to me at Quiribri Island when I stopped things from progressing between us?"

I licked my lips. "That I was afraid if we didn't seize our chance to be together, we'd never have another."

He pushed away a lock of my hair with infinite tenderness. His eyes were focused on my lips, his presence surrounding me. "I do not know what will happen when we go before the Matriarch. But if things go wrong, I do not want to lose this chance."

My sluggish mind took a moment to reorient from the way his

fingers were trailing down my throat over the swell of my breasts. To take in what he was saying. Part of me was incredulous. Here? Now? In this house of horrors?

But the much stronger part of me was certain he was right. That if I missed this chance, I'd never forgive myself.

So I seized the collar of his shirt and kissed him. He wrapped his arms around me and pulled me flush against him.

I poured everything into that kiss—my doubt, my fear, my hope and love for him. And by the urgency of his kiss, I knew he was doing the same. If this was all we had left, we would make it count.

Konstantin needed no extra encouragement. His lips crushed against mine.

Hot and hungry, my hands roamed up the lean landscape of his shoulders and back down, seizing his tight ass.

He let out a throaty chuckle and broke off the kiss. "Find a new favorite part?"

Every part, I wanted to say. But I replied, "How can I tell without a proper inspection?"

"I know you've been eying it." He found the hem of my shirt and pulled it up over my head in one quick motion.

"Does it come with the vampire DNA?" I asked breathlessly, even as he trailed kisses down the side of my throat.

"A fine ass?" He chuckled. "Right. It's a tradeoff. Ravenous, unyielding hunger in exchange for a tight butt." I tilted my head to the side, allowing him better access.

My fingers were finding the buttons of his shirt of their own volition, trembling in anticipation.

"My ass was just as nice when I was human," he said as his fingertips trailed over the tops of my breasts, tracing a line of fire along the line of my bra.

"And so modest." I reveled in the sight of him as his shirt came off.

"Modesty is overrated. And you know what else is overrated?"

"Clothes?" My eyes were fixed on the creamy stretch of his skin, his perfect stomach.

"Talking," he growled. He seized me under my ass pulled my legs up around his waist. His lips silenced me with a bruising kiss, but I reveled in it. Sensations washed over me—the awareness of him—of his every touch. The low thrumming terror of what would happen if someone walked through the door barely registered. It didn't matter. He was the only thing that mattered. And us.

A knock sounded on the door and we both froze.

With a sad sigh, Konstantin broke off his kiss. Setting me down, he pressed his forehead to mine. "It seems this chance was never ours."

12

The Matriarch's audience chamber had not changed in five hundred years. Not its columns flanked by crumbling tapestries depicting scenes of vampire savagery. Nor its stale stench of dust and blood.

Konstantin had been here once before, during a conclave of Authentic vampires gathered to deal with a threat from some unaffiliated males. That rebellion had been quickly and savagely crushed. An example had been made. He still remembered those bodies in cages, swinging above the wall at sunrise. Left there to slowly starve to death, until all the life drained from them and they became dry corpses. He couldn't help the shiver that ran through him at the memory.

A wizened old woman stood at the front of the room, her blood-red eyes glittering dangerously. Her hair was snowy white, and her gnarled hands gripped a silver-topped cane, but she looked anything but senile. Power radiated from her.

The Matriarch. The oldest known living Authentic vampire.

"So," she said. Her raspy voice carried a strange harmonious quality. It was compelling. "You come before me to cement your Claim to this one?" The Matriarch walked slowly down the steps, quirking her head at Zariya. "She is unique."

Zariya met the Matriarch's gaze boldly.

The Matriarch curled her lip. "It seems as though that she does not yet know her place."

"Her place is beside me," Konstantin said. "And I would appreciate your confirmation of it so my Maker will cease interfering with our lives."

It was Iona's turn to sneer. "This is a sham. He Claimed her only to in an attempt to spare her from the righteous punishment she deserves."

"What is her crime?" The Matriarch asked.

"Being born to the man who killed my daughter."

"Had you a blood feud with this other family?"

"No," Iona admitted.

Konstantin cut in. "Zariya deserves no punishment. She's done nothing wrong. Please, can we proceed?"

The Matriarch nodded and motioned to one of her attendants.

The black-clad vampire stood before the Matriarch, holding out a large, flat wooden box. The Matriarch opened it and retrieved from within it a large object—almost like a glass mirror, with gold gilt edges. It was fashioned in the shape of an eye. He recognized the design. It was the Eye of Ra—an Egyptian symbol.

"The Egyptians," the Matriarch said as she regarded the object in her hand, "are the only advanced civilization as ancient as our own. Hathor, their goddess of love, was a friend of mine."

Zariya glanced at Konstantin.

He gave her an infinitesimal shrug. Was this Matriarch thousands of years old? Had she lived during the time of ancient Egypt? He couldn't say.

"Hathor is also known by another name. The Eye of Ra. It was a form she took from time to time. This Eye has a gift—it sees the bonds of love. You will stand on either side and look through at each other. If your love is pure, the glass will grow clear. You will see each other's faces."

"And if not?" Iona asked.

"Then the horrors they will see in its surface will drive them both mad."

"I'm sorry, what?" Zariya leaned forward, a hand to her ear. "Like our faces will melt *Indiana Jones* style?"

One of the vampire attendants snickered.

The Matriarch turned with a quizzical look. "I do not know what you refer to. But yes. It is the punishment you must pay for making a false claim before me."

Konstantin's mind stopped and started. Maybe she was bluffing. This could be all part of the mythology surrounding the Claiming. But if not... There *were* magical objects that could corrupt the mind. Could they risk it?

He looked around, evaluating. They were surrounded. How had he let them become so completely boxed in? No exit. No backdoor. They could only hope that the love between them was real.

Zariya shrugged. "Well, I'm ready if you are." Her voice was surprisingly steady.

He felt his heart swell. Even without Vizol's memories, Zariya was brave. She faced the unknown like a warrior. "I'm ready as well."

The Matriarch held out the Eye. "Take the mirror. Stand on either side and hold it up between you. Hathor will judge the truth of your heart."

Konstantin's stomach twisted and swooped. But he took a step forward and seized the mirror. They faced each other. And began to look.

AT FIRST, I saw nothing. Just the blank stretch of mirror—silvery as a still pond at dawn. But then there was movement. A rippling and swirling that began to coalesce into something.

The danger around us fell away, one by one.

Iona.

The Matriarch and her vampire guards...

None were as important or compelling as the object before me.

I gazed into the Eye of Ra with rapt fascination. Something was taking form. The outline of a face. Masculine. Rugged...

A bright flash emanated from the mirror and burned my eyes. I squeezed them closed, looking away. When I opened them again the mirror was as clear as a pane of glass. It hadn't been an image forming. It had been fog clearing.

Leaving me looking directly into Konstantin's perfectly blue eyes. I couldn't help it. I smiled. "Hey, you."

"Hey, yourself." He grinned back.

The wizened Matriarch moved lightning-fast—suddenly, she was behind Konstantin, peering through the mirror at me.

"Konstantin—" My voice was full of warning. I didn't know what this meant. Had we passed?

"The Eye of Ra shows us our truest heart's desire," she rasped. "That it has shown you each other tells me your love is true. Konstantin Bauer, your Claim on this woman is upheld. It must be respected by all vampires, Authentic or Derived."

My shoulders sagged in relief even as the Matriarch turned to Iona, whose face had twisted into a mask of rage. "She shall not be harmed by you. Or you will have much to answer for."

"Yes, Matriarch," Iona said stiffly.

One of the Matriarch's vampires took the relic from us, leaving Konstantin and I facing each other. Awed. He stepped in close and took my face in gentle hands. "I have never been a man of flowery words and poetry. So I will only say the words that have been written on my heart these past weeks. I love you, Zariya Chanji."

I swallowed the huge lump growing in my throat. Konstantin loved me. This vampire—this powerful warrior, fierce and fearless and ancient—he had chosen me. "I love you too." I found that tears were glittering in my eyes, turning his chiseled features into a refracted prism.

"I never could have guessed that the loss of my dear friend would bring such joy into my life."

At the mention of my father, my elation dimmed. I looked at Iona, my eyes narrowed. My goal from the very beginning had been to avenge my father's death. I had traced the conspiracy through MASC, the Collectors, Warrick Mason, and now here. To Iona. The Authority.

We'd escaped her clutches, but I couldn't just walk away from here and let her go free. She needed to suffer for what she'd done. A low snarl escaped me and Konstantin pulled me into an embrace, enveloping me in cool and calm.

"She will pay," he murmured into my ear, so quiet, I almost missed the words. "Trust me."

So I would. I had to. Because I had no plan myself.

He released me and turned to Iona. "We need to return to the DRC immediately. Matriarch, thank you for your hospitality."

She inclined her head at us. "Your reputation has traveled, Konstantin Bauer. I hoped I might meet you again someday. Are you certain you wish to remain working for this...Veil Force? You could do great things here, for me. You'd finally know real power."

I stiffened, but Konstantin nodded magnanimously. "I thank you for your kind offer, but my place is with the Mythical Alliance. Life has set me on a different path."

"So it seems. Very well. Iona, do as he asks. Escort them back to that little cesspit you call a city."

"As you wish," Iona choked out. She hadn't stopped glaring at us since the Matriarch had announced the results of the test.

Iona stepped into the middle of the room and threw down the Chinvat Gate. She touched the pendant around her neck—the key— and the gate began to pulse with purple light.

My stomach seized at the sight of it, not eager for another trip plunging through space. But I definitely didn't want to linger here any longer than necessary. Someone might decide that I smelled like a tasty appetizer.

The gate roared to life and Konstantin took my hand. "You first." He nodded to Iona.

She bared her teeth. "You think I would defy the Matriarch's order by sending you somewhere...unpleasant?"

"I know there's no end to your creativity," he replied simply. I shivered and he squeezed my fingers.

"Fine." Iona nodded to the Matriarch, strode across the room, and made a graceful leap into the glowing light.

Konstantin and I quickly followed.

My relief was palpable when we emerged back in Iona's throne room. Konstantin's comment had set my mind racing, filled me with images of all the horrible places a person could be deposited by a magic portal. The middle of the Sahara Desert. The bottom of the Mariana Trench. Inside an active volcano.

Konstantin smoothed his hair and turned to face his Maker. "Release the rest of my team. We're leaving."

Iona's blood-red lip curled back. "You and this...*thing* are free to go. But the Matriarch said nothing about the rest of your sorry excuse for a team. They will be remaining with me. Indefinitely."

My mouth dropped open. "They didn't do anything wrong. They broke no laws. You can't just keep them forever!"

"They are agents of a foreign governmental organization infiltrating my city. And in this city, I can do whatever the *fuck* I please!" she bellowed.

I stumbled back a step.

"Iona, please, be reasonable." Konstantin's voice was even. As if he weren't the least bit surprised by her outburst.

"Veil Force ordered the mission that killed my daughter. If I can't have her"—Iona pointed at me—"then I might as well have the rest."

That bitch! What were we going to do? We couldn't leave the rest of Phoenix Team here, trapped in her clutches.

"Iona, can I speak with you alone, please?" Konstantin asked.

"What?" I looked at him with barely veiled panic. We couldn't be separated, not in this place. "No, Konstantin—"

He looked at me gently, squeezing my hand. "She can't hurt you. I need a minute with her alone. Please." There was something else written in his blue eyes that made me pause. That brought to mind his whispered comment to me. *Trust me.* Konstantin had a plan.

"Fine." I just really hoped his plan didn't involve kissing her again.

Iona waved a hand to one of her lackeys, the bald-headed vampire. "Escort her to the sitting room. She'll wait there until Konstantin and I are finished."

Quickly, the two guards closed around me and ushered me out of the room. I looked over my shoulder and saw Konstantin watching me go.

Everything would be okay. He had a plan. We'd find a way to get the guys out of here, and then one day, we'd come back to end her. Like Dad had always said, sometimes you had to retreat and live to fight another day.

I was so caught up in my thoughts that I hadn't noticed the path we took. Until we turned into a black tiled room that dead-ended. An industrial shower hung over the damp floor. Despite the fact that the room had clearly just been washed, my nose detected an underlying scent—the copper tang of blood. My senses roared into awareness. I turned on the two vampire guards, mustering every ounce of disdain and authority I had left. "What are we doing here? Iona said to take me to a sitting room."

"That's what she said out loud," the grinning vampire guard with the mohawk said. Slowly stepping forward. Herding me into the room.

"But we got other instructions," the bald one said.

"What is this place?" My imperiousness was quickly wilting, giving way to fear.

"This is where we drain the blood to feed the vampires of this place. We don't always have time to take it fresh from the vein, though that is our preference, of course."

I took several more cautious steps back. "The Matriarch said I must not be harmed. It would be a violation of vampire law." My voice sounded shrill. Breathy.

"We can't harm you," the first vampire said. "But accidents happen."

With a flash of speed, he circled around behind me.

I whirled in time to see him taking an iron grate off a large drain in the corner of the room. "It would be such a shame if you fell somewhere you weren't supposed to. Tragic."

"Tragic," the other vampire echoed.

I bolted for the door.

But the bald vampire was faster. His arms circled around my waist like iron bars, my stomach lurching. He pulled me back flush against the stone-hard surface of his body even as I flailed against him.

I snarled and thrashed, trying to twist in his arms to scratch or bite him. But he was so strong, and Dad's memories had left me, leaving me only with my training as a kid. And nothing in the dojo could have prepared me for this.

I reached back and made contact with his face, my fingernails gauging furrows through his skin.

He bellowed.

"Shove her in!" the other cried, seizing my wrists. Together, they positioned me over the open drain, shoving me down towards the blackness of the hole.

I kicked and fought them, but my legs slipped through. With a gasp, I caught myself on the ledge, dangling out over blackness, my fingers just gripping the slick tile.

The last thing I saw before I fell was two macabre vampire faces grinning down at me. "Oops," the first one said gleefully.

And then his boot came down with a crunch on my knuckles.

13

I splashed into cold, fetid water and came up spluttering. It was perfectly dark in this place, the inky black of empty space. I opened my glands, questing out around me for infrared signatures. I registered a few small signatures, rats likely, but nothing larger.

I was safe.

For now.

I threw an arm up to my face, doing my best to muffle the stench that permeated the air. Rot and death and sewage... I let out a whimper as my mind spiraled into thoughts of what unmentionables might be floating in the water I stood in. I needed a way out of here.

And then I would come back and rip that Authentic bitch's head off.

A splash sounded in the distance.

I froze. Questing out with my senses, I searched farther for what I might have heard. My eyes widened. There was a new form in these sewers with me. Something *big*.

And it was coming right at me.

My breath came in quick bursts as the huge bulk of the creature drew nearer. I looked around with my glands frantically for a weapon, but there was nothing. I had only my hands, my venom, my wits. Those things that Manasa had gifted me with. They would have to be enough.

The creature was only yards away.

On the other hand...maybe I could hide. I fumbled my way to the side of the tunnel I stood in, pressing myself to the cold, slimy wall.

What kind of creatures inhabited a hellish labyrinth like this? Rabid, vampire-blood-gorged crocodiles? I sure as hell didn't want to find out.

But then I heard something strange. A high, female voice, murmuring low in the dark.

I blinked and refocused on my infrared sight. I'd missed it before amongst the bulk of the other, but there were in fact, two bodies coming towards me. One huge, and one small and slight.

I held my breath and listened. I could hardly hear over the sound of sloshing footsteps, but the female voice said, "We're nearing the turn to the dungeon grate."

"You sure we'll find them there?" A deep male voice rumbled. That voice...it was so familiar. Where had I heard that voice before?

"Not sure, but it's likely. We can start our search from there."

"I can't believe you're willing to go back into this place."

Yes, I definitely recognized that voice! The tone, the tenor...

"It's the least I can do. They saved me."

"Yani?" I whispered into the darkness. I couldn't believe it. It was our troll contact. The one who'd betrayed us to the Authority. But then he'd warned us, too. Why was he here?

The sloshing footsteps froze, leaving a heavy silence soon broken by a muffled click. The sound of a gun being cocked. "Who's there?" he replied.

Praying I hadn't just made a terrible mistake, I sloshed into the center of the brackish water, facing them. I held up a hand to block the flashlight illuminating me. "It's Zariya."

"Zariya?" Yani exclaimed. He uncocked his gun, much to my relief. "What in God's name are you doing here?"

"Iona." My shoulders slumped. "She couldn't kill me outright, so they dumped me down here."

"Lucky for you they don't know there's a way out of here. And back in," the female voice said. I squinted at the outline of the slim form at his side. Who was it?

"Zariya, this is Mandri. The dryad whom Konstantin saved."

My mouth dropped open. "You're all right?"

"Thanks to your vampire friend, I am. Yani took me to a healer and nursed me back to health."

"And now you're what, rescuing us?" I narrowed my eyes at Yani's bulk, not that he could see it in the darkness. Or maybe he could. I didn't know if trolls could see in the dark. "Feeling guilty for turning us over to Iona?"

"Yes. You have to understand, the Authority rules this place. She'd put out a request for intel on your team before you'd even contacted me. When you showed up at my door, I knew that keeping you from her was risky beyond belief. I liked your dad, but I wasn't sure I owed him that kind of loyalty. And then I thought I saw your vampire friend Konstantin kill Mandri, and I lost it. I turned you in. But I realized quickly what a mistake that was. I knew I needed to do what I could to help."

I considered. Yani *had* been in a difficult position. And frankly, he was here now. That was all I cared about. I didn't need grudges, I needed allies. "All right. The team, minus Konstantin, are locked in the dungeon. Can we get to them? Free them?"

"You're sure your boy can take down the Authority?"

"Absolutely," I said with much more certainty than I actually had. I had no idea what Konstantin's plan was.

"Then we're in. Let's go get your team. And rain some hellfire down on that bitch."

I didn't think I'd ever heard more welcome words.

~

KONSTANTIN WISHED he had his comm. He'd needed this moment alone with Iona, but he was desperate to know that Zariya was safe. Iona was as poisonous as a spider. He didn't trust her for a second.

He needed to end this. End her. The poison he'd procured from Merhzad was still tucked safely in his pocket, but he was no closer to finding a way to administer it.

Iona drank only from the veins of fresh young blood donors, and she was never alone. There was no way he'd be able to slip the poison into something she'd consume. He needed another plan.

And he thought he had one.

But it was risky—and foolhardy.

It was the only way to claim his freedom, once and for all. To end Iona's reign of terror.

"What now, Konstantin?" Iona let out a longsuffering sigh. "Isn't it enough that you flaunt your love before me?"

"You brought us here," Konstantin pointed out. "You tried to kill Zariya, forcing me to make a formal Claim to her. If there's any fault here, it's yours."

She sneered. "Yes, with you, everything was always my fault. Poor Konstantin, forced by his Maker to do such horrible things. Never mind that you delighted in them as much as I."

"I did not," Konstantin roared, advancing on her. "You tried your best to turn me into a monster, but still my conscience persisted. I knew what I was doing was wrong, and that knowledge ripped a hole so wide in the fabric of my soul that it almost ended me."

She didn't back down, her tiny chin held aloft in defiance. "Yet here you stand, stronger and prouder than ever. A true vampire. Everything I made you."

He stepped in close. He towered over her, though she faced his wrath without a glimmer of fear. "Everything I am today, I made myself. I scraped and clawed my way out of the black despair you shoved me into and put myself back together as best I could."

"Do you want a fucking prize, Konstantin? Vampires give no medals for being weak, mewling things plagued by conscience."

"I want nothing from you other than what I've always wanted. For you to leave me the fuck alone!"

"None of this changes my decision. You can have your whore, but the rest of your team is mine."

He let his head drop. Feigned frustration and defeat. He put his hands on his hips. "I can't leave without them, Iona."

"Then it appears we're at an impasse."

"What if... What if you could have me instead?" Konstantin looked up. Choked out the words. "Would you let them go then?"

"What are you suggesting?"

"The Maker's Kiss." He felt some measure of pride, that he could say the words without disgust. That he could hold his voice firm.

Iona's dark eyebrows flew up. "You would bind yourself to me with the Maker's Kiss? Your will would be mine as surely as it was when you were first made. But not for a decade. Forever."

"I know what the Maker's Kiss is." Konstantin ground his teeth. It was an ancient ritual, as ancient as the Claiming. He would drink her blood, binding him more tightly to her than the day he'd been made. Then she would complete the ritual by drinking his blood. Cementing her power over him.

Except he'd have poison flowing through his veins.

He'd turned it over a dozen different ways in his mind. Each potential method of administering the poison came with the same problem: He couldn't be sure that Iona would be fool enough to drink.

Except from his own veins.

She'd always had a weak spot when it came to him. The prospect of claiming his will once again would be too tempting to resist.

So many things could go wrong.

The poison might take him too. But he wasn't an Authentic vampire, so perhaps his human physiology would be different enough to allow him to survive.

Maybe the poison wouldn't work on her, in which case he'd truly be bound to her for the rest of his unnaturally long life.

But one saying chimed in his head—trite yet undeniable. *Desperate times call for desperate measures.*

14

Yani hung from the dungeon drain, his huge torso stuck halfway through the hole. Mandri and I tugged on his arms, panting with effort.

"You have to suck in," Mandri said.

"I'm sucking as hard as I can." Yani groaned.

"Okay, on three," I suggested. "We pull, he sucks."

We were making an awful racket. At any moment a guard would come in, and we'd be totally exposed.

"One...two...three!" I pulled with all my might at Yani's shoulder as Mandri pulled on his other side. Yani's face purpled...and then he slipped free, half-tumbling, half-sliding up out of the grate onto the dank dungeon floor.

We lay in a little pile, gasping and laughing. "Oh thank god." I closed my eyes for just a moment.

A gunshot cracked.

My eyes snapped open to find Yani holding a smoking gun.

Across the room, a Derived vampire guard looked down at the blood blooming from his chest with shock.

"Come on!" I scrambled to my feet, offering a hand to Mandri. "They know we're here now."

Yani pulled another gun from a holster in his boot, twirling it to hand it to me handle first. I wasn't a crack shot, like I had been with Dad's memories to guide me, but I knew how to use it. Point at bad guy. Boom.

I raised it, and just in time, too. Another two vampires appeared and we took them out.

"What's in these bullets?" I asked.

"New synthetic compound. Kills Deriveds on contact," Mandri said. "PharMagus tech. Only the Authority has it. I stole a few of these before I was caught."

I scowled at the mention of PharMagus, led by the douchebag Parker Kensington. He and I had a score to settle someday.

"The main cellblock is through here," Mandri said.

I knelt by one of the fallen guards and retrieved a ring of keys.

We hurried through the stone corridors and came out in a large semi-circular room filled with cells.

The sight of my teammates brought the sting of tears to my eyes.

"Six? Is that you?" Daevin was the first to notice our sudden appearance.

I jogged over and began to test out the keys.

Luiz poked his head out from the next cell with a grin. "I have never been so glad to see your fine ass slither in."

I grinned back. "I had some help."

Daevin's cell door opened and he stalked out, standing face to face with Yani, anger radiating off him. "This traitor?"

"He's sorry," I threw over my shoulder as I headed for Luiz. "And we need him."

Galu called from a cell over, "Report? Where's the boss?"

"He's with her. I don't know what's going on, but he wanted to be alone."

"He had a plan for coming here," Rex said from two cells down. His calm words made me grin even more. I'd missed these guys. "We have to assume he is executing it as we speak."

"So long as *she's* not executing *him*." Daevin turned.

I finished letting them out of the cages, and we exchanged quick hugs.

Galu rubbed his chin. "Rex has a point. If we go in there guns blazing, we might ruin Konstantin's plan."

"Nothing's gone according to plan," I pointed out. "We've been improvising all along. Even Konstantin. As it currently stands, she's bound by vampire law to let Konstantin and me go. But she plans to keep all of you indefinitely."

"Hard pass." Luiz shuddered.

"So we run? Leave Konstantin to fend for himself?" Daevin shook his head. "No way."

I knew how he felt. "As much as I hate it, right now, you're the one bargaining chip she holds over him. I think it's best if we remove that leverage. Trust Konstantin."

"I agree," Rex said.

The guys exchanged looks. "I guess we should have done that from the beginning." Galu sighed. "All right. We take ourselves out of the equation."

Mandri was standing by the door keeping watch. "There's someone coming! Hide!"

There was no way whoever was about to walk in wouldn't notice four prisoners missing.

"Got more of those bullets?" I whispered to Yani as we pressed ourselves to the wall.

He nodded.

Two Derived vampires strolled in. I recognized them both—they were the two who had ambushed us in the taxi. "I can't believe the fool has agreed to the Maker's Kiss. The great Konstantin Bauer, brought low. And she wants his team to watch? She's a cruel bitch."

"That's why we love her," the older vampire replied before his eyes fell on the open cell doors. "What the fuck—"

Yani popped the older vampire in the back.

I took down the other.

They both fell, and I surged forward, rolling over the vampire with dreadlocks. "What are you talking about? The Maker's Kiss?"

He sneered at me, taking in all of us standing above him. Then he spit in my face.

I closed my eyes to the flecks of blood. Wiped it slowly off. *Gross.*

"Konstantin...Bauer...is binding himself to her. For eternity." The vampire's head fell back, his dark eyes vacant. He was gone.

I surged to my feet, turning to the others. A pit of dread was growing in my stomach. "Do any of you know what the Maker's Kiss is?"

Mandri's lovely face had gone pale. "I do. It's a ceremony—they drink each other's blood. It's supposed to connect them as tightly as when a vampire is first made. But it doesn't wear off."

"Why would he agree to that?" My voice quavered.

Galu set his jaw. "To free us."

"We can't let him do it. Not when you're already free!" I said.

"Hell no," Daevin said.

Luiz nodded. "New plan. Stop the madness."

I turned to Rex. "Are you with us?"

"Of course," he replied. His golden eyes flashed. "The situation has changed."

I threw my arms around him.

Konstantin glowered at Iona, who stood smirking at him. Her sycophants had carried out a ceremonial stone table, stained red with the blood of former victims. In the four corners of the table were iron shackles to hold a person's wrists and ankles.

"Is this strictly necessary?" Konstantin waved at it. "I already told you I'd do this freely."

Iona pouted, sashaying over and running a finger up his arm. It was all he could do to resist a shiver of disgust. "You used to appreciate theatrics. You're so boring now. That's the first thing I'll train out of you."

"As you wish." Konstantin had one focus now. He needed to ingest the poison before they shackled him to that table. It had to be flowing in his veins before Iona sank her teeth into his neck.

"Your chariot awaits, sweet Konstantin." Iona walked to the table, lovingly stroking its pockmarked surface.

"Give me just a moment to ready myself." Konstantin turned and strode across the room. There were no windows, but he imagined that he could see the tangled city beyond. His last glimpse of freedom.

The future branched before him as he retrieved the tiny vial from his pocket.

The end.

Eternal servitude.

Or perhaps, freedom at last.

He had to trust his old friend Merhzad. If he said this poison would end an Authentic vampire, then it must be so.

Quickly, Konstantin drained the vial into his mouth, swallowing the sweet draught down. It tasted faintly of apples.

He turned back, shoving his hands in his pockets. Walking back towards what might be a gallows of his own making.

Iona was leaning forward, her elbows planted on the table, her chin on her hands. "Ready, my darling?"

"Ready."

Konstantin rolled up his sleeves and eased himself onto the table. He lay down and Iona herself closed the cold iron shackles around his wrists.

He looked at the vaulted ceiling so as not to see the glee written on her face. She was so certain she'd won.

The ceiling bore a fresco of two vampires twined around a desperate human subject. It was horrible. He latched on to it. This was why he'd done what he'd done. This was why he'd risked every-thing. Because the Authentic vampires, Iona especially, were true monsters. Devoid of humanity. A plague upon this Earth.

A flush of heat washed through him, followed by a cold wave that raised goosebumps on his skin. The poison. It was clearly affecting him somehow. Maybe it would take him too. He needed to hurry.

"Come," he said. "Let us be done."

Iona stood beside the table, looking down. She reached out one pale wrist, laying it just above his mouth. "Drink."

God help him. He surged upward and latched on, burying his teeth in her flesh. Letting the sweet, copper tang of her blood flow into him. Even as he wanted to spit it out, he forced himself to swallow.

Her head lolled back in delight.

When he released her wrist, she looked down at him, her eyes as bright as cherries. She bared her fangs.

"Stop!" came a shout from across the room.

Konstantin looked up, craning his neck.

It was Zariya. Wet, bedraggled, a gun in her hand. With his team behind her. Come to rescue him. The most beautiful sight he'd ever seen, even though he knew she was too late.

Iona pounced.

15

———

It happened so fast. And then so slow.

Iona, bent over Konstantin's body like a lover.

Iona, burying her fangs in his neck like a predator.

The Maker's Kiss.

Binding Konstantin to her for all eternity.

My teammates surged forward—Galu and Rex, Luiz and Daevin—attacking her vampire guards with fierce abandon.

But I was transfixed to the spot—pinned by her triumphant gaze like a butterfly spread beneath the scientist's pin.

Finally, almost languidly, Iona uncoiled herself from Konstantin's neck, straightening before us, her lips stained red. She unlocked Konstantin's shackles and he rose from the table onto unsteady feet, leaning heavily against it.

Oh, God. She was going to unleash him against us. Against *me*. "Konstantin—" Iona began, but she paused.

Coughed.

Konstantin himself was pale, still bracing himself against the stone table. His features looked like they were sketched in shadow, an artist's harsh charcoal lines where cheek and nose and jawline should be. Something was wrong.

The snarls and commotion around us had fallen still as my team-mates laid low the remainder of Iona's guards.

Iona's hand wavered, then flew to her stomach. She doubled over, and with a retching cough, vomited crimson blood onto the stones.

Konstantin was moving towards me now, hand over hand, bracing himself against the stone table. As if he couldn't stand on his own. What the hell was going on?

"What...did you do?" Iona snarled as she wiped her mouth with the back of her hand. She swayed on her feet and staggered to the side, falling hard to her knees.

"I knew you wouldn't be able to resist the Maker's Kiss," Konstantin panted. He lurched towards me and I grabbed him under the arms, staggering under his weight. He was heavy—all muscle and sinew.

Rex appeared at Konstantin's other side and wrapped our leader's arm around his shoulder, taking some of his weight.

Buoyed, Konstantin fixed his glacial-blue eyes on Iona again. "So I knew the only way to poison you was through my own blood."

"Poison?" Iona shrieked. But then she fell silent as her hand flew to her mouth. Her shoulders heaved and she vomited again.

"Poison?" I echoed, meeting Rex's gaze over Konstantin's sagging head. That meant...Konstantin had dosed himself with whatever the poison was, knowing she would ingest it through his blood. "Konstantin, the antidote. Where is it?"

He let out a low groan. "There is no antidote."

I swore my blood froze in my veins. No antidote...

"There has to be." Iona growled. She tried to crawl towards us, her hands slipping in her own bodily fluids. My stomach roiled at the sight. Her skin was graying, cracking. Blood dripped from the corners of her eyes, snaking down the planes of her cheeks in crimson rivers. She'd been a monster, but this—this was a was horrifying way to go. Even for her. "You would kill yourself just to end me? Do you truly hate me that much?"

"I love my team that much," Konstantin shot back. He turned his head slowly to look at me, as if that very move pained him. "I love you that much, Zariya. To see you free from her."

Tears stung my vision. "You didn't have to do this, Konstantin. There had to be another way. We have to find a cure."

Konstantin turned to me and Rex released his arm. I nearly fell as I took his full weight, his arms draped around my shoulders. His lips were as white as snow, and black veins shot through the whites of his eyes. "This was the only way."

No. Hell, no. This wasn't happening. I found my cheeks slicked with tears. "Don't give up, Konstantin. We'll find an antidote. Signe and Verte. Oliver. They'll save you." I flashed a glance at Iona, who lay prone on the floor. Unmoving.

She was dead. The poison had worked so fast. How long did Konstantin have? "Iona is gone, but you're fighting it. Keep fighting!"

Konstantin raised a shaky hand and caressed the line of my scales from temple to neck. "I consider it the greatest honor of my life to have had the chance to love you. I only hope I loved you well enough."

"No!" I cried. I pressed a shaky kiss to his dry lips. "No, you didn't love me well enough. How can you say that? We only just found each other! I need years. Decades. Konstantin...fight it. Fight it for me."

"Zariya." Galu's voice cut through the fog of my desperation. I searched through refracted tears for him. He was standing in the doorway, holding something in his hand. The Chinvat Key.

"We need to get him back to base," Daevin said. "They can save him."

Konstantin's eyes rolled back in his head and his legs collapsed beneath him. We began to topple, but Luiz and Rex were there to catch him.

They lowered him to the ground.

Rex's golden eyes flashed as brilliantly as two tiny suns, and an iridescent glow surrounded Konstantin's prone body.

"What are you doing?" Luiz asked.

"I can manipulate time as well as matter. In small doses. I created a stasis field to keep his condition from worsening until we get him medical attention."

A tiny amount of tension unwound from my shoulders. I looked down at Konstantin, lying still as the grave. Panic flooded back in, hot and unrelenting. An ache had settled deep in my chest. This couldn't be happening. I couldn't lose Konstantin. Konstantin was immortal. Ageless. Fearless and fierce. This was wrong. "It doesn't look like he's breathing— Rex, why isn't he breathing?"

I surged forward to check him, but strong hands seized my shoulders. Galu held me back gently but firmly. "He's frozen in time."

"Like a princess in a fairy tale," Daevin added. For once, without sarcasm.

"We'll find the cure, and you'll wake him with a kiss," Galu said. "Don't worry."

"How could he do this?" I sobbed. "Poison himself?"

Galu handed Rex the Chinvat Key and Gate. "You know how to work this thing?"

"I can figure it out."

Galu led me gently to the stone table, where Konstantin had been strapped just minutes before. So alive. And now, there was only a spark of life in him, kept alive by Rex's magic. Galu maneuvered me to sit on the table and I obeyed, like a child, my mind and body unresponsive to my commands.

I watched numbly, tears streaming down my face, as the rest of my team took charge of the situation with brisk efficiency. Some part of me took it all in. Daevin checking to make sure Iona was dead. Luiz talking quietly to Yani and Mandri, who had appeared at the doorway. Shaking their hands. Rex setting up the Gate. But another part of me—most of me—was numb. As frozen as Konstantin.

Galu sat by my side the whole time, his arm wrapped around my shoulder. Anchoring me and lending me a semblance of calm I didn't feel.

Rex, Luiz, and Daevin gathered round us, and I half-listened as they discussed how to safely transport Konstantin. They decided that

Rex would do it, as he was the strongest and the least likely to disrupt his own magical field.

I said nothing. Their words felt far away. As if I were listening underwater. I could only look at Konstantin lying on the ground.

I wondered what would happen if we couldn't find a cure. Wondered what my life would be like if he never woke up. Losing Dad had almost broken me. I had only just come back to life. Phoenix Team—this mission, these friends—they'd been my salvation. Shown me that there was still a life worth living.

I couldn't lose Konstantin. I knew in my heart that his loss would shatter me into pieces too small to ever put back together.

"Come on, Six." Daevin stroked my hair, and I startled.

The others were gone from my side, standing around the circle of the Chinvat Gate, which projected lavender light onto the ceiling above us.

I let Daevin take my hand, his palm warm and comforting in mine. Let him lead me to the edge of the Gate.

"Ready?" Galu asked.

I nodded.

And we jumped.

16

***

Cyriaque Broussard pounded the punching bag with unyielding fury.

Hook. Jab. Cross.

Again.

Again.

Again.

Things were falling apart here at Veil Force. He had an entire team MIA. The MASC Under-secretary was riding his ass about tracking them down.

But he didn't know if he wanted to. Because he had a powerful suspicion why Konstantin Bauer had taken his team off the radar.

Bauer knew Cyriaque was working for the enemy.

It was only a matter of time before Bauer appeared, pointing his righteous finger. And then Cyriaque would be taken away in hand-cuffs. Never again to run free under the light of the moon.

Who was he kidding? He hadn't been free since Antares. Since the Authority had twisted new loyalty out of him.

After days of torture, his addled brain had been sure it would be easier to just comply. Slip a little intel to the Authority and her

Collector dogs. He hadn't known how far she'd take it. What it would mean to be owned by her.

The punching bag creaked and fell to the ground before him with a heavy thump. He shook his head in surprise, searching for the issue. Ah. He'd punched it so hard that the metal rings holding it up had separated. It seemed his workout was done for the day.

His phone buzzed in the pocket of his athletic pants, and he pulled it out. "Broussard."

"Cyriaque," an unfamiliar male voice said. "So nice to finally talk."

"Who's this?"

"I'm calling on behalf of our mutual friend. The Authority."

Cyriaque froze for a moment. And then he turned on his heel, striding out of the base gym towards his office. "She's no friend of mine." He growled low.

"Semantics. I know you worked for her."

Cyriaque narrowed his eyes. *Worked.* Past tense? "Who are you?"

"I represent a very ancient, very powerful organization called Leviathan."

"Never heard of it," Cyriaque said as casually as he could. Goddammit, the last thing he needed was another asshole playing supervillain trying to own him.

"No matter. I'm calling because I'd like to help you."

"Help me with what?"

"Your little Konstantin Bauer problem."

Cyriaque froze just outside his office door. "What do you mean?"

"So coy, Cyriaque. Fine. I will spell it out for you. Konstantin Bauer is onto you. He and his team have proof of your connection to the Authority. To Leviathan."

Proof? Fuck. He'd been so careful. What could it be? "I have no connection to Leviathan."

"But you do, Cyriaque. You see, Iona worked for us. So you work for us, too." Again, past tense. What was going on?

Cyriaque sank into his chair, swiping the sweaty hair from his forehead. Jesus Christ Almighty. "I'm done, okay? I'm fucking done with your bullshit demands—"

"Easy, boy," the caller snapped. "I said I'm here to help. As we speak, your intrepid little Phoenix Team is preparing to return to base. They'll be demanding your arrest and resignation within the hour."

"I'm sorry, why isn't the Authority telling me this?"

"Because she's dead."

Cyriaque leaned back in his chair. His shock was quickly replaced by satisfaction. Good fucking riddance. Though now apparently he had to deal with this asshole.

"Okay. Great. Well, thanks for your 'help.' I'll remember it fondly from fucking prison."

"Oh, Cyriaque, you're far too valuable to go to prison. We have big plans for you. Check your email."

Cyriaque wanted to tell the caller, this Leviathan person, to go fuck himself. But that had never gone well with the Authority. He'd always ended up doing her bidding anyway. So he opened his laptop and navigated to his email.

A new message sat in his inbox—from an unknown email: gray@leviathan.org. "Are you Gray?"

"Some call me by that name. Download the attachment."

"This better not be fucking malware or something," he muttered. But Cyriaque did as he was told.

The voice on the line sighed. "Trust me, Cyriaque, we have better things to do with our time than engage in amateur computer mischief."

"Never can be too careful," Cyriaque said. He leaned forward as the attachment opened. It was a black-and-white surveillance video of a room. "That's the Tartarus Base evidence locker." He examined the footage. But the angle was wrong. It came from a different corner than the regular security cameras. The ones he'd disabled to steal back the Chinvat Gate for the Authority. "What the fuck is this? If you're trying to blackmail me, you're a little fucking late—"

"Just watch," the voice commanded.

On the video, someone walked into the room. Looked over their shoulder surreptitiously.

Cyriaque leaned forward. It wasn't him. It was Konstantin.

He watched, his mouth hanging open, as the video showed Konstantin unlocking and opening the cage that held their evidence. Showed him removing the Chinvat Gate and Key.

"I assume by your silence that you now see?"

"I don't understand. How...? What...?" Cyriaque opened and closed his mouth.

"The wonders of modern technology. Video editing capabilities have truly advanced by leaps and bounds in the last few years."

"This is fake," Cyriaque said. Still dumbfounded. Why would this Gray person help him? Though as soon as he thought it, he understood. To keep his inside man. So he could continue to pull Cyriaque's strings and effectively control Veil Force.

"You know it's fake. I know it's fake. But the MASC Under-secretary doesn't know it's fake. In approximately five minutes, the entirety of Phoenix Team will come through the Chinvat Gate into Tartarus Base. You'll be waiting for them when they do. And you'll arrest them all for treason."

USA TODAY BESTSELLING AUTHOR
CLAIRE LUANA
MYTHICAL ALLIANCE
PHOENIX BETRAYED

1

We emerged from the Chinvat Gate into the familiar halls of Tartarus Base. But everything was wrong. Instead of arriving home as heroes, ready to arrest our director, Cyriaque Broussard, for his crimes against Veil Force, we stumbled through the magical portal with our leader, Konstantin Bauer, near death.

I hit the ground hard, banging my chin and my knee. But the pain was nothing compared to the thrumming panic I felt.

I hadn't been able to help Dad before he'd died. I hadn't been there. But I was here now, for Konstantin, and I was going to do everything in my power to see him safely healed.

I shoved to my feet and offered a hand to Galu. The nereid, now in command, clasped my wrist with blue-tattooed fingers and hauled himself up.

Rex had managed to come through the portal mostly on his feet, cradling Konstantin's unconscious body in his strong arms. He wore his jackal-furred head—its tall, pointed ears and sloping snout reminiscent of ancient Egyptian hieroglyphics. Of all the Phoenix Team guys, Rex was the most enigmatic. He was the descendant of Anubis, the Egyptian god, and had mysterious god-like powers himself. I knew little beyond that, except that I trusted him with my life. And more importantly, Konstantin's.

"We need Oliver." I panted, trying to fight my lingering nausea. "He should be in his lab."

"Signe and Verte too. If anyone can find a cure for the poison Konstantin ingested, it'll be them." Luiz darted for the hallway, but before he rounded the corner, he came up short, his handsome face a picture of confusion. "Easy, boys." The incubus slowly raised his hands.

Next to me, Daevin, Phoenix Team's caco-demon, pointed his rifle at whatever was rounding that corner opposite Luiz.

Galu did the same, after quickly returning the Chinvat Gate to its normal size and shoving it into his cargo pocket.

I didn't have any weapons, but my muscles tensed just the same, ready for a fight. What was going on? Had Tartarus Base been breached while we'd been gone?

Luiz's opponent came into sight around the corner and I snarled. Cyriaque Broussard pointed a modified AR-15 directly at Luiz's heart. Our werewolf director wore standard-issue black camouflage pants, leather boots, and a black T-shirt that stretched over his bulging muscles. His brown, curly hair was wild, and his lean cheeks were unshaven. He looked a far cry from the neat, orderly supe in gray slacks who'd given me my shot to join Veil Force. It seemed the past weeks hadn't been easy on him, either.

Good.

Just a small taste of the punishment he deserved. There was a special place in hell for men who betrayed their brothers and sisters. Daevin had even confirmed it.

More figures followed Cyriaque. More armed Veil Force Phantoms. A few I recognized. The huge, towering bulk of Commander Strongroot, the Sequoia dryad who ran Aquila Team, was unmistakable. He was Alviya's team leader.

More familiar faces followed. The dainty blonde form of Signe, one of Veil Force's two norn Demi-goddesses. Leilani, the kapua shifter and Draco team commander. Kiki. These were our teammates. Our friends.

"What's going on, Director?" Galu asked, the barrel of his gun drooping. "Konstantin needs immediate medical attention. He's near death."

"We'll make sure he gets the care he needs." Cyriaque nodded to Strongroot. "Arrest him."

Galu's gun barrel went back up, and we tightened into a line before Rex and Konstantin. Luiz fell in beside me.

"What are you doing, Director? I'm telling you, one of your commanders is dying. He needs care *now*. Why are you arresting him?" Galu asked.

"Konstantin Bauer is under arrest for the theft of the Chinvat Gate from the Veil Force evidence locker. And for treason, in supplying it to a foreign, enemy force." Cyriaque's voice was hard, his back rod straight. He didn't appear concerned that two weapons were pointed directly at him. He had to know that with the other Phantoms around, we weren't going to shoot unless absolutely necessary.

A disbelieving laugh escaped me. "You have the fucking nerve to accuse Konstantin of stealing the Gate? *You* stole it." I jabbed my finger at him.

Cyriaque crossed his thick arms over his chest. "You can't believe that. When clearly, it's how you traveled back here. Konstantin took it. Konstantin had it."

"We have it because we took it from the Authority after Konstantin killed her. Konstantin caught you on camera stealing it. You're the mole! You're the one who's been working with the Collectors and the Authority all this time. You're the one who set up my dad. You're the reason he's dead!" My voice was growing high and wild.

Cyriaque exchanged a look with Strongroot that was almost pitying.

Luiz's hand locked around my forearm, and I looked down. I hadn't realized I'd been surging forward to pummel that smug look off the bastard's face.

"Did Konstantin ever show you this supposed video of me

stealing anything? Or did you just take his word for it?" Cyriaque asked.

I frowned. I didn't want to admit that we hadn't seen it. We just hadn't had a chance, with all the madness in the DRC. Right?

Cyriaque smirked. "I thought so. Well, I actually *have* a video of Konstantin taking the Gate. And they've all seen it."

That wasn't possible.

"You're lying," Daevin said. His gun was still pointed at Cyriaque's heart. The barrel hadn't wavered.

"He's not," Commander Strongroot rumbled. "We watched it in the briefing before coming here. It was clearly Commander Bauer. I'm sorry, child."

No. No fucking way. "He's doctored the video somehow! It has to be. Cyriaque is the mole, not Konstantin. This is all part of his plan to deflect the blame onto Konstantin."

Across from us, gazes softened, mouths twisting. They didn't believe me. They felt...sorry for me! Like I was some love-crazed girl who'd been brainwashed by her evil genius boyfriend.

And while we all stood around and had a chat, Konstantin was slipping away from us. Which was exactly what Cyriaque wanted. If Konstantin died, there was no one to get us the real footage. No way Konstantin could defend his name. No way to get to the bottom of this.

"Let us take him." Cyriaque held out a hand. "We have no reason to believe any of the rest of you were in on this. Unless you resist us now. And then I'll have no choice but to assume you're collaborators. And arrest all of you."

"Give us a minute to discuss," Galu said. "You have to understand; it's not easy for a team to hand over their commander, even if it's to their director."

Cyriaque nodded. "One minute."

Daevin kept his rifle trained down the hall at Cyriaque and the other Phantoms while we huddled up.

"There's no way we can let Cyriaque take him," I said under my breath. "He'll let him die."

"Oliver would never let that happen," Galu murmured.

"He could have sent Oliver on an all-inclusive vacation for all we know," I shot back.

"I agree with Six," Luiz said. "No way we're handing Konstantin over. This smells dirty."

"We have to consider Konstantin's condition," Rex said. "Do we have the resources to heal him if we flee?"

Fuck. No. We needed Tartarus Base. Oliver. Signe. Smart supes who knew about magical medical treatment. "Okay, so we fight our way into Oliver's lab, barricade ourselves in, treat Konstantin, and then run," I suggested, even knowing as I said it how impossible it would be.

"I don't see how we have any choice," Galu said. "Konstantin needs medical treatment."

The threat of tears stung my eyes. "If we let them arrest him, he's as good as dead. I feel it."

"Your time is up," Cyriaque called out. A bit too gleefully for my liking. How had he known about the video Konstantin had made? And how had he doctored one to show the other Phantoms and get them on his side?

I supposed it didn't matter. We were no closer to finding a solution. We had to turn Konstantin over and hope for the best. A weight settled in my chest, smothering my lungs. Konstantin was going to die. I was going to lose him too.

"Breathe, Six," Luiz murmured as my tears started flowing.

Galu turned back to Cyriaque to give him our decision. Resigned.

"There is one other option," Rex said quietly. "Out of MASC's reach, with medical aid for Konstantin."

"Where?" I asked eagerly. "Let's go!"

Rex looked down at Konstantin, hanging limp in his arms. Konstantin's color had faded even more. He was as white as death, his breathing shallow. "I do not know if I will be welcomed back there—"

"No more stalling, Galu," Cyriaque barked, drawing our attention back. I think he understood that something had changed. That he was losing our attention.

"Please, Rex," I begged. "I can't lose him."

"Do you trust me?" Rex whispered. He was clearly addressing each of us, his glowing amber eyes like burning embers.

We responded with a chorus of affirmatives.

Rex handed Konstantin's limp body to Galu and then turned to the wall. A honey-colored glow burst from him, filling the concrete hallway like a sunrise.

I squinted against the brilliance and held up a hand to shield my eyes.

"Stop them!" Cyriaque shouted.

There was a brief moment of hesitation, but the Phantoms followed orders. They opened fire.

But the light surrounding Rex was growing—swirling large enough to embrace the six of us clustered together.

Streaks of golden light shot by before my eyes, enveloping us. Awe filled me. This wasn't the twisting, gut-wrenching travel of the Chinvat Gate. This was something wonderful.

Everything outside the light seemed to slow. The movement of Cyriaque and Commander Strongroot. The deadly paths of the bullets.

It all stopped.

My hair whipped around me, and I turned just in time to see the world fall away.

2

Rex had not traveled this way in a long while. Not since he'd left his homeland and sworn never to return. Yet here he was, breaking his promise.

But if one had to break a promise, he might as well break it for a friend.

He could have taken them back through the Chinvat Gate. But then Broussard and the Phantoms could have followed. And that would not have solved the urgent problem of Konstantin's fading condition.

This has been the only way.

He'd feared the way was closed to him—that his family had cut him off after he'd run. But traveling was as easy as ever, as if something was guiding him home.

And now he'd brought his supernatural team with him. To this secret, ancient place forbidden to mortals. Well, his father was already going to be furious with him for leaving. One more thing wasn't likely to put him over the edge.

They emerged into the shade of a palm grove, the huge, orange sun filtering through the leaves. Ra, the Sun God, hung closer in this realm. He was always near.

Rex's magic drained into the ether, leaving his teammates gasping and coughing. It was not a comfortable method of travel.

Rex turned to look at Konstantin cradled in Galu's arms. He put a hand to his commander's neck and exchanged a troubled look with Galu. Konstantin's pulse was weak. He was slipping away. "We have to hurry."

"Where are we?" Zariya held up a hand and surveyed the sun-drenched landscape.

Rex suppressed a smile. Zariya was so young and impetuous. Hot-blooded and passionate. But courageous. And as protective as a lioness, as fierce as his aunt Sekhmet. How quickly she'd taken over their little pride. She was like a little sister he'd never had—half the time frustrating him, the other half worrying him. Life on Phoenix Team had certainly not been dull since she'd arrived.

"Rexy?" Daevin nodded across the stone path before them. "Please tell me those are friends of yours?"

Two muscular men with fearsome crocodile heads and sharp spears were striding their way. The welcoming committee.

The two guards drew to a stop before them. Their broad, strong chests were bare, and they wore white pleated shendyt skirts about their waists, bound with elaborate belts of leather studded with gold and malachite. "Rexsis. Your father has requested your presence. Immediately."

"I will come. But one of my companions is near death. Is the goddess Sekhmet about? We have need of her healing arts."

"She will be summoned. Now come."

Rex resisted curling his snout in a snarl. The guards had always been little better than brainless sheep. He supposed it was not their fault they were bred to follow orders without question.

"Your father?" Galu asked. "Rex, where are we?"

Rex turned. "Welcome to Phairo. The last bastion of the Egyptian gods."

He trailed after the guards, not waiting to see if the rest of the team followed. They would. They'd stick close to him in this place.

"Do you think they have alcohol here?" Zariya whispered. "Because I really need some."

"No kind of heaven if they don't," Luiz replied.

Rex shook his head. "Technically, this is not a heaven. We're on Earth."

"Um, pretty sure the travel guides would have mentioned this place," Zariya countered.

"We're in a mirror realm. Tied to Earth, but not exactly in it. Or at least not completely."

They all fell silent after that.

Phairo looked no different than the day he'd left. It was a city of exquisite beauty, the walkways flanked by columns carved with ornate hieroglyphics, sheltered from the sun above by lush vines fragrant with jasmine blossoms. Courtyards and fountains, gardens and libraries—he'd clambered over every inch of this place as a child.

The stones beneath them shuddered. "What was that?" Zariya squeaked.

"The entirety of the city—well, it's a large palace compound, really—floats atop the Nile River, held in place by the most ancient of magic," Rex replied.

"Fascinating," Galu said.

Rex glanced back. The others seemed less enthusiastic about the prospect of a floating island—Daevin especially was looking at the ground beneath his feet as if it might reach out and bite him. "It's quite sturdy," he assured them.

But he couldn't distract himself with his friends' reactions forever. He was about to confront his father again. And he wasn't at all ready.

They walked into the shadowed coolness of the palace, through hallways painted in glorious frescoes. Some of the Egyptologists he'd known at Oxford would have killed for just a few moments in this place. A place where history lived on.

He had gotten out as soon as possible.

The guards led them into the massive receiving chamber, its vaulted ceiling inlaid with gold.

Behind him, Daevin let out a soft whistle.

But Rex's eyes were fixed on the figure before him, standing tall in center of the room, where a beam of light from the roof spilled in a molten puddle around him. His father. Anubis, god of the dead. He'd always been a lover of theatrics.

"Father." Rex kept his voice strong and indifferent.

Anubis turned and fixed Rex with his glowing yellow gaze. But then his ears perked up, and he opened his eyes wide. "My boy! Returned to us at last." And then he crossed the room and pulled Rex into an embrace.

Rex stifled his surprise as best he could, patting his father on the back awkwardly. "It's good to be home." He pulled back. "Father, where is Sekhmet? My friend is grievously wounded."

"Yes, she's coming." Anubis waved a hand.

"Father, please—"

Zariya whispered something, and Anubis's ears swiveled. He turned his attention to her. "Yes, young human?"

Zariya paled, but to her credit, didn't back down, even when confronting the Egyptian god of the dead. "I said that I can see where Rex gets his good looks."

Anubis threw back his head and laughed, revealing his straight, white canines. "Oh my, Rex, such wonderful companions. You must be tired after your journey. Shall we have some refreshments?"

"Father, my friend—"

"Rexsis, always so impatient," a female voice said.

He turned in relief to see Sekhmet striding across the room, wearing her golden lioness's head. On her human body was draped a violet silk gown, trimmed with gold and cinched with a gem-studded belt. She'd always been beautiful.

Sekhmet took his head gently and kissed each of his cheeks. Rex was glad for his dark fur so his blush didn't show. "Good to see you too, Rex."

"Yes, good to see you. My friend has ingested poison designed to kill an Authentic vampire. He's Derived, but it has harmed him anyway. He is near death."

Sekhmet turned to look at Konstantin and her eyes widened. "I know him. And you!" She pointed to Zariya. "I have seen you so recently. In Hathor's mirror."

Zariya recoiled. "You could...see us?"

"Have you taken such poor care of your beloved that he's already lost?"

"I—It's a long story." Zariya's face twisted. "Please, can you help us?"

"Of course. You will come with me. Lay him down," she instructed Galu.

"I can carry him—" Galu offered, but she gave a sharp shake of her head.

"Down."

Galu knelt to put Konstantin gently down on the tiles, but Sekhmet wrapped his body with her magic until Konstantin floated in the air, as if lying on an invisible table. "Never fear, Rexsis. Your friend will be well. Now take refreshment with your father. You've been away too long."

Zariya looked over her shoulder at him with doubt in her eyes.

Rex nodded at her encouragingly.

The gods could be fickle, vain creatures with their own agendas, but he trusted Sekhmet to keep Konstantin and Zariya safe.

He hoped.

3

I followed Sekhmet through the frescoed halls. Konstantin, wrapped in glowing yellow light, floated beside me like Sleeping Beauty in her glass coffin—but he didn't look serene or peaceful. He looked dead.

"Is he—" I choked. "Shouldn't we hurry?"

"The magic acts as a stasis field. It will freeze his condition while I work."

"Okay." All I could do was take her word for it. I felt helpless and desperately out of my league. I was still smarting from the loss of Dad's memories and the extra confidence they'd given me. I didn't know if I could face this alone. Konstantin near death. The team on the run. No doubt we were all at the top of MASC's most wanted list by now. Who knew what sort of smear campaign Cyriaque was painting against us? How the hell were we going to sort this out?

We turned into a sunny room lined with cabinets and shelves. Several stone tables dotted the room, and Konstantin's body settled onto one, seemingly of its own accord.

"Your anguish is quite distracting, my child," Sekhmet said without looking my way. "Take a breath. And a seat. All will be well."

I looked around and spotted a chair of brown leather in the

corner. With shaking legs, I collapsed into it. And, much to my embarrassment, started to cry.

It all burst forth at once—in sobs and racking breaths. The stress of the last few missions—getting shot, kidnapped, sold, cursed. Almost dying on more than one occasion. Falling in love and having that love nearly torn from me. Finding the truth about Dad, swimming in memories that had made me feel closer to him than before he'd died...and losing those too.

It was all too much for one person to bear.

I was breaking.

I loved Phoenix Team. I loved Galu's compassion, and Daevin's stupid jokes. Luiz's brotherly hovering, and Rex's frank dependability, shot through with dry humor even better for its rarity. But most of all, I loved Konstantin—his brilliance and his bravery and the tenderness that only I got to see.

I loved being a Phantom. But I couldn't ignore the reality staring me in the face. It wasn't healthy for me. As much as I loved Phoenix Team—it was going to be the thing that killed me.

But how could I give it up? How could I let the team down?

If we even got through this at all.

A cleared throat startled me, and I looked up.

Sekhmet was standing over me, holding a cup that looked to be carved from a horn of some kind. "Drink this. It will make you feel better."

"What is it?" I took a sip. It was fruity, with a slightly bitter undertone.

"A special tonic made of crocodile testicles."

I gagged, spitting it back into the cup.

Sekhmet laughed, a pleasant, deep sound. "I jest. It's hibiscus tea with apricot."

I swiped my tears away and took another sip. "You got me." I did not expect the Egyptian goddess to have a sense of humor.

Sekhmet turned back to Konstantin, her head bowed in concentration as she examined him.

I tried to give her quiet to work, but I was desperate for answers. "Can you help?"

"Yes, I think so. His blood will need to be drained of the poison. Once it is removed, his natural immunity should take over and heal him."

"How do you drain his blood?" That sounded painful.

"Leeches."

My stomach flipped. "Is that another jest?"

"No, child. It is an old remedy, much misused over time. But effective when properly directed." She crossed the room and opened a little wooden cabinet, pulling out a jar that glowed faintly. "Besides, these are not ordinary leeches. Would you like to help?"

I'd sworn to the uncaring universe that I'd do anything to help Konstantin, but I'd never imagined myself picking out slimy, glowing leeches and attaching them to his pale, perfect skin.

But Sekhmet directed me where to place them, and I found myself falling into an easy rhythm. My roiling emotions calmed as my mind fixed on the task before it.

"You have a steady hand," Sekhmet remarked.

"I studied to be a doctor," I admitted. I used to do this—help people. I had wanted to be a doctor since I was a kid. I wanted to heal people, not tear them apart with bullets and bombs.

"And now you have chosen a different path?"

I shrugged. "Or it chose me? I don't know. It's a long story." I'd been so desperate to find Dad's killer, and so broken over his death, I hadn't given a passing thought to the fact that joining Veil Force meant giving up my dream and the years of study I'd put into realizing it. But now, here with Sekhmet, raw and wrung out over our string of disastrous missions...that dream surfaced again, an ache nestled deep in my chest.

"You have a healer's spirit. I'm not sure that path will surrender so willingly."

I didn't know what to say. I'd made my choice. Hadn't I? I placed the final leech and surveyed my work. "He's so weak. Are you sure he'll be able to withstand it?"

"His body is weakened, but his heart is strong. He has something to live for," she replied. "We should let him rest. Shall I return you to your companions?"

"I'd like to stay with him, if that's all right."

She nodded.

"You said you saw us in the mirror. How?"

"Ah." Sekhmet crossed the room and poured herself some tea as well, then came to sit beside me. This was freaking weird. I was having tea with a real, Egyptian goddess. Her lioness head had been strange at first with its tawny fur, rounded ears and perfect whiskers, but I was already growing used to it, like I had with Rex.

"Hathor is my sister, and our powers are deeply intertwined. Her mirror is one of our most ancient relics. It was a surprise to feel it in use, after so many centuries. And even stranger to find that those that looked into it were the companions of our long-lost Rexsis. Fate can be surprising, even for the gods."

"I didn't realize Rex was lost," I said carefully. Even when I'd had Dad's memories, I'd known the least about Rex. He had always been mysterious, holding himself a bit apart from the rest of us. I knew that he'd studied and worked at Oxford, focusing on antiquities and ancient civilization. An obvious choice, I supposed. But even Dad had had no idea how an Egyptian demi-god had ended up in the realm of mortals.

Sekhmet sighed. "Rexsis had a hard childhood here. His mother was a mortal servant, and many of the gods looked down upon him for his mixed heritage. He was teased mercilessly, and some of the other gods were unnecessarily cruel. Anubis...he tried, but not hard enough."

Sympathy filled me. I knew exactly what it was to be treated as an outsider. Living half in one world, half the other. Belonging in neither. Why had I never seen that Rex suffered in the same way? I supposed he had seemed so confident to me. So aloof. But maybe that confidence had been its own kind of defense mechanism. Hold everyone at a distance, and there's no risk of getting hurt.

"He renounced his powers and left Phairo one night after a

terrible fight with his father. I thought of him often. I do hope Rex found the acceptance he was craving in the human world."

I knew that Rex had approached Veil Force after he had been refused tenure for a third time. Obvious supernatural prejudice, as the quality of his research and scholarship was unrivaled. It hadn't been easy. But he had found acceptance, of a sort. Like I had. With Veil Force. With our team.

"He's an integral part of our team. We care for him deeply," I said.

"I can see that, child. And that brings me great joy. And sorrow."

I frowned. "Why sorrow?"

"Because he will not be able to return with you." Sekhmet cocked her head at me.

I set my drink down. "What? What do you mean?"

"Rex had to renounce his powers to leave here. He was young then, and they were not fully formed. But now that he has returned, they will return too, even stronger than before. He cannot live in the mortal world with such forces at his disposal. It's not safe for anyone. You didn't think he had his full demi-god powers, did you?"

"Well...he was able to manipulate matter...and light..." I trailed off. Yeah, I supposed that adjusting stolen outfits so they fit my ass better likely was not the extent of Egyptian magic. But what was she saying? Rex was...stuck here? No. No way. "If he relinquished his powers once, he can do it again," I countered. "We're grateful to be able to rest here, but he's coming back with us when this is all over. He's our friend. Our teammate."

Sekhmet shook her head sadly. "I'm afraid not. Rex left when he was a teen. But once his powers come in fully, they'll be permanent. Like all of us, he'll be bound to this place. Forever."

4

———————

Rex stood in the northern courtyard, looking out over the railing into the river beyond. This had been one of his favorite places as a child. It was shaded and quiet, away from the watchful eye of Ra and his other kin.

The servants of this place had shown his friends to rooms where they could sleep. But he found himself restless. He rarely slept as it was. The night was quiet, without distraction—perfect time for reading and his research. Even when he went to bed he mostly rested quietly, allowing his brain to fall dormant.

"I wondered if I'd find you here." His father's voice sounded behind him.

Rex turned and watched as his father met him at the rail. "We are creatures of habit."

"That British accent," Anubis remarked, his snout curling slightly. "I'm not sure I'll ever get used to it."

Rex let out a sharp laugh. "I was trying to fit in when I first arrived at Oxford. It stuck."

"And did you?" Anubis cocked his head.

Rex looked back out at the churning, muddy river. "No, I don't think I ever did. Not there, anyway."

"I'm glad you're home. The humans are multiplying so quickly. They encroach on this place with their technology and satellites and radar. We need all of our power to hold the borders."

Rex pursed his lips. "I didn't mean to come home. It was an emergency. To save a friend."

"And now you're stuck with us?" Anubis asked. "Will you be moody and ill-tempered all of your immortal days? I do not relish a return to your tantrums."

Rex turned on his father. "I was a child. If a half-human offspring was so inconvenient for you, perhaps you should have thought of that before you took a servant to bed."

"We are gods. We take what we want."

"Perhaps in the old days. Now you huddle together in this relic of the old times while modern civilization presses in around you. It is no way to live. It is not a way I wished to live."

"You speak as if we have a choice. You know that our power, if unleashed in the mortal world, would be too much for the fabric of this reality. It would warp and tear. We exile ourselves here as a sacrifice. And you would begrudge us some small degree of pleasure."

"I care little what you do, Father," Rex snapped. "I just know that this was no place for a half-human child to grow up. The other gods ignored me or tormented me. Sekhmet and Hathor were the only ones to show me kindness."

"And so you left. Was the outside world so kind to you? Was it worth it to give up your powers—to delay them as long as you could?"

Rex leaned his forearms down on the railing, looking at the water below. "Yes. Father, the outside world is imperfect, but it is vast and colorful and full of stories. I found..." He trailed off. Would his father even believe him? He was so set in his ways. If Rex told him he had a way to get them out of the pampered prison that was this infernal place, would they come? But didn't he have to try? Otherwise, he'd be stuck here, right along with the rest of them. "I found something, Father. An artifact. A necklace, created by the Hebrew god for his angels. So they could walk among the humans without their power being detected. If I could just get that necklace, I think it could control my full powers. Neutralize them safely so I could be in the mortal world without harming it. If I could fabricate more, then you all could travel freely as well."

Anubis stepped back. "You meddle with what you cannot understand, son. This is the way it has always been, and it is the way it must be. I understand you resent your lot in life, but it is your lot nonetheless. Now I want no more talk of necklaces or leaving this place! You are here to stay." Anubis spun and stalked off across the stones.

Zariya emerged from the far doorway and had to scramble out of Anubis's way as he ducked inside. She looked at Rex with wide eyes. "Good talk with Dad?"

Rex closed his eyes briefly. He admired the way Zariya could cut to the heart of a matter with humor. Daevin used jokes to deflect and diffuse as well, but Zariya had a way of doing it in a manner that showed she cared. That addressed, rather than dismissed. He appreciated that about her.

She walked slowly across the courtyard to take up the spot his father had just vacated. "Sekhmet said I could find you here. Do you want to be alone?"

"No, I appreciate the company. How is Konstantin?"

She bit her lip. "She said he's going to be all right. I think I believe her."

"If she said it, then it's true. The gods here don't have the empathy to create a comforting lie. A benefit and a curse of this place is the honesty."

"I see where you get it." She patted his arm. "So...what were you and your father arguing about? You don't have to tell me—"

"I don't mind. It might be nice to have a friendly ear. We were arguing over me staying here."

"Sekhmet explained to me that your powers will come in fully, now that you're home."

"I left to halt the development of my power so I wouldn't be stuck here. But what was more, I was certain there were answers in the mortal world. It's why I went to Oxford. Why I studied antiquities. I was convinced I could find a solution. A way to live in the mortal world with my full powers. But come back here as well. I never wanted to be cut off forever. I struggled here growing up, but these are still my people."

"Did you find what you were looking for?"

"I did. A necklace that I believe should control my full powers, rendering them safe. It's called the Nephilim's Knot. It's why I joined Veil Force."

"What do you mean?"

"The Nephilim's Knot is in MASC's possession. Held in the vault in the headquarters at Turtle Bay."

"Are you serious?" Zariya exclaimed. "Let's get it! I'm sure when we explain the situation, they'd prefer to have it benefiting a Phantom, rather than buried in some vault."

"That was what I thought, and it's why I joined. But unfortunately, it's not how the Under-Secretary felt. My request for the necklace was denied. I would be even less likely to obtain the necklace now, with us labeled as traitors."

"Well, that sucks," Zariya grumbled.

"Precisely."

They fell silent, Zariya looking out over the landscape. "I've been thinking, Rex. About our Cyriaque problem. He's turned Veil Force against us. Maybe MASC too. If we have any hope of bringing him to justice, we need to go over his head."

"You're talking about the MASC Under-Secretary-General? Convincing her that Cyriaque is the true traitor?"

"Exactly. It's the sort of conversation you'd want to have in person. So maybe we solve both problems at once. Infiltrate MASC headquarters. Talk to Under-Secretary Pérez and show her the real video. Not the doctored one showing Konstantin stealing the Chinvat Gate. And while some of us are having that conversation, the rest sneak into this vault and snag your necklace."

"Robbing MASC is hardly the best way to convince them we're not traitors."

Zariya grinned. "That won't be a problem."

"Why do you say that?"

"Because we're not going to get caught."

5

Konstantin blinked, his eyes scratchy and dry. It was a peculiar sensation. His mouth was dry, too—and a foul taste coated his tongue.

His surroundings were unfamiliar. He lay on a hard stone slab. The vaulted ceiling above him was hewn of warm sandstone. So he was no longer in Iona's castle. And he was alive. Those two facts alone were quite promising. Perhaps his desperate scheme had worked.

A shuffling across the room drew his attention. He turned his head slowly, his neck stiff with disuse. His body was sluggish to respond to his commands. It felt almost like he was human once again. Across the room stood a figure in white. He squinted, unable to make out the details.

"Who's there?" he rasped. His voice was hoarse.

The figure turned. "You're awake!" A female voice. "Excellent." She came to stand at his side and Konstantin's eyes widened. Her body was that of a willowy human female, stylishly wrapped in white linen trimmed in gold. But her head—it was the tawny, furred head of a lioness. She was like...like Rex.

"Here, drink this." She slipped a cool hand beneath his head and helped him angle up to drink from a shallow bowl. "It's nectar from one of our sacred plants. It will help you regain your strength. Your body went through quite an ordeal filtering out all of the poison you ingested."

"It's gone?" He let his head drop back, panting slightly.

"It is. I drained it all from you. But it was a powerful toxin, and it was in your system for longer than I would have liked. I fear it may have done some permanent damage."

Konstantin let his eyes close briefly. "You saved me. That's more than I expected." He'd had many lifetimes with super-human strength. He could learn to live without. Though...what did that mean for Phoenix Team? He couldn't lead missions if his body was too weak. And what would it mean for him and Zariya? She'd fallen in love with him while he'd been strong and powerful. Would she want a lesser version?

As if his healer heard his thoughts, she said, "Your lover refused to leave your side. I finally made her go get some fresh air. To see how Rex was doing."

"What do you mean, how Rex was doing? Is he injured?" Konstantin tried to sit up, and his head swam.

"Slowly, now." The lioness grabbed him under the arm and helped him to a seat. "He's well, but there have been...developments. Why don't I show you to a guest suite where you can rest further and have food brought to you. I'll find Zariya and send her to you."

"I don't need further medical treatment?" Konstantin asked. Looking around, he had deduced he was in this place's version of a hospital room.

"I've done all I can for you. You'll need lots of rest, good food, and gentle exercise to help you regain your strength."

He nodded.

"Do you think you can walk?"

"Let's find out." Konstantin eased himself onto legs as shaky as a newborn lamb's. But the goddess held a strong hand under his arm, supporting his weight. "What's your name?" he asked as they began shuffling across the room.

"Sekhmet." She smiled.

"Thank you, Sekhmet," he said. "Perhaps you can fill me in while we walk. Since it seems it will be a slow trip."

I BURST into the room Sekhmet had pointed me to, desperate to see the truth with my own eyes. Konstantin was awake. Konstantin was alive.

He was sitting on the bed, his hair around his shoulders, his skin pallid. He looked tired and frail, but I didn't fucking care.

I threw myself into his arms, tumbling us both back onto the bed.

"Whoa!" Konstantin let out an exclamation of surprise as I fell atop him, my forearms framing his head, my curls forming a curtain around us. "Hello, you."

I peppered him with kisses—across his eyelids, his cheeks, his jawline. "You...are...the...most foolish...bravest...man...I have...ever known."

He brushed my hair back with both hands. "I know." He drew me down to a kiss, slow and tender.

I figured I shouldn't totally crush him, so I rolled onto my side on the bed. He did the same, scooting up slowly so we lay across from each other. Our fingers intertwined. "I was so worried. I thought I'd lost you."

His smile faltered. "It was the only way I could think of to end Iona."

"It was too risky."

"I couldn't have her hanging over our lives together like a dark shadow. I couldn't let her hurt you."

"So you hurt yourself?"

"It was the only way."

I shook my head. "You're an idiot." I leaned in and kissed his nose. "But you're *my* idiot."

He smiled, his eyes as bright and blue as the sea. And then it was like a cloud passed over them. "Sekhmet thinks there might be permanent damage. I may never be the same. My abilities. My strength. If it changes things, I wouldn't blame you—"

"Shut up," I said. How could he ever think that after what we'd been through, I'd let anything come between us? I pressed my lips to his, tasting some lingering sweetness on his mouth. Reveling in the sweetness of the fact that he was *mine*. "I don't love you for your strength. Or your power."

"Why do you love me then?" He raised one eyebrow in challenge.

I offered a devious smile. "For your money, obviously."

A bark of laughter escaped him.

"Kidding. I love you for the way you protect those who can't protect themselves. For how you love and care for your teammates like family. For your ten-language-speaking smarts."

"Eight," he corrected.

I rolled my eyes. "For how totally not a know-it-all you are."

"What is it the kids say? It takes one to know one?" That eyebrow again.

I grinned. "I love you for your stupid old man jokes. And because you see me. Like I'm enough."

"You are more than enough," he said gently, his nose nuzzling mine. "You are remarkable. And brave. And sexy as hell."

An undeniable heat flooded me, and suddenly, I was desperate for him. We'd been denied so many times. "Just how sick are you?"

He stroked a line down my scales—temple, to collarbone, around my shoulder, and down the curve of my waist. "Sekhmet says all I need is rest and gentle exercise, and I'll be as good as new."

"Gentle exercise?" I rolled him onto his back and straddled his narrow hips. I drew my shirt up and over my head, tossing it at his face.

He caught it with a low growl. So his reflexes were still good. "I'm not sure I'll be able to keep things gentle."

I pushed my hands under the hem of his shirt, sliding my palms over the ripples of his abs. Reveling in his perfect form. "I'm willing to take that risk if you are." I tugged his shirt up, and he sat up to allow me to pull it off. I ignored the bruises that marred his skin where the leeches had attached themselves. It didn't matter. He was perfect.

As for Konstantin, it seemed he'd found a second wind. With a swift motion, my bra came off. Konstantin murmured in appreciation before raining kisses across one breast and then the other. He circled my nipple slowly with one rough thumb and then the heat of his tongue.

I couldn't help the sound that escaped me. Animal. Desperate. I tipped him back and crawled off him, unbuckling his pants and pulling them off. The heat in his gaze could have melted gold. I tried to savor the moment as I pulled off his black boxer briefs, but I wanted things too desperately. When the firm length of him sprang free, my mouth went dry.

God, he was beautiful. Arrayed before me—naked, glorious. A flicker of shyness crept through me and I squashed it viciously. Now was not the time to be timid. Boldness was the only choice. To take what I wanted. And what I wanted was him. I wriggled out of my own pants and he seized me by the waist and twisted me onto the bed.

The heat of his kisses trailed down low, to the place where I desperately ached for him. I gasped as his tongue connected with the most sensitive part of me and he began to work in earnest.

I had never felt anything like it. I could tell, even as he worshipped me, that I would be ruined for all other men. I hoped that there would never be another man. That I could just live and breathe in this moment with Konstantin.

As tremors of pleasure rolled through my body like waves, everything else fell away. The team, the Authority, the bullshit and lies beneath it all. This was something pure and shining, something worth fighting for. Something worth living for.

My breath came in ragged pants as he crawled back above me, as his body gently lowered onto mine—skin on silky skin. I felt the exquisite length of him fill me even as his presence filled my awareness, as my every sense reveled in him. I kissed him, unafraid that the venom of my fangs would harm him. We were made for each other.

And then Konstantin began to move with a rhythm that was only for me. I found myself teetering on the edge of a cliff—a cliff of rainbows and sparkles and goddamn unicorns. And as I tumbled over the edge, Konstantin was right there beside me.

6

Zariya lay at Konstantin's side, her beautiful breasts heaving, one arm thrown over his stomach. She wore a languid grin on her face.

Konstantin drank in the sight of her, the stretch of her graceful scales curving from delicate ankle, over hip and waist and shoulder.

Part of him wondered if he should have given in—they knew next to nothing about what permanent damage the poison had wrought in his body. He didn't want to shackle Zariya to an invalid. But he was done holding back.

He'd lived his life being cautious. And then he'd lived his life with vicious abandon—those years he had been driven near to madness by Iona's control over him. Then he'd lived with grief and self-hatred and sorrow as a sliver of his humanity had poked through and reminded him of what he had become. And then he had lived for others. Devoting his life to serving his country and fellow man, those who were less fortunate. It had been so long since he'd lived just for him. Since he'd had a piece of beauty in his life all his own.

His love for Zariya felt like it was bursting with potential. Their love was a seed. The beginning of something good and rare.

Zariya reached up and brushed his blond locks back from his

forehead. She was watching him, her slitted green eyes fixed on his face. "What's going on in that big brain of yours?"

He took her hand and kissed her palm. "Just thinking how rare this is. How precious. I wish we didn't have to go back to reality."

A shadow passed over Zariya's face and she sat up on her elbow, looking down.

"What?" Konstantin asked. "What is it?"

"Maybe we should put some clothes on for this."

KONSTANTIN WALKED SLOWLY at Zariya's side, a low, burning rage fueling his shaky movements. Sekhmet had found him a cane, and he leaned heavily on it now. His and Zariya's earlier exertions had left his muscles tired and burning. God, he hoped he recovered more than this.

Sekhmet had pointed them in the direction of a shady courtyard, and they found the rest of the team lounging beneath a wooden pergola threaded with flowering vines. Well, Luiz was lounging. Daevin and Galu were playing cards. Rex was standing at the far balcony, looking into the river. But he turned when they arrived, the first to notice their presence.

"Boss!" Galu sprang up and jogged across the stones to help Konstantin to a seat.

He waved him away. "I've got to learn to do it myself."

"You almost died—" Galu trailed off as Zariya shot him a look.

"Male pride and all." Zariya rolled her eyes.

Konstantin managed to sit on the sofa next to Daevin without totally losing his balance. He let out a groan of relief. A thin sheen of sweat had broken out on his brow.

Daevin clapped his leg. "Welcome back, boss. You look good."

"Liar." Konstantin closed his eyes briefly, sucking in a breath. "What, no clever jest?"

"Well, I was going to say you look like Anubis, the God of Death, ran over you with his car, and then backed over you again for good measure...but I thought that might be in poor taste." Daevin grinned.

Zariya pinched the bridge of her nose. "You think?"

"I've always appreciated honesty, Daevin," Konstantin said. "But I might need to rethink my position."

Luiz was looking from Zariya to Konstantin, a thoughtful look on his chiseled face.

"What?" Zariya asked.

"You two look different." Luiz pointed from him to Zariya and back again.

"No, we don't," Zariya insisted.

Luiz started to nod and a delighted smile broke across his face. "Yeah, you do. You two boned! About fucking time!"

Zariya's face flushed. "Luiz, what are you, a fifth grade boy? No chill. You have absolutely *no* chill."

"I'm just excited! I've been shipping you two since our first mission."

Konstantin's brows furrowed and he exchanged a look with Zariya. "Is he speaking English?"

Everyone laughed. Zariya patted him on the shoulder. "I'll explain later."

Rex had joined the circle, coming to sit on a leather stool across from the couches. The expression on his face was troubled. "As excited as we all are for this important development in the life of Phoenix Team, should we perhaps discuss our collective problem?"

"Who's going to be best man at the wedding? Obviously, I would give the funniest toast," Daevin said.

Konstantin dropped his head into his hands to hide his smile. Good to see the team's morale hadn't suffered too much.

"What?" Luiz scoffed. "Love is my business, man. I would kill that speech."

"*Sex* is your business," Galu pointed out. "Not sure that's what they'd be going for. Besides, they don't call me Phoenix Two for nothing—"

Rex ground his teeth. "I was *talking* about how we are all

international fugitives wanted by every law enforcement agency in the world."

They all fell silent.

"Hometown Rex is a bummer." Daevin shook his head.

Rex sucked in a breath and blew it out. "I'm sorry. Yes, being here puts me on edge. I'd like to discuss a plan to return our lives to some degree of normalcy."

Zariya put a gentle hand on his shoulder. "We know how much you sacrificed to bring us here."

"What do you mean, Zariya?" Galu asked.

She turned. "Rex's divine powers were suppressed in our world. But now that he's back, they've been unleashed. Unless we find a solution, he can't return to Earth. He's stuck here."

Shocked silence blanketed the space.

Konstantin pressed his lips together in a thin line. He never would have asked the demi-god to sacrifice himself. Rex should have just let him slip away. His life wasn't worth Rex's freedom.

When Konstantin looked up he found Rex regarding him. "I know what you are thinking, Konstantin," Rex said quietly. "And I would do it again in a heartbeat."

Konstantin swallowed thickly.

"We may be able to pull this one out of the fire." Zariya quickly outlined the plan she had already gone over with him. Her idea involved breaking into the MASC Headquarters at Turtle Bay, somehow getting Under-Secretary Pérez alone and showing her the real video...all while someone else stole an ancient Hebrew artifact from the MASC vault. It was madness. But he had no other ideas.

When Zariya was finished, the rest of the team sat, digesting it.

Galu spoke first, carefully. "The plan has some minor wrinkles to work out."

"Minor?" Daevin scoffed. "It has more wrinkles than a linen suit after a fourteen-hour flight."

Zariya groaned. "I know, I know! I need everyone's help to figure out how to make this work."

"I'm afraid showing the Under-Secretary our video won't be

enough," Konstantin said. "If Cyriaque has a video that's as compelling as you say, they could just accuse us of faking ours. And say that theirs is the real one."

"We could use a computer forensics person to analyze the videos," Galu suggested. "There have to be markers of tampering."

"We need Kiki," Zariya muttered.

"I still think we'll need more evidence against Cyriaque." Konstantin shook his head.

Luiz offered, "He must have been in contact with Iona somehow. Mason before that. That would be the proof we need. Phone records. Emails."

"We need Kiki," Zariya said again.

"We still have the issue of the cameras inside HQ and getting into the MASC vault. We don't know what kind of security the vault has," Galu said.

"We need Kiki," Zariya insisted.

Konstantin nodded. "We need Kiki."

"You're right, boss." The corner of Daevin's mouth twitched as he held back a smile. "Great idea. I wish someone had thought of that sooner."

Zariya threw a pillow at him as the rest of the team busted up laughing. "Fucking mansplainers!"

7

I stood next to Rex, my heart thundering in my chest.

We'd decided it was best for the two of us to go alone. Me to talk to Kiki, Rex to get us in and out of this strange dimension. Less chance for the rest of the team to get captured or compromised. The rest of the guys hadn't liked the idea of staying behind one bit—especially Konstantin. But I'd convinced them.

Rex and I were leaving from the bedroom Sekhmet had given Konstantin. Hoping to stay under the radar.

"Are you sure it's all right you're heading back to Earth? Now that your powers are growing?" I asked.

"Since they haven't fully returned yet, a short trip shouldn't disrupt things," Rex said. "And if I learned one thing from living among humans, it's that it's better to ask for forgiveness than permission."

"I hope Anubis agrees."

"Me too." I took Rex's hand and got a little electric shock.

"Sorry." He offered me a small smile. "Ready?"

"As I'll ever be."

I braced myself, but there was no way I could ever really be ready for the world to spin sideways. The room fell away and all that was left was the firmness of Rex's hand and the blinding glare of golden light.

When I blinked the light away, I found us standing in a familiar space. My apartment. My bedroom. I wanted to weep with the familiarity of it. My striped duvet cover, photos of me and Dad, of me and Kiki and Alviya—my clothes! My phone—which I'd left plugged in on my bedside table when we'd headed to the DRC. That felt like an eternity ago.

I gravitated towards it, but Rex grabbed my arm. "We don't have time."

I nodded reluctantly. The only thing on it was probably a hundred missed calls from Auntie. As much as I wanted to rip off the strange Egyptian dress I'd changed into and put on jeans and my White Snake tee—I needed to focus. Kiki. I was here for Kiki.

I opened my glands and took in the heat signatures in the apartment. Three. Me, Rex, and a small form in Kiki's room. I breathed a sigh of relief. We'd chosen to come at night in the hopes that she'd be here and not on base. It seemed we'd guessed right.

"She's here. Wait here, okay?"

Rex frowned but nodded.

I stepped into the hallway quietly and tiptoed to just outside her door. I quested out with my mind. *"Kiki? It's Zariya. Can I come in? I need to talk."*

"Zariya?" I winced as her surprised voice shouted in my head. *"What are you doing here? Everyone's looking for you!"*

"Please, I need your help. We're innocent."

Kiki jerked open the door and we stood face to face for a moment. Kiki was wearing an oversized Care Bears shirt that hung off one slender shoulder, her black hair messy. And then she grabbed me in a hug, squeezing the air from me. "I'm so glad you're all right."

Relief welled in me. "It's really good to see you."

She released me and ushered me into her dark room, filled with glowing computer screens. She moved a stack of electronics off a chair, spinning it around for me. "Where have you been? Tell me everything. After you got back from Quiribri Island, you all just went AWOL."

"We needed to rescue Konstantin." I explained what had gone on in the DRC with Iona and trailed off when I got to us ending up in Phairo. Laid out our haphazard plan to try to convince the Under-Secretary of our innocence. "I'm telling you, Kiki. Cyriaque is the traitor, not Konstantin. We need your help to get into Headquarters to talk to the Under-Secretary—"

Kiki cut me off. "Zariya, I've seen the footage. It's definitely Konstantin. And he just took off—"

"Because his team was being threatened! Konstantin has a video of Cyriaque taking the Chinvat Gate!"

"Have you seen it?"

I paused. "Well, no, there hasn't been time, but—"

"Zariya, I like Konstantin, and I've always trusted him. But I feel the same way about Cyriaque. Are you so sure that it's Cyriaque playing you? Not Konstantin?"

I let out a grunt of disbelief. "Yes! Iona *told* us she turned Cyriaque."

"The same Iona who's Konstantin Maker? Couldn't they have been working together?"

I squeezed my eyes shut. Cyriaque must have really done a number on her to make her believe him so unquestioningly. What was going on back at Base? "No. Kiki, Konstantin nearly died to kill Iona. They were not working together. Konstantin is not our enemy. He's a good person. Kiki, I love him."

Her dark eyes were sympathetic. "Can you see why that might mean you don't have the best judgment when it comes to him?"

I stood up in a rush. "You don't believe me? Do you think *I'm* a traitor?"

Kiki stood too, putting her hands out to placate me. "Of course not, Zariya. But I do think it's possible that Konstantin has been manipulating the whole team. Can't you admit it's a possibility?"

I shook my head. This couldn't be happening. "Not unless you admit that Cyriaque being the traitor and framing Konstantin could be a possibility."

She sighed. "Yes, it is a possibility. Though I've seen no evidence of that—"

"I have." I punched my chest with a finger. "I have, Kiki. Believe me. Look into Cyriaque. If nothing else, to assure yourself I'm wrong and that I'm really being manipulated by the criminal mastermind Konstantin Bauer. But I'm telling you, you're going to find that it's Cyriaque who's the traitor. He worked with the Authority to kill my dad. His own best friend. And I'm not going to let him get away with it."

"*Okay*," she said quietly. "*I'll look into it.*"

It took me a moment to realize that she had spoken in my mind. "*Why didn't you say that out loud?*" I looked around as warning bells went off in my mind.

"I'm sorry, Zariya."

I opened up my senses and sent them shooting out, taking in the entirety of the building, the city block around it. There was a concentrated mass of figures barreling up the stairwell a few floors below. More outside.

My eyes flew open as outrage kindled to life within me. "You turned me in?"

"I didn't!" Kiki cried. "They thought you might come here! They rigged a sensor on the apartment to detect magical activity."

"But you could have warned me! Rex!" I turned and ran into the hall. "Rex, we've gotta go!"

Kiki followed and grabbed my arm, whirling me around. "Stay, Zariya. Come back to Base and tell them everything. You don't have to run. You didn't go anything wrong except follow your commanding officer. We'll get this sorted out."

I rounded on her, spitting my words. "I don't abandon my team. And I don't betray my friends. I thought I could count on the same from you, but I guess I was wrong."

The front door shattered inward on its hinges and Commander

Strongroot, all seven feet of him swathed in black tactical gear, barreled into the living room.

I spun and bolted into my bedroom, form tackling Rex, who was already glowing gold. I looked over my shoulder and Kiki's face, painted in misery, was the last thing I saw before we swirled into the abyss.

~

WE TUMBLED out of Rex's glowing portal onto the hard stone floor.

I groaned as I came to a stop on my back and cradled my head. All of this dimension hopping was going to give me a migraine.

"How'd it go?" Galu asked carefully.

I just lay there, my hands over my eyes. "Terrible. She didn't believe me. Strongroot almost got us." And I'd told her our plan to break into base. Which meant that Cyriaque now knew exactly how to oppose us. Motherfucker.

"Well, that's wonderful," Luiz added in a strangled tone. "Glad we risked it." What the hell was up with the guys?

I opened my eyes and shoved to a seat. And then froze. Crocodile-headed Egyptian guards lined the room, their spears lowered threateningly.

I looked around at the rest of the team, who sat gingerly around the room, backs ramrod straight.

"What's going on?" I asked weakly.

Rex stood slowly and dusted off his hands. His visage had changed—he wore his jackal head, and he stood with his spine stiff, his shoulders rolled back. "I suspect this has to do with me."

One of the guards stepped forward, his curved teeth clacking as he spoke. "Rexsis Ahmad, by order of Lord Anubis, you are under arrest."

Cyriaque massaged his temples in a futile effort to banish his headache.

Following Aquila Team's unsuccessful attempt to capture Zariya and Rexsis, there had been questions. So many damn questions.

Though Kimiko and the others seemed to accept what he'd told them—that Zariya's accusations were all part of Konstantin's plot to discredit him and divide Veil Force—he could see the seed of doubt in their eyes. That seed had been planted. And it would begin to grow.

The situation here was getting out of hand. For the hundredth time, Cyriaque wished he and Vizol had never gone to the DRC on that mission. He wished he had never headed to that card game. He should have stayed in his room, staring at the ceiling. Vizol would still be alive. And Cyriaque wouldn't have to live with the knowledge that he'd had a hand in his best friend's death.

It wasn't good for a wolf to be alone. His father had been a bastard, ruling his pack like a dictator. Cyriaque still had the scars on his back to show it. He'd begged his mother and his wolf brothers to leave with him, but in the end, he'd been the only one with the balls to go. Maybe he was the only one naive enough to think he could make it alone. Without a pack.

But he'd found another pack. His special forces brothers. And then his Veil Force teammates. And yet somehow, he'd become just like this father. A dictator. A liar. A traitor to his own people.

His mind spun hopelessly for a solution. He should just turn himself in. But his wolf wasn't meant to be caged. He'd die in prison. And he wasn't ready to die. He could run—just pack up and disappear. That might buy him a few weeks, months at best. But with their resources, MASC and this Leviathan organization would find him. It would only be a matter of time.

Ring!

Cyriaque looked at his phone like a poisonous snake. He didn't want to answer.

Ring!

He had to. He snatched the receiver up. "Hello?" He already knew who it was. He had a feeling.

"Director, good to speak to you again." The smooth voice of the man he knew only as Gray came through the line. The Head of Leviathan. Since their last conversation, Cyriaque had done what covert digging he could on the organization, and he hadn't found much of a footprint.

Leviathan barely existed; it was little more than a whisper in the intelligence circles, a word overheard in intercepted phone calls but not understood. In this day and age of modern technology, it was hard to be invisible. Nearly impossible, in fact. That convinced him of Leviathan's true power more than Gray's boasting ever could.

"I'm not in the mood for pleasantries," Cyriaque responded.

"Tell me about our Konstantin problem—is it taken care of?"

Cyriaque pursed his lips. He was furious with himself—with his men—for letting Phoenix Team slip though his fingers. But how could he have anticipated Rexsis Ahmad having a teleporting power even more powerful than Enigma's? Had he been holding out all this time? It didn't make sense. "I have intel on his team," Cyriaque said. "They're fighting back."

"Of course they are. You wouldn't have trained them very well if they just gave up. It's always good to have a worthy adversary. Much more satisfying when you crush them."

This guy had a serious super-villain complex. "They plan to plead their case directly to Under-Secretary Pérez. To convince her the video was a fake."

"Hmm. Not the most creative approach, and one easily countered. Now we know where to expect them."

"We're already in place to apprehend them if they try to get into headquarters."

"Or," Gray mused, "we could seize this opportunity for our own purposes. A higher purpose."

"What do you mean?" Cyriaque asked slowly.

"The Under-Secretary. She has been a thorn in our side. Unwilling to compromise on our key policy issues."

"You mean she can't be bought." That actually gave him some measure of comfort.

Gray ignored him, continuing. "If some tragedy were to befall her...if a rogue agent took her out during a wild mission and then was tragically killed in the process... that would be an unfortunate scenario that we could turn to our benefit."

Cyriaque sat for a moment, disbelieving. Was this guy for real? "You're talking about killing her and blaming it on Konstantin?"

"People get injured in firefights. Accidents happen. Mistakes. Munitions blow in the wrong place at the wrong time."

Cyriaque licked his dry lips. "I don't want anything to do with this. I won't be part of this—"

"Just relax, Cyriaque. I'll handle everything. You won't need to get your pretty claws dirty."

"It's wrong," Cyriaque protested. This was all so fucking wrong. He should just turn this guy in right now. Confess everything. How much blood could one person have on their hands before it drove them mad? He needed to find a fucking way out of this Gordian knot he'd landed himself in. "How do you know that the next Under-Secretary wouldn't be worse?"

Gray chuckled. "We have enough sway at MASC to ensure that the next nominee is sympathetic to our cause. In fact, I have just the person in mind."

Cyriaque knew he should let it go, but he couldn't help himself. "Who?"

"You, Cyriaque. What would you think about being Under-Secretary-General of the Mythical Alliance of Supernatural Creatures?"

Cyriaque sat for a moment in stunned silence before letting out a bark of laughter. "Me? No fucking way. I'm not cut out for politics." And he had no doubt his current predicament would seem like a dream compared to the situation if he became Under-Secretary. Who knew what horrible things they'd try to manipulate him into doing.

"I beg to differ. I think you'll be perfect. The job would come with significant privileges. Financial. Political. Just sit with the idea for now. No need to make any decisions."

Cyriaque opened his mouth to give another refusal, then closed it. This might be his only opportunity to get information on Leviathan —straight from the horse's mouth. Information that could be traded for leniency if he decided to give himself up. "If I'm going to even consider being Leviathan's puppet inside MASC itself—"

"Not puppet, Cyriaque. Trusted ally."

"Whatever. For me to think about doing this, I need to know who Leviathan really is. What are you after?"

Gray chuckles softly. "Our mission statement? It's simple, Cyriaque. Leviathan wants nothing more than to usher in a utopian era for supernatural life on this planet. Where all mythical creatures enjoy equal opportunity, security, and abundance."

"Oh, is that all?" Cyriaque snorted. "And how exactly do you plan to do that?"

"That's simple. Through the complete eradication of the human race."

9

———

I stared down the Egyptian God of the Dead. My intense eye contact had always worked on Dad.

Anubis seemed less impressed. Maybe he had never had a daughter.

"You can't arrest Rex," I said again. "He didn't do anything wrong."

Konstantin and I stood in the great receiving chamber where we'd first met Rex's dear old dad, who now sat before us on his ornate throne. The rest of the team was waiting outside, as we hadn't wanted to come in too hot and make Anubis feel like we were threatening him.

"You are wrong, naga girl," Anubis rumbled. "Rexsis left this place against our specific orders, knowing the danger that his growing magic posed to the mortal realm. His disobedience cannot go unpunished."

"He was following my orders," Konstantin protested. He stood next to me, his shoulders thrown back, but there were shadows beneath his eyes and his face looked ashen. He needed more rest. He should be in bed. A pang of guilt hit me as I thought about our earlier...activities.

Way to jump the guy when he's not even out of his hospital bed, Chanji.

I mentally kicked myself. I needed to do what was best for Konstantin. Because knowing men in general and Konstantin in particular, he thought he was invincible and would run himself into the ground if I let him.

"I see what you try to do, vampire," Anubis said, "and I will not let you take the blame from my son. He is a free creature and I know his mind. These actions are his and his alone."

"At least let us see him," I begged. "We have a lead on something that could help him travel back and forth between worlds. Isn't it worth letting us look into that? Do you truly want him to be a prisoner here? Perhaps this could benefit all of you. Aren't you tired of sitting in this palace?"

Anubis stood, his eyes flashing. "You know nothing of what you speak, child. This is how it has always been. And it is how it always will be."

Konstantin shot me a warning look, but I ignored it. Typical old dude patriarchal thinking. Fuck that. "That's small thinking," I said. "That's how you grow stagnant and obsolete. Great leaders think creatively. They plan for the future and adapt. And most of all, they think of the needs of their people. And that includes Rex. You can't trap him here unnecessarily. We're his family, too."

Anubis's snout drew back in a snarl, but Sekhmet laid a hand on his muscled forearm.

"This need not be decided now," she murmured. "Let them see Rexsis. He wears the Set's bracelet, which will keep him from transporting himself to Earth. It is safe. Perhaps seeing his friends will help him come to terms with his situation."

Anubis glared at me but gave a curt nod. "Very well."

"Thank you." Konstantin gave a polite bow.

I just glared back.

∽

Sekhmet directed some guards to take us to the chamber where they were holding Rex. It wasn't exactly a cell. The room was spacious, the furniture ornate and comfortable. There were no bars to be seen. But there were no windows, either. And guards lined the hallway outside the thick door.

My brilliant plan to spring Rex out fizzled. This would not be easy.

Inside, Rex was sitting serenely on the sofa.

"Are you all right?" I went to sit next to him, threading my arm through his. Rex had always been the most enigmatic member of the team—the one I hadn't quite managed to connect with. But seeing him here, with his family, I was getting a glimpse of the real Rex beneath the polished, calm exterior—the Rex with chinks in his armor. And I felt like a protective mother hen.

"Yes, I have not been mistreated." Rex patted my hand. "I'm surprised they let you see me."

"I can be very persuasive." I grinned, eyeing the ornate golden bracelet that now tightly circled his wrist. This must have been the bracelet Sekhmet referred to. The thing keeping him here. It was pretty—for a shackle.

Konstantin snorted. "She was about as diplomatic as the church during the Inquisition."

Galu rubbed his temple. "You seriously need to update your metaphors, boss."

I chuckled.

Konstantin sat down in one of the chairs across from us, leaning back with a groan. "Nonsense. I'm just a...living reminder of the importance of history."

"Right. Like the mummy from that movie," Daevin said. "What was it called?"

"*The Mummy*." Luiz shot Daevin an incredulous look.

Rex shuddered. "The historical inaccuracies in that movie are appalling."

"Not to mention I'm much better-looking than that mummy," Konstantin said, then he frowned. "At least I was before that poison drained the life from me."

I stood and crossed the room, dropping into Konstantin's lap. His arms curled around me, locking me into his embrace. I kissed his nose. "You're still much better-looking than a two-thousand-year-old mummy."

"Low bar. Low. Bar," Galu muttered.

Konstantin smiled, his eyes fixed on me.

"All right, now that we've gotten that disgustingly sweet display out of the way, can we talk strategy?" Daevin asked. "Specifically, how the hell we're going to get into MASC headquarters?"

"I've been thinking," Galu said. "We don't have Kiki. We need someone else who can give us access to the security system. At the least, we'll need to divert the cameras while we infiltrate and talk to the Under-Secretary."

Konstantin nodded. "I'm still in contact with Rocky. He and Cyriaque always butted heads. I bet he would help."

"Who's Rocky?" I asked.

"He was Kiki. Before Kiki," Daevin said. "He's good."

"How are we planning to get into HQ?" I asked.

"You can't teleport in or out. The place is warded," Luiz said.

I shifted in Konstantin's lap so my elbow wasn't digging into his side. I was probably cutting off circulation to his legs, but I didn't care. I was still reveling in the fact that I was allowed to be here. That he was mine. "Rex, do the wards affect your power? Would you be able to teleport in from here?"

"If I wasn't being detained by my own family?"

"Naturally, if not for that."

"Yes. But there is no way for me to break free of this bracelet without the key. The magic threaded through it is too powerful. And my father's concerns over my growing powers twisting reality on Earth are founded. Until we have the Nephilim's Knot, I do not think it is safe for me to return. Unfortunately, you will have to execute this mission without me."

Shit, that really sucked.

"What sort of impact would your powers have?" Konstantin asked.

"Massive distortions of space and time. We originate from a

higher dimension that exists outside linear time. My presence could create pockets of time that untether from the greater timeline. It's not pretty."

"How did the gods live on Earth back in the day then?" Galu asked. "Without warping time?"

"It did warp time. Think about the miracles and accomplishments of Egyptian civilization—so far advanced beyond the technology of the surrounding cultures—and not always explained through carbon dating techniques. Egyptian civilization is in fact much older and lasted much longer than we think, because that area was not entirely in phase with the rest of the world's timeline."

Silence fell over the room.

"Damn, man. And I just thought it was cool that you could put on a different head," Daevin said. "And now we find out you're like an alien time-lord or something?"

"Only half an alien time-lord. No need to oversell it," Rex said with a straight face.

"Okay, so no risking the fate of time and space. Rex is out. Where does that leave us?" Konstantin asked. "We can't use the Chinvat Gate if the wards are up. Going in the front will be a nightmare now that they're expecting us."

Thanks to me being a complete idiot and spilling our whole plan to Kiki. I cringed internally.

Luiz tapped a finger on his chin. "What if we could bring the wards down long enough to teleport in?"

"That would be great. But none of us can do that," Galu pointed out.

"We can't. But Isobel can."

I raised an eyebrow. Luiz hadn't mentioned Isobel, the Crescent Moon battle witch who had helped us free the captives on Quiribri Island, since that mission. But we'd been kind of busy, what with infiltrating the DRC, being captured by the Authority, and then fleeing our own organization in a weird Egyptian sub-dimension. "You think she'd help us?"

A smile floated across his face. "I think I left an impression. I could ask."

"I imagine she'd need to get inside to disable the wards?" Daevin asked. "She needed to on Quiribri Island."

"A witch going into MASC headquarters alone might look suspicious," I pointed out.

"It would be better if she went in with a group. Easier to stay under the radar," Rex suggested.

Konstantin shook his head. "There's no way any of us could escort her in. They're going to be looking for us."

"You're right. We need someone who they don't know," Luiz agreed.

"Melusine." Galu looked up. "No one knows about her except us. We didn't mention her in the Inverness briefing. They wouldn't connect her to us."

"That's not a bad idea." Konstantin nodded. "Okay, so would they go in as guests?"

"Actually, I've got that one covered," I said. "I have a MASC keycard. We could have them go in the service entrance as staff."

"Why do you have a MASC keycard?" Konstantin raised an eyebrow.

"From back when everyone I knew and loved was lying to me in a massive conspiracy to bury the true reason behind Dad's death." I flashed my fangs.

Konstantin winced. "I had hoped you forgot about that."

I smiled. "Nope. You still have to make it up to me somehow."

Konstantin's thumb stroked hypnotically along my thigh where his hand rested. "However shall I do that?"

I kissed him. It was meant to be a quick peck, but his tongue parted my lips and desire roared to life inside me.

A cleared throat drew me back to reality. I broke off the kiss reluctantly.

"That's a bit much even for the incubus," Luiz said, though he was grinning. "Can we get back on topic?"

Right. Infiltrating MASC headquarters. "Where were we?"

"We were discussing your pilfered keycard," Daevin suggested. "So Melusine and Isobel, assuming they're willing to play ball, will sneak in the back. Isobel will disarm the wards, and we'll teleport in using the Gate. We'll split into two teams, one to get this Nephilim's Knot, the other to talk to the Under-Secretary and convince her to spare all of us and arrest Cyriaque. Where is this knot thingy again?"

"It's kept in the vault on the bottom level." Rex shook his head. "I'm not certain it's even possible for you to get it. Certainly not advisable. The vault is heavily guarded."

"Of course we're going to get it," I said. "Can't we teleport directly into the vault?"

Rex shook his head. "There was a time, after Under-Secretary Pérez denied my request for the artifact, where I looked into the possibility of...*borrowing* it myself."

"Rexy, you devious dog." Daevin elbowed him in the side.

Rex continued, unfazed. "I concluded it could not be done. The vault is designed to neutralize any magical objects or magic. With so many artifacts packed in a closed space, they didn't want something going off that would trigger the magic of all the other objects. I do not believe the Chinvat Gate will work inside."

"So we'll need to go through the front. That's all right. We'll just do our best to minimize casualties," I said.

"What if we did our infiltration in the dark?" Galu asked. "Knock out the lights?"

"They'd definitely know we're coming then," Luiz objected.

"There's a backup generator as well," Rex said.

"We'll just have to take our chances," I said.

"Or...what if there's an artificial night? Localized?" Daevin suggested.

"How would we do that? We won't have Rex," I pointed out.

"Yara. She can throw shadows, blanketing the place in darkness. We use our night vision, take out the guards, and break into the vault."

Galu nodded. "That's not bad."

"That might work for the vault, but I like that plan less when it comes to the Under-Secretary." Konstantin frowned. "It might put her on the defensive—less likely to believe we're friendly."

"Fair point," Galu said.

"So how do we get to her? She'll have bodyguards close at all times," Luiz asked.

I looked up with a grin. "Ladies' room. No bodyguards. And it's the perfect place for a heart to heart."

It took two days to gather the help they needed. To send teams out in the Chinvat Gate to sweet-talk and return with Melusine, Yara, Isobel, and Rocky, a red panda shifter and former member of the Tartarus Base staff. All had agreed to help, though Isobel's agreement was grudging and came with conditions.

Konstantin had stayed with Rex, directing the team's forays back into the real world. It was strange and uncomfortable to stay back while his team was in the field—potentially in danger. But his body was still weak. He *was* growing stronger with rest; he could already walk without assistance and stand for more than a few minutes at a time. But he was a long way from full strength. It was best to let his team handle things until absolutely necessary. It didn't mean he liked it.

At least the food and the company were good. He spent his days with Rex, exchanging stories about history and the old ways. His nights were devoted to Zariya—more specifically, worshipping her beautiful body in every creative way in his arsenal. He longed to free them from the dark cloud of these charges hanging over them. He wanted to stroll through the city with her, hand in hand, stopping at Sarge's Delicatessen for bagels and coffee in the morning, the steakhouse he liked for dinner. He wanted normalcy and safety. For both of them.

But the only way they'd get their life back was to claim it for themselves.

The team had gathered in Rex's large room, digging into a spread of pita and hummus, glistening olives and succulent melon. Rocky sat and chatted with Rex, his brilliant red hair standing in short spikes. The man had retired from Veil Force because the hours weren't conducive to having a family, but Konstantin had always liked him. He'd already been hugely helpful, getting them detailed blueprints of the building and guard rotations, as well as tapping into the security feed so they could control it when the time came.

"All right." Konstantin spoke over the chatter, clapping his hands. Part of him didn't want to interrupt the moment. Despite the circumstances, everyone was here. Happy. But they wouldn't be able to stay in Phairo forever. "Today's the day. We know Under-Secretary Pérez will be leaving tomorrow to spend a few days in Geneva for the United Nations Climate Summit. This is our window."

Zariya settled in the chair next to him, a gold Egyptian dress stylishly wrapped around her curvaceous form, a crystal glass of mint tea in her hand. She gave him an encouraging smile.

"First, I know I've said it before, but it's worth saying again. Rocky, Melusine, Yara, and Isobel. Thank you for joining our cause. This doesn't concern you, and you're taking a risk to be here. We're grateful."

"I couldn't very well let Galu be locked up for life after we've just been reunited." Melusine patted Galu's knee. Her blue hair was threaded into several long braids that trailed over her shoulders, and her tattooed marks glowed faintly with power.

"Agreed," Yara said. "I've spent too much time standing silent, unable to stop the injustices around me. You all freed me from that." She looked at Daevin with a smile on her lavender-skinned face. "I'll help Phoenix Team anytime you call."

Konstantin looked at Isobel, who lounged back in her chair. She had changed out of her gray battle witch attire on arrival, and her black hair with its white streak was pulled back in a neat bun. Isobel shrugged. "Luiz promised to take me to dinner, and he can't very well do that from prison, can he?"

"I promised you dinner *and dessert*," Luiz purred at Isobel.

Zariya chortled.

Rocky stretched, the stocky little man at ease amongst these more deadly supes. "I'm just here for the falafel."

The team chuckled.

Zariya leaned forward, intent on Rocky, her lower lip between her teeth.

Konstantin shook his head in warning, but she ignored him.

"Rocky, I know this is so uncool to ask you...but..." She looked at Melusine and Isobel, who nodded encouragingly. "Would you shift for us?"

Rocky snorted as Konstantin dropped his head into his hands. Asking another supe to demonstrate their abilities was definitely *not cool*. Zariya knew that. She shouldn't risk alienating Rocky—

But Rocky had already stood, shouldering off his black bomber jacket. "It's okay, Konstantin. You'd be shocked how often I'm asked this. I will shift, on one condition." He pointed at Zariya, then the other women.

"Anything!" Zariya said eagerly.

"Absolutely no cuddling. I'm a married man and the mate gets territorial about cuddling."

"But—" Melusine started, then sighed. "Fine."

"What about one pet?" Zariya said. "On your head? Is that okay?"

"Zariya!" Konstantin scolded.

She ignored him.

Rocky rolled his eyes. "Fine. One pet each. On the head!"

The women nodded solemnly. "One pet only." Zariya crossed her heart. "Swear."

Konstantin exchanged a look of amusement with Daevin and Rex as the telltale tingle of shifter magic filled the air. Then Rocky was gone, replaced by what Konstantin had to admit was a fucking adorable furry red panda.

Zariya literally squealed with delight, falling on her knees next to him.

Rocky stood on his back feet, his furry face distinct with the signature markings of his shifter breed—black eyepatches, white face, pricked ears. He looked a bit like an Ewok from those Star Wars movies.

Zariya lay a careful hand on his head. "He's so soft!" she cooed in delight.

Melusine, Yara, and Isobel gravitated across the room, crowding around Rocky.

Then Luiz got up.

"What are you doing?" Konstantin asked him.

"Look how fucking cute he is! I want to pet him too."

Konstantin threw back his head and stared to laugh.

"Damn it." Daevin stood and followed Luiz.

By the end, tears were streaming down Konstantin's cheeks. Everyone had pet Rocky except him. Even reserved Rex.

Rocky ambled a few feet to stand in front of him, his striped bushy tail flicking back and forth. As if to say, *Come on. You know you want to.*

With a roll of his eyes, Konstantin reached out a hand and stroked the soft, thick fur on Rocky's head.

The rest of the team cheered.

Rocky returned to his seat and shifted back to human form, leaning down to pick up his pants. He was grinning. "I don't know about you all, but I think we just bonded."

IT DIDN'T FEEL right to leave Rex behind, but they had no choice. Rex would monitor the mission from his chamber in Phairo.

On their trip to pick up Melusine, they had also done an equipment run, securing weapons and comms, though not the special kind used by Veil Force.

They had used the Chinvat Gate to transport into an empty apartment just a block from MASC's Turtle Bay headquarters.

"So we all know the plan," Konstantin addressed the team. "Isobel and Melusine will go in the back using Zariya's keycard and find a safe place to take down the wards. We will use the Gate to transport into the stairwell in the center of the building. Zariya, Isobel, Yara, and Daevin will proceed down to the vault. Melusine, Galu, Luiz, and I will make our way to the fourteenth floor, where the Under-Secretary's office is located. Then we'll talk."

"We've got it," Zariya said softly. "And Rocky still hasn't been able to find any additional evidence of Cyriaque's treason?"

"Unfortunately, no," Rocky said. "But I did receive an encrypted packet from someone named Kimiko Nakamura. A friend of yours? I'm still decrypting it, but it looks like she may have uncovered Cyriaque's private email server."

Zariya's eyes lit up like Christmas. "I knew she'd believe us!"

Relief flooded him. Konstantin hadn't been so certain, but it looked like Kiki had come through after all. "Decrypt it as fast as you can and send it to me. That with the video showing Cyriaque taking the Chinvat Gate should be enough to make her listen. The authentication we had done shows that the tape hasn't been tampered with."

"It'll work." Galu nodded encouragingly.

"Is everyone ready?" Konstantin looked around. Besides Melusine and Isobel, who wore service uniforms pilfered from the MASC laundry, they were in plain clothes, with guns concealed under their jackets or in pant legs. They couldn't risk going in with obvious armaments.

"Ready." Zariya nodded, and the rest of the team echoed the sentiment.

"Ready here," Rex said over comms.

Isobel nodded and gestured to Melusine. "Let's get this started."

Melusine gave Galu a thorough kiss.

Luiz raised his eyebrows at Isobel, who just snorted and headed out the door. Melusine quickly followed.

"Now comes the waiting. The worst part," Daevin said under his breath.

"We won't have to wait long." Konstantin settled into a chair to conserve his strength.

Zariya came up next to him and stroked his hair. "You sure you're up for this?"

He nodded. "We agreed. I'm the only one who knows Under-Secretary Pérez personally. And this revolves around me. I need to go. I'll be fine."

Zariya huffed. "Typical man, thinking everything revolves around you." But she leaned down and kissed the top of his head.

"We're in," came Melusine's voice over their communication link.

"That was quick," Luiz said.

"How long did Isobel estimate it would take her to dismantle the wards?" Galu asked.

"Five minutes." Luiz hit his watch. "We should be ready about—"

"Got it," Isobel said triumphantly.

"Or five seconds," Luiz amended. He turned his watch off. "Ready for this?"

Zariya looked at Konstantin, her eyes shining with love and utter trust. Konstantin prayed that trust wasn't misplaced. "Let's go."

11

R ocky had announced we were cleared to transport ourselves into the stairwell sooner than I'd expected. Isobel and Melusine had made quick work of taking down the wards.

I still wasn't quite sure what to call it when we traveled through the Gate. Portaling? Jumping? Gateing? Whatever the name, my stomach refused to get used to the process.

The Chinvat Gate hurled us up over its round edge into the landing of a concrete stairwell. I twisted and landed hard on my knees, managing to avoid a hard stair jamming directly in my side. It was tight in here—but we all poured out before the Gate winked shut.

Galu picked up the artifact, which had shrunk back to its petite size, and shoved it in his cargo pocket.

Isobel's voice crackled over comms. "We're headed up the stairs to meet you."

"All right." Konstantin nodded. "Vault team, head out. We'll rendezvous back at the safehouse."

My gut clenched as I realized this was it—Konstantin and I were separating. If things went sideways with the Under-Secretary, he could end up arrested. Worse.

He seemed to have the same thought. Konstantin threaded his hand through my hair and pulled me in for a rough kiss to the sound of quiet wolf whistles and whispered cheers around us. It seemed the team hadn't grown used to Konstantin and me together. Neither had I. The thrill of kissing him hadn't started to fade—not by a long shot.

I pulled back a few seconds later, breathless, my heart in my throat and my whole body tingling. I pressed my forehead to his. "I'll see you soon."

"That's a promise."

Daevin and Yara were smirking at me as we turned and started down the stairs. "Shut up," I mock-grumbled, but I couldn't keep the grin from my face. Even with treason charges and the threat of a firefight against our own organization hanging over my head—Konstantin made me grin like a fool.

"Didn't say a word." Daevin held up his hands innocently.

"There's a first for everything," I shot back.

Yara snorted a laugh.

We met Isobel and Melusine a few floors down and Melusine jogged past us to join the other team.

Isobel fell into step with us, nodding. She said she had a spell that was going to unlock the vault for us without triggering the alarms. It was useful to have a witch around, especially one who had more in her repertoire than Enigma, the one-trick pony. I wished we could recruit her, though I doubted that Svetlana Morikova, High Priestess of the Crescent Moon Coven (still pissed at Luiz) would let us poach her best battle witch without putting up a fight.

"Both teams clear in the stairwell to their target floor." Rocky's voice sounded in my earpiece.

Sweet. This was going surprisingly well. But I wasn't going to get cocky. Things could still go sideways in a blink. Like they had in every other mission.

We made our way down to the bottom floor, where the vault was located, deep beneath the streets of New York City. I paused at the door, sucking in a breath. "We ready?"

Yara cracked her knuckles. "Ready."

Yara, Daevin, and Isobel pulled down night vision goggles. I opened my glands, sensing into the space beyond the stairwell door. "Two guards flanking the vault door, like we thought."

Daevin held up three fingers and counted down while Yara grasped the door handle. Three... Two...

On one, we exploded out of the stairwell. Yara unfurled a wave of shadows that swallowed the whole hallway in darkness. Even expecting it, the effect was disorienting. It took me a second to adjust, and by the time I was aiming at the guards, Daevin had already popped both of them with tranquilizer darts. We had real bullets in our sidearms, but we were hoping to avoid any MASC casualties. These were our colleagues, after all.

I straightened and lowered my gun. "Nice."

Daevin motioned us forward. "Yara, can you hold the shadows out here in case anyone comes down?"

"No problem," she replied.

We approached the vault door and paused while Isobel pointed her wand, murmuring in a language I didn't understand. The wheel on the huge steel door ticked and began moving counterclockwise. And then it stopped.

"Is that it?" Daevin asked.

"That should do it," Isobel replied.

"That was easy." I grabbed the wheel and pulled. Too easy?

The door swung open and revealed a massive vault, lined with row upon row of objects.

Yara whistled softly.

"Let's find this knot thingy and meet up with the team." Daevin strode inside like he owned the place.

Tension uncoiled from my shoulders. Good. Part of me had expected a secondary alarm to go off when he entered. But Isobel must have really disarmed everything.

We spread out through the vault, scanning the objects. "Is there any sort of order?" Isobel asked.

"Not alphabetical," Yara replied. "Because this scimitar is next to a monkey's paw."

"Geographic region?" Daevin asked.

"I think so," I said. "Look, there's some Hebrew writing on the stuff in this corner."

I crouched down, checking the low shelf. *Knot, knot... Where are you, Nephilim's Knot? Ah-ha!* Tucked in the back corner, nestled on a velvet pillow, was the golden Nephilim's Knot, just like Rex had shown me in ancient biblical images. "I found it!" I reached back and grabbed it, but as soon as my fingers touched the metal, the room shook.

I looked up. "What was..." I trailed off as I realized. The door had slammed shut.

"Shit." Yara hurried over towards the door, but the gears were already turning, engaging the lock. She grabbed it and tried to hold it still, but the mechanism was too strong, practically wrenching her sideways. The huge lock clicked back into place.

I stood on wooden legs, the Nephilim's Knot in my hand. "Shit." Suddenly, this room felt very small. Very deep.

A hissing sound filled the vault. I whipped my head up and saw where it was coming from—some sort of white gas was pouring out of tiny jets in the four corners of the room.

Yara, Daevin, Isobel, and I looked at each other in horror, saying in an echoing chorus, "Shit!"

CYRIAQUE PACED the short span of his office.

Something was wrong. His wolf senses could feel it.

It had been three days since he'd talked to Gray—three days of bad sleep and a churning gut. When he tried to shift, the transformation was slow and painful. Like his wolf was fighting him. Like his animal self didn't want anything to do with the piece-of-shit human Cyriaque had become.

Was he really going to stand by and let the Under-Secretary of the Mythical Alliance be assassinated? He'd talked to Ximena on more than one occasion—he liked her.

When the Collectors had set up the hit on Vizol, they'd kept the truth of their intentions from Cyriaque. True, he'd provided Vizol's location, but he hadn't known what they'd planned. He'd thought they'd just wanted the intel to keep their criminal operations out of Vizol's way. After his best friend had died, he'd comforted himself with the thought that if he'd known, he would have stopped it. He wouldn't have let them go through with it. No matter what it would have cost him.

But here he was again. No, it wasn't his best friend in the crosshairs, but it was a supe he liked and respected. And whom he had sworn to protect.

Cyriaque picked up his phone with shaking fingers. Dialed the number for Under-Secretary Pérez. Already, tension was sloughing off him like a too-tight snakeskin—he took his first deep breath in a week. He was going to do the right thing. What he should have done a long fucking time ago.

The phone rang four times and then went to voicemail. He frowned. Maybe Kiki could get through to her. She was in danger. He couldn't wait.

Cyriaque strode out of his office, through the hallways of Tartarus Base. The place he and Vizol had built. The base had once been a fallout bunker for MASC, and he still remembered when he and Vizol had moved their ragtag team in, going to work cleaning cobwebs and repainting crumbling cement halls. He let his hand trail along the wall as he rounded the corner into the Ops Center. Once it came out that he'd been working with the enemy, he'd probably never see this place again.

Kiki was on comms, her fingers flying over the keyboard. "Okay, stay with the Under-Secretary. I'll let you know if there are signs of movement."

"What's going on?" Cyriaque drew up next to the screen, which contained a satellite image of the MASC headquarters across the river.

Kiki turned, her eyebrows knitting together. "Uh, I'm overseeing the Aquila Team mission?"

"Who ordered Aquila Team into the field? What's their mission?"

"What—" She paused with a shake of her head. "Wait, what? Director, you did. You authorized the mission to protect Under-Secretary Pérez. You said there was a credible threat."

Every hair on Cyriaque's body stood on end. "When did I give the order? How?"

"You called a few hours ago. Ordered Commander Strongroot to mobilize his team and get over to HQ right away." Kiki cocked her head. "Director, are you all right?"

"I didn't give that order," Cyriaque said quietly.

"Then who did?"

Leviathan. It had to be. No one else knew, no one else had the capability of feigning a phone call from him. Gray had planned to frame Konstantin's team for the murder of the Under-Secretary. So why would he want another Veil Force team there—potentially in a position to stop it?

But then Gray's words on the phone swam to mind. *Accidents happen. Mistakes. Munitions blow in the wrong place at the wrong time.*

His eyes went wide. The Under-Secretary wasn't the only target. Veil Force was. If an explosion went off near the Under-Secretary, if Gray timed it right...it would take out all of Phoenix Team and Aquila Team too—half of Veil Force's Phantoms gone in one blow. The organization would be devastated. And it would be all his fault.

"Kiki, call them back." Cyriaque surged forward, his hands gripping the desk.

"But—"

"Do it!"

Kiki spun in her chair, her hands on the keyboard, but the screens arrayed around them went black. Strings of white code began streaming across the screen. "We're being hacked!" Her fingers flew over the keyboard.

"Can you contact Strongroot? Tell them to fall back! It's a trap."

"MASC HQ is shielded from psychic interference and remote viewing. I can't get to them if I can't use comms. And comms run through our network, which is currently..." She tapped furiously. "Totally fucked."

"I need to get over there. Where's Enigma?"

"You gave him the day off."

"What? No, I didn't!"

Kiki didn't turn around, still hammering at the keys. "What's going on, Cyriaque?"

"What's going on is that Veil Force is under attack. And the Under-Secretary is in danger."

He didn't hear Kiki's reply because he was already running. He pulled his shirt off, unbuckling his pants as he barreled through the hallway. His wolf form was ten times faster than his human form. And time was running out.

The Fourteenth floor was empty as Konstantin's team emerged from the stairwell.

Above them, the steady *whoop* of an alarm had been ringing for the last sixty seconds. "Rocky, what's going on?" Konstantin asked.

"I've lost contact with Daevin's team. I think we can assume this has something to do with the vault break-in. The hallway outside is still pitch black. I can't see shit on camera."

"Damn it," Konstantin swore. He turned. "Galu, get out the gate. We need to help them."

Luiz held up a hand. "Konstantin, the best way to help them is to convince the Under-Secretary we're all innocent. We have to trust them to take care of themselves."

Konstantin ground his teeth.

"I could go, with the gate," Galu offered. "Check it out?"

Konstantin shook his head. "Luiz is right. The four of them are capable of getting out of this. I'm not sending you into a potential ambush. We stick to the plan until we know more." He hit his comm. "Rocky, you tell me the second you have intel on Daevin's team."

"Roger that," he replied. "I think the alarm might help you, though. The building's being evacuated and the majority of the Under-Secretary's guards have headed out to respond. She should be minimally guarded."

"Good. We don't have time to wait anymore for her to come to us. Let's go." Konstantin waved his team forward, shoving off the wall where he'd been leaning. His body was fatigued—he'd been feeling stronger these past few days, but he was tiring so quickly. It didn't matter. He'd get through this with adrenaline and sheer grit if he had to.

They moved silently though the empty corridors lined with offices that had apparently been hastily vacated. There was a still steaming cup of coffee on one desk; on another, a phone beeped as its receiver sat half off its cradle.

The Under-Secretary's office was at the end of the hallway, behind two closed mahogany doors.

"Konstantin!" Rocky's voice shouted through comms. "You've got company!"

Konstantin and the team pulled to a halt—weapons up, just as the double doors swung open to reveal a familiar figure.

And another.

Konstantin's heart dropped into his chest. It was Veil Force's Aquila Team. Commander Strongroot—sequoia dryad—towered in front. Sofia—Italian siren—stood with her twin blades drawn. Alviya —the valkyrie's black eyes glared from her scowling face. Ahmir, an ifrit, Brak, the tall, eerie Watcher, and Tsara, the tiny pink-haired pixie.

Behind all of them, in the shadow of the great dryad, stood the Under-Secretary, Ximena Pérez, brown-skinned ciguapa with impossibly long, glossy violet hair. She didn't look happy.

"Stand down, Bauer," Strongroot rumbled.

Konstantin knew each of these Phantoms, had worked with all of them. Mentored them. Laughed and shared beers with them. He couldn't fight them. It was over. Their best chance now was to negotiate and hope Pérez would listen.

"Konstantin—" Rocky's voice exploded in his ear.

Konstantin raised a hand, touched his comm. "I see them."

"No! Behind you!"

A gun went off.

Konstantin whirled to see two strange supes standing behind them. Wearing plain clothes like his team was, similar comms in their ears. Like they were *with* them. *What the fuck*? Who'd been shot?

"The Under-Secretary!" someone shouted.

Konstantin turned back, just in time to see the Under-Secretary stagger and fall.

REX SAT with his eyes closed, his mind questing out for answers. Ever since arriving back in Phairo, his powers had been expanding rapidly, and that included precognition. Being outside of time allowed him to see events on the linear timeline before they happened. It was a disconcerting feeling when the flashes of future flickered by—he would have to ask Signe and Verte how they managed it.

He let out a soft snort. No, he wouldn't. Because he'd never see Signe and Verte again. He'd never leave this place ever again.

Despite this sobering thought, Rex didn't regret coming back here. He'd saved Konstantin, and likely the rest of the team. He'd known, on some level, that he couldn't stay away forever. He was grateful for the time that he'd had on Earth. The experiences and adventures. Most of all, the friendships.

His only regret was not finding the Nephilim's Knot. He had come so close to securing real freedom for himself, and perhaps for all of his kin, if they could recreate the lost magic of the Knot. Well, it was not meant to be.

A shooting pain lanced his temple and Rex gasped. A vision struck him, capturing his mind so completely that it was like he was there himself.

He didn't recognize the inside of the building, the neutral office walls with quiet cubicles. It must be MASC Headquarters, as the vision revealed to him a view of his friends—Konstantin, Luiz,

Galu, and Melusine. But there were more Phantoms there— Commander Strongroot and all of Aquila Team faced off again Konstantin.

He found himself shaking his head. No, it wasn't supposed to be like this. Konstantin was supposed to talk to Pérez alone—to convince her that Phoenix Team had been set up. It couldn't come down to a firefight.

He jumped as a round went off and the Under-Secretary fell, red blood welling from a wound in her shoulder. Chaos erupted as Aquila Team retreated inside the Under-Secretary's office and Konstantin's team withdrew into the cubicles to address the threat behind them.

Shots and shouting paused momentarily as a massive brown wolf skidded into the hallway and tore the head off one of the men arrayed behind Konstantin.

The wolf transformed into a man—Cyriaque Broussard. Rex furrowed his brow. Come to help? Cyriaque shouted something that Rex couldn't make out. He squinted in his mind, trying to draw nearer to decipher his words, when a blinding flash whited out the entire scene.

Rex gasped as the vision left him and he found himself leaning against a chair in his room in Phairo, puffing in great gulps of breath. There was no doubt about what he had seen. A bomb. A bomb was going to go off and kill all of his friends.

Unless he stopped it.

Rex yanked the door open and barreled into the hallway. Two shocked crocodile-head guards tried to stop him, but he pulled one of their swords from its sheath and made quick work of them. The other guards lining the hallway turned in surprise—one pulling his sword half out.

"I go to speak to my father," Rex stated. "Try to stop me and you die."

The supes pressed back against the walls, out of his way. It seemed none of them wanted to go the way of their comrades.

Rex exploded into the throne room where his father sat lounging on his great chair. Sekhmet was playing chess in the corner with Thoth, whose ibis head swiveled at his entrance. Sekhmet stood.

"Release me from this," Rex held up his wrist with the cuff as he strode to stand before his father. "My friends are in grave danger. I have only moments to stop a catastrophe!"

Anubis looked at his fingernails and sighed. "Son, mortals are always in danger. There is always one catastrophe or another. I cannot release you."

Rex felt his power swelling with his anger, its heat and light and energy breaking through the last of the mortal bonds that had held it. Until it raged within him, hot as a sun. "Release me!" Rex bellowed as his form swelled and grew. Shadows and light raged around him, whipping the throne room with a howling wind. "Release me or I will tear every stone of this place to the ground!"

Anubis stood then, his dark eyes flashing black. He strode towards Rex and began to grow as well until they stood nose to jackal nose twenty feet in the air, crackling energy mirrored from father to son, arcing and snapping. "You forget who you talk to, *son*. Your power is middling here. The answer is *no*."

So be it. If his father wanted war, he would show him war. Rex drew his magic inward, gathering it to himself—only to find it draining from him, like water from a bathtub. He began to shrink and looked down in surprise. His father was shrinking too, his power dissolving.

Sekhmet strode up to them with an annoyed expression on her furry face. "Are you two idiots just about done?" In her hand she held a piercing ball of golden light—the magic she had somehow drained from both of them. With a motion, she disbursed it into the air around them, charging the room with electricity before it began to dissipate.

"How dare you—" Anubis began, but she cut him off.

"Rex may not be able to destroy this place, but he can sure as hell be a misery to live with for the next thousand years. Let him do this last thing for his human friends. You will be quick, won't you, Rex?"

He nodded.

"And when you are done, you will return to us with the full understanding that your days on Earth are finished?"

He swallowed thickly. "I will."

"His presence will distort the space-time continuum," Anubis protested.

"You know that we may visit Earth for as many as four minutes without permanently harming things. Let him go. Rex knows how important it is to return."

Another vision flashed before him and he groaned, holding his temples. This time, the image was of Zariya and Daevin, along with Yara and Isobel. They writhed on a metal floor as white gas flooded the space around them. Falling still.

Tears sprang to his eyes. Not like this. He couldn't lose all of them.

Rex looked at his father, the being who was a near stranger to him, with pleading in his eyes. *Let there be some good in the god. Let there be some humanity.* "Please."

With a sigh, Anubis reached out and touched the gold cuff. As it fell off Rex's wrist, he was already opening a portal. Rex prayed he was not too late.

13

I hunkered down against the metal shelves of the vault, one arm thrown over my mouth. White smoke was rapidly filling the space, stinging my eyes.

"Do you think this is knockout gas or...?" I trailed off with a cough.

"I don't think we can wait to find out," Daevin replied.

"Isobel, can you spell open the door?" I asked.

She knelt on one knee before the huge vault door, blinking away tears. "I'm trying. I'll try everything I can think of. But we might need a Plan B."

Plan B? We didn't even have a Plan A!

"What about the objects?" Yara motioned to the shelves. "There must be something that can get us the hell out of here!"

My vision swam and I shot out a hand to grab a shelf. "Rex said the vault neutralizes the magic of the objects because they didn't want them all reacting with each other."

"Right." Yara shook her head, coughing.

The vault shook as one of Isobel's spells ricocheted off the thick door, rocking the objects on the shelves.

She turned to us, a little dazed, her dark hair blown back. "Uh, sorry."

"Did it work?" Daevin asked, his hand over his mouth.

Isobel gestured to the still-closed door with exasperation.

But it gave me an idea. "Isobel, is it a spell that's dampening the magic of the objects? Like a ward?" A fit of coughing overtook me and I put my hands on my knees. It was getting hard to breathe in here. "Can you—"

But she was already on it. Isobel had whirled and was gesturing in the air like a conductor, murmuring under her breath.

A shockwave of sorts punched through the air, setting my teeth on edge. It left quiet in its wake. The hissing of the gas had stopped; the air in the vault was thick with the stuff.

But something else was rising up—a swelling tumult of magic of all different shapes and sizes. Whispered voices, subtle pressures, pulsing energy surrounded us. Overwhelmed the space. The magical artifacts were kept in here because they were some of the most powerful objects in the known world. And we'd just unchained them all at once.

I swallowed thickly as the four of us exchanged worried glances. "I think that might have been a mistake," I found myself whispering.

Isobel coughed, a hand to her head. "They're all clamoring for me to use them."

"Can you put the wards back up?" I asked. "Corral the objects again?"

"What does that get us?" Daevin was reaching out towards a gently pulsing mask of black onyx, his eyes transfixed upon it.

Yara slapped his hand down.

"If we can find something to get us out of here, we can bind the rest," I suggested through a cough. The gas still choked the room, but it seemed it wasn't strong enough to knock us out. Or perhaps one of the freed objects had stopped it—as if it knew that if we were unconscious, it wasn't getting out of here. That was disconcerting. "Let's work in pairs. No one touch anything."

Yara slapped Daevin's hand again, just inches from a jeweled fork.

"Ow," he complained.

"*Baby.*" She scoffed, but I saw their tails were curled around each other, a subtle sweet gesture that swelled my heart. We needed to get out of here. I needed to get to Konstantin. We needed to get the Nephilim's Knot to Rex.

I turned back to the shelves, resolute. There was something in here we could use. There had to be.

KONSTANTIN HUNKERED behind a pockmarked cubicle wall, sending another spray of bullets at the supes who had appeared behind them.

Who were they? And why were they dressed just like his team? How had they known what was going on here?

Galu was closer to the Under-Secretary's office, where Aquila Team had retreated with the injured supe. The windows into the interior office were completely shattered thanks to the flying bullets. But Konstantin didn't think she was dead. He prayed she wasn't dead.

"Strongroot!" Galu shouted, pounding on the office door before ducking back down, out of range of the strange team's gunshots. "They're not with us! They're not with us!"

But if he were Commander Strongroot, he wasn't sure he'd believe them, either. No doubt Cyriaque had painted them as the villains—traitors to Veil Force. And then they'd appeared here, an armed force trying to take out the MASC Under-Secretary-General. How was he going to get his team out of this one? At least for now, Aquila Team was firing at the enemy, not Phoenix Team.

"Daevin, come in." Konstantin tried his comm again, but there was nothing but static on the other end. The vault team had totally disappeared from comms. Konstantin had a bad feeling about what was going on downstairs.

Not to mention a bad feeling about what was going on here. They'd taken down half a dozen of the unknown supes, but they just kept coming.

And there was one who had darted into the cubicle one row over from him and hadn't reappeared. What was the supe doing?

Three more supes turned the corner into the hallway before the office, barreling their direction. Konstantin got his weapon up—when a huge brown wolf thundered into the three from behind, tossing them all off their feet.

The wolf shifter was fierce and fearless. In quick succession, he ripped out one man's neck and crunched the wrist of another one. A bullet flew from the office and caught the third enemy right between the eyes. Konstantin glanced up to see red hair disappearing back below the windows. It had been Alviya's shot.

The wolf pulled his attention back. It had to be Cyriaque. Konstantin wasn't the best at telling shifters apart when they were in their animal forms, but who else knew what was going on here?

Then, confirming his suspicions, the wolf morphed into a very pissed, very naked Cyriaque Broussard.

Konstantin's eyes narrowed and he aimed his gun right at the supe's heart. This mess was all Cyriaque's fault.

"Phantoms, listen up," Cyriaque bellowed. "There's a bomb somewhere on this floor about to blow. We have to get out now!"

No one moved. Konstantin caught Luiz's eye across the room, where the incubus was hunkered behind another cubicle. Luiz shook his head.

Konstantin agreed. It could be a trap. The minute they stood up, Aquila Team would take them out. "Aquila and the Under-Secretary evac first," Konstantin called. "We'll bring up the rear."

"Nice fucking try, traitor," Commander Strongroot bellowed. "I'm not getting shot in the back by you today."

Cyriaque threw up his hands and strode into the sea of cubicles, his nostrils flaring. Konstantin kept the Director in his sights.

Konstantin wished Rex were here. His own nose for explosives had never been as finely-tuned as Rex's. He realized, with a pang, that Rex would likely never be on a mission again.

A shot went off and Cyriaque recoiled. The enemy soldier who'd disappeared down the aisle—

Cyriaque snarled and dove, and another shot went off. Cyriaque stood back up, one bloody hand to his stomach. The other hoisted a detonator with blinking red numbers.

7.

6.

5.

14

———

My eyes scanned the vault shelves with desperation. I wished Rex were here with us. His knowledge of magical antiquities would come in pretty fucking handy right now.

"I don't know what anything is," I admitted, hating the despair in my voice.

"What about this?" Daevin pointed at a silvery cup covered with what looked like Norse runes. A foamy substance had welled up in the center.

"What is it?"

Daevin reached out and seized it.

"Daevin!" Yara cried.

He sniffed the liquid and then threw his head back, draining the cup dry.

"Daevin!" all three of us shrieked, waiting with bated breath for his skin to melt off or for something equally horrifying to happen.

The cup was already starting to fill again.

"I think it makes unlimited beer." Daevin smacked his lips. "A nice lager. At least we can get drunk before we die."

I balled my hands into fists. "So not helpful." I turned back to the shelves with a huff.

"I don't know. I already feel better," he replied.

"What about this thingy?" Isobel had crouched down and was looking at a low shelf, towards the corner of the vault.

My eyes widened. Was that—something I recognized? "It couldn't be."

"What?" Daevin and Yara crowded around. Daevin had handed the cup to Yara, and with a shrug, she took a sip.

The object in question was shaped like a long, golden staff, but with a huge bulbous end. It looked exactly like a weapon I'd seen in hundreds of paintings and depictions. "It looks like the Ekasha Gada."

"The what whata?" Daevin said.

"The Ekasha Gada. It's the mace of the Hindu god Shiva. One hit from the Ekasha Gada was said to be the equivalent of the power of a million elephants."

Isobel looked back at the door. "That should work." Before I could protest, she seized the mace and stood up. It was nearly as tall as she was, and it took both her hands to hold it. "It's heavy."

I covered my mouth. If it truly was the Ekasha Gada, it was total sacrilege to even be touching it.

Isobel staggered over to the vault door, just barely keeping the tip of the mace from dragging on the floor.

"I can't watch." I turned away.

"Brace yourselves," Isobel cautioned.

I grabbed one of the vertical poles holding the shelves up.

"One...two..."

An explosion rocked the room, throwing me against the shelves so hard, I rebounded off and crashed to the cement floor. The tang of copper blood filled my mouth.

"Everyone okay?" Yara asked from her position splayed on the floor next to me.

"I spilled my beer." Daevin groaned.

I looked at the vault door. It wasn't dented in the slightest. How was that possible? "It didn't work?"

Isobel was slouched against one shelf, her fingers probing around a gash on her forehead. "No. I didn't even hit the door. That explosion wasn't me."

❧

REX EMERGED from his portal to a world of fire and flame.

An explosion had gone off.

No. An explosion—*was* going off.

Time was like a river around him, a river he could see and taste and touch. The other gods had told him that time would flow differently around him once he gained his status as a full demi-god, but being told such a thing in the abstract and seeing it with his own eyes were two very different things indeed.

With infinite slowness, the power of the bomb was billowing outward in all directions with concussive force. As if frozen in time, Konstantin and Luiz, Galu and Melusine, were running for their lives from an enemy that couldn't be outrun. The rest of Aquila Team too —Commander Strongroot holding an unconscious supe in his arms —were just behind, even closer to the blast. In just nanoseconds, his friends and colleagues would be obliterated.

He couldn't let that happen.

Rex couldn't turn back time; that was beyond his power. He could only protect them as best he could. He ran towards the center of the inferno, gathering his power to himself. His father was the God of the Dead, but all the gods shared power, and he drew on the power of the god Ra now, the magic and energy of the sun. Only a sun could absorb such power unflinchingly.

He would be their sun.

Golden light enveloped Rex as he drew on every bit of his heritage and magic—as he fully embraced who and what he was. He'd run from it for so long. But no longer. In Phoenix Team, he'd found friends who had embraced and accepted every part of him. It was time that he accepted himself.

Rex closed his eyes as the power raged around him—as he drew the energy and power of the explosion into himself. More violent power poured into him and he sucked it all into his essence, taming it—transmuting it. Until it was all gone.

When he opened his eyes, the room was still, but for the infinitesimal movement of the rest of the people in the room as time still ticked by impossibly slowly. The carpet beneath the bomb had burned away, and the cubicle walls and chairs had tumbled outward, as if from a central crater. But the place was intact. And his friends were alive.

With a frown, he focused on the stream of time, struggling to pull it faster—speeding it up until the rest of the people in the room were almost moving at full speed.

"Rex?" Konstantin's blue eyes were wide with shock. "What did you do?" His words were still stretched like taffy.

The reality pained him. He couldn't stay here long. He had only a few minutes more before his presence would permanently warp the space and time around him.

"I felt that something was wrong," he said simply. "I had to come."

Konstantin pulled Rex into a hug, pounding him on the back. "Thank you, brother. I know what it must have cost you."

Rex let out a long sigh. "It was worth the price."

Rex drew back and saw that Director Cyriaque Broussard was there—naked. He had righted a chair and sank into it, one hand gripping a wound in his stomach. Rex shrugged out of the sleeveless tunic he wore and handed it to Cyriaque. He still had his shendyt skirt underneath.

A commotion across the room drew his attention. Rex saw that Aquila Team had gathered around the Under-Secretary, who lay on the floor as blood leaked from a wound in her shoulder.

"Can you help her?" Konstantin asked.

Rex merely nodded.

The team parted for him as he approached—no, that wasn't right.

Shied away. He knew the full power of the Egyptian gods was intimidating, even for such accomplished supes as these. He couldn't blame them. He set aside those thoughts and knelt down next to Under-Secretary Pérez, placing his hand on her wound. The bullet had passed cleanly through her shoulder, and it was a simple enough thing to create a tiny temporal anomaly, speeding up her body's natural healing process just in the area of the wound.

She gasped and opened her eyes, her violet irises fixing on Rex. She coughed, then took a deep breath, testing. "Does someone want to tell me what the fuck is going on?"

Relieved laughs rounded the group and Alviya and Strongroot helped her to her feet.

Konstantin looked warily at Strongroot, then turned to Cyriaque. "I think I know who can tell us."

Cyriaque raised his weary head, then stood, straightening, tightening Rex's tunic around his muscled form. "Under-Secretary, we've been targeted by an underground criminal organization that goes by the name of Leviathan. These men who planted the bomb and shot you worked for them. Their plan was to frame Konstantin Bauer and the rest of Phoenix Team for the crimes." Cyriaque exchanged a glance with Konstantin. "As they framed him for the robbery at Tartarus Base."

Under-Secretary Pérez pursed her full lips. "And how do you know all this?"

Cyriaque cleared his throat. "Because up until about fifteen minutes ago, I was helping them."

Stunned silence blanketed the room, followed by a cascade of expletives.

But Rex felt peace. So the Director had finally done the right thing. Good. Now he could return to Phairo, knowing his team and the other Phantoms would be safe.

He turned to go.

"Wait—" Pérez's voice cracked like a whip. "Where are you going, Phantom? No one goes anywhere until everyone is fully debriefed and this mess gets sorted out."

Rex turned back. "Unfortunately, I cannot comply. If I do not leave within the next ninety seconds, my presence will permanently damage this realm."

Pérez recoiled slightly.

"It's true, Director. Let Rex go. We can fill you in on the rest," Konstantin said.

Luiz and Galu strode over and Galu offered his hand. "It's been an honor."

Rex shook it, nodding.

"Come here, Rexy." Luiz pulled him into an embrace. "Don't be too serious now. Find yourself a lady with a cute snout and make adorable cosmic babies."

Rex chuckled despite himself.

"It has been a privilege to serve Veil Force." Rex nodded and pulled open a golden portal.

"Wait!" came a shout.

A disheveled Zariya sprinted across the room, her chest heaving as if she'd just run up fourteen flights of stairs. Which, if she'd come from the vault, she had. "Wait," she gasped as she slid a leather thong around his neck.

As the pendant settled onto his chest, the portal winked out, and the taffy-slow nature of time snapped back to normal. Zariya had done it. She'd found the Nephilim's Knot.

15

———————

Konstantin closed his laptop with a groan. Writing that debrief had taken much longer—and had been significantly more painful—than he had anticipated. The events of the last few days were a whirlwind. Their time in the DRC —in Phairo... None of it had been sanctioned by MASC. He'd made the necessary decisions at the time, but in retrospect—on paper—he looked totally out of control. He wouldn't be surprised if he ended up cleaning out his desk within the week.

A knock on his office door drew him from his spiraling thoughts. "Come in."

Signe popped her head in. "There's someone here to see you."

Under-Secretary Ximena Pérez walked in behind Signe, and with a nod, Signe closed the door behind her.

Konstantin suppressed his groan.

"Don't look so happy to see me," Pérez said sarcastically, settling into one of the chairs across his desk.

Konstantin gave her a weak smile. "I was hoping I'd have another few hours to brace myself for this conversation."

Pérez had changed into a fresh charcoal suit after the events of that morning, and her long, violet hair curled in glossy waves around her shoulders. She was quite lovely, with wide intelligent eyes and a curvaceous figure. Konstantin wasn't surprised. Ciguapas were known for their compelling beauty—used in the old days to draw and trap unwary travelers. "I find it's best to just rip the Band-Aid off."

Konstantin grimaced. "I'm glad to see being shot hasn't had any lingering ill effects."

The Under-Secretary rolled her shoulder. "Feels good as new. Your Phantom, Rexsis Ahmad, is it? He did quite a job healing me."

"I'm glad. It's the least we could do—"

"After you annihilated my office?"

"That wasn't just us."

"Leviathan. Like we need a new shadow to hunt down." Pérez gave her head a rueful shake. "You're lucky Cyriaque Broussard confessed to everything. It helped significantly with sorting this mess out."

"He's in custody now?"

"Yes, and it will stay that way until he can be tried by the MASC Council."

Konstantin nodded. "So you understand that everything we did was to convince you of the truth? To warn you?"

She gave him a tight smile. "Not exactly *everything*."

"What do you mean?" Konstantin played innocent. He'd hoped the events in the vault might fly under her radar. It seemed he would have no such luck.

"Sending a team into our vault was extremely dangerous and foolhardy. Your witch neutralized the enchantments keeping those magical artifacts safe. They'd already started to stir up trouble by the time we got down there."

"I'm sorry. It was critical that we secured the Nephilim's Knot for Rex. You saw how important."

Pérez sighed. "Yes, I see his value."

"Will he be allowed to keep the Knot?"

"It belongs to MASC." Her eyes flashed. "But...I suppose I do owe him something for saving my life. As long as he works for Veil Force, the Knot may remain in his custody. That's enough to allow him to remain on Earth, if I understand correctly?"

Konstantin felt an immense weight lift off his shoulders. "Yes. Thank you. Truly."

"But you tell that demon of yours I want Odin's Chalice back."

Konstantin blinked. Daevin had taken something? "Of course. If they removed something else, I'm sure it was just a misunderstanding."

Pérez harrumphed.

Konstantin hesitated. He should take this opportunity to give her the other bad news. In the madness of the firefight on the Fourteenth floor, the Chinvat Gate had fallen out of Galu's pocket. And was now missing. He had to assume Leviathan had it.

But he didn't want to go down that road right now. She could read it in his report. Konstantin stood. "I'm grateful for your understanding. Thank you for coming. I should have come to you."

"Sit down, Bauer. We're not done here."

Konstantin's ass thunked back into his chair as his stomach dropped. Here it came.

"Your fingerprints are all over Veil Force's messes these last few weeks. Phantoms kidnapped, cursed, injured—I understand you yourself almost died."

How would he say goodbye to this place? How would he tell his team? Who was right to lead Phoenix Team? Who would put up with Daevin's shit and see through Luiz's bluster and not take for granted Galu's gentle support and Rex's silent strength? And who would take care of Zariya? Help her be as good a Phantom as her father had ever been?

Pérez was still talking. "Yet you saved an iconic mythical creature, took out an entire poaching and trafficking ring, and destroyed one of the most dangerous Authentic vampires in the world."

Konstantin blinked. Wait, what was she saying?

"Vizol Chanji rarely played by the rules, and this place flourished in his care. Vizol never wanted Cyriaque Broussard to succeed him. He wanted you."

A stab of grief flashed through him at the honor. *I miss you, old friend.*

"I appointed Cyriaque as Director because he had seniority and I didn't think he would stay if we passed him over. I made a mistake not trusting Vizol's judgment, and I won't make that mistake again."

His mind was swimming. "What are you saying?"

"I'm saying that I want you as the new Veil Force Director."

REX WAS PLEASANTLY TIPSY.

He rarely drank, but some times called for it. Particularly in celebration.

The rest of Phoenix Team, minus Konstantin, lounged around the team's cages, happily munching the last of three pizzas they'd ordered.

The delivery guy had been ridiculously confused as to why he was dropping off food in the middle of a park, but Luiz had just given him a big tip and a bigger smile and sent the man off a bit dazed.

"Pass that thing over here." Luiz waggled his fingers for the magical cup Daevin had snagged from the MASC vault.

Daevin tossed it, showering him with beer.

"Not cool." Luiz took a sip from the already refilling artifact. "Do you think this thing can fill with other types of booze? Lager will get a little boring. Maybe some tequila? Or a good cachaça?" He groaned in delight at the thought.

Zariya snorted. "Sorry, I think you'll need to find the ancient chalice of a Brazilian deity for that."

"None of the Egyptian artifacts are this fun," Rex mused. "They're all for summoning plagues of locusts or stopping the implosion of space-time."

Zariya giggled. "Bo-ring."

"Indeed."

Galu got up with a stretch. "All right, amigos. I'm headed off. My presence has been requested at home."

Luiz whistled and Daevin gave a little catcall.

"Tell Mel thanks for all her help," Zariya said, tipping her chair onto its back legs and looking sideways at Galu. "Seriously. She's the shit."

"I know." Galu smiled and left with a wave.

"That guy is *whipped*," Daevin said.

"Oh, whatever!" Zariya threw a leftover pizza crust at Daevin. "Mr. Yara This, Yara That. She's got her tail wrapped 'round you tight as a boa constrictor."

"I don't know what you're talking about." Daevin held out a hand to Luiz, who passed back the cup of endless beer.

"Will Yara join Veil Force?" Rex asked.

Daevin shrugged. "Depends on the new Director. I think she'd like to."

"She should. She'd be bomb." Zariya nodded, as if that were that. She turned to Luiz. "Did Isobel head back?"

"For now." Luiz examined his fingernails.

"But...?" Zariya said.

Luiz grinned, looking up. "But I'm making her dinner on Friday." More hollers filled the room.

Zariya turned his way. "Now we just need to find Rex a lady."

Rex shook his head. "I've had more than enough excitement for one lifetime." He wasn't against the idea of finding a partner, but he wasn't in a hurry. It just felt good to finally be free of the sentence that had been hanging over him. Phairo and Earth were both home to him now. It was a blessing to be able to travel freely between them. Well, assuming Anubis would forgive him. Upon returning to base, he'd sent his father a message informing him that he'd found the Nephilim's Knot and wished to remain on Earth for a time. He'd be looking into ways to recreate the Knot so his brethren could travel freely as well.

Zariya was chattering on, though, about finding him a girlfriend. "I'm thinking a sexy British librarian. Maybe a brunette, curly hair... glasses...kinda old-fashioned style..."

Rex rolled his eyes. "You're just thinking of the female character from the movie *The Mummy* again."

Zariya's eyes went wide. "Oh, shit, I am."

Luiz and Daevin cracked up. "Busted."

"There is *actual* Egyptian cinema, you know," Rex suggested. "I think it's high time I introduce you to some real culture."

"Movie night at Rex's!" She grinned.

The door opened to reveal Signe striding across the room towards him. "It seems everyone thinks I'm their messenger pigeon today." She held out her hand and he looked down. Resting in her palm was a shimmering indigo scarab beetle.

Rex sobered up immediately. A response from his father. "Thank you." He took the insect from Signe's hand, and it immediately opened its hard carapace, revealing a folded message. With hands that shook, he opened the note and read the scrawling script. He could almost hear his father's grudging voice as he read the words. "Do what you must. The door is open."

Relief flooded him, and he couldn't fight the smile that insisted on forming on his lips.

"Well?" Zariya asked. She was sitting up. "What did he say?"

Rex understood the subtext beneath his father's brief words. And it meant everything to him. "He said he forgives me. And I'm welcome home any time."

16

———

My apartment looked exactly the same as it had when I'd left it to head on our mission to Quiribri Island. Yet everything was different. *I* was different.

It was like the world had shifted underneath me.

Alviya was picking up takeout Chinese and beer and Kiki had sworn she was on her way home. So I took advantage of the opportunity to shower and change into a comfy pair of jeans and a black tee. Konstantin had promised to call me once all his paperwork was done. Would he invite me over to his place? The thought made my stomach clench with nervousness. I thought Konstantin and I were on the same page since we'd seen each other through the Matriarch's mirror, but we still needed to have the *talk*. Where did we go from here? What if after everything, he decided he didn't want something so messy and tangled? He was still my commander, after all.

Unless I quit.

I'd hardly had time to come up for air this past week—I'd been so busy getting shot at and kidnapped and cursed and almost killed. Without Dad's memories, I wasn't exactly cowardly, but I didn't have the fearlessness I'd felt those first days as a Phantom.

Maybe I could go back into Dad's memory palace and have him

re-download his memories—the day Cyriaque's goons had kidnapped me outside of Auntie's house, she had found Dad's talwar abandoned on the sidewalk. So that was an option. But did I truly want that? Or did I want to start making memories of my own?

My time with Phoenix Team had burned off the fog of grief and brought me back to myself. And now that I remembered who I was, I realized how much I wanted to finish what I'd started. I wanted to finish medical school, and I wanted to become a doctor. I wasn't cut out for killing people. I was meant to be saving them.

I toweled my hair off, lost in thought. Could I really abandon the guys? Luiz and Daevin, Rex and Galu—they'd become like brothers to me. I didn't want to break their hearts by leaving so soon. But I couldn't stay in the wrong place just to shield their feelings. That wasn't right, either.

A knock sounded on the door. "Just a minute!" I hurried through the kitchen and looked through the peephole. Auntie?

I pulled the door open and she breezed inside, a long black case tucked under her arm. She gave me a kiss on the cheek, smelling of oranges and incense.

"What are you doing here?" I asked.

"You wouldn't return my calls, so I had to come and make sure you were still alive."

"Auntie, you know I was on a mission." Several, actually, but she didn't need to know that.

"That doesn't mean you can't pick up my phone calls." She set the case on the kitchen counter. I recognized the case—Dad's talwar was inside. Sometimes having an aunt with psychic abilities came in handy.

"Actually, it's exactly what it means." I ran my fingers over the case's worn leather. "Do you want to stay for dinner? Alviya's getting Chinese."

She clucked her tongue. "Don't any of you cook? Food is supposed to be crafted lovingly with your own two hands."

I shrugged. "I *eat* it lovingly with my own two hands. Does that count?"

She pretended to knock me upside my head. "Your generation is hopeless."

"I'm aware." I sighed. I wasn't in the mood to discuss the supposed millennial-induced decline of civilization. "Why'd you bring the talwar?"

"It's yours. He gave it to you." Auntie blinked at me with a wide-eyed innocence that I suspected was not entirely genuine.

"You know I lost Dad's memories."

"I had a feeling. Your grief at their loss was palpable. I felt its echo."

I nodded, blinking back tears. "It was awful. But..." I trailed off.

"Maybe it's for the best."

I looked up at her. "Do you think so?"

"Your father always wanted you to have your own life. You should feel no obligation to follow in his footsteps. His path is not yours."

"I would miss everyone so much if I left Veil Force," I admitted. "They feel like a second family already. But I just don't think I'm cut out to be a Phantom. Not for the long term."

"Does Veil Force not need doctors? Your father used to come home with all sorts of injuries."

"They already have a base doctor."

"Maybe they need two. Whatever you decide, curlicue, Veil Force has embraced you now. They will not turn their back on you."

I nodded. "I hope you're right."

"Will you go back into the memory palace?" Auntie asked.

"Yes. But not right away. I need to figure some things out on my own before I'm ready to see Dad again."

Her dark eyes were bright with tears. "My smart, beautiful girl. I am proud of you."

Cue lump in throat. "Thanks, Auntie," I managed.

The front door flew open, revealing Alviya in her winged glory hoisting aloft Chinese food and beer like the slain heads of her enemies. "Tada—oh, hi, Auntie."

Auntie patted my cheek. "I'm headed out. You girls have fun."

Kiki arrived as Alviya and I were setting out plates around the tiny table. "You animals better not have touched my Kung Pao Chicken."

"Didn't feel like suffering agonizing mental torture today." I handed over the takeout box to her.

Kiki grinned. "I've trained you well."

We filled our plates and collapsed into the chairs. "What a fucking day," Kiki said.

Alviya nodded vigorously, talking around a bite of street noodles. "Hey, remember that time that my team and Zariya's almost killed each other, only to be almost blown up by some evil bad guys we didn't even know about?"

I laughed. "I have some vague memory of that incident."

"I'm glad you weren't upstairs with us." Alviya affixed me with her black eyes. "It was hard enough to point my sights at Luiz and Galu and Konstantin. If you'd been there…" She shook her head. "I don't think I could have done it."

"We're lucky it didn't come to that," I agreed.

"These Leviathan people are buried deep," Kiki said. "With the hours I spent recovering the base network, I didn't have time to do much digging, but they seem to cover their tracks well."

"I guess it would be too much to ask for a few days of peace and quiet," I said. I thought about telling them my doubts about staying on Phoenix Team, but something held me back. I needed to talk to Konstantin first. I owed him that much.

"Seriously. We're headed out on another mission tomorrow," Alviya said. "We got an anonymous tip about a drug smuggling operation out of Miami."

I frowned. "An anonymous tip? Is that common?"

"Not common, not uncommon," Kiki said. "This one seems to check out."

"No rest for the weary." I took a bite of my egg roll.

Kiki set her chopsticks down and raised her beer bottle. "I'd like to propose a toast. Our friendship has been through a lot the past few weeks, and I, for one, am fucking proud that we made it out stronger. I love you guys."

Awwr. "Hear, hear," I said. "May nothing come between us ever again."

"Skol," Alviya said, and our bottles clicked together.

My phone buzzed on the counter and I leapt up to grab it, breathless. It was a text from Konstantin. *Want to come over?*

I squealed. "I gotta go, you guys."

Alviya was still holding her beer aloft. "Let nothing come between us except hot vampire ass."

The sound of their laughter followed me out the door.

KONSTANTIN'S PENTHOUSE apartment was even more stunning at night. The floor-to-ceiling windows displayed a glittering expanse of city skyline that threatened to steal my breath as I stepped off the elevator.

"Konstantin?" I called into the vast space. You could play a wicked game of *Marco, Polo* in this place.

"In the kitchen!"

I found him by the sleek, industrial chic island, pouring a glass of red wine. "Want one?"

"Sure." I drummed my fingers nervously on the white quartz countertop. Holy shit, this felt awkward. Did he feel awkward?

Konstantin was showered and dressed in jeans and a thin maroon T-shirt that hung like a dream over his muscular form. His blond hair was loose around his shoulders. He was still moving more slowly than normal, as if the lingering effects of the poison hadn't quite worn off. He handed me the wine glass and I couldn't help but revel in his beauty. "Let's sit in the living room." He nodded in that direction.

I pressed my hand to my heart as I followed, sucking in a deep breath, trying to banish the physical ache I felt in his presence. I wanted to be with him *so badly*.

Thoughts raged through me as I settled onto the worn leather couch, doubts and fears and desperation. If I told him I didn't want to be a Phantom anymore, would it drive a wedge between us? Could I risk it? I did my best to smother my wild urge to say anything to make him love me. I was done living someone else's life. I needed to honor my truth. My path.

"Konstantin—"

"Zariya—"

We chuckled nervously as we spoke over each other.

"You go ahead," I said.

He nodded. "I'm feeling much stronger after returning from Phairo, but I'm still not back to full my strength. I'm not sure I ever will be. I think I could be a liability in the field."

I blinked. This wasn't what I had expected. "So what are you saying?"

"I spoke with Under-Secretary Pérez. She asked me to be the new Veil Force director." He looked up. "And I accepted."

"Are you serious? That's so great! Congratulations!" I leaped forward and pulled him into a hug. When I retreated, I realized my jostling had spilled Konstantin's wine across his chest.

"Oh, sorry." My face turned scarlet.

"It's all right. I knew I wore red today for a reason." Konstantin wiped at the wet spot absentmindedly. "It means I'm no longer going to be Phoenix One. I'm recommending that Galu take over."

"He'll be great at it." I nodded. It made sense.

"If I'm no longer your commander, it solves some other issues. We won't have to worry about upsetting the team dynamic in the field."

"Right." I nodded. Okay, this was good. "Because…" I trailed off.

Konstantin smiled, the corners of his blue eyes crinkling adorably. "Because we're together now?"

"We are?"

He cocked his head. "Aren't we?"

I felt like this train was running off the tracks. I hurried to explain. "Of course that's what I want. We just never, like, decided anything." I kicked myself even as the words tumbled out. I sounded like a middle school girl wondering if we were officially boyfriend and girlfriend.

Konstantin took my wine glass from me and put both glasses

down on the table behind him. Then he turned to me and took my hands in his. "Zariya Chanji, you are fierce and beautiful and brilliant. And those are just the parts I've had the privilege of seeing these past few weeks. I want to get to know each and every bit of you. I want to spend my life with you. I want to be your partner, for as long as you'll have me."

My smile grew so wide, it practically broke my face. "I want that too."

Konstantin took my chin in firm but gentle hands and kissed me. It started out sweet, tasting faintly of the fine Bordeaux he'd poured us, but it quickly morphed into something fierce and hungry.

Konstantin broke off the kiss, pushing me away gently. "Wait. You had something you wanted to say too."

"It can wait." I surged forward to claim another kiss, but Konstantin darted out of the way, standing up. "I said *every* part of you, Zariya. Come on, what is it?"

I pouted for a moment.

"The sooner you tell me, the sooner we can proceed to the bedroom..." He grinned, pulling the hem of his shirt up to reveal a stretch of rippling abs.

I squeezed my eyes shut. How was a girl supposed to think with that beautiful sight tempting her? "I don't want to be a Phantom anymore. I want to be a doctor." I opened one eye tentatively.

Konstantin had lowered his shirt. "Of course, Zariya. I'll support whatever you want to do."

"I don't want to leave Veil Force, though," I admitted. "I wish I could work at base, like Oliver does. But I know you don't need two Olivers."

Konstantin laughed. "God knows the world couldn't handle two Olivers. But I happen to have an in with the new Director, and that handsome beast has some intel that could benefit you. But it's going to cost you."

"Oh, yeah?" I stood up, stalking towards him. "What's the price?"

He clasped his hands around my waist. "Your heart," he said quietly.

"Then we've got a problem. Because I already gave it away."

Konstantin kissed me again before pulling me into an embrace, burying his nose in my hair. He let out a deep, satisfied sigh. "Oliver doesn't want to work at base anymore. He wants to go back into the field."

I pulled back with a squeal. "Are you serious?"

"Would I joke about something like this?"

"No, you only joke about things like butter churns and coats of arms."

Konstantin's mouth dropped open in mock outrage. "Was that an age joke, Ms. Chanji?"

"So what if it was?" I grinned.

"Then I'll have to show you what this old timer can do!"

I let out a shriek as Konstantin reached down and flipped me over his shoulder, carrying me towards the bedroom.

I, for one, couldn't wait to see what he could do.

EPILOGUE

Konstantin strolled down the hallway at Tartarus Base, a whistle on his lips and a cup of fine coffee in his hand. It was past ten A.M. He hadn't gotten to work this late in, well, decades. Centuries?

But there was something about having Zariya's lithe body stretched out next to him in bed that robbed him of all motivation.

Probably not the best way to start his tenure as Veil Force Director, but he figured almost dying had earned him a respite. Besides, he was the boss now. So who was going to tell him otherwise?

They were still in the process of cleaning out Cyriaque's office, so Konstantin headed towards the Ops Center. He'd call a meeting that afternoon to make the announcement that Pérez had named him Director and get down to work, but for now, he just wanted to float. How long since he'd just walked around base, chatting with his co-workers? Without some purpose or task in mind? He'd need to be better about that as Director. Make sure he was connecting with his people—addressing their concerns.

"Konstantin!" Kiki's shout in his mind nearly made him drop his coffee. He winced.

"Here."

"Did the Under-Secretary appoint a new director?" Kiki shouted.

"Yes. Me." He pursed his lips. What was going on?

"Then get your ass to Ops now!"

Konstantin dropped his cup in the nearest trash and sprinted down the hallway, skidding around the door to the Ops Center. He was still much slower than he had once been, but he was getting some of his lung capacity back.

The scene flickering on the screens above Kiki made him recoil. A blazing inferno—a building afire, viewed from above.

"What is that?"

Kiki's voice was strangled. "That is the building where Aquila Team was investigating a drug smuggling ring."

His blood ran cold. "Aquila Team is inside that?"

"They...were." she stammered. "I can't—I can't reach any of them."

"We need to get that fire put out so we can get inside—"

"I deployed Daevin and Enigma," Kiki said.

"Good. Quick thinking."

As they watched, the flames on the screen began to dim. The building still smoked horribly, obscuring their satellite shot.

Daevin's voice sounded over the microphone. "Flames are out."

Konstantin picked up a headset. "Daevin. It's Konstantin. Get in there and find them."

"Roger that, boss. Those flames weren't natural. They didn't want to go out. I'm afraid this was a targeted attack."

Kiki's face was pale. "We got an anonymous tip about the site. I ran it down myself; it all checked out. It was consistent with our other intel from the FBI and MASC sources. But I should have looked closer. I must have missed something—"

Konstantin put a gentle hand on Kiki's shoulder. "This isn't your fault. It was a trap. They designed it to look as tantalizing as possible."

"Is it Leviathan?"

"I don't know who else it would be. We foiled their plot to kill the Under-Secretary. And they lost their inside man. This must be payback."

Kiki's hands covered her mouth. "Alviya was in there."

Konstantin's heart seized. Alviya was Zariya's roommate, too. She'd be devastated if something happened to her friend. "She's a valkyrie. They're allies of death. She could have escaped this."

"I don't feel her," Kiki whispered, shaking her head back and forth, her dark eyes wide with unshed tears.

When Daevin spoke again, Konstantin could hear the uneasiness in his voice. "It's real rough in here, boss. I found some bodies, but..."

"Is it our people?" Konstantin asked, praying the answer was *no*.

The silence stretched long. "I can't tell."

Konstantin sank into a chair before his legs gave out. All of Aquila Team, wiped out in an instant. Six Phantoms. He hadn't even been Director for twenty-four hours, and Veil Force had suffered the biggest tragedy in its history.

It was a long time before Konstantin spoke again. "Is it safe for Enigma to go in there? We should bring the bodies back here. We owe it to them. And their families."

"Yeah, it's cool enough he should be fine. I'll get him."

Tears were streaming down Kiki's face now.

Konstantin wanted to comfort her, but he found himself numb. He'd seen so much death in his long lifespan, felt so much loss, he'd thought himself immune from this kind of sorrow. He wasn't sure whether to be grateful or angry that his heart could still break over lost soldiers.

"Wait!" Kiki sat up. "I feel something. Someone's still alive."

"Daevin, we have a survivor," Konstantin said excitedly.

He looked to Kiki. "Can you direct him?"

"On the bottom floor, southwest corner," Kiki said.

"Can you tell who it is?"

"I detect..." Kiki closed her eyes, as if trying to concentrate. "She's female..." Her eyes snapped open. "It's Alviya. Daevin, it's Alviya! But she's slipping. You have to get to her. Enigma, get in there!"

Konstantin and Kiki sat on the edges of their seat as the seconds seemed to stretch impossibly long.

"Daevin, report," Konstantin barked when he couldn't wait any longer.

"There's no one here." Daevin's next words were shaky. "Just a charred body. A husk. There's no way this person survived."

"She's alive," Kiki insisted.

"I'm sorry, Kiki. It must be an echo—"

Enigma's horrified words sounded then. "Daevin, look. The fingers—she's moving. I don't know how, but she's still alive."

THE SECOND SEASON of the Mythical Alliance, featuring Draco Team, will be launching in 2021! Sign up for my mailing list at http://claireluana.com to make sure you don't miss it!

IF YOU LIKED the Mythical Alliance, you'll love the Faerie Race trilogy! Keep reading for a sneak peek of book one, *The Sorcery Trial*!

SNEAK PEEK OF THE SORCERY TRIAL...

Welcome to The Faerie Race—an epic adventure through a realm as compelling as it is deadly...

Fame. Fortune. Your most extravagant wish granted. These are the prizes promised to the team that wins The Faerie Race, the first and only reality television show to venture into the dangerous realm of the fae. But that's not why Jacqueline Cunningham wants in. She's after any sign of her sister—who vanished without a trace into the faerie world two years ago.

Jacq thought getting into the race would be the hard part. But she didn't count on the other competitors—who will stop at nothing to finish first. Or her distractingly-handsome jerk of a partner, who seems to be hiding secrets of his own.

Plunged into a world where everything wants to kill her, what starts as a hunt for the truth turns into a desperate contest for survival. Now that Jacq's in the race, it will take all her wits to make it to the finish line alive.

The Sorcery Trial is Book One in *The Faerie Race*, a nail-biting, edge-of-your-seat thrill ride through a realm unlike you've ever seen.

~

CHAPTER ONE

I NOTICED two things in quick succession. One—the tips of his ears tapered to a delicate point. And two—his white button-down had been soaked in a tidal wave of coffee. The first meant he was a faerie. The second meant he had the misfortune of running into me.

My hands shook before me, empty of the carrying tray and the four venti quadruple shot Americanos I had just bought with the intention of ferrying them back to the studio headquarters. My pulse pounded like a jackhammer in my ears, adrenaline coursing through me.

The perky woman behind the counter goggled at us, adding to my unease.

I narrowed my eyes at her, hoping she would get the point that I didn't really need an audience right now. We were in Hollywood for goodness sakes—huge stars of the screen frequented this coffee shop day in, day out. Of course, if it was merely a famous actor I'd thrown coffee all over, my heart wouldn't be beating like a marching band, and none of this would be an issue. No, the male in front of me was no actor. He was a faerie. Here. In Los Angeles.

I took a deep breath and tried to keep my breakfast on the inside. Down on the floor, the four now-empty cups with my name misspelled on all of them—Jack instead of Jacq—mocked me, swimming as they were in a sea of black and pale brown liquid.

The faerie male was hissing in and out, his hands pulling his wet button-up away from his body, rivulets of steaming coffee running down his dark jeans onto wingtip shoes. "An oracle for a cousin, and I did not see that coming!" He barked a laugh, shaking off his shock. "If I wasn't awake before, I am now. I just expected to get my caffeine hit by drinking it."

"I'm sorry," I stammered, my thoughts racing almost too fast to catch. In the blink of an eye, I took him all in. His honey-gold locks falling over his forehead with a tousled elegance even a Disney prince would envy. Tan skin, tawny and glowing. Angled cheekbones, square jaw, and teeth as straight as a white-picket fence.

I had seen pictures of faeries every day for the last ten years. Since the existence of the fae and faerie realm had been exposed to all of humankind, they'd been news. Internet headlines, network stories, and viral videos. They were everywhere. And nowhere. Because faeries couldn't be in the mortal world, not without a visa from the ICCF, the International Coalition for Cooperation with Faeries. And mortals couldn't go into Faerwild.

I knew of their ethereal beauty in the way that you know a wildfire is hot. But that knowledge doesn't compare to standing next to the inferno and feeling it burn.

To be face to face with one in real life was terrifying. Exhilarating. No, definitely terrifying, I corrected myself.

"It was a most unfortunate accident," the faerie said. He looked young, maybe only a couple of years older than me. Twenty? Twenty-one? But I knew that looks were deceptive when it came to those of a faerie persuasion. He could be a hundred. He could be a thousand. However old he was, he was at ease in his skin in a way that few mortals managed. Even drenched in coffee, he was relaxed, friendly. He didn't *seem* dangerous. And it was that fact that scared me most of all.

"It was," I managed. "It was my fault. I wasn't looking where I was going." It wasn't technically true. It'd been like a slow-motion movie crash. Once I had caught sight of him, once I had realized what he was…I'd been unable to avert disaster. I could see him there, but my mind refused to believe it. So I just kept walking.

"I'm more worried about the depth of your coffee addiction. Can a human even drink that much caffeine and live?"

I wrinkled my brow, silent for a moment before I realized he was teasing me. The murderous creatures could joke?

Years of resentment and pain bubbled under the surface, so close it made my skin itch. Yet, he seemed so normal. If it wasn't for those ears of his and that weird aura of confidence that so few could pull off…I wouldn't have even known he was a faerie in the first place.

"They weren't for me. I work at the studio," I managed, nodding my head in the direction of the headquarters, where right now my high-strung bosses were, no doubt, wondering what was taking me so long to deliver their next caffeine hit. They were not the kind of people that liked to wait, and as I was the lowest monkey on the Hollywood ladder, I was extremely expendable. A fact that I was reminded of on a daily basis.

"Cool. What do you do?" he asked, shoving his hands in his pockets, seeming to have forgotten the aromatic liquid still dripping down him.

"I'm a gopher."

He cocked his head. "You're not like any gopher I've ever seen. I'd be very impressed to see a human turn into a small woodland creature. Not even most faeries could pull that off."

I ran my fingers through my blonde ponytail, a nervous gesture from childhood. "Is that another joke?"

The faerie chuckled. "If you have to ask, it means it wasn't a very good one."

"Not gopher. Go-fer. Like, go get stuff. I do random odd jobs. Coffee, errands, whatever punishment my boss can dream up for me. It's just for now." Everyone in the industry knew what a gopher was. The fact that he had to ask marked him as even more of an outsider.

"I want to do stunts," I blurted out. As soon as the words left my mouth, I wanted to swallow them. Why was I even telling him that? It wasn't as though I was embarrassed by my job. Plenty of stars started their Hollywood careers in much the same way.

"You're going to be a stunt woman?" His green eyes widened and crinkled up at the edges. He seemed genuinely impressed. I guess there wasn't much call for stunt people in Faerwild. "What kind of stunts do you do?"

I weighed the question, wondering if he was genuinely interested or if his question disguised some sinister intent. It was so hard to tell. I decided that it didn't really matter if I told him. It was hardly a state secret.

"Whatever they want. I can drive, I can ride horses, I can fight. I'll do it all." I managed, though I still couldn't believe his curiosity was genuine. To a faerie, I was as important as a woodland creature. As an insect. That's how faeries saw us mere mortals. Something to play with. And to squash when they got bored.

"Sounds like you're attracted to danger." A mischievous smile played across his handsome face, and warning bells rang in my mind. That's what I expected. That's what I needed to watch out for. That's what got Cass.

"I should go," I said. "I need to place another order and get back to work. I'm really sorry about your clothes." I wasn't *that* sorry. His clothes looked expensive—perfectly tailored to fit his lean, muscled form. He probably had a leprechaun slave or something who could make him another set.

"Don't worry about it," he said. "In fact, I can fix it right up."

His hands were out of his pockets before I could protest, moving in an unnatural motion. My heart seized in my chest as his lips moved, mouthing strange nonsense syllables. He was doing magic.

Every fiber within me told me to run, to flee from him, and not look back. But I was rooted to the spot, fascinated and horrified in turn. I hadn't been around magic for two years—not since Cassandra and her coven were playing around in the attic with candles and runes. Since she started sneaking out to meet some guy, a guy who happened to have glowing golden eyes and pointed ears. Since she disappeared into the field behind our ranch with him and never came back.

At the thought of my older sister, my heart squeezed in my chest like a vice. Even as the coffee cups and carrying tray were floating back into the air, the dark coffee pooling and flowing back into them like real-life CGI, I thought of her. I held her in my mind, reminding me. Why, no matter how beautiful they appeared, or enchanting they seemed, I hated them. All of them.

The girl behind the counter was full on staring now, which somehow irked me even more. It was a detail to focus on. A safe, human detail.

The blond faerie seemed ridiculously pleased with himself as he took the tray of full Americanos and handed it back to me. "You're welcome," he said with a wink.

I pushed past him, even the words *thank you* sticking in my throat.

I hurried back through the lot, past the parked golf carts and a gaggle of extras clad in Viking attire. It wasn't until I passed into the glass door of the headquarters that I realized I hadn't even thought to ask the faerie, why was he here?

DOWNLOAD THE SORCERY TRIAL TODAY!

FROM THE AUTHOR

Thank you so much for taking the time to read the *Mythical Alliance: Phoenix Team*! I hope you've enjoyed reading about Zariya's adventures as much as I've enjoyed writing them!

I envisioned this serial series like a tv show; the six Phoenix Team books are just the first season! The second season, Mythical Alliance: Draco Team, will be launching in 2021. If you're interested in receiving updates on the Mythical Alliance series, participating in giveaways, and requesting advanced copies of upcoming books, sign up for my mailing list at http://claireluana.com.

As a thank you for signing up, you will receive a free ebook!

Lastly, reader reviews are incredibly important to indie authors like me, and so it would mean the world to me if you took a few minutes to leave an honest review wherever you buy books online. It doesn't have to be much; a few words can make the difference in helping a future reader decide to give the book a chance. Thanks!

ABOUT THE AUTHOR

USA Today Bestselling author Claire Luana grew up in Seattle reading everything she could get her hands on and writing every chance she could. Eventually, adulthood won out, and she turned her writing talents to more scholarly pursuits, going to work as a commercial litigation attorney. But it turns out that's not nearly as much fun!

Since returning to her more creative roots, Claire has written and published five fantasy series: the Moonburner Cycle, the Confectioner Chronicles, the Mythical Alliance, the Knights of Caerleon, co-written with Jesikah Sundin, and The Faerie Race trilogy, co-written with J.A. Armitage. She is currently writing a new epic fantasy series called the Annals of the Seven Realms.

She lives in Seattle, Washington with her husband and two dogs. In her (little) remaining spare time, she loves to hike, travel, binge-watch CW shows, and of course, fall into a good book.

Connect with Claire Luana online at http://www.claireluana.com

facebook.com/claireluana

twitter.com/clairedeluana

instagram.com/claireluana

OTHER BOOKS BY CLAIRE LUANA

Moonburner Cycle

Moonburner, Book One

Sunburner, Book Two

Starburner, Book Three

Burning Fate, Prequel Novella

Moonburner Cycle, Box Set

Confectioner Chronicles

The Confectioner's Guild, Book One

The Confectioner's Coup, Book Two

The Confectioner's Truth, Book Three

The Confectioner's Exile, Prequel Novella

Confectioner Chronicles, Box Set

The Knights of Caerleon, with Jesikah Sundin

The Fifth Knight, Book One

The Third Curse, Book Two

The First Gwenevere, Book Three

Gwenevere's Knights, Box Set

The Faerie Race, with J.A. Armitage

The Sorcery Trial, Book One

The Elemental Trial, Book Two

The Doomsday Trial, Book Three

The Faerie Race, Box Set

The Mythical Alliance: Phoenix Team

<u>Phoenix Selected</u>, Book One

<u>Phoenix Protected</u>, Book Two

<u>Phoenix Captured</u>, Book Three

<u>Phoenix Trafficked</u>, Book Four

<u>Phoenix Revealed</u>, Book Five

<u>Phoenix Betrayed</u>, Book Six

<u>Mythical Alliance: Phoenix Team</u>, Box Set

<u>Orion's Kiss</u>